Sun River

————◆————

Bannack

Sun River

———◆———

Bannack

Richard S. Wheeler

A Tom Doherty Associates Book / New York

SUN RIVER AND BANNACK

Sun River copyright © 1989 by Richard S. Wheeler

Bannack copyright © 1989 by Richard S. Wheeler

A Forge Book
Published by Tom Doherty Associates, LLC
175 Fifth Avenue
New York, NY 10010

www.tor-forge.com

Forge® is a registered trademark of Tom Doherty Associates, LLC.

ISBN 978-0-7653-7853-8

Forge books may be purchased for educational, business, or promotional use. For information on bulk purchases, please contact Macmillan Corporate and Premium Sales Department at 1-800-221-7945, extension 5442, or write specialmarkets@macmillan.com.

First Edition: September 2014

Printed in the United States of America

0 9 8 7 6 5 4 3 2 1

Contents

Sun River

For Win and Martha Blevins

Chapter 1

Eager for information, the Reverend Cecil J. B. Rathbone hurried diagonally across the dusty parade ground of Fort Laramie, past the two-storied officers' quarters known as Old Bedlam, and on to the sutler's store at the far corner.

Inside that low, wide building, and hovering amidst the piles of tarpaulins and ropes and clothing and barrels of foodstuffs, lurked a sallow clerk. That would not do, Rathbone thought. He wished to speak to Bullock himself.

"Where, sir, might I find the sutler?" he asked.

The clerk said nothing, but gestured toward a far corner. The Reverend Mister Rathbone nodded, and found a bearded man there doing his accounts at a crude plank desk.

"Mr. Bullock, sir."

"Why yes," said the man. "May I be of service?"

A Southerner, the reverend supposed.

"I am told on good authority that you can direct me to a certain Barnaby Skye. The guide."

"Mister Skye," said Bullock.

"Why yes, Barnaby Skye."

"*Mister* Skye," the sutler repeated. "He permits no other address." He carefully blotted ink from his nib pen, and set it on a lined ledger. Then he rose, a tall and courtly man. "I am Colonel Bullock," he said. "And whom do I have the honor of addressing?"

"Cecil Rathbone. I'm a clergyman. My party and I wish to employ Mister Skye to take us to the Blackfeet."

"Blackfeet? Bug's Boys?" The sutler was visibly startled.

Rathbone grinned. "Scares the bejabbers out of me, too."

Bullock stared out of his small window toward the low June-greened bluffs that rimmed the Platte Valley. "Skye won't take you. I can tell you that now. There are certain Blackfeet who'd kill him on sight. Old blood, bad blood . . . Maybe I can find you someone else to transport you to your doom."

Cecil J. B. Rathbone laughed. "I say we'll prosper. We made it this far, haven't we? In spite of the troubles?"

The sutler glared at him fiercely. "Indeed you have, suh. The work of innocents or fools or madmen. I suppose you're with the wagon train that just rolled in. Probably the only one we'll see in 1855, with the Sioux in an uproar and Harney gearing up to a fight . . . not to mention bloody troubles in Oregon, and all the rest. I must say, suh, you and your good missionaries took a desperate risk. And the worst is yet to come."

Rathbone laughed easily. "It's been a perfect trip. Lots of grass because there is no one ahead of us. No waiting at the fords and ferries."

"I can imagine," said the sutler dryly. "The luck of the innocent. An odd year. Last year we counted over five thousand wagons. But that was before that popinjay, Lieutenant Grattan, got himself slaughtered."

Time was wasting, Rathbone thought. "Now then, Colonel, if you'd be so kind as to steer me toward Mister Skye . . . ?"

"How many are in your party?" Bullock asked.

"Ten. Five men, three women, two children. Four wagons."

"Wagons? There's no road whatsoever to the Blackfoot country. You can't take wagons. You can't take women or children either."

"We intend to," said Rathbone. "Now, sir, if you could direct me?"

Back in Independence they had told him that Bullock was the man who'd put him in touch with Skye. He felt a little irked. What was it about being a missionary that caused people to assume he was fragile as an egg?

"Far as I know, Mister Skye's available. No one's hired him this year. He came in a few days ago. Bought a new slant-breech Sharps. But I can tell you, Reverend, you'll have no more chance of engaging him than a snowball in, ah . . ."

"His whereabouts, Colonel Bullock?"

"Why, he keeps a lodge up the Platte some. Two, three miles above Squaw Town. Beside a stand of cottonwoods."

"Thank you kindly, Colonel," said Rathbone, offering his big, frontier-hardened hand. The trader pumped it, shaking his head.

The reverend walked quickly through the store and out into the blinding sun of the parade. God love 'em, they all thought that Indians were unteachable; that the savages would sooner or later be exterminated, and probably sooner, to make way for settlement. And any attempt by missionaries to civilize and settle the tribes must be the work of muddleheads, fools, and religious crackpots. Cecil Rathbone intended to show them otherwise. His plan had seemed hopeful and plausible enough to persuade the Methodist Board of Missions to approve, and spring a few miserable dollars.

He liked Fort Laramie, but he knew no one else in the party would. It was, really, a desolate outpost, many hundreds of weary miles beyond the Missouri frontier, bleak and almost treeless, set improbably at the juncture of the Platte and Laramie rivers, a fur-trade post until 1849. Now it baked in a late spring sun, its bunch grass greening early in the arid climate. The bedraggled adobe fur-trade stockade still stood, a magazine and storage area now. And the army was desultorily building around the parade. Long barracks. Cavalry stables. Married officers' quarters. Innumerable outbuildings, thrown up crudely. The commanding officer had been a green West Point brevet lieutenant—until the Grattan affair last year. That woke up the army, and now an experienced officer, Brevet Lt. Colonel William Hoffman, commanded, and the post flexed its muscles for war.

Unlike most clerics, the Reverend Mister Rathbone paid heed to all of that, noting the sentries, the two howitzers and their limbers strategically placed to protect the weak fort with a wall of grape since it lacked a stockade. Mister Rathbone approved. It seemed an unfinished place, like the business of life, with some buildings started, and others half raised.

Mister Skye, he thought, lived well beyond the fort's protection, alone in a skin lodge up the river. And between him and the fort lay Squaw Town, the camp of the loafers and ne'er-do-wells and—he thought piously—those squaws sunk in vice. Most of them were Oglala Sioux, he'd heard, but some were Brulés, the very band Grattan had tangled with; the band General Harney was preparing to punish.

Skye was plainly a man to reckon with, living beyond safety like that. It jibed with everything he'd heard about him, too. He had made inquiries back east in St. Louis and Independence and St. Jo. Who could take his party, his wagons, his women and children, safely to the Blackfeet? No one can, was the answer. Veteran fur traders along the Missouri frontier looked at him aghast even for asking the question. And had smirked. But even as he had asked, the name Skye emerged. One man, one man alone, a legend of a man, Barnaby Skye, might do it. Not that Skye would consent to such folly, they had hastily added. But he could do it. He could even move missionaries.

Rathbone grinned at the memory. Moving missionaries was a sort of ultimate wilderness test. And Mister Skye would be the man to do it. On lanky legs the reverend raced on down past the fort to the meadow beside the trail where the wagons were parked. In normal years it was bare, littered ground, every blade of grass mashed under by a thousand wagons and oxen and mules and horses and hordes of people heading west. But this year it remained lush, and the missionary herds—oxen, horses, mules, milch cows—grazed contentedly.

Cecil Rathbone managed to wear his black broadcloth suit through most of the journey, as a sort of badge of office, although he felt more comfortable in homespuns, and the lean hard legs that had walked him from frontier Illinois to the Wesleyan college in Boston were more at home in soft denim britches and big square-toed boots. He would saddle up the mare and ride out to Mister Skye. Persuading Mister Skye did not worry him. Paying Mister Skye did. There really were no other candidates. He had noted how trappers' eyes softened at the name: Skye? Ah, yes, Mister Skye. How well I remember . . .

The reverend wondered whether the man was real, or merely a legend, another frontier tall story, the sort of yarn old Jim Bridger loved to spin for greenhorns. He'd find out soon enough. Mountain men had peculiar notions, and some of their raucous kind were esteemed not because of any known virtue, but because they had survived in a brutal wilderness. Skye might be that type—a lout in stinking, dirty buckskins, a man so murderous that he thrived on terror. The thought made Cecil Rathbone uneasy. He did not want to employ a guide so repellent that he outraged his own party of missionaries, or violated its ideals, nor ride into the northern Blackfoot land in the company of a man who personified evil among them. On the other hand—and this was where Cecil Rathbone believed he differed from the others in his party—one had to be flexible, and manage the practical compromises that would ensure success. Where would Mister Skye fit?

The wagon train slouched haphazardly in the meadow, all discipline broken down in the safe lee of the fort. There were twenty-eight wagons, of which four belonged to his missionary group. The rest were owned by men—there were no women this wartorn year, save for the missionary wives—bound for golden California beyond the far western mountains, or Oregon and the Willamette Valley where, people said, anyone could grow anything in such abundance that it staggered the imagination to think of it. How often he had listened to them, and their shining dreams and great hopes, on the trail! After some rest and refitting at the fort, those wagons would lumber up the Oregon Trail. These were small wagons mostly, the sun-bleached canvas stretched and sagging over the bows, and the undercarriage and boxes showing wear and grit. Many of the owners had drifted to the fort, the sutler's store in particular, seeking news and companionship and sometimes supplies, or a trade or two. Worn oxen for fresh, a heavy bedstead or dresser for a barrel of flour; two saddlesore gaunt horses for a rested fat one.

The three wagons and light carriage of his own party looked even less trailworthy than those of the others, for there had been little money, and the missionaries had acquired the oldest and meanest available, and had prayed that they would do; that the battered hubs and spokes and wheel-rim felloes and tongues and axletrees would somehow last them. Cecil Rathbone was not content with prayer. He held that God always demanded the best from his people. So Cecil had pulled out his broadaxe, his draw knife, his saws and chisels, and had set to work on the old wagons, replacing weak wood with fine strong hickory or ash or birch, and somehow the wagons had survived. The rest of the party had thanked God, and attributed a minor miracle to him. Cecil thanked God too, and smiled as he touched the new spokes and axles he had hewn and cut and shaved.

The Newtons in particular had thanked God, rather than Cecil. And that was good enough, thought Cecil Rathbone. Henrietta Newton was his daughter; Alexander, his son-in-law. He loved them, but knew their narrow letter-perfect faith was radically different from his own. The pair of them was pious, intense, and—the Reverend Mister Rathbone sighed—sour-natured. It worried him. How would they react to the savage Blackfeet? Still, he loved them, and they had bravely joined the Rathbones in this great enterprise.

He looked among the wagons for his own Esmerelda, and didn't find her. Like the rest, she had drifted off to the fort, no doubt, in her black skirts, to gaze upon this place of war and arms with good-humored prudishness. But the Newtons lounged beside their wagon, resting in camp chairs and flapping small folding fans. It amused Cecil to see them thus. He and his brown-eyed Esmerelda were thin as sticks, while his daughter Henrietta and her husband Alex were plump as autumn turkeys, and both sandy-haired and freckled.

"Have you seen the Samples?" asked Alexander in his

nasal voice that could rattle the back wall of a cathedral. "It's past the nooning and the Samples have drifted off."

"Around the fort, I'm sure," said Cecil amiably. "You might fetch your own meal this time." Clay Sample, his wife Alice, and two children had come along to launch the mission farm and eventually to teach agriculture to their charges. Cecil admired them as he did all Yankee yeomen of hearty and courageous manner. On the trail Henrietta and Alexander, pleading exhaustion, had soon taken to sharing the Samples' table, and now had come to expect it.

"That's the trouble with the world and the thing we must preach against," added Henrietta. "People running off, not caring about the needs of others, selfish in their own pursuits, heedless of want. I wish we had brought a more responsible couple."

Cecil didn't like the drift of this. "It's a holiday," he said. "A celebration; the end of the first great leg of the Oregon Trail. Why don't you make a holiday of it yourself? I hear the sutler has a splendid eggnog."

"Daddy, it's too hot. And besides, I'm unwell," she added pointedly, referring to her delicate condition.

"The Samples will have to contribute more to the mission if they want my esteem. We've no room for ne'er-do-wells in a hard wilderness," Alexander said. "And they scarcely even understand Methodism. God relies on us to spread his message; and we are forced to rely on the Samples for better or worse."

All of this stretched Cecil's patience. Prior to this long hard journey he'd scarcely given a second thought to the character of his daughter and son-in-law. But now, far removed from the world they all had known, he was discovering—or perhaps they were first revealing—traits that disturbed him.

"Good news," he said cheerily. "Skye's available, the

sutler thinks. I shall go find him. He lives in a skin tee-
pee out beyond Squaw Town a couple of miles."

"I've heard about Squaw Town," said Alexander. "May
God smite them all, with their unspeakable vices, and I
suppose this famous guide is a part of it, in his filthy
buckskins."

"I don't think so," said Cecil mildly.

"I think we should have an army escort take us. The
Republic owes it to the missionaries who bring light to
the savage breast," said Henrietta. "I have no stomach for
a hard journey led by some barbaric pig of a man."

Cecil smiled again. "Perhaps it would be best to with-
hold judgment," he said mildly, and chastised himself for
not adding that Christian charity might help.

"Yes of course. You don't need to lecture, Daddy," she
said. "And if you see the Samples, direct them here at
once."

The Reverend Cecil Rathbone ignored his daughter
and set off to find his horse, a ribby bay mare, gaunt
across the haunches, and venerable of age, if Cecil was
any judge. Still, she had come this distance and had not
become sorefooted. He had ridden her as much as possible
to take the strain off the oxen dragging the overburdened
wagon.

He found her in the loose herd of the wagon train, several hundred yards east, where grass grew lush and green.
There was no guard whatsoever—the entire complement
of the train had bolted toward the fort, leaving no on to
watch the herd, a laxity that worried and astonished him.
He had been too long on the frontier of western Illinois to
suppose such a thing didn't invite trouble. The Newtons
were on hand; perhaps he could prevail upon Alexander.
But then he thought better of it. The Reverend Alexander
would not be prevailed upon. Cecil threaded casually

through the oxen and milch cows and mules, until he came nigh to the mare, but at the last second she spun away.

"Blast it, Magdelene, are we going to go through this again?" he muttered, easing after her. He thought perhaps if he paused and invited the Lord to stop Magdelene in her tracks, he might catch her, but he scorned that. He'd do his wily best first, and only after that, if all else failed, would Cecil J. B. Rathbone bend a petitioning knee.

"Come along, Magdelene," he crowed amiably, with a tone of voice he reserved professionally for recent widows. And he laughed. Her name was his delight, mainly because it had shocked the Newtons, and had even troubled his dear wife Esmerelda. A preacher riding a horse named Magdelene indeed! A school for scandal. "Come along now, Magdelene," he repeated in a quavering funereal basso that caught her ear. She paused delicately. He haltered her and led her back to his wagon, where a tattered saddle and battered bridle with woven horsehair reins awaited.

"It gets harder and harder to catch Magdelene," he said in passing to the Reverend Alexander Newton.

Newton sniffed knowingly.

"The herd is quite unguarded. I don't suppose, from Christian duty, you'd care to walk over there and keep a watchful eye, Alexander?"

He looked remarkably pained. It was like asking him to wash dishes. "I don't suppose anyone will take them," he replied. "But I will petition God about it."

Cecil Rathbone nodded, and turned the mare toward Skye.

Chapter 2

The way threaded through Squaw Town, which turned out to be a chaotic jumble of lodges, crude huts, brush arbors, and makeshift livestock pens lying loosely along the riverbank on a meadow hemmed by cottonwoods. The Reverend Mister Rathbone stared, curious and appalled, at bronze women with bold stares, drunken men, naked brown children with moon faces, and gaunt hard-used Indian ponies. Here troopers and infantrymen could find most anything, from women to buffalo robes and winter capotes. Here were the Laramie loafers he'd heard of, the fort's own Sioux, who ran errands, guided, sometimes supplied buffalo meat and hides, worked in menial jobs at the fort, and made small livings from it, which they exchanged for powder and lead and strong spirits. The place was a fact of life, and did not dismay Cecil, though he pitied its dissolute denizens.

But he knew the others in his party, the Newtons, and Silas Potter who had come west to teach, would find it loathsome and stark proof of the damnation of the red races. Cecil sighed, wondering how the mission would fare if its staff harbored such obdurate contempt of the people whose lives and souls they hoped to change. There were noisome odors here, and lurking disease, and no doubt some of his fine white colleagues would hold it all against the redmen, not understanding that this degradation was a product of a white man's fort. In their distant villages the Sioux did not live like this.

After a few minutes Cecil found himself on the far side of Squaw Town, on open meadow uninhabited save for some loose Indian ponies in various colors, paints, brindles, roans, spotted animals, buckskins and bays and whites and blacks, and some boy herders.

Leisurely he threaded up the river, in a wide sunny valley dotted with stands of cottonwood. The fort disappeared from sight as he rounded a broad curve, along with Squaw Town. The missionary was quite alone in a wilderness six or seven hundred miles from the frontier. Then at last he spotted a solitary lodge of buffalo hide, its smokehole and flaps blackened by long hard use. As he approached he realized it was a small lodge, perhaps ten feet at its base, as if its owner was a man on the move and wanted no roots. Grazing beyond the lodge was a small herd, consisting of two heavy ebony mules in good flesh; several nondescript Indian ponies of varied hue, and a monster of a horse, a giant blue roan that struck Cecil Rathbone as the ugliest brute he had ever seen. Closer to the lodge, a fresh-killed mule deer carcass hung from a limb. He saw a pleasant brush arbor supplying shade. And under it, the figure of an Indian woman in buckskin, working a hide. Just what she looked like he couldn't say; she was too far away for his poor eyes.

As he approached, a man emerged from the lodge. At least, Cecil thought, it appeared to be a man, for indeed it was the strangest apparition imaginable, and gave him a fright that not even all his frontier experience could allay. As he drew up Magdelene he found himself gaping at a veritable Falstaff, a man of great height, built like a hogshead. From top to bottom the man looked bizarre. He wore his iron-gray hair loose and shoulder length, in the manner of the mountain men, which the reverend had anticipated. But on top of his head sat a black silk stovepipe hat, jammed down hard and dimpled from hard use.

It rested slightly akilter, to portside, making him look unballasted and likely to list in a hurricane.

In the center of all this was a square beardless face, with a massive, pulpy, twisted nose of a magnitude beyond the experience of Cecil Rathbone; a majestic prow that had obviously been smashed and mauled in a thousand brawls. From behind this formidable stem stared two small, icy eyes, perhaps blue but so buried in folds and creases of flesh that the reverend couldn't tell. A jagged white scar ripped across his right cheek, and a pucker scar dug into his forehead above his nose. Cecil thought that if God wanted him to hire this man, God had better send a sign.

At the base of a thick neck a fine buckskin shirt with fringes on its sleeves barely contained the barrel staves of the man. All this mass rested on stout, slightly bowed legs, encased in fringed leggins and a red-beaded breechclout. On his feet were not moccasins, but heavy, worn, square-toed boots largely hidden by the leggins. Only then did the reverend notice a shining new rifle resting easily in brutish brown hands the size of summer squash. So electrifying was all this that he scarcely glanced at the woman who placidly scraped hide under the brush arbor. This was, he thought wildly, a most alarming sight, half devil and half Viking berserker, and not fitting for ladies or gentlefolk. Surely this could not be the man . . .

"Mister Skye?" he croaked.

"Yaas?" thundered the man. With one word he had sounded like a den of grizzlies, whose shiny gray claws indeed he wore in a necklace.

"You are Mister Skye, the guide?"

"I am Mister Skye," the man said in a voice that rumbled like an earthquake. "May I be of service to you?"

The question—or rather the elegance of it—startled

Cecil Rathbone. Was this brute educated? Housebroken? "Why . . . why, I believe you can. I'm, the, ah, Reverend Cecil J. B. Rathbone."

"Ah," said Mister Skye, "a divine. One who does not wear the collar of Rome. You have come west to tamper with the heathen."

"Methodist," said Rathbone shortly. He had detected something—was it mockery?—in Skye's comment. He would turn around right now and hire a human rather than a grizzly, he thought. This man would be utterly impossible, especially among the women of the mission. "I was, ah, looking for a guide, but I don't think—"

"To where?" asked Mister Skye.

"To the Blackfeet."

"For what?" demanded Mister Skye.

"Why . . . why . . ."

"To turn them into white men. And probably do a bloody poor job of it."

"Not exactly," Cecil stammered. "All by degrees. A farm. A school. Practical things first . . ." Cecil began to warm to his topic, his vision. "Christian religion doesn't catch in a savage. They have been vaccinated against it . . . by savage living . . . We have to civilize them first and then they'll understand religion."

"The Blackfeet are nomads and roam a land the size of several New Englands," said Mister Skye. "Will you roam with them?"

"No, no, not at all. We've heard of a place called Sun River. Wide, flat, fertile valley east of the Rockies some; a place to set up our farm, our school, our headquarters. The advice we got was Sun River, and we'd like to employ you to take us there."

Mister Skye stared up at the reverend, and then at his

gaunt horse. "I will consider it," he said at last. "How many are there of you?"

"Ten. Five men, three women, a boy of fourteen and a girl of eleven. Three wagons and one carriage. Some oxen, mules, and two milch cows."

"Wagons," said Mister Skye.

But he said no more, and Rathbone was surprised.

The man studied Cecil. "What did you say your name is?"

"Cecil J. B. Rathbone."

"What does the J. B. stand for?"

Cecil felt skewered, and hastily blurted his response. "Nothing. Nothing at all. I added it when I entered the ministry. Ah, just vanity. When I entered Wesleyan, I was plain Cecil, from Galena, Illinois. When I graduated and was ordained, I became Cecil J. B.—John Burnside, I tell people. More clerical, I fancy."

For the first time Mister Skye grinned. Cecil felt nonplussed. He had confessed something that not even dear Esmerelda knew, his own little pettifoggery and conceit. What sort of man was this, who elicited such things? A dangerous one, surely.

"And who are the others?"

The Reverend Rathbone felt rattled. "My daughter Henrietta, ah, now Newton. Married to the Reverend Alex Newton. Ah, Silas Potter, a lay brother and divinity student—our teacher. James, a mulatto escaped slave from Louisiana. Fine strong fellow. Ah, the Samples. Clay Sample, good Yankee yeoman who'll tend our farm. His wife Alice, sturdy stock. Their son Alfred, almost a man. And a daughter, Miriam, old enough to help with everything."

Mister Skye waited, disconcertingly, for the reverend to continue, but Cecil had already blabbered more than he intended. Then the giant nodded. "This is Victoria," he said. "She is a woman of the Absaroka, the Raven people, the Crow. I named her for the Queen, God save her bloody life. She has another name in her own tongue. She tends the camp, tans fine buffalo robes, makes the elkskin clothes I wear, guards the horses, fetches wood, shoots her percussion lock rifle better than I can, takes scalps, mutilates the enemy"—Mister Skye's eyes glinted at that—"swears bloody oaths, tells bawdy jokes that make preachers swoon, makes spirit medicine to heathen gods, is a real medicine woman and healer of the Crow people, builds my sweat lodges, rides buffalo ponies, and is second-in-command when I'm, ah, incapacitated."

Cecil turned for the first time to look at her. So galvanizing had Mister Skye been that he had quite forgotten she was present. She was tall and gaunt and her black hair was well shot with gray. Though her walnut flesh was withered, she looked almost as strong as her consort. She smiled gently, and turned back to the hide scraping, which she did with a curious black iron and wood tool. Could she really do all those appalling things, or was the guide funning him? Cecil suspected that the woman could and would do everything on that dismaying list.

Cecil grinned back, and nodded to her.

"She also swears like a bloody sailor, and if you don't do what she says, mate, she'll turn you into a tenor."

Cecil nodded. Take orders? From her . . . ?

"Do you shoot?" asked Mister Skye abruptly. "I see no arms at hand."

"I do," said Cecil. "I have fed our party this trip, in fact. Pronghorn, deer, several rabbits."

Cecil expected him to ask whether the missionary would shoot at humans, at redmen, in self-defense, but the question never came, and Cecil felt vaguely relieved.

Instead, Mister Skye said, "My fee would be five hundred dollars in advance—if I accept, which I have not made up my mind to do."

Cecil was stricken. "Why, sir, that is what a man makes in a year!"

Mister Skye nodded almost imperceptibly.

"We haven't it," Cecil said, relief flooding through him. "We reserved two hundred maximum, a draft on the Methodist Board of Missions, but hoped to do for less."

Cecil felt giddy with escape, and turned Magdelene to go.

"Wait," said Mister Sky. "I will go with you. I never make up my mind until I have examined the party."

"But we can't possibly afford you!"

"We shall see," said Mister Skye. "Belay yourself. I'll gather my horse and be with you right smartly."

He whistled in some earsplitting fashion, and that terrible blue roan's head lifted and he trotted toward his master.

"I can pipe him in," Mister Skye said amiably. "His name is Jawbone."

"Were you perhaps a sailor, Mister Skye?"

"I was. Royal Navy. Pressed in, until I deserted."

"I have it that you were a brigade leader with Astor's American Fur."

"That too, Mister Rathbone."

If Mister Skye was an apparition, Jawbone was twice an apparition to Cecil Rathbone. Never in a life spent among horses had he seen such an animal as this. Jawbone was a horse sired by the devil on Moloch, and the reverend piously resisted the impulse to cross himself or run.

Never had an uglier horse been spawned among the

gentle creatures of earth. Jawbone towered seventeen
hands but looked lean as a starved wolf. His enormous
bones projected through flesh everywhere, making him
all ridges and bumps. He stared at the world with cruel,
intelligent yellow eyes set narrowly on a long Roman
nose that rivaled his master's. An ear was half torn off.
Everywhere, his battered blue and white hair bore the
scars of a thousand battles. Across his chest lay a long
puckered slash. In a dozen places were hairless circles
where arrows had buried themselves. His rump was con-
cave and laced with ridged, proud flesh, sites of countless
blows from lances and knives. His legs looked straight
but battered and knotted. Long sinewy muscles rippled
and corded through his stifle and shoulder, suggesting raw
strength. Even as the reverend gaped, horrified, Jawbone
bared his long, cruel teeth. He clacked his molars re-
soundingly, and Cecil Rathbone felt faint. But at bottom
it was not the physical aspects of this monster that appalled the reverend; it was his malevolence, burning in
his eyes from the throne of hell with an intelligence that
was almost human—or demonic.

"Where . . . where did you get a horse like that?"

"Pulled him from a dying mare, suckled him on a she-
bear, raised him the way I wanted," Mister Skye replied
as he threw an apishamore over the stallion's back, and
then cinched down a light battered rawhide thing that
could be called a saddle.

Mister Skye looped a horsehair rope loosely over the
monster's nose and knotted it underneath, a single line of
it running back along the neck.

"Better stand back, mate. You and your party must never
come closer than ten or twelve feet."

"Does he kick?" asked Cecil.

"No, he kills."

Involuntarily Cecil Rathbone edged Magdelene back. Jawbone clacked his teeth from the sheer joy of it.

"How—how can you steer a horse with only one rein?"

"He knows."

With that, Mister Skye bounded effortlessly into his saddle, lifting his vast weight the seventeen hands as easily as stepping over a hound, and holding that gleaming new rifle to boot. Then they rode off, Mister Skye taking the lead, straight through Squaw Town, parting its gaping denizens like a bow wave, while Mister Rathbone on Magdelene trailed like a dinghy in the wake. Squaws and squaw men and breeds stared, half afraid, and Cecil Rathbone saw respect and more. There in Skye's wake, he never felt safer. That was a novelty: he hadn't felt truly safe, this year of wars, ever since they had left Independence.

On the meadow at Fort Laramie a squad of infantrymen were practicing with their bayonets, learning to feint and stab while a drill sergeant with a long staff tutored. As Mister Skye approached they stopped and stared, resting the butts of their Springfields in the battered grass.

Who was this to make the United States Army gawk? Cecil asked himself. Then they rounded the north corner of the parade, and Cecil saw the wagons.

"Over there." He pointed toward the knot of wheels and canvas and people comprising his missionary group. It looked from that distance like his party had returned from the fort and the sutler's, though with his infernally bad eyes he couldn't be sure.

Mister Skye nodded and imperceptibly steered Jawbone in that direction, while Cecil's nerves tightened. What on earth would they think of a man such as this? It was not going to be easy. Could they understand that here was not menace, but safety?

A sharp breeze lifted Cecil's hair, and he wondered whether it would pluck Mister Skye's black silk hat and set it sailing. But it didn't, and the hat, still askew, seemed anchored to his skull over his flowing white-shot hair.

Then they were there. Mister Skye reined up Jawbone, and stared, first at the assembled missionaries, one by one, from eyes so small and buried that no one could meet his gaze. Then his eyes raked the equipment. The horses and mules and oxen first, and then the wagons, lingering on the hubs, spokes, hounds, felloes, axles, tongues, and singletrees. Then at last he smiled. Jawbone raised his head to the heavens, bared his terrible teeth, and screeched. Several people jumped.

In all this awful silence Rathbone's party stared back, dismayed and alarmed, their eyes darting from man to horse, resting on Mister Skye's awesome nose, studying the scars on his weathered face, darting to the wounds and lumps and ridges of the horse he sat, peering disapprovingly at the bit of brown thigh flesh between Mister Skye's beaded breechclout and his leggins. Miriam Sample, pale and toothy and thin, slid around behind her mother and hid but young Alfred stood his ground bravely. No sissy was he.

The Reverend Cecil Rathbone thought that the stretching silence had gone on long enough. He cleared his throat. "I would like you . . ." he rasped, "I would like you to meet Mister Skye, who may become our guide to the Blackfeet."

Mister Skye nodded amiably.

Cecil continued bravely. "This is my daughter Henrietta and her husband, the Reverend Alexander Newton."

The pair nodded curtly, indignation rising in their plump soft cheeks.

"Next to them, my dear wife Esmerelda."

She managed a darting smile, and Cecil was pleased.

"Over there now is James, James Method," Cecil continued, nodding toward a powerfully built tall mulatto of perhaps thirty, with tawny flesh and yellow eyes. "He fled his native Louisiana, and we have taken him in. We don't hold with slavery here. A good man, and a fine addition to our party. We gave him the surname, Method."

James Method grinned easily. He alone was not dismayed by the barbaric power of the guide. He stood easily, muscles rippling through his homespun shirt that was tucked into denim britches. "Ah think you'll do in a tribulation, Mister Skye," he said. "You look like safety itself."

The mountain man stared, smiled, and nodded. "Likewise," he rumbled. "You remind me a heap of Jim Beckwourth, a trapper friend of your color, and an adopted Crow headman."

"And these are the Samples. Clay here, who can make things grow in deserts; Alice, his wife, and the young 'uns, Alfred and Miriam."

They too managed smiles. Mister Skye's eyes lingered on Clay in particular, and then the others, and he nodded.

"And lastly, our fine teacher, Silas Potter. William and Mary College and Dartmouth too, before he began his studies at Wesleyan for the missionary field."

Silas Potter was frail, pale even after weeks on the trail, and nearsighted. He wore gold-rimmed spectacles. Now he stood rigidly, his soft young lips drawn into a pout, his eyebrows furrowed into contempt.

Silas Potter swallowed, and his Adam's apple bobbed up and down. Then he said, "I will not travel a mile with this unholy barbarian. We are people of God, not the devil."

Chapter 3

Mister Skye had a way of sizing men up in a hurry. He had refined that gift as a brigade leader in his trapping years when his very life depended on the sort of men he had around him. He knew at once that he would take this group up to the Blackfeet. What might happen to them after that was not his business, but he would get them there.

Now, as he eyed the group, Jawbone restless under him, he turned again to James Method, and liked what he saw. The ex-slave had seen the worst of life, and the worst of human nature, and that made him a realist. But one who had not gone sour or stoked his soul on hate. That sort of embittered man could be a menace in the wilderness, where sticking together often meant the difference between life and going under. He was muscular too, and probably had a journeyman's skills with tools as a result of his slave chores. Strong. He would do in a corner.

"You can shoot that?" he asked, alluding to a battered percussion lock rifle lying easy in the man's hands.

"Ah thought you might ask whether ah could aim it," James replied. "Do you want to see?"

"You'll do," said Mister Skye.

Even while the rest of them wrangled about him, he surveyed them one by one. Clay Sample would do, too, but seemed less bright and in need of a leader. The Reverend Rathbone was made of sturdy stuff, frontier stuff, and would be an asset, unless attacked by some sort of scruples. So would his doughty wife.

The Newtons were a question mark. Soft, arrogant, disdainful on the one hand, but with strong wills. They might shape up. He'd reserve his opinion of them. And then there was Potter. A loss and liability out in the wilds. But every brigade and caravan had a few of those, he thought. The man's flapping mouth would be the problem, rather than his physical frailty. That mouth could breed dissension, division, hatred, and weakness. As for the rest, Mrs. Sample and her children, assets.

"Mister Method," he said. "Are you as handy with a shovel as you are with that rifle? We have roads to make, cutbank streams to cross."

The man grinned.

"It doesn't matter whether he is or not," Silas Potter snapped. "We have decided not to employ you."

"I have decided to take you," said Mister Skye. He addressed Cecil Rathbone. "Reverend, you just hand me that letter of credit on your mission board, and we'll be off."

"Why, I was about to do it."

"Daddy, I do believe this requires more discussion," broke in Henrietta Newton.

"It's all discussed," said Cecil. "You might bend a knee about it, however."

"I think we're being hasty. We'll let you know in the morning, Skye. We have other candidates to interview—" said Alexander Newton.

"Mister Skye."

"Well, whatever it is."

"Newton. All the years I was a slave on a British man-o'-war I was Skye. Now I'm mister. Have we come to an agreement about that? Yes, Newton?"

James Method grinned.

They fell to wrangling again, and Mister Skye watched them, learning much. Cecil Rathbone was the senior man, and in command, in some fashion. And that was good. If

Newton or Potter had been senior, he would have long since turned his back. But Rathbone was a man to reckon with, plain enough.

The money wasn't much. He'd turn the letter of credit over to the sutler, who'd collect, and put it on account meanwhile, so he could draw on it. There were no other prospects this year, with the Sioux aflame across the prairies. Two hundred would do. It would mean only a little less strong spirits, he thought ruefully. Even so, the two hundred would buy him a cask.

He addressed Potter. "What is it about me that offends you, mate?"

"Why . . . why, your immodesty for one. You haven't the decency to wear britches, and your exposed limbs are a disgrace. In front of women, too."

"And what else?"

"Why—you have a squaw. You live in sin with a woman of the red race."

"You don't know the half of it," said Mister Skye. "And what else?"

"Why—you are the very apparition of war, and we come in peace and brotherhood. Your very presence among us belies our entire mission and purpose."

Mister Skye smiled. "Your peaceful presence, Mister Potter, will assure you of a peaceful journey through the lands of the peaceful Sioux and Cheyenne and Crow and Blackfeet."

"My faith is in God's providence, and not that instrument of murder in your hands."

Mister Skye understood the silence that followed. Potter had evoked the sword of God, and that meant much to these people. He didn't scorn it. Indeed, at sea as well as in this ocean of wilderness, there had been the inexplicable, the unexpected succor, the safe passage through the bowels of hell. No, far be it from him to scorn it.

"We'll meet you here at dawn," he said quietly, "and be off after breaking the fast. You'll have the rest of this day to reoutfit, rest your stock, trade off the gaunted ones. We'll be making road where there is none, so I'll want a shovel for every man, woman, and child. A pike pole and a sledge would help."

"We haven't the means," said Cecil.

"Find the means. Or forget your wagons and walk. I'll collect that letter of credit now, Reverend."

"Surely," said Cecil eagerly. He hastened to his wagon, found a black pigskin valise, extracted it, and started to hand it to Mister Skye.

"Don't step closer," said the guide sharply. He slid off Jawbone, who stood stock still, ears laid back, and collected the letter from the minister, glancing at it briefly.

"We are agreed then. Be ready at first light."

"But—" said Silas Potter. The word died in the breeze.

Cecil J. B. Rathbone looked pleased.

"Be ready," said Skye, touching Jawbone's flanks. The horse knew he was going to the sutler, and took him there. Jawbone was not a horse to tie to a hitchrail, and not a horse to leave in any intimate proximity with other beasts, two- or four-footed. So Mister Skye simply dismounted and left Jawbone to his fate. Jawbone, in turn, turned rump toward the store, stood guard, and eyed the world murderously, as Skye knew he would.

He found Colonel Bullock at his desk, and with a carrot-haired visitor wearing the collar of Rome and a suit of black broadcloth. He handed the letter to Bullock, who read it slowly.

"They've engaged you, then."

Mister Skye pondered. "More like I engaged them."

Bullock read it again. "It'll take a half a year to collect this," he said. "But I'll advance you a hundred eighty on account, taking twenty to negotiate this."

"Fair enough," said Mister Skye. "I will make a list. What have you by way of spirits? I am as dry as a Methodist sermon."

The red-haired priest grinned.

"Is it grain alcohol you want, or whiskey?"

This was always a profound dilemma. The grain alcohol, properly diluted, and with a twist of tobacco in it and a few peppers, was the great lubricant of every trappers' rendezvous he had ever attended. It tasted bygod awful, and drove redmen to vast excesses, not to mention white men; but it wasn't the stuff of his parched desire. Good aged corn whiskey was. Alone among life's terrible dilemmas, this one flummoxed Barnaby Skye.

"Well . . . well . . . twenty gallons of alcohol. No! The bloody whiskey, Bullock. A ten-gallon cask if you please. I'll have Mary and Victoria pick it up, and the rest."

"I perceive you have an unrequited thirst, Mistuh Skye," said the sutler.

"I do, I do."

"Let's see here. I have advanced you almost a hundred dollars of credit for the slant-breech Sharps, which this mission draft will cover and leave you with about ninety. The cask will run you twenty-eight. Not much left for a year's outfitting, Mistuh Skye."

Mister Skye groaned.

"But I have, in fact, a bit of business for you." The sutler smiled at Skye through the combed white strands of his full beard. "This, suh, is the Reverend Father Dunstan Kiley of the Society of Jesus. He's headin' your direction."

At that, Skye took a closer look. Father Kiley was a

big, rugged, florid, freckled Irishman, perhaps forty, with observant eyes, taking in what there was to take in about the mountain man.

"Where might that be, Father?"

"Why, to the Bitterroot Valley, Mister Skye. To Fort Owen, which used to be St. Mary's Mission, established by my friend and colleague Pierre de Smet some years ago."

Skye knew of the place. Father de Smet had built it in the 1840s to minister to the Flathead Indians and other nearby tribes. But funds were not available, and it had been closed and sold to David Owen, who had forted up there and become the first white settler in that area.

"But there's nothing of the mission now—"

"Of course, of course. My task is to bring the holy sacraments to our Indian converts there, teach as much as I can this summer, and let them know we'll return when we can."

"A long dangerous trip for that."

The priest shrugged. "Obedience is a Jesuit vow. But I am bringing something precious to people who have asked for it, asked for us to return. And that is reason enough."

"How'd you get here? You're a long way from the states."

"I had intended to come with the wagon train—the only one leaving this year. But I was delayed, and came along alone, hoping to catch up. At times these last days it was in sight ahead of me, but I never quite made it."

"You came all that way alone? Without protection?"

"I am told that we are everywhere respected among the plains Indians. The blackrobes . . ."

Mister Skye laughed.

So did Father Kiley.

"Are you armed?"

"I'm armed, but only to make meat. If it's my fate to become a martyr, then that is my fate."

"How are you traveling, mate?"

"A light cart and a dray. And I'm on a saddle horse. I thought to abandon the cart here, and pack from here on."

"A sound idea," said Mister Skye. He leaned forward. "Now tell me, Father Kiley, how you will deal with the Methodists, the missionary party I'm guiding."

The priest turned somber. "It's in the hands of God," he said quietly. "Let us hope for the best. The evening campfire usually draws people close. But if not, holy silence. Perhaps I shall camp apart. Certainly I can manage my own meals. If they object entirely, I will go my way alone. Perhaps you will give me some idea where I am to go?"

"You're coming with me, mate. Objections or not from the Methodists, I'm taking you as far as I can, which means to the Yellowstone and west. I have friends among the Crow you can engage to take you to Bitterroot Valley."

Father Kiley fussed with a pipe, tamped tobacco in it from a black pouch, and lit it with a sulfur match. "We haven't discussed your fee, Mister Skye."

"Nay, we haven't. I usually charge what the traffic will bear."

"And what might that be?"

"Why, a quart of Mister Bullock's finest."

The sutler laughed.

"I fear I would be leading you to perdition, Mister Skye."

"I've already been there and back more times than I can count, Father Kiley."

Father Kiley sucked his pipe noisily a moment. "A most satisfactory arrangement," he said slowly. "But one proviso . . ." He paused, a glint in his eye. "Share and share alike."

"Done!" cried Mister Skye. "A wet Jesuit in a party of dry Methodists. A man of faith and sauce. We shall make the prairies sing, Dunstan Kiley. We shall make the buffalo bulls bellow, the wolves bark, the ducks quack, and the rattlesnakes rattle."

"I *have* led you to perdition," chafed Father Kiley.

"The water's warm there," said Mister Skye. "We are leaving soon after dawn. I'll introduce you then." He arose. "Now I must put my squaws to work. There's a heap to do . . . Colonel, they'll be along presently and strip your shelves."

"That's what I'm afraid of," said Bullock.

"Squaws?" said Father Kiley.

"Mary and Victoria."

The priest stared.

Alexander Newton sat patiently in the chill dawn on the seat of his wagon, waiting for the oatmeal that Alice Sample was boiling up over the morning fire. He scorned coffee as a stimulant of the flesh, and therefore sinful, but the use of it was so common among others that he kept his silence about it. Someday, from a proper pulpit, he'd condemn it. The wagon swayed under him as Henrietta squirmed into her skirts underneath the canvas-covered bows. The air felt moist and sharp here in the bottoms, but he bore that patiently as well, doing his devotions as he waited.

The trip had been just short of an ordeal, and many was the time he wondered why he had volunteered. Perhaps because his father-in-law had been so enthused and persuasive. Neither he nor Henrietta shared that enthusiasm, but they perceived the need for a mission to the Blackfeet, and considered it a matter of high duty. There were benighted souls throughout the wild savage places of the west, and the church's mission was to reach them all.

Unlike his father-in-law, Alexander had no roots in the frontier. Quite the contrary. He had matured in amiable circumstances in Trenton, New Jersey, a settled, shady, civic-minded place. That perhaps was why these hundreds of miles through a desolate prairie in a bouncing wagon had seemed an ordeal. There was not even a privy for comfort and privacy, an ordeal for poor Henrietta. But they had a fiery faith, he and his Henrietta, and the pair of them intended to be torches, beacons, fires upon the hills, for generations to come.

Silently Alice Sample handed him a bowl of oatmeal gruel and a large spoon.

"Thank you, my dear Alice," he said. "You should smile, I think. God has given us a glorious day to begin the next leg of our mighty exodus."

But she didn't smile, and indeed turned her back to him and began to feed Miriam and Alfred, who had helped her gather wood and build the fire and now stood waiting.

"There's no need to be cross," he said. "We must all smile."

Across the meadow the buildings of the fort loomed, misty and lavender in the dawn light. Once in a while, the call of sentries had drifted to them in the night.

At another fire the Rathbones bustled, along with Silas Potter and James Method, and the smell of sizzling side-pork drifted toward him, annoying him because Alice Sample served only gruel, and that without salt or season.

He noticed laughter over there too, for the Rathbones were
early risers, unlike himself and Henrietta, and came
alive almost from the moment they awakened and poured
steaming coffee into themselves.

Well, God forgive them such fleshly exuberance, thought
Alex. Henrietta emerged, and thumped silently toward
the river brush for her necessary needs. Why couldn't
man be born without bodies—and just be ethereal spirits? he wondered, puzzling as he often did about disgusting bodily functions that kept the soul from flying freely
into the realm of heaven. It was a puzzle, why God fashioned men with bodies that made demands, hurt, required
attention.

He finished the oatmeal and silently dropped the bowl
and spoon into a kettle of boiling water that Alice Sample
had over the coals for that purpose, and stepped down
into the dewy grass. Time to find James and have him
harness the oxen. There were three yoke to gather.
The heavy, carved wooden yokes had to be dropped over
the necks of each pair, and then the tugs attached. Alex
had tried it once or twice, but it all was beyond him so
he had gotten the mulatto to do it. Which was just as
well, he thought. It permitted him to engage in spiritual
exercises and devotions that, he was sure, brought the
whole party closer to the Divine, and kept them all safe in
the midst of all sorts of storms. Each to his own best labor.

No sooner had he collared James at his in-laws'
campfire and set him to work than he noticed Skye—
preposterous of the man to call himself mister, like some
lord of the wilderness—and his entourage toiling toward
them from out of the dark west. The burly guide he recognized easily enough, astride that terrible blue roan monster. And behind him, riding two ponies, were two Indian
women, which surprised him. As they hove close he saw

that one was gaunt and gray, while the other one was young and full-figured. Behind her on the little mustang sat a child, a boy he supposed. They sat scandalously astride, with their skirts hiked high and their brown calves brazenly displayed. He decided he'd have a private talk with Skye about that. Such things were not permissible. Behind them came two giant black mules, each heavily laden with canvas manties bulging with supplies, hitched down with taut ropes forming diamond patterns. And bringing up the rear was another pony dragging a travois with some sort of burden of skins tied to it.

Nor was that the whole of this strange parade. Beside Skye rode a man on horseback who looked very like a Romish priest. In fact, he was obviously a priest, in a suit black as sin, and a white collar that could only choke out all goodness. And beneath the flat-crowned, wide-brimmed black hat was a florid square face, and a bit of hair as orange as the rising sun. And behind the priest came another packhorse, this one lightly laden.

Skye stopped the infernal blue roan an appropriate distance from the missionary fires, and surveyed the whole party and its preparations.

"I see you are not yet ready," he said. "Very well then. Henceforth at this time, and by this light, we will all be ready."

Alex Newton resented the tone of command in the wildman's rumbling voice.

Skye continued. "These are my wives. The younger is Mary, of the Shoshones, and the older is Victoria, of the Crow. And behind Mary is my son Dirk."

"Oh dear," said Henrietta.

Then the guide's voice rumbled through Alex's reveries again. "And this is the Reverend Father Dunstan Kiley.

He's a Jesuit. He will accompany us much of the way and has engaged me as his guide."

A Papist, thought Alexander Newton. A bigamist, if that was the word for living in carnal sin with two squaws. And now a black Papist. The whole mission party would be in the grip of the prince of darkness, he thought wildly.

"I won't move an inch in this company," cried Silas Potter.

But Cecil J. B. Rathbone had started to laugh.

Chapter 4

For four days Mister Skye led them along the ruts of the Oregon and California Trail, angling ever northwest on the south bank of the Platte. Because of the rampant Sioux, there was no other traffic. Swiftly, under his keen eye, the party had settled into a successful routine.

Mister Skye rode in the lead on his great blue horse, his silk stovepipe a black landmark for all to see. Close to him rode his younger squaw Mary, a striking woman, and with her their four-year-old son Dirk, a burly child like his father but with the warm dark features of his mother. The older squaw, Victoria, scouted lithely on the right flank, often ranging a mile or so from the party, and frequently out of sight. On the left flank, also far removed from the party, rode James Method, recruited by the guide because of his natural wilderness skill and keenly observant eyes. On occasion Mister Skye himself rode ahead to the crest of a hill or beyond, looking for surprises and finding none.

The Reverend Cecil J. B. Rathbone, observing all this as he walked beside his lead yoke of oxen, found himself satisfied by it. Mister Skye was not for a moment careless, and ceaselessly maintained a casual but potent discipline in his entourage. Cecil was a happy man. With each step he came closer to bringing Light to the benighted Blackfeet, a tribe that had fascinated him since his youth because of its ferocious and warlike ways.

Sometimes Esmerelda trudged beside Cecil, lightening the load in the heavy wagon. She had become as expert with the bullwhip as he, and could often relieve him for a spell when he grew weary. She didn't exactly share Cecil's dreams—what woman would?—but wherever Cecil went, she would go too, and enjoy herself if she possibly could. If she could no longer entertain women in sewing circles and reading societies, why, she'd have the Blackfeet wives over for tea and talk. And perhaps slip into the gossip a word or two about the faith, and the joy, and important things of life and death. She might be middle-aged, but she knew she had a gem in Cecil Rathbone, and her constant concern for his happiness and comfort was a pillar of her life.

The three yoke of oxen tugged a heavy load, the stuff of Cecil's dreams, for in addition to the necessaries of the trail, they hauled a new one-bottom plow, scythe and sickle, and seed—corn, wheat, oats, and all the things he supposed he would need to teach the Blackfeet about farming and turn them into civilized sons of the soil. It pleased him, that vision, and he had chosen his supplies with care. He even included apple and cherry saplings that would spring into an orchard, grape cuttings for a vineyard, and in the loose herd behind, two milch cows for butter and cheese and cream. These things, leading to a settled agricultural life, would be the salvation of the

Blackfeet, and wean them from their warlike ways. As they grew more pastoral, their minds would open to God, he hoped. Thus it pleased Cecil Rathbone to haul this precious cargo across an unknown continent, and he guarded this special load as carefully as if it were the Ark of the Covenant.

Cecil's wagon was a small one with upright bows, but the Newtons' wagon, directly behind, was larger, with flared sideboards and bows that overhung the box fore and aft, similar to the majestic Conestoga, but smaller. Henrietta was hauling furniture, unwilling to part with it for the sake of the oxen. Cecil knew that only the mercy of abundant grass this unusual year, keeping the trail-worn oxen in tolerable shape, made it possible to haul that highboy and bedstead and little pump organ. Alex guided his oxen grimly, unrelieved by Henrietta, who mostly lounged inside the wagon or perched on its front seat. Cecil gave him credit for that: it wasn't Alex's nature to walk across a continent beside slow oxen, but he was doing it. Cecil felt faintly ashamed of his own Henrietta. He resolved to speak to her at a proper moment.

Behind the Newtons came the mule-drawn carriage driven by Silas Potter, and carrying the small supplies that he and James Method required. And behind them rolled the Samples' wagon, pulled by three span of big mules. Alice usually drove, handling the jerkline running to the fractious mules as easily as Clay. Their children on foot, as well as Clay on horseback, brought up the rear, herding the loose stock along. They had one spare yoke of oxen, and one spare span of mules among the loosely herded animals. It seemed a good arrangement, Cecil thought, and one that Mister Skye had insisted on.

But that was not the whole of the party, Cecil knew. There remained the alien presence of Father Kiley, the blackrobed Jesuit, in one sense a colleague, but in a more profound sense a rival and a menace. They rarely saw the man, for Skye had made him a hunter and scout. The priest's laden packhorse, following dutifully behind the guide's mules up near the younger squaw Mary, was the only concrete evidence, hour after sunny hour, of the presence of Rome. Cecil felt faintly envious: he would much rather have been out hunting—dangerous as it was in a high prairie that was home to the Sioux—than plodding along beside his lead oxen all the dusty hours of the day. Each day the priest had returned with meat. Once an antelope, and twice doe mule deer, each shot with a single, well-placed bullet and—Cecil supposed—only after a careful survey of the surrounding hills.

Mister Skye knew men, Cecil thought, and it was quite shrewd to keep the priest out beyond the horizons, where his presence would not fester in the minds of the Newtons and Silas Potter, or—Cecil admitted—in himself. For he scorned the Romish persuasion and all its ritual and arrogance, and he scorned above all this order of Kiley's, the Jesuits, that had been so merciless as the soldiers of the pope. He thought of Kiley as an emissary from the old world, a power that had no rightful place in this new one that freemen were creating here on a virgin continent. Still, Cecil thought, the priest had been civil enough, almost a shadow in the evening campfires, withdrawn and buried in his breviary while the long June light held. The truth of it was that he'd like to try his theology on the man, and taste the priest's—but he doubted that Father Kiley would seriously consider any of the ideas that Cecil entertained, and would dismiss him as a heretic. Well, Cecil thought tartly, maybe the Jesuit was the heretic.

It grew hot. Cecil wondered how the priest stood the dry, furnacelike winds in his black broadcloth and tight white collar. Cecil sweated freely in the June sun, his own suitcoat off and great dark patches spreading under his armpits. The oxen slavered and foamed, and sweated heavily over their shoulders, where the cruel wooden yokes dug into their flesh. Far above, an eagle circled, and then glided toward a hazy horizon. The bronze prairie had grown rugged and rocky, cut defiantly by the swift and murky Platte.

Esmerelda joined him, matching his stride with hers, looking cooler in her brown dress and numerous petticoats than he felt wearing half as much. It was her thinness, he supposed.

"You look done in," she said. "I'll drive for a while; lend me the whip. You go fetch a cup from the cask. It's still cool."

"I believe I will."

She took the bullwhip. "Gee!" she cried. "Giddap!" She cracked the whip smartly, producing an expert pop. The weary oxen tugged a bit harder.

She grinned ruefully at Cecil. "The teamsters have a much better vocabulary," she said. "Sometimes I am envious."

"You probably learned it from me."

He stood gratefully while two yoke of oxen passed by and the wagon rattled up, and then found the dipper and lifted mildly alkaline water from the river to his lips. He was filled with the impulse to thank God for water, the succor of life itself. Refreshed, he waited quietly for Alex and his lead yoke, and then paced amiably beside his sweaty son-in-law.

"Henrietta has the heatsickness," Alex said. "She's

resting. I've never known such heat. You'd think Skye would stop and have mercy on the beasts. Look at the poor creatures."

The unfortunate oxen that were dragging Henrietta, her organ and other furniture, were indeed in trouble, their tongues lolling out and spraying foam as they went. They were dehydrated, Cecil judged. Normally three yoke of oxen could walk, rather than pull. The pulling had exhausted them. But so heavy was the Newtons' wagon that these three yoke never stopped pulling, and Cecil doubted that even four yoke could walk and not strain into their wooden collars. How the beasts had survived this long he couldn't imagine.

"And what does Skye do? He sends that papist priest out on easy hunts when the man could be helping, spelling us, doing his share. I say we should get rid of Skye. This trail's ten yards wide and smooth as a turnpike. Don't see as we need a guide . . ."

Cecil nodded. It was talk. The Reverend Alexander Newton knew perfectly well that soon enough they'd leave the trail and plunge into land known only by mountain men and guides, and still terra incognita to the United States Army.

"Even if the road was clear all the way to Sun River, we'd need Skye, or one like him, to deal with the Indians," Cecil said.

"We can hire someone else. Go on to the Platte River crossing and find someone else, and be done with this devilish bigamist and his wanton women and the half-breed brat. It's a scandal."

Cecil nodded cheerfully. Let the man talk, as long as they were plodding steadily toward the land of the Blackfeet.

"And that priest . . . I've been talking with Silas about

it. We think you're playing with fire, Cecil. There are things that godly people don't accept; lines to be drawn. We've stepped across those lines, Cecil, and we can expect the wrath of God upon us. This devilish heat is just the beginning. I say we meet tonight after supper, and vote on it. I think the Samples are with me. I'm sure Henrietta is. James isn't; he is much taken with that barbarian, but he doesn't count."

"If there is a vote, his will be recorded," said Cecil sharply.

They had been climbing slightly, and now they struck a long downgrade into a broad coulee that stretched down toward the Platte. The gulch looked dry now, but could carry a heavy wash when it rained. And down below, the trail dropped into a rocky white streambed, twisted sharply and scaled the far side of the coulee at an angle. Cecil hastened forward to relieve Esmerelda, for steep slopes were tricky and dangerous. Now, instead of dragging the deadweight of the wagons, the oxen would act as brakes, especially the wheel oxen, whose yoke supported the wagon tongue between them. These beasts in particular bore the looming weight of the wagon pressing behind them. Cecil pulled a heavy chain from the wagon box and rough-locked a rear wheel by running the chain between the spokes and hooking it to the undercarriage so that the wheel skidded rather than rotated. With a wheel skidding, the looming wagon no longer pressured the faltering oxen. Sometimes it became necessary to chain some sort of drag, usually a log, behind the wagon to slow its descent or attach a special clawed shoe to the locked wheel. But Cecil judged that the grade would be soft enough this time to handle with a rough lock and the slowest possible traverse.

Esmerelda plucked up another chain and headed for

the off side, where she could slip it between the spokes in an emergency, while Cecil gazed at her fondly. Through this whole trip she had been everywhere, contributing quietly to the well-being of all. There was scarcely time to wonder how Alexander was faring, or to hasten Henrietta out of that wagon in case it broke loose. But even as Cecil worried, he saw Mister Skye sitting aboard that terrible horse beside the trail, his gaze raking Cecil's wagon first, and then fixing upon the Newtons'.

"Your wagon's overloaded, mate."

Alex did not deign to answer.

"Lock a wheel while you can."

"I beg you to remember who is employer and who is employee," said Alex irritably.

Skye ignored him and addressed Henrietta, perched on the front seat. "You'd better get off and walk now, and be prepared to lock the wheels."

"I don't know about such things," she replied shortly.

The lead oxen were heading downslope now, the heavy wagon perched on the crest of the grade. Reluctantly Henrietta descended and began to trudge through the fierce heat. Then the groaning wagon rolled onto the downgrade, and pressed at once against the weary oxen, making them mince and drag their hoofs in the dust.

Mister Skye watched, but said nothing.

The locked wheel on Cecil's wagon proved to be the right medicine, and he negotiated the grade successfully. It bottomed with a sharp drop into a sandy streambed, and careened up an equally sharp rise on the far side, even as the trail twisted to the right to traverse the opposite grade obliquely. On the upgrade, past the turn, he unlocked the rear wheel and hung the chain back on its pegs, even as he grew aware that the Newtons' wagon was rolling downslope too fast, the trembling wheel oxen barely holding back their burden. Swiftly Cecil whipped his lead oxen forward, making room on the upslope, and then ran back to the gully to help if he could. The Newtons' wagon was not out of control, but neither was it descending at a safe speed. He saw Henrietta throw a small wooden chock in front of a rear wheel. The wagon tilted, slowed, and then righted itself as the iron wheel rolled over the chock. Then they hit the sandy bottoms, the front wheels bouncing sharply as they dropped into sand, even as the weary lead oxen whipped to the right to ascend the far bank and the angling grade beyond.

The tongue snapped as it was yanked violently to the right. The heavy wagon careened a few more feet into the sand and stopped. The three yoke of oxen, dragging the broken tongue, trotted a few feet up the far grade and stopped, trembling and slavering. The Reverend Alex Newton, red of face but containing his temper, stood staring at the wreckage. Cecil sighed. Mister Skye rode close, surveyed the damage silently, and rode upslope toward his own packmules and the waiting Mary. There he slid off Jawbone, opened a pack, extracted a heavy axe, and rode down the coulee toward the Platte a quarter of a mile distant. There were cottonwoods along its bank.

He will cut a new tongue, Cecil thought. Clay Sample arrived, toting his mechanic's box, and began at once to unbolt the tongue fragment.

"We're lucky the kingpin didn't go," he said as he loosened the shattered piece from the hounds.

"This wouldn't have happened if you had helped us at the top," snapped Henrietta.

Clay paused to stare at her.

"I am sure that Clay had his own problems, Henrietta,"

Cecil said hastily. "It was up to you and Alex to handle your wagon."

For an answer she clambered into the tilting wagon and pulled the flaps shut.

Cecil stood. "Let us thank God the matter isn't worse," he said gently. This bickering of godly people shamed him.

"It's another warning," cried Silas Potter. "When we traffic with devils, we must expect this and worse."

"Where's James? Why isn't he here helping?" demanded Alex.

Cecil spotted James on the distant ridgetop, sitting easily, rifle across his saddle. And on the rear ridge was gaunt Victoria. The pair of them were their sentries out upon the prairie, now that they were caught in these coulee bottoms.

"Guarding us well, I believe," said Cecil mildly.

"He's loafing is what he is. Turning lazy on us, thanks to your Mister Skye."

Clay Sample hammered the last bolt, and Cecil pounded the splintered tongue free. "Cottonwood won't make much of a tongue, but it's what we have," Clay said as he rolled out from under the wagon. From down on the Platte came the whacks of methodical chopping as Mister Skye felled a cottonwood limb. While they waited for him, Esmerelda circulated among them with a dipper of cool water.

"Alex," said Cecil, "you might profitably drive your yoke down to the river for a drink. Here. I'll help you unhitch the tongue."

"I was just going to," snapped Alex. Together they drove the tired animals down to the riverbank and let them drink their fill. Mister Skye had dropped a well-chosen limb, and was clipping the branches off of it.

"We're just in time to drag that back," Cecil said.

Skye nodded. Sweat blackened his buckskin shirt. He stared long and hard at Alex, but said nothing. Then his gaze roamed the ridges, settling first on James, and then on Victoria, until he seemed satisfied that nothing was amiss. The priest was nowhere in sight.

Mister Skye's silence seemed somehow even worse than his occasional snarls. When the guide issued his quiet commands, the whole party understood him and obeyed. But this silence! It made Cecil shiver. Who knew what somber thoughts Skye was entertaining? The things he did not say to Alex Newton—or perhaps himself—screamed in Cecil's ears.

They chained the cottonwood log to the tugs, and a red-faced Alex Newton hawed the three yoke back up the coulee. In two more hours Clay Sample had expertly barked and squared the limb, hewed it into shape, and bored the bolt holes through it with his auger and bit. In another hour the new tongue was bolted in place and the oxen hooked up. The mishap had cost them half a day, and Cecil supposed they'd camp soon, as they strained their way up the long grade and out upon the high plains again, driving straight into a low and blinding sun.

He worried about the evening's camp. There'd likely be blame and temper, and somehow the whole trouble would be laid to Mister Skye and Mary and Victoria— and the priest. God spare us that, he thought. He intended to use a strong hand if he must, and resort to his rare rebukes. High time this surly group looked up to the great heavens and thanked the good Lord for this Mister Skye.

The supper hour came and went, but Skye pushed on, and they followed in sullen silence. They were all trail-hardened, having come seven hundred miles across empty prairie, and they endured it quietly. Then at last they descended a long grade into the bottoms of the Platte, and a halt was called close to the river. The oxen and mules and horses were set out to graze, with young Alfred Sample detailed to keep an eye on them, and the surrounding hills. Later the beasts would be driven into a rope corral which Skye had devised, with the three wagons and the buggy forming its four corners. That was familiar to them too. In the larger train from Independence the wagons had been formed into a defensive circle each night, and the animals kept within, to keep them from the cunning hands of Omaha and Pawnee horse thieves.

Even as the party plunged wearily into its evening tasks, Father Kiley rode in, this time with the tongue and hump ribs of a buffalo cow wrapped in canvas behind the saddle on his nervous bay horse. There would be a treat for all when the tender hump meat was done. The priest gave meat to Alice Sample and Esmerelda, who did much of the cooking because Henrietta felt indisposed. The rest of the meat he gave to Mary and Victoria, for Skye's mess, which was also his own. He smiled quietly, walked off to the river to wash, and seemed to vanish into the dusk from whence he had appeared minutes before.

When at last the meat had browned and the keen fragrance of dripping fat on the fire wafted through the evening air, Cecil drew them together and blessed the food and praised God for this abundance. Skye, Mary and Victoria, and the priest ate separately, but on this occasion he stood beside the Reverend Mister Rathbone during his grace.

"We're at Bridger's Crossing," Mister Skye said abruptly. "This is where we leave the Oregon Trail. The crossing is no easy matter. The water's high and we may have to build rafts. Or tack canvas or hide over the beds of the wagons and float them. Either way, we have work ahead. From now on, there's no trail. If you insist on taking these wagons, we'll shovel our way down every cutbank, and shovel our way up the other side." He paused, staring at Alex Newton. "Your wagon is overloaded, mate," he continued. "I don't know what's in it, but this is where it stays. We're going out upon a land with no trails, with rocks and holes and gulleys. That wagon won't last ten miles. Your worn-out oxen even less. That ballast must go or we capsize."

"I brought my pump organ, bedstead and highboy seven hundred miles and I'm not going to surrender them now," Henrietta Newton retorted shrilly. "The organ is for the church. I play it; that's my gift to God and the people we will redeem. If it stays on this riverbank, then I . . . why, I must stay."

Mister Skye didn't argue. He walked back to his own fire, where Mary and Victoria and the priest were waiting.

"It's come to a head," whispered Silas Potter. "Now we will free ourselves of that barbarian."

Chapter 5

Silas Potter quietly disapproved of the Reverend Cecil J. B. Rathbone. And Esmerelda Rathbone too. The pair of them were too lax, too spiritually loose, to command an important mission. He had his doubts about the entire mission, and particularly about Rathbone's plan to show the Blackfeet pastoral ways and turn them into civilized and educated farmers before stressing the Gospels.

Silas had been hired as a lay teacher, to instruct the savages in grammar and arithmetic, in reading and writing, and science and the wisdom of Western civilization. That was all well and good, he thought: he had a bachelor's degree that proclaimed his ability to do so. But he also had a year of divinity school, and he regarded himself as a keeper of the faith, destined to celebrate its orthodoxy and drive out heresies and bad thinking. And in his estimation, Cecil Rathbone was trafficking with evil now.

Grudgingly he respected Father Kiley, for he saw in the Jesuit his counterpart, the pope's soldier enforcing the faith. Of course they were corrupt and wrong, those people, and Silas was careful not to carry the analogy too far. Nonetheless, he saw himself as the Methodist Jesuit, his mission to save other Methodists from weakness and sin, and keep the faith pure. Toward this end he studied the Scriptures assiduously, underlining passages, comparing texts. He knew that in theological debate he could be acid and biting, even withering in his contempt for those who strayed.

Potter was a humorless young man, thin and weak, not from illness—he was in blooming health—but because his scholarly life had cloistered him indoors, and his muscles had atrophied. He was fair, and could burn to a crisp in minutes under a summer sun, and this had always been his rationale for avoiding the great outside. At least until now. He wore a broad-brimmed flat hat that kept the sun off his face, and under it small rimless glasses that gave him the distant vision he lacked. Even protected by the hat, his face had grown red and chapped under the fierce western sun and wind.

Unlike the Newtons, who indulged their corpulent flesh and foisted off the labor of the trail on others as much as possible, Silas did his share without complaint, being careful to go a shade beyond what was required of him as a matter of virtue and general principle; he considered sloth a sin. His helpfulness was not inspired by any sympathy for the burdens on others, such as the Samples, but by a sense of sublime duty. To do his share and more was virtue, and the virtuous were close to God. So in all matters he acted with care. He treated James Method cordially, as was his duty. Not that he, a considerable scholar, had anything in common with James, an escaped slave. But Method was a child of God, and therefore worthy of proper treatment. And so the pair of them shared a tent and wagon amicably and politely, though they could scarcely be called friends.

He addressed others gravely, often blinking behind his glasses. So far he had not been smitten by a woman, though he was not immune to their attractions. That had been a matter that troubled him terribly, and led him into moments of secret despair. For in the night he sometimes lusted, vague images of feminine faces floating through his mind, young women he had seen once, or met a time or two. Worse, in the night his mind turned to their figures, the exquisite forms beneath their petticoats and skirts, and he knew this to be lust and of a devilish nature, for all the appetites of the flesh were, in his eyes, sinful and only the things of the spirit were of God. He prayed he might be free of his body; that it might become an inert thing so that his soul could enjoy the pure rapture of the spirit. He did not perceive these lusts to be the natural hungers of a young man, but rather an alien appetite instilled by the devil, and many a time, startled awake out of his lustful dreams, he prayed fervently for release from the devil, who plainly possessed him or a part of him, and was his private torment.

This had happened two nights in a row. His mind, half asleep, had entertained visions of Skye's young squaw Mary, dark and comely and voluptuous in the loose buckskins she wore. She never braided her lustrous blue-black hair, but let it fall loose over her shoulders and breasts. Her brown eyes were as warm and inviting as a doe's. From time to time she had looked thoughtfully at Silas, sizing him up. She had stared with equal curiosity and intuition at the other white males, but Silas was certain that he had somehow galvanized her particular interest, and that her interests were wanton. Certainly she had smiled at him, and had been careless in her dress, often revealing her young honey-colored arms and neck and graceful shoulders to him. Perhaps later she would become stocky, as so many of her people did, but now she looked lithe and supple and a man's dream of fleshly paradise. And cheerful as well, with shy smiles toward them all, and adoration in her eyes when she gazed at Mister Skye, which Silas often caught her doing, to his annoyance.

Brazenly she rode her horse astride, exposing smooth knees, a portion of female limb that Silas had never seen. It had made his heart pound. In the night, tossing in his bedroll, he had imagined himself performing the marital act, the sacred business, with her, she beneath him wide-eyed and smiling. It was too much. Trembling, he had awakened and walked through the camp under the icy stars, to purge himself. Now, he knew, he must drive Skye, his dark concubines, and that whore of Rome out of this place, for the sake of them all, or surely God in his wrath would turn this trip into a journey through hell.

Now the chance had come. Skye had issued an ultimatum of sorts about Henrietta Newton's furniture—even the pump organ, which would grace the little church they would erect on Sun River! There would have to be a meeting, apart from the demonic ears of Mister Skye and his women and that priest. And they had to overrule Cecil Rathbone. If not, if the head missionary persisted, Silas intended to take the dissidents—himself, probably the Samples, and surely the Newtons—back to Fort Laramie. They could establish a mission right there in the safe lee of the fort, and there would be work enough for ten missionaries among the soldiers and the lost creatures of Squaw Town. That might be better anyway than this wild plunge into a frightening wilderness to minister to a tribe noted for its ferocity and evil.

After their buffalo hump supper, Silas had demanded a private meeting of the mission group. Surprisingly, Cecil obliged at once: they would gather after the dishes had been washed and the chores done, beyond the herd along the riverbank. Cecil even volunteered to tell Mister Skye of it, and that it would be confined to the missionary party.

In a lavender twilight they gathered quietly, except for the Sample children who had slipped into their bedrolls.

"Pray, what is on your mind, Silas?" asked Cecil amiably. His very kindness enraged Potter. Why couldn't the man simply be unreasonable, instead of merely wrong?

"Some of us feel it's time for changes," he began tartly, his fevered eyes focusing on one and another of them. "Henrietta has brought her organ seven hundred miles, and there is no reason to abandon it now. It's unbearable, this instrument we have brought so far to praise God with song, lying here on the trail, to be smashed to bits by savages.

"Another thing. We must dismiss this wicked and sinful guide and his concubines, and rid ourselves of that priest. We are trafficking in evil. Skye will start wars, murder redmen whenever we meet them. I despise the Jesuit, but he and his kind have roamed the far west in their black robes, unarmed, and have had little trouble with the savages. We don't need guides like Skye. We must establish our peaceful and friendly intent and trust in Divine Providence instead of murderous weapons."

He turned nervously to James Method, wondering whether the African would carry tales back to Skye. "Most of us oppose your policies, Cecil. Perhaps we have more faith than you. We believe we can carry that organ to Sun River, and the rest of Henrietta's furniture too. And we wish to do it without Skye. The longer we keep him near, the more we provoke God and invite his wrath. Already there have been signs, the unnatural heat, the snapped wagon tongue. Much worse might come if we persist in our faithless ways."

There settled an uneasy silence. Silas knew he had not minced words.

"Why, perhaps you're right," said Cecil. "Let us take a silent moment to seek guidance, eh?"

Silas did not pray. He raged at the senior missionary for being all too accommodating. He wanted matters to shatter right then and there, so that he and the Newtons could turn around and head for Fort Laramie, and holy work there.

Then Cecil said, "Alex, how do you and Henrietta feel about this?"

"Why, perhaps Silas has stated it a bit strongly. But something must be done. We would grieve to abandon the organ, and the few small amenities we have hauled so far, through such a terrible wilderness. And of course Skye and the priest trouble us. He parades his sinfulness before our eyes. And issues commands as if we were his servants. Frankly, Cecil, we think he's loathsome. Surely there are other guides within reach."

"Clay?" asked the Reverend Mister Rathbone.

"Well, I tell you. We're doing right fine, except some overworked, I reckon. Seems like Mister Skye has got us this far safely. I figure he's right about that extra weight."

Silas Potter felt betrayed. The trouble with those yeoman farmers was that they never thought for themselves.

"James?"

The black eyed the others nervously, He was not used to being consulted, and it plainly troubled him. "Ah feel safe as a frog on a lilypad with Mister Skye keeping track. If he says we should lighten up the loads, I guess that's what we should do."

Silas had expected that. The half-civilized African had little sense of sin or virtue, goodness or evil.

"Henrietta?"

"I have no intention of abandoning that organ. Or anything else," she said. "Except maybe this hare-brained trip to nowhere. I wish to return to Fort Laramie. There's work for us there."

Silas Potter felt delighted. He had primed her to say that. Cecil J. B. Rathbone cocked an eyebrow when he heard his most cherished dream being called hare-brained by his own daughter, but he showed no other sign of distress.

"Alice?"

She smiled, making dimples in her cheeks. "I'm in the middle, I guess. I think Mister Skye is really a comfort. But if he's objectionable in some way . . ." her voice trailed off. "I know how much the furniture means to Mrs. Newton," she added, folding and unfolding her hands.

Silas smiled. The woman would accept any course of action.

"And my dear Esmerelda?"

"Why I was thinking we might redistribute things between the wagons, and then Henrietta and Alex could keep the furniture." Mrs. Rathbone's practical bent irritated Silas. Compromisers always ended up compromising their faith.

But Cecil picked up on it. "Well, there's something to it. The wagons are lighter than when we left Independence. Lots of food used up. Suppose we work something out. Mister Skye's quite right, the Newtons won't get ten miles with that load going overland. I imagine, Henrietta, if you abandoned the heavy highboy, and we and the Samples divided the bedstead between us, and we put a hundred pounds or so of the Newtons' supplies on one of the spare mules, we might make a stab at it—"

"I will not surrender anything," snapped Henrietta. "Least of all the highboy."

"My dear, your oxen are near collapse. The spare yoke we've been rotating are trailworn too, gaunted down. There's really not much—"

"If we have faith we'll perform miracles," said Silas Potter.

"Perhaps we could slow down and let the animals graze more. Maybe five miles a day," suggested Alex Newton.

Cecil Rathbone sighed. "It is almost July. We are only halfway. Seven or eight hundred miles more, I reckon. At five miles a day, we'd arrive at Sun River in late November. A northern wilderness devoid of shelter, in late November. It'll be bad enough making a road up there . . ."

Agitated, he paced back and forth, hands clasped behind him. Then he halted.

"We will unload the furniture here. All of it. Perhaps

Mister Skye will help us cache it so we can recover it later. There must be ways. Then we'll redouble our efforts. If the oxen tire, we'll abandon a wagon, too. If the oxen die—and they might—we'll pack what we can. We'll do what we must."

Cecil stared at them, waiting for them to defy him and his authority as the senior missionary. No one did.

"Mister Skye is our safe passage across this wild land. Indeed, his conduct is deplorable, and one bridles at his ah . . . peculiar marital circumstances and all the rest. But he's a man, a man to get us through. As for the priest, he's not our business. He's supplied our meat and has been an able scout, keeping watch. He'll be leaving us anyway, on the Yellowstone. I pray that you accept these matters, and tomorrow we'll be on our way."

He was done, then. Silas fashioned a riposte in the silence and nerved himself to begin.

"No," he said. He hated the shrillness of his own voice, which seemed to echo across the murky river to the brown bluffs beyond.

"Unless we discharge Skye and proceed with the furniture, the Newtons and I are going to return to Fort Laramie. They need us there, a mission to the soldiers and the lost souls of Squaw Town. I'm sure the Samples will join us, too. There in the safe valley of the Platte."

"I see," said Cecil slowly. He looked melancholy for a moment, but then he brightened. "Sleep on it, and we'll discuss it in the morning."

"A night won't change anything," Silas cried. "We won't traffic with evil."

Cecil stared at his daughter and son-in-law, and they looked away. He glanced at the Samples, who seemed caught and unable to decide what to do. And then a sadness settled upon the old minister's craggy face. "Perhaps

Esmerelda and James and I might go on . . . if James is willing. I have a dream. A dream of a peaceful land, of a people finding God's grace, of farms and fat cattle and tall haystacks and young Blackfeet building a new world . . ."

Nothing more was said, or needed to be said. As the shattered party trudged back to its camp, Silas Potter felt pleased. It had been so easy. James Method walked beside him, back to the tent they shared.

"Reckon we'll be saying goodbye come morning," he said softly. "Ah'm a man to stay with Mister Skye. And with the Rathbones."

They stood quietly, watching the Samples gather the grazing herd together to contain it for the night in the rope corral. The animals had had less time to graze this evening because Mister Skye had pressed on, almost to sunset. But they were docile, having watered at the riverbank and spread out over the lush grass of the bottoms. Jawbone was not among them. Skye kept that violent animal separate, close to his lodge, where he usually grazed all night. Even in the dusk Silas could see that the oxen and mules looked gaunted. All the more reason to return to Fort Laramie, he thought tartly. Then the last of the stock drifted inside the rope, and Alfred tied the line tautly to the Samples' wagon.

A milch cow bawled once. A horse nickered, and then silence settled. Silas stood outside the tent—he needed to make water but never did so until the others were retired, out of some natural delicacy—and admired the long streak of blue light riding the northwestern horizon, slightly sawtoothed to suggest that there were mountains there, far across the brooding and mysterious high plains. Then he found the moment to relieve himself, and turned in. James Method was already asleep in his roll, breathing through his open mouth. The ground felt hard, but at least dry, and Silas refused to complain. Complaining was an act of self-indulgence. Eight nights, coming across the plains, they had made a wet camp, and set their bedrolls down in soft, cold, damp ground that moistened his blankets and numbed him. Two of those nights had been pouring rain, and there had been nothing for it but to shiver in his sopping roll, and pray for a warm dawn.

He drifted into a troubled sleep. The bare earth always kept him restless, and not even the exertions of the trail, day after weary day, brought him the kind of oblivion at night that he craved. He began to dream again, the sinful images of Mister Skye's squaw, warm-skinned and voluptuous, drifting through his misted soul. She laughed and invited and beckoned, and he grew tempted, though a stern voice from heaven itself warned him, warned him not to surrender—

A rush of hoofs on grass outside his tent awakened him. Then the thunder of a small stampede, squealing horses, bawling oxen, braying mules. And then a piercing "Hiyah, hiyah," the nasal cry less human than animal, and harsh as wilderness. And then a booming shot. The rattle of other shots. A harsh zip as something seared through the canvas above him. Another boom, and Mister Skye's roar, and the crackle of the lighter rifles of the squaws. And then silence.

Silas Potter quaked in his robes. "You all right?" came the soft slur of James. "We been having our stock stole."

Stock? In horror now, Silas pulled his wire-rimmed spectacles over his ears, and peered out, fearing the bash of a tomahawk cleaving his brain. But it was quiet. Dawn light streaked the east, and he supposed it might be four or five, this time of year. In the murky gray light he searched for the stock. He could see not an animal. The corral ropes curled on the grass between the wagons.

Every ox, every mule and horse, were gone. He knew instantly what had happened: this was God's punishment upon them for employing Mister Skye. This was exactly what he had warned of, the wrath of God, leaving them out here in these gray wastes, helpless, abandoned, without so much as a pony to take them back to Fort Laramie.

He spotted Cecil standing beside his wagon, disheveled and shocked, in his bare feet and nightshirt.

"I told you so," cried Silas. "I warned you."

Then the rest were up, carrying rifles, nightshirts stuffed into britches, women peering modestly from the puckerstring holes of their wagons. And not a horse in sight.

Out of the gray murk Mister Skye loomed, in his buckskins and some moccasins, oddly calm although his shining new Sharps was crooked in his arm at the ready.

"Gone! The thieving redskins stole our stock," cried Alex in his grating nasal voice.

"We'll get them back," said Skye quietly.

"And how do you propose to do that?" snapped Silas. "Every animal we possess has been stolen. Why weren't you guarding?"

Skye looked surprised. "Should we have posted a guard? Aren't we on a peaceful journey, our intent plain to others? Would you have stood guard, you and Mister Method, and Mister Newton, and Mister Sample, and Mister Rathbone, two hours in the middle of each night? Ready and willing, of course, to shoot raiding Indians on sight?"

"You didn't ask us. You're incompetent as well as immoral."

From beyond the far hills came an unearthly whinny, and Barnaby Skye smiled.

Chapter 6

The neighing had sounded like the cry of a ghost horse cantering across the sky, but Mister Skye knew it was Jawbone. He could see very little. The sun had not yet torn loose from the shoulders of the prairie to the east, and the gray gloom obscured the terraced bluffs to the south of the river, that still rose step by step into pale night, miles of dark grasses.

The missionary party looked stricken. They wandered disconsolately from wagon to wagon, wagons that seemed anchored to earth like frigates without canvas rocking at the end of a hawser. In a moment of time these schooners had turned into useless hulks. The priest emerged from his small tent, dressed in black as usual, but without his white collar. He had started a beard, and now the red stubble blurred his jawline and made him look disheveled. He stared at the empty animal compound, saw that his horses, too, had been taken, and then trudged toward the river to begin his ablutions.

Again they heard that terrible shriek, the scream of the ghost horse clattering over the clouds of heaven, making the grassy hills cringe into their rocky bones.

"What was that?" cried Alex Newton.

"Your salvation," rumbled Skye.

"I have never heard a sound so . . . demonic," said the Reverend Rathbone.

Mister Skye laughed. "It's from the devil, all right."

Cecil drew himself up. "Well, Mister Skye, what are we to do? We are marooned in this sea of grass, as surely as sailors on a sandy isle."

"March back to Fort Laramie," snapped Silas Potter.

"I warned you of God's wrath. I warned you! Now we have no choice but to walk whatever it is, seventy, a hundred miles."

"More like a Cheyenne horse-stealing party, mate, than the wrath of God. Four or five of them. Not enough to slaughter us in our beds, but enough to snatch a few horses."

"You may see worldly events as merely that, Skye, but I see God's purpose in all things."

"It's Mister Skye, mate."

James Method grinned.

"We need a miracle," Silas Potter said, "and I doubt that you'll supply one."

"We do need that," Cecil agreed somberly. "We are a long way from anywhere. And with women and children in our party."

The northeastern horizon, far across the Platte, vibrated with golden light now, and then the top of the sun emerged like a golden caterpillar crawling along the far blue ridges, throwing long light, slats of fire, across the wide land and into the western dark.

Now Skye saw them, five tiny gold coins cantering over the crest of a hazy ridge miles away, and off to the left, a sixth shining coin he knew, even from that vast expanse, was Jawbone. Then his horse stopped and neighed once again, closer this time, like the shriek of werewolves.

"What *is* that dreadful sound?" cried Henrietta.

It drew their eyes to its source, and now the six running animals became visible, tiny dots of light, now in sight, now plunging into blue coulees not yet lit by the horizontal sun. Closer they came, while mortals stared, fascinated, by the flight, and by the skillful herding of the giant blue roan that drove the rest.

"I don't suppose that's miracle enough for you, mate," said Mister Skye, addressing Silas Potter.

The young man paled. "The Scriptures say that evil spirits can perform wonders."

"Some devil," said Cecil acidly.

Then the animals clambered down a steep slope into the river bottom. They were, precisely, Mister Skye's own creatures: Jawbone, the two giant black mules, and the three wiry Indian ponies. Those, and no other.

Then at last they stood, sweated dark and trembling from long miles of running, while Jawbone slavered and heaved.

"It looks like any miracles you come up with are strictly for yourself, Mister Skye," Alex Newton said.

He ignored the remark. "Start to tar or canvas the wagon boxes," he said. "Get a move on now. We're going to float them across soon."

They gaped at him.

"Get along with you," he growled. "Have faith."

Victoria and Mary slipped horsehair bridles onto two ponies, and led them toward Skye's lodge.

Jawbone stood panting, legs stiff and head lowered. Skye walked to the great horse, who pressed his head into the guide's chest, while the man ran his thick hands down the great roan's knotted neck, beneath his mane. It was a reunion. "Aye, you did it again, lad," whispered Mister Skye into Jawbone's ragged ear. The horse sucked air, and butted him gently.

"Who might they have been, sir?" Cecil asked.

Skye shrugged. "Cheyenne most likely. Sioux. Arapaho."

He hurried toward his lodge, Jawbone following of his own accord, breathing more quietly now. Skye hated to put the sweat-stained animal to work, but there was no helping it. He dropped the apishamore over Jawbone's back, and then the light pad saddle of the Crow people over it, and cinched it tight, and clambered aboard.

The missionaries had done nothing, only gaped at him as he steered Jawbone southward, up the layered land and out of the Platte Valley, into a choppy sea of grass. He was in no hurry, and let the blue horse pick its way easily, resting at a walk. Now the long sun gilded the grasses, cutting shadowed trenches in the prairie, glowing off east-facing bluffs.

Southward he rode, his new rifle cradled loose in his arms, his vision on horizons that receded before him like the very curve of the earth. The oxen would not be far, he knew. They could lumber along only a little, and then would have fallen behind. He hoped only that the horse-stealing party hadn't stopped to slaughter them, driving arrows into the hearts of the white men's buffalo. As for the mules, they'd run longer, be farther along before dropping out, unless the raiders made a point of keeping them. But what warrior of the northern plains lusted for mules? In the end, the raiders would have the horses—the Jesuit's two, and the Methodists' four—the ones ridden by James Method, by Cecil, by Clay Sample, and the spare. He'd get those six too, if he could. They would be needed.

Now the sun brightened the great massif of the Medicine Bows to the west, the first great chain of the Rockies which would ultimately funnel the raiding party south, up and down vast ridges. This land close to the mountains reminded him more of the ocean than did the flatter prairies to the east, as if the mountains were tidal waves, and the great ridges the churning of the mutinous seas. He rode easily, at home in this stretching place. The seas had given him that.

He had been born in England in comfortable circumstances, his father a successful merchant trader who sent his barks to the ports of Portugal and Africa and back.

At the age of fourteen, looking ahead to a time at Cambridge and then his father's trading house, he had been idling near the company docks on the Thames when he was suddenly surrounded by several of His Majesty's sailors, rough sorts, who cornered him and pinned him easily.

"Why here's a powder monkey," said one. "Come along, matey."

And they had dragged him bodily, the boy sobbing and fighting, aboard the H.M.S. *Jaguar,* and down into its stinking cramped hold, into a brig so low he couldn't stand up. He never saw his family, or England, again. He didn't even see daylight, or the sun, until the frigate rode the sea, sailing south by southwest, bound for Portugal and a load of limes that the admiralty had belatedly employed to prevent dread scurvy, and on down the coast to South Africa.

A powder monkey he had become, and a roustabout who cleaned slop pails and scoured decks with holystone . . . and starved. For at the mess, larger and meaner men stole his food and laughed, and if he protested at all, cuffed him and sent him sprawling. No one cared, least of all those fancily dressed officers who captained the vessel and seemed to run it with terror and whip and the threat of bodily harm. He weakened and knew he would not last long, and as he performed his bitter chores, wrestling heavy kegs of acrid gunpowder up precarious passageways from the bowels of the ship to the upper decks where cannon filled each port, he did not know whether he cared to live at all. But some youthful spirit raged, a boyish will to live, and one day he walked to mess with a wooden belaying pin wrapped in a sack.

That time, when a particularly brutal sailor and bullyboy named Larch mocked him and grabbed at his gruel, he swung the pin and knocked Larch cold. They leapt on him in an instant, pulverizing him with their horny rope-scarred fists. Even in his weakened condition he clobbered one and another with the belaying pin before they pinned him to the deck and poured slop over him.

But after that no one stole his food. And slowly he filled out, grew burly and strong. There was a lesson in it. From that point on, win or lose—and he lost more often than he won—he fought whenever he felt himself trespassed. He became known as a brawler, and half the time he nursed injuries, a nose mashed and mashed again, torn ears, ripped flesh, bruised kneecaps where belaying pins had shattered them. The officers looked upon him with distaste, and sniffed at the young sailor, and never inquired into his origins or how he came to be aboard King George's vessel of war. He came to know the ship's foul brig intimately, and every cockroach in it. Those above him were called mister and sir and even lord, and wore clean clothing and slept in private quarters, and had property, while he slept in a miserable hammock in the pitching, rocking fo'castle and owned utterly nothing but his own body. Someday he would be mister, like his father, and unlike every humble tar grinding out life in the bowels of the ship.

They knew him for a potential deserter, and never let him off ship at port that first year. Later, when the Royal Navy plunged into the Kaffir War of 1819 against the native Xhosa, Barnaby Skye finally set foot on land, closely watched. He never forgot what it felt like to stand on solid earth, momentarily free from the tyrannical confines of the hull that had oppressed and degraded him. He would be free. The moment didn't come until 1826, when the H.M.S. *Jaguar* braved the dreaded bar of the Columbia River, on the far-off Pacific coast of North America, to visit the new Hudson Bay post, Fort Vancouver. There, in the fog, the powerful man Barnaby Skye had become jumped overboard carrying only a wooden belaying pin, and emerged, dripping, on the cold south bank of the river, in a disputed land the Americans were starting to call Oregon. That belaying pin was all he needed. All his years as a sailor he had brawled with one, and now he could throw it with such accuracy that he could kill small game, and defend himself with it, even against a man with a knife. He survived, found succor, and hated the land of his birth, though not entirely. And from that moment, he permitted no man to address him as Skye. He became Mister Skye, an awesome man of the mountains, harder and more daring than others, cautious, wily, but a terror in war. He soon led the fur brigades of Mister John Jacob Astor, and later Monsieur Pierre Chouteau of St. Louis, becoming, insensibly, a legend among the mountain men, and even more a legend among the Indian tribes that had the misfortune to run into him.

This vast continent was better than the sea. And he steered his own ship, Jawbone beneath him, down the plain trail of broken grasses, hoofprints, and excrement that marked the exodus of the missing animals. A party of young Cheyenne horse stealers, he thought, not knowing why he thought it. He had simply become so alive to the land, so attuned to its spirit and its wild people, that he knew without knowing why he knew.

The carcass of an oxen hulked on a rise, and when he drew close he recognized it as one of those worn hard by the Newtons. The last of its precarious energy had been consumed in this pell-mell run. Over the brow of the next divide he found two more, one dead, the other still alive, breath staggering in and out of its lungs spastically. He let it go. If it got to its feet soon, it might survive the wolves. If not, it might be eaten alive. Three gone. The trail ran relentlessly up and down ridges, crosswise of the water courses, so that he never knew what he would find as he topped each ridge. He held Jawbone to a walk, letting him rest after his long harsh run. He knew approximately what Jawbone had done, herding his own animals away from the flanking braves, and he knew what he might find ahead.

In the next long swale he found the oxen, still dark with sweat and dirtied over from rolling their soaked bodies in dust. Some lay on the ground; others stood still, head down, legs propped, refusing to sink to earth. One quiet one looked dead or dying. Four gone, two yoke. There in the same swale but farther down were the mules, which had lost ground to the fleeter horses. The run had been easier for them than for the oxen, and now they grazed. Six mules, all belonging to the Samples, all suffering no more than a winding.

Mister Skye did not stop, but let Jawbone carry him farther, over the brow of the next ridge. The trail grew smaller now, but still plain in the early sun, a path of bent and crushed grass leading ever southward. Now he could make sense of it, and thought there were about five raiders, five young warriors on their ponies, several miles ahead. From the crest of the ridge he stared down a long gravelly slope broken by outcrops of layered tan rock and occasional copses of cottonwoods. Jawbone pricked up his battered ears. There down the slope, near the bottom, lay a dark form on harsh fragmented shale rock. It looked human. Now Skye paused and scanned the wide land, dwelling particularly on the copses of cottonwoods and the rocky outcrops that might conceal other life. He took his time. He always took his time, and survived because of it. Beyond the form on the ground, the trail continued onward, broken grasses shining in the slanting sun, over the next long shoulder of sagebrush-covered land. Here is where it had happened; where Jawbone had fought his own war. The horse beneath him seemed to expand at the recollection, some evil pride making him mince as his rider eased him downhill, far more alert for trouble than previously.

It was a young Cheyenne, scarcely sixteen, Mister Skye thought, staring lifelessly at the sky. He had bled to death from a compound fracture of his right leg, and another of his right forearm. Cheyenne fletching of the arrows still in the quiver on the young man's back. Cheyenne warlock. Each tribe had its own way of making moccasins, and these were Cheyenne. Just above the boy's right ankle there were toothmarks, a circle of broken and bloody indentations in his smooth flesh. That was where Jawbone had thundered close and clamped his massive teeth over the leg and had yanked the youth to his doom. This was where Jawbone had made his move, while it remained almost dark and the copses of cottonwoods and the outcrops would enable him to drive Mister Skye's own horses and mules away from the running herd and kill the flanking Cheyenne boy on the left in the process, simultaneously clamping the boy's leg while lunging crazily into the Cheyenne pony, making it stagger and fall, pitching the boy off at a lope or even a gallop.

They might be back at any moment, looking for the boy. Skye walked Jawbone to a thick grove of cottonwoods forty yards distant, slid off Jawbone in deep shade, and waited. The boy had died an honorable death, young but in the midst of a successful horse raid. He would be honored in the lodge of his family, for there was no shame in the accident that killed him. Mister Skye settled down to wait, confident that the whole party would return. Jawbone stood like a gray ghost behind him, head low, dreaming his evil dreams in the shade.

Some while later—he didn't know how long exactly— the rest of the Cheyenne party rode cautiously over the far shoulder single file, looking for the missing boy. Two rode ahead, then the loose horses, and two behind driving them slowly. From the shoulder they spotted the dead boy and wound slowly into the bottoms, negotiating patches of shale and thickets of sagebrush. When they reached the body they stared, and pointed, and looked fearfully at the ridges and the glades, and began to sing sad songs. It saddened Skye as well. For all his brawling, and for all the death he had seen, the death of the boy still saddened him. The boy had probably died on his first horse-stealing raid, at the very dawn of his warrior life. Even as he had died at the very dawn of his own life as a Cambridge scholar and then a merchant in old England.

The boy's pony was missing. Perhaps Jawbone had demolished it, too. These young Cheyenne youth would recruit another horse, one of the stolen ones, to carry the sad burden back to their village. But Mister Skye would prevent that. The horses belonged to his clients. He slipped onto Jawbone quietly, and rode out of the thicket and was spotted at once. None of them had rifles, but they all swiftly nocked an arrow . . . and then lowered their bows. They knew. Most of the tribes of the plains knew of this man and this demon horse, with a medicine so evil it made them quake inside and hide their eyes from the sight. The blue roan riveted their attention, and Jawbone knew it and responded, baring his terrible teeth and uttering small screeching noises and mincing as he walked forward, murderously alert.

Skye stopped Jawbone and stared, not unkindly, but with the bore of his shining rifle gliding carelessly from man to man. He knew the tongue, and wouldn't need signs this time.

"I am sorry that your brother has died," he said. "It was a good death in a moment of honor. His pony is missing. But I will not give you one. You will have to make a travois and carry him behind one of yours. When you make war, and go to steal ponies, you must pay the price." He stared at them, one by one. "Bury him with honor. Mister Skye has said it."

One, on the far right, meant to try him. There'd be no greater glory for a young warrior than counting coup on Mister Skye or Jawbone. To wound Skye, or kill him, or even touch him, would make any warrior a great man among his people. It came suddenly: the boy whipped his bow back. Mister Skye's Sharps thundered and the boy's hand bloomed red and the bow clattered to earth. He screamed. Jawbone plunged into the others, screeching and biting and flailing with murderous hoofs, even while Mister Skye arced the Sharps, now a terrible club, knocking two more warriors off their plunging ponies as they drew their bows. And then it stopped as fast as it had started, with one gasping at his hand and two more writhing in pain in the dirt.

"Bind up his arm," Skye rasped to the remaining two, who were watching the screeching and plunging Jawbone with terror.

Two of their ponies were limping. One bled hard where Jawbone had ripped flesh from its chest. The others danced in panic.

Mister Skye reloaded the Sharps as he watched them care for the wounded. In the grass, one of the writhing warriors stopped writhing, and was out cold. The wounded youth, gray from pain and loss of blood, fainted as the others stanched the flow with his buckskin war shirt, and fashioned a tourniquet.

"You will need two travois," said Mister Skye, eyeing the inert one he had clubbed.

They stared a moment, then headed for the cottonwoods to cut poles, while Mister Skye watched. They built two crude travois—the cottonwoods were poor material—loaded up their dead and wounded, rode quietly south, over the shoulder, and were gone. In the bottoms, grazing, were Father Kiley's horses and four more belonging to the missionaries, all sweated black with dirt and drying foam. Leisurely he herded them north.

In the next valley he herded the oxen and mules and began the slow push forward, four miles of walking the exhausted stock. At midday he drove them over the last layering ridge and down into the Platte Valley, and on the riverbank the missionary party gaped. They had never expected to see their stock again.

Chapter 7

White people were mystifying to Victoria. Even Mister Skye was sometimes mystifying, although she understood him much better than she understood other whites. He was a leader of men, and that made him a chief in her mind, and not a mister. There were lots of misters among them, and none of them a chief.

Even more mystifying were these white medicine men and their wives—Victoria had scarcely seen a white woman before, so they fascinated her and she studied them surreptitiously. Right now, for example, no one made medicine. In fact no one did anything. Jawbone had returned with some horses. Mister Skye had saddled Jawbone and had told them to prepare the wagons for the crossing of the Platte. But now, an hour after he had ridden into the hills, these white people had done nothing. They had not even cooked a morning meal, but stood around with long faces, as uncertain as newly weaned colts. Had not Chief Skye told them to get busy? Had not Chief Skye told them he would bring the wagon cattle back, the lumbering white men's buffalo? And the mules too?

She watched them narrowly as she busied herself around her small fire. The priest, at least, had sense enough to feed himself. As soon as Mayree—the Shoshone wife's name was hard to pronounce in her Crow tongue—had finished spooning the buffalo stew into Dirk, Victoria would clean the pots and load the packhorses and tie the lodgepoles and lodgecover to the travois, and then they'd be ready. And Mayree would have the ponies saddled, and Dirk dressed in soft doeskins and up on a pony's withers, clutching its mane.

What was the matter with these medicine men? The long-robed one, at least, looked ready. But not even he believed he'd ever see his horses again. All of these whites seemed to think that Chief Skye had simply bragged, made giant boasts, when he said he would come back with the stock. It irked her. Not even the sensible one, old Rathbone, seemed to do anything but sit on his wagon seat, as if he had given up his medicine. Didn't these whites believe in their own medicine? Here they had come a long way to bring the medicine to the vile Siksika—the thought appalled her but she kept her silence—and now when trouble came they ignored their own medicine, God they called him. It was odd medicine, asking just one God for different things, when everyone knew that all the spirits had different tasks, and you had to find the right spirit helper to get things done.

She would put a stop to it. Rathbone was the chief medicine man, and she would tell him to get busy. So she went to him.

"Sonofabitch," she said. "How come you ain't doing what Mister Skye says? He says make the wagons float. Get ready. You ain't even cooked the damn stew yet."

He stared at her shocked.

"Get your ass off the seat. You ain't got all day."

From over at the next wagon Alex Newton stared, turned red, and closed his eyes. Henrietta, horrified, ducked into the protective darkness of her wagon.

"If you ain't got medicine, you go home. Beat it from here."

Esmerelda absorbed all this without wincing. "She's right," she said to Cecil. "We must have faith. We must do our chores. We must have our breakfast and prepare, just as if the stock were here."

"Do believe you're right," Cecil said.

"Hey you!" Victoria was yelling at James Method. "How come you ain't guarding? Cheyenne maybe come down the slopes into this here river bottom and kill us all. Just because you ain't got no horse don't mean you stop being the eyes and ears of this here camp."

"Ah think you're right," he said. He picked up his rifle from the plunder scattered around the buggy, and began walking upslope to a crest where he'd have a clear view of the country. "Bring me some of that chow."

Victoria headed for the Samples, singling out Clay. "Hey

you," she bellowed. "How come you ain't got them damn wagons ready for floating?" She waggled a finger at him.

Clay brightened. "Don't think it's necessary," he said slowly. "I thought Mister Skye had it wrong, telling us to make the boxes watertight."

"You do what he says. He's the chief."

"No, now wait just a minute, Victoria. Maybe we can block up the boxes and get over. I reckon these wagon bottoms stand about two and a half feet above ground. You figure that river's two and a half feet? I can block them up, too. Lift the box beds up a foot by putting blocks on top of the axles. You think that water's three and a half feet?"

This subdued her. She didn't understand it all. But at least this one was still thinking about the trip and not wandering around like a wrung-necked chicken.

"Hokay, you fix them wagons."

Clay scratched his ear uncertainly. "Sort of need your help," he said. "Need to borry your pony and ride into the river and see how deep she goes. Maybe take a pole."

Victoria grew indignant. "Ain't nobody rides my pony. Ain't nobody touches my pony. She's big medicine pony, buster."

"You ride then," Clay persisted. "Go see how deep."

"All right I will," she said. "Only then you get them wagons fixed up plenty fast, or Chief Skye get mad."

She spotted Silas, smirking happily near his wagon. "Hey you!" she bawled.

"Save your breath," he replied. "I don't intend to do your bidding. We are returning to Fort Laramie, and on foot, and I see no need—"

"You go over there and pull that heavy stuff, that stuff Skye says don't go up the trail—you and that preacher, Newton, you pull it out of that wagon."

"I have no intention—"

"If you ain't got no intentions, do it anyway." She glared at him. "When Skye comes back, you better be ready, or I make you dance fancy."

With that the old crone stalked back to her camp, and slid a horsehair Indian bridle over the head of her spotted buckskin and brown pony. Then she pulled her heavy skin skirts high and clambered up on the barebacked horse, turning it toward the river as she settled herself. She steered it toward the turbulent water.

"The river will be cold, Whistling Arrow," she said in her own tongue to her horse. "But you will go in, and we will see how deep."

The horse entered unhesitatingly, and the flow tugged hard at its slender legs as it stepped carefully, deeper and deeper. At the center of the river the water rippled around its thighs. Victoria kept on. "You see, Whistling Arrow? It is not so bad. My legs are cold too, but soon they will be warm."

Then near the far bank they hit the main channel, and the horse plunged suddenly, boiling water edging up on its belly, nearing its withers. But with the next steps, it grew shallower. She turned her pony around and rode back to the deepest part. The water sucked and pushed dangerously at the standing horse, but she took the measure of it, lapping just below the withers, almost to her pad saddle, and then urged the pony back to shore.

"Hey you," she said to Clay. "The water comes upta here." She flattened her hand on the pony's shoulder.

"I dunno," he said slowly. "Wisht you'd taken a measuring stick. But I reckon it'll do. We'll block up the wagons, and save us a big piece of work."

She eyed him narrowly. "You disobey Skye, just to make lazy, and it don't work, I'm gonna make you dance."

"I reckon it'll work," he said. "I'll fetch my double bit, and cut me some blocks."

The women were stirring at last, Alice and Esmerelda building a breakfast fire, the children hunting wood. They found little because emigrants had stripped the whole place bare of it in previous years.

She spotted Silas Potter, lounging beside his buggy, reading his Bible. "Hey you!" she bawled. He looked up calmly. "I tell you to pull that truck outa that wagon, you do it, hokay?"

He blinked at her patiently through his thick spectacles. "You are perfectly rude," he said nastily. "But let me tell you something. I don't know whether it will sink into that wooden head of yours, but I'll try. I have resigned from this party. I don't recognize your authority, or Skye's authority over me. The Newtons have resigned as well. We are going back to Fort Laramie."

Henrietta watched all this from the puckerstring hole in the back of her wagon. "I have no intention of walking a hundred miles back to Fort Laramie," she shrilled. "Not in my condition. I'm staying right here until oxen are brought here and I can ride."

"I don't care what kinda stuff you say. You get your ass over there and pull that plunder from the wagon like Skye says." Victoria squinted at him. "Or else I cut you up," she added, pulling from the folds of her skirt a shining Green River knife. "Slice you good, fingers and toes first, then better stuff." She grinned maliciously.

The knife glinted in the new sun.

Silas stared at it, at her, and then carefully closed his Bible and stood. He looked faintly annoyed.

Cecil approached. "I'm truly sorry that's your decision, Silas. And I grieve that we've lost my own daughter and son-in-law, too. I didn't know things had progressed this far. I imagine I'm to blame, not listening very well . . . I wish you'd reconsider, and seek guidance . . . But until you quit this camp, I reckon you're necessarily under my authority as the senior man here. We cannot permit a camp to tear itself apart in a hostile wilderness. And I've chosen Mister Skye and his people to guide us. So, until you quit us—and I'm sure you'll reconsider, my young friend—until you quit us, we'll have no anarchy here. Understood? . . . She's instructed you to help unload the Newtons' wagon. We're going to do it, you and I."

He turned to Victoria. "We are God's people here, and that knife is not helpful."

There was something in the man, Rathbone, she liked and respected, and she slid her knife into its buffalo-hide sheath at her waist. "I leave him to you. You fix him good, and move all the truck."

Silas fumed. From her pony Victoria could see rage in him, twisting his face, driving his arms and hands in small angry movements. But he was obeying, with a look of long-suffering patience painted falsely on his face, like white victory paint on a warrior after a losing battle. He followed Cecil Rathbone to the Newtons' wagon.

"Alex, please lend a hand. It'll take the three of us to lower these things."

"No!" cried Henrietta. "Daddy, what're you thinking of?"

From her saddle seat Victoria could see that the wagon was chockful of trunks and barrels. The furniture hulked at the rear. Toward the front, on a false floor, lay a straw-filled tick they used as a bed.

Cecil peered in, while Alex watched in icy rage. Then Cecil walked to the rear, undid the puckerstring, and pulled the canvas back until it fell free of the rear bow. He nodded to the others, and clambered in. The fine black walnut bedstead came easily. Cecil handed the head-board, footboard, and runners to Alex and Silas, who laid them on the grass. The walnut highboy was harder. Even after they had removed the drawers, each stuffed with clothing, it remained a heavy and cumbersome piece. But eventually the two reverends and the teacher eased it to the ground. Irritably Henrietta yanked clothing and linens from the drawers and stuffed it all into gunny sacks.

Then they confronted the organ. As organs went, it was a small one, with foot bellows. But it was a monster on the trail, and filled much of the wagon. Getting it out meant lifting it over the sides of the box and lowering it safely to the ground. And that proved to be plainly impossible, at least until Clay could join them and skids could be built. It was scarcely possible for the three men even to lift the organ for a few moments, much less lower it from the wagon side to the ground.

"This will have to wait," Cecil said to Victoria. He was winded. "I'll have Clay cut some runners. Perhaps Mister Skye can help us . . . I never imagined the Newtons were carrying this much weight . . . or that it could be dragged this far."

Victoria nodded. She would have pushed the thing, whatever it was, over the side and let it crash. What good was it? It would sit here anyway, until someone busted it up for firewood. But that would not be the way of these people.

"Hokay, I'll have Skye come do the damn thing."

She saw that the white women had a meal ready. "You go eat and then you get them wagons fixed up for the crossing."

From the women at the cookfire she got a small iron pot of oatmeal gruel and a wooden spoon, and then rode up the long rocky slope to the black man's sentry post.

"Here's the slop," she said. "You see nothing?"

James Method shook his head. She didn't trust his vision, so she squinted out across the prairies, spotting several small groups of antelope and some almost invisible mule deer. But the sun-kissed steppes seemed to hold no mortal terror at the moment. Still, she peered again, having lived through murderous ambushes several times. Nothing.

The man downed his oatmeal hastily.

"Slop is what Skye calls it. He tells me don't cook it unless there ain't nothing else to cook."

"Ah've had worse by far," said Method. "Lots of times Ah've had nothing."

"Don't they feed them slaves?"

"Lots of times they don't."

"How come some of them white people got slaves and some don't."

Method shrugged. "In the north they're against having slaves, and in the south they're for it. I got runnin' out of the south."

"We got lotsa damn slaves," she said. "The Absaroka people capture lotsa Siksika women, Lakotah women, make them dandy goddam slaves. I don't know how come them white medicine men are against it."

"Beats me," said James Method. "It's plenty bad for some black men, especially the cotton pickers. They get whipped all the time, and die quick if they run away. I had it easy—what they called domestic service. I just run around and chop wood and haul slop and such. They even taught me reading and writing, and I got to play some with the young masters at first . . ."

"Then how come you ran away?"

Method smiled. "Read too much, I guess."

She sniffed. "Maybe so Skye should make you a slave again. I could use you good."

Method's eyes grew cold. "He monkeys with me, and I'm going to fight. Maybe I'll die trying, but I'll fight."

"You'd make one helluva warrior," said Victoria. "When Skye comes, you tell us. Don't fire that piece, just wave, hokay?"

Victoria rode down the slope, puzzling about white men. In one part of their land they had slaves, and in another part they didn't. And they had longrobes, like that priest she'd been feeding, and shortrobes, like the rest of these medicine men, and they never could agree. The longrobes never touched a woman, and the short-robes did. It scandalized her that the longrobes scorned women. That was plainly crazy. But maybe it made big medicine. Bigger medicine than the shortrobes had. She didn't know. They were all strange, even Skye.

Back in camp she dropped the empty pot at the cook-fire, and scanned the whites. They were bustling about, and that was good. The big one, Clay Sample, had a wagon bed jacked up and was sliding blocks under it, between the bed and the axle. The women packed their plunder. Even the spectacles one, Potter, packed up his gear. Sat-isfied, she rode back to her own fire. Mary had long since made ready. They could leave in a minute.

Unless maybe that blackrobe wasn't packed and ready.

She found the priest on the riverbank, fishing with a pole he'd cut, and some string.

"Them fish ain't good to eat. Makes you weak and puts poison in you," she said.

"All the things of the earth are good," he said. "They are given to us by God."

She sniffed. "How come you don't touch no women? Eh? Sonofabitch, you blackrobes are crazy."

His wild orange hair and freckled face fascinated her. She hadn't ever seen freckles. Maybe that was because he had black and white parents, or maybe ones spotted like a trout.

He laughed easily. "It's so that we can give our entire loyalty to our Lord. All our time and effort, instead of looking after a wife."

"Sonofabitch, that's big medicine. Hokay, what do you do when you want to crawl between the robes with a woman. Ain't that a distraction?"

He scanned the horizon dreamily, until she thought he wouldn't answer. "For me, a lass is always a distraction. But I'm a poor priest. For the best, the ones with— medicine . . . that part of us is dead. The body's dead, and we live a life of pure spirit."

"Ain't that crazy," she muttered. "How come them shortrobes over there don't like you, eh?"

"Who's to say they don't like me, old mother? You must know more than I know."

"I don't know nothing about white man medicine, only Skye, he gets you away from camp, and you eat from our pot."

"It goes back a long time, almost three hundred years . . ." he said, and slipped into silence. The pole twitched, and he lifted it, but nothing had bitten. "We're all fishermen," he said.

There was some shouting behind them. She peered up the slope, and saw the black man waving. Far to the south, she saw a herd of driven animals wend its way down long slopes.

"Sonofabitch, here comes Chief Skye," she said happily. "Now you get your goddam horse back."

He stood slowly, not quite believing, squinting into the glare of the day with the wind riffling his carrot hair.

"I'm a poor priest, mother," he said. "Aye, a poor priest."

Chapter 8

Somehow, the return of the stock was not an occasion for joy. Shock, rather. No one had expected it. Even as the weary animals spread out to graze along the river-bank, the missionary party stared mutely. Only Father Kiley showed any pleasure. He gathered up his pack and riding horses and curried them.

Cecil J. B. Rathbone felt the pang of guilt. He had been faithless. And the division among them was far from settled. This miraculous recovery of the stock might even make matters worse, he thought.

Mister Skye stared at the camp from his perch on Jaw-bone, his gaze first upon the blocked-up wagons, and then upon walnut furniture sitting forlornly in the grass, and then upon the carriage, which had been emptied because it rode too low, the few possessions of Silas and James now aboard the Samples' wagon.

Satisfied, he said, "We'll cross now and then rest the stock on the other side. Use the mules, not the oxen, to cross all the wagons."

Cecil realized there were fewer oxen.

Mister Skye caught him staring. "Lost four," he said. "All of them Newtons'. They ran themselves to death. Only two yoke of theirs left and no reserves for them or for you. Your three yoke made it."

The remaining oxen looked desperately weary, and unable to pull wagons a mile farther, but the mules were in good condition.

"We will have to lighten on the other side," Cecil said.

He spotted blood on Jawbone's muzzle, and the sight of it disturbed the preacher.

As if reading his mind, Skye said, "Cheyenne. Five young ones on a horse-stealing raid. Looking for a little glory."

"You met them?"

"Aye, I did."

"And was it peaceable? Did they suffer any . . . losses?"

"Let's get these wagons across, mate."

So then there had been trouble, Cecil thought. Perhaps dead and wounded. For the love of God, he had hoped to avoid that.

The crossing of the north fork of the Platte was routine. The mules did heavy duty, pulling one wagon across, and swimming back for the next until all were over. The oxen were hazed across and swam so wearily that they drifted well downstream before they found footing on the north side. Silas and the Newtons were oddly subdued, offered no resistance, and did not threaten to take themselves and their goods back to Fort Laramie. The loss of so many oxen would have made even that hundred-mile retreat impossible. And in their wagon, bare inches above the lapping water, sat the heavy organ, its fate uncertain.

The far side offered good grass and a better supply of firewood in the river bottoms, and they made a good camp. Cecil wondered, though, if half a day of rest would suffice to strengthen the gaunted oxen and tired horses. But he would leave that to Mister Skye, who seemed more and more to reveal some commanding ability to get along in this vast land. The guide sent Victoria and James Method on long horseback scouts, and detailed the priest to hunting nearby. Skye didn't want any shots fired more than two or three miles from camp. Father Kiley's horse seemed none the worse for wear, and jogged off northwest, out of the bottoms.

"Your woman Victoria is a very effective leader. She had us hustling," said Cecil amiably.

"Aye, and why was it necessary for her to do it?" the guide answered tartly. "And why aren't you out finding a wagon road, mate? There isn't a road over here for wagons. From now on someone's got to hunt out a level path and avoid the worst grades and coulees, and find a way around cutbank streams, and have shovels handy to dig roads past ditches, and axes handy to cut through sagebrush and thickets and all the rest. You thinkin' it'll be easy now, mate? The hard part's scarce begun."

Seven hundred miles left, Cecil thought, and no road. Not even a rut. There'd be dead ends, backtracking, boulder pulling, shoveling crude paths down cutbanks and up the other sides. He shrank from the thought, and wondered what madness had set him upon this endless journey to the lands of dangerous Indians. He suddenly understood the yearnings of the Newtons and Silas Potter to hasten back the way they had come, to some small snatched security and comfort at the fort.

Mister Skye was watching him. The guide hunkered easily, squatting on two feet, a position the mountain men seemed able to enjoy for hours, but one which cut off Cecil's circulation and swiftly made his legs tingle.

"I'll go with you; I don't want you getting too far from camp and picked off by some Sioux. Grab a shovel, mate, and we'll go make a road."

They trudged up a long gentle shoulder with some sort of path on it, whether made by Indians or buffalo or other wild animals the Reverend Rathbone didn't know. He carried a shovel; Mister Skye bore his new Sharps, and a holstered Army .44 Colt as well. At its crest they left the river bottom behind. Ahead rose a vast tawny prairie, fairly flat, and stretching aching distances, clear to the horizon and beyond, to some unknown lip of the world. Far to the northwest lay a low strip of blue mountains, scarcely visible.

"Those are the Big Horns," said Mister Skye. "We'll keep well to the east where the going is easier. Maybe up the Powder. There are creeks all across here, headwaters of rivers that join the Yellowstone. Beyond the Big Horns we'll strike the Yellowstone and follow it west a way, and then cross it, drive north through a gap—Judith Gap—and head northwest toward the Missouri . . . and Sun River."

"Why," exclaimed Cecil, "this doesn't look half bad. Level enough for a road. No trees or brush to cut through."

"There are cutbank streams, some of them running down small canyons, to work past," Mister Skye warned. "And Indians. This is game country—buffalo, antelope, deer, bear. They come here to hunt—Cheyenne, Sioux, Arapaho mainly, but also Crow, Shoshone, Gros Ventres, Assiniboin, and sometimes others."

"It looks like it'll swallow armies. Like it'd be sheer chance if our tiny caravan might be discovered."

"We'll be found and watched," said Mister Skye grimly. "Probably are already, mate."

"Are you expecting a fight?"

"I always expect a fight. Especially here."

"There seems little enough road-building as far ahead as I can see."

Skye grinned. "Wait until we're out in it, Mister Rathbone. The prairie hides its hellholes until you're hard upon them."

Cecil didn't doubt the guide. Far to the west he saw a solitary horseman, who appeared, antlike, along a rise and then disappeared from sight. James Method probably, or the priest. Appearing and disappearing on what seemed to be level prairie. Cecil sat down to rest, and Mister Skye squatted beside him.

"Mister Rathbone, there are things you aren't telling me. Victoria says there's division in your party. I must know of it. I must know everything—for the safety of us all."

Cecil sighed. A division indeed, and there was the other thing too. Weary oxen, enough for one wagon maybe, but not two.

He hemmed around in his mind, backed and filled, softened and harshened, and then settled on plain talk, since honeyed smooth words would clang like cymbals at dawn.

"Mister Skye," he said, "there's some who want us to discharge you, and think you're—ungodly." He smiled wryly. "I didn't put that true. Potter thinks you're the devil's own creature, and maybe the Newtons do too. Lust and blood and bigamy upon you, and a horse that is hell on earth. Maybe I'm not so far from that notion myself, only I got my own reasons . . ."

He waited for some reaction, some disclaimer from Mister Skye, but the guide only nodded.

"They were all set to hightail back. Seventy miles back to Laramie, but they're calling it a hundred. Henrietta's plumb determined to haul that organ to Sun River, or quit us. That and all her truck."

"Organ?" Mister Skye had forgotten about it.

"Their wagon's got a little pump organ in it. So heavy we couldn't even get it out to ditch it. And she ain't going anywhere without it. Says she'll set it up in our Sun River church and play the daylights outa it."

Unconsciously Cecil had drifted back to a frontier tongue he had abandoned in his youth when he walked east to school.

"The oxen are so worn we hardly got enough for one

wagon—five sorry yoke. Some footsore, too. So we've got to ditch a wagon, too. And that means we lose the Newtons. Lose my own daughter. Crack the whole mission apart."

"Well then, let's take the organ," said Mister Skye. "I'm going to deliver one bloody organ to Sun River."

"But . . . but . . ."

"From now on we'll take one ox-drawn wagon. Yours because it's lighter. And it will contain one item—the organ. You and Mrs. Rathbone will ride the buggy. Mister Method is out scouting all day and needs only a tent. Mister Potter will learn to walk. You'll abandon your plunder, except for food and a tent; the Newtons will abandon theirs, except for the bloody organ. And we'll trust that five wornout yoke can haul your lighter wagon with one organ inside of it."

"But that's—mad," Cecil cried. "I'm bringing tools, a plow, seed—to teach . . . I can't leave that, just leave that. It's the heart of the whole dream, the vision—"

Mister Skye shrugged. "You can buy some of that at Fort Benton. Not far from Sun River. That stuff isn't important, mate. That ain't worth a diddlydamn. Now that organ, that's what's important. You get Henrietta pumping that in your mission church, and that'll cure whatever ails the bloody Blackfeet."

"I can't let you do this!" Cecil cried. "I spent months—years—culling and selecting and discarding, until I fitted everything into my wagon—everything to start a farm, teach domestic sciences . . ."

Mister Skye stared. "Everything for a farm, sure enough, mate. And nothing for a mission. We're hauling the bloody organ."

"But that's not the way . . ." Cecil's voice faded. Was this heathen and heretic measuring Cecil's faith and dedication and finding it wanting? The thought tore through him like a barbed arrow. "Oh, Lord," he muttered.

"If I don't get Potter busy pushing his feet forward, he'll cause trouble," Cecil added quietly. "It's all set then."

They turned back then, Mister Skye rolling along with his sailor's gait. The earth could buck and heave under him, and not slow him down a particle. And the Reverend Rathbone behind, once again feeling like a dinghy towed by the man ahead. On the soft zephyrs came a muffled report, far to the west. Mister Skye paused a moment, sorting, and then continued on.

"Father Kiley has a deer," he said mysteriously, and Cecil wondered how he knew. And hoped, for once, Mister Skye might be dead wrong.

Back in the bottoms, the guide explained the new order of things, with a series of short sharp commands, and astonished people hastened to obey. Esmerelda laughed, and pecked Cecil on the cheek. Together they tugged everything out of their wagon until it lay in heaps on the grass, and the wagon bed looked oddly naked. Then she began to sort out the necessaries, with a ruthlessness that Cecil didn't possess, while he groaned silently within, watching his plow and harness and seed and hoe and scythe end up in the discard pile, while food and clothing survived the holocaust.

Over at the Newtons' wagon, a similar process had begun, though more anguished, as they wrangled to hang on to things. Henrietta cried occasionally, and Alex wondered out loud why he did this, why he was here, why he took orders from a brute and a heathen. But it was the organ, the vision of the organ arriving safely on Sun River, that compelled them onward. To get her organ to Sun River, Henrietta would bear any cross.

Silas Potter had withdrawn into a shocked petulance

ever since Skye returned with the stock, and in that condition he lacked will. Mindlessly he emptied the buggy
of its tent and his few books and clothes, and let Mister
Skye show him how to make a mule-pack of them, absorbing the lesson with dull eyes and bare interest. In the
grass of the Platte Valley the heap of discarded things
grew. It was nothing new. All along the Oregon Trail they
had seen remnants such as this. Some had been salvaged
by those who came behind, or by Fort Laramie scaven-
gers, who collected it far and wide and took it to the fort
for furnishing. But much more lay in ruin beside the
great artery across the continent. At least there was one
thing that pleased Silas Potter, and he took pains to
express his pleasure: the organ would go, and Cecil
Rathbone's farm implements wouldn't.

The Samples were unaffected by this great sweat-
down, at least until Cecil cornered Clay and begged him
to take just one small barrel, containing various seeds,
and one little hoe, and a few orchard cuttings. Clay grinned
and found room. His mules had weathered the trail well.
They looked ribby but trail-hardened, and seemed strong
enough. There were ten of them: three span for his wagon,
a pair for the carriage, and two spares, which would henceforth be carrying packloads of the Newtons' goods. The
spare horses would carry the meager possessions of Silas,
and James Method.

"May the Lord bless you," cried Cecil. "And don't tell
Mister Skye."

Later, all the men in the camp helped to transfer the
organ. They positioned the Rathbone wagon back to back
with the Newtons', and rolled the canvas off the bows of
both. Then, with Mister Skye and James Method on one
end, and Clay, Cecil, Alex, Silas, and young Alfred on
the other, they hoisted it over the solid rear wall of the

larger wagon, and down into the smaller. They stripped the Newton wagon of its canvas—which would become a tent at Sun River, while they built dwellings—and abandoned it. It sat forlornly, its naked bows hard against the sky. The sight of it saddened Cecil. It had come halfway, sheltering his daughter and Alex and all their worldly goods, which now lay scattered in the tall grasses, unclaimed, for any wild child of the plains to take.

The only thing in Cecil's wagon other than the organ was the Newtons' tick. They would sleep there nights; the tick added nothing much to the weight. Alex stalked the camp, red-faced and angry, while Henrietta pouted and complained that her feet would swell and she wouldn't be able to walk. Cecil had a remedy, if it came to that: Henrietta and her mother would ride in the buggy, and he would ride Magdelene.

Ruefully he gazed at the rear seat of the carriage, piled high now. The canvas salvaged from the Newtons' wagon filled most of it, and what little space was left was given to food and a few items of clothing. He and Esmerelda would arrive at Sun River with scarcely more than the clothing on their backs, an axe, and a few tools.

Esmerelda saw him staring at the small desolate load in the buggy, and knew the thread of his thinking. She took his hand.

"We're going for a walk, you and I, Reverend," she said, and tugged him toward the riverbank, and down the stream through cottonwoods and brush, until the camp disappeared and only the silence of sunny nature lay around them, black and white magpies flitting from tree to tree, and corrugated clouds high overhead to the south. He felt her strong warm hand in his, leading him somewhere, and did not resist, though he worried about slipping too far from the safety of the camp.

Then at last in a sunny glade where the grasses grew emerald and the river gurgled just beyond a wall of brush, she stopped him and turned to him.

"Cecil Rathbone," she said. "We don't have much left, but we have each other." And then she hugged him, and he felt his own hard hands and skinny arms fold around her and pull her lean warm figure tight. They kissed.

"We have that, and we're rich," he said. "Plumb rich."

She smiled, comfortable and warm in his arms. "There's not a dream ever dreamed by mortal man that has not been battered and changed as life went along," she said. "We'll make do with whatever God gives us. Is that not right, Cecil?"

He sighed. "Hate to give up dreams. I get to thinking I'm giving some kind of gift to God, bringing a whole tribe of people to Him, and then He upsets my apple cart."

Cecil Rathbone laughed, and Esmerelda joined him, and they hugged in the quiet, and were reluctant to let go. There had been so few stolen moments clear across the plains.

"The organ won," he said, and they laughed softly together. "But Clay's carrying my seed, and a hoe."

They kissed again, and then walked arm in arm back through the golden quiet, sun filtering through the young cottonwood leaves, aware of each other, and danger out here, and sudden fate.

There had been some imperceptible change in camp. The abandonment of their worldly things had been some sort of shriving that had cleansed them and drawn them closer. Even Silas Potter smiled thinly.

Cecil hunted down their guide, for it somehow was Skye's doing. He found him, and Father Kiley, skinning a doe that hung from a stout cottonwood limb, and taking care about it because Victoria wanted the hide.

Cecil watched awhile. The priest was an expert, peeling and cutting delicately, yanking the hide down in clean, effective jerks.

"Mister Skye," Cecil said at last. "We have the organ, and we've ditched almost everything else except for the clothing on our backs. And I daresay tempers are sweet for a change. Now how is that?"

"Well, mate, it has to do with flags. Do you know about flags?"

"You have me there, Mister Skye."

"During the Kaffir War, the man carrying the Union Jack fell, and fast as he fell, we marines—the bloody Royal Navy turned us into marines for a bit, down there—we fled. It was a godalmighty rout. Until a bloody tar grabbed the Jack and lifted her up, and all the bloody tars saw it again and rallied with a shout that still rattles me ears. And we turned around, mate, and overran them bloody Kaffirs."

"I'm still not following you, Mister Skye."

"Well, Reverend, men will follow flags and guidons through hell on earth. But men ain't going to be brave for the sake of plows and seed and hoes."

"You're saying I failed to inspire my people?"

"No, Mister Rathbone, I ain't saying that at all. What I'm saying is, that pump organ of Mrs. Newton's—that thing is your flag, and all your folk are rallying to her."

Father Kiley grinned. And for the first time he and Cecil took amiable measure of each other.

"Perhaps our Lord prefers organs," he said, and Cecil chuckled.

Chapter 9

For nine days they toiled north by northwest, sticking to the ridges and shoulders because they were easier on the wagons, with fewer boulders and gullies. They crossed several small streams without difficulty, finding wide sandy places with easy slopes. Two creeks gave them trouble, and they had to shovel their way down sharp dropoffs and throw earthen ramps together on the far sides, so the wagons could roll up to the grassy slopes again. And uncoiling behind, mile after mile, were the tracks of wagons, cutting grass and indenting the virgin earth, tracks anyone could read.

The exhausted oxen that had dragged the Newtons' heavy wagon clear to the crossing of the Platte were not used at all. The three yoke that had pulled the Rathbone wagon were in better condition, and now they continued to pull it and the organ inside of it. The strife that had torn the Methodist party was gone, or at least much subdued, as far as Father Kiley could see. The ones least equipped for this wilderness travel, the Newtons and young Potter, were quiet and self-absorbed, perhaps humbled by the vastness of this virgin land.

Dunstan Kiley had been here before, several times, as one of the several Jesuits who had helped Pierre de Smet bring the faith to the northwestern tribes, most particularly at St. Mary's Mission in the far Bitterroot Valley. Father Kiley had first seen this incredible land in the fur-trade days, and it awed him no less now than it did then. He imagined, as he rode perhaps three miles ahead and to the west of the missionary party, that it could easily hold the whole population of the earth in one small cor-

ner of it. The red-hued earth and limitless land, stretching over the lip of the horizon, contrasted starkly with
the verdant, misty, intimate vales of his native Ireland. It
had frightened him once, as a man who has never been to
sea is frightened when there is no land in sight, and every
lapping swell seems a menace. But now he knew precisely where he was and where he would go. Each day
the blue bulk of the Big Horns off to the west and north
grew larger, and visible now was a vast barrier ridge,
dark and foreboding, where God had cleaved the great
plains from the mountains.

Everywhere here he found game. Rarely an hour went
by that Father Kiley did not see something or other, deer,
antelope, elk, and even a bear or two. But these he ignored
for the choicer meat of a young buffalo cow. The great
brown beasts had not gathered into a giant herd here, but
grazed the bottoms in small groups guarded by a fierce
old bull or two. Whenever Father Kiley approached the
top of a ridge or shoulder, he paused, his head barely
above its crest, and he surveyed the open lands beyond
not only for succulent buffalo, but for Indians as well.
But of the Indians he saw none.

Now, in this cloudless early afternoon, he found what
he was looking for, a herd of a dozen buffalo grazing
quietly in a shallow dished valley with a small creek and
a few cottonwoods lining its bank. The west wind would
be ideal, for he was to the east. And the cottonwoods
would supply cover enough for him to stalk close and
select a good cow with care. He traveled lightly, and without a packhorse. His bay gelding could carry an antelope
or even the hind quarters of a doe as well as himself, if
the distance to camp wasn't too large. It never quite grew
used to the brass smell of blood, and carried its burden
with subdued alarm. Buffalo were a different matter. For

these he needed a packhorse, and usually went back to the party to fetch his spare, leaving his packload temporarily in the wagon carrying the organ.

Father Kiley rode quietly toward the group, screening himself as much as possible behind the cottonwood groves. The old bull that stood apart from the others, and guarded this group, twisted its massive head until it peered straight into the cottonwoods, and then looked away again. Its weak eyes saw nothing, and the west wind brought him no scent of danger. Even so, he turned his body so as to stare continually toward the copse where Father Kiley sat his horse. Easily the priest slid off and unsheathed the old Hawken percussion lock rifle he had acquired years ago from a young mountain man whose two children he had baptized. It was a good weapon, with a short heavy barrel and a ball large enough to drop a buffalo with one well-placed shot.

But Father Kiley needed to get closer. He crouched two hundred yards distant, and he preferred to shoot from half that. There lay a crease in the sere land that would permit him to edge closer if he crept, and kept his head low. He did not wish to crawl. That would besmudge the heavy black suit he always wore, even now, in the heat and on the hunt. He had learned to carry a smock in his kit, and this he wrapped around him when he butchered or shouldered meat. That suit and its white Roman collar was his badge, his joyous prison.

He selected the cow he wanted and edged closer. But the guardian bull was restless now, and it puzzled Father Kiley, for the bull stared not toward him but toward the east, on his flank. The cow was still too distant, but he decided not to wait. This herd grew restless now, and ready to run. He lined up the sights of the Hawken until he stared at that place behind her shoulder where the ball would tear through lungs and heart and she would take a step or two and drop. And then he felt, as he always did, a grief about the taking of life, for his Irish heart was tender and his spirit exulted in the life he saw in the shining eyes of God's creatures. Even as he aimed he remembered for a moment that some Indians thanked the creature they had slain for the use of its body, and to bless it on its journey to the spirit world. He could not do that; he could not address a prayer to an animal or commune with its spirit, but he wished he could.

He fired. The throaty boom of the Hawken echoed out upon the wide land. The shot went true, and the cow coughed and slowly folded, sinking to the warm earth even as blood frothed from her nostrils. And then another boom erupted, lighter than his Hawken's, and a third, and two other cows were wounded. One began to run, and made twenty yards before she sank to her fore-knees, her head low, refusing to collapse and die for as long as her will permitted. And then she fell. The other cow had collapsed, and now lay on her side, her legs kicking spastically.

Father Kiley was astonished. He stood. And as he stood, mounted Indians poured out of a defile, a crease to the east that the priest scarcely knew was there. More and more of them poured into the valley, until at last he counted twenty, a sizable party, all of them naked on their ponies except for breechclouts and moccasins. They alarmed him, for he had no way to escape. But they were not painted. This was not a war party, as far as he could see. These might be hunters, or more likely, a group out to make mischief, steal horses, count coup wherever there might be enemies . . .

They ignored the three slain buffalo and the retreating herd, and instead rode straight toward the priest, fanning out, arrows nocked in bows, and the black bores of several rifles and fusils pointing at him. Some wore their black hair shoulder length; others wore it in two braids. One wore his long hair in a single braid that fell clear down his back and over the right stifle of his pony. Except for the quivers on their backs and the small medicine bundles hanging from a thong around their necks, they carried nothing. His heart hammered. Sometimes in his fancies he had dreamed of becoming a holy martyr, and going straight to God, in all honor. But now death chilled him. He didn't want to be a martyr, at least not yet, not yet . . .

They studied his black suit, and the white collar tight around his neck, and the small burnished wooden cross hanging on his chest, and then they pointed and gestured and stared. One leapt off his pony and approached, his eyes gleaming like agates, and Father Kiley had no notion what the warrior might do. The priest stood quietly, forcing himself to stand with a calm he didn't feel, while the powerful short warrior stepped close, raised a hand, and then fingered the white Roman collar, feeling the tight fabric that imprisoned the priest's neck. He grunted then, and Father Kiley had no idea what it meant.

They argued among themselves in a language he didn't know. He didn't even know what tribe they were, not having mastered the subtle differences between them, as Mister Skye had done. Father Kiley could recognize Nez Perce, Shoshone, Flatheads, and Blackfeet, all tribes that usually roamed well to the west and north of here. But these Indians were none of those. And yet . . . the headman, the one with the unusually long single braid and a single eagle feather tucked into the top of it, awakened some memory in him, some campfire knowledge exchanged with a hundred men of the mountains he had sojourned with. This one had scars on each arm, torture

scars shaped like three chevrons that made puckered
white lines in his umber flesh. Like a sergeant's stripes,
the priest thought wildly. And if this was the one he had
heard of, the one who wore those scars, then this was a
subchief of the Cheyenne named Wolf-That-Circles, and
a more erratic and sometimes dangerous man did not exist on the prairies. Father Kiley blessed himself. If he
was to become a martyr, he hoped he would find the
courage within himself to endure it grandly. But oh, God,
spare him that . . .

For what seemed an achingly long time to Father Kiley,
nothing happened. They stared and muttered and pointed.
Then, at a sharp command from the one with the long
braid, two of the warriors set off to find the priest's horse,
and another was sent to the crest of a nearby hill to act as
a sentinel. In short order they found his bay and brought
it close. Then the powerfully-built leader—Father Kiley
was sure it was Wolf-That-Circles—opened the priest's
saddlebags. He found little inside. A white stole, a small
tin of wafers not yet sanctified, a flask of oil for anoint-
ing, a breviary, a flint and striker for fire-starting, balls,
powder, and caps, and some jerky. The chieftain flipped
the tissuey pages of the leather-bound breviary, as if to
read, and threw it to the ground, a useless thing.

Father Kiley didn't know what else to do, so he talked.
"I am Dunstan Kiley, a priest of the Jesuits and a brother
of Pierre de Smet, whose name you probably know," he
began.

They listened, but without understanding, as far as he
could see.

"I'm on my way west, passing through here to go to
the mountains, to bring my . . . medicine to tribes there
who ask for it."

They watched him talk, even as they pawed through

his few simple possessions. One of them took the flint and striker and began to build a fire, gathering dry cottonwood sticks.

"I have killed that cow; you have killed the others. I will butcher mine now, and you can butcher yours. Perhaps we can have a feast, and then I must leave," he said to no one in particular.

He still had his Hawken in hand, but now Wolf-That-Circles wrenched it violently from him. Father Kiley thought to smash the chieftain with his big freckled fist, but thought better of it. He wasn't a bit frail, but neither would he be a match for that war-leader, who'd kill him in an instant.

Instead, he stood upright and made the sign of the cross, knowing in his troubled heart that he was not invoking God's blessings, but employing theater, medicine, to save his life, and he felt ashamed.

They stared. Again he blessed them, this time trying desperately to invoke the blessings he sought.

"You have my rifle now as a gift. I'll just leave now. You have the cow I shot as well," he said, walking hastily toward his bay horse.

But at a barked command, arms grabbed him roughly and spun him to the ground. He grew frightened now but determined not to show it, and again he blessed them with a sweeping slash of his hand, and even from the ground gazed at them steadily, one by one.

He didn't expect what happened next. They undressed him, taking great care not to rip his clothing, as if these items of clothing were medicine itself, and might impart medicine to whoever wore them. The white collar was most prized. Wolf-That-Circles took it and hooked it in place on his own bronzed neck, and paraded happily with it. They took everything from him, and Dunstan

Kiley felt violated, naked before his enemies, his freckled white flesh bared to them and the sun. One of them tried on his black broadcloth suitcoat and found that it fit, except that it was too long in the arms. Another pulled on his black clerical shirt. Another his black pants. Another the black-dyed boots he had specially made for this trip into the wilderness.

Then they lashed his hands behind his back, and his legs as well, and left him in the grass. He felt utterly helpless and his heart hammered and he could not pray. At last the Latin seeped back into his brain, and he began to chant it from some wellspring of memory. He recited the Mass.

Several of them were gathering wood, bringing armloads of it from the copses. He supposed they would have a feast of delicious hump ribs and tongue, or liver and boudins, while they decided what to do with him. Where was God? Where had God vanished? His mind riveted upon the preparations before him, and he could not pray.

But there was something wrong with his hopes, for none of them butchered a cow, peeling back hide, cutting out the succulent hump ribs or severing the choice tongue. No, they were gathering long dry sticks and placing them in the fire like the spokes of a wheel, watching their ends flare and burn hot.

And then Father Kiley knew. They would test the medicine of this priest of the whites, this shaman of the whites, with burning brands twisted into his pale flesh, and see for themselves whether this holy man was vulnerable and mortal, or whether he might magically resist, or laugh, or heal himself as fast as the brands were thrust into his flesh.

Father Kiley groaned, a dread engulfing him beyond any dark feeling he had ever experienced, and for a moment he hallucinated, thinking himself back in the cool green vales of his home, seeing his good mother and father at the hearth of their cottage, smiling, seeing the softly smiling Virgin in her niche at his parish church . . .

Wolf-That-Circles eyed him intently, his eyes bright with curiosity. He would begin the honors. From the fire he selected a thick stick, its end a glowing orange coal and blazing. With this in hand he approached the priest, tied hand and foot on the grass. The chieftain had dark gray eyes, and these peered deeply into Father Kiley's own. And then the burning stick drew close, not toward the priest's torso, but toward his face, closer and closer, and then Father Kiley knew. The blazing stick was coming toward his eye, his left eye.

"No!" he shrieked, and twisted violently to one side and the fiery brand drove home. It missed, singeing his ear. He yanked and twisted violently, flipping and jack-knifing on the grass, his mind gone mad with terror. Powerful hands pinioned him from behind, jamming him back to earth, brutal weight across his shoulders. More hands caught his flailing legs and pinioned them. Still more hands caught his writhing body and held it down.

"Mother of God," he cried, imploring.

And then the fiery brand came again, faster and harder now, searing his face, into his eye, burning and grinding unspeakably. White light exploded in his head, white and blackness, the smell of burning flesh, mad pain in his eye, blackness. He screamed and didn't know it. Then the other eye, burning fire, sizzling flesh, white and black light, stars of yellow, sun and midnight, and then blackness. He fainted, then came to, then his spirit wove in and out of himself. Blackness.

But they weren't done. Now smaller brands jabbed

into his chest and thighs, convulsing him wherever they touched, stinging pain and ache, mortal ache, and blackness. Then a hot coal touched his private parts and he shrieked and not even ten hands of five powerful warriors could subdue his writhing body. Then the coals touched the bottom of his feet and he flew out of himself into madness, muttering and yowling like a rabid wolf.

A rifle boomed but he scarcely heard it. Blood splattered across his burned and raw chest, but he scarcely felt it. A body fell on him, even as the rifle boomed again, and other rifles, but he scarcely knew of it. The torture stopped but the pain still burst through him, waves of lava that exploded in his head, one after another. Then no one pinioned him. Blackness. He could not see. He hoped he might die fast. His breath came in gasps. His heart pattered, too fast, bursting itself within him. It slowed, and he caught a hoarse breath. More shots, volleys of them. God, let him die, let him die . . .

Someone beside him. "Easy, mate, easy," said Mister Skye. "We chased the scurvy bunch of them. Killed four, bad medicine for them."

"Shoot me," begged Father Kiley.

He felt small feminine hands on him, cutting the thong that bound his arms and legs, and in the midst of his pain he remembered he was naked.

"Cover me," he cried.

"Easy, mate," came Skye's voice. "It's nothing to them and they have washing and salving to do. Mary and Victoria are here; James Method's here. Clay Sample's here. Alfred too. Wagons are on the hill yonder, and the preachers are guarding."

"Where are my clothes?"

"Scattered about, mate. Bad medicine. Three that wore

your things died, and Wolf-That-Circles is dead. We took your collar off him."

"Kill me, I beg of you. I cannot see."

"Nay, mate, we'll be doing none of that."

The priest felt a powerful rough hand hold his. Pain lacerated his head and muddled his thoughts, tearing his mind to pieces. He saw God and then he didn't. He touched his brow area and felt wet pulp. His nose was a blistered hill, dripping fluids. The only reality was the ghastly pain, and the big rough hand holding his own in the middle of midnight.

He grew feverish and slipped in and out of awareness. At last he felt a blanket around him, torturing him wherever it rubbed one of his burns, and then strong gentle hands were carrying him, laying him on a tick, covering him.

"You're in the wagon with the organ," Mister Skye said. "Your face is in a bad way, but the rest of you isn't so bad, a dozen burns that'll heal up. Aye, you'll live, Father Kiley, whether you want to or not."

"Pray God that I will not," he begged.

He heard the voice of Cecil Rathbone speaking. "Can't say that it's the end, Father. Can't say that at all. Not from the standpoint of heaven above. Might just be the beginning. Only, was I in your shoes, I'd figure it the end for sure. Don't know how you took it. I'd a gone plumb mad. You got some kind of holy fire burning away in you, I'd say. No, Father, it's no end."

He heard Esmerelda. "Dear Father Kiley," she cried. "How my heart aches for you. How I wish . . . how I wish . . ." She wept. Her hand found his and clutched it.

But he could think of nothing to wish for.

Chapter 10

For two days Father Kiley was out of his head. The wagons toiled northward over gigantic shoulders of land that reached out from the westward mountains, all the while to the somber groaning and cries and babbling from within the covered wagon. They were all subdued by that ever-present reminder of suffering and terror and the suddenness of death in this wild land.

Mister Skye detailed James Method to provide meat for the small caravan, and to scout as well to the west, or mountain side. They passed close to Pumpkin Buttes to the east, and then struck the Powder River and worked north in its valley a way. In the lush wide valley of the Powder the going was level and the animals rested after the up and down strain of negotiating the surrounding slopes. But the Powder was a favorite place among the hostile Sioux and their allies the Cheyenne, and Mister Skye did not want to tarry there long. Victoria, who became his principal scout, felt nervous all the while. She had seen several smokes, and her keen senses told her they were never far from other parties. Tomorrow they would cut northwest over a high prairie divide, to Crazy Woman Creek.

Each morning and evening Victoria tended the raving man, making poultices of roots and herbs known only to herself, which she collected, ground to powders, and carried with her in small skin sacks. She had dealt with innumerable wounds in her day among her own people as well as Mister Skye and Jawbone, but nothing she had ever seen was as ghastly as the oozing carnage of Father Kiley's eye sockets and the blistered dripping red flesh that surrounded them. Still she cleansed the wounds while the priest raved, and packed in the wet mash of her medicines and then bound his head again. The other burns, while festering and painful, were not mortal or even dangerous unless they infected badly.

For Father Kiley there were no longer days and nights, and he raved and sobbed at odd hours, deep in night as well as noon. Little of it sounded coherent, but Mister Skye thought the priest was addressing, variously, his mother and father, a brother, the Virgin, the founder of his order, St. Ignatius, and others beyond deciphering. In his more rational moments the priest begged to die, prayed God to slay him. And always there was the priest's red pain maddening him; a pain that never lifted. The man was feverish as well, his tortured body hot and dry, and frequently each day Skye stepped off Jawbone and gave the priest a dipper of water. He had seen terrible things in his day, but this was one of the worst, and it built in him an awesome thirst he knew he could not long resist.

Of the others, only Cecil and Esmerelda approached the sickbed. The Newtons somewhat grumpily pulled their tick from the wagon and began to camp outside nights. Alex and Cecil took turns driving the oxen hauling the organ and the priest, but the groaning cargo was more than Alex could endure, and he fled from the task as much as possible. As for Silas Potter, he had a sharp and unsympathetic opinion of the whole matter, and voiced it to anyone within earshot, including Mister Skye. He pitied the poor priest, blinded forever, but it had clearly been the wrath of God, unloosed upon the minion of Rome among them. Of those who contemplated the priest's suffering, Esmerelda was affected the most, for she had a practical and loving bent that foresaw a bitter life for the blinded man. She would have nursed him but for Victoria, who seemed better able to cope with those ghastly wounds and a raving spirit. And beyond the endless suffering there loomed the question: what would they do with this helpless man out here? Where would they take him? Wilderness stretched in every direction. He could not be dropped off somewhere, turned over to someone's care. This Irishman, this Jesuit who wore the collar of Rome, had suddenly become their burden.

Then, after three days of raving, Father Kiley became himself. Victoria, who was tending him at the time, was the first to know it.

"Is it day or night?" the priest asked. "Who am I talking to?"

She summoned Mister Skye, who was eating buffalo cow ribs succulently prepared by Mary.

"It's evening, mate, and Mister Skye here, and my Victoria."

"I could eat a little," he said. "If I can sit up. I hurt so much I don't know whether . . ."

He started to lift himself up, but fell back weakly.

"You'll be getting well fast now, Father."

The priest sighed. "I don't want to. Forever night. I don't know why . . . Why must I suffer this? It was because I wasn't brave. I didn't have faith; I didn't endure . . . I cried and begged them, most shamefully."

"You have nothing to be ashamed of," Mister Skye retorted harshly.

"I failed in every way a man given to our Lord can fail. They wanted to see whether I had medicine. They tested my medicine. Religion for them is medicine, power. And I had none, none at all, only weakness of body and a faithless soul . . ."

"Father Kiley, I'll not have you torturing yourself, tormenting your soul along with your body. Let me tell you something, mate. We came over the ridge and saw what it was all about, and began shooting at once. I killed three of them. This new Sharps with its paper cartridges reloads fast, mate. And Victoria killed one, and Mister Method injured two, all before they reacted much. Then they fled. The dead ones were wearing your clothes. Wolf-That-Circles was one, shot through the head. You know what the rest did? They stripped off your priest clothing from the dead. That stuff had medicine, big medicine, bad medicine. The story of that medicine, Father, that story is going to fly from campfire to campfire, to every tribe on the plains, and I doubt that any of your folk, wearing your collar, will ever be menaced again. They hadn't ever seen medicine like that and they aren't going to forget it."

The priest sighed. "Medicine. That's not what I came to bring them. Not what I wanted . . . superstition . . . just coincidence that your bullets hit the ones who wore my things—you didn't shoot at them for that reason, did you?"

Mister Skye shook his head, and then realized that the priest couldn't see. "No, it was just something that happened. But it's big medicine for them. From now on, they'll leave priests alone, mate."

Father Kiley sighed. "It means nothing."

"You're wrong. It means everything. All religion is medicine, the quest for power and control, whether you want to admit it or not."

The priest didn't respond. Then, "Are you a believer, Mister Skye?"

"I don't know what I am. I think about it, like most men. Read about it too."

"You read?"

"Whenever I can lay me hands on a bloody book."

The priest lay quietly, exhausted even by these few words. Then Victoria returned with warm broth and a horn spoon, and slowly fed the priest a little, then more.

"That's enough," he said. "My head bursts with every swallow."

"I don't know the mystery of religion, Father. I'm too old, and a bloody scoundrel, and beyond knowing, I'd say. But I'll tell you, mate, things happen. Things that can't happen naturally. I've seen strong and haughty men struck down at the height of their power. I've seen weak, miserable, hopeless ones lifted up, find courage, dare the impossible, and succeed. I've seen too much o' that not to respect it. At sea, and here in the wilds. The Indians call it medicine, and I'd call your faith medicine too, but of another kind."

"I can't talk anymore," Father Kiley said. "Even to form words is too much and sets my head afire . . . more than I can bear. Never goes away . . ."

Mister Skye knew what he'd do, then. For himself more than the priest.

"I've got just the painkiller," he said. "The very jug of sour mash you bought at Mister Bullock's."

The priest nodded. "I'll try anything," he said. "Anything to slow this pain down."

Skye clambered from the wagon and lumbered heavily toward the mule-packs beside his lodge. Victoria watched him, knowing. Jawbone watched him, knowing. He yanked the cords loose and rummaged within until he found the brown jug, stoppered with a cork. This he twisted out sharply and threw aside. This jug would not be returned to its niche in the pack goods half emptied. Then he lifted it, letting the fiery liquid gurgle from the neck and into his mouth until he burned, and his eyes watered, and still he didn't stop. Then finally, a pint later, he wiped tears from his small eyes, stood quietly, the demon pressures gone, and returned to the wagon where Father Kiley lay.

"Try this, captain."

The priest held up his hands feebly, searching for whatever was proffered, and Mister Skye realized he must help the man.

"Right here, captain," he said, placing the jug in Father Kiley's hands.

"Just a little," said the priest. "Enough to stop the pain. Oh God, enough to damp it a wee bit."

The jug was heavy, and he barely managed to lift it, and lift himself up enough to swallow. He coughed. Mister Skye watched him hawklike, ready to catch the jug, ready to snatch the precious juices in it.

"Ah," said the priest. "Ah . . . just a little. I am a weak man, Mister Skye. I should endure all this and more, but I am weak."

He sucked again, and coughed, and Mister Skye rescued the brown jug as it slipped.

"That is enough," Father Kiley said. "I am sinking into the pits."

His body drooped and then relaxed, and his ragged breathing steadied. But Mister Skye scarcely noticed. He lifted his jug regularly, feeling fire in his belly that spread out to limbs and made his head light.

Victoria peered in. "Come to the lodge. Sonofabitch, this here is a granddaddy coming. You git your ass to the lodge. Them missionaries all looking now, too, and ain't that trouble."

Mister Skye did as he was told. He usually managed that, managed to get to the lodge when Victoria demanded it. She would take over, she and Mary and Jawbone, while he took a voyage of his own.

They were staring, he knew, icy glares as he wended his way from the wagon to his lodge, but it didn't matter. Once in a while it was good that nothing mattered. Not anything. Not Methodists for sure, not the priest, or himself. Maybe Dirk, his little son, born of Mary.

He settled back into his buffalo robes and sucked regularly, feeling the warmth spread to his toes and fingers.

"That's the way the stick floats," he muttered. "Here's damp powder and no way to dry it . . ." and then, after a fine satisfying belch, "God save the bloody Queen."

The priest lay quiet that night, and for that the Reverend Cecil Rathbone felt grateful. For three nights the priest's sobs and groans had rended the dark and spawned terrible night-thoughts in them all, pouncing upon them when their aloneness in the dark lay deepest. On the other hand, from Mister Skye's small lodge there had emitted awful sounds all night, like a bull's bellow or an elk's bugle, and for these Cecil was not grateful. Their guide was drunk. Nay, more than drunk: he had departed from them into some world of his own, bawling like a newly weaned calf.

So the night was sleepless like the previous three, and at dawn the mood turned sullen among them. Even tireless Esmerelda showed signs of strain and fatigue, he thought, watching her as she busied herself at the cook-fire.

Alex Newton approached, looking unkempt and haggard. "Your Mister Skye has become a drunken lout, leaving us unprotected and unguided," he said acidly. "We seem to have little choice but to turn back. Preferably alone, leaving that swine and his squaws here to meet their fate."

The thought had occurred to Cecil, but he resisted. He possessed a dream. "Let us wait and see," he replied mildly.

"Perhaps this will pass in a day. We could all use some rest, and a quiet day given to repair of ourselves, and given to God—it's Sunday, I believe—might serve us well."

Over at Mister Skye's lodge there erupted a great bellow, and the guide emerged, shaking his head from side to side. He wobbled unsteadily ten yards, and then dug at his breechclout and relieved himself. The white women turned their faces away.

"We cannot permit this," snapped Alex. "The man's everything that is barbaric and pagan and unholy, and now he has offended our womanhood."

Mister Skye rolled unsteadily back to his lodge, but it was no longer there. Victoria had yanked it down and was folding the lodgecover. So he teetered over to Jawbone, but the evil horse laid back its ears and clacked its teeth and then butted Mister Skye, who tumbled to the ground and growled.

"Mercy!" said Esmerelda.

"Now his true character emerges," said Silas Potter coldly. "I saw it from the beginning and tried to warn . . ."

Something in the young man's smugness annoyed Cecil. Something of instant judgment and impossible standards and holy rectitude that felt as cold as a grave.

"I think we should hold a meeting here and now and decide what to do," Silas continued. "We obviously must do something. Skye is scarcely among the living and can't guide us. I don't suppose he could even say which way is north. And no protection at all. What if the savages fell on us? And we have that mad priest to cope with too—"

"He is not mad," said Esmerelda tartly.

Silas Potter stared coldly from behind his thick lenses. "Blinded then. He is now physically what he and all his ilk have always been mentally. I think there is a kind of justice in it. At any rate we have that to deal with, and I suppose we're stuck, unless we simply leave him here with the drunk and his loathsome squaws, and we return to Fort Laramie . . . picking up the other wagon and the Newtons' furnishings, if they haven't been demolished by passing savages. If our party is dirtied, it must wash, and the way to cleanse ourselves is to scrub away the filth and return to holiness."

Both Alex and Henrietta agreed, adamantly. The Samples, as usual, tended to their business and avoided the controversy. James Method was out scouting.

Cecil wasn't ready to surrender. "We'll wait a day. Take your rest today. We will see how things look in the morning. I'm not going to throw away a thousand miles of hard travel just because of a temporary setback. Mister Skye has kept us out of harm's way and delivered us here, and I'll not quit now. I am going to conduct some small Sunday service in an hour, when we are done with chores. I intend to invite Father Kiley to join us."

The look on Silas's face told Cecil a lot about the young man. Too much. He knew instinctively that he had chosen the wrong man to come west and teach the Blackfeet. The man was a holy hater, without a saving humor, and Cecil went cold at the thought of putting the Blackfeet, who would be both suspicious and eager to absorb the religion of the whites, in daily contact with Silas. And there'd be no help for it. This deep in the wilderness, the die was cast.

He watched Victoria clamber into the wagon to succor the priest. She was burdened with her bag of medicines, an iron pot, and a brown jug. Somehow the woman had brought Father Kiley along, tended to his needs, cleaned him, helped him through his bodily functions, and all of it kinder and more Christian than anyone in his camp. Cecil felt ashamed.

He walked to the wagon and found her spooning a buffalo meat stew into him.

"This is Cecil Rathbone, Father. I trust you are better?"

The priest remained silent. Then, "I couldn't say."

"It's Sunday, and I'm going to have a little service. A psalm, some Scripture, a prayer or two, maybe a little sermon. Thought maybe you'd like to sit in . . ."

He was met with silence.

"Or maybe I could read to you some, from your book, your, eh, breviary . . ."

"No."

"Well, if I can help—"

"No. I failed and am an outcast. Thrown into the darkest corner of hell, Reverend."

"Sonofabitch, you're crazy, blackrobe. You just getting your sight now, medicine sight inside. You're gonna be big medicine man before you know. Goddam, you ain't got sense."

She set the pot aside angrily and began cleaning his wounds.

"You!" she bellowed at Cecil. "You go away. You go get your people ready to move. Too damn much daylight gone by. We're all ready. All set to hop on ponies. Mary, she got us packed up."

"This is our holy day and I've declared a day of rest," said Cecil firmly.

"We ain't gonna stop. This here place ain't safe and we're gonna git out, see?"

"Without Mister Skye?"

"He's going to get on Jawbone. Mary and me, we'll lift him up. He's gone away awhile but he'll come back. Meanwhile, I'm the chief, you see? Sonofabitch, we don't stop for nothing. Me and Mary and Jawbone, we are the chiefs now."

"I think you have your marching orders, Mister Rathbone," said Father Kiley.

"I am going to have my services," said Cecil stubbornly. "But after that we'll go if you insist."

Victoria glared. "Make 'em fast. We got to go. This is a bad place, see? Too damn many Lakotah around the Powder River."

There was something in all this that delighted Cecil, and he agreed. On this day they'd do another fifteen miles or so, trek that much closer to Sun River.

"I will tell them," he said.

"You, blackrobe," said Victoria, proffering a jug to Father Kiley, "you drink some firewater I stole from Skye. Make pain go away. Drink before he come get it."

The priest found the proffered jug, swallowed and coughed, and swallowed again. "It helps," he said softly.

Two hours later the small caravan rolled out of the valley of the Powder and toward some high, rugged prairie ridges. When Cecil told his missionary party that they'd travel that day as usual, immediately following a brief service, they stared back harshly. All except Esmerelda, who laughed with delight. But they had silently packed and prepared, and silently listened when he conducted his service. And before they decamped, Esmerelda, as well as James Method, had stopped at the wagon and quietly held Father Kiley's hands, giving what they could.

Ahead rode Mister Skye, jug in hand, and listing twenty degrees to the right. Cecil Rathbone could not imagine how that black silk hat stayed on the guide's head.

Chapter 11

They toiled slowly this day because the land was rugged, and the towering shoulders of prairie were riven with gulches and thickets of chokecherry and buffaloberry brush. Victoria watched impatiently as the white medicine men behind her dug the earth with their shovels so the lumbering wagons and the carriage could ease into a dry gulch and groan up the other side. Sweat rivered from them, and their chief, Mister Rathbone, had finally taken off his black clothes and put on faded blue britches.

Victoria did not scout today: it fell to her to lead the caravan, because Mister Skye was in his own world for a while. She sent Mary out to the right, and the powerful black man, James, out to the left, and hoped they would see the world as well as she did. Before her, on the withers of her pony, sat Dirk, as much at home with Victoria as with his mother. She had no doubt about Mary's scouting. Mary had Indian eyes and could see and stay hidden herself. But the black white man, James, she worried about. The whites didn't see. That had become obvious to her over her long life. They could look straight at trouble and not see it. Often they didn't see it even when they looked at it through the magic eye-that-makes-things-bigger. The first time she had looked through Mister Skye's magic eye, she had jumped. The doe she stared at was so close she could almost touch it. The whites had strange and wonderful medicine, and the magic eye was one of those things. But they had to have medicine like that because they were so inferior in other ways. Any Absaroka person could see things that the white missed.

They were a strange people, the whites. They had lots of words, but some of them could not be said. She grew aware that the medicine men and their women recoiled when she said some things, as if she was saying something terrible. She had learned the English words from the trappers who stayed with the Crows each winter in the days of the beaver-catching. Lots of good English words filled her mouth full and rolled over her tongue like honey. Sonofabitch! they'd say, and she liked the sound of it better than the Absaroka. Mister Skye had lots of words, and she mostly used the ones he used, which were a little different because he came from across the big water and the other trappers didn't. She liked his better. But these medicine whites made sour faces, like eating green cherries, when she used the words, and so she knew these whites had good words and bad words. More than ever, the whites mystified her. These medicine men should be able to use all words, not just some. The Absaroka used all their words, and the shamans were the word-givers, not the word-hiders.

Victoria did not relish being in command today, because this was dangerous country, and the Lakotah lurked everywhere. Some of the Lakotah, the Brulé and Oglalla, were at war, but some not, but that didn't make much difference. There were always war parties out this time of summer, hunting prey, hoping to jump enemy hunting parties or steal horses from villages. A small party of whites like this would be great sport for any of them.

Mister Skye would be away from the world for another sun or two, she knew. He had finished the jug the blackrobe had given him, and was now into the ten-gallon cask he had bought from the sutler. He sat on Jawbone swaying gently and hugging his jug. Whenever he listed too far, Jawbone snarled at him, and he set himself right for

a while, only to lean the other direction, until Jawbone
snarled at him again. Jawbone didn't like to have Mister
Skye out of the world, and he walked with his ears laid
back and murder in his eyes and was twice as dangerous
in these times. He let Mary and Victoria lift Mister Skye
on and off his back, but that was all.

The trouble with this land of great shoulders was that
whole war parties or villages could be hidden just beyond any ridge, and it worried her. It was ambush country. It would take a dozen scouts, not two, to check all the
possibilities for trouble. To make matters worse, the wagons had to travel along the smoother ridges rather than the
coulees, so they were visible for miles in these uplands. So
Victoria rode, expecting trouble and maybe death at any
instant, and constantly seeking out defensive places as
they went along, where they could instantly shelter themselves from arrows and the occasional fusil or rifle of the
Lakotah or their Cheyenne allies.

When Mister Skye was in the world he would show
himself to enemies, and maybe treat with them, and his
medicine and Jawbone's medicine were so great that
usually there would be no battle. The Indian people of
the prairies knew that to fight Mister Skye or Jawbone
was to invite death. But they had never caught Mister
Skye out of the world as he was now, and Victoria worried that they might at any time, and kill him, and then
the rest of the party.

They struggled over the crest of a dry divide in the
middle of the gusty day, and stared down upon the long
green basin of Crazy Woman Creek miles distant. The
going was steep, and they had to lock wheels once again.
An hour later they reached a flat filled with shady cottonwoods and watered by a purling spring, and here Victoria called a midday halt to rest and water the animals,

and unlock the wheels of the wagons. Mary appeared, but Mister Method did not. Victoria, who was Mister Skye's sits-beside-him wife, listened to Mary detail the dangers ahead. She had seen nothing but she knew there were war parties ahead. It was something she knew. It was something Victoria knew too, and she wished Mister Skye were back in this world. She feared for James Method. He might be caught. He might give away their position to the Lakotah.

But all remained silent. A red-tailed hawk soared above the protected valley. She spotted crows, the symbols of her people, hopping from limb to limb among the cottonwoods. She could feel trouble, but could not see it. Together she and Mary lifted Mister Skye from Jawbone and let the horse graze. Skye relieved himself and sat upon the grasses, muttering and sighing and cradling his shining new Sharps in his big hands, and staring into the prairie hills.

The medicine people busied themselves with the livestock and the wagons and a simple noon meal. They were all quiet, knowing that Mister Skye was not in the world with them. The blackrobe groaned in the wagon, so Victoria took the jug away from Mister Skye and gave some of the spirits to the suffering priest.

"Is this Victoria?" he asked. "I am glad to have a sip. My head, my face . . . everything seems more painful than ever today."

He sucked the raw whiskey and gasped, and sucked again.

"I never knew how it is to be helpless and hopeless and plunged into hell. And to depend utterly on others for everything, the food I eat and the needs of my worthless body," he said. "I wish a good Sioux arrow would take me."

Victoria had no answer for that; there was none.

A half mile to the south James Method burst over a ridge on a sweated horse and raced recklessly downslope to their camp, and Victoria knew that the trouble had come. Jawbone laid his ears back and snarled, and in one gigantic shaking heave pitched Mister Skye's loose-cinched saddle off him and prepared for war. Mister Skye rocked slowly and then stood up, weaving like a dying top.

James Method rode fluidly, staying with the horse even as it plunged down a hard slope creased with gullies. It was no small feat of horsemanship, and Victoria momentarily admired it. But then the ridge above him filled with riders, bronzed warriors naked save for their breechclouts, ponies dancing along the ridge, a great horde of them, twenty, thirty, finally maybe fifty, she thought, all stripped for battle or the hunt. Not painted for war but plainly looking for prey of any sort, the great summer war games of the plains Indians. They lined the ridge, a terrible sight spread far to the left and right, dancing their sweated ponies, taking the measure of the small party below with its astonishing wagons where none had ever rolled before.

They were waiting, plainly, for some signal from the tall warrior who sat his white horse quietly about in the middle of the line. Then some of them were pointing and gesturing at Jawbone, and at Mister Skye, who rotated on his feet and peered at the blur ahead of him. Victoria hoped that it might be enough; that his mere presence and medicine might stop the slaughter. Mary stared, gathered Dirk to her, and began to sing her Shoshone death song. Victoria shuddered. Soon she would sing her own, and then join the others who had gone across to the other side.

But not yet. "Sonofabitch!" she cried. "You!"—she gestured at Cecil Rathbone—"get them damn horses and mules into the cottonwoods. Get them damn rifles out. Get them damn women in the wagons if they ain't gonna shoot. Get them damn wagons rolled around to make a fort along the cottonwoods. You git ready to shoot lotsa Lakotah. Mebbe Sans Arcs, mebbe Minneconjou."

They unfroze and began feverish preparations. Henrietta burst into tears and fled into the wagon. Clay Sample and his son Alfred drew their rifles and found cover in a thicket of cottonwoods. Alice and Miriam Sample shooed the oxen and mules and horses into the woods.

"Oh dear," said Esmerelda. "I think I'm going to find a rifle and I think I am going to shoot."

She did find one in the carriage.

James Method raced up and jumped from his lathered horse.

"They're a-coming," he said to Victoria. "And there's more than I ever seen. I guess I ain't gonna be a freeman very long." Then he grinned. "Bet they ain't ever took a scalp like mine before."

He found an excellent defensive position behind a fallen cottonwood trunk. It even had a notch in it where his blue rifle barrel poked its deadly bore toward the ridge.

"You!" Victoria bellowed at Silas Potter, who blinked whitely behind his spectacles. "You get your rifle and guard the rear. Them Lakotah is going to run to the side, see? You git over to them cottonwoods over there and cut them off, see?"

He stared. "I don't take life. I will retire to the Sample wagon and invoke the divine blessing that will preserve us. Meanwhile, I trust you will proceed to make peace."

"Sonofabitch!" Victoria roared. "You and that other one,

Newton. You git your rifles and git into them cottonwoods and see that them Lakotah don't come from the sides."

Red-faced and frightened, Alex Newton demurred. "I think you should treat with them first. You know the hand signs and all . . . Tell them we are missionaries. Medicine men. Peacefully passing through to do the works of God, eh?"

"Sonofabitch, you git them rifles and plenty of powder and ball."

Neither of them did as she bid. And now the leader, up there on the ridge, was putting on his warbonnet. Its white and black eagle feathers caught the sun and whipped in the wind. Its red tradecloth trimming looked as bright as new blood. Its tasseled ermine skins framed the face of the chief. The long bonnet-tail of feathers whipped sideways and fell over the croup of his dancing white pony. But still they pointed and argued up there, and it was Mister Skye's presence they argued about.

For his part Skye yawned, belched, lifted his new Sharps, and fired into the heavens. A hawk plunged to earth, losing feathers as it fell, Victoria gaped. How could he do such a thing? Within seconds he loaded a new paper cartridge and primer. Whites stared. Skye belched.

Above, young warriors were arguing heatedly with the chief, and Victoria knew exactly what they were saying: there is Mister Skye down there, and Jawbone. We are over fifty and they are few. Now at last we can count coup, take the scalp of Skye, kill the terrible horse. And whoever kills Skye will be the greatest warrior on the plains. And each of the young Lakotah, she knew, dreamed the dream of glory, of Skye's scalp on the tip of his war lance. They would come even if the chief forbade it; the young warriors would sweep down and around, seeing only glory against such a puny party below.

And they would succeed, she knew. Who among these missionaries could even shoot straight? Then they stopped arguing, and the warriors on the ridge began a fierce war chant, wheeling their restless ponies, gathering into three attack groups, one for each flank and one down the center, even as the chief directed with sharp strong gestures up there.

Jawbone, ears back, returned the howl, with an unearthly shriek. Mister Skye was not in the world and not in the saddle, so he would need to fight alone. Mister Skye peered boozily up the slope and decided to saddle up. Languorously he lifted his saddle to Jawbone's back and tightened the cinch, fumbling a little. It gave Victoria some small hope. Skye's actions were so deliberate that he seemed contemptuous of danger. From above, where the warriors were milling and watching fascinated, Skye would seem to have a superhuman nonchalance. Still, Victoria thought, it was nothing. Nothing against so many crazed young Lakotah. This would be her deathsong day. And all these missionaries, too. They would die whining the way whites usually did.

Behind her Henrietta Newton was doing something crazy, pawing desperately at the puckerstring of the wagon. Then she had the canvas loosened at the rear of the wagon and pulled it over the bows until the organ in the rear of the wagon was in plain sight. It puzzled Victoria. Maybe Henrietta was just showing the warriors on the ridge what useless plunder lay in the wagon, that big wooden thing that did whatever it did. Victoria shrugged.

Then they came. With an ear-shivering howl they flowed down the long grassy slope, shining bronze bodies glinting in the afternoon sun, wild ponies plunging and dancing beneath them, lances in hand, bows nocked with arrows. Above, the chief sat still on his white horse, watching. There were two headmen with him, ready to convey his messages.

Jawbone shrieked but Mister Skye held him, weaving gently in his saddle. Even out of this world, Mister Skye was an awesome force, and with Jawbone beneath him, a danger to the clot of warriors pouring toward him. Victoria knew what Mister Skye would do, and Jawbone knew it too. At the right moment they would plunge up the slope directly toward that war chief on the ridge.

Behind her Henrietta was still fussing with that organ thing. Now she sat before it and pulled out small white-capped things. What a useless business. At least the woman was not cringing in the bed of the wagon the way some white women did in war. Then her hands pressed down on the organ thing, and thunder rose up from it and shivered through the valley. "A Mighty Fortress Is Our God," she sang in a quivery voice even as the organ sent thunder out into the ranks of the howling warriors, now only a hundred yards off.

"Sonofabitch," yelled Victoria.

"Jaysas," muttered Mister Skye.

Several warriors pulled up their ponies and gaped. Victoria sighted down the barrel of her carbine and squeezed, and one fell off his pony.

The music bellowed out now, as majestic as a cathedral hymn, with Henrietta's tart soprano in accompaniment. What new and terrible medicine was this? Victoria didn't know. Mary, hand to her mouth, peered at the organ wagon, terrified. A shot racketed from James Method's rifle and another warrior who had stopped in his tracks to fathom the thunderous organ fell.

An arrow hissed toward Henrietta but missed. She was oblivious to danger anyway, spellbound by her own recital. Several of the milling Sioux renewed the charge, but Clay Sample's rifle barked and then Alfred's. Esmerelda, crouching behind the carriage, aimed and fired and a pony faltered, sagged and collapsed, the young warrior on it jumping free. And still they milled, terrified of this thunder-music. Some saw that it was only noise and tried to rally their brothers to battle. But others saw the medicine of the sky spirits in this white woman's hands and knew the day would be evil unless they fled at once. More arrows hissed, and one burned past Victoria slicing her sleeve and drawing blood on her arm.

"What's happening?" cried Father Kiley.

"The Sioux are attacking," said Henrietta primly as her hands continued to press the keys.

"I will stand then and pray for an arrow," he said, rising in the wagon beside Henrietta and the organ. He wore his priestly clothes again, which were none the worse for wear except for some bullet holes in them. And then the warriors were pointing at him as well, the man in the black suit and white collar, with a heavy bandage over his eyes, tall and blind and exposed to whatever arrow or bullet came.

Far up on the ridge the chief in the warbonnet barked something to his lieutenants, and the subchiefs rode down the slope, signaling. It seemed all over, at least for the moment. Victoria did not lower her carbine. There might still be some Lakotah warrior itching to count coup against Mister Skye. Jawbone shrilled insanely, pawing the earth.

Henrietta finished "A Mighty Fortress Is Our God," and started "Rock of Ages," still warbling along with the thunderous organ.

"Jaysas," growled Mister Skye. "My head."

Cecil rose from under a wagon. "Henrietta, dear," he said. "I think you have inspired us enough for the moment."

She played on, though, unable to stop, afraid the silence would bring renewed howls of war and death. Father Kiley held his hands to his ears, and then sat down weakly in the wagon again. And then at last Henrietta finished her solemn hymn, and stood, glaring at the world.

"Thank God," said Alex, but he didn't say for what.

From his vantage point high on the ridge, the chief elaborately pointed his rifle into the sky and fired. Then he slowly picked his way down the slope, his powerful bronze torso impressive even from Victoria's distance. His authority lay upon him. A nod, a gesture, won instant respect among his warriors. She knew he was a great chief of the Lakotah, a dread enemy of the Absaroka people. Easily the man rode, straight toward Mister Skye, who squinted through blurred eyes while Jawbone snarled. Mister Skye handed his jug to Victoria, and she knew he would come back into the world again. Jawbone watched Mister Skye pass the jug, and he no longer laid his ears back.

Then, at perhaps fifty yards, he waited. Mister Skye squinted, weaved, and roared like a grizzly.

"Man-Afraid-of-His-Horses!" he roared. "It is you."

"And it is you, Mister Skye."

Mister Skye dismounted from Jawbone, who watched the encroaching menace with murderous intent and bared teeth.

But Mister Skye wove forward with open arms now, and the great war chief of the Oglala Sioux did likewise.

And then they were together, Mister Skye quietly pressing the chief's hands, and Man-Afraid-of-His-Horses likewise. From the ridge the Oglala watched suspiciously, angry about their dead, and from the scattered shelters of the wagons and cottonwoods, the missionary party watched narrowly. What sort of turn of events was this? Victoria lowered her carbine as a sign of peace, but not all the way.

Chapter 12

Under crisis, Mister Skye's mind cleared swiftly, although he was reluctant to abandon his whiskey-journey. He knew Man-Afraid-of-His-Horses well. Many times the Oglala chief had come to Fort Laramie, and had visited with Mister Skye. Now they would smoke the pipe, and there would probably be a feast, unless some fool among the missionaries, or some refractory Lakotah warrior, caused trouble.

Even now Man-Afraid-of-His-Horses was pulling the sacred calumet from its soft-tanned bag, and summoning his lieutenants. Mister Skye recognized one of them, a tall craggy warrior in his early thirties named Red Cloud. He stared up at both of them. The Sioux leaders were tall men, though he was wider.

He thought to summon his own lieutenants to this parley. "Mister Rathbone," he called. "Bring Father Kiley, and leave your rifle behind."

He glanced at Victoria, who swiftly concealed the whiskey jug in the mule-packs, and at Jawbone, who had settled into resigned toleration of these enemies. Victoria and Mary would see what lay ahead, and erect the lodge nearby, for this would be an all-night affair.

He spotted James Method standing behind a cottonwood

log rampart. "Mister Method, you will join us," he said. "We are going to have a party; lay down your rifles, all of you. Your lives depend on it."

He watched as Clay and Alfred Sample reluctantly slid their rifles into the wagon, and Esmerelda Rathbone lowered hers and grinned. Alex Newton hefted a rifle as well, but seemed almost paralyzed at the sight of so many warriors so close.

"Mister Newton," Skye roared.

Slowly the reverend lowered his weapon, and sought out Silas, who stood stiffly, white and staring, a Bible in hand. Those two would be the ones most likely to cause trouble, Mister Skye thought. He nodded to Victoria, who understood his purpose at once. She always did. She would keep her hawk's-eye on them.

Cecil Rathbone led the priest to the growing circle of headmen sitting in the meadow grass. Even as the priest sat down, shakily, beside Cecil, they were staring and pointing at the priest's bandaged eyes, but also at the bullet holes in his black coat and black shirt. Victoria had washed the priest's garments, purging the bloodstains from them, and Mister Skye knew exactly what the Lakotah were thinking—that the blackrobe's medicine had prevented the bullets from piercing his body. They themselves had sacred war shirts they believed turned bullets. They were almost as fascinated with James Method, although a black man of the whites was not new to them. From the fur-trade days, there had been several, including the dreaded Crow subchief, Jim Beckwourth.

"We shall smoke the pipe," said Man-Afraid-of-His-Horses, tamping tobacco into the bowl and igniting it from a glowing ember one of his warriors brought to him solemnly. The chief held the pipe before him, and then saluted the cardinal directions with it, and Mother Earth, and Wakan Tanka, and puffed solemnly. He passed it first to Mister Skye, who repeated the small ritual, and then passed it around the circle until all present had smoked the pipe of peace, and the charge of tobacco had been entirely consumed. Then he knocked out the ash and leisurely slipped the sacred pipe back into its elaborate pouch.

"Now then, Mister Skye," the chief said in Lakotah, "I will introduce my chiefs and you will do the same, and then we will talk. Our hearts are heavy because two of our young men lie dead, and one horse. Our hearts are afraid because of the bad medicine of the thunder-music-maker. And our hearts are curious about the blackrobe with the bullet holes in his clothing and the bandage upon his eyes, and the black man here, of a kind we have seen only once or twice in all our winters."

Then he introduced his headmen while Mister Skye translated for the whites and James Method. Mister Skye stared at Red Cloud, knowing in his bones that the craggy warrior with the proud demeanor would become a great Sioux war chief, perhaps against the whites someday. Mister Skye then introduced his own men.

"This is the Reverend Cecil Rathbone, a holy man who is taking his medicine people to the north to teach the ways of his medicine.

"And the man without eyes is Father Kiley, of the blackrobes, who is bringing his medicine to the people of the west. He is a brother of the blackrobe you know, Pierre de Smet. A few days ago he was caught by a hunting party headed by Wolf-That-Circles, and they put his eyes out. But Father Kiley's medicine was very large, for no sooner had they done that thing than Wolf-That-Circles died, and so did others among them who had taken his clothing."

The Oglala headmen gasped. This was news indeed.

"What did you tell them?" asked Cecil Rathbone.

"That Father Kiley is a man of great medicine; that those Cheyenne who took his clothes all died."

"I have no medicine," said Father Kiley wearily. "I didn't want to teach them medicine. I came to bring them other things. You are misleading them, Mister Skye."

The priest spoke in a voice so small and tired that it seemed to fade even as he finished.

"Leave this to me, mate," Mister Skye said. "Who says you haven't got medicine? Will you say it wasn't the hand of God, eh?"

Red Cloud followed the exchange closely, and Mister Skye suspected he knew English.

Man-Afraid-of-His-Horses broke in. "We have two dead and even now I hear my warriors chanting the songs of death behind me. We have a dead pony. What will you pay us for this? We want many horses and powder and lead, and we wish to hear the thunder-music-maker if you will assure us it is not bad medicine."

Mister Skye turned harsh. "You lost your young men in war, attacking us. We did not attack you. They died honorably in battle and will be celebrated in the lodges of the Lakotah for dying bravely. We will give you nothing. We will not reward you for making war upon us. And you must never do it again. If we make the thunder-music you will all fall away like leaves after the frost comes."

The chief nodded solemnly, and then conceded. "It is as you say. Our medicine is bad because of the wagon that makes noise. We are not at war with medicine men. We wish to learn of this thing you have here. We have no word for it."

The priest surprised Mister Skye by responding in a

hesitant Sioux tongue. "My good chiefs, it is called an organ, and it has no medicine in it. Only the One Above has medicine. It is the same thing as the flutes you have, only larger. It is used by whites to praise the One Above, mostly, but it is nothing but wood and metal and leather. If Mister Skye tells you it has medicine and you must fear it, then he misleads you."

Mister Skye was astonished.

Man-Afraid-of-His-Horses stared at him sharply, and Red Cloud did also.

"Mister Skye," said Father Kiley in English. "I'm a poor priest. I'd be an even poorer one if I let the Lakotah here believe that the organ has medicine powers for good or ill. I will not encourage them in their idolatry."

Red Cloud, who seemed to understand some English, listened sharply.

"What is all this about?" asked Cecil Rathbone. "Have you threatened them with the organ?"

"Aye, mate, I have. Medicine is life or death here."

Cecil pondered it. "And so are other things life or death, Mister Skye. Please tell the chiefs and headmen that Henrietta will be pleased to present an organ concert of hymns offered to God."

Mister Skye did, pondering all the while the strange courage of Father Kiley. And for that matter, the strange courage of Henrietta Newton who responded to bullets and arrows with hymns.

Man-Afraid-of-His-Horses nodded. "We will listen to the woman play the organ," he said. "We will have a feast. We killed two fat buffalo cows and that will be enough. We will listen to the organ make music to Wakan Tanka. And then we Lakotah will dance for Wakan Tanka, so that you may see our music as well. The black-robe, Father Kiley, speaks well and with a good spirit, and has eyes inside of his head that see light. We will honor this blackrobe, Father Kiley, as a friend of Lakotah, and of the Oglala people this evening, and we will give him a name. You, Skye, have great medicine, but medicine goes bad, and someday your medicine will not be enough for you."

Mister Skye translated most of it for Cecil Rathbone and James Method, while Red Cloud watched intently.

The chief stood, and with him his headmen, and with a nod he retreated to his warriors.

Cecil Rathbone helped the priest to his feet. "I don't know what all that was about, not speaking Sioux lingo, but I got the gist of it. Must say, you got courage, padre."

"No," Kiley said slowly. "It is not that. It is that I have nothing, and therefore have nothing to lose. I would welcome an arrow, Reverend. My Lord has taken everything away from me, and surely I have been punished. I am a poor priest, but I could be a poorer one if I didn't speak out against idols."

Mister Skye did not have time to ponder the strange turn of events. There was a feast to prepare for, camp to be made. And cobwebs to shake out of his head. Silently Victoria handed him a cup of coffee, and he drank the hot bitter liquid thinking of medicine and power and living and dying, and the warning of Man-Afraid-of-His-Horses.

"Mister Method," he said. "Some of the younger Sioux will no doubt try to steal the horses. They don't care about mules or oxen, though they might drive the mules off just to keep us from going after them. They're likely to try it even though the headmen have smoked the peace pipe. So . . . hobble them. And picket them close to the wagons. And you and the Samples keep guard. Shoot if you must."

"Ah'll do it."

"And, Mister Method. They've scarcely seen a black man. They'll be curious. You tell them what you want. They have slaves of their own, so they'll be interested in how you got away."

"Not very often Ah'm the center of attention."

"Well, enjoy yourself. They mean no harm."

Mister Skye wanted to talk with Silas Potter. If this feast under the peace pipe turned into a slaughter, it would be Potter's doing. He found the young man slumped behind the Samples' wagon, staring whitely at the bustling Sioux warriors, jaw clenched.

"Need to talk with you, mate."

"Are you drunk, Skye?"

"No, but I'm not cold sober either."

"I do not heed the depraved."

"You'll listen to me, mate. Your life depends on it. Stand up now. I'll not talk to you sitting down, like a man addressing a mutt."

"Is that what you think I am, a mutt?"

"Stand up."

Angrily and deliberately the young teacher stood, contempt written across his face.

"I do not intend to be at this party of yours. I will not watch heathen savages dance to their heathen god. I will not tolerate naked savages in the presence of our women."

Mister Skye scarcely knew where to begin, he had so much to say. He would have preferred a chop to the jaw that would lay the bloody fool down for a few hours.

"I'll start with a little warning, Potter. If you start trouble, any kind of trouble, I'll truss you up and gag your mouth and throw you in a wagon."

"That's about the way I've assumed you'd behave, Skye. All force and power and diabolical strength. No reason, no persuasion, no holy restraint. You're as barbarous as these savages. Do you know what preserved us a few minutes ago? Henrietta's hymns. The invoking of Divine Providence, and not your drunken confrontation with fifty or sixty armed Sioux, with a few rifles here."

"Medicine," replied Mister Skye. "Thunder-music, bad medicine for the Lakotah."

"Henrietta's faith; divine intervention."

Mister Skye was not one to mock God. "Perhaps you are right, Mister Potter."

Self-righteous Silas was not one to be gracious in victory. "Your demon medicine is nothing, and you have no authority over me. I intend to stop the heathen dance to their heathen god."

"Will you listen to reasons and arguments?"

"I've no intention of listening to any of your talk. You are Satan or one of Satan's."

Mister Skye shrugged. "That's what I thought, mate. We'll be watching you."

"Poke my eyes out and jam burning brands into me!"

"You envy Father Kiley, do you?"

Silas Potter looked pained. "The church of Rome is a whore," he said.

Mister Skye shrugged. There were other things to do, and he hunted for Henrietta, who sat quietly with Alex.

"That was a fine brave thing, Mrs. Newton," he said.

"No thanks to you," Alex intervened shortly. "With a drunken guide she had to do something."

"Aye, mate, I was that," Mister Skye agreed. "My women run a camp better than I, and you were bloody fortunate they were in charge."

"I don't believe in guns and war. We would have all been slaughtered," she said. "I played the hymns to rally us, remind us of our purpose, bringing God to the savages rather than fighting them. I played so that our missionary party would lay down our guns and trust in God."

Mister Skye grinned. "It was a brave thing, madam. The Sioux have requested a concert, and I have told them you would oblige. Play what you will, but play."

"I will do that," she said quietly. "Perhaps if they hear sacred music, they will be converted."

"They're going to dance, you know. They want to show us how they dance to Wakan Tanka. They have no drums or rattles, because they're traveling light, for war. Maybe you could do a drumbeat while they dance."

"I don't know—a heathen dance . . ."

"Mrs. Newton, what they call Wakan Tanka is their perception of God. A dance to Wakan Tanka is not the same as their dances to the animal spirits, buffalo dance, deer dance, rain-maker dance, and all the rest."

Henrietta looked at Alex, uncertainly.

"Well . . ." she said.

"I think not," said Alex. "Their nakedness offends our women. They're doing a heathen dance. No, when they start we shall all retire and not witness evil."

"I can scarcely imagine a graver insult to them," said Mister Skye.

"Mister Skye," said Alex in a pained voice. "We are people of God. We don't traffic with heathen things."

Mister Skye sighed. "I don't know what you'll do when you reach the Blackfeet—if you reach them, Reverend."

There was no arguing with them, so he left them. He'd truss and gag them too, if he had to, if they invited a massacre. Off a little, the Sioux had several cookfires burning. Guards had been posted on a ridge, and herders watched their ponies. He counted fifty-seven of them. One small incident, and he and all his charges would be slaughtered. The warriors had finished skinning the buffalo cows—usually women's work but this was a war party—and brought the prize cuts, hump ribs that tasted better than a beef standing rib roast, to Mary and Victoria and the white women. He hoped the whites understood the courtesy of the Sioux, presenting them with the prize cuts.

The shadows lay long across the hills when at last the buffalo meat was cooked perfectly and the feasting began. There were three feasts, really. One composed of the Sioux warriors, off by themselves, some of them nursing anger toward the whites who had killed two of their number. At another fire sat a smaller gathering of the whites. But around a separate campfire between the others was Man-Afraid-of-His-Horses, his headmen, and invited guests, which included Mister Skye, Father Kiley, James Method, and Cecil Rathbone. Mary, Victoria, and Esmerelda sat outside of this circle, according to Sioux custom.

They ate heartily. The buffalo meat was as tasty as any that Mister Skye could remember. There was little time for talk although the ones next to James Method were curious about him and plied him with questions, which Mister Skye tried to translate from across the circle. The former slave enjoyed the attention. When at last they were all full and heavy in the belly, they wiped their hands in the grasses or at the spring beside the cottonwoods. And then the chief addressed those around his fire, in the twilight.

"I wish to give the blackrobe a Sioux name," he said, while Mister Skye translated. "He has a true tongue and is a brave man who has endured torture and pain. He's worthy of my people. Please bring him forward."

Cecil led the priest around the fire and settled him on the grass before the chief.

"I have decided on a Lakotah name for you," said Man-Afraid-of-His-Horses. "I have chosen a name that describes your great medicine. I will name you Man-That-Sees. From now on, among my people, you will be Man-That-Sees, and you will be welcome in any Lakotah village or camp, and all the Lakotah people will hear of you and know you are a brother."

Father Kiley nodded. "I am honored by the name," he said softly. "You have given me vision again. May I see in your behalf, and may my vision be true and pleasing to the One Above."

One by one the Sioux in the circle clasped his hands and gave him their names, the chief last, and it was done.

"Now we would like to hear the thunder-music again. We would like to see the woman make the music that praises the One Above."

The chief stood and beckoned his warriors, and in time they gathered quietly around the wagon with the organ in it. The canvas had been stripped away from its bows so that all might see Henrietta play. She sat down gravely, choosing a Bach recital first, before the hymns. When the first deep notes thundered into the lavender sky and echoed off the wild lonely hills where no such sound had ever been heard, the Sioux shivered and covered their mouths or held their ears, and even Mister Skye felt an odd twinge as the vibrating music lost itself in the wilds the way the rays of fire were dimmed by distance. Henrietta played determinedly, no longer from the sheet music before her because it was growing dark, a white-faced rigid figure. She did not play particularly well, Mister Skye thought, but with force nonetheless.

She turned to her hymns then, all of them majestic and slow. No one sang. The warriors stared, absorbed by this novelty, half afraid at first but gradually relaxing. Across the flickering light Mister Skye watched Silas Potter and Alex Newton carefully, wondering what was going through their heads. And then Henrietta finished. She stood stiffly, bowed slightly, and clambered down from the wagon.

The chief stood. "Now my young men will dance," he said.

Mister Skye waited, on edge. A Sioux dance could involve almost anything, including a display of scalps. That, indeed, proved to be what this dance was about: a scalp dance, invoking the blessings of the One Above in the taking of many scalps from many enemies. The chosen dancers assembled around the fire, each carrying a lance dressed with scalps, or carrying war shields with scalps dangling from them. He saw excited whispering over among the whites, and pointing, and pained expressions, and Mister Skye feared the worst.

He leaned over to the chief. "I believe I can make the organ sound like a drum. Send me a drummer, and we will make the organ thunder like drums, fast or slow as your drummer says."

The chief spoke, and an older warrior, honored by the chief's request, sat down beside Mister Skye on the organ bench. He showed the warrior how to pump the bellows with his feet and how to tap the lower keys, and he returned to his place between the chief and Cecil. Then it began, harsh chanting, pounding organ beat, sticks on logs, and the rhythmic spastic movement of almost naked bronze men circling a fire, waving lances and shields adorned with human hair. Two or three minutes of that were enough for Silas Potter and the Newtons, who stared angrily and turned to leave, herding the Samples with them. That's what Mister Skye had feared, a calculated insult and a deadly gesture. He arose, intending to herd them back again or box them into submission, but Cecil caught his arm.

"Would our Sioux friends mind if I joined the hoedown?" he asked. "I haven't had a chance to kick up my feet since I left Illinois. Methodists frown on dancing, you know, but I feel a bit wicked tonight." He laughed heartily, even as his eyes followed the retreating backs of his missionary party out of the firelight. His eyes were not alone, for now every Sioux watched and muttered.

"Hurry!" said Mister Skye.

Cecil leapt up and headed straight into the circling warriors and began a nimble imitation, as spirited as anything the Sioux did. Laughter and excitement rippled among the Sioux. Cecil was grinning, leaping and dancing in his black suit, enjoying himself. Out at the edge of light, the Newtons and Potter and the Samples gaped, horrified.

Esmerelda stood. "Come, Father Kiley, we shall dance too, and I'll lead you. In their own way, they are dancing to God, and so shall we."

The priest shook his head at first, tired and afraid, but the cataract of her laughter caught him and his face brightened beneath the heavy bandage. He stood, and was led into the firelit circle and gently, with Esmerelda leading the priest, they circled the fire with quiet dignity. The warriors stood and howled with delight. The drummer working the organ speeded up the heartbeat. Man-Afraid-of-His-Horses smiled and leaned over to Mister Skye.

"There are some among your medicine men who are friends of the Lakotah, and some who are not," he said. "And so it shall be, before Wakan Tanka."

Chapter 13

Crazy Woman Creek proved to be the toughest obstacle they had yet encountered. It ran between cutbanks in a rugged arid prairie valley, and it was running high because of heavy June storms in the Big Horns, combined with the last of the spring snowmelt. James Method rode over a mile in each direction from the point where the small caravan struck the creek, but the best he could come up with was a place somewhat to the north where the east bank was gentle enough to carry the wagons, while on the west side there loomed a ten-foot cutbank of tan gumbo clay. It would mean a lot of shoveling.

For three days after their encounter with the Sioux they had toiled down a long grade into the wide dry valley of the Crazy Woman. Mister Skye resumed command, keen-eyed and cold sober after giving parting presents of tobacco and shot and powder to Man-Afraid-of-His-Horses, and watching the Sioux war party trail east toward its Powder River village. James Method rode at his usual position, scouting forward and to the west, while Victoria scouted ahead and to the east. James had also become the principal hunter, something he did with ease and caution, never felling his game until he was certain there were no hostile parties within earshot. He favored buffalo, which grazed this up-and-down country in small groups, but when luck failed him, he could usually find a deer, and once an elk. He had a chance at a sow grizzly with a cub, but chose to avoid the dangerous animal.

All the long day the men of the party, mainly Cecil Rathbone and Clay Sample, along with Alfred, Silas

Potter, and sometimes Alex Newton, took turns with a pike and shovels cutting a notch in the far cutbank that would serve as a ramp for the wagons. Alex Newton, soft and corpulent, swiftly blistered his hands and complained continuously. Silas Potter worked grimly, though his thin frail body kept him from achieving much. The real burden fell upon Clay Sample, who worked the pike into the hardpan, and Cecil, who shoveled the loosened earth away. Mister Skye helped occasionally, although he had the larger responsibility of keeping this party guarded and safe while it labored.

By the end of this hard day, with only a pitiful cut in the far bank to show for brutal labor, Alex began to complain about James Method, off scouting and hunting and lazing in the June breezes, instead of turning his powerful young body to the hard task of hewing out a wagon road. The black scout was unaware of it until he rode into camp at the end of the day bearing a heavy load of hump ribs, tongue, and liver he cut from a young cow.

"We employed Method because he's a strong young man and can do these things. I'm a minister of the Gospel and not made for such things. But you send him off lollygagging each day . . ."

"Mister Method is my choice," said Mister Skye bluntly. "Who else is there? Father Kiley can no longer do it."

"Yourself or young Alfred," Alex replied. "Maybe we don't need a scout at all. Your younger squaw could do it, keep an eye out . . ."

All of this was a peculiar and petulant argument coming from a man who had dug into the far cutbank less than an hour and had then pleaded blisters and fatigue. Even as Newton complained, Clay and Alfred Sample and Cecil Rathbone continued to chip away quietly and patiently.

Method had scarcely returned to camp when he felt
Alex's glare, not to mention the frosty gaze of Silas Potter,
and he wondered about it. The teacher's frozen gaze he
was used to; he had rarely seen the frail white scholar
smile or laugh. But he felt discomforted by the Reverend
Newton's probing stare.

Then Mister Skye enlightened him. "Mister Method,
they'd like you to help shovel. I suppose I'll have you do
that in the morning, and I'll scout myself. After the nooning, we'll switch."

"Ah'll shovel," he said. He didn't mind. He'd let his
lithe, powerful body work up a fine sweat. "Oh, Mister
Skye, there's been another storm boiling up over the Big
Horns, and flashing lightning I can even see from here,
and Ah expect this river's going to flow hard soon enough."

The guide nodded.

Method turned over the meat to the women and
stopped, as he did each evening, at the wagon where
Father Kiley lay. "How goes it today, Father?" he asked.

"Is that you, James? I wish I could tell you better, but I
can't. The pain never stops, and sometimes I think it's
worse than ever. Victoria tells me there is lots of, ah,
drainage from my eyes—from my eye sockets. I am rec-
onciled to blindness, but Lord help me, this pain . . ."

"Ah'm sorry. Ah was hoping for better news."

"Tell me about your day," said the priest hastily.

"Ah saw something strange, and thought you'd know
since you've been here a lot, or maybe Mister Skye . . . It
was maybe two valleys over to the west, toward the Big
Horns, still in this dry country and on a little creek Ah
could jump across, with a lot of cottonwoods along it . . .
good camping place. Ah dropped the cow buffalo right
there, an easy shot, the wind right, and no sound carrying far out of that little bowl . . . And when Ah rode up,

that cow was lying in some ceremonial place that gave me the shivers. There was twenty, thirty human skulls all in a circle, facing out, with signs of old paint on them, and some kind of rock pile with a stick in the middle, and paint-pictures on the stick, and other things, totems and amulets . . ."

"A ghost place," said Father Kiley. "Some village or some tribe lost a lot of people there, probably from ambush or war. They believe the spirits still haunt it. It's a taboo place where they never come. If I saw it, I could probably tell you what tribe. They all leave their marks. If you shot that buffalo cow in the middle of it, you'd better not tell Mary or Victoria, because they'll think that cow had one of the ghosts inside it. They'd no more eat that cow than shoot themselves."

"Ah thought it was a fine camping place. Would other tribes stay there now?"

"No, never. That's a place of terror, spirits haunting and lurking in the night, terrible things. No."

"Ah felt it, even in broad daylight, lots of sun, and the blue mountains with their white peaks just a little away. Ah got the shivers cutting her up."

From the campfire perhaps fifty yards away and far out of earshot, Victoria was staring at him and at the meat. It was not over the flames, but lying untouched in the grass. Then she walked to him in her fiesty way.

"Sonofabitch, that meat is no damn good," she snapped. "Where did you shoot it?"

"Nice little valley over west."

"What was there?"

"A few buffalo."

"It gives me damn bad feelings. That is bad-medicine meat. You get that damn meat out of this camp, way out, down the river and let it float, see? No good."

"That's fresh meat. Ah didn't even shoot it until a couple of hours ago."

"You get that damn hump meat out. I got the doe still hanging and we're gonna have that."

"Perhaps you could explain, Victoria," said Father Kiley softly.

"Nothing to explain. That cow got bad spirit in it. I stare at the ribs and I see old grandma Absaroka woman there. Sonofabitch, she's been dead ten, twelve winters now. I know her, that one in the meat."

"Surely you were imagining—"

"I see what I see. Now go get that dead Absaroka spirit woman and take it away or we all die."

There was no resisting her. She had the same sort of frantic power he had seen once before in an old black fieldhand at the plantation he had fled.

"Ah'm coming, grandmother," he said. Meekly he picked up the day's offering, wrapped it in a small tarpaulin, and carried it out of the camp, Victoria glaring at him all the while. Mister Skye noticed, and angled after him as he plunged deeper into the cottonwoods and away from camp.

"What was that all about?" Mister Skye asked.

"Victoria said the meat was evil, said she saw a ghost in it, and Ah have to remove it."

"Where'd you shoot that cow?" he asked sharply.

"Few miles west. In a place with some skulls in a circle. Ah confess, Ah didn't tell her that."

Mister Skye nodded. "I know the place. That is a place no Indian goes if he can help it. There was a slaughter there, whole Crow village wiped out, almost, by Arapaho wandering north of their usual haunts. Caught them at dawn, with the young warriors already gone after buffalo. If you saw a rock cairn and a marked stick and a

few other things, that was Crow medicine there. But
there's not a plains Indian who'd go near the place knowingly."

"Ah felt it, felt the evil, Mister Skye."

"Who can explain it, eh?"

"Ah don't understand Indian religion."

"Mister Method, I've been here in this wild land almost twenty years and I don't understand it either. But I
respect it. Makes my hair stand sometimes. There are
plenty of times when it's no good at all. The shamans
will say good medicine is coming and then there's a disaster. But there are other times, mate, so help me, one of
them has a dream, and they go to a shaman to have it interpreted, or they simply declare what is going to happen
in the future, and then it happens exactly as they dreamt
it. How do you explain that? I can't."

"Ah think there's earth spirits and heaven spirits, and
maybe the Indians know the earth spirits. Ah remember
where Ah come from, there was an old woman, fierce old
woman, one of the field darkies living in a shack, with
wire gray hair and hot brown eyes and a thick nose, and
all bent over and frail from a hard life picking cotton all
her days, and she had it, the knowledge of the spirits and
the future, and the power to change things. Ah was lucky,
a house boy for the master, always living easy . . . But
Ah used to sneak off and visit her down there and listen
to her angry talk. She never just said something; she spit
it out, made it snap out of her teeth. Ah'd take her the
stuff Ah snitched from the big kitchen in the big house,
sweets, leg of fried chicken, good stuff, so she liked to
see me. She told me things then . . . she told me where
Ah come from. Ah didn't know who my pappy was. Ah'm
lighter so Ah thought maybe it was some white man, but
the old woman said it was the master himself—and Ah

was half-brother to the white boys Ah played with. She told me lots of things that were true. She told me Ah'd escape when Ah was older, and Ah did. Ah got a good education reading books and studying on the way the masters lived there in the house, and Ah had saved a few pennies and what all, and some castoff clothing, so Ah got a black suit and a boiled white shirt and a Bible one day, and Ah got a stagecoach ticket—they wouldn't let me sit inside because Ah was a darkie—but Ah sat on top in my suit and white shirt and cravat with a Bible in one hand and a valise in the other, and rode away and no one stopped me. Ah was Reverend Isaac Horne . . . Oh, Mister Skye, it was good to get free. The masters treated me right kindly—Ah was lucky—but still they owned me, could sell me or my children, and Ah couldn't go anywhere because that slave collar was around my neck, invisible but real . . . That old woman told me it was going to happen. She told me lots more, too . . ."

James Method suddenly remembered another story told by the old grandma down in the shack, and his heart lurched.

"You and I were both slaves, mate. I was press-ganged by the Royal Navy at age fourteen, just a few blocks from my parents' house near London. Never saw them again. A slave in the bowels of a warship for years, until they thought I wouldn't try to escape, and then I did, yonder to the west where the Columbia River nears the Pacific . . . Jumped over in fog, so the watch couldn't see me, nothing but a belaying pin . . . Oh, it felt good, even though I half starved for a month . . ."

But James Method wasn't listening. He had remembered still another of the prophetic stories the sharp-tongued angry granny spat out at him in the shack beside the cottonfield . . . a story with skulls in it and a storm, and something else . . . something that would transform his future.

"I suppose we've hauled the buffler meat far enough to satisfy Victoria, mate. We'll leave it here for the wolves and coyotes. They'll start a chorus tonight, eh?"

"Maybe Ah should take it back to the place where the skulls are," Method said suddenly.

"You seeing the ghost spirit in it too?"

Method shrugged. "Ah think maybe she's right; that's not buffalo at all."

Mister Skye looked exasperated. "You want to haul it a quarter mile back and put it on a horse and haul it back to the valley of the skulls, do you?"

"Ah think Ah do."

"That must be fifty pounds of buffler."

"Ah still think Ah do."

"Leave it," said Mister Skye.

Method shrugged, and they walked back through a loose growth of cottonwoods along the creek bottoms. But his mind wasn't in the present; it slipped back a few years, trying to remember what the fierce old granny in the shack had told him, what she had said would happen at a place with a circle of skulls that would give him the shivers . . . There were so many stories, and he couldn't quite remember this one. But he knew what he would do.

Back at the camp beside the Crazy Woman, the hostility grew so thick he felt it physically. Victoria squinted at him and muttered as she sliced a haunch of deer. The Reverend Alex Newton looked flushed and angry, and glared at him as if he were responsible for the blisters and the hard labor. Silas Potter, whose perfunctory courtesy had usually made tent-mate life easy for them, peered owlishly at him, bursting to criticize but not saying whatever it was that burned in his eyes. It was something James felt, and rightly or wrongly, he knew, they would turn their grievance into a racial thing: he had been sent by Mister Skye himself out to hunt and scout, but he knew that they were turning it into something else in their minds, darkies were lazy, darkies avoided hard work. He laughed within himself, thinking of the field-hands in the blazing sun of the cottonfields, doing brutal stoop labor because they'd be whipped or even killed if they didn't.

Well their opinions didn't matter. That was the magic of this wilderness, this vast somnolent country a thousand miles from the rim of civilization and organized life. Here he felt free in a way that not even freemen were free back there. Nothing could stop him from doing what he would. If he could survive, find food and shelter and friends, he could live here in perfect freedom all his days, forever beyond sheriffs and slave auctions and whips and masters and murder. So he smiled, said nothing this evening, and waited.

Only Mister Skye sensed anything, and now and then the guide stared at him with hard eyes.

It turned into a rumbling night as distant storms over the Big Horns flashed and growled, and the tendrils from them blotted out the stars. The growling of the heavens made them all uneasy. The Newtons, unused to camping and irked to have no wagon to sleep in, fussed with their tent and ran trenches around the side of it to carry rainwater off. Alex handled the shovel easily enough, blisters or not. Silas Potter also battened down, hoping to fend off water so that it didn't soak his bedroll, and James lackadaisically helped out. The Samples would sleep in their wagon tonight, high and dry. As for Mister Skye's lodge of carefully smoked cowhide that would turn any rain, the squaws always erected it in a place that would shed water well. That was a part of the Indian heritage and intuition of Victoria and Mary, and it had been done without a conscious thought. James watched Silas nervously anchoring the tent with extra ropes against the harsh winds that would rise in the night. Silas was too busy to notice James casually loading his gear in his saddlebags, or slipping his saddle and carbine sheath out into the night, or carrying his bridle off to the herd.

The horses and mules were restless and ready to bolt. A night like this could scatter their stock over vast areas. Clay headed out into the herd, bridles in hand, but the mules turned skittish and dodged him. He tried a horse, only to have it rear wildly as he approached. He called for Alfred to help, and then the rest of them. James grabbed a halter and a picket line. Alex and Cecil did too, cautiously circling the nervous animals. Several horses burst into a restless trot, and then stopped a hundred yards distant. Mister Skye, bareback on Jawbone, stood there, blocking passage. Cecil caught Magdelene and bridled her; then the others caught horses. The mules proved more difficult, but at last they too were picketed. There were not hobbles enough to go around, so only the better horses were hobbled, and at last the camp was ready for a stormy night. James drifted back to his tent, feeling strangely isolated and restless as he shifted more gear to his hobbled horse.

From his usual station near the lodge, Jawbone watched him narrowly, and James wondered if he'd shriek. Jawbone had been their night guard. Nothing approached the camp, four-footed or two, without Jawbone making a terrible racket. But would the demon horse permit a departure?

Then at last the campfire dimmed and the missionary party abandoned itself to sleep and silence. But the night muttered and roared and threatened. James did not wait long. After an hour or so he slipped out into the gusting dark—the stars were obscured so there was awesome blackness—and found his old bay horse. After saddling and loading, he set off into the night, leaving the sleeping camp behind him. Trusting the instincts of the horse because he couldn't see, he steered it north along the riverbank toward the spirit meat, and more by instinct than by senses found it untouched on the sand spit beside the creek where they'd left it. He wrapped it in burlap and lifted it to his overburdened horse and forded the creek through belly-deep water. The bay scrambled up a steep bank and then they were out, a jolt of lightning revealing the peaks of the Big Horns. He hadn't the faintest idea how to find the place of the circle of skulls, but he would try.

The ride that should have taken twenty minutes took hours. When he became utterly lost he rode to a ridgetop and waited for the lightning to give him a single blinding glimpse of the land, and in this way he wandered westerly, over several ridges. It began to rain lightly, and he dreaded the lightning when the storm was overhead. Still he pushed onward, his horse edgy and afraid between his legs. It was not his horse, really, but the missionaries' animal, lent to him for the journey, and that made him feel bad. But this seemed familiar. The storm was part of it, part of the old granny's story that was hissed out at him in harsh sibilants long ago. And in the story no harm came to him because of the storm. Still, the eerie rattle of lightning and the thunderous roars, and the hiss of light forking the black frightened him, and he wondered if the old granny was evil. Evil, leading him to his doom now. And then suddenly a flash revealed the place of the skulls down below. Rain pelted hard now. He felt the cold water sliding through his clothes, draining into his saddle beneath him, slithering down his neck. Another flash revealed the dead buffalo cow. He slid from his bay and undid the meat and returned it to the cow, reverently fitting it as close to its place in the carcass as he could, and when he looked up she stood there.

Chapter 14

A stride Jawbone, Mister Skye stared at the buffalo cow carcass and the replaced meat. It had not been touched by wolves or coyotes or magpies, as if the animals, too, knew this place of the skulls was taboo. He looked for hoofprints, a trail, but knew there'd be none; the rain had washed everything away. Method was gone, vanished into thin air. Not an uncommon thing in this wild and lonely land.

"Bon voyage, mate," he said aloud, and turned Jawbone back.

His party had become smaller and more vulnerable with Method and his steady courage gone, and Father Kiley blinded and helpless. What would he do with the priest? Take him to Fort Benton up on the Missouri? And what would they do with him? Skye didn't know. There were no answers for a question like that.

When he left the camp the men were gouging the gumbo clay bank on the far side of the creek. The going became easier because the rains had moistened the soil for a foot or so, and the pike could work large chunks of it loose. But it still looked to be a labor of several days. He rode north, thinking that there was no particular need

to cross just there, and maybe he could find a good ford
at some place well below where Method had hunted.

It was a fine cool day, and the water beading on grass
and leaves glinted in the sun. The air, washed of its dust,
looked transparent. The brutal summer heat, which had
made the digging such an ordeal, had temporarily gone.
He pushed along the west bank of Crazy Woman Creek,
beyond where he knew Method had scouted, hoping to
find a crossing. Two miles yielded nothing but then the
land flattened and the valley widened. Three miles north
of the camp, he found a place. A rough one to be sure,
but passable. The water flowed high from the rain, but
the bottom was hard under Jawbone's feet, and the banks
would not be an obstacle for double-teamed wagons. The
river bottoms yielded their secrets to his keen vision—how
often people in the wilderness looked but didn't see, he
thought. Especially porkeaters, greenhorns from the east.
He rode to the west lip of the valley and studied the country. It looked passable for wagons too. Then he turned
back to the camp to share the welcome news.

He found Cecil, along with Clay, hard at work cutting
the notch in the bank.

"Any sign of James?" asked the minister, leaning wearily on his shovel.

"Yes, some sign. He replaced the meat he took from a
buffalo cow yonder to the west, and then vanished. Rain
wiped out his tracks."

"It sounds like hoodoo," Cecil said. "Will we ever see
him again?"

"I have no more idea than you do, mate."

"Was it the heathen religion? Why would he take buffalo meat back?"

"To undo what he had done, I suppose."

"It's paganism, Mister Skye. I never would have guessed it of James. He's lost to us."

"I think he was killed or hurt by the lightning," said Clay.

"No. He made it to the place of the skulls and returned the meat. There was no sign of trouble between here and there, mate."

"It was the devil at work," said Silas Potter.

Skye paused. "The things we don't understand aren't rightly the devil's work," he said slowly. "A man follows his own music. I will wager he's alive, and I'll wager he is doing what he must."

Cecil sighed. "He's gone, whatever the reason. A good man gone, and I'll miss him. Now we're a man short."

"Oh, I'll miss him so!" cried Esmerelda.

"Well, could be you'll meet up with him soon. That's a thing about this big country. It's not that people vanish in it, but that people reappear, show up when you're not expecting it."

But Cecil and Esmerelda looked crestfallen.

Silas was aflame with righteousness. "It's good riddance," he snapped. "He heeded the powers of Satan, and we must drive him from our midst."

"Pack up your gear and get ready to roll," Skye roared, cutting off Potter. "There's a crossing about three miles north."

They stared at him.

Cecil blinked. "Almost hate to give this up. This little cut in this bank has taken a day and a half of our lives, and now we're leaving it half done." He sighed. "Good labor and honest sweat gone."

"You should have found the crossing earlier. Or James should have," snapped Silas.

"Mate, hindsight is a fine thing, and makes us wise after things are over. Now if James hadn't disappeared and set me to wandering west and north, you'd—ah, Clay and Cecil—still be digging here for another day or two."

He turned Jawbone away, angered.

Late that afternoon they crossed Crazy Woman Creek with little difficulty and rolled another five miles over barren rolls of prairie, and made camp in a swale beside a small chokecherry and buffaloberry-lined spring. From their protected valley they could not see the Big Horns looming to the west, but the great mountains were ever-present now, brooding over the western reaches of the great plains.

In his lodge that evening Skye relaxed in the soft glow of a tiny fire that served for light rather than heat. Mary had arranged the robes into fine beds, as she always did, and played with young Dirk in the flickering light, laughing with him as he drew stick-figures with charcoal on a piece of smooth bark. Skye looked at her warm flesh in the soft light, and the shining braids of her jet hair, and her young curves beneath her dotted calico blouse, and he wanted her. Later, when the fire had died a little more, he would have her, and she would be glad, as always. He looked at his boy, who seemed to thrive under her care, and displayed the warmth of her flesh and darkness of her people, but his own blocky shape and squinting pale blue eyes.

Victoria busied herself with the last of her packing—she was always ready to travel at dawn, or in any instant in danger. And then she sat back, close to Mister Skye, because she was his sits-beside-him wife and had that privilege.

"Tell me about the black man," she said. "Tell me all the things you have not told me."

Skye grinned. "Mister Method shot that cow buffalo in the Place of the Forty Skulls," he began.

"I knew it!" she cried.

"Cow landed right in the center, near the cairn and stake."

"Ah!" she cried. "That was a spirit buffalo cow. The spirit of old White Buffalo Cow Woman was within her, and he shot it. Truly, I saw her face in the hump ribs, and so I knew!"

"Sometime just before the storm or during it, he left here, picked up the meat, and took it back there. I don't rightly know how he did it, unless the lightning helped. But it was there, the meat, placed as close and as reverently as possible to the carcass."

"Ah!" she cried again. "Now I know. The spirit of White Buffalo Cow Woman was pleased that it was no longer roaming in the air looking for a home."

"But it is a dead home; it's still a carcass," objected Mister Skye.

"Yes, but the spirit is happy, and perhaps it entered into the breast of James Method."

From across the fire, Mary objected. "But there cannot be two spirits in one breast, Crow Mother."

"Ah! Who knows? Perhaps Mister Method is following the spirit to its new home. That is what I think. He is going to a village of the Absaroka, the village of White Buffalo Cow Woman and the chief, Many Coups."

"You think he's heading toward the Crow, eh?" Mister Skye asked.

"I am certain of it. We shall see him shortly, but things will be different for him. I do not know what the spirit of the Absaroka grandmother will bring to him, but it will be something good for bringing back the meat of the spirit cow that he took."

With that she would say no more, and rolled comfortably in her robes, the top one the softest albino buffalo cow hide and ideal for summertime.

"Bring me Dirk," he said, and Mary lifted the sleepy boy into Mister Skye's lap. He always enjoyed these moments. He was old enough to be a grandfather many times over, but this was his first and only child.

"Ah, my lad," he said in English. "You know the words of your mother, mate, but not those of your pap. It's time I teach you the poems and the stories and the songs of my people."

"I want the English words," Dirk said, "but I'm sleepy now."

"Go to sleep, mate," Skye said, handing the boy back.

Mary flashed a smile. In a moment the boy would be sound asleep in the cool air, and in another moment she'd slip out of her calico, and she and Mister Skye would lie together in the robes.

He never said a word. She always knew. She aroused him as no woman ever had with her lithe young beauty. Let the missionaries howl, he thought. Let them rage. He was a happy man with Victoria and Mary, and what was not permitted back in civilization was of no consequence here. He was a savage now. A British press-gang had seen to that when they started a chain of events that brought him in middle years to this warm lodge high on the steppes of North America, where a beautiful and fiery woman now awaited him.

The guide grew ever more dissatisfied with his party. Just beneath the surface lay cauldrons of bubbling hate. In a time of crisis, they would all fall apart rather than hang together, and that might cost all of them, himself included, their lives. At the heart of it was Silas Potter, whose contempt for the others writhed inside of him like a snake. Ever since Cecil had joined the Sioux scalp dance, Silas had refused even to talk with the senior missionary. Just as bad, he avoided Esmerelda or glared at her, and was uncivil, if not rude, to Father Kiley and almost oblivious to the man's distress and blindness.

Alex Newton had become the other dissident and troublemaker, nursing a rage that his wagon had been abandoned and his body comforts reduced because of it. And, like Silas, appalled by the conduct of his father-in-law, who seemed to grow more boorish and barbaric the farther they penetrated the wilderness.

Though things seemed amiable enough on the surface, and the business of the day proceeded with polite and distant courtesy, surface courtesies were not unity, and Mister Skye wanted and needed unity here. Under pressure from hostile Indians, or weather, or most any calamity along the way, they would go their separate directions. Even Clay Sample seemed to be harboring antagonisms as the caravan pushed its way north and west.

The footsore oxen, rested again while the party dug at the cutbank of Crazy Woman Creek, were pulling the wagon with the organ and Father Kiley in it. Clay Sample's mules, though gaunted, showed no sign of failing. And the span of mules pulling the carriage made easy work of it.

But all was not right. Mister Skye stopped Jawbone and waited for Potter, who rode a horse regularly now as eastern foodstuffs dwindled and the loads lightened.

"Mister Potter," he said, "I'm about to go out on a scout. You'll come with me."

The young man's face flamed.

"You don't even ask," he snapped.

"If I'd asked, you'd say no, and I mean to have you come, mate."

"I'm not the slightest bit interested in scouting."

Jawbone snapped his teeth at Potter's saddle horse, and the animal hurried along beside Mister Skye, no matter that Potter tugged on its reins.

In twenty minutes they were half a mile north and west of the wagons, riding up and down long swales and shoulders, with Potter sullenly following, a pained look stamped on his face.

"First watch the ridges, mate. Trouble usually sits on a ridge out here, and what may look like a small rock may be a head peering from the other side. And then watch the brush and the stands of trees and the banks and the coulees, all of which are hiding places, places where deadly men lurk to surprise us."

"I'm sure you do your job adequately, Mister Skye. This is unimportant to me."

"You might feel differently about it if fifty warriors boiled out of that draw over there, and came for your scalp."

"That's what you're paid for."

"Do you dislike me, Mister Potter?"

The young man rode silently for a while. "Let's say I don't approve of some things."

"Disapprove. Yes, that's the exact word, I think."

"I don't dislike you. Some of your conduct I deem improper."

"I imagine you do," said Mister Skye. "What do you disapprove of? My two wives? My taste for whiskey? My camp and trail discipline? My buckskins? This evil horse I ride? Or is it that I'm a white savage, armed with rifle and revolver here, and a pair of knives to boot? Perhaps it's because I'm a killer, a killer of human beings who may or may not intend to kill me. Or is it that I'm not of your denomination, and damned because of it?"

Silas Potter chose silence. Skye let him brood awhile, and then started in again.

"You're not even speaking to Cecil. He and Esmerelda danced a heathen dance, so you disapprove of them. And you disapprove of his plans to better the lives of the Blackfeet. Does the man set in authority over you offend you that much? You talk only to Alex Newton, but you disapprove of him, too. He's self-indulgent and a shirker. And Henrietta you dismiss as self-indulgent also, and mindless. Neither do you visit with the priest. You disapprove of him so much that you barely feel his tragedy. Don't you suppose Dunstan Kiley would welcome a little comforting? If you had been blinded and tortured by some Cheyenne, and lay helpless in a black world in a bouncing wagon, would you welcome some kindness? And what about Mister Method? He was scarcely gone before you were saying good riddance. Did you disapprove of him also? Perhaps you felt the African was beneath you and lacked your intellect?"

Silas looked pained. "You don't understand, and I doubt that I could explain it to you because you lack the . . . the . . . ah, scholarship. I merely uphold the loving standards of church and civilization. I'm afraid if I elaborated them, it would be beyond you."

"Try, Mister Potter."

"I'd rather not."

"Well, mate, if you won't, I will. And you'll be my captive audience, eh?"

"Go ahead. You disapprove of me. I uphold the laws of God, so you will heap whatever abuse on me you will. The more you condemn me, the more I serve God. I'm not interested in your opinions—not yours or Cecil's or anybody's. I'm interested in what is true and holy and good, but I don't expect you to understand that."

"Am I keeping you here against your will?"

"Yes."

"That happens in life, doesn't it. I was a prisoner for nigh onto eight years, and bullied about by people who were called sir, or lord, or mister. Now you're my prisoner for a hour or two, Mister Potter. I suppose you can't suffer me because I'm an uncouth sailor and a ruffian and violent man.

"Or maybe it's my drink. A true weakness, Mister Potter, and one you are free of. I get a fine edge to me, and over I go—at least when the nectar of the gods is available, which isn't often in this vast wilderness. Now there is a weakness. I abandoned you to your fate, and failed to guide and guard you. But not entirely, Mister Potter. For those squaws you privately scorn are better and wiser on the trail than I am, and this horse beneath me is worth ten guards and guides, and they are all more faithful than I am.

"Or perhaps it's this new Sharps and this Army Colt, with which I am always prepared to commit murder. This Sharps is a killing machine, sir. I can load a paper cartridge in it almost as fast as I can discharge the Colt. I am very good at it, Mister Potter. I have killed men in multiples of ten, and so I can understand your disgust. It disgusts me, too.

"And my lovely Shoshone, Mary, I take to bed and she builds a fine lust in me, just as she does in you, Mister Potter."

The young man reddened.

"Oh, those things don't hide themselves, my friend. Those glances, those trips to the creeks when Mary is bathing, the heat rising from you as your eyes dog her. No,

Mister Potter, your lusts are no secret, except maybe to yourself. What bothers you is not that I have a second wife who is beautiful and half my age, but that she inspires your lust, and that ruins your notion of yourself as the keeper of the flame."

"I am pure," Potter cried hoarsely. "It is the Tempter, not I; the Tempter I wrestle with."

"Why, that's as good a name for a stiff as any, mate."

"You don't understand. I don't want your dirty squaw. I have nothing to do with her."

Mister Skye stared. "You don't command your own ship?"

Silas Potter glared hotly. "I can't explain it to someone who doesn't even have the rudiments of theology."

"Well, friend, you and your Tempter leave Mary alone, or I'll break your bloody neck."

Silas turned to ice. "I told you I have nothing to do with . . ."

Mister Skye was amused. "Nothing to do with any of us."

"—Nothing to do with certain episodes that gave the unfortunate appearance of, ah, misimpression that . . ."

"I know a dozen young ladies in the Crow villages who'd be enchanted with even you, Mister Potter. I will make certain arrangements. Oh, those Crow girls! You and your Tempter will have a high old time . . ."

"Are you done with your ravings?"

"Yes, that's all."

Mister Skye smiled.

Silas stared at him, not quite believing it, and then yanked his horse toward the wagons. And Jawbone let him do it.

Chapter 15

He caught a glimpse of her in the flickering blue lightning and then blackness closed again. He supposed he had imagined it. He was soaked now, chilled to his bones, and eager to return to camp if he could make his way back. In the arc of one lightning bolt he had glimpsed a young Indian woman, her black hair parted and braided, her skin clothing black with water and hanging heavily on her slim figure. And that was all. He waited for another flash, more curious than afraid, but it did not come.

It was just an image in his head, he thought. He fretted. Why had he come here, and why had he felt such a compelling need to return the meat to the cow buffalo here?

Another blinding bolt, chattering and then booming, and he saw her again and she was closer. She said something and beckoned but he hadn't the faintest idea what she said.

"Who are you and what do you want?" he asked.

He heard a soft reply in a tongue he didn't know. He had some notion she was handsome, maybe even beautiful, but he dismissed it. She was saying something, but his thoughts were upon finding his way back, or maybe finding shelter until the storm was over.

Then her hands reached to the bridle and she tugged the reins, saying something. She wanted to take him somewhere. All right, then, maybe she has a shelter. He gave the reins to her and mounted, and let her lead the horse where she would. What had the old granny said? *This was how he would find his woman.*

He felt the horse walking beneath him through a black void, going in a direction he didn't know. Was this woman a demon carrying him off to hell? He thought of Cecil Rathbone and his faith in one loving God; and he thought of old Mattie in her shack, angrily invoking the spirits of rocks and trees and frogs and telling him what his future would be. James felt himself slipping away from Cecil and Esmerelda—the others he cared little about, sensing they didn't care much for him, an intruder in their white caravan. No, he thought, that wasn't quite right. He cared about the Jesuit, Father Kiley, and he could not fault the Samples, who put him at ease. But now in this wild night he felt the Rathbones and their faith slipping away, and Father Kiley grow distant in his mind, even as the spirits of the earth-things rose before him. He felt the spirit of the horse beneath him, and the magnetic pull of the woman who led him through utter blackness. And the anger of the heavens, and the arrows of lightning and the rage of thunder, seeking him out but not finding him because this was not his time to die. He wondered whether he would slip away from all the white things, the civilized things, he had absorbed in the master's house, and return to the African life. His grandmother and grandfather had come from there, herded in the bowels of a clipper ship and barely alive when they landed on the Carolina coast and went to the auction block and were sold naked, both of them to the father of his master.

For a moment he hated all whites, even the Rathbones who had been unfailingly kind and not at all patronizing either. But that passed. He had few grievances. All the while he was a slave, he had been treated well, save for the fact that he was property that could be bought or sold. Still, he was drifting away. God and the gentle Jesus they had taught him about were sliding away, and he felt fierce and attuned to every tree and drop of water, and especially the silent woman leading his horse.

They were climbing a long gulch with water running in it, he sensed. The hoofs struck rock, and the horse occasionally pulled up over low ledges. How the woman knew where to go he couldn't imagine. Ahead flickered a tiny light, and he wondered how a fire could prosper in a deluge like this one. Then its light reached out and he could see the silhouette of her ahead of him, and could even see his horse and its ears before him. The fire illumined a yellow hollow of rock in a cliffside, with a ledge over it. And it illumined another Indian woman, an older one, standing in its light.

It seemed warmer under the shelf of rock, and the gusting air didn't penetrate here. He dismounted and stared. The older woman stood tall and lithe, much taller than the younger one, whose figure was fuller. The older woman was dry, and had a green trade blanket drawn around her doeskin-clad body. Her black hair was shot with white, and on her face were several disfiguring scars. She smiled gently but there remained a fierceness about her that was palpable to him. He gazed at the young one, then, the one who'd brought him here. She seemed perhaps twenty, with a fine golden flesh and eyes that shone in the firelight.

"We were expecting you," said the older one in fluent English. "This one"—she pointed at the girl—"had a vision. Four times she dreamt the dream, and then came to me with it. I am Pine Leaf, a medicine woman of the Crow people. And before my medicine came to me, I was a warrior of the Crow. But I will tell you of that later. This is Gliding Raven. She does not speak your tongue, but she will learn."

"Ah'm James Method," he replied uncertainly.

"Ah, James. That is a name I know. You are wet. Take off your clothes and I will dry them at the fire."

He stared. "But Ah'm . . . Ah can't . . . You're women!"

"There is a fine, soft, well-tanned buffalo robe there for you to wrap in. There's another robe here for Gliding Raven."

"But Ah . . ."

"You whites don't have any sense. Do you want to shiver in those things?"

"Ah'm not exactly white . . ."

"You were a slave of theirs, like my friend Jim Beckwourth."

It struck him funny: hours ago he rode with a party of puritanical missionaries, and here he was about to peel off his shirt and britches and boots. He laughed easily and pulled off his sopping gray readymade shirt, and then felt stricken by modesty and turned his back to them and pulled off the rest. Someone behind him laughed and gently wrapped a fine buffalo robe over his shoulders.

When he turned, the girl stood naked, stepping out of soaked skirts, and the sight of her warm flawless flesh, her tawny breasts in the firelight, her lean and supple legs, lit fires in him, punched him until he felt breathless. But then she wrapped her own robe about her, and peered shyly at him from the brown curly hair of her soft robe. She laughed too, as shyly as he had laughed, and they seated themselves around the fire. But the image of her burned in his mind and prodded at his body, and he did not sit easily.

Pine Leaf wrung out the clothing and propped it up on sticks she cleverly arranged into a drying rack, and then sat down between them. James Method's heart pounded.

"Gliding Raven is a beautiful woman, yes?" said Pine Leaf, and that didn't help James at all.

"The most beautiful Ah've ever seen," he replied hotly.

"She will be yours," said Pine Leaf solemnly.

He could scarcely imagine it. Even now visions of her poured through him. He wanted her. This would be his life. Gliding Raven and himself, a thousand miles from white men's civilization.

"Listen to me, James Method, for now I must talk of things sacred to the Absaroka people, and of your future, and of Gliding Raven's vision that brought us here, far, far from our village where the Big Horn River, as the whites call it, meets the Yellowstone."

James could barely listen; his glances slipped to Gliding Raven and her golden bare throat and shoulders that gleamed in the firelight.

"Four times did Gliding Raven have a medicine dream. In it she saw a black man kill White Buffalo Cow Woman in the place of forty skulls. Four times the spirit of White Buffalo Cow Woman came to Gliding Raven and told her to come here at once. And bring to our village the black man, who would become a great warrior for our people, and would bring us knowledge of the whites, who are coming more and more, and tell us how we might live with them in peace. I won't tell you the rest of her medicine dream yet, but it is a good vision, good medicine. Gliding Raven told me her dream, and I saw that it was good for the Absaroka people and that she must travel a long way, seven camps, to come here so that her medicine would happen. I decided to come with her. We would like to take you back to the Absaroka village."

"Ah'm ready," he said.

"You must not touch Gliding Raven even though you

want to," Pine Leaf said solemnly. "First you must become a brave warrior. When you have counted coup, or taken a scalp, or have stolen horses from the enemies of the Absaroka people, especially the Siksika, the Blackfeet, and give one of them to Gliding Raven's father, he will declare a great feast and will give you his daughter."

James Method was amazed. "Marriage?"

"Yes. But first you must become a warrior. Then you will be named Seven Scalps and you will have Gliding Raven. She is very eager to have you. Her eyes shine and her body hungers for you, James Method. But that time has not yet come."

All of this happened too fast and he thought perhaps he should get back on his horse and strike out for the wagons in the dying storm. And then he looked at Gliding Raven, and knew he wouldn't. He'd been smitten with something, love or lust or both.

"I am Pine Leaf, and now I will tell you about me, and about my friend Jim Beckwourth, who became a great warrior of the Crows, just as you will be . . .

"I myself am a warrior of the Absarokas, and sit high in the councils of our people. When I was young I vowed not to marry until I had taken a hundred scalps of the Siksika. I took many scalps, but not a hundred, so I have not married. I fought in many battles, and if I was not as strong as some warriors, I was faster, and deadlier with my bow, and I could make my ponies run the fastest of all. My medicine is strong as a woman warrior, and now it is strong as a prophet, and many come to me with their dreams and visions, and I see what is to be seen.

"Among us lived a trapper, Jim Beckwourth, who became a great warrior, and we gave him the name Antelope in honor of his deeds. He looked like you, and was my friend in battle, and I shared his robes for a while. He taught me your language. When I saw you, I knew the Absaroka people would have another great warrior among us, and that White Buffalo Cow Woman had sent for us to come welcome you."

"Ah've heard of Beckwourth. Our guide, Mister Skye, has told me many a tale of the beaver-trapping days around our camps at night—of Beckwourth and Bridger and Broken Hand Fitzpatrick, and the Sublettes and many others . . ."

"Skye? You've come with Skye?"

"He's taking some missionaries to the Blackfeet."

Pine Leaf pondered that. "He has many enemies among the Siksika. And he has always been our friend and ally. Why does he take these white people to the Siksika?"

"That is his business now—taking people where they want to go."

"That is not good," said Pine Leaf. "We will not let these people take their medicine to our enemies. They must share the white medicine with us first, so we may have the magic of powder and guns and the eyes that make faraway things close."

"Ah'm not so sure Ah want to go to your village. Ah broke free of them just a little ago, and Ah want to sort things out. Ah've never been free before. There's nobody to tell me Ah can't do anything. But here you are, telling me Ah have to go join up with you Crows and become your warrior and take scalps. Ah've never taken a scalp in my life and Ah don't intend to start . . . In the morning Ah'm going to ride right out of here, and maybe Gliding Raven'll come with me."

Pine Leaf shook her head solemnly. "You will come with us. The spirit of White Buffalo Cow Woman has spoken."

The glitter in Pine Leaf's eyes told James she meant it, and meant to enforce it, and probably could. She smiled slightly, as if reading his thoughts. "I am large for a woman, but not the size of a man. Perhaps you would like to test me in battle? Any kind of battle?"

He shook his head. These two had his life planned out for him and called it medicine. Still . . . what spirits had inspired them to come to the place of the skulls and find him? They had come perhaps two hundred miles from their village, maybe more, just for this. He thought life as a Crow slave would be less free than the life he had in the south. For a moment he wished he had the protection of Mister Skye, who had taught him how to live in freedom, but now he was on his own, with two Crow women who consulted hoodoo spirits to guide them. He stared first at Pine Leaf, standing resolutely, a quick reach from her bow and quiver and lance; and at Gliding Raven, who was, he knew, the very woman, golden and black-haired, that the old granny had spat and raved about in the shanty. She lounged in her curly-haired buffalo robe, wrapped carelessly about her so that her amber thighs glistened in the firelight.

Something within screamed at him, warned him not to trifle with the earth spirits of these people, but to love the one God. But it was too late. The image formed of Alex Newton glaring at him; of Silas Potter's frost and politeness, and of the others' indifference. He sat in his robe, tugged two ways. Then he thought, who is God, if he let Father Kiley be blinded even while the Jesuit was doing God's work? This God he had grown up with seemed weak. The medicine of these Crow women was not weak. Had he not felt the call of the old woman's spirit? Hadn't these women glimpsed the future, coming here to escort him?

He peered into Pine Leaf's eyes, and found her watching him alertly.

"If you make a slave of me," he said softly, "Ah'll fight you, even if Ah die. Ah will not be a slave again. Ah'll not be the least among you, either. Ah'll be a man among you . . ."

Pine Leaf laughed easily. She sat down and lifted his old percussion rifle and carefully dried it while he watched distrustfully. The fire dimmed, and she did not renew the tiny blaze with more sticks.

"We have a long way to travel," she said.

In the dark, sleep didn't come. The clouds cleared, and the uncurtained sky paraded its stars. So much reeled in his head: what was medicine, what was God? Were they the same, or different? What was the devil? Was medicine the same as Satan? Who was Gliding Raven, and what would she be like? The image of her firelit brown body and jet hair and black eyes lit blazes within him. She lay there, a few feet away.

Then in the dark a form drew close. "It is Pine Leaf. Take me, and then you will not think about Gliding Raven," she whispered.

She was agile and firm and fiery, and soon he lay exhausted, slipping into a troubled sleep at last.

In the morning he found Gliding Raven dressed in her dried doeskins, preparing a small breakfast from jerky and a few roots. Elkteeth and quillwork decorated her dress. Her necklace was of polished hollow bone. By day she was even more beautiful than she had been at night, and he could not help but follow her with his gaze. She grew aware of it, and smiled at him shyly. There came to him a determination to have her, to wait for her, to win scalps for her, or whatever he must do. Her tawny flesh looked not so different from his own, but her jet hair hung blue and straight.

Pine Leaf had their ponies ready, and had saddled his as well. "I will scout ahead," she said, and slipped toward a nearby ridge, while James and Gliding Raven walked their mounts side by side. They had not spoken a word. He knew no way to communicate with her. He had not learned the sign language of the plains tribes. Then at last he decided to teach her the words he knew, and perhaps learn her words. And so they traveled, each of them pointing at something, eyes, nose, horse, water, and supplying the word, sometimes laughing at bungled pronunciation, but learning all the while. Pine Leaf acted as their eyes and ears, and they rarely saw her.

Once she rode back swiftly and steered them into a thick stand of cottonwoods, and a while later they could see mounted figures, tiny on a distant ridge, heading west. They were not discovered.

Each night they made camp in a well-selected place where Pine Leaf supposed they might find some safety. It was a giant country, with great swells of prairie running limitlessly to far horizons. Always the Big Horns loomed to the west, blue and inviting during the hot afternoons. Some nights Pine Leaf came to him; other nights she chose not to. It felt good, but not what it would be with Gliding Raven, whose image lay always in his mind now.

They made thirty or forty miles each day, traveling with caution because this was a land hunted by many tribes, most of them enemies of the Crows. On one occasion Pine Leaf led them by night, explaining that they were circling around a large Lakotah party to the east, warriors who would enjoy nothing so much as torturing James and two Crow women to death.

Between the language sessions James brooded about medicine. What empowered Pine Leaf to know the things she knew? How did she know of enemies she had merely felt but not seen? How did she know this trip would be safe? Was medicine stronger than God? Pine Leaf seemed to know everything, including what James and Gliding Raven were doing, and the words they had exchanged. The graying medicine woman paid homage here and there to things she considered sacred, an arrow buried in a cottonwood at one place; at another, a small cairn of rock, with vermilion daubed on one rock.

By the sixth day they were rounding the northern end of the Big Horn Mountains. So adept had James and Gliding Raven become with each other's words that now they made simple talk. She was teaching him, as well, the sign language of the prairies, and he knew the signs for friend, and peace, and food, and other helpful things. They rode in the basin of the great Yellowstone River now, Pine Leaf said, and in the heart of the beautiful lands of the Absaroka people, who roamed a country of towering mountains, rushing rivers, vast prairies teeming with buffalo, all of it blessed by a warm dry climate.

Then on the seventh day, Pine Leaf led them into the great village of the Kicked-in-the-Bellies band of Crows.

Chapter 16

There was only night. Dunstan Kiley's world had shrunk to the bed of a jolting wagon that bounced and rolled him hour after hour, until the day's journey ended. He had learned to tell day from night. By day, birds sang and temperatures rose, and sometimes he felt the hot summer sun heating his black clothing. And by day people came to him: Victoria to feed and clean him, Mister Skye to talk occasionally, and the Rathbones, who tried to bring cheer but could not, because he'd fallen beyond cheer. The little Sample girl, Miriam, came regularly too. James Method came also, until he disappeared. They told him Method had simply vanished the night of the heavy storm, leaving no trace, but doing a heathenish thing, taking meat back to the buffalo cow he had killed.

Like the darkness, the pain never ceased. He suffered an endless ache in his eye sockets, and it had become a part of Victoria's daily ministration to clean away the suppurating flow from them and wrap new bandaging. Each day she washed the soiled bandaging wherever there was water, and reused it because there was little cloth to be had. She had applied powders and ointments of her own devising, and muttered frequently when they failed to heal. On occasion Father Kiley saw blinding white flashes that scorched the inside of his skull, but these came infrequently and only punctuated the blackness.

His fate appalled him. He was alive, but useless, and a total burden on others. He had no notion what he would do, where he might go, or how he might relieve these people of the need to care for him. He thought of suicide, but that would be a grave sin. He thought of continuing his priestly duties, but that seemed impossible. He couldn't even read to say the Mass or perform other offices. He thought he knew them all by heart, but now his mind rebelled and blanked. He could not be a priest.

The sky was black, as it must be in hell, he thought. For surely hell must be the same as blackness, a place of no light. He tried to imagine the throne of heaven, the faces of saints, the look of his parents in Ireland, but the images were fleeting and laced with pain and lightning.

He thought especially of the Virgin, in her blue gown, smiling gently, but her image diffused and vanished in his aching head. He thought he had a duty to perform, forgiveness of Wolf-That-Circles and the other Cheyenne whose names he didn't know. But the war chief had died, and Father Kiley found himself beyond forgiveness or anger, beyond hate or love in his extremity. He had come to believe that the Cheyenne were inspired not by malice, but by curiosity. Like all the plains tribes, they had heard much of the religion of the whites, who seemed to have medicine beyond anything the Indians had ever imagined. And so they had tested it, tortured the white holy man to see the medicine with their own eyes. See whether he would be immune to pain and fire and death. If he were ever to minister to Indians again, could he resume his holy offices without hatred or fear? He didn't know. And now he knew only the awful present; future and past had vanished into the night.

Day by day the small party rolled north. He sensed approximately where they were: a little east of the Big Horns, and up at their northern end now. Perhaps near Goose Creek. It was a land of vast shoulders and long coulees which became palpable to him as the faithful oxen dragged his wagon up long slopes and down the far sides, the wagon pressing into the breeching of the wheel yoke, or sometimes skidding downslope upon chain-locked wheels.

One morning immediately after Victoria had given him breakfast, Mister Skye came to him. "Are you well this morning?" he asked.

"I no longer know what sick and well mean," the priest replied. "My head always throbs; the rest of me is the way it always has been."

"I thought I'd take you scouting with me, Father."

He shrank from that. "On a horse? Blind on a horse? Unable to see what's ahead or steer the animal?"

"I've got him saddled up. You've a Santa Fe saddle with a Spanish horn on it, something to hang on to if you need it. Do you good. I thought I'd lead you with a halter rope."

It sounded terrifying. "I couldn't—" he began.

But Skye's big hand was lifting him up and drawing him across ground he couldn't see.

"Now, mate, you're beside your horse. I'll put your foot in a stirrup and get you settled."

The priest paused. "If this is unbearable, will you bring me back when I ask?"

"Perhaps. I might cheat a little and leave you in the crow's nest a little longer than you want."

"Crow's nest?"

"The little platform at the top of the mast of a sailing bark. Even in a calm sea it'll swing twenty or thirty feet as the ship rolls. There's many a sailing lad who'd rather go on bread and water in the brig than be put up there in a storm."

The priest smiled wanly. "I think I shall have to re-name my horse Crow's Nest."

He felt Skye's hands guiding a foot into a stirrup, and then he swung up, finding the saddle horn with his hands. His free foot probed for the other stirrup, and then was guided into it by an unseen hand.

"I fear to bring this horse close to your terrible Jaw-bone," Father Kiley said.

"Nothing to fret about. Jawbone's as mannered as I want him to be."

Then they rode, and he felt the horse swaying under him. He gripped the horn desperately. "I hope this ordeal won't last long."

Mister Skye replied gently. "Father Kiley, getting back to the business of living is going to be nothing but ordeals. I had a notion that this might be a little first step. Here's your hat. You'd better wear it against sunburn."

They rode quietly awhile, and after a few minutes the priest's dread of it lessened. He found he could stay on the horse, even when it gathered its muscles to leap a small crease in the grassy hills. The sun bored in hot upon his black broadcloth suit.

"We're north of Goose Creek, heading north," Mister Skye said amiably. "The blue Big Horns jutting up to our left. We're about a mile ahead of the wagons. We're rolling along pretty smoothly now. Few days and we'll be in the Crow camps. They're Victoria's people, and have always welcomed me and my parties."

"I have stayed among them," said Father Kiley. Once when he had been traveling with Pierre de Smet, they had stayed with the Crows awhile, and had been appalled by them. Never had he experienced such a bawdy and licentious people.

"I expect to find James Method there," Mister Skye said.

"Why? What would he be doing there?"

"Big medicine."

Medicine was a word the priest had come to dread and loathe. It was testing medicine that had blinded him; medicine that kept these western Indians blinded to his teaching and purposes.

"It's a pagan thing," he muttered.

Mister Skye said nothing for a while. Then, "There's a ridge ahead I'm going to climb and scout. Leave you here for a moment. You just hold your horse. I'll be back when I can. You're in a grassy wide valley. There's no cover here. I'll hand you the halter rope now. If your horse wants to follow, just pull hard on it until you twist him into a tight circle."

The priest felt the halter rope thrusting into his hands, and he took it, suddenly afraid. The horse turned, wanting to follow, and he pulled the rope. The horse circled, and sidled ahead, and he knew he was being taken somewhere. He thought to cry out, but didn't. Silence was vitally important when scouting, when trying to see without being seen. The horse kept drifting, and he grew afraid. The horse continued to drift, and he knew he was edging away from the place where Mister Skye had left him. Then came the nightmares—being lost or abandoned, helpless, blind in utter wilderness, wandering and stumbling to his death. Never had he felt so alone.

"Lord have mercy!" he cried, and knew at once what to do. He simply dismounted, sat down in grass, holding the halter rope in his hand. And waited. If Mister Skye didn't return, he'd remount somehow and let the horse drift. There'd be a good chance the horse would rejoin the wagon herd.

The throbbing of his heart slowed. He could hear his horse cropping grass close by. In blackness there is little time, and he lost track of it, not knowing whether Mister Skye had been gone minutes or hours.

"I am a weak Christian," he said to no one. Here he could talk to the wind and the sky. "I have little faith."

He waited he knew not how long, then heard the swift pulse of hoofs in grass, friend or enemy, coming death or coming life.

"Get up fast," said Mister Skye softly. "Yonder beyond the ridge is a whole village moving. Don't know what, but likely 'Rapaho, on a buffalo chase."

Father Kiley leapt to his feet, found his horse, felt for the stirrup, and pulled himself up and poked around with his free foot for the other stirrup.

"We're going to have to run, Father. Find cover before their scouts, their wolves, find us. Yonder half a mile's a crease in the land, a coulee full of brush, and that's where we're going. We're going to run, and you'll have to hang on."

He heard Jawbone plunge away in a hard gallop. He kicked his horse, and it leapt ahead, almost yanking him from the saddle. Then he was galloping through a black tunnel, his hand locked to the saddle horn, faster and faster, in a whirlwind of terror. The horse leapt over something, perhaps nothing but a crease in the ground, lifting him high, and when he landed he careened to his right. But he held on, death gripping the horn.

His heart thudded, and he knew a fear almost as terrible as the fear of torture. Then he thought: why am I afraid of the death I hunger for? What will be, will be . . . and he formed a small helpless prayer on his lips, even as the wild horse thundered down the black tunnel. He calmed. Brush whipped his legs. Ahead, he heard Jawbone slowing. His own horse slowed as well and then stopped, its sides heaving. He reached forward to its neck and found it soaked.

"We're here, Father," said Mister Skye quietly.

But Dunstan Kiley was unable to talk. He trembled on the trembling horse.

"We're in a draw full of chokecherry. I think we made it. I should be seeing their scouts along the ridge anytime now," Skye said, so quietly his voice carried only a few yards. "I don't rightly know what that village was. But it wasn't Crow. I know Crow on sight. They're moving west to east ahead of us. Should pass ahead of our wagons by two, three miles. Likely they'll spot the wagons, unless we're lucky."

"Blind on a galloping horse. Blind and no reins on a galloping horse," Father Kiley muttered.

"Be glad you didn't have reins."

"What now?" asked the priest.

"We wait. I'm going to slip off Jawbone and hold your horse. Don't want him whinnying."

There came a long silence. Then Mister Skye spoke, even more quietly. "Three of their scouts on the ridge. Half mile."

Another long silence. The priest sat helplessly on his horse, blackness around him, danger approaching. "Mother of God," he muttered, and it became a prayer, too.

"Quarter of a mile." The priest felt Skye's hand on the muzzle of his horse, ready to pinch the animal's nostrils.

"Quietly, smoothly, slip off your horse," whispered Mister Skye.

The priest hastened to do so, stepping into crackling brush.

"You were too high."

The silence pulsed like a heartbeat.

"One's coming down here, dropped off the ridge. That run of ours left tracks. Broken grass, hoofprints."

There was another aching silence.

"Gros Ventre."

Bad news. They were a wandering people, closely allied with the Blackfeet, and murderous enemies of all whites. The Gros Ventres could show up almost anyplace.

"He's picked up our tracks now."

"Where are the others?" the priest asked.

"One's up on the ridge watching. Other's gone, other side of it. Can't talk anymore. His horse knows we're here, but he's not looking at his horse."

The silence stretched out. No birds of summer sang on the breezes. A stick cracked somewhere ahead. The priest peered into black horizons. His horse jerked as he leaned upon it, and he felt Mister Skye's hand clamping its muzzle.

The priest waited for the cry, the arrow, the rattle of hoofs, the shot that would end his nightmare. Nothing.

A horse whinnied, just a few yards ahead. Another whinnied far off and higher. He felt Skye wrestling with the muzzle of his horse.

Skye's breath was in his ear. "He's onto us," the guide whispered. "He's got the other one up on the ridge coming down. We're in a jackpot, mate. If I kill them, I'd bring the whole Gros Ventres village down on the wagons."

"Mister Skye," whispered Father Kiley, "my life is nothing to me. I'm going out."

He didn't wait for a response. He found the halter rope and mounted, presumably in plain sight now of the warrior, wherever he might be. He turned his horse in the direction of the sound of stalking, and rode forward, crashing through brush, waiting for the fatal arrow. None came.

He held one hand high over his head and rode, he didn't know how far. He guessed fifty yards, until the brush stopped scraping at his legs.

He lowered his arm, and sat upon his quiet horse, reciting in Latin the Pater Noster. All was darkness, but in his soul he saw light ahead, blinding light.

He discerned voices now, harsh sibilants of two men talking. He felt a hand upon his coat, a finger finding the bullet holes and the undamaged flesh beneath them. Hands gripped his head, and he felt hands untying Victoria's bandages, first the outer leather casing she had contrived, and then the cloth pads over his draining eye sockets. The pads were pulled away. He felt dry air reach into the holes where his eyes had been.

"Ayaaah!" exclaimed a low voice.

He heard a furious jabber of low voices. The language was Algonquian; he knew that. These would be the Atsina, then, one of two tribes the French trappers called Big Bellies, Gros Ventre. He knew little of this tongue, but he knew the one word that came to him over and over, medicine.

Would he live because of medicine? He didn't want that. He didn't want to survive because of medicine but because of—faith.

"I have no medicine," he said to them in English. "You are wrong! Wrong! There is but one God!"

Silence then. He sat tall in his saddle awaiting the blow. The arc of an axe; the thrust of a lance; the jolt of a war club, smooth rock bound by rawhide to a handle.

He felt the horse beside him again, felt legs brushing his, hands grasping his head. The pads were pressed back into his eye sockets; the leather wrapped over his forehead and tied again in back. Then the stir of horses. He did not know whether he was being taken. To find out he dismounted and held tight to the halter rope of his horse. The sound of hoofs diminished.

"There is only God," he cried after them.

He did not know where he was. He stood quietly, holding the horse, feeling the sun burn into his black clothing. He was very thirsty. Perhaps Mister Skye was dead. It didn't matter. He would mount his horse and let the horse take him where he would; no doubt to water eventually. He would wander alone until he died; of thirst, of starvation, of exposure . . .

He waited what he thought might be five minutes and then began to mount.

"Wait just a minute, mate," came a low voice from behind. "They're not yet over the ridge. I'll be with you in a minute."

He waited then. He felt an insect on his hand; others hummed around his face, landing at the edges of his leather bandaging. Then hoofsteps, and the felt presence of Mister Skye.

"You're a brave man, Father Kiley," said the guide. "You've saved us all; saved that whole missionary party."

"I cannot claim such a thing. I sought only to die."

"Medicine," said Mister Skye. "That story about Wolf-That-Circles got around fast. Stories do, you know. Within a fortnight it was probably known to most tribes on the northern plains."

"That's the last thing I wanted."

"It was medicine, mate, big medicine. They poked their fingers into the bullet holes. They had themselves a look at your eyes. Big medicine, Father Kiley. They hightailed out as fast as they could and left you strictly alone. Left our whole party alone, I imagine."

"You can't imagine how that grieves me," Kiley said. "I'm grateful we are safe, but not by medicine . . . not with heathen belief . . ."

In fact the encounter had plunged him into a terrible despair. God had spared him. But for what?

They were traveling again now. It grew very hot, and Father Kiley shed his suitcoat and managed to tie it behind the cantle of his saddle. Mister Skye was leading his horse.

For a half hour or so Mister Skye said nothing. Father Kiley grew weary beyond endurance, and he focused upon one thing, the luxury of the buffalo robe in the shaded bed of the swaying wagon.

"Have you thought of your future?" asked Mister Skye.

"I have none. Take me to Fort Benton, I suppose. Perhaps I can catch a river packet."

"To where?"

"To wherever I am sent. The Society will take care of me. One thing we Jesuits are is obedient. We are soldiers."

"Are you sure that's what you want?"

"I don't want anything, Mister Skye."

Mister Skye was silent a long time. Then, at last, he spoke. "I don't rightly know where I stand about religion. I think on it; read Scriptures now and then. Makes my head ache. I suppose I'm a pagan, but I wouldn't claim it. Things happen. I respect faith. I've seen miracles. But none ever happened to me. When I was pressed into the Royal Navy, I tried to pray. I prayed my heart out. I was a slave, mate, a powder monkey, and a young lad, and my prayers never netted me a thing. God abandoned me. I had to survive other ways, mostly by giving a harder licking than I took . . . But you're different, Dunstan Kiley. Call it Irish courage. Call it blind courage. Call it Jesuit courage. I can't rightly say, but for sure it's Dunstan Kiley's courage. Are you so set on going back to the states? I'm not much of a believing man, but seems to me maybe God has other plans for you, Father Kiley. Hope you'll think on it before we get into Blackfeet country and Fort Benton."

"We were rescued by medicine and superstition, not by our Lord, Mister Skye."

"Don't know that I agree with you," said Mister Skye. "I think God's love is upon you."

Chapter 17

Pine Leaf pushed them at a pace that James Method had scarcely believed possible. They made forty or fifty miles a day, he guessed, and yet the horses showed little sign of weariness. He was learning from her. Frequently she rode well ahead of Method and Gliding Raven, peering over ridges, disappearing into cottonwood bottoms, reappearing miraculously beside them when they least expected her. He studied the old Crow warrior woman, hoping to learn how to traverse the vast country almost invisibly, as she did.

Whenever his erstwhile friends in the missionary caravan encountered deer or antelope, the animals would race over the nearest ridge and disappear, sometimes leaving behind them a distant sentinel to monitor them. But now somehow things were different. Frequently they rode close to a herd of antelope without triggering flight. The deer seemed a little more edgy, but from safe distances they, too, stood their ground while Pine Leaf, Gliding Raven, and James Method passed in silence.

The limitless land had its effect on the former slave as well, and he felt himself shedding cocoons and growing day by day. It was July now, and the blush of spring-green was fading in these arid lands. He had not known that the earth was so vast. For days they had ridden north, and the whole while a single range of mountains loomed in the west, snowcapped and blue. Frequently they forded cold rushing creeks fed by the mountain snows.

He surveyed the aching distances, the hundred-mile vistas, and felt free. He had scarcely known what freedom was. He was finding that the vast land, without

fences, without barriers, without forests, without civilization, taught him about liberty. For here he could travel
unimpeded in any direction farther than the eye could
see. In the South the cottonfields had been hewn out of
dense lush forest and there was scarcely a hill high enough
to afford a view. The damp hot land was itself a prison,
the forbidding forests were the walls of his slavery. On
occasion a slave would disappear into the dank woods.
Usually he was caught, but sometimes one or another
managed to live semi-free, a hunted creature of woods
and swamps. But James Method knew that wasn't freedom; it was slavery amid the dripping woods. The south-
land had reduced his vision, made him believe that all
the world, whites too, was enslaved after a fashion. He
had not dreamed of freedom, because he scarcely understood it. He had dreamed of escape, running away so that
he could possess himself, own his body and shape his
mind as he saw fit.

But here on the sunny, somnolent high prairies he understood liberty. He became his own master, yes. But
more than that, he could travel in any direction or climb
the majestic mountains with a purpose in life—a wife,
riches, horses, land beneath his feet that was not the
master's. Almost daily he shed cocoons as they traveled,
finding his own will, riding through a world without
walls. As fast as he learned survival skills from Pine
Leaf, his confidence fleshed out within him, as if liberty
required command, power over nature and will. He
thrilled to it. One evening Pine Leaf had taught him how
to use her bow and arrows. In time he would master that,
and be able to bring down game without the telltale
boom of his rifle, echoing toward unfriendly ears. She
taught him things he thought he knew, but didn't; how to
skin game swiftly, how to build a fire with nothing but

the flint and frizzen of his rifle, plus a tiny fuzzy bit of tinder.

Something else, too, was transforming him. His two companions were people of color. Pine Leaf's umber flesh, weathered with age, was darker than his own. Gliding Raven looked lighter, almost golden. They accepted him completely. He had never felt that among the whites. The Samples had been courteous. His tent-mate, Silas Potter, had been painfully pleasant. The Newtons simply distant. Only the priest, the Rathbones, and Mister Skye himself seemed not to care. He was certain of the goodwill of these people, but at bottom, uncertain whether he was an equal. Sometimes they seemed to monitor their tongues as they spoke to him, simplify words—as if they were telling him that he was a product of darkest savage Africa, and they the product of a refined complex culture infinitely superior to his own. But that too had vanished here. The two Crow women did not patronize him in the slightest.

Another thing was affecting him. Years earlier the mulatto Jim Beckwourth had come to live with the Crows, and had become one of their great warriors and sub-chiefs. James had heard of Beckwourth, who still roamed the West, and still spent time in the villages of the Crow. So a man of his color had gone before him, and these women were perfectly familiar with him and at home with him. Pine Leaf had shared the buffalo robes with Beckwourth, even as she sometimes came to James Method's bedroll in the middle of the night.

All of this was swiftly transforming the former slave into a freeman enjoying liberty and acceptance such as he'd never known. That seemed to him the miracle of the American West. He knew that eventually the tide of whites would flood here, too, but he hoped it wouldn't be in his lifetime. He hoped he might be a freeman, in perfect liberty, for all of his days.

He grew aware of yet another side, a side that crowded into his mind only in the night. Where there were no laws and rules, there were no barriers to the evil in men's souls. He was free, but also at risk. Any passing party of Sioux or Cheyenne could capture and torture him or make him a slave. He could not own land by title and deed, and he could hold his possessions only by power and domination of others, because there was really no such thing as property in a wilderness, or even in the villages of these people. Like Father Kiley's eyes, everything could be taken away. He would need medicine, big medicine, to enjoy his new liberty. For the poor, the weak or sick, the unfortunate, the widowed and orphaned, this liberty he was experiencing could be the liberty of death. Who would care for him, he wondered, when he grew old and sick and perpetually tired, like the bitter old granny he visited when he was young. The master had fed his old slaves, even her in her shack beside the cottonfields.

Now at last the bulk of the Big Horns diminished in the West, and Pine Leaf steered them westerly across a rolling arid land dotted with silvery sagebrush. Gliding Raven's eyes danced with excitement, and she managed to tell James that soon they would be in the village of her people. He could never look at her without the stirrings of desire. And the longing in her eyes and the touch of her hands told him she felt all this too. He was, after all, her intended. The medicine had made it so, and who among them would resist that mysterious power they called medicine?

Pine Leaf had told him something of this power her

people called medicine. It was more than power over nature and events. It was spiritual insight, healing force. It could be used for good or evil. Those who resorted to bad medicine were destroyers, casting evil upon the lives of others, enjoying power and control. There were few among the Absaroka people who did that, and they were feared and despised. The shamans, the medicine men, were sacred and holy people, who asked nothing but to help those who came to them with needs or hungers or fears. A person who had medicine, who interpreted dreams, helped others to find their spirit helpers, named others with good medicine names, was a respected elder whose counsel was sought in all grave matters, including peace and war.

Now they pierced deep into Crow country, and Pine Leaf relaxed her scouting a bit, and rode beside him more and more, answering his questions, translating for Gliding Raven. Through Pine Leaf, the young people learned each other's thoughts and hopes. Gliding Raven wished him to become a great warrior and a person of high repute among the Absaroka people. She wished to bear his sons and daughters, as numberless as the winters of life. She wished to make him fine clothing of soft-tanned elkskin, trimmed with red tradecloth and beads and porcupine quills. She wished to scrape and tan prime buffalo hides that he could trade at the post of the whites for new weapons and powder and lead, and iron cooking pots, and sharp iron arrow points, and four-point blankets.

All day they rode northward along a river Pine Leaf said the whites called the Little Big Horn. Actually they stayed clear of the stream and rode along the western lip of its wide, shallow valley, ready to disappear from hostile eyes in an instant. That night they camped at a tiny tributary splashing out of the low hills that were all that remained of the great Big Horn range.

Pine Leaf sat down beside him after they had filled themselves on a haunch of antelope.

"Tomorrow," she said, "we will reach our village. We will leave this valley and go west over the hills, and down into the valley of the Big Horn River, and there will be the village of the Kicked-in-the-Bellies band, the people of Gliding Raven and myself. I will present you to our people. I will tell them of the medicine that brought us to you. Already they know of Gliding Raven's dreams. Now they will see that her dreams were true and good. There are things you must tell me; things I must tell my chiefs and my council. Tell me again about the people you came with; the people who have Mister Skye with them. Why are they going to the Siksika? Why are they taking their white medicine to the enemies of my people?"

"Ah'm not sure Ah can explain it very well," he said. "They're a kind of medicine people, just like you're a medicine woman. They have a vision, Ah'd call it, to bring their beliefs, their faith, their God, to all the people on earth. They've selected somehow the Blackfeet to bring it to."

"Why them? They're dogs. I have taken many of their scalps and maybe I'll take more. Why not us? We want the medicine power. The whites have things we need now—iron pots, iron arrow points, wool blankets, many kinds of guns . . . power."

"Ah can't say," he said, perplexed. "That's what they had a vision to do."

"Who?" demanded Pine Leaf.

"Why, Cecil Rathbone. He's a good man. He and his wife. They are good people, straight as your arrow flies."

"Why is Mister Skye taking them? His wife is one of us! He betrays us! And he hates the Siksika. He has almost been killed by them many times. And one among the Siksika has vowed to kill Mister Skye, has sworn the oath at their Sun Dance to kill Mister Skye. And yet he takes these people to our enemies. I don't understand this, and neither will my chiefs, my council."

"Who is this Blackfoot that will kill Mister Skye?"

Pine Leaf hesitated. "His name is Moon-Hides-the-Sun. There is no more terrible name given to any man. Moon-Hides-the-Sun was born the day it happened, when all the world was shadowed and we thought the end of all things had come. It is the most terrible name ever given. I am afraid of only one person in all the earth, and that is Moon-Hides-the-Sun. He has evil medicine that I do not have. It is said he has the strength of seven warriors. He could kill me, and maybe will. He is not a chief. He refuses to be a chief of the Kainah, the Bloods, of the Blackfeet. He has said that to be a chief would destroy his medicine, for he would be responsible to others. No, he stalks alone, no one knows where, striking anytime, anyplace, even here in the middle of the land of the Absaroka. So powerful is his medicine that the children of our people dream of him coming and wake up in the night crying. I do not understand why Mister Skye goes to the land of Moon-Hides-the-Sun."

"Ah can't say, but Ah imagine you could ask him directly when he comes here."

"I am sure we will. And if the answer is not good, I know my chiefs will not permit them to go north."

They rode over the low divide, over hills serrated by coulees, scattering coyotes that denned there. At a promontory they paused to gaze into the wide valley of the Big Horn, not far north of the canyon it cut between the Big Horn and Pryor Mountains. Below them lay the great Crow village, somnolent in the afternoon sun. The tiny dark cones of two hundred or so lodges, grouped in concentric

circles, were visible. The village horse herd grazed quietly
in the lush meadows beside the Big Horn River. A faint
blue pall of smoke hung over the village.

Gliding Raven's eyes glowed proudly, and she sought
Method's eyes, to let him know of her pride and pleasure
in her people. Pine Leaf touched the flanks of her brown
pony and they began the long descent. They were spotted
below, and the camp guards, the wolves, boiled out to greet
them even as the village crier raced among the lodges
announcing their arrival.

To Method, the lodges looked much alike, smoke-
blackened at the top, around the windflaps, but golden at
their bases, where the buffalo cowhide retained its original color. Some of the lodges were painted with medicine symbols, suns and moons and other designs. One
lodge seemed larger than the others, and he supposed
it belonged to the chief. He found other structures here
too, brush arbors resting on poles planted in the earth,
to provide a welcome shade and relief from the midsummer sun.

By the time they rode into the village, great crowds
had materialized, along with barking dogs and scattering
naked children. Everywhere in this year of 1855 was the
evidence of extensive trading with the whites. Many of
the women wore light, patterned calico skirts. Before
many lodges hung black cast-iron kettles. A few of the
very old clutched striped trade blankets, even in the heat
of high summer. Scarcely a male wore anything more
than a breechclout and moccasins.

This was, Method realized, a happy occasion, and
people danced and pointed and chattered about them as
they rode past. He was plainly an object of great curiosity, and he met their stares with a dignified nod of the
head. All of this was medicine. Had not Gliding Raven

dreamed just such a dream as this? Had not the great medicine woman, Pine Leaf, declared the truth of it? Had these two worthy women not gone many sleeps away to bring the black man to this village, where he would become a great warrior, and husband of Gliding Raven? What more proof did anyone need of the medicine vision of these two? And so they rode with honor through the chaotic village, with old and young streaming along beside them on their way to the chief and the elders, who were gathering before the lodge of the chief.

James Method relaxed. It had seemed an alien thing at first, this village and these savage people, so unlike his white masters and the civilization that had enslaved him. These Crow were not handsome at all, plain-featured, ill put together. That made Gliding Raven's incredible beauty even more unusual, he thought. Ahead was the great lodge, and the chief, wearing his ceremonial bonnet, with other headmen beside him. James felt a little uneasy now. He had come into the far west with a party en route to the Blackfeet, mortal enemies of these people. Would it be held against him?

Beside him, Gliding Raven cried out and steered her horse into the crowd, and then slipped off it. Her parents stood there, and she hugged them. They stared at James, and he at them, these two graying people who would become his in-laws, his family, because the medicine proved true. Then they were lost from his sight. Pine Leaf beckoned him to come to dismount, as she did, before the village elders.

The chief was speaking, and James understood little of it. But then Pine Leaf translated. "Many Coups, chief of the Kicked-in-the-Bellies, welcomes you to our village. He praises me, and praises Gliding Raven, for our great medicine, and for bringing us a great warrior who will be like Antelope, Jim Beckwourth . . . You and I are to come into his lodge now to smoke the pipe."

"Tell him Ah'm glad to be here in this great land of the Crow, and this great village which has taken me in. But tell him Ah know nothing about war and fighting; Ah don't know about this warrior business."

Pine Leaf hesitated a second, and then translated.

The chief replied. "It does not matter what you were; it matters what you will be," Pine Leaf translated. "You cannot go against your own medicine."

With that, Many Coups and his elders filed into the great lodge, and Method and Pine Leaf followed. He was beckoned to sit down in a place close to the chief, a place he supposed to be of honor, Pine Leaf beside him to translate. But Many Coups was extracting a long pipe, its bowl made of some sort of red stone, and its wooden shaft decorated with raven feathers and small talismans. It grew very quiet. The light fell mellow gold, piercing through the translucent cowhides. Not even the raucous noise of the village seemed to penetrate here. Slowly the old man with the seamed cheeks and crow's-foot eyes tamped tobacco into the long pipe, and then lit it with a brand from the tiny fire at the center of the lodge. He puffed quietly until the tobacco glowed and its fine aroma filled the lodge. Then he saluted the east and west, the north and south, the earth mother and the sky father. Solemnly he passed the pipe to James Method, who didn't have the foggiest idea what to do, so he did exactly as the chief had done. Not until the pipe had circled the council, ten elders plus James and Pine Leaf, did anyone speak. Many Coups asked a question of Pine Leaf.

Beside him, the graying medicine woman began to speak. It took a long time, and he realized she was supplying the council with her story of the journey. At various times their eyes rested on him. Then the tone of her voice changed, and she was explaining something else, and now their eyes settled searchingly on him, and he heard the word Siksika mentioned, and supposed she was telling what she knew of the mission party.

Then she asked him a question. "They wish to know how Many Quill Woman is faring."

That mystified him.

"Victoria," she said. "Mister Skye calls her Victoria."

"She is well and happy. She feeds Mister Skye and scouts, and cares for the blinded Jesuit."

The who? That was news to them. This blackrobe Dunstan Kiley they knew, and the other one, Pierre de Smet, but surely Kiley had eyes?

James realized that these people did not know the story of Wolf-That-Circles and Dunstan Kiley. So he told them the story, Pine Leaf translating.

"Ayaah!" they cried. "That is news. That is great medicine. Blind and filled with medicine. It is a holy thing, worthy of great respect. Soon we will honor this great blackrobe."

Then came the hard questioning, and Pine Leaf struggled to convey answers. Who were these missionaries, shortrobes with wives? Why did they choose to take medicine to the Siksika dogs? Why was Mister Skye guiding them to the enemies of his own wife? Why was Mister Skye braving the terror of Moon-Hides-the-Sun? Why, why, why?

All of this James Method answered as best he could. Before he was done they had his life history, his escape from slavery, the help of these Methodist missionaries, who he named and described, one by one. As best he could, he explained the white men's faith, the purpose of missions, conversions, and the changes of habit and life they hoped to bring to the Siksika.

"It is beyond my understanding," said Many Coups. "If they bring their medicine to the Siksika dogs, why do they expect them to stop making war?"

"Perhaps the blackrobe, Father Kiley, can explain it to you, Chief Many Coups. Ah can't. Or maybe the head-man, Cecil Rathbone."

The chief nodded solemnly. This would be a matter of high policy for his council. For a while they debated among themselves, and none of it was translated for James. But he knew it concerned the missionaries, and whether to prevent them from heading north. There seemed to be many opinions, and none of them prevailing among them.

Then at last the chief called a halt with an uplifted hand, and turned to address James Method.

"You are welcome in the village of the Absaroka people," Pine Leaf translated. "You will be my guest in this lodge for a day and a night, and then a guest of the parents of Gliding Raven, her father New Lance, and her mother Iron Kettle Woman. You will live in the lodge of Gliding Raven, and her brothers, and her parents, until it is the time of your medicine. In the time of your medicine, as it was dreamed by Gliding Raven and pronounced by Pine Leaf, you will in time take seven scalps. And that is now your name among us, Seven Scalps, according to what she has perceived from the hidden side of the world that is open to her because of her virtue. When you have counted coup, or stolen the horses of our enemies, then will New Lance give his daughter to you. And until then you will not touch her."

He smiled gently and dismissed them all, save for James Method and Pine Leaf. While his three wives prepared a buffalo hump roast, along with wild onions and herbs, he questioned Method further; indeed, well into the twilight. And when James Method fell into the robes given him, he felt that the chief knew every scrap of information about him there was to know. And as he drifted off, he felt free.

Chapter 18

They struck the Big Horn River in mid-July and found no sign of the Crows. Mister Skye scouted to the north as far as the Yellowstone, while Victoria scouted south. When she returned that hot evening, she had information. Her village, the Kicked-in-the-Bellies, had indeed camped some twenty miles upstream, but were no longer there. The grass for miles around the village had been grazed to the roots, and the village had moved to new pasture and a cooler place. She was quite certain where that would be, a creek the Absaroka called Arrow two or three days travel to the west, that white men had come to call Pryor, after a sergeant in Lewis and Clark's Expedition. It was a sacred place of the Absaroka people, she said, for a little to the south rose three small conical peaks, the medicine place of her people. The center of these three low, matched peaks was the place of the vision-quest, where Absaroka youths went to discover their spirit helper, and their adult names, and their role in life.

To the south of these peaks lay the Pryor Mountains, long blue hulks split by a gorge, and teeming with the wiry mustangs that formed the foundation of the magnificent Absaroka horse herd. The way there was almost level, no obstacle to wagons once the Big Horn River was crossed. But the river itself was a formidable barrier that would require the building of a raft. Its silt-laden water ran cold and deep and swift as it approached the Yellowstone, and the deepest channel of the river in some seasons flowed eight or ten feet deep. The banks here were flat and gravelly, and that would be a blessing. Also, they'd find abundant cottonwoods that could be cut into giant logs. These, lashed together, could raft wagons from the east side of the river to the west.

Cecil Rathbone wondered whether between them they had enough rope to lash a raft together and provide a guy across the river, so the rafts wouldn't be swept downstream. There was no help for it but to set to work, and the next day he and Clay Sample hewed heavy limbs from giant cottonwoods, while Alex and Silas yoked oxen to them and dragged them to the shore. It took a day of hard chopping in blazing summer heat to cut and trim enough limbs for the raft. Mister Skye helped when he could and scouted and hunted for meat the rest of the time. Game was scarce here, where hunters from the great Crow village had scoured the country.

They were desperately shorthanded, Cecil thought. Alex Newton and Silas Potter between them equaled less than one hardened frontiersman. Method had vanished. The Jesuit lay helpless. Someone had to make meat, especially since the stores of food brought from the east had been eaten, and there was only Mister Skye to do it, and Victoria to guard the camp against surprise. Fortunately, young Alfred Sample pitched in, and seemed almost a man. It fell to the boy to lash the logs together in a shallow eddy of the river, and to guard them zealously against the reaching fingers of the swift current.

In the late light of a brutal day they completed the raft,

and anchored it tightly to shore. Tomorrow they would cross. There was nowhere near enough rope for a guy from shore to shore. They would have to yoke oxen into teams and swim them across, pulling the raft, three round trips, one for each wagon and the carriage. And they would have to drive the entire loose herd across, and hope for the best.

Mister Skye rode in when the sun lay low, without meat. Nothing. Antelope and deer had vanished. No buffalo. Elk fled to the mountains this time of year. For men who had hewn and cut and dragged themselves to exhaustion, that was the hardest news of all. Cecil felt his stomach cave in as he watched Mister Skye unsaddle Jawbone.

"Sorry, mates," was all he said.

No sooner had Mister Skye returned than Victoria and Mary disappeared. Mary handed her boy, Dirk, to Esmerelda, muttering something she took to be a request to look after the child, and then the two Indian women disappeared into the lush growth along the river.

"What have we left?" asked Cecil.

"I have a little flour and salt. There must be some tallow. I think I could manage some sort of fry cakes."

"That sounds as splendid as a rib roast right now."

Dirk stared at them solemnly, understanding a little of his father's tongue. He was a quiet child, as stoic as his parents. Cecil admired the uncomplaining boy, even as Silas and Henrietta and Alex approached.

"What are we going to eat?" snapped Silas. "You'd think he'd have the foresight to gather game back a way, rather than wait until we got to this hunted-out area."

"Would have spoiled fast in this heat."

"Maybe Alice Sample has something," Henrietta said crossly.

"I'm sure Alice needs everything she has for her own very hungry family, dear," said Cecil.

"Are there fish in that river? I despise fish, but I'll eat a dozen tonight," said Alex.

It was a moot question.

Cecil saw the priest sitting quietly on the dropped tailgate of his wagon, and thought to let the man know of their distress.

"We're short of chow this evening, Father."

"So I gathered."

"We've a little flour. Esmerelda might manage some simple cakes if we can find some lard."

"I need nothing," he said. "I've sat here quietly all day while the rest of you have labored. Some water, and I'll be filled. For you I'll ask for loaves and fishes."

The thought struck Cecil then. Had he lost faith? Had he failed to ask?

He wandered back among his people.

"All along I've opposed this incompetent, demonic guide," snapped Silas Potter sourly, "but no, we had to go ahead, had to have him, and now he's left us to starve on the banks of a river many hundreds of hard miles from help."

Cecil placed a gentle hand on the young scholar's shoulder. "No, son," he said. "We are never far from help."

"Piety won't fill my stomach," Silas snapped. "This whole mission has fallen to pieces. Where's that lazy Method? Gone! What does a hard, powerful man like Skye do, when we have a heavy raft to build? Take his leisure on horseback, allegedly hunting for us. What do his squaws do all day? And now even they've vanished, heaven knows where."

Alex chimed in. "This is unbearable, Cecil. When we reach the Crow village, let's see who we can hire. Surely we don't want to employ this bumbling Skye anymore."

Cecil thought for a moment to lead them in a prayer,

or a hymn, but thought better of it. They'd become so sullen their hearts were not open. He stopped briefly at the Sample wagon and Alice smiled wanly at him. They had, it seemed, almost nothing either, and the children were cross and even Clay sat sullenly. He spotted a small rise a few yards away, and repaired to it, wondering whether its rocky, striated top might harbor rattlers. But he found none, and sat down, feeling the day's heat rise from the yellow sandstone. And there in the deepening shadows he prayed for loaves and fishes.

Below him Mister Skye had lit a small fire near his lodge, and Cecil wondered at that. Heat hung thick, and there was no food to cook. He had taken Dirk back from Esmerelda, and was playing with the boy, laughing and roaring, while the child chattered like a squirrel, somehow impervious to the gnawing hole in their bellies.

Cecil resolved to show the same fortitude, and decided to ignore the howl and growl of his belly and go pass time with the lonely and alone priest, whose spirit Cecil had come to admire. But as he rose and stretched, he spotted Skye's squaws toiling down the riverbank toward the camp, each burdened with unidentifiable things in bundles and bags.

The others stared sullenly, lost in self-pity, but Cecil grew curious and trudged over to them. Victoria was laughing, and Mary grinning.

"More damn vittles than we can gather," Victoria said. From the bags they pulled quantities of roots, carrot-like but white, and scores of small bulbs Cecil recognized as wild onions. There were other greens he supposed were herbs, and indeed their fragrance lifted to him in the evening breezes. Gently wrapped in Victoria's brown shawl were scores of wild asparagus, each cut with her Green River knife. In Mary's hand was a small pot with sur-

prising contents: ripe, red, lush raspberries. And another
bag bulged with some berries of a variety Cecil didn't
know.

"Sarvisberries," said Mister Skye. "Chokecherry and
plum coming along, but still too soon."

Over the guide's campfire water boiled in a large
kettle. It had mystified Cecil before, but now he understood. Swiftly the women cleaned the roots—breadroot,
Skye explained, an Indian staple collected by them in
large quantities—and the onions and dropped them into
the kettle. Next came various herbs, and finally Victoria
dipped into one of Mister Skye's parfleches and extracted
several handfuls of buffalo jerky, which also went into
the stew, whose aroma now galvanized the famished
company. While the great stew bubbled, Victoria and
Mary cleaned the berries, reserving the raspberries for
the children, and the tart sarvisberries for the adults.

The hungry company demolished the whole kettle of
stew, and the berries as well, pronouncing it the finest
meal they had had during their whole exodus. But not
before Cecil invited Dunstan Kiley, who was led to the
feast and was sitting quietly beside Mister Skye, to say
grace. Esmerelda watched him, and wept.

At dawn the Indian women took the white women with
them in search of another meal from nature's providence.
Even Henrietta, inspired by her brush with hunger, was
eager to go, and to learn. Cecil walked to the riverbank,
to study the wide, rippling, quiet river in the long light of
the new day. It seemed peaceful enough, wending its way
through silent shadowed hills. But he sensed its power, its
strength-sapping coldness, its cruelty, and once again he
wondered at his own folly in coming here with wagons.

Had he been crazy in his zeal to do God's work? Here, in these lapping waters, lay grave jeopardy again. The wagons, perched on their high wooden wheels, were top-heavy. A ripple, a wave, a gust of air, could capsize them, and if they tipped, they would spill the essence of his dreams, the tools, the Bibles, the organ, into the swirling river, and it would all end.

He had met and conquered rivers before. What man on the nation's westering frontier hadn't? Each stream was a separate problem. Each wreaked its havoc its own way, and only the canny observer might hope to anticipate and deal with the troubles. So he had come here in the utter stillness to meet his enemy. God gave him brains to deal with life's hard moments, and he intended to use them. To trust in God's providence, yes indeed, for that was part of it. But also to use himself and his skills and intuitions too. There was, he thought, too much of the other thing in the world—declarations of trust and faith that really masked indolence and foolishness. Hand in hand with it went the wrong kind of humility, the kind that avoided trying and striving. Cecil had the other kind, that came upon him after he had thrown himself at a knotty problem and failed. That gave him some sense of his outer boundaries, his folly, and that was where his kind of humility began. That was the river where he met God. He feared he might really be arrogant, insisting on trying, striving, pushing himself beyond his former limits. Had he not read of saints who trusted God more, and simply became God's instruments? He admired them, but he wasn't that kind. He was God's unruly servant, and now he had a river to tackle and a cottonwood raft, and some oxen to pull it.

He threw a small stick into the water to measure the flow. It vanished into the dark north swiftly. He trudged downstream to see how the banks lay a quarter, half a mile that way. The crossings would not be straight across but at a long angle, driven by the current. It looked good. The river bent east slightly, driving its current gently toward the far shore. But the shore was thick with brush, and passage might have to be hacked through it. He guessed the river ran seventy or eighty yards wide here.

He closed his eyes a moment, trying to visualize what might happen. They'd haul the wagon onto the raft and lash it. They'd double-team the oxen and hook the tugs to the raft. But how would they do that? Drive the oxen into the current and hope for enough shallow water so the oxen could stand while being hooked up? He decided to take a horse and just measure depth a bit. The more he knew, the more he could avert catastrophe. Then what? Someone riding a horse, riding a swimming horse, would have to whip the oxen. And then what? Why, that cold current would whip the raft downstream, swinging the oxen, pointing them away from the far shore, until the whole team was swimming upstream against the current, until it grew exhausted and the end came to the oxen, the raft, and all within it.

He knew then what not to do.

Instead he would take advantage of that gentle curve that threw the mainstream toward the far shore a few hundred yards down. There were willows here, and he'd cut some fine flexible poles from them, and he'd put the men on the raft, poling hard until they lost the bottom. He'd tie the last of the rope to the raft, too, about fifty feet of it, ready to be thrown to horsemen down at that curve where the current swept ten or fifteen yards from shore. As for the stock—the oxen and mules, the horses and milch cows—they'd swim free, with no lines to entangle them.

Only then, after he had envisioned his plan with whatever shrewdness he possessed, did Cecil J. B. Rathbone submit it all to God. "This is my best thought," he said. "Now show me your way and let me be humble enough to receive it."

He waited quietly in the somnolent dawn light, and then walked back to camp. While the women cooked he found his axe and began to cut long willow limbs and trim them until he had four or five poles, running two or three inches thick and ten feet or so in length. He was ready for the day, though there was one more river still to cross, the stream that separated his thinking from that of others.

After the meal he assembled his people and explained his purposes, and his reasoning. He would put the men of the party on the raft with poles; he would ask Mister Skye to cross the river and wait on the bend of the far shore, to catch the rope tossed to him and, on Jawbone, draw the raft to safety.

As he expected, both Silas and Alex thought it was madness. "Why," asked Silas petulantly, "float the raft free when there is all the power of the oxen to draw it across?"

And Alex, who abhorred the hard work of poling, added, "What if we miss the far bank? There we'll be, stuck on a raft and no way to get off and whirling down the river—clear to New Orleans."

Mister Skye said nothing, but saddled Jawbone and rode down the river a way, studying it. Ten minutes later he returned with his verdict. "It'll work," he said. "Best plan there is."

That settled it. Clay Sample, having weighed it all, announced in favor. But he had a question.

"We've got to cross that raft three times. How are we going to get it back for the next crossing?"

Cecil saw the answer at once. "The oxen will pull it

back this way, slanting upstream into the current to get here. They won't be fighting the raft coming this way. We'll drive them across first, and throw the harness in the first wagon over."

And that was the way they tackled it. Mister Skye doffed his leggins, and in his breechclout swam Jawbone over and trotted on down the far shore. Victoria swam her pony, and continued up the far side to a distant ridge to do sentry duty there. Mary swam with her, with Dirk clinging behind. The Samples' wagon was eased down to the riverbank and laboriously levered up onto the rough cottonwood logs and lashed down. All the party's harness was thrown into it. Alice and Miriam nervously chose to go too, hoping to stay dry.

They hazed the oxen into the water, cracking whips and prodding with their poles, and watched the heavy beasts swim toward the far shore, drifting downstream as they did. A few minutes later they clambered up a muddy slope and shook themselves heavily and began to spread into the brush there.

Following Cecil's example, the men doffed their shirts and shoes, except for Alex Newton, whose corpulent body rather embarrassed him, and who chose to remain, as he muttered to himself, decently clad. Cecil, Clay, young Alfred, Silas, and Alex each grasped a pole and heaved the heavy raft into the stream, scraping bottom a way. Then they slid clear, poling furiously, sweeping downstream toward the curve. For a brief while the poles touched nothing, and they stood helplessly. But the raft angled the right way, drawn by its momentum and the current, and Cecil soon found his pole touching a soft bottom again, and he pushed hard. Mister Skye sat on Jawbone, belly deep in the eddying water, waiting a hundred yards downstream. It was easy. As they drifted close,

Cecil tossed the rope. Mister Skye plucked it from the water, and set Jawbone toward shore, pulling mightily, helped by the poling. The raft bottomed somewhat sooner than they had expected, ten yards out, and the jolt sent Alex Newton careening into the cold water. He sputtered and stood, mad at creation, his black suit drenched. The laughter didn't settle his temper any. Cecil himself jumped off, wondering what sort of bottom they had. It was mud rather than the gravel he'd hoped for, but not muck. They could offload the Samples' wagon and drag it out with the oxen, cutting a path here.

It was well past noon before they had crossed the Big Horn, but Cecil's plan had worked, and they had no losses, though there had been a bad moment when a milch cow mysteriously turned around, halfway across, swam back awhile, got confused, turned into the current again and was swept far downstream. They found her alive and safe on the west bank a mile down. On the last trip across they rafted the other wagon, with the organ and Dunstan Kiley in it, and Cecil took time to explain to the blind priest what they were doing and why.

"I can pole," said Kiley.

"I'm sure you can," replied Cecil, "but you've got other rivers to cross."

By early afternoon they had reassembled their caravan and rolled toward the village of the Crows, Victoria's people, and the old woman's eyes shone bright in the July sun.

Chapter 19

On Arrow Creek, hard by the cool slopes of the Pryor Mountains, James Method waited uneasily for the arrival of Mister Skye and his erstwhile colleagues. One glance at him would tell them much: he was attired now in breechclout and leggins, and fine elkhide summer moccasins all made for him by his future wife, with the help of her mother. Around his neck hung a sacred medicine bundle that Pine Leaf had given him, saying she would explain its contents to him in time, as he came to understand the Absarokas and their medicine.

Daily the great woman warrior instructed him in the uses of bow and arrow, lance, battle axe, and knife. She taught him how to ride his horse lightly and to jump off of either side and other things about horses and horsemanship he'd never known. Once she told him that her people needed a great leader, for their numbers had dwindled because of white man's smallpox, and many of them had succumbed to whiskey from the trading posts, and fallen into filth and degradation.

She met his gaze then and told him that he might be the very one who would restore her people to their former numbers and courage. Gliding Raven had brought a great gift to the Absaroka people. Perhaps it was so. In less than a moon—he was thinking in Indian terms now—he had become a new person. He felt ready now to join a Crow war party, and do the things that would win him Gliding Raven. The Kit Fox Society, one of the most esteemed of the warrior groups, had invited him, and the invitation was a great honor. It all showed in his eyes, and the way he walked, and the assurance of his words. In scarcely half a year he had ascended from slave to uneasy companion of westering whites, to free warrior, on the brink of triumph among the Crows.

Mister Skye's party rode into the large village one afternoon, announced by the crier and escorted by the wolf warriors, village guardians and policemen, cavorting children, yelping dogs, and all of the curious. James stood well back among them, watching the fearsome bulk of Mister Skye in his black silk stovepipe hat, riding his terrible blue horse. And Victoria, greeting friends and relatives with joyous cries and hugs, and the Shoshone Mary, with the boy, smiling quietly from her pony at these occasional allies of her people. Behind them came the missionaries and their wagons and loose stock, staring at the Crows and being stared at in turn, curiosity and pleasure on Cecil J. B. Rathbone's gaunt and homely features, fear on the faces of the Newtons, and taut loathing radiating from the rigid pale face of Silas Potter. Behind them came the Samples, a little afraid, quiet, and self-possessed.

But it was Father Kiley who drew the stares and nudges now as he sat on an improvised seat at the front of his wagon. He had been known to them as a blackrobe colleague of Pierre de Smet, and now the story of his encounter with Wolf-That-Circles was familiar to them all, and they stared and pointed, and wondered what lay beneath the leatherbound bandages wrapping his upper face. Crow warriors stared thoughtfully at the white shaman whose medicine was so powerful that it felled Cheyenne right and left.

Victoria spotted her venerable and widowed father, and leapt lightly from her pony and into his embrace, and then the embrace of her stepmother. James Method stood near, and he could not yet understand the rapid Crow chatter of their reunion, but he could sense its joy and the love these people radiated. Victoria embraced not only her father, but those of her Sorelips Clan kin, sisters and cousins all, united in a powerful tribal faction.

As Mister Skye rode by, a man so terrible that there was always a notable space around him where others feared to penetrate, his small obscure eyes spotted James and held him in his gaze, instantly absorbing all that had transformed him. Then, faintly, he grinned, acknowledging it and approving of it. James felt suddenly that in Mister Skye's eyes, he had increased in stature, had come into a kind of manhood, an inheritance of the free western lands. He felt a kind of warmth, and even nostalgia about all the months of the trail, and Mister Skye's canny guidance came back to him. He had won manhood.

At the great smoke-darkened lodge of Chief Many Coups, this slow cavalcade halted. There the village elders and medicine men gathered, along with its esteemed medicine woman Pine Leaf, in whose austere lodge hung fifty-eight scalps of the enemies of her people. The chief gripped his raven feather-bedecked ceremonial coup stick, a badge of office, and studied this strange party brought by his friend and ally Mister Skye. And it lay in the chief's face, James thought, that these were odd white men and white women. The Absaroka women had scarcely seen a white woman, and now they crowded around Esmerelda and Henrietta—who looked like she might scream—and the Samples, fingering the cloth of their dresses, observing styles and stitching, boldly examining high-button shoes, poking at skirts to discover white petticoats. Only Esmerelda enjoyed it, and that perhaps was because she was studying the dress of her Crow sisters, the finely-wrought moccasins decorated with beads or fur trim; skin skirts and blouses worked so soft that they were velvet; hair parted into dark braids, with carmine paint down the part and on the cheeks, and trade ribbons in rainbow colors gaily tied to the braids.

Cecil, dressed in his Sunday-best black broadcloth, which seemed less and less appropriate to his gaunt frontier-hardened frame, drew up beside Mister Skye, before the chief and subchiefs and great men of the village. Many Coups raised a hand and addressed them in the Crow tongue, while Mister Skye translated softly. They were being welcomed, he said. Next would be a smoke. He and Cecil and Dunstan Kiley would sit with the elders in council; the rest were welcome to the village, and were invited to make camp at a place that would be designated, and to turn their stock over to the Crow herders.

Now at last Silas spotted James, stared icily, and nudged Alex and Henrietta, who simply gaped. James nodded amiably, seeing at once an impenetrable barrier forever between him and these whites. Esmerelda and then Cecil spotted him too, but in their gaze was curiosity and finally small grins of delight in reunion, while the chiefs and Mister Skye exchanged greetings according to the great protocol of the high plains.

Then Mister Skye turned to his party. "These lads here will take you to our place here, mates," he said. "We're among friends and allies. Many know English. The trappers—Beckwourth, Bridger, and a score of others—have stayed among them. The Absaroka are the finest warriors and horse thieves on the northern plains, and will take special care of the livestock of their guests, for it would bring dishonor to them to lose even one animal of any guest in their village . . . You'll have no need to cook a meal, for you'll be guests at great feastings this evening, and all the while we're here.

"Now, mates, some of us will smoke the pipe with the chiefs and elders. Mister Rathbone and Father Kiley and I, as well as our lost and found friend there, James Method"— the Samples, who had not yet spotted him, gawked—"are invited to counsel with our hosts. We'll be along in a while. There are many here who'd like to enjoy your company, mates, so welcome them at your wagons."

With that, he dismounted from Jawbone, and left the horse standing in its own pool of space, untouched by any Crow, who well knew the medicine powers of that awesome animal. His new Sharps rifle lay in its saddle sheath at Jawbone's side. Way was made in the crowds, and the others turned their oxen and their wagons and drove them off down the creek a bit, accompanied by the flocking curious among these people. Esmerelda glanced fleetingly at Cecil, with a look that said she wished she might stay and be with him, and then followed the others. James waited until Cecil and Mister Skye had led the priest into the chief's lodge, and then ducked through the east-facing door himself.

"Well, mate," said Mister Skye, wrapping a brawny arm about Method's shoulders. "I knew it, and I know what's been your good fortune. If you've got Pine Leaf for a sponsor here, you've got a fine life ahead of you."

"Is Mister Method here?" asked Father Kiley.

"I am beside you, Father."

The priest said nothing, but grasped James's hand warmly.

They were seated according to custom, having carefully walked around the central firepit. James was familiar with the smoking ritual now, but waited impatiently as this ceremony of peaceful intention and hospitality unwound, and Mister Skye had presented his hosts with twists of tobacco, powder and ball, and vermilion paint, treasured things all.

Then there came silence. James became aware that Many Coups was assessing the two white medicine men across the circle from him, his shrewd eyes first upon Father Kiley, and then upon Cecil J. B. Rathbone. The priest sat quietly, unaware and waiting. With some frontier aplomb, Cecil sat quietly as well, and met the chief's steady and penetrating stare with a direct gaze of his own, obviously aware that upon his conduct here rested the fate of his long exodus. When at last the chief spoke, Mister Skye translated.

"Mister Rathbone," said the chief, "your purposes have been made known to us, but we would have you tell us in your own words. The taking of your sacred medicine to our ancient enemies, the Siksika, has caused controversy among us. There are some here who say you insult the Absaroka people. Others say you are the enemies of my people. Others ask why you do not bring your medicine here to us and stay among us. Others— our great woman, Pine Leaf, especially—say that you have no real medicine; it is false and weak and evil, and if you want to take it to our enemies, then go and do it, for it will diminish them and make fools and old women of their warriors, and destroy their nation. I haven't yet made up my mind. I'll hear you and hear my friend Mister Skye, and then I'll decide what to do, after talking with my chiefs and elders."

It would be a long afternoon of theology, then, Method thought uncomfortably. And so it turned out to be.

Cecil Rathbone plunged in with a robust enthusiasm and a poignant innocence, describing the things he hoped to bring to the Blackfeet, the ways he hoped to transform them from warlike nomads to plowmen and ranchers, raising grains and fruits, and herding cattle. He would erect a church and a school, and introduce them to a loving, caring church and Lord who'd look after his Siksika children and keep them from harm and who, in turn, required submission, love, loyalty, virtue, and praise. He'd teach them to read and write, and some figures too so they could calculate, and with that they could do what whites do, manufacture what whites produce. When the Blackfeet no longer waged war, or caused turmoil or raided whites, then the Lord of Creation would pour his medicine upon them and help them endure all things, and bring them to Himself and no matter how they suffered on earth, their next life would be spent with Him in perfect happiness.

The chief then turned to Father Kiley, who had an altogether different message and interpretation of the faith. Quietly the Jesuit addressed his unseen audience, droning on, as if reading from his missal or reciting a homily, seeing his words on the screen of his mind. The anguished priest began at once to separate the purposes of God from the magic possessed by whites, cleaving the things of the spirit from guns and powder and the power to find metal and turn it into pots and bullets and arrow points and knives. Father Kiley's narration turned to stranger things, long suffering, submission, obedience, and love freely given to God, redemption through the sacrificed Son Jesus, born of the Virgin, baptism, the spiritual and the carnal, the schism between the reformers and the original church, orthodoxy, divine love for all God's creatures, Crow and Siksika and Sioux and white alike, miracles, sin, sacrifice, confession . . .

To all of this the chief and his elders listened solemnly,

more bewildered by the conflicting strains of this white man's religion than comprehending. Sometimes the things the Reverend Rathbone and Father Kiley said struck the familiar. Was not this God similar to the One Above, the Great Spirit, or even Father Sun? But Father Kiley's narration became a mystery to them: why worship and love this God if there was no medicine to be found in it? He had talked much of suffering, purging the soul, enduring grief, being humble and meek. Why become groveling dogs and miserable crawling creatures, worse than the Digger people far to the west who lived naked in deserts and ate grasshoppers and lizards and ran from others?

Pine Leaf, great warrior and medicine woman, drove these points home, in a voice laden with scorn. The Crow were a great warrior people, strong, the terror of their neighbors, powerful because they stayed true to their medicine and heritage as the people of Absaroka, the raven. If these white medicine people wished to take their strange faith to the Siksika, and turn them into fools and weaklings, so much the better! Let them go do it, so the Absaroka nation might triumph!

At last Many Coups turned to Mister Skye. "Why is it, my old friend, that you take these white medicine people to our enemies? By marriage, you are one of us, friend and ally, and many times over many winters, you have fought these very Siksika at our side. Have you now a change of heart?"

Mister Skye replied in Crow, and this time Pine Leaf quietly translated for James.

Mister Skye was a law unto himself, and diplomacy was a thing that had been beaten out of his very soul by a hard life, brutality, slavery, and ultimately his force of will. So his words were not chosen for their effect on his listeners. James sensed he spoke with the force of truth, rather than expediency.

"I was brought up in the Christian religion," he said, "and I respect it, for in my youth I saw its effect upon many people whose tongues were true and works were good and kind and loving. But I was ripped from my nation, and thrown into another world, and in my time of worst trouble, my religion failed me, and I became a man of no religion. I make my own medicine. Since then I have learned of your medicine religion, and have seen its mysterious force, even as I have sometimes seen the miraculous force of the faith I abandoned. I have come to your medicine men with gifts, seeking to know my future and what will make me strong, and I have found them keen and wise, and somehow able to look into the beyond and see what is to come, or the spirits of those who have gone to the other side. They are holy men—and women—and I honor them. I am taking these missionaries to your enemies and mine, the Siksika, and I think they will benefit. I will support myself and my family by doing it. I think the missionaries will give the Siksika something good that the Absaroka do not have and will need when the buffalo are gone."

"The buffalo gone?" asked Many Coups sharply.

"The buffalo will all go, and when they go, the buffalo medicine of the Absaroka will go with it."

There was anger and scorn among the elders.

"The buffalo are as thick as rivers and beyond numbering," said Pine Leaf to them all. "They are the brothers and sisters of the Absaroka people."

The chief stood. "We have heard you. Now my elders and chiefs and medicine men will talk."

Mister Skye and Cecil Rathbone led Father Kiley

through the flap door and into blinding low sun, and James followed. Pine Leaf stayed within.

Mister Skye mounted Jawbone. "Mister Method," he said, "I'd like to powwow with you. Bring Father Kiley when you come. His wagon is no longer here."

James slid his arm around the priest's and led him slowly toward the missionary encampment downstream a bit.

"Well, James," Kiley said. "I would guess that you have come to stay with these people."

"Ah am," he said. "Ah'm free, and Ah'm going to become a leader among them."

"I can understand that. Though I regret it."

James thought to steer away from that. "And how are you, Father?"

For a long time the priest didn't answer. "The pain is lessening," he said. "My headaches are fewer. But I have a long dark wait until I am released. I hope I have the courage not to offend my Lord while I wait."

"You have many years, yet."

"My misfortune."

He took Dunstan Kiley to his wagon and helped him in, and settled him upon his buffalo robe. Cecil hovered near, animatedly telling the other missionaries of the council and the unsettled future.

"Mister Method," said Mister Skye. "Let's go yonder to the shade, and palaver. I don't know what the others are seeing, but I'm seeing a bloody new man."

The guide listened gravely while James described the strange, compelling need that had driven him to take the cow meat back to the place of the skulls during that storm, and all that transpired after that.

"Thought something like that," Skye muttered. "You're a free man, on your own now, mate. I think you're where you should be."

None of the others approached him, sensing from the things he wore, and the change in his demeanor, that he had crossed some divide of the soul and was no longer one of them, no longer a black citizen of a white world. Silas Potter stared icily, as if James's transformation were a personal affront. But the rest were simply distant, intimidated, perhaps, by what they saw. He stayed there, curious about the fate of these people and the council's decision, but he hovered close to Mister Skye's lodge and Mary and Dirk. Victoria was with her people.

The answer came at sunset, borne by Pine Leaf. "My chiefs have decided," she said to Mister Skye, "not to stop you. You may take these medicine people and their poisons to the Siksika. Let them rot. It might have been otherwise but for your talk about the buffalo going away. They laughed at such a thing. I laughed too. Those were strange prophecies, Mister Skye, and your medicine is bad. Take these people to our enemies.

"But I have foreseen something else. You will have troubles from our enemies along the way north. Not the Siksika dogs, but one of the others, perhaps the Assiniboin. I saw this in the smoke of the sweetgrass burning. Your party is weak because of these spirit men among you, who will not fight or defend their wives. I will go with you a way, and I am taking Seven Scalps, James Method. He must prove himself a warrior to us, so that he may have Gliding Raven, and we may see his medicine. With your people, he will have his chance. I am no longer young, but I have not forgotten how it is to draw a bow."

Mister Skye nodded. "Your presence among us is the same as many warriors, Pine Leaf."

She nodded. "My chiefs are making a feast. Bring your people when it is just dark, and we will feed you buffalo hump, the meat of the sacred buffalo sister that you say will depart from us. It will never go away! And bring the great wooden many-flutes that James described to us. We would hear it. We have never seen such a thing. Tell the woman to make the sounds."

"Her name is Henrietta Newton, and I will tell her. The Lakotah feared it. Will the Absaroka people also be afraid?"

"The Lakotah warriors are afraid of everything," Pine Leaf snorted. "The Absaroka fear nothing."

Chapter 20

From the Crow village on Arrow Creek they struck west across a vast arid land, skirting the Pryor Mountains hulking like a tilted table to the south. In the hazy west rose vast and jagged mountains patched with white, even though July was upon them, and of a looming majesty that not even the Big Horns possessed. They looked to be the roof of the world, and Mister Skye confirmed that these Beartooths were a main strand of the Rockies.

Cecil and Esmerelda exulted in the wild windy land, exclaiming at the prospects from every prairie ridge they traversed. Even Silas Potter was enthralled by this incalculable wilderness the Crow people called their home. He perceived it as a country that was too harsh for settlement by whites. It would be beyond civilization, the permanent province of savage peoples, an island of barbarism in a civilized world. He had grown skeptical of converting these heathen people, or teaching them the ways of white civilization. Unlike Cecil, whose boundless frontier optimism led him to believe anything was possible, Silas had a sense of limitations. He knew he had a much more acute intellect than Cecil; he could foresee disaster, and he was sure the only proper course for this party was to admit defeat and retreat to the east.

The overnight visit to the Crow village had confirmed him in his belief. He had a scholar's eye for detail, and a student's ability to find meaning in all that he observed. What he saw, as he peered owlishly through the lenses of his spectacles, was heathen savagery. These Crow people hadn't even the decency to dress their boys, who ran naked, though he admitted even the smallest girl wore a little deerskin dress. If the Crow were as bad as this, the Blackfeet could only be worse.

The buffalo hump roast tasted fine, but other Crow food was odd, and he wondered what was in it. Strange roots. Henrietta's organ concert had been edifying. They had rolled the wagon into a central area near the chief's lodge and stripped back the canvas from its bows, and she had played fine hymns, such as "Rock of Ages." At first terrified children and some of the women had held hands to ears, or run away screaming as the organ thundered. But they had crept back, with wide eyes. Henrietta told him she regarded her playing as the beginning of a great conversion of these people, and that inspired her to strenuous efforts. Silas doubted that; doubted that the organ hymns were anything but a fearsome novelty within the savage breast.

She had played until the dark thickened and her hands and feet were worn out, and then stood and bowed. But the heathen had built fires and were assembling for a dance of their own, and the evening that began with correct and sacred solemnity turned into a savage, howling, unspeakable saturnalia. The heathen Crow men and women danced in a great circle, undulating toward each other, and back, flaunting their bodies and behaving in a matter most improper and carnal, he thought. He saw umber glistening flesh everywhere in the amber firelight, Crow men prancing in their breechclouts, women lifting their skirts. It was too much for Silas. It all evoked wild and forbidden thoughts of Mister Skye's Mary in him, so he fled to his bedroll in loathing and disgust, and demanded of God that He put a stop to such things.

Now their caravan rolled westward again, augmented by James Method, and that heathen medicine woman beside him. It was bad enough, he thought, that Method had reverted to utter savagery, wearing Crow skins, the tops of his tawny thighs in plain sight above his leggins. But the heathen medicine woman and warrior woman wore even less, a breechclout and a fringed skin shirt, her long fine legs straddling her horse and scandalously bare. Like Mister Skye, she had a shining rifle of the modern breechloading type in a decorated saddle sheath, and a quiver upon her back. A bow she always carried in hand. She stood almost man-tall, and her black hair, glinting blue in some lights, hung loose. For a middle-aged woman, she seemed amazingly lithe and young.

It was bad enough that they had the Romish priest with them. But now they had a Crow priestess as well, what any good Christian would call a witch, and an African who had defected to that side. Had Cecil Rathbone gone mad? Silas peered around him. In this missionary party the only acceptable people were the Newtons, perhaps the Samples, and himself. Rathbone had strayed, making common cause with heathens. It was time, he thought, to put a stop to it. He'd form a faction: Newtons, Samples, himself. Meet in secret and decide what to do—return east, separate themselves from these people of perdition, whatever. He would think on that.

One possibility was exorcism. He had not seen such a thing, but had heard of it. They could capture that priestess, Pine Leaf, tie her down and perform the rite. There were rituals in the Catholic and Anglican churches for it, bell, book, and candle, but he didn't know what reformed churches did. He would consult Alex Newton, who was a considerable scholar. Kiley, the Jesuit, might know, but Silas had no intention of consulting him.

They made excellent progress that day, over land without barriers, and that night they camped in the bottoms of a considerable river Mister Skye called Clark's Fork of the Yellowstone. After the meal of venison, from the spike buck the Crow priestess had easily brought down with an arrow, Silas watched narrowly, and was rewarded for his vigilance. The woman had actually unrolled her buffalo robe next to James Method's and it became plain what their relationship was.

"Have you noticed it?" he whispered to Alex Newton.

"I have. I have only sorrow in my heart for James. The Crow medicine woman I pity in her ignorance, but I hold nothing against her. I am not sure one could call such a thing evil. One must know the laws of God before one can understand evil. Saint Paul argued just such a thing in Romans, I think. She knows no better."

Alex's temperate answer annoyed Silas. "We are missionaries on a sacred enterprise. We can't permit such things," Silas snapped. "It is pure evil, right in our midst."

Alex sighed. "We succeed or fail as apostles by being a shining light among them, not by avoiding them or scorning them," he said. "Sorry, Silas. We're among the people of darkness, the ones we want to reach. These are ones who have never heard the Word. We surely can't thrust the benighted from us, or exclude them from our love and caring."

"You mean you tolerate it, like your father-in-law," snapped Silas.

"I think you will want to reconsider that harsh indictment," said Alex. "Prayerfully, and with love of all men. Think about love," he added.

Silas spun away angrily. So then, he thought, I am alone here! I alone uphold the laws of God, without compromise! I am the only one left in this small and faithless congregation! They are all lukewarm, and I am a pillar of fire!

That restless night in his blankets, staring out upon the chipped ice of heaven, Silas Potter knew who he was. He was a prophet of God. He would be a voice crying in the wilderness. He would be a brother of the other pillars of fire, Jeremiah, Isaiah, Ezekiel, Malachi . . . ! He would cry out at their wantonness and idolatry, and be driven from their midst for it! He would be their lost conscience, and the voice of God, and be exiled and persecuted for it!

He drove the thought of Mary's nakedness from his vision, where it had crept, with fierce contempt, and then slipped into the easy sleep of the righteous. In the morning he would no longer be a soft-spoken scholar and theology student; he'd be an acid-tongued wasp, stinging right and left, shaming and chastising them all, a hornet of God.

With the dawn Silas was a transformed man. He peered about him with burning eyes, finding wickedness everywhere. It was a lovely place, a meadow turning golden, rimmed by cottonwoods beside the river. Meadowlarks trilled, but Silas didn't hear them. He had thought to anathematize Pine Leaf and James Method, because their hot sin of the night would be lingering upon them, but both had slipped from camp and were out scouting and hunting, even while the rest ate and prepared to cross the wagons over the bouldered bottom of Clark's Fork. Still, there was Mister Skye and his wives, and he would begin with them.

They camped apart. The cookfires of Mary and Victoria nourished Skye, the Jesuit, and now Pine Leaf and Method. Silas found them in a merry mood, Victoria full of laughter and chatter, for she had seen her people and this was the heartland of the Crow nation, and she had the greatest of Crow women, Pine Leaf, here with her. Silas watched her and Mary laughing, and scolding Dirk, all with a pounding pulse. And there was Skye off near Jawbone, and urinating in plain sight.

With a quickening pulse he approached, steering wide of the evil blue horse, that followed him with bright malevolent eyes.

"Mister Skye!" he said hoarsely.

"Yaas?"

"You are a bigamist and a sinner. Set aside your younger squaw and stop using her. You are a transgressor against God. Repent of your ways!"

Mister Skye was taken aback. From the cookfire the squaws stared, not so much because of what they'd heard, but because of Silas's odd and imperious tone of voice.

Mister Skye laughed heartily, his beefy frame convulsing with it, and his silk hat darting in spastic circles.

"Mate," he said, "if a couple of kings like David and Solomon could have lots of wives, I imagine the good Lord will spare me my two."

Silas hadn't expected that from the man. Hadn't even known Mister Skye could read.

"I see you're familiar with Scriptures. The Gospels say—"

"Mister Potter, do you know what a good woman is?

She's a bloody miracle. She's a joy and a blessing. I'm an old vagabond roaming the wilderness and all I can give a woman is a hard life and a lonely one. But yonder's my Victoria, who does for me, lifts my spirit, makes me laugh, serves me like I was King of England, Scotland and Wales, lord sovereign of Canada, Australia, India, and the rest. She treats me as if the sun never sets upon me. And yonder's my Mary of the Shoshone, beautiful creature, warms an old man's flesh in the night, hugs a man who needs hugging, raises our son Dirk, of our union, fills my lodge with her youth and vitality and warm smiles. And the pair of them fight like warriors in a scrap, rescue me, nurse me, heal my wounds, and all for the hard life I give them. That's called love, mate. Go find some yourself."

Silas drew himself up with dignity. "Love is all well and good. But the Scriptures say that to love God, you must keep his law."

With that he stalked off, faintly alarmed by Skye's heckling bellow, but delighted with himself for getting in the last word, the true Word. Now there were others to reform, and he would be the sword of the Lord . . .

Next he pounced upon the Rathbones, who were breaking camp and stowing their few small things in the carriage, and readying themselves for the day's travel.

He felt feverish now with the heavy sword he carried, and he wasted no time in holy rebuke, beginning with Cecil's wrongful concern about the bodies and livelihood of the Blackfeet and his unconcern about their spiritual life, and jumping from there to Cecil's derelict conduct on the trail, hiring Mister Skye and his bigamous squaws, welcoming the Romish priest, tolerating sin and evil, weakness and shame, and all the rest.

As he accused he felt an excitement, his voice rose and sharpened, and he felt it cutting like a stiletto into the burning souls of his listeners. He was opening their eyes, awakening the Rathbones, firing them up to duty!

The outburst took only ten minutes, and when at last he quieted, he waited for Cecil to argue. But against this Silas was armed with Scripture. He would cite chapter and verse for all that he had said, verses to rebuke the derelict cleric who had led this party to perdition.

But all Cecil said was, "You're perfectly free to go back east, Silas. I'm sorry you feel that way. You contracted to come with me, but of course I won't hold you to it, feeling as you do about Esmerelda and me."

Silas felt faintly disappointed. He wanted to throw verses like thunderbolts, and Cecil wasn't defending himself. But that was the same as admitting his guilt, so he knew he had triumphed after all. There were others here now. The Newtons had been drawn to this by the keen high pitch of his voice, and the sharp slash of his condemnations. They, too, watched him quietly.

"I have no intention of going east," he said, as loftily as he could, so they might understand his high purpose. "While I put my trust in Divine Providence, and would be safe enough, it doesn't suit me to return alone. My mission is to correct—to rectify—all that has fallen into evil here. But I will do this: as a symbol of my separateness, I intend to travel a ways behind you, the conscience in your ears. I will be with you but not of you, making straight the ways of the Lord."

"As you wish, Silas," said Cecil easily. "Esmerelda and I would like to enjoy your company at our campfire this evening. You'll be there, eh? I'd like to hear more of what you have to offer us."

Silas felt excited. At last they would listen!

"I will think about it," he said. "There will be certain conditions."

He knew then what it was to be intoxicated. He was dizzy with delight, floating on air, feeling a strange power within him, an invincibility, a high exaltation he ascribed to God, to some mystic joy that was the gift of God.

There was yet the priest of Rome to scourge, and now he swept toward the wagon where the Jesuit sat in his black suit and Romish collar, an affront to decent men.

"I heard you, Mister Potter," said Dunstan Kiley as Silas approached.

It surprised him. In blindness, the priest's hearing must have become acute.

"I'm glad you did," he cried. "We don't want you among us. You belong to a faithless church, with leaders that live like kings and princes, and charge money for God's gifts. And your order has persecuted millions, and spread lies. We don't want you among the godly. Your wounds are nothing but the wrath of God!"

Dunstan Kiley said nothing. Then, softly, "I have a small favor to ask, Mister Potter. Somewhere in this wagon are my things. Everything is in two packsaddle panniers. Would you find them for me?"

Silas paused, wanting to go on with his great indictment, yet compelled to comply. Wordlessly he clambered into the wagon and dragged the panniers toward the priest.

"In one of them," said the priest, "is a small valise of black pigskin. Would you find it for me, please? And one other small favor, if you would. Would you lower the tailgate of the wagon?"

Silas dug in the panniers, mystified and suspicious. He found the valise and handed it to the priest.

"What are you going to do with that?" he demanded.

"Why, I thought to say Mass. I haven't, you know. It's been many weeks. Even though it was all as familiar to me as the back of my hand, it vanished when I was blinded. But now . . . now I wish to say it. I think it'll come back, once I start.

"You will curse us all the more with your Latin mumbling."

"I rather hope to bless us. I am most bewildered, lost you might say. A priest needs the Mass as much as any communicant, you know. It is friendship and reconciliation . . . for us."

Silas hadn't noticed the approach of Mister Skye.

The booming voice startled him. "Take your time, Father. We'll be busy crossing the Clark's Fork for a while, and we'll take this wagon over last. Mister Potter, we'll be needing you now to help drive the livestock."

"I do not recognize your authority."

But the priest was unlatching his small valise and removing things. First a white stole, which he placed around his neck, and then a small silver chalice, and a silver plate. Feeling his way, he edged to the rear of the wagon.

"I believe the tailgate is still up?" he said softly.

Silas stared at him coldly, and then walked over there and lowered it.

"There you are."

"For a little while, it will be an altar," the Reverend Father Kiley said.

Silas didn't know what to say to that, so he left. He still felt a fervent exaltation, a wild ecstasy. He peered behind him and saw the squaws, Victoria and Mary, settle near the priest.

Let them see the show, he thought. They won't understand a word of it, and the lost can lead the lost.

He thought better of his rejection of Mister Skye, and

decided to help with the livestock. A prophet must be stainless and fulfill every duty asked of him. He suddenly felt terribly alone. He was acutely aware that being the sword of God had cost him friends, simple companionship, something that was hard to come by here, over a thousand miles from even the westernmost reaches of the frontier. Well, he thought, that would be the price, the great price paid, the burden borne, by those few mortals elected by God to chastise a fallen world.

Cecil and Alex toiled among the oxen, dropping the heavy yokes over their shoulders and pinning them, attaching the tugs. Near them Clay labored, slipping heavy collars over mules, tightening surcingles, slipping on bridles, buckling breeching for the wheel team, running the long lines through rings, and leading a pair at a time to his wagon. How oddly distant they looked to Silas, all of them strangers going about their business.

Mister Skye forded the river on Jawbone, back and forth, sounding the bottom. Mary and Victoria had already packed Skye's mules, this time piling the skin lodge on top of one for the crossing, rather than tying it down to a travois. They all seemed distant, and he was alone.

He climbed the east rim of the river valley until he stood on a low promontory and could look over the tops of the green cottonwoods, off to the Beartooths ahead, and the blue Pryors behind, vast and lonely and silent reaches of a land unknown to man—almost, it seemed—a land unknown to God. A land that oppressed him and held him prisoner in its iron grip.

"Do you love me?" he asked.

Chapter 21

The next day they ran into buffalo. There seemed to be only a few at first, until they topped a grassy shoulder and peered into a basin that was black with them. This prairie between the Beartooth Mountains to the south and the Yellowstone River to the north hindered their progress. Massive shoulders radiated from the mountains, and the humped earth broke the sweeping country into endless valleys and hollows, most of them pierced by cold creeks that collected into larger streams.

It brutalized the oxen and mules, this land of grades. Sometimes they toiled most of a day upslope, only to toil downslope after that, hard work with the heavy wagons looming behind them, pressing into the wheel-team breeching. In each of these hollows buffalo grazed, or lay in the grass, rising hastily, rump first, as the caravan clattered into view. Close to the cows spring calves gamboled, and out on the ridges stood the sentinel bulls, half blind but with keen ears and a good sense of smell. Usually the herd in a valley burst away, led by a dominant cow, as the caravan approached, and with it went the slinking gray forms of the wolves that preyed upon the buffalo, striking the wayward calf or the injured and lamed with bloody frenzy.

This vast herd seemed beyond numbering, but not the black river of buffalo they had seen once on the flat prairies of central Nebraska. The corrugated land divided them all into villages, cities of buffalo. That whole day they traveled among them, and not until evening did Pine Leaf kick her fine buffalo runner into a wild gallop, draw up beside a fleeing young cow, and unloose a well-aimed arrow deep into the heart and lung cavity.

The animal staggered, ran awhile more spraying blood, and slowly sank to its knees, a half a mile from the Stillwater River, where they would camp that night. Even as the cow fell, wolves watched from the distant ridge. Pine Leaf slid lightly from her heaving pony and stood beside the trembling animal, and lifted her arms to it.

"What is she doing?" Cecil asked Mister Skye from a distant vantage point.

"Praying to the cow she killed. She's asking its forgiveness for killing it, and thanking it for the meat she has taken to sustain our lives."

Cecil was quiet. "I can understand that sentiment," he said at last.

"Let's go help her butcher."

Pine Leaf and James Method had already begun the hard bloody work, slitting up the belly and releasing gray steaming entrails across the parched grasses.

"Boudins," Mister Skye said. "Life-giving water in there, for any man dying of thirst. We'll go for the liver now—try it raw, Mister Rathbone. It's a treat that every trapper relishes."

Cecil was horrified.

"Does something good. Gives a man strength. The Indians know it. A man eats that liver, and he's made new by it. There's some that say the buff, with the liver and the boudins, is a complete food, and a man needs no more."

Pine Leaf sawed at the tongue, severing it at last and placing the bloody hunk on a piece of hide that James had industriously ripped in violent jerks and occasional flashes of knife from the carcass. Then at last the choicest parts lay exposed, the hump ribs, and the fine, juicy, fatty tenderloin of the buffalo. These they cut and hacked loose, set them on the warm hide, and then wrapped it all into a bundle and hoisted it to the back of Cecil's nervous horse, all in all some two hundred pounds of prime meat and hide. They were not far from the others, setting up camp beside the sparkling shallow river. A feast tonight and a feast for breakfast. Even as the party walked the last quarter mile to camp, the wolves, gray wraiths in the late light of day, edged closer to the carcass.

"Seems a waste," Cecil said to Mister Skye, "taking so little. All the rest for the wolves and coyotes and magpies and crows."

The reasons were obvious, and Cecil knew them as well as any frontiersman could, so Mister Skye said nothing. Tomorrow there'd be another buffalo for supper, and maybe another the day after that. Victoria would grieve because they were on the move and she couldn't stake out the fine light brown summer hide, flesh the inside, scrape the hair off the outside, tan it, and repair a rotting hide in their lodge with it. If they had a more permanent camp she'd be at the carcass, hacking meat from it and drying strips into jerky on high racks that reached toward the fierce sun.

They spent a restless night, hearing the bark and howl of wolves and the cackle of coyotes that sometimes seemed to rise from the very edge of their camp. Once in the night they awoke to an ominous roar. Somewhere near, countless of thousands of buffalo rumbled through the dark, driven by some unseen menace. At times the earth shook with them, as animals weighing a ton and more trotted from somewhere to somewhere else. The whole night grew alive with noises. Somewhere downstream, there was a great splashing in the Stillwater. Once Jawbone whinnied softly, his warning, and Mister Skye prowled the moonless dark to no avail, his Sharps in hand.

The horses and mules were restless, itching to join the flowing movement nearby. Mister Skye nudged Cecil, who was awake anyway, and between them they hobbled some horses and hoped the mules wouldn't drift with the buffalo herd. The exhausted oxen lay quietly in the darkness.

Dawn was extraordinary. An eastern cloudbank turned rosy, and its reflected light turned the Beartooths red and salmon, so that the looming peaks just south turned into a wall of fire. They all rose early from want of sleep, and gaped. For Mister Skye there was only joy. Of all the grand vistas of the west, this place was among the dearest to him. Here was a land so breathtaking it drew him here, and he always looked for business that would take him here to this heartland of the Crows. The sun caught the prairie hills now, lighting flanks of the earth except where jackpine made black patches along amber ridges. Here and there the sun caught the tops of aspen and cottonwoods, igniting the leaves into glowing emeralds. He stretched, enjoying the clean cool air, the tang of the silvery sagebrush and the resinous ponderosa pine that encroached everywhere here upon the prairie grasses. Victoria came to stand beside him, exuding joy, for this was home, and other villages of the Absaroka people camped nearby, perhaps in the awesome valley to the west where the Yellowstone River ran south and pierced into the rafters of the world.

One of the oxen had died in the night, the previous day's brutal toil up and down the shouldered prairie too much for the weary, gaunted creature. Cecil and Mister Skye and Clay examined the rest, concluding that they'd have to rest soon. The wagons were in bad shape, too, after thirteen hundred miles of overland travel, jolting along where no road went. The iron tires rolled loose on the felloes because the dry air had shrunk the wood of the wheels.

"In two or three days we'll strike the Yellowstone, mates, and we'll cross at a place I know of that's wide, shallow, and gravelly, with some islands. West of Sweet Grass Creek, which we'll follow north to the Judith Gap. On the north side of the Yellowstone's a fine flat with good grass and cottonwoods, and we'll rest and reoutfit there."

For two days more they drove through buffalo. Once a stream of them flowed toward them, running between the wagons and the carriage, panicking the oxen, causing horses to buck, turning the mules frantic, and sucking the loose herd with them. Had the buffalo been stampeding, galloping instead of trotting, they would have demolished them, perhaps killing most of the small party. As it was a milch cow disappeared, and it took hours of sweaty riding for them to gather stray horses and mules.

They'd never seen such a land as this, and they exclaimed at the yawning vistas at every ridgetop, sucked up the sweet-scented air, sniffed the cool distant pine forests of the mountains, enjoyed the exploding scent of sunhot sage, and drank water so sweet and clear and cold it seemed pure snowmelt. In every creek trout darted.

The buffalo thinned out at last as they turned down a valley Mister Skye called Jim Bridger's Creek. He took them north, through sage-dotted hills, toward the Yellowstone until one evening they emerged in its wide lush valley hemmed between cliffs of gray rock here, though downstream the yellow bluffs gave it its name. It felt warmer in the protected bottoms. Mister Skye and Pine Leaf redoubled their scouting, for this was a great avenue for all sorts of travelers, many of them intent on horse stealing, but some much more dangerous than that.

The next afternoon they crossed the Yellowstone easily. The river was braided here, running in small channels and rivulets through a bank of gravel with an island in the middle. On the far side Otter Creek debouched into the river, and just east of that lay a flat where Mister Skye chose to rest the weary party.

There was much to do. Not least of the problems was the condition of their boots, virtually soleless and torn from the continental hike. The women set to work on the boots, cutting buffalo-hide soles and piercing them with awls so they could be sewn to the uppers. Clay Sample and Cecil set about repairing the wagons. Each wheel had to be removed and wedges driven between the iron tires and the felloes. In one wheel of the Samples' wagon there was a broken spoke that would need replacing with whatever hardwood they might find here, which turned out to be none, so they fashioned one of tough cedar, the alternatives being aspen, willow, cottonwood, and ponderosa. It would be a brutal job that involved pulling the iron tire off the wheel. There were cracked hounds to replace, worn bolsters, ragged harness to repair with rawhide or anything else at hand. The weathered, bleached wagon tops were torn and needed sewing up. Their clothing, too, had gone to rags, except for Father Kiley's. Some skirts and petticoats were beyond repair, and some of Clay's and Cecil's britches had gaping rents in them.

The footsore oxen and mules spread out upon the grass, closely watched by the Sample children. Pine Leaf and James Method scouted and brought buffalo meat into camp each evening. Through all of this Silas remained distant and icy, not deigning to talk with any of them, taking lonely walks, Bible in hand, a man set apart by his own will. He volunteered no help now, and made no repairs even though his boots were in worse shape than most, and his dark prim clothing was shredded. He had become a burning-eyed figure in rags.

After two days of repair and rest, they had visitors. There rode into camp one evening a party of eleven rough men, grimy and grizzled, black-bearded, sallow, armed with greasy muzzle-loading percussion lock rifles, and long cruel knives sheathed at their sides. Pine Leaf and Method came too, a rifle-shot away. The visitors rode in silently from the west, their dark eyes taking in everything at once with total knowing, lingering long on the women. Mister Skye watched them come, knew they were French-Cree breeds from the north, famous for their volcanic and mercurial tempers and ruthlessness, and knew he and his missionary party, the women especially, faced grave trouble.

From the corner of his eye he saw Victoria and Mary slip into the lodge, and knew two rifles would soon be poking from the doorflap, ready to fire if any of these strangers lifted a weapon toward himself. The others had paused in their work, Clay standing next to the dismantled wheel, Cecil and Alex rising from the pile of harness they were mending. From a little distance, Pine Leaf and Method sat their horses, rifles in hand. And he held his own Sharps in the crook of his arm. Jawbone stood restlessly, primed to bull among them and ruin their shooting. But it would not be enough. Not against eleven razor-edged feral animals.

"*Bonjour*," said one in front, with a sagging eyelid and a shining scar from the corner of his mouth to his right ear, just above his full black beard. His lips were smiling, but his opalescent pearl-colored eyes didn't.

About five of the rifles were a fraction of an arc from pointing at him. The others, not so carelessly, aimed loosely at the other males among the missionaries.

"It is a pleasure, *oui,* a pleasure to find company. The

wagons! We have never seen the wagons in this land. We will make the feast, *oui*? Across the river are many buffalo, and we shall make the feast. Tonight will be a ball, a promenade, *oui*?"

Mister Skye said nothing.

"You don't talk? You don't understand, maybe? But you are Yankees, *oui*? What gallant women, what beautiful creatures you have brought to this feasting place. What manner of people are these, so far from home?"

His pearl eyes were upon Alice Sample and young Miriam.

Mister Skye studied the ensemble, knowing what he would find. He saw no pelts on their packhorses, and if they had traps, they were few. He saw no signs of vocation, no array of axes that would signify woodcutters supplying the occasional steamer that braved the Missouri to reach Fort Union far to the east. They were not hunters, making meat for some larger party, for there were no spare packhorses. They were creatures of prey, plundering whatever they happened upon in this vast and lawless land, for whatever wealth there would be—canvas, horses, mules, firearms, and women . . . who would be used brutally awhile and discarded when dead or dying.

They probably had Cree mothers and French trapper fathers, these Canadians. That mix seemed to splinter two ways, the better among them becoming substantial frontier citizens, albeit unruly and resenting British rule, and nominally Catholic. But the others . . . Mister Skye stared at these, seeing the offscourings loathed by the Crees, and loathed by the French. It could go two ways: they'd take over swiftly and begin a brutal bacchanal, especially after finding the whiskey. Or they'd wait until the small hours, slit the throat of every sleeping male, defile the women, plunder the wagons, and steal the livestock.

"I'm Jacques Spratt, my friend, and you do not speak, eh?"

There was nothing to say. Mister Skye surveyed them one by one. Spratt was built like a bear, but next to him slouched a wiry one on a dun mustang, the blue stubble on his cheeks suggesting he once had shaved. He stared blankly at Mister Skye from under the rim of a greasy felt hat that had been tan. He had killer-eyes. Mister Skye was familiar with killer-eyes. The ones with killer-eyes would kill humans with no more compunction than killing a mouse. This one's hand gripped a revolver rather than a rifle. In a sheath hanging from his saddle pommel was another.

On the other side of Spratt sat a fat one, oddly fair-skinned, with ruddy and chubby cheeks and a vacant, moronic look that suggested he might be the deadliest of them all.

The others, bunched behind, ranged from ones who seemed pure Cree, with high cheekbones and flesh the color of rust, to a few who looked French. Their eyes were not upon him, but focused on Alice and Miriam, and Henrietta and Esmerelda, and sometimes at the lodge where the voluptuous Mary had vanished. It was plain to Mister Skye.

"No," said Mister Skye. "You will be on your way."

Spratt grinned. "We will have a feast," he said. He nudged his black stallion forward. "I will send a man to shoot the buffalo, and your squaws will get the wood."

"No," said Mister Skye.

"I do not hear your name, monsieur. And who are these others you bring here in this place by the river?"

From the wagon Father Kiley emerged. The breeds stared, first at his bandaged eyes, then at his black robes. He wore his cassock now, black with red piping, and he had found his crucifix among his things and now its silver glinted in the late sun.

"Mister Skye, if you will talk a bit I will find my way," said the priest.

"A blind priest," said Jacques Spratt. "A father sans eyes, who cannot see us. Now isn't that an entertainment? He will bless us and he cannot see what we do. We will eat buffalo before him, and laugh, and he will not see us. Maybe he will dance with us, *oui*? It will be a great joke, dancing in front of the blind father. Was there ever such a night? Ah, the things his eyes won't see!" Spratt laughed easily.

Mister Skye felt unhappy with it, but the priest was there.

"You are the French children," the priest said easily. "You've been a long time away from the sacraments. My friends, I will hear confession and then I will say Mass."

Jacques translated this to the others, and they laughed amiably. The fat one snickered.

"Father," said Mister Skye, "they've heard you now, and perhaps you can find your way back to the wagon . . ."

"I'll stay here, Mister Skye."

"Mister who? Who are these? A blind priest, and my eyes tell me the others are the heretics. We have never feasted with heretics before."

He nudged his horse forward again.

"It might be bad medicine for you," said Mister Skye.

"Medicine? Now we have it all—the medicine, the heretics, and the priest." He laughed.

"Your medicine is bad," said Mister Skye. Pine Leaf and James Method had edged closer now. She had slipped

her rifle into its saddle scabbard and held a bow and
nocked arrow.

"It will be a fine evening. We will listen to the prayers
of the heretic women. We like prayers," said Jacques. He
swung his rifle toward Mister Skye, and kicked his horse.

The other breeds lifted their weapons, grinning.

Skye shot Jacques through the heart with his cradled
Sharps. The noise rattled through the clearing.

Jacques Spratt gaped, his eyes clouded, and he began
to slide off his horse.

Mister Skye danced sideways to distance himself from
Father Kiley.

From his lodge two shots boomed. One caught the
skinny one in the head. The other missed, but seared a
horse across the neck. The horse squealed and pitched.

Jawbone shrieked insanely, and catapulted violently
into the massed riders, biting and kicking and squealing.
Horses careened and danced and sidled, spoiling aim as
breeds attempted to fire.

Pine Leaf rode in like a wraith, loosing an arrow that
struck one breed in the thigh, and loosing another arrow
with blinding speed.

James Method shot a breed at the rear of the party
who had steadied his horse and was aiming at Skye.

Mister Skye dropped his Sharps and plunged into the
middle of them with his Army revolver in hand. He shot
once, putting a ball into another breed.

Then one of them clubbed his arm, paralyzing it. The
revolver fell. As it fell Mister Skye plucked a Green River
knife from his waist and in the space of a heartbeat plunged
it into the withers of a horse, slicing it around and across
the thigh of a breed, leaving gouting blood in its wake,
and threw it at another, burying it in the man's chest.

Then he pulled a breed off his horse and kicked him

as he fell. Mister Skye's silk hat fell off and was trampled by a pitching horse.

A shot creased Mister Skye's left arm, and red blood blossomed there.

Jawbone kicked and bit. His teeth clamped over the arm of a breed and the horse yanked the man to earth and stomped on him.

A bullet grazed Henrietta, tearing hair and dazing her. She fainted.

Three of Pine Leaf's arrows plunged into horseflesh.

A breed's shot put a bullet into Jawbone's stifle. He shrieked and began to gout blood.

And then the remaining breeds careened away.

It was quiet. They all gaped at Skye.

Silas Potter stumbled forward, his eyes crazed.

"You killed him in cold blood. We all saw you. You are a murderer," he said.

Chapter 22

Barnaby Skye ignored Potter.

Cecil came running.

Skye caught Jawbone, who was shrieking and pitching. Gouts of blood pulsed down his offside stifle. He held the horse by the neck, calming it, stroking it with big, rough, loving hands. Then he examined the wound, a clean one with entry and exit holes at front and rear of Jawbone's powerful thigh.

Mary arrived, holding a weapon on dead and dying French-Crees. Victoria ran too, bringing a steel needle and thread.

"It's going to hurt, mate," Mister Skye said, grabbing each of Jawbone's ears and twisting them slightly.

Victoria was afraid, and so he swiftly hobbled Jawbone's rear legs. Then he held the horse's ears again and braced himself against the wild animal while Victoria sewed furiously, jabbing the needle in and out of flesh. The gouting from the entry hole slowed, and she turned to the larger and messier exit hole. The horse flinched and shied at her slightest touch. She couldn't sew, and the bleeding was dangerous.

Mister Skye flipped his knife, red with human and horse blood, to Cecil. "Heat it in the fire, mate," he barked. Cecil grabbed the vicious knife and placed the blade over live coals. The blood on it hissed and burned and stank. Victoria pressed a cloth pad into the wound, stanching the flow a little.

As Cecil waited he noticed Mister Skye's own arm sheeted with blood, and a hard grimace etched into the guide's face. Seconds, minutes rolled by.

"Bring it, mate."

Cecil tried, but even the handle was fiery to the touch, and he yanked his burned hand back. Mister Skye let Jawbone go and grabbed the knife, which seared the flesh of his hand.

The horse shrieked as the flat of the blade pressed into the exit wound, cauterizing flesh and lifting a nauseous smoke into the air. Jawbone quivered and hopped, and at last broke free, dancing madly, but the job was done; the bleeding fried to a halt.

"Take him to water," said Mister Skye to Cecil.

The minister was terrified. "I can't . . . he'd kill me."

The guide threw an arm over Jawbone's mane, and whispered something in his ear, and the horse quieted and permitted himself to be haltered.

"He'll be fine, mate."

Victoria started slicing Skye's shredded buckskin
shirt off to get at the vicious slice in his upper arm. He
grew gray from loss of blood and pain, and sat quietly in
the grass, clenching a stick, while she dashed water into
the wound and began to sew, her fingers and the needle
and thread red with Mister Skye's blood.

Then finally it too was under control, and he lay back
in the grass, while she bandaged the long slice tightly.

"Whiskey," he muttered.

"Sonofabitch, that would kill you."

"Pour a little on the wound. Some say it stops the mortifying."

"I got better," she snorted.

He glared at her but said nothing. She brought him
water instead. "Drink it all," she commanded. "Then I
make some damn good stuff with herbs, make you happy
and stop fever and sweats."

Cecil returned from the river, with the badly limping
horse lunging along behind him, and released it near
Skye's lodge.

He stared, finally, at the bodies. One twitched periodi-
cally. The others lay inert and lifeless. There were four.
Four more human beings dead because of his mad enterprise, his idyllic plan to bring peace and harmony and
God's love to these far-flung peoples. As he watched,
Mary systematically gathered weapons and piled the
possessions of the dead into a small heap. They had very
little, but she found a pair of good boots on Spratt. She
unlaced them and pulled them off. The others wore moccasins.

Cecil glanced toward the wagons and the other campsites. His dear Henrietta was sitting up, and Esmerelda
holding a compress to her daughter's head. Pine Leaf

and James Method stared at the bodies, one in particular, the one James Method had shot.

"Ah don't know how to do it," he said.

Pine Leaf said nothing. She slipped a small skinning knife from its sheath at her waist, and knelt beside the body, grasping a fistful of black hair. The knife slid around the skull, just above the ears and forehead. Then she yanked hard. There was a soft sucking sound, then a pop, and the dripping scalp hung free in her hand.

"It is yours."

"I can marry Gliding Raven now."

"Yes, if you wish. But this is not what New Lance would hope for, this scalp of this dog. It is a scalp, but it is beneath her. Bring a scalp of the real enemies, the Siksika, the Assiniboin, the Lakotah . . ."

Cecil watched, fascinated, faintly sickened.

Mary scalped the rest, including the one not quite dead, so they would arrive in the spirit land bare-skulled, their medicine taken from them. She did not keep the scalps, but threw them into the bushes.

Pine Leaf stood, lithe and strong, two retrieved arrows in her hand. "We will hunt the others now. Perhaps they are not far and we can send them all to the spirit land."

Method nodded, and the two mounted and rode off.

Clay Sample came to stare at the bodies, having prohibited his children from approaching. Alex hovered at a distance, peering at the carnage but not wanting to come close. And Silas Potter was present, peering feverishly first at Mister Skye, then at the bodies, bursting to say things.

Cecil looked at Clay. "Let's bury them. Lot of work," he said. "Perhaps Father Kiley can give them some sort of service."

The priest was sitting in the grass. "You will have to tell me what happened," he said.

Silas Potter elected to do it. "Skye killed their leader in cold blood. Then these other savages killed three more and wounded others. We are in the hands of bloodsoaked savages. We are in the hands of demons, we have taken a peaceful mission and soaked it with murder and every carnal sin, bigamy, lust. I anathematize you. I declare the wrath of God upon you."

From the grass Mister Skye peered grayly up at Silas. "In two or three more seconds you would have been disarmed. Every man here tormented, tortured, and eventually murdered. Every husband forced to watch the debasement of his woman. They would have had special fun with Father Kiley, because the weakened are particularly fun . . ."

Cecil blanched, realizing how close they had come. Still, he grieved. Lost life, war, blood, injury. What more might happen in this wild land where there was no law of God or man, and bands like these roamed freely to prey where they could?

"It never would have happened if you all had bent a knee and called upon God. Submitted yourselves unto the Lord and his Divine Providence. Trusted! Offered faith and peace!" Silas cried.

Father Kiley sighed, wanting to say something but not saying it. Finally he murmured, "The Church holds that it is no sin to defend one's self and loved ones from mortal danger."

"Your church is faithless!" Silas cried. "You are all far gone in evil. There was no danger. They wanted to have a feast."

Cecil felt torn. A part of him lay on either side of the bitter issue. Mister Skye was right. Silas Potter was right. That priest was right. And everything that had happened was wrong, a mission soaked in blood and led by murderous heathen through a wilderness that usually smiled but could suddenly become deadly.

Clay found two shovels. He and Cecil hunted for soft earth, and found some near the river, a wet loam. No one came to help them. They dug and hacked and lifted the damp umber soil into a heap, and Cecil tried to make sense of life and death, of faith and Divine Providence, and self-defense, and couldn't, and it ragged him as he shoveled and sweated. No one came, no one watched, no one appreciated. At last they had hacked out a hollow in the earth about three feet deep and as much wide, and just long enough for the short breeds. Wordlessly they set their shovels down and carried the bodies one by one, Clay gripping arms and Cecil legs, and dropped them into the ground, cheek by jowl.

The more Cecil shoveled, the angrier he became, but he couldn't focus it upon anything. It was just anger, a hot resentment of death and blood, of division in his mission, of danger and bare escape. And then as he set his shovel down, he knew. He felt angry at God, who had permitted all this. God who had sent suffering instead of help to this mission that had set out to glorify Him and spread his Word. He had been angry at God before in his life, and knew it for the evil it was, his own impatience, and weakness.

"Let's get Father Kiley. These were probably his people, baptized Catholics. Perhaps he would welcome . . . words . . ."

Clay nodded. The sweat-stained pair of them trudged back to the meadow, where the priest still sat, Mister Skye still lay gray in the grass, and Jawbone stood with his injured leg cocked, glaring yellowly at the world.

Cecil knelt beside the priest. "We have them in a trench. Not covered yet. We thought you might want to say a word."

The priest nodded. "They were probably baptized," he said. "Let me get my—no, never mind. Just take me there."

They guided the Jesuit through the brush to the place near the riverbank.

"They're in front of you now, two steps," Cecil said.

Father Kiley peered sightlessly into heaven, and blindly into the earth.

"Little children," he said. "We do not know your names, but our Lord does. He has loved you from the beginning, and loves you still . . ."

Quietly the priest talked of love and forgiveness and reconciliation; of hell, purgatory, and heaven. Of the baptized and the unbaptized. Of the sins we do from our own will and pride, and the sins that we would rather not do, but do anyway. Of Christ's judgment. Then the Lord's Prayer in Latin, and he was done. Cecil and Clay shoveled earth over the French-Crees, and stood quietly a moment.

Cecil trudged wearily back to the wagons, where Esmerelda waited. He took her hand. "I need to go sit on that bluff up there. Would you join me?"

They walked together, hand in hand, he sweaty from his shoveling, she floating with relief. They found a warm sandstone outcrop on the bluff, where they could peer down into the meadow and the wagons, and see Mister Skye's lodge, and the people there.

"I suppose we could laugh," she said.

There was nothing else to do, so they did. They sat upon their rock and laughed heartily, and all the questions and doubts that had been flooding his mind seemed to diminish. If anyone heard them down below, he didn't care, and neither did his bride.

Then they said nothing, and let the sweetness of being alive seep through them. He drew the sweet August air into his lungs and exhaled and considered the act sensuous.

Below, Victoria helped Mister Skye sit up, and then gave him a bowl of broth and a horn ladle. He swallowed slowly.

"The two who saved us were hurt badly," Cecil murmured. "I saw it all happening but I was too dumbfounded to help, to act. In the space of a heartbeat, it would have gone the other way."

"How do you now that?"

"It is a lesson of the frontier. I cannot say just why."

"Some will condemn Mister Skye."

"I will encourage them to leave us," he said, rising. She took his hand again, and they talked softly.

They rested six days more. Mister Skye recovered quickly, and his grayness disappeared. But Jawbone limped terribly as he hobbled through the succulent grasses. Even the switch of his tail to drive away the flies brought a shiver through his rump. He slept lying down, on his good side, which was something he never did.

The oxen and mules ate constantly and fattened in the cloudless cool days. In two days they completed repairs. Clay assembled the wheel with the new spoke in it. Worn harness was repaired. Oxen shoed. Clothing restored. Boots and moccasins resoled. Only Silas did nothing. His clothes were tattered and the uppers of his boots had torn loose in places. The boots of the dead Jacques fit him, but he refused them violently.

After that they waited for Mister Skye and Jawbone to heal. Or rather, Cecil did. The Newtons and even Clay Sample avoided the guide, and loathing filled their eyes. Then Mister Skye pronounced himself fit, and they rolled off the next morning. Cecil was itching to be on his way:

they still had shelters to build before winter at Sun River, and even now the days grew short and the night air sharp.

Mister Skye walked. Jawbone limped painfully behind, untethered. He had a sailor's roll, as if even this continental prairie pitched like a bark on high seas. From their camp on the Yellowstone he took them north through rolling brown prairie, just west of Sweet Grass Creek, with the jagged Crazy Mountains always looming blue on their left.

The oxen and mules pulled eagerly after their rest and they made good time, finding splendid camps in the creek bottoms each evening. One night frost nipped the grass but by day the air was cool and invigorating. At a point where the Sweet Grass swung west into the Crazy Mountains, Mister Skye abandoned it and took them over a low prairie divide into the Musselshell drainage.

Three days later they reached the Musselshell, and camped in its cottonwood-choked bottoms. On the north bank rose sandstone bluffs, but they were broken, and reaching the high prairie beyond would pose no problem. To the north rose two ranges Mister Skye called the Belt Mountains and the Snowies. He said they would travel between them, through a gap. They were now, he said, in Blackfoot lands, though the Musselshell was also a haunt of Crows, Assiniboins, Gros Ventres, Flatheads, Crees, and others because it was prime buffalo country. Indeed, they found buffalo traces everywhere: along the small river were hoof-cut avenues winding like twisting highways through the sandstone bluffs. Increasingly the prairie ridges were dotted with dark jackpine, long-needled and twisted. The dry pitch-laden pine made fine fires for the buffalo hump meat that James Method and Pine Leaf brought to camp each evening.

They found grizzly sign along the river, but they saw none of the great and terrible bears, and were grateful. One old Ephriam, as Mister Skye called him, had scratched his mark perhaps nine feet up the trunk of an old cottonwood. They crossed the river easily the next morning, and toiled north along a rising prairie that seemed limitless except for the distant ranges. Already the Snowies wore a cap of white along their flat crowns. Never had Cecil experienced a land so vast, so limitless, so silent. It gave him a sense of security. He was sure he could see a hundred miles, and hear movement almost as far.

Mister Skye began riding Jawbone again, but not all day. The horse favored its wounded thigh but was game for anything. There were two cookfires each evening now, and they reflected the schism that had befallen the party. At one were the Samples, Newtons, and Silas Potter, who grew more ragged and brimstone-eyed each day. The other served Mister Skye and his family, the Rathbones, and Father Kiley. More and more, James Method and Pine Leaf were at neither, eating privately out somewhere in the beyond. Faithfully they brought meat and scouted, but they grew apart. Each time James Method rode in, Cecil noted that he seemed more Indian. They reported horse-thieving parties in the area, but so far the travelers had not been molested.

One evening when they camped midway between the Little Belts and the Snowy Mountains, some of the women went berrying. A long coulee twisted sinuously northeast, running a tiny trickle along its bottom, and was laden with buffalo bush, the leather-leaved hairy shrub whose berries were nourishing and a staple in pemmican. With Victoria showing them what to gather and how to strip the berries fast, and Esmerelda and young Miriam Sample following, the trio toiled its way up the coulee and around a bend and out of sight of the camp.

At twilight they didn't return. By full dark there was no sign of them, and Cecil grew alarmed.

"They should have been back long ago," he said to Mister Skye.

The guide began to saddle Jawbone. "It's best that I go alone," he said. "I am used to night work."

Mister Skye's voice sounded so calm that it quieted Cecil. Perhaps, he thought, the women were treed by a bear that was also gathering berries.

"Could they be in trouble?" asked Alice Sample.

"Aye, ma'am, they are in trouble."

With that he rode silently from camp. Blue afterlight lingered in the west, but it would be a moonless night.

From the campfire he saw Pine Leaf and James materialize, and ride off with Mister Skye up the dark coulee. That was good, he thought. Pine Leaf would have Indian-eyes, have that ability to pierce into the night and see the way a cat did. Cecil wasn't at all sure there was such a thing as Indian-eyes, but it was a common frontier belief, and it comforted him. Pine Leaf would see through the deepening dark.

It became a long wait. For an hour, at least, the missionary camp was unified, and beside the fire before Mister Skye's lodge they sat, Mary and Dirk, Cecil, Clay Sample and Alfred, and his own dear Henrietta and Alex, each silent and filled with a deepening dread. Silas lay in his bedroll, unaware of trouble.

It was close to midnight, Cecil judged from the position of the Big Dipper, and growing sharply cold when the searchers returned, slipping so quietly into camp that it startled them. There had been nothing, no sound, and then they were there.

Mister Skye lumbered over to them and hunkered down beside the embers of the fire.

"They've been taken," he said. "Captured. Pine Leaf says Assiniboins. Horse-thief bunch. She says not many, maybe ten, plenty of fresh sign, heading east toward the bend of the Musselshell. There's probably a village of them within a day's travel. We're going to pack up now, mates, and follow."

Chapter 23

There were seven. There had been nothing but peaceful twilight as they gathered berries, and then they stood there, materializing out of nothing. They looked shorter and stockier than the Crows, and had yellower flesh. Seven young warriors in breechclouts, six with bows, one with an old flintlock fusil. They rode small dark ponies, with shaggy manes and tails that hung to the ground, horses the proud Crow would have scorned.

Esmerelda stared, her heart suddenly thumping. Miriam, beside her, unconsciously slid closer to her side. Victoria stood nearby, rooted to earth.

"Assiniboin," hissed Victoria. These were enemies of her people, but a weaker tribe than the Blackfeet. The Assiniboin lived along the upper Missouri to the east and were a long-separated branch of the Dakotah Sioux.

Most were youths, but there was one with graying hair and deep seams in his brow, and a cruel arrogant stare. Upon his chest lay a strange necklace with long objects hanging from the beadwork. Esmerelda saw that they were desiccated human fingers, eight of them, each perhaps taken from an enemy in battle. She swallowed. The necklace was great medicine. Did she have any medicine to match it?

The headman stared at the three of them at length, dismissing Victoria the Crow woman, and focusing on Esmerelda first, and then Miriam, with flat, expressionless eyes. The girl shrank under his unblinking gaze, and hugged Esmerelda.

Like Cecil, Esmerelda believed that life must be tried and tested. Even now, there was no surrender in her. How many times, in how many lives, had opportunity slipped away because someone had been afraid to try?

"Come along, Miriam dear, we shall walk back to the wagons."

With that she took the girl in hand and turned her back to the menace behind her, and they set off, with the berry basket half full. Thus it went for a hundred yards. She did not look back, though she wanted to, and the muscles of her back rippled with the anticipation of an arrow.

Then an arrow did hiss by, into the dirt before them. She did not stop. There was yet a half a mile to the wagons, and she would not stop. Her legs would move steadily, rhythmically.

She heard the soft crunch of hoof behind her and then a hand as hard as strap-iron grasping her dress and tearing it. She turned, and the flat-eyed one, the one with the dangling human fingers on his breast, was leaning over his horse. Their eyes locked and she saw mockery in his, but the face was as immobile as ice. He leapt off as lithely as a panther, and lifted her as if she were weightless, setting her on the small animal. Then he lifted the struggling Miriam and dropped her on the withers of another pony ridden by a young warrior. That pony had chalk-white handprints blazoned on its chest.

"I don't want to go," cried Miriam fiercely.

But they would go. Victoria, too, now sat on a horse, her doeskin skirt hiked high up her legs. Esmerelda felt the headman settle himself behind her, and steel arms grip her carelessly, and they rode off, trotting silently up the long coulee. When they topped out a mile or so east, another warrior joined them, making eight. It grew dusky, and colors faded from the world, prairie and the nearby Snowy Mountains alike turning gray. Soon it would be night.

Now at last the implications of this seeped through Esmerelda a little at a time. Captivity. It had happened often enough. Her fate—could be anything. But one thing she knew now; she was being taken farther and farther from Cecil with each step of the pony, across an empty land. Unrolling behind them would be tracks, broken grasses, horse sign, leaving a thread of a highway to follow, mile after mile, so long as it didn't rain or snow. She didn't know where she would be taken—this was an endless land, a sea of rolling grass that stretched beyond horizons. How would Cecil find her; how would Cecil free her, even if somehow he found the place, the dot, the pinprick in this endless universe, where she would be?

The horse felt uncomfortable beneath her, its sharp withers grinding upon her thighs. But she was imprisoned in this precarious spot by bands of steel, so she endured because it was the only thing she could do. It grew dark now. She heard Miriam weeping, poor little girl, a tiny life suddenly torn apart. And still they rode. When night settled she spotted the Big Dipper to her left, and the North Star, and knew they were trotting east, always east, farther and farther from Cecil.

It came to her she might never see Cecil again. It had been a good marriage. She was only forty-four, and had hoped for many years, decades, more; growing old together. Doing the work the Lord had given them to do. Seeing grandchildren soon, when Henrietta gave birth. Bringing Light to those in darkness . . . even the darkness of soul she felt hard against her back.

It grew cold, and a biting wind sprang up, and she wondered how these Assiniboin, and all the plains warriors, could ride nearly naked in chill weather. All through the jouncing night Cecil grew more distant. They never stopped. She grew desperate to relieve herself, and the suffering turned into anguish, but they never stopped. With each passing hour Cecil drifted away, growing smaller and smaller. Her own Cecil. She yearned for the familiar contour of his lean body and the blankets that covered them both, but he was not here.

She turned to her faith and prayed, but the thoughts and words came hard. Then she began to talk out loud to her captor. "I beg you to take us back," she said. "We have come into this land to do God's work, and not to hurt anyone. We . . . we . . . I trust you will treat us kindly. I am, I've been a good and faithful woman. I do not want another husband . . ." She thought she would cry, but refused. She would not cry. But even the most timid review of her future brought a shudder. Violated. Taken as a squaw. As a slave. Tortured. They loved torture, didn't they. Loved to see how brave a white woman might be. If she cried and screamed, they'd mock her. If she remained silent and defiant, they would say her spirit went to the Other Side with honor and courage. She grew afraid she'd weep piteously.

Sometime before dawn they stopped at a tiny creek running southward from the Snowy Mountains. The tiniest fraction of a moon had finally risen and lit the place with ghost-silver. She was dropped rudely from the pony and permitted to slip into the darkness. There were no bushes. Near her were Victoria and Miriam. They all walked then, and the movement of her legs felt good in the harsh night air. The air felt icy. Ever eastward they walked, and then after a half hour of it they mounted again, even as a thin line of light cracked the horizon. Now, on mounting, she felt tired, and the nervous energy that had propelled her through this nightmare had vanished. She slumped. If she fell off it didn't matter, but whenever she slid, iron hands clamped her straight again. And now her captor snarled when she slid. She was weary beyond experience, and thirsty and hungry as well. During their brief stop the horses had been carefully watered, but not the prisoners. She closed her eyes, slumped into herself, and tried to rest.

The black world turned gray again and the long mountains on her left became a ghostly presence. They loomed lower here, and tailing down, petering out into a long high ridge. Their captors angled ever closer to them, and now they started into the foothills, following a pine-dotted ridge. The sun burst in the east and painted the land orange. Now she could see Victoria riding resolutely with a warrior behind her, and Miriam, sleepy, her eyes burning black. Her thoughts turned to the child. Surely they would not harm her, a girl who had not yet budded. But she didn't know. Those things seemed to be a question of whim.

Esmerelda thought of that tiny, fragile trail unwinding behind them across the miles and leagues, that fragile thread that was the sole link between her and Cecil. They climbed steadily, and now the weary pony heaved, and its neck and withers were drenched with wetness even in the cold air. Steadily they rode upslope, attacking it at an angle. It was park and forest country now, ponderosas and grasses, with the trees becoming steadily thicker until they rode into true forest and topped the long ridge. On the north slope they quickly emerged into grassy benchland again, and before them was a wide valley running east, and west, with a silvery creek glinting in its bottom. And in this valley, but far to the east, was a village of seventy or eighty lodges, blue smoke hovering in the long orange dawn light.

For a moment the warrior carrying Victoria rode close; close enough for Victoria to say, "Flat Willow Creek, what the whites call it. Sonofabitch."

The fist of the warrior she rode with smashed into her face.

Esmerelda had never heard of Flat Willow Creek. But it was a name, something she could write in charcoal upon bark and leave to be read somewhere. Even now she was thinking of sign, and wished she had thought of it sooner. There were things she might have done, petticoat she might have ripped and dropped, piece by piece, petticoat to say she lived. Petticoat to tell Cecil she loved him.

They jolted down benchland, plateaus, and cliffs, and into the bottom of Flat Willow Creek, lush with bunch grass turned golden now as August faded. And just ahead rose the cones of the village, the dogs and ponies, and the welcoming Assiniboin people, who rushed out now to greet the raiding party of young and inexperienced warriors under the tutelage of the greatest warrior of the Assiniboin, Killer.

They rode toward the center of the village, where there was a clear space, a sort of village square, surrounded by tall lodges with their windflaps opening to the east. Just outside the village stood high racks upon which countless strips of buffalo meat were being dried into jerky. They were met first by a pack of snarling curs, yellow and gray, half wolf or coyote, that snapped at the heels of the horses. On either side of the headman's lodge near the center of the village rose tall slender poles topped by sun-bleached human skulls, with tufts of hawk feathers dangling beneath, to tell the world that this was a man of great medicine.

Straight toward the center of this village they rode, followed by the clamoring mass of newly awakened people, who were enjoying this victory celebration even before they had breakfasted. The young warriors raised their thick buffalo-bull shields high to announce the capture of slaves, a valuable asset to this small band. Here were women to flesh buffalo hides and bring wood, and a girl to bring Assiniboin children into the world someday. Only the capture of horses would have been a greater victory for this horse-starved people.

At last they stopped before the chief's lodge. Esmerelda shrank from the sight of it, for every totem here spoke of death; black-haired scalps dangling from lances thrust into the grassy soil; buffalo skulls set ritually around a space before the lodge; and those human skulls on the poles . . .

Her captor lifted her and dropped her unceremoniously to the ground, where she fell to her knees because her legs had gone numb. The village women swarmed about her, and she realized she was perhaps the first white woman they'd ever seen. There were a few white women at Fort Laramie, an infinity away, but these were northern people whose home was largely in Canada, and the sight of her amazed them. She tried to stand, but a horde of women pinned her to earth, plucking at the fabric of her dress. She had worn that day a silk taffeta, her best dress, because her ginghams were worn and she hoped to find time to mend them. But the shiny taffeta was a marvel to these women, and they fingered and plucked at the lustrous brown cloth with fascination, and then began ripping it, wanting it to decorate themselves.

Some of them had bone daggers or fleshing knives, and now they began ripping and slicing. Esmerelda felt her bodice tear, and saw the small buttons fly to earth. Then she felt terrible rips that tossed her one way and another, savage tugs at her skirt, the sound of fabric shredding, the murmur and cry of these women as they stripped her. And they didn't stop at the taffeta. She felt the cool morning air upon her chest, and white things disappear from her. She pulled herself into a ball and hugged herself but still the ripping continued, and now the points of the bone daggers found flesh and drew blood from her arms and thighs and buttocks, and she knew she was naked, and eyes of all sorts were upon her, staring at the whiteness of her thin body.

She didn't cry. She sensed her utter helplessness. There was no contortion of body or cry of her mouth that might help her. The women stabbed and jabbed with knives now, to see how this white woman bore the sting of them, fascinated. They'd peel her flesh, burn her with glowing brands snatched from cookfires, see to it that she died slowly, she knew.

She blanked her mind to the pain. The only flight open to her was the flight of soul, of mind, into some other place, and by some miracle she succeeded in that. She chose her wedding day, the day of her union with Cecil. She saw her big, homely frontier minister, very young, standing beside her. She heard the drone of the minister, and saw Cecil slip a ring upon her finger . . . . and then she plunged back in the now, and felt her fingers being crushed, and some old crone of a woman yanking at the plain gold ring and finally sliding it over unyielding joints . . .

A sharp nasal command halted it all, and the women

slid away from the sport, clutching whatever treasures
they had managed to rip from Esmerelda. She lay alone
on the earth, bleeding from a score of pricks, ghostly
white. She huddled into the smallest ball she could make
of herself. But even that protection of the sheltering earth
was not to last. Her captor lifted her bodily to her feet.
Beholding her was virtually the entire village, men,
women, children, packed densely around the space of the
buffalo skulls before the lodge of the chief. She felt a
helplessness such as she had never known.

But she would not die! She'd fight to live, to survive, to
count the days until she could be with Cecil again. And if
he didn't want her because of these . . . these shames . . .
she'd live anyway, find a life, remember the warm sun,
the love of God . . .

She stood erect, eyes closed, watched but not seeing. Her
captor let go of her arm. If this is what the universe gave to
her, then she would stand erect. She had nothing left to
hide, so she did not cover herself. She opened her eyes and
found herself staring into the flat agate eyes of the headman, who was watching her with interest. Never had she
seen such a face. He had half a nose, the other part of it
having been hacked away in war, and indeed his name, she
would find out, was Cut Nose. He was missing most of an
ear as well, and terrible jagged scars creased his torso. The
lips looked thin and cruel, cheeks hollow and cheekbones
prominent and skeletal. But his eyes transfixed her. She
had seen eyes like that in rattlers, unblinking and deadly.

She peered around now. Victoria and Miriam were nowhere in sight. Victoria would be an ordinary prize for
these people. They might torture and abuse her, and work
her like a horse. But Miriam's fate she couldn't imagine.

The chief, dressed only in his breechclout and fringed
leggins, plucked a war lance from the ground beside his

lodge, and leveled it at her, and then stabbed delicately at her belly. It pricked, adding to the blood that smeared her. She felt death upon her. So this would be the end, then. Gutted here, so far from Cecil, still almost young . . . But the chief withdrew the lance, his lips forming a small cruel smile, and nodded to her captor, whose iron clamp upon her arm pulled her off, through the gawking crowd, past the nipping curs, toward a lodge larger than most. He was followed by two proud young women, obviously wives of this the greatest warrior, and displaying their status with every step. There were four good ponies tethered here, Assiniboin wealth, and painted on the lodgecover was the story of Killer's exploits: Killer counting coup with his lance, Killer with his bow drawn. Killer on horseback among a dozen prone bodies, all of it painted in black and carmine stick figures.

She was pushed hard through the doorflap and into the gloom of the lodge. Thin light pierced here through the cowhide cover and the smokehole, but it was a shadowy place. Around the firepit at the center, cold now because the women had been cooking outdoors, lay fine buffalo robes and parfleches. Medicine totems hung from the lodgepoles; a doll, although there seemed to be no children here; and a stuffed ferret, the medicine animal of this high-caste warrior. He followed her inside, and the squaws followed after, their eyes alight with the fun of what would come. Esmerelda peered into their moonwide faces, seeking sisterhood and sympathy, and finding none, but only the flat-eyed pleasure she had seen in those outside. She thought she should have been grateful for this relative privacy, but it no longer mattered. She crawled to a robe and lay curled in it, feeling hunger and thirst now. She'd had nothing for as long as she could remember, when the world turned upside down.

She saw an earthen pot of water. If she was given no help, then she must find help in her own actions. Something as simple as taking water might yet preserve her. She reached for the bone ladle, and drank. No one stopped her. She dipped it and drank more, the cool water welcome in her parched throat and body. She drank a third time, and felt better.

"I would like food and clothing now," she said. They stared.

"If I am to be your slave, then dress me and I'll be about it. Someday, I will be free. Someday, you will know the love and lash of God, even though you don't know Him now."

The two young women squatted at the far side of the lodge, waiting for something.

She peered up at her captor, and read his intent. It grew very plain. Not that, she thought, God spare me that. God spare me for Cecil . . .

But even as her heart cried against it, she knew it would happen, she saw it happening. And they would not even be alone, but it all would happen before his other—his wives. She wished she might go mad, be transported out of reality, away from this place. But she knew it could not be. She was strong, and her mind rode upon the troubles of life serenely. Perhaps that was why Cecil had been drawn to her, had married her. She had been a full match for his own frontier strength and character and that is why the marriage had been so good, so good . . . She felt strong, and her mind would not crack and break. She would experience what was to come with all her faculties, with the strength she had been born with.

If she closed her eyes, she could pretend it was Cecil, but it wasn't Cecil and she couldn't pretend.

Chapter 24

I t began with a wrangle. Both Cecil and Clay insisted on coming along. Mister Skye would have none of it. He wanted only Pine Leaf and James Method with him, plus two spare horses to bring the women back.

"Look, mate," he said to Clay. "If all of us go, there'll be no one here to protect these people, protect Mrs. Sample. I'm leaving this camp in the hands of my Mary, and I trust you'll obey her. But she may need help." He left unsaid the obvious, that neither Alex nor Silas Potter would defend themselves and others with arms.

Clay Sample pondered the thought of his wife here with so little protection, and reluctantly agreed, anguish written across his face.

"And that goes for you, Mister Rathbone. They need you here. Your daughter and son-in-law need you. Every man counts here. I'll add, mate, that we don't want to be slowed down. Every minute counts."

"Esmerelda is my wife," said Cecil. He plunged into the darkness and found his hobbled Magdelene and freed her. He would come along, Mister Skye realized, unless he was hogtied. The guide didn't like it. Not even a frontiersman like Cecil would know what his wife's fate was likely to be.

The four of them rode into a bitter cold night, up the coulee. No moon shone. At the head of the coulee, two miles east of camp, Pine Leaf slid off her pony and studied the ground on her hands and knees, smelling because she couldn't see.

"I do not know," she said at last. "I have not found it."

They spent the next hours making a wide arc, with

Pine Leaf on foot, pausing every few feet to hunker next to the earth. They swung southerly first, and arced north, and at last she gave up.

"It hides in the night," she said.

Mister Skye had a decision to make—wait here, or go. To go the wrong way might result in more delay. But he had not lived life like that. "We will go east," he said.

They rode east through the night over rolling prairie with a wind at their backs. When a cloud mass blotted out the heavens, they rode by dead reckoning through an awesome inkiness. Mister Skye hoped the wind hadn't changed. The breath of it on his neck had given him direction. He wondered about Cecil, riding silently beside him. Had the man any idea of what to expect? The minister had said nothing, but neither had he shown the slightest sign of despair or remorse for having embarked on this perilous journey.

When dawn cracked the northeastern sky, they were twenty miles or so to the east of their camp. To the north, the Snowies began to glow like ghost mountains. They paused to rest the horses and to chew on some jerky from Mister Skye's kit. He thought the Assiniboin, if that's who it was, would likely be on the bend of the Musselshell, another day east. But now would be the time to patrol north and south and cut sign if they could, rather than risk going farther astray. They paused another ten minutes until it became possible to see, and then Pine Leaf and James Method swung north, while he and Cecil swung south.

Mister Skye walked so he could study the ground. It was time to rest the wounded Jawbone anyway. He spotted nothing. The undisturbed prairie grasses and umber earth stretched endlessly south with no mark of passage other than buffalo trails.

"It's the needle in the haystack, isn't it," said Cecil. "I had not understood the size of this land until now."

"Not that bad, mate. Where people and horses go, they leave tracks."

Cecil walked silently, studying the ground a little to the left of the guide. "Tell me, Mister Skye, the exact truth. What is my wife's—their—fate?"

He did not want to answer that. "Bad," he said. "If it's the village of Cut Nose, worse."

"Then let us hurry."

But they found nothing. For two hours they walked south, spotting no sign of recent passage. Once they found an old trail, windblown hoofprints, brown-dried dung, and studied its direction, but it meant nothing. Then Mister Skye turned back to see what the others had found, riding now but studying the ground still, in case they had missed a clue.

James Method was waiting for them at the place where they had split. "Ah don't believe we have anything, but Pine Leaf asked me to come back here and fetch you. She's inclined to believe they're over beyond yonder ridge."

"Little Snowies," said Mister Skye. "We'll follow her then, mate."

At midday they found her. She seemed to materialize from nowhere in the root ridges of the mountains. And she was standing squarely on fresh tracks of several horses.

"Eight," she said. "I have studied them."

Mister Skye knew they were lucky. They had gained nothing from the night march, and would have been here before this in far fresher condition had they slept out the night back at their camp. But they had the trail. They silently followed it up into country dotted with pondero-

sas, and finally into forest, and topped a ridge. A half
hour later they stood their ponies on a promontory overlooking the valley of the Flat Willow. And in the hazy
eastern distances, where the creek valley bellied out
upon plains again, lay smoke.

Pine Leaf sat beside Mister Skye, seeing what he saw.
"Have you a plan?" she asked.

In truth, he hadn't. Ride in, find out if he could if the
abducted women were there, bargain. If they bargained
at all, he knew what they'd want. And so did Pine Leaf.
"Let's tie the spare horses here," he said. "Or down a little,
as close as we can hide them."

"It is a good day to die," she said. "I have taken many
scalps from them, and they will want mine now. But I
will live. While I waited for you, I closed my eyes and
permitted the medicine vision to form. I saw what I
needed to see. I will live, at least for today. I will be very
strong, as I was when I was young."

Skye nodded. He, too, had taken the lives of these
people, while fighting them beside the Crows. They angled
eastward now, staying upslope in the trees for cover and
coolness against the midday sun, and when the trees
petered out they tied the two spare horses.

The village lay ahead, but too far for details to emerge.
They were in range now of its patrols, the police warriors
who were responsible for its security at all times. Mister
Skye stared at Cecil, wondering how the minister would
bear the burden, but found him resolute and set-jawed.
And he stared at Method, the young untried warrior tasting freedom now, but perhaps not yet aware of the price
of this wild freedom of the plains. Then they rode.

He rode with his Sharps across his lap, wondering
whether to go in with it in hand. To ride into a village
with the weapon in hand, and not sheathed, would be a

warlike act. It would be countered by village warriors, who would have lances and bows in hand. Even to lift the Sharps to fire it would result in a dozen lances piercing him before he got off a shot. To ride in with weapons sheathed would be a sign of peace and parleying, but also a sign of weakness in the eyes of this peculiar chief, Cut Nose. He sighed, and slid the rifle into its beaded saddle scabbard. At the same time, he unloosed the thong that held his Colt in its holster. Behind him, the others followed suit. Pine Leaf returned an arrow to her quiver.

There would be, he reckoned from the lodges in sight below now, seventy or eighty warriors, and they would all be waiting. Indeed, an advance guard of greeters was boiling out of the village below to escort them, or fight them. So they had been seen now, and what followed would be fate, or medicine, or the will of God, he thought, his mind running through the beliefs of these three beside him.

Of all the villages he hated to ride into, this was the worst. He would even prefer to ride into the villages of the Blackfeet who were his enemies, knowing that the proud Blackfeet would behave in the protocols of the plains, than into this village where Cut Nose and his lieutenants, including the dreaded Killer, ruled by cruel whim and trickery.

The greeting party consisted of ten warriors, all in breechclouts and nothing else save a band across their foreheads to hold their long flowing hair in place. One wore a single eagle feather and was graying. Mister Skye knew the man, and dreaded his presence. It was Killer, legendary warrior of these people, whose whole life consisted of living up to his name.

Now they were arrayed in a line ahead, and Mister Skye and his colleagues stopped. Killer smiled faintly.

"We have come to parley with the great Cut Nose," Mister Skye signed with his hands.

Killer's gaze rested not upon him, though the warrior knew him and knew of his horse, Jawbone. It leveled instead on Pine Leaf, recognizing her and anticipating everything to come, with seventy of his kind beside him, and only one Absaroka woman to contend with.

Mister Skye's hands flashed again. "These are white medicine people. The white man here is a medicine maker, like the blackrobes. Pine Leaf of the Crows is now a medicine woman of her people. The darker man is a warrior of the Crow, but came with the white medicine people."

Killer nodded faintly.

"We have come to get our women. You have taken my wife Victoria." Now at last Killer's agate eyes focused on the famous Mister Skye and the terrible blue roan horse that carried him. "You have the wife of this white medicine man, who comes in peace. We will take his wife back. And you have a girl, daughter of the white medicine people."

All this Pine Leaf followed with her eyes as Mister Skye made the signs with his hands. The others all followed his hands too.

"What women?" asked Killer. "We have no women. Come into the village and see. We will show you."

Mister Skye did not answer.

He touched heels to Jawbone, and they rode quietly into the village, past staring, unfriendly people. Flanking them were the warriors who had met them, each carrying a bow with an arrow nocked in it, a sign of contempt and trouble. Villages bore the stamp of their leaders, and Cut Nose ruled by terror. Maybe, Mister Skye thought, it would end here. But not before he put a bullet through the heart of Cut Nose and a knife into Killer. It would be a good day to die.

They drew up before the chief's lodge and found him standing before it, a rifle cradled in his hands. There would be no smoking of the pipe here. He peered up at them with the flat beaded eyes of a rattler, and beneath those eyes was the remains of a nose hacked off on one side.

Mister Skye chose English: these people had traded for years at Fort Union, the old American Fur post at the confluence of the Missouri and Yellowstone. Since they had been greeted without the protocols of the prairies, Mister Skye chose to return the insult.

"We have come for our women."

"What women? We have none of yours," Cut Nose replied.

"They are hidden in the lodges. Bring them at once and we will leave peacefully."

Cut Nose smiled, a grotesque smile because the scars across his face twisted his lips.

"Peacefully. I see four of you. Are there more?"

Mister Skye said nothing.

"I see a great enemy of the Assiniboin, the warrior woman Pine Leaf. She has taken many scalps. I am glad she brought herself to us."

"She is a medicine woman now. Her visions told her she would live through this day."

"Perhaps today," Cut Nose said, smiling. "Perhaps not tomorrow."

Cecil caught Mister Skye's eye, and pointed. Among the silent spectators was a squaw wearing the bodice portion of Esmerelda's brown taffeta dress. The sleeves were gone, and so was the skirt.

"I see the clothing of our women worn by yours," said Mister Skye. "Will you lie again?"

It was as much an insult to an Indian as to a white.

"Perhaps the famous white warrior would like to look in our lodges?" Cut Nose replied evenly. "I have decided that you will be our guests. We will have entertainment. We will take care of your horses, and I will keep your weapons in my lodge."

"I think not."

A silence stretched.

"You are four," he said at last.

"It is a good day to die." He sat on Jawbone waiting, ready, cold inside. He would have time to shoot once. Jawbone's ears laid back, and he tensed murderously. The horse's medicine was well known to these warriors.

Cut Nose eyed the horse contemplatively. "It is a good day for sport," he said. "We will have contests."

"We have come for our women."

Killer stepped over to the chief and whispered something. Then he said, "The women for the horses. I myself want the medicine horse of Mister Skye. I will have his medicine, or I will kill the horse with this arrow in my bow. With such a horse, the Assiniboin will be rulers of the prairies. Four horses for the women."

Mister Skye stared. "I know the famous Killer who speaks. But surely, with all the warriors here, you will have the horses anyway when you kill us? No. We will have the women now and leave."

Cut Nose waved Killer aside. "We will have sport," he said. "We will test the medicine of the great Crow warrior woman, who says she will live through this day. Here are two of our enemies, two Crow warriors, the woman and this one we have never seen, with flesh the color of the grizzly bear. We will let them run, and if they outrun my warriors they will be free. We will take their moccasins first, and if their medicine is good they will run away. The warrior woman, Pine Leaf, is reputed to be the fastest runner among all warriors."

"She is a medicine woman, not a warrior, and her hair is turning gray."

"That is good. We will see if her medicine is good. Otherwise, we will torture them. These are Crow enemies of my people."

Pine Leaf laughed scornfully. "We will outrun all of your warriors," she said. "This one with me is Seven Scalps, and his medicine is as great as mine."

She slipped lithely off her horse. James Method uneasily followed her.

Cut Nose was delighted. "The Crow warriors will start here," he said, indicating a place beside the creekbank. "My warriors will start there." The place he chose was scarcely fifty yards distant.

Lazily Pine Leaf unlaced her moccasins. James Method followed suit, looking troubled. She handed them to Mister Skye, and then her bow and quiver. She had for a weapon only the small skinning knife at her side—and she'd need it, Mister Skye thought. The spare horses were three miles distant. If they made it to the horses, cut the tielines, they might escape. Still, he did not like this. That left only himself and the minister here.

The Assiniboin warriors clustered happily at their starting point. They dropped their bows and arrows and chose lances, fine weapons to throw at a fleeing target just ahead, deadlier than bows and arrows. By Mister Skye's count there were over fifty.

"When I spear the earth with this lance," called Cut Nose, "you will go." To his own warriors he said something in his own tongue, and they laughed.

"Don't wait," hissed Pine Leaf to James, and he nodded. Now the whole village crowded to the starting points beside Flat Willow Creek. Mister Skye studied the village. Perhaps this would be opportunity. In the chase would be every warrior, save for the police society of the Assiniboin, who would as always guard the village. Ten or twelve might stay; the rest would run.

It looked like certain death for Pine Leaf and Method, barefoot, a few scant yards ahead of the howling pack of warriors trained to run and run. And Pine Leaf lithe in her breechclout and shirt, but graying . . . She walked indolently toward their starting place, not deigning to look behind her, but James did. He was already sweated with anticipation and fear.

Pine Leaf sprang. Method looked momentarily confused, then sprang after her. The Assiniboin warriors, enraged, howled after them, lances in hand. Pine Leaf raced straight for the spare horses, as Mister Skye knew she would, but it was plain they wouldn't make it, not even running for their lives. As they grew distant to his vision, he could see the warriors steadily closing the gap. One paused and threw his lance, wanting to count coup before the others. It sailed close to James. Mister Skye slid off his horse unnoticed by all around him, and slid his rifle from the saddle sheath. Now the police society warriors were watching, but he didn't care. He clamped a hand over Jawbone's ear and issued a quiet command. Then he let go of the rope he used for a rein.

The horse shrieked, and plunged furiously toward the pack of running warriors, now stretched out over a quarter of a mile with the slower ones dropping out of the race. The sight of the horse plummeting after the runners enraged Cut Nose, who turned to find Mister Skye's rifle bore pointing directly at him, though the rifle was cradled in Mister Skye's arms.

"I thought I'd even up the medicine, Cut Nose."

The runners and Jawbone all disappeared beyond a shallow ridge, and Mister Skye knew he wouldn't see them for some minutes, if at all.

"We'll take the women, now."

Cut Nose stared at the rifle, and then stared beyond. The village was far from being disarmed. Eight warriors of the police society remained, and all of them surrounded Mister Skye and Cecil now, with nocked arrows in their bows, or lances at the ready. Even the old men held drawn bows, another dozen missiles aimed at him.

Mister Skye laughed. "It is a good day for you to die, Cut Nose. The bullet will pierce your heart and send you to the Other Side before any arrow or lance touches me."

But some crept behind Mister Skye, and he could not watch them all. Cecil saw it, and turned his horse to face them, his own old percussion lock rifle at the ready. Still it would not be enough. An arrow pierced Mister Skye's silk hat and set it sailing. Mister Skye dodged sideways, and an arrow intended for him struck Cut Nose in the arm, piercing the biceps and running half through without striking bone.

The chief roared something, and the arrows stopped.

"You and your women will die. As slowly as we can torture them, and you," he snarled.

Chapter 25

Cut Nose looked pale and in great anguish, slipping toward shock.

"Your medicine is bad," Mister Skye said.

One of the chief's three squaws ran to help him, a

leather thong for a tourniquet in hand. Skye waved her away.

"Your medicine is bad today, Cut Nose. The spirit helpers have abandoned you. The One Above looks away from you. You saw it in your own visions. Taking the women was bad medicine. You saw it. The things in the medicine bundle around your neck won't help you now, Cut Nose. Evil is upon your village. Killer should not have taken the women. There will be no good medicine here until you give them up."

Near Cut Nose, an old shaman lifted a hand to his face. Cut Nose glanced uncertainly. Mister Skye understood medicine and used the knowledge ruthlessly among these dreaming, vision-questing tribes of the plains. Now he saw, in the gesture of the old one, that he had struck a nerve.

"Let the women go and tomorrow your good medicine will return. You have offended the spirit helpers and the One Above."

Blood leaked from the pierced flesh of Cut Nose's arm.

Then he barked a command to two of his warriors. They turned toward some distant lodges. Mister Skye eyed the far hills, wondering when the main body of warriors would return and give Cut Nose new courage, new medicine. So far, he had no inkling of what was happening out there.

They brought Esmerelda first, naked. She walked with her head low, her gaze fixed upon the earth. Dried blood smeared her. Cecil's breath exploded from his lungs. Then another pair of angry warriors brought Victoria, who was dressed and seemed none the worse for wear.

Mister Skye did not know where to look. He did not want to look at gaunt, violated Esmerelda, or at Cecil. He looked at the chief, who was paying the prisoners no attention. He nodded to a squaw, and she leapt to Cut Nose and began the task of extracting the arrow.

Esmerelda was brought to within a few feet of Cecil, but could not look up at him.

"Esmerelda," he cried softly.

Victoria was brought to Mister Skye. "Sonofabitch," she muttered.

His old wife looked unharmed, and he felt a surge of relief. They smiled at each other. She had been something the Assiniboins understood, a good Crow slave woman. But Esmerelda . . .

"Cover her," said Mister Skye.

Victoria wrested herself free of the guard pinioning her, and stalked resolutely past two of the chief's squaws and into Cut Nose's own lodge. Moments later she emerged with a fine doeskin dress. She handed it to Esmerelda, who took it but did nothing.

"Put it on her, Victoria," Mister Skye said softly. Victoria did, and somehow Esmerelda was transformed by it into a dignified beauty with averted eyes, the dyed quillwork and other rich-colored decor on the dress magically illumining her.

The guide spotted returning warriors on a distant ridge. Time was running out, if it hadn't run out long ago. Cut Nose saw them too, as he sat on the grass while his squaws worked on him.

Cecil finally nerved himself to say something, after clearing his throat helplessly. "My darling. I'm glad you're safe," he croaked.

"You don't want me."

"That is not true, God is my witness."

"It will never by the same," she murmured.

"What happened wasn't your doing!"

"Nothing will ever be the same."

Tears slid down Cecil's cragged cheeks. Mister Skye could not watch a thing so terrible.

"I will help you upon this horse," Cecil croaked, slipping off the animal. She did not respond, but let him lift her up.

"Where's the girl, Cut Nose? Bring us the girl," Mister Skye roared.

The chief peered up at him malevolently, sensing perhaps that his medicine wasn't all that bad today.

"You will not have the girl. She will be a squaw in a year or two, and bring children to the Assiniboin. You will not have the girl. We will keep your horses and the girl. You will leave with your squaws. That is my final word."

Even as he spoke those warriors who understood a little English led away Pine Leaf's and James Method's horses, and prodded Esmerelda with nocked arrows. Listlessly she slid off and they led Cecil's mare away.

"We will take the rifles, too," said Cut Nose.

"Whoever touches our rifles is dead," said Mister Skye. The bore of his was aimed directly at Cut Nose again. "Your medicine is worse now. We will take the girl. Now."

The gray-fleshed chief didn't reply. With every passing second the situation deteriorated. Now the whole body of the village warriors came into sight, and at least one was being carried. Some limped, hanging heavily on others. Jawbone had scythed through them, then.

"See, Cut Nose, how your warriors are hurt. The village medicine is very bad."

But the chief saw it differently. "Perhaps I will change my mind when they get here. Go now or die. Maybe you will die anyway," he said tautly. The women had withdrawn the arrow after cutting off its iron tip, and had stanched the blood.

Mister Skye pressed hard. "Cut Nose, American Fur will not let you trade at any post as long as you have that girl. They will hear of it soon enough. You know that. You will have no place to get powder and lead and iron pots and iron arrow points and blankets. You will be beaten by all your enemies because you have no guns."

"I have said what I have said," replied Cut Nose angrily. "Say no more or you will die! And the rest will die too, after we have tortured them all!"

He barked a command and two of the police society warriors beckoned Mister Skye's party. These would be their safe-conduct past the returning Assiniboin warriors . . . perhaps. Mister Skye debated a moment . . . and acceded. With Jawbone gone, he lacked choice. He nodded.

There was one last delay, while Cecil tenderly laced Pine Leaf's moccasins upon Esmerelda's legs, and then they walked, Mister Skye, Victoria, carrying Pine Leaf's bow and quiver, Cecil, and Esmerelda, between the two stony-faced warriors. There would be a bad moment, very bad, when the group collided with the returning warriors, Mister Skye knew. The two escorting warriors would kill them at that precise moment.

The two parties converged. Mister Skye made his decision. He'd go for the two escorts first. Each of them had trade tomahawks and lances and could murder the four of them in the space of a heartbeat or two. Next he'd shoot Killer, returning now with the other warriors and in a rage to see his captives released. The seconds ticked down. The others were staring, lances poised. They came within arrow range, then lance range . . .

On a far ridge Jawbone screeched, and it sounded like the howls of a thousand wolves. They all stared at the terrible horse pawing ground. It was big medicine, frightful medicine. And then next to Jawbone, riding the spare horses, Pine Leaf and James Method appeared, long black objects in hand. Mister Skye guessed they were sticks being held the way one holds rifles.

The escorting warriors shouted something at the other warriors and the groups passed in knife-edge silence. Among the Assiniboin were four walking wounded, some bloody from Jawbone's terrible teeth and hoofs. And they carried one, dead or unconscious, bleeding and with an arm hanging unnaturally. And so they passed, and after Mister Skye's group broke clear, the escorting pair abandoned them and turned back.

Mister Skye watched them narrowly, expecting surprise, but nothing happened. A few minutes later the four met Pine Leaf and James, and he took the measure of things. They had lost three horses and Miriam Sample. Jawbone had a bloody slice along his chest, where a lance had glanced by. It had not been a good day. His Victoria was fine, but what about Esmerelda, who peered vacantly into an alien world?

What would he say to Clay and Alice Sample when there were no words? Lovely Miriam gone, perhaps to reside there, perhaps to be traded again and again, north to the Crees, south to others. Some captive women had even ended up in Mexico. They would not violate the girl. Indians as a rule loved children, and would probably care for her very well. But it still might shatter the child, drive her to madness . . .

"What happened yonder?" Mister Skye asked James, handing him the rifle he had rescued in the village.

"Ah ran until my lungs and heart were on fire, and still they came on. Some lances came so close they caught my clothes. Pine Leaf was a little better, ahead. My feet stopped hurting and turned to ice. But there was one, just a few yards behind, fixing to throw and my shoulder blades were prickling when I heard the screech and it gave me heart.

"Jawbone, he came a-roaring. They were throwing lances at him but he snarled and attacked them, and knocked them over, and then got the one behind me with a wild bite . . . and then he turned and faced the whole bunch of them, pawing and screeching, and it scared them off. Only Pine Leaf and Ah, we didn't quit running . . . Ah don't rightly know how a horse can tell friend from enemy and do that."

"He picks it up from me. Everyone's enemy at first, until people have been with me awhile. The first week or two after we left Fort Laramie, I couldn't have sent him out like that. He wouldn't have separated you from the others."

"He's a smart horse."

"More a crazy horse," said Mister Skye. "And I have made him so."

They walked westward all day, made camp at the spring south of the Snowy Mountains, and walked most of the next day, with only Esmerelda regularly mounted. The rest took turns walking and riding. Pine Leaf's feet had been scratched and torn and bruised by the long desperate run; Method's too, and each step tortured her until Mister Skye thought to remove Pine Leaf's moccasins from Esmerelda, who rode horseback the whole way. She put them on gratefully, but there was nothing for James Method. He walked grimly, leaving small spots of blood in every print in the clay earth.

There was only silence among them and a sense of defeat because sweet Miriam had been lost. Victoria seemed the least harmed, and the food gathering fell to her. They took no meat, but she industriously gathered roots and berries as they trudged through early September chill, into the jaws of northern autumn. And then as the sun sank that second day, they stumbled wearily down the long fatal coulee, and into camp.

They were all staring.

"Mother!" cried Henrietta and rushed to Esmerelda, only to fall back confused at the sight of Esmerelda's face.

"What happened? Tell us!" Alex demanded.

Only Silas Potter seemed unperturbed, a faint knowing smile on his face. By the fire, Father Kiley sat quietly, listening.

Mary read everything at a glance, and soon she and Victoria were chattering.

But it was Clay and Alice Sample, with Alfred beside them, who concerned Mister Skye most. They stared as the party straggled in, and then looked behind, as if Miriam might be a little back from the others, and then came the terrible dawning.

"Oh, God," Alice cried.

Clay stared resolutely, awaiting news.

"Sis isn't here," said Alfred sharply.

Mister Skye stepped down from Jawbone. He did not want to say what he had to say, but it was something to be done.

"Miriam's alive, a captive of the Assiniboin. We tried hard to free her, but could not."

"She's alive?" Clay asked.

"I believe so. We didn't see her."

A terrible silence settled while they absorbed that. Then Clay asked, "Can we get her back?"

"It's possible they'll trade her for goods at some American Fur post. The company won't deal with bands that have a white captive. So, yes, there's a chance . . ."

"And if not?"

Mister Skye stared into twilit hills. "Don't count on seeing her again," he said softly.

Alice wept. "Why did we come, why did we come?" she sobbed. "No, no, no . . ." She slumped into the grass and wept desolately, her small hands clenching and unclenching. "She was such a good girl. Sweet and helpful. She never complained. I don't know why God wants to punish—to punish a girl . . ." Wetness seeped in sheets down her face now. "Miriam, oh my Miriam," she cried, choking and trembling. Mary knelt beside her and slid brown arms around her, but Alice Sample was beyond consoling. The muffled sobs continued, haunting the hills. "I have so little," she said, her voice muffled on Mary's breast, "I've never complained . . ." she whispered. "Oh, God, Miriam . . ."

Clay knelt beside her. "I'm going after her now," he said resolutely. "I'll fetch her, Alice."

She seemed not to hear. He stood and headed for his horse.

Mister Skye caught him by the arm. "You'll only give Cut Nose another scalp for his medicine tripod."

"I can't stand here and do nothing. I'll take a little gold, all I have."

"They'll take the gold and your hair and laugh. Mister Sample, you must stay and care for Alice and your fine son."

"Doesn't seem right. I've got to do something. Must do something!"

"Aye. We'll do something when we get to an American Fur fort. The traders have ways, mate. Ways that we don't have."

"I must do something!" But Clay's resolution was

seeping from him as he stood in this prairie place so far from help and civilization. "Do something!" he said, but it was an echo.

Mister Skye slipped a thick arm around his shoulder and steadied him until his breathing changed. Alfred stood nigh, and he grasped the boy's hand in his own big blunt-fingered one. It was small and clammy. The boy took courage from it for a while and then returned to his mother, who wept softly.

"May I talk with you, Mister Skye?" asked Clay. Together they walked into the dusk, far from other ears.

"First, tell me what happened. The whole thing. Then tell me something that is heavy on my mind—will Miriam be . . . abused?"

Mister Skye related the story, and then addressed Clay's question. "Unlikely she'll be abused, Clay. She's not yet a woman. Most Indians love children and delight in them. This group though . . . a bad chief, a bloody chief, poisons a band and its traditions, like a bloody bad king poisons a realm. Possibly some squaws will treat her meanly, half starve her. They want her for a squaw, Clay. They want more people in that small band. Likely they'll be decent enough to her and wed her off when she's at marrying age. They might trade her, though. Slaves, white women, get traded. Sometimes the trade is good because the new owners trade the woman for goods at some post or other . . ."

Clay sighed heavily. "I'm not encouraged."

"I didn't want to encourage you falsely, mate."

Clay's eyes turned moist. "We had a fine farm, rich soil, in the Ohio Valley, a place that prospered us. I've known Cecil a long time, and when the call came, I answered. We sold the farm, and put what we had into some fine mules and the wagon and a few things. Have you ever heard of Cincinnatus, Mister Skye?"

"Not rightly, Mister Sample."

"Cincinnatus was a great patriot of the old Roman republic. A great soldier and leader, who despised power, and for that reason was entrusted with it. They came to him one day, when the republic was besieged, and asked him to save them. He loved his farm, but he answered the call. Some say he left his plow standing in the middle of that field, and went off to war. He answered the call, Mister Skye. He was a patriot, and when he was called, he didn't dally; he answered . . . and soon enough he'd rescued Rome, gave up his dictatorial powers and went back to his farm. He's my inspiration, sir. I'm a patriot not only of this Republic, but of the Kingdom of God, and when Cecil's call came, I answered."

Mister Skye found himself admiring the man.

"I can't say as I left my plow in the middle of the field, but we sold out. Alice fretted some about it, but we came along to plant the Christian flag out here . . ."

"I am sorry it came to this," Mister Skye said roughly.

"It is worse, sir. We had six children, but cholera took four after a trip to the river. Jonathan was the eldest and we lost him. And the three younger, Sara, Artemus, and Josiah."

Mister Skye could not imagine what to say.

"Mrs. Sample will be wanting to go back, I'm sure. Alice has borne more than a woman can bear. I have no mind for it. We have no money to purchase good bottoms again. What would you suggest, Mister Skye?"

"No man can make that kind of decision for you, Clay."

"I was called and I must answer," he said resolutely.

The camp was morose that night. Some had been saved, but one lost. And another so wounded of soul that perhaps she'd never be the same. Only Silas talked, and his talk didn't help anyone. "It is the whip of God upon the sinful!" he cried, until Clay finally cornered him and asked bluntly what sins Miriam had committed that had led to her fate.

"It is the sins of the fathers upon the next generation," cried Silas.

"There are those here who grieve," said Clay bluntly. "Will you not comfort them, and me?"

"The voice crying in the wilderness does not come to comfort, but to discomfort."

"Then be silent," Clay snapped. "Or I will silence you with my fists."

Father Kiley stood. "Mister Potter! You are crucifying our Lord! My heart breaks for the Samples."

Mister Skye observed that with a certain pleasure. The condition of his party was worrisome. It was gravely weakened by a lack of horses, and demoralization, and he knew they'd be no match at all for any of the wolves, two- or four-legged, in this land. Pine Leaf and James were out scouting, on mules because the remaining horses were worn down.

Cecil seemed lost in his own world. He had wrapped Esmerelda in blankets and then slipped into the twilight, doing something that puzzled Mister Skye. Cecil plucked the last of the fall flowers, those that had resisted the frosts, and these he gathered into a great bouquet. Then he sat down beside the small cookfire and braided them, losing a lot of the petals of the asters and daisies as he did. Then, when he had a crude garland completed, he awakened the dozing Esmerelda and slipped it over her shoulders. She sat up, still wearing the beautiful doeskin dress of her captors, and stared at the garland about her neck.

"That's my wedding necklace for you," Cecil said.

Then, one by one he summoned the others to the fireside. The Samples did not wish to come, having retreated to their wagon, but he sternly bade them. He brought Father Kiley as well, and seated him, and beckoned Mary and Dirk and Victoria. He asked Silas to join them, but the young scholar refused.

"You have no authority over me," he said.

Then Cecil stood in the dusk. "We will pray now," he said. "First for the mercies of God; next for his blessing upon Miriam and the Samples; and last for my bride, my Esmerelda, and our joyous union and reunion. But let us first remember that Miriam Sample is not alone now; Almighty God is by her side, and hears our pleas."

And so they did for a half hour. Mister Skye watched quietly from beyond the firelight. He never felt comfortable at night close to a fire. But he saw, in that space of time, the renewal of courage and hope among these missionary people, and he approved.

At the end, Esmerelda wept, and Cecil leapt at once to her side, his scrawny hard arm around her, clutching her blankets to her. The others slipped away, permitting them their privacy. Esmerelda wept for a while, and then fell silent.

"Hold me, Cecil. Hold me and don't let go. If you hold me, I know I will be all right."

Chapter 26

The deeper they pierced into Blackfeet country, the more dour Pine Leaf became. James scarcely recognized the woman he had come to know in the land of the Crows. They were poorly mounted now because the Assiniboin had taken her swift Crow horse, and James's fine bay as well, leaving them only Cecil's spares, or mules.

"We will steal good Siksika horses," she said sternly, and from then on her efforts were devoted less to protecting Mister Skye's party than to hunting prey, a Blackfeet hunting or raiding party that could be jumped in the night. That such a thing was at cross-purposes with Cecil's missionary hopes did not enter her mind, or if it did she had dismissed it contemptuously.

It worried her, this lack of a good horse between her legs, and now it made her fierce and angry as she stalked through the Judith Gap and into the lush Judith basin with the eyes of the hawk, and the cunning of a lion, seeing everything before she was seen. She barely talked to James or tolerated his presence.

He knew her story now. She had told him some of it. Mister Skye had confirmed and elaborated it. At the age of twelve her brother had been killed by the Blackfeet, and she had made a most sacred vow never to marry until she had taken a hundred scalps of the enemies of her people. She grew lithe and swift and graceful as a puma, and tall for a woman. When she insisted on going out on war parties, the warriors laughed at her, but humored her wishes, only to discover that she was fierce in battle, making up in swiftness—she was a brilliant horsewoman—what she lacked in strength. And she became absolutely fearless.

She was also the fiercest of all Crows, haranguing her people into battle, and performing such feats of daring when it came to stealing horses and taking scalps, that she rose high in the councils of her people, becoming in time the third-ranking person in their midst. She never won her hundred scalps, and never married, but she eventually had lovers, including Antelope, Jim Beckwourth.

Now, in the grasslands of her enemies, the old flame burned hot again. She ejected James from her buffalo robes and ritually purified herself for war. Her temper turned hot and smoldering. James didn't mind. He had tasted death a few days earlier, felt its breath on his back, and if the Crow woman beside him was transforming herself into a dervish, that would be all the better. Her very ferocity was transforming him into a fierce counterpart. He thought she was beautiful, tall and perfectly formed, and as lean and graceful as a girl.

All this Mister Skye saw, but said nothing as far as James could tell. Pine Leaf and James stayed in the camps briefly, only to bring in buffalo hump and tongue, and then rode off again, stalking ahead of the caravan.

They rode through an awesome land of lush tawny grass and rushing cold creeks full of trout. The Snowy Mountains formed a smooth white wall to the southeast. To the west lay the Belts; to the east the pine-clad Judiths; to the north the Moccasins and Highwoods. And not far beyond lay the great Missouri, and the mouth of Sun River, near the great fall. After entering this northern empire, Mister Skye turned just north of west, and the wagons toiled over country so thick with buffalo that sometimes long processions of the great animals in their dark winter fur paraded right through the wagons, scaring everyone. This was a different country, somehow even more limitless than before, with dizzying views that ended in blue infinity.

Here Pine Leaf knew she'd find what she wanted, a hunting party of the despicable Siksika, and she searched now not for buffalo, but for humans, like some great stalking cat. And the second day into the Judith country, she found them. Violently she pulled James from his horse and hid the animals in a grove of long-needled ponderosa. At this point they were fully twenty miles west of the wagons and Mister Skye. Far ahead were nothing but tiny dots to James Method's vision, but to Pine Leaf's they were mortals. Some wild anger radiated from her.

"Siksika!" she hissed.

And so they proved to be. About a dozen men were preparing to run down their prey on buffalo ponies. They had crept up on a band of buffalo, mostly fine big cows, staying downwind. And now they were mounting the fleet buffalo runners, specially trained fast and daring horses that would close on a running buffalo, narrowly avoiding its horns, until their riders had loosed an arrow into the chest cavity of the buffalo. They had to be fleet, because buffalo could run with astonishing speed and pull away from all but the best ponies. Leaving their packhorses in the hands of a herder, the hunters plunged into the wild chase, and instantly the band of buffalo broke into a trot, and then a lumbering run as the Blackfeet swept in among them, their cries drifting down the wind, pumping one after another arrow into the animals. One cow with an arrow in her swerved and the buffalo runner did too, but a second too late and a horn gashed its flanks.

From their vantage point at the crest of a low grassy hill, Pine Leaf muttered and chanted Absaroka words that James didn't understand. The stampeded herd swept a quarter of a mile away, but still Pine Leaf never moved. She was studying each hunter, one by one, mastering his habits and daring. James thought she was probably measuring their scalps as well for the cutting. His own heart thudded. Soon he would be taking a Blackfeet scalp— the scalp he needed to present to Gliding Raven's father— and bringing fine horses too. He would begin his Crow life rich in horses, all stolen from the Blackfeet, and there would be prize buffalo runners among them.

When it was over there were twenty-three black carcasses humped in tawny dried grasses in the space of a mile. The hunters dismounted from the winded buffalo runners, and brought up the packhorses to carry the precious cargo of prime hides and hump meat and tongue back to their camp. There would likely be women in camp too, who would follow with knives, and take more meat for drying into jerky. The hunters were jovial after their success, and James could hear their shouts sometimes on the soft breeze. Twilight came, and still Pine Leaf did not move, but merely muttered the fiercest of incantations, summoning medicine. James felt hungry. He wanted also to return to the wagons with meat before it grew dark, check in with Mister Skye and let them know there were Blackfeet nearby. But Pine Leaf shook her head.

"Tonight," she hissed, "we will do what we came for. We will take Siksika scalps. We will steal horses. And then we will go back to my people. We will fly to the south, and you will have scalps. You will kill one night-herder, and I will kill the other. We will each take a scalp. And then the horses!"

"Ah'd like to say goodbye to Mister Skye. Ah'd like to shake the hand of the others, Cecil Rathbone especially. Ah'd like at least to let them know . . . Victoria's one of your people, Pine Leaf."

"Yes she is. But Mister Skye always takes care of them. We will go south as soon as we have made our raid."

"But Ah'm afraid those hunters will find the missionaries and blame them for—"

"Maybe that is good! Maybe they shouldn't take the white medicine to the Siksika!"

James didn't like that, didn't like abandoning the missionaries to a large group of vengeful Blackfeet.

"Ah'm going to go warn them. Ah'll be back here before we raid," he said. "And return our horses here to Cecil Rathbone."

She glared fiercely. "If you go anywhere, you will die. I will take your scalp back and tell my people you were against us."

She was fully capable of it, and that subdued him. It also made him feel all the worse. He had never before betrayed friends.

Even as they lay quietly behind the crest of the hill the wind picked up out of the northwest, and a vast cloud mass blotted out the stars and the last of the twilight. The temperature plummeted and it grew so cold that James longed to run, move, warm himself. But still Pine Leaf lay in the grass, like stone, impervious to discomfort. When he could no longer bear the cold knifing at him around his leggins and across his neck and face, and up the sleeves of his buckskin shirt, he stood anyway. It was pitch-black now. Even as he stood he felt the needles of sleet sting his face, and smelled snow on the cold damp restless air.

"If it snows we'll leave a trail of prints in it a mile wide that they can read," he said unhappily.

"All the better," she snapped. "It will lead south to my village. And they will know we did it. The snow will save me an arrow that I planned to leave among them, so they would know that Pine Leaf is not yet too old to make war."

James groped his way back to the horses and untied a small buffalo robe that he carried behind the cantle.

"We might as well get comfortable," he said, offering her space in it.

290 RICHARD S. WHEELER

But she scorned it. "It is good medicine to suffer. If you are warm you are soft and sleepy. If you sting with the snow and the cold of the Man of the North, it is good and your medicine will be strong."

It snowed then, the flakes streaking horizontally into James's face. He ignored her and wrapped the warm robe tight about him, and sliding his rifle into its protection as well. In that fashion he endured more hours, until at last Pine Leaf shook him roughly and bade him mount. He had no idea what time it was, but he knew that the hunters would be long asleep in their robes. There might not even be any herd-guards on a night like this, and that would make the whole thing easier: take the horses, kill some Blackfeet in their robes . . . that thought repelled him.

He settled into the icy saddle and they rode off into the teeth of the blizzard.

"We will use knives, or my bow and arrow," she said. "Be silent! The rifle will awaken them all."

How she knew where to go through that tunnel of black snow he couldn't imagine. No stars. The night was pitch-dark. They rode thus for perhaps ten minutes, though it seemed an hour to James. And then their horses caught a scent and their rhythm changed. Their heads were up and alert, and he hoped the animals wouldn't betray them.

"We will need to saddle the good Siksika ponies and leave these," she whispered. "So we will unsaddle these just ahead. I don't need a saddle at all, but you do. If these ponies follow us, that is good. If not, we will leave them."

So, thought James, they'd need time to saddle the horses they would steal; and Cecil and Mister Skye would be short two more horses. In the depths of himself he suddenly didn't want to be a Crow warrior. He wasn't

at all sure he wanted to marry Gliding Raven. He wanted
to head back to the wagons and camp and comfort in this
fierce September storm.

But Pine Leaf had already slipped from her horse, one
of Mister Skye's packhorses, and was loosening the cinch.
James sensed dimly they were next to a grove of pines,
of the type that dotted this country. He stared hard, trying to orient himself, but couldn't. Then she led him
forward, their moccasins treading an inch or two of
snow, straight into the needling wind. That was the only
orientation he had: getting back to his horse meant going
with the wind rather than against it.

They topped a low rise, and the hunting camp lay before them. The wind plucked sparks from the remains of
a fire, and around that pinprick of warmth lay inert forms
wrapped in dark, snow-covered robes. Beyond loomed
the horses on a picket line to keep them from drifting
ahead of the wind. Pine Leaf paused, waiting. After an
icy eternity, the faintest shadow of a horse and rider
circled out of the inkiness, faintly illumined by the occasional flare of flame.

"He is for you. We will see if there is another," Pine
Leaf whispered, her voice lost in the gale.

James grew numb. He had never felt colder, and he
wondered whether his numbness was a matter of the heart
as well as his blizzard-buffeted body.

And still they waited. Another came then. This one
rode close to the fire, slipped numbly off his horse to
warm his hands. He cradled his rifle in the crook of his
arm and held his hands to the orange embers.

Pine Leaf studied him. "It is the same one. They have
only one guard. They think no one will come because
the Cold-Maker has come tonight. We will show them
the Absaroka come anytime!"

She rose and nocked an arrow in her bow. "I will kill him. But first we must circle around and cut the horses free, and drive them so the Siksika cannot follow us. Then I will kill the one at the fire, and you will kill one of the sleeping ones and take his scalp. And you will count coup on the others."

James nodded. They arced around through darkness, until they came close to the horses, dark hulks with snow catching on their backs. They were alert, heads up. Pine Leaf stalked close, catlike, murmuring some incantation that seemed to calm the animals, then her knife flashed silver in the dark, and horses pulled loose and drifted downwind. One snorted. The guard peered into the blackness, seeing nothing through the driving snow. But he seemed to sense something, and stood up, rifle in hand, finger curled around the trigger.

He was crouched like that when Pine Leaf's arrow drove into his chest. He coughed, began to fall, and his finger pulled spastically on the trigger. His rifle banged thunderously, and in an instant the others sprang up, grabbing their weapons from their robes. But they saw no target, only a whirling wall of snow, and blackness beyond.

From out in the blackness Pine Leaf cried out, like the bark of wolves. James knew enough of her tongue to understand. "It is Pine Leaf, warrior woman of the Absarokas," she cried. "I have taken your horses. I am holding your horse, Moon-Hides-the-Sun."

That terrible news chilled James even worse. Which one of those ghostly forms, now shooting into the blackness where Pine Leaf's voice had come, was the most dreaded of all the Blackfeet? He didn't have time to worry about it because now they were spreading into the night in pairs, and one pair stalked directly toward him.

He shot one and darted to one side, knowing the other

would shoot or drive an arrow into the place where his muzzle had flashed. He saw the one dark silhouetted form drop. There were more shots, and he heard a horse snort and cough, and a heavy thud. A horse had been killed, then. Now others glided toward him, drawn by his shot, but he dashed sideways and crouched low in the grasses, hastily pouring powder into his hand, digging in his pouch with numb fingers for a ball and a new percussion cap. It took forever. His fingers wouldn't work. He dropped a ball into snow. Half the powder lay on the ground rather than in his barrel. He couldn't even feel the caps he dug for. And then it was too late. Out of the blackness came a rushing form, with glinting steel in hand. James clubbed wildly and struck a solid blow as the stock of his rifle slammed into the shoulder of the warrior. The man staggered and came on. James leapt sideways again, and clubbed a second time as the Blackfeet warrior whirled after him. This time the rifle connected with skull, and the man went down with a thud. But others were coming. Wildly James dug for his knife. Violently he caught the hair in one hand and slashed a circle around the skull with the other and pulled. The scalp popped off and James tumbled back into the snow, just as three others loomed near. It was enough. He had his Blackfeet scalp. He crabbed back, and when blackness enfolded him he paused to sense the direction of the wind, his heart clawing.

Downwind. He had to get downwind. He was lost now but Pine Leaf and the horses would be downwind. He was sweating, even in the bitter night. At every quarter he felt the looming presence of Blackfeet about to rush him, like ghosts, like hobgoblins, like the creatures that old granny had hissed about in the long ago.

Somehow he had lost his rifle. He had his knife in one

hand and the scalp in the other. He didn't pause to hunt for it in the snow, but ran now, with the snow, through the night, alone and without a horse and surrounded by vengeful Blackfeet, including the most terrible of them all. Then, far off into the left of blackness, Pine Leaf was laughing. "We have stolen your horses, Siksika dogs," she cried.

Shots racketed again from behind. But James veered sharply in her direction. The taunting was really for him, summoning him to come if he still lived. Now he ran, the white earth rising before him. He hit a tree branch and it slashed murderously across his face.

"You are careless, Seven Scalps. You were afraid, even though we have taken their horses."

"Pine Leaf!" he gasped.

Now he could see the dark bulk of drifting animals ahead, a great many of them.

"You have a scalp," she said. "That is good. But where is your rifle?"

"Lost it. Clubbed with it."

She led him fast to a place where black trees loomed.

"Here. I have saddled two. For myself I saddled the one that was owned by Moon-Hides-the-Sun. It is my prize. I am the greatest warrior of the Absaroka."

James fumbled into the murk, found the horse and his saddle and swung up. Beside him, Pine Leaf had already mounted.

"Now we must herd them," she said. "Fast for a little while. They cannot follow until daylight, and then they will run on foot after us if there is not too much snow. They will run down our trail, hoping to catch us, hoping we will be careless."

He could not see what they were herding, and marveled at her night vision. Occasionally a sharp word from her reached him through the tumbling snow. He felt less cold now, running with the wind. But a great quaking limpness filled him, and he hung weakly to the pommel. Thus they fled through the night.

Dawn came so imperceptibly in the overcast he scarcely noticed its arrival, but at last he could fathom the world around him. Ahead of them, making a great swath through a foot of snow, were seventeen, no, nineteen, ponies, some of them fleet buffalo runners. A little to his left rode Pine Leaf on a great gray horse. As the light grew, he saw the hulk of mountainous country to the south. They were probably traveling east because that part of the low cast-iron sky was slightly brighter.

And there was something wrong with Pine Leaf. She held an arm unnaturally to her side, and her fine buckskin shirt was soaked with dark blood.

Chapter 27

When dawn was nothing but a gray pencil of light across the breast of the prairie, Mister Skye saddled up Jawbone, shrugged into his blanket capote, and set off to the west. Pine Leaf and James hadn't shown up last night. Perhaps they had holed up in the blizzard, but he doubted it. They should have been back in camp before the blizzard started.

Behind him the camp was awakening to acrimony. Alex and Henrietta had a blazing fire going to warm up, and were haranguing Cecil, not only about the night's miseries but about their destination.

"It's too late in the year!" Alex snapped. "We won't

have time to build houses and make meat. We have a whole northern winter ahead of us. We must make for Fort Benton at once, Cecil."

Mister Skye didn't tarry to find out the result of that. He was in Blackfeet country and he hadn't heard from his scouts and the whole party would be in danger. It would be a miserable day, he thought. The sky was cloudless. A hot September sun would turn the snow to slush and bog the wagons. There was no spare stock now, and the skeletal oxen and mules would make only a few miles through the mud before giving out. Pine Leaf had been riding Victoria's horse. Method had ridden Mary's. There were no more spares, thanks to the Assiniboins. Not only were his scouts missing, but two precious horses.

He turned Jawbone northwest, the direction the caravan would go today, if it went at all. Victoria would whip them into action if she could, and she and Mary and Dirk would walk beside the remaining horse and mules carrying the lodge and their supplies.

Jawbone made easy work of the snow, except where it had piled up and Mister Skye found himself in two-foot drifts. He rode an animal that seemed all the more energetic when the going became hard.

A half hour later the sun cracked the east, sending long yellow light across a vast undulating plain. A snow-capped distant square butte suddenly bloomed in the light. He saw nothing; no sign of Pine Leaf and James. No sign of human passage anywhere. Then, an hour out from the wagons, he spotted movement off in the hazy southwest. He stopped at once, knowing his very immobility might prevent him from being seen. Jawbone froze beneath him, and together they watched a small dark mass of animals toiling toward them rapidly. Twenty minutes later he could tell it was a group of perhaps twenty ponies, and there were two riders herding them.

He waited patiently, still immobile. Let them exhaust their animals in the heavy snow; he would save his. At a half mile he knew it was James and Pine Leaf, not because he could make out their features, but because he knew how they sat. But Pine Leaf slumped. A raid, then, he thought, Blackfeet ponies, and a scalp or two for James.

They saw him now. He steered Jawbone toward them, watching the steaming breaths of the hard-driven ponies as he closed. It is not an easy thing to stop a driven horse herd, so Mister Skye fell in beside James and Pine Leaf. Her left shoulder was soaked with frozen blood, and she looked ashen. Hanging from James's pommel was a fresh scalp, frozen red blood around the lip of black hair.

"Congratulations," said Mister Skye.

"Ah didn't expect to see you again."

Mister Skye nodded.

"Your two horses are here," said Pine Leaf.

Mister Skye had already seen them.

"Take another if you need it," said James.

"That would be incriminating," said Mister Skye. He turned to Pine Leaf. "Would you pause long enough to be bandaged?"

She stared at him gravely. "There is one hole, not two. It is above my heart, and it no longer bleeds. I am dead, but not until we have taken these ponies, and these scalps"—she had one too, he noted—"to my people."

Mister Skye stared at this graceful, legendary woman.

"I believe I know the horse you ride. He was a colt when I saw him last, and that scar across his withers is one I made."

"I took him from Moon-Hides-the-Sun."

"Is he alive?"

"We do not know who we killed."

Behind them lay trampled snow, winding off into the cold haze. As they talked, both Pine Leaf and Method glanced to the rear every few moments. But they saw nothing but the blue haze of September there.

"I will say goodbye, then," said Mister Skye. "I will sing the song of Pine Leaf whenever I am with her people."

She nodded solemnly. She would live for a while because she willed herself to.

"I saw this in the visions," she said. "And I am ready."

"Mister Skye, Ah want to—would you shake my hand?"

"I would, mate," he replied, and they did. James tried to say something, but couldn't. "You have your freedom, mate. And you'll have a fine wife soon. But it is the freedom of the wild, Mister Method. From this day on, there'll be a whole tribe of Piegans wanting your scalp. And what they want, they usually get."

"How will they know Ah raided their horses, Mister Skye?"

"The songs that are sung in one camp echo in another, Mister Method."

Mister Skye slid Jawbone into the herd, parting it as it flowed southward. From his kit he extracted a ball of thong, and with it fashioned a catch-line for his two horses. Leaning over Jawbone he tethered one animal, and then the other, and pulled them away from the herd. He held them still as the dark ponies, mostly winter-haired now, slipped past, along with his two Absaroka friends.

"Adios, Seven Scalps," he muttered.

It was quiet. He headed back toward the wagons, leaving behind him the tracks of three horses, blue-shadowed cups in the snow. Now he, too, peered into the northwest, looking for whatever might materialize upon the brow of a distant swell of prairie.

He had things to think through. Behind him were tracks through the snow that linked him to the horse raid. And which endangered his missionary clients. Still, none of the stolen ponies would be found among the missionary stock.

Moon-Hides-the-Sun would be somewhere ahead. And in a rage because his great horse had been stolen. Mister Skye considered that man, that fearless and cunning and ruthless fighter, as one more formidable than himself. And motivated as well by the searing memory of a previous encounter that had cost him his medicine. Moon-Hides-the-Sun had come down the mountain from a vision-quest and announced to all his people that he would kill Mister Skye at Fort McKenzie. Skye had been there—that part of the vision was true—but when it was over, Skye had taken his medicine pouch, snatched his medicine feather, broken his medicine shield—which had a black moon in its center with sun rays of white emanating from it—and had sent the warrior into the dreamland for two weeks with a blow of a belaying pin about the ear. But it had been luck and would not happen that way again. To get his medicine back, Moon-Hides-the-Sun would do anything, including ambush from cover.

When Mister Skye returned, the wagons had not moved.

"Sonofabitch," said Victoria, viewing the horses that Mister Skye brought with him. She and Mary threw their saddle pads over them while Mister Skye briefly described his encounter with James and Pine Leaf.

"Sonofabitch. Tonight I will wail for Pine Leaf," she muttered. "Now you make these crazy-medicines go. I cannot make them go. I got damn mad and still they don't go."

She clambered up on her pony then, and off scouting. He walked over to the other fire, where the missionaries huddled trying to stay warm.

Cecil seemed cheerful, as always, but the others were surly.

"Did you find them?" Cecil asked.

"I did. They are heading back to the Crow Village. I have my horses back, and they have others."

"Will we ever see them again?"

"Not this trip, mate."

"Oh dear. Oh dear," cried Esmerelda. "He's gone? I do so wish we might have said goodbye. I am so fond . . ."

"He cared for me on every occasion," said Father Kiley. "Oh, how I'll miss that good young man."

"He took a shine to you, Father. But he's a Crow now, Crow in his soul, Crow in his faith. And a Crow in war."

Cecil pondered that. "The Blackfeet will be wrathful, and we may be in harm's way," he said at last. "We have a division here, and I pray we can resolve it amiably. The storm has been very hard upon my Henrietta and Alex, and all of us have suffered. It's melting now, but that seems to make no difference. Briefly, the Newtons and the Samples and Mister Potter wish for us to turn north for Fort Benton and winter on the Missouri. They say—and there's truth in it—that we haven't time left to build shelter on Sun River, and lay in supplies and food."

"We're saying more than that," snapped Alex. "Those of us who wish to go to Fort Benton will go, no matter what the rest of you do. Alone if necessary. My dear Henrietta is now only two months from her time. I insist that we make for Benton, so that she may be delivered in comfort and safety."

Mister Skye nodded, and turned to Father Kiley, who sat near the fire huddled in his blankets.

"What of you, Father? Have you thought of your future?"

"Mister Skye," said the priest. "I am in the hands of God. Since I no longer have a life of my own, there is only His will. I have that at least. In the weeks since the blinding, I have come face-to-face with His will."

"Fort Benton would be a place to shelter, and then be taken down the river. You'd be looked after."

"My Lord will take me to where He wants me, if He has any use for me."

Mister Skye peered off upon the vast white prairies, now blinding in the fierce sun. The sky looked almost black with blueness.

"I don't know whether you are surrendering your will, or surrendering your life," Mister Skye said.

"Only will, Mister Skye." The priest smiled. His bandages had been replaced by a leather patch that Victoria had devised.

Mister Skye returned to the fire where the mission party huddled.

"All right, mates. I've not brought you this far, so close to Sun River, to steer you elsewhere. You've toiled your way across a continent to build a mission at a place only sixty or seventy miles distant. Cecil Rathbone had a dream, and once you all were lifted up by it.

"But you're right, mates. There's not time to build a mission and lay in meat and go to Benton for supplies before the real cold and snow sets in. But there may still be two months of good weather before winter closes.

Time to locate your mission and begin to build it, hew down the logs, put up your corrals, cut some prairie hay.

"You preach faith, mates, but you have little of it now. I'll take you to Sun River, leave the men to start the work, and take the women to Fort Benton. American Fur will shelter you all through the hard weather, and the presence of you women will brighten that post. My friend Alexander Culbertson, the booshway there, will be glad to have you. And of course Father Kiley will find the help he needs there. He can be taken downriver in the spring, on a mackinaw first to Fort Union, and then by steamer."

He did not wait for objections.

"Harness up, mates. It'll be hard going for the mules and oxen, especially when the ground goes soft. Harness up now, and we'll have a warm camp in the evening."

Slowly they stood, half shamed by Mister Skye's criticism, half inspired by the thought of Fort Benton. And in a while they rolled off, the weary ill-fed oxen struggling in the slop and soft earth, and the ribby mules doing just as poorly. The day itself turned golden and pleasant, with the sun slaying the snow until bright grasses lay exposed again. They stopped frequently to let the burdened animals rest and feed.

They came upon the remains of the stolen traffic, now an avenue of rotting snow piercing west by northwest, and Mister Skye turned onto it. The going was slightly easier, but heavy in the thoughts of them all was where this avenue might lead.

Late in the afternoon Victoria slipped over a prairie ridge, and rode straight to Mister Skye.

She sat hard and wizened and motionless in the saddle, and her brown eyes blazed. "Siksika," she hissed to Skye. These were the ancient and dreaded enemies of her people. "A whole band, Kainah, the Blood tribe, in a buffalo camp. They are as many as ants. Maybe there are a hundred lodges."

Not as many, Mister Skye thought, as some years earlier, before the smallpox darkened so many of the lodges of the Blackfeet. And not so formidable, now that whiskey had cut its terrible swath through their numbers, whiskey from American Fur, in exchange for the exquisitely tanned Blackfeet buffalo robes.

"What of the hunters whose ponies Pine Leaf and Seven Scalps stole?"

"That is where the village is, where the Kainah dogs all camp. The whole village came to the camp of the hunters, where the snow trail ends. The buffalo are upwind to the west."

Making meat first, Mister Skye thought. Making meat for winter while the buffalo were near, and then they'd head on down toward the Crow country for revenge.

"We will go in," said Mister Skye.

"Sonofabitch," she said in English. "If I go in there and come out, I will build a lodge and purify myself for four suns."

"Do that, Victoria."

Late in the day, a dozen or so warriors boiled over a ridge and stared at the first wheeled vehicles they had ever seen, the two wagons and burdened carriage toiling slowly toward them.

Mister Skye rode ahead to meet them, and soon the Kainah warriors gathered around him, knowing him, knowing his medicine horse. They were older men, powerful and graying, the Buffalo Bull Society, the ones who guarded the various bands of these people. They were not painted for war or looking for it. If anything, they were intensely curious about these wagons furrowing the muddy prairie, and what might be inside.

Moon-Hides-the-Sun was not among them.

"Who speaks my tongue?" asked Mister Skye. It would be easier to talk than to flash the hand-signs of the prairies.

An older warrior who was made of slabs of tawny flesh welded into a powerful frame spoke up.

"I have spoke it some at Fort Benton, and before that at Fort McKenzie. You are Skye, and who are these that come?"

"Medicine men," said Mister Skye. "Shortrobe medicine men of the whites, and a longrobe medicine man."

"A longrobe? Has the longrobe Point returned?"

"Not Father Point, but a brother. The longrobe Father Dunstan Kiley."

"Ah!" said the warrior. "I have heard of him. He has great medicine. I am named Bull Elk With Locked Horns, but at Fort Benton they call me Locked Horns. Has this blackrobe come to bring us more of the white medicine?"

"The shortrobes have," said Mister Skye. "They have come to bring medicine to the Piegan and the Kainah and the Siksika."

Mister Skye remembered Father Nicolas Point, a French Jesuit colleague of Pierre de Smet. The good father had stayed for many months at Fort Lewis in 1847, teaching the Blackfeet and baptizing them. Now they supposed he was returning, or one like him, to give them the white man's medicine at last, the medicine to command thunder and heal the sick. Father Point had left at last, gloomy about his labors, for the powerful Blackfeet had shown little sign, except for the crosses they wore as totems, of abandoning their fierce ways and turning to a Christianized life.

There was much muttering among these Bull Society men, and at last Locked Horns addressed Mister Skye.

"We will take the medicine people to our village. But there is one among us who has vowed to kill you, and him we cannot control. And on this day he is very angry."

"Moon-Hides-the-Sun," said Mister Skye. "But his medicine is bad. I will give him a new name: Stolen-Horse Man. Tell him that I have said it; that his medicine is bad."

Locked Horns stared. "How did you know of the stolen horse? Was Pine Leaf of the Crow among you?"

"For a while," said Mister Skye. "Pine Leaf and Seven Scalps. But they have gone from us and are returning to their village with many horses."

"Ah! We will kill her. We will have revenge. We will steal more horses than she took! I myself will drive my lance through her!"

"You are too late."

The news shocked Locked Horns. "Is it so?" he said at last.

"It is so. She lives, but will die soon from a Kainah bullet."

"Is it known whose bullet made this great medicine?"

"It is not known."

"Maybe it was a bullet from Moon-Hides-the-Sun! Maybe his medicine is good!"

"You will know when he tests it upon me."

They rode then into the great village comprised of three bands of the Bloods, and all of the village gaped at the wagons they had heard of but never seen, and the white women they had never seen. Where the white warriors and trappers kept their women had been a great mystery among them, and some had said the whites had no women of their own. But now such women were here, two of them in the carriage and another in one of the white-topped boats of the prairies.

No Indians were handsomer, thought Mister Skye, even in the soiled clothes they wore to butcher buffalo and scrape hides and make jerky and pemmican. This village spoke of pride and power, with well-kept lodges of new cowhide, vividly painted, and signs of great industry everywhere, in ground-staked buffalo hides drying in the sun, and great racks of drying meat.

Mister Skye glanced behind to see how his missionaries were taking it; indeed, how Victoria and Mary were faring in this place of enemies. Esmerelda looked drawn, and clamped tightly to Cecil, but enduring. The Blackfeet women peered into her face curiously, cheerfully, fingering her dress and even pressing a finger to her soft fair cheeks. In the carriage Henrietta endured, more fascinated by her first encounter with the people she had come across a continent to proselytize than afraid. But Alice Sample seemed the worst off, pale and unsmiling, and no doubt finding no differences between these Blackfeet and the Assiniboin. Of the men, Cecil and Clay and Alex seemed calm enough, though young Alfred peered about in near panic. And Silas Potter, in his ragged clothing, shuffled along arrogantly, his disdain for these heathen stamped across his face and plain to every one of his hosts. Men, women, and children of the amiable Kainah stared thoughtfully at him, and said nothing.

Mister Skye resolved to watch Silas closely. There would be trouble there. The camp was on the Judith River and sheltered by abundant cottonwoods now turning gold. The buffalo, he surmised, were four or five miles west, within easy reach of hunting parties that rode out each morning to slaughter as many as they could for the meat, and hides now coming to prime. He peered sharply at these people, looking for his ancient enemy Moon-Hides-the-Sun, but did not see him at first. Not, anyway, before they pulled up before the Kainah chief and headman, who waited patiently before the chief's lodge, which was blazoned with yellow sunbursts.

The young chief, whose name meant Moose-Bellowing-in-Water, looked as taut and skeletal as a drawn bow. He had eyes that weighed a man for war, and a cast of lip that showed arrogance and cruelty. He stood measuring Skye for caskets and holes in the earth. And next to the chief stood Moon-Hides-the-Sun, he of burning eye and glowering face, a giant of bronze fully a head taller than Mister Skye, and riveted of strap iron.

"You are someone we know, Mister Skye. But we do not know these others. We are told they are white medicine people, shortrobes and the longrobe who slew the Cheyenne. Some among us favor the white medicine they learned from the longrobe Point, many winters ago. But I scorn it and trample on it. The ways of the People are sacred. Some say we will be stronger if we learn the medicine of the whites, but it is old-woman medicine that tells us to do woman's work, plowing and toiling. I will not permit it here. Tonight you will stay; tomorrow you will leave—if you are still alive. Beside me is one you know, and he has made a vow."

"I know Moon-Hides-the-Sun and I know of his vow to kill me, and I give him now a new name: Stolen-Horse Man, because his medicine is still bad," said Mister Skye.

Moon-Hides-the-Sun snarled and turned his back upon them.

"Is your medicine good, Mister Skye? I will not stop him. No Kainah will stop him from keeping his vow."

"See how he has turned his back. He is afraid. He has

become a slinking coyote because his medicine is bad and he knows he will die."

Moose-Bellows-in-Water smiled malevolently. "If you kill the great warrior, Moon-Hides-the-Sun, in the village of the Kainah, you will face others."

Chapter 28

Victoria huddled under her robes all night waiting for the Siksika dogs to kill her. She was ready, Green River knife in hand. Let the doorflap open a crack, or a knife start to saw through the lodgecover, and she would spring up like a lion.

Jawbone loitered at his usual station outside, ready to shriek his alarm, but she doubted the horse was a match for Moon-Hides-the-Sun. Mister Skye slept easily near her, his black silk hat parked to one side, and just beyond his dark hulk lay Mary and Dirk, all asleep. But Victoria knew the heart of the Siksika dogs, and the perfidies and murder in all of them, so she kept her vigil through the night. It had been different with the Assiniboin. She slept soundly through her captivity, because they were beneath contempt, not demons like these raiders of the north.

Yesterday, their chief, Moose-Bellows-in-Water, had insulted Mister Skye, refusing to smoke the peace pipe with him. Later, from within the lodge of the chief rose the snarl of angry elders and she caught enough of it to know that some among them wanted to murder Mister Skye and his whole party. Moon-Hides-the-Sun had vanished and was preparing himself to kill Mister Skye because he had made a vow. But others of the Kainah had

come to sit beside the uneasy cookfires of the evening to
talk with the white medicine men. Some of them had
been baptized by Father Point in 1847 and still wore cross-
totems around their necks as a part of their medicine
bundles.

Dawn was visible through the smokehole, though inside the lodge it remained night. Victoria uncurled from
her robe, her knife still in hand. She was not tired from
the sleepless night. Many times she had thus guarded
Mister Skye. But she was eager to be off this morning, to
escape the village of these Siksika dogs. She peered out
the doorflap, and saw nothing; only gray mist rising from
the Judith River where the frosty autumnal air breathed
over it. The Siksika dogs called this stream Otokwi Tuk-
tai, Yellow River. She stepped outside. Mary joined her,
and Dirk, still sleepy from his long night's rest. He was a
good child, quiet and happy.

Mary took the boy by the hand and led him to the river
brush for their morning ablutions. Victoria watched narrowly. There was no one else awake. The Siksika dogs
still slept, and so did the missionaries in their wagons
and tents. No sooner had Mary and Dirk gone to the
stream than Mary's shriek pierced the morning quiet.
Victoria ran. Behind her she glimpsed Mister Skye,
struggling through the lodge door. Partly concealed by
chokecherry brush was Moon-Hides-the-Sun, his powerful arm arcing down, the stone-headed war club landing
with a dull thud upon something there. Victoria raced,
frantic with fear. She rounded a bend and saw Dirk, scram-
bling into the brush, and Mary staggering backward, a
terrible gash gouting blood above her ear.

"Ayahhh," Victoria cried.

Moon-Hides-the-Sun sprang toward Mary as she began to topple, and again the bloody club smashed through

the dawn gray. But Mary cringed sideways at the last second, and the club did not find her skull. She fell heavily. He wheeled toward Dirk, smashing his war club into the brush to brain him, but the brush held, and Dirk scurried deeper. Victoria sprang at him, sliced hard with her knife, but he blocked her arm and his own war club snapped close. Then he spotted Skye and he laughed and trotted away into the awakening village, dancing among the lodges, his feet burning on the scorched earth of fear, and his head hitting the sky of his vow.

Mister Skye, dressed only in his breechclout, rumbled through the brush and beheld the carnage, paralyzed. Mary writhed on the ground, her head a mass of bright blood that was matting her sleek black hair. Alive. Victoria reached her, plunged to her knees, and cradled that wounded head in her lap, crooning, singing the chant of death. Mister Skye said nothing, his breath steady in the morning air, his powerful barrel-body gathering up a lion's strength inside. Then he sprang back to the lodge and dug through a parfleche, extracting a thing he always had with him, something he took in hand only when he went berserk.

He called it a belaying pin. It looked like a war club, but made of lathed hardwood, one end flared wider in diameter than the other. He had told her that when he rode the seas in great boats, the pin was used to anchor long ropes. He said the water warriors who rode the giant boats used belaying pins as clubs.

And truly they did, for she had seen him use one, and in his hands it was a lethal, balanced club and better even than a knife, and he could stun limbs and brain enemies with it. Now she saw him punch through the doorflap and into the dawn to begin his deadly search for the Siksika dog who had attacked his wife and son. The village was stirring. A headman had found Dirk and Mary and Victoria now, and was rushing to the chief.

Mary's spirit hovered above her, so Victoria stood, and followed her man. So too did Jawbone, his long ears laid back, his yellow eyes murderous and his teeth snapping. But Mister Skye sent him back with a harsh growl, and walked with a roll, walked as if he were upon a heaving deck of a great boat, stalking the killer. He had no weapon other than that wooden belaying pin. Moon-Hides-the-Sun had two—a glinting knife in one hand, and the bloody war club in the other. Mister Skye was a man turning gray; Moon-Hides-the-Sun was yet in his prime.

Victoria followed, ready to kill and be killed, but Mister Skye didn't see her. He saw only the retreating, prancing figure of the murderer ahead. Moon-Hides-the-Sun never stood to fight, but always slid away, dancing around lodges, bursting through knots of spectators, edging past the headmen and finally past the chief himself, who stared.

"Your medicine is bad, your medicine is bad, Stolen-Horse Man," said Mister Skye softly, so softly that the hush of his voice was deceptive. Still did Moon-Hides-the-Sun edge backward, avoiding the trap of the creek but slipping out now upon the meadows near camp, with a swirl of Blackfeet, still wrapped in the night's blankets and robes, trailing after him. The warrior was edging toward the horses. He would dash for them and run away, and Victoria understood it perfectly. His medicine was bad. Moon-Hides-the-Sun knew he would die unless he escaped.

But he hadn't reckoned with his chief. This was a shameful thing, this wild dancing retreat. Had any Siksika, had any Kainah, ever brought such shame to a village? Victoria watched rage build in the chief as he beheld the flight of Moon-Hides-the-Sun. Mister Skye had calmly cut off his retreat to the horses, and now the bad-medicine warrior pranced backward once again, and the whole village was ashamed. Squaws wailed and pulled at their hair. Never had they witnessed such a thing. Bad medicine. Worse medicine than the Kainah had ever known. Neither had Victoria seen such bad medicine, so shameful a thing as this. The giant warrior was no longer a man, but a caged thing caught between a vow and bad medicine.

Angrily Moose-Bellows-in-Water snarled a command, and jammed his own lance into the soft earth, where it shivered from the blow. The Kainah warriors came running, lances in hand, forming an arc behind Moon-Hides-the-Sun until he could no longer retreat without impaling himself on a Kainah lance. Other warriors, including the angry chief, raised their lances to complete the circle of murderous points surrounding Mister Skye and Moon-Hides-the-Sun. Jawbone shrieked, but Mister Skye growled at the animal. Some feral flame lit the chief's face, and his lance throbbed in his hands.

And so the pair danced alone in the death-ring.

"Your medicine is bad," muttered Mister Skye, still stalking forward with a strange rolling gait as if the earth were heaving under him, the hickory club poised easily in his right hand.

Moon-Hides-the-Sun stopped retreating and suddenly bulled ahead, feinting with his glittering knife while smashing his war club into the space where Mister Skye would be.

But Skye parried. The knife struck hardwood with a crack and the stone war club whipped air.

He kicked as it arced past, and the blow collapsed the warrior's leg momentarily. The belaying pin smashed brutally across the warrior's elbow, sending a streak of pain through his arm, and the stone war club sailed free of his spasming hand.

The warrior ripped upward with the knife, just nicking Mister Skye's thigh, leaving a line of red.

"Ayahh," cried spectators.

Jawbone shrieked.

Now the warrior thrust and jabbed, spun and sliced upward, mincing from side to side. Mister Skye didn't dance. He stood quietly on the balls of his feet, his eye on the knife, the belaying pin parrying and blocking, the wide girth of its top protecting his hand from the whipping blade. The blade hit wood with clicks that rattled like grapeshot.

"Medicine is bad," muttered Mister Skye. He let the blade glide past him and whipped his bare foot brutally into the warrior's gut. As the warrior doubled up the belaying pin, propelled by biceps of spring steel, caved in his skull. Moon-Hides-the-Sun was dead before he hit the grass.

Victoria peered around her wildly, ready to kill the first Siksika dog that raised a lance. But the chief had lowered his, discovering something in Mister Skye's berserk eyes that terrified him, and the warriors lowered theirs. Beside her she discovered Esmerelda sobbing, and Cecil Rathbone clutching her. Across the ring of warriors stood Silas, wild-eyed and scornful.

"You have committed murder, Mister Skye," he shrilled. "The devil will have you."

Mister Skye was not winded, though Victoria thought she could hardly find enough breath. He peered silently at Silas, and then at the chief, and walked slowly toward the chokecherry brush where his family lay. Victoria followed him, and so did the others, in utter silence.

The boy had crawled from the brush and was hugging his mother, who lay inert, flies gathering in the matted mess of blood and hair. Mary stared up at Skye, her eyes open, and Victoria supposed she was dead, too. But she was not.

"Take me to our lodge, Skye," she whispered.

He lifted her gently, carried her as lightly as he might a bird with an injured wing. And he wept. Slowly he walked to his small lodge, his wet eyes peering first at the chief, and then one by one at the others of this Kainah village. He laid her on the tawny grass before the lodge, and Victoria hastened inside for a buffalo robe and her kit of herbs and medicines, and began at once to wipe blood and hair away from gouged white bone. Mary's skull was not broken; only the surface flesh had been lacerated by the glancing blow. She slipped into a muttering delirium again, but Victoria knew she would recover unless she got the brain fever. Mister Skye took his son's hand in his big one and led Dirk to her. He sat solemnly beside his mother, contemplating the blood.

For the rest of that morning Mister Skye sat cross-legged before his lodge, with Mary's head in his lap. He did not move until her breathing became normal, and she peered up at him with unfocused eyes.

The drums thumped at about the pace of a heartbeat, their fleshed hide membranes drawn taut over the wooden barrels and vibrating to the soft rhythmic strokes of the four drummers and singers who beat them. The thumping was not loud, but it penetrated, and it seemed to pluck at Victoria's own heart and govern its pace. The Siksika dogs were holding their sacred buffalo dance, giving honor to their father Sun for the good hunt. It was a fine afternoon under an azure sky. Later there would be a feast of hump roast and tongue, along with all the delicacies, such as buffalo brains, raw liver, soft nose gristle, and bone marrow.

They had been in the village two days, more or less prisoners, although none of the Kainah had attempted to disarm Mister Skye. While the great hunt continued and the men rode out each morning to the buffalo herd and the women butchered meat and fleshed hides, the chief and his shamans debated the fate of the white medicine men, and Mister Skye. There were those, the chief included, who wanted to torture and kill them all and show the whole village once and for all that the medicine of the whites was false and weak and contemptible. But there were others who feared Mister Skye and Jawbone, and who argued that the traders at the fur posts might retaliate, and the annuity goods coming from the Grandfathers in Washington might not be given them. In the chief's council were none who welcomed the white medicine or thought it would benefit the people.

Mister Skye was in no hurry to leave. Mary remained too weak to be moved. The slightest movement of her head set her to groaning. A bouncing wagon bed would be torture for her. Each day the chief had painted his cheeks with vermilion slashes, blood-red insignia of war, and had thrust eagle feathers into his hair, and had paraded past the missionary party, his embered eyes boring into them all. The missionaries had met his evil with good, offering small presents and smiles. How strange these missionaries were, soft as the breast of a dove, smiling at the one who would slaughter them. Victoria spat. Sonofabitch, she thought, how evil it was to be caught in this camp of Siksika dogs. Not even Mister Skye felt at ease among these people he called Bug's Boys, and he never stirred about without his Colt at his hip and his Sharps in his arms.

Some few who had been instructed by the Jesuit Father Point in 1847 had come to talk with the missionaries as much as language barriers permitted. Especially, they came to see Father Kiley, and touch him, and hear the Mass he finally offered when they pressed him to. But they were few, a handful in a village that clung to the old tradition of the Siksika.

Now she watched the impressive buffalo dance, beside Mister Skye and Dirk. The throb of drums was too much for Mary, and she slept in the lodge. On the other side of her sat the white missionaries, even Father Kiley, except for the strange one, Silas Potter, who roamed fiercely among the spectators, unkempt and in rags. The young scholar stormed toward Cecil.

"They are performing a pagan rite. You are watching a heathen religion. The worship of idols. Have you no loyalty? Will you continue to betray God?"

"Silas, Silas, lad, to watch something is not to participate in it," Cecil said mildly. "And they are going to do it anyway. Sit and learn. What you learn of their religion will help you teach them about the true one. Have a seat, friend. This is a thing to enjoy."

"Satan stalks the earth; demons dance here," Silas cried.

Cecil nodded. The sacred dance was throbbing before them. Virtually every boy and warrior in this long riverside village was circling the Buffalo Woman at the center. Each of them carried a ceremonial quiver, beaded and fringed, and a strung bow, and at certain climactic beats, they all loosed imaginary arrows at Buffalo Woman, who trotted her own small circle in the middle of the seething ring of hunters. Each hunter in turn stopped and proclaimed his successes, the cows and bulls he had killed, the gifts of meat and hide he had made to the poor and widowed of the village. It was a merry celebration for the hunt had been good and all the lodges were fat with comforts.

Victoria envied the Buffalo Woman, for she had won a great honor. Like the medicine woman who was chosen each year to conduct the sun dance of midsummer, the Buffalo Woman had to be a woman of impeccable virtue, esteemed by the whole tribe for her faultless conduct, and the gifts she bestowed on others. This one was a beautiful young matron with glossy black braids, wearing a dress of soft white doeskin and bone necklaces. Her face and shoulders were invisible, covered with an albino buffalo head, so that the Buffalo Woman seemed almost a living thing, staggering with each flight of imaginary arrows.

Thus they celebrated and thanked Sun for the bounty, with a nasal chant that rattled the windows of Silas Potter's soul. Restlessly he stalked around the dancers, at one point raising his Bible over his head, and stretching his arms toward heaven. He looked shabby and distraught, his pale flesh hard-blistered by outdoor life. Then with a violent cry, he forged his way through the line of dancers, walked slowly toward Buffalo Woman, stood before her as she danced her small circle, and seemed to gather his breath.

"In the name of God, I command you to stop!" he cried.

The spectators, curious now, stood up and watched breathlessly, half amused, half appalled by this sacrilege. But nothing happened. The dance continued, after a fashion, the drummers softly drumming and chanting, and the dancers watching the crazy one in their midst. And then Silas whirled, smashed into Buffalo Woman, and knocked the sacred albino buffalo head, used only in Sun ceremonies, to the earth. She reeled and fell.

"You are worshiping the golden calf," he cried. "I proclaim unto you the day of the Lord!"

With that he kicked the sacred albino head violently, breaking a horn, and again, mashing a nose. Buffalo Woman scrambled to her feet and fled.

Victoria clasped a hand to her mouth. She had never seen such a thing, such a sacrilege. Even if these were despicable Kainah dogs, she felt offended by Silas Potter's insult.

They grabbed him, the warriors of the Raven Carriers Society, whose dance this was, and pinioned him. Cecil leapt up, but Mister Skye dragged him down.

"If you so much as move a muscle, you'll die, mate," he whispered.

Victoria clutched her Green River knife, and peered narrowly about her, ready to kill and to die.

They dragged the shouting Silas before Chief Moose-Bellows-in-Water. He stood slowly, a cruel curl to his lips.

"Repent," screamed Silas. "Demons, you worship demons. I proclaim the Gospel of the Lord. Repent and listen!"

The chief waved a hand, and an iron arm clamped across Silas's mouth. He bit it. The Kainah chief growled things to the Raven Carriers, and they dragged Silas back to the place where Buffalo Woman had woven her graceful steps. Here they tied his arms behind his back with a thong, and here they lowered the sacred albino buffalo head over Silas. And then the dance resumed.

The drummers again began their heartbeat rhythm, and the hunters again praised Sun and sent volleys of imaginary arrows into Buffalo Man. Then the drums quickened, and along with the pulse, so did hearts, and along with hearts, feet and legs of the dancers, whirling wildly, madder and madder, pulsing and throbbing . . .

Then silence. It became a terrible silence, loud with heartbeats, stretching beyond the horizon, longer than any silence Victoria had ever known. Then, magically in unison, each hunter reached into his quiver and withdrew an arrow. Every arrow in that great flight of arrows went true. None missed, to sail past Buffalo Man and into the Kainah on the other side of the circle. Most of the hundred arrows pierced clear through Buffalo Man, riddling his chest and abdomen like the quills of a porcupine.

And still Silas stood, not falling and not falling.

"I proclaim the day of the Lord!" he cried, and fell. The albino head cracked as it landed, and rolled away.

"Oh God, oh God," sobbed Esmerelda.

"Not you, Silas!" muttered Clay.

Alice Sample sobbed wildly, coughing and trembling.

Alex stood abruptly, gaping at the twitching corpse, and Mister Skye yanked him down. "But he—but he—but he came to serve God and Man," gasped Alex.

"Tell me!" cried Father Kiley. "For God's sake, have they killed him?"

"Murder," muttered Cecil.

"I had such hope that he . . . he'd settle down when we got here. We loved him, loved him . . ." wept Esmerelda.

Across the circle Moose-Bellows-in-Water licked his lips.

"Silas, my Silas," Cecil muttered. "Were you a prophet and a martyr, or were you mad?"

Chapter 29

Five chill days later they reached the wide Missouri at a place where it ran north and south between dun prairie bluffs. That morning they had steered their tired wagons down a shallow coulee, and by noon they were in the Missouri bottoms. They stared silently at the throbbing river and its clear mountain-fresh water, and knew they had one last ordeal.

They had toiled through these last days in deep silence, doing what had to be done but living inside of themselves. Mary lay in the wagon she shared with Father Kiley and the little organ, improving steadily but not yet able to sit up for long because the concussion made her dizzy.

The party had acquired a new member, Weasel Nose, a slim cheerful youth of about twenty winters, who had asked to come with them and learn the ways of the whites from them. Cecil was glad to have him, and set about at once learning the Blackfeet tongue from him, while giving him English words.

The very afternoon that Silas Potter had died with a hundred or so Kainah arrows piercing him, the village packed up and fled that bad-medicine place, its shamans deathly afraid of what sort of white man's medicine might befall them all.

They buried Silas where he fell in that meadow beside the Judith, and Cecil scarcely knew what to say over his shallow grave. He brushed off his worn black broadcloth suit and put it on. He'd lost so much weight on this continental voyage that it no longer fit. And he picked up the worn Bible, bound in fine-grained pigskin, and talked about love, perhaps because love was the thing Silas Potter never found in this life, and the thing, Cecil believed, he had found now in the other. Father Kiley stood beside Cecil in his long black cassock, saying nothing but sharing wholly in the bereavement and farewell.

"Oh, how we'll miss the boy," said Esmerelda afterward. "He wanted love. Just a few more miles, and he'd have reached our place, our mission. And then he would have been all right. Then he would have remembered love, divine and human." Her sorrow was shared by them all, and seemed somehow fitting.

Then they drove the wagons four or five miles in utter silence before the darkness came, through a heavily grazed swath where the buffalo had been and where wolves still prowled.

Cecil felt grateful for Weasel Nose's company. All the others had turned into themselves. The Kainah youth bestowed names upon the features of the land. What Mister Skye called the Belt Mountains, Weasel Nose called Mapsi Istuk. What Skye knew as the Highwoods, looming to the north, the boy called Sitosis Tuksi. The boy was the gift of God, and Cecil dreamed of the day when he could deliver a simple sermon in the tongue of the Blackfeet.

Now, on the bank of the Missouri, Mister Skye was uncertain.

"Sun River flows in here somewhere above the falls, but I don't reckon just where, Cecil," he said.

"Weasel Nose might know," Cecil said. "If we can get him to understand what we're looking for."

Mister Skye's fingers and hands flew in the language of the signs, and eventually the youth nodded. "Kaksistukskwi Ituktai," he said, pointing north. His hands said Point-of-Rocks River.

They crossed the river right there, for want of a better place. The autumnal stream ran languidly between gravelly beaches. The unburdened wagons were floated across, pulled by weary yokes and spans of oxen and mules. What few goods that water might harm were slung under the bows, while the tools were simply permitted to get wet. The waters leaking into the boxes rose several inches into the organ, and Henrietta fretted about the bellows, but there was no damage.

On the far side they toiled up a coulee and out upon a great benchland of tawny frostbitten prairie. An hour later they peered into a wide, shallow scoop in the prairie, with a goodly blue stream coiling in loose bows in its bottom.

"Sun River," said Mister Skye gently, from his seat on Jawbone.

They were perhaps two miles above its confluence with the Missouri, gazing into a gentle valley that stretched westward across a vast flat land, vanishing into a country of buttes to the southwest, and the low blue wall of the Rockies far off upon the sunset horizon. It seemed a barren place, with only a few cottonwoods in the bottoms, their leaves blazing golden now, to soften the tawny expanse and the endless emptiness of this land.

Cecil stood on the lip of the benchland and stared. To this place they had toiled over fifteen hundred miles, from far Independence, in their wagons, on foot, or riding their horses and mules. Esmerelda drew close to him and slipped her arm into his, and squeezed it gently. A few feet off, Alex and Henrietta Newton, she big with child now, peered into the valley. And beyond them the Samples, Clay, Alice, Alfred and . . .

It was late in the October afternoon, and the long sun lay golden upon the brown grasslands, making an unearthly light that seemed to pluck up buttes and ridges a hundred miles distant and make them blaze. It was a limitless land, somehow more vast even than the endless slopes of Nebraska. It was a strange, mystical land, a place of dreams and dreamers.

"So few trees," whispered Esmerelda.

"But endless sun, and a big sky," said Cecil.

"We will make it home," she said, "and build a home for God."

"Was it worth it?"

"I don't count my trials," she replied. "But I ache for the Samples. And I try hard to remember Silas, who came with us so far. We have our work cut out. We endured whatever was set in our path, but that's the past, and there is only the future and our mission. Cecil, we're the torch-carriers, bringing Light to the people we've come to bless. Now we'll begin."

Cecil smiled.

"It's so—desolate," said Henrietta with an edge in her voice. "You mean to say that we came all that way, walked all that way—for this?"

"Cecil, I'm not sure this is much of a place. We were misled. Let's think about this, eh?" Alex said cautiously. There was disappointment lancing his words.

"Surely you didn't expect homes and gardens and a church and a parsonage, Alex."

"I didn't expect there to be—nothing!"

"We'll build. Tomorrow we'll find a site and conse-crate it. Alex, nothing of value was ever built without a cornerstone."

"I'm not a mason or a carpenter," Alex muttered. "And I hope that dear Henrietta may have some comforts."

"Tomorrow we'll begin," Cecil said.

In the morning they unloaded the organ and set it under canvas in a sweetgrass meadow near a band of cotton-woods. Cecil saddled up the mare and plunged along the river clear to its junction with the Missouri, splashed across and plunged up the other side, all the while dismounting and poking and prodding the land and soil and rock like a child. Then at last he made up his mind.

"Here," he muttered. "Here's rock and wood and good soil and river water. We can dig a shallow well too, in this bottom land. Look at this soil! Not black, but soft and rich, with good grass. We'll put the church here. The school over there. Build some houses along this way to have the view and stay out of the wind."

They watched him amazed, tagging along, sensing their fate and comfort in his hands as he circled the land like a horse getting ready to roll, muttering, crying to himself, kicking dirt, peering at highwater marks on Sun River.

"Here's the rock!" he cried. "Alex, fetch Mister Skye so we can move it!"

Men and horses dragged the speckled boulder to a gentle rise, and planted it in soft earth there, in a sunlit place that gave a noble view. Cecil stalked around an oblong, driving stakes into corners. "Now gather around!" he cried, some wild delight in his features.

They consecrated the mission there, blessed the cornerstone, remembered those who had fallen or vanished along the way. Alice Sample cried. They sang a hymn while Henrietta played her organ. Cecil's voice sailed sonorously into the wild that was already his home, blessing the land here and the church and all that it might accomplish. It wasn't long, a half hour, and they were done.

Father Kiley stood to one side quietly, and when all was done and this place consecrated, he blessed it.

All that took a day, and early the next morning, after tearful goodbyes, Mister Skye and his family, Esmerelda,

Alice and Henrietta, and Father Kiley left for Fort Benton, taking two yoke of weary oxen and the nearly empty wagon. Even as the wagon drew away, they could see their husbands and friends sharpen axes and swing them into the cottonwoods in the deepening distances. The women wept and talked of turning back and enduring the cold and hardship with their men. But they didn't. Instead they tended Mary, who lay in the wagon still sick and weak from her concussion, and ministered to Father Kiley, who now rode horse in blind ease beside Mister Skye each day. They steered well north of the Missouri to avoid the giant coulees and claws of rock that sliced down into the river bottoms. The nights grew bitter, and stars were chips of ice.

Fifty miles and three days later they skidded the wagon, with locked wheels, down a steep grade and into the outpost, dominated by the log and adobe fort built by American Fur in 1847 and rebuilt nearby later. It had first been called Fort Lewis, but renamed Fort Benton, after the Missouri senator and patron of the expanding west, Thomas Hart Benton. In a great sprawl around the fort lay rude cabins of married engagés, as well as the smoking lodges of assorted Blackfeet and other tribes. The crude village lay hard upon the Missouri, backed by a towering yellow bluff that protected it from north winds.

"We are at Benton," said Father Kiley.

"We are, Father."

"And you're wondering what to do with me."

"It passed my mind."

"I can draw upon the credit of the Society of Jesus to some extent. I will need to be taken down the river."

"There might be a mackinaw or two going, Father. That'd mean sitting in an open flatboat loaded with buffalo hides and freezing. If you'd like my advice, I'd say get to Fort Union before hard winter if anyone's going and will take you—that's fancy civilization compared to here—and winter there. Catch the fur company steamer down the river next summer."

"That's a long time," said Father Kiley desolately.

The place throbbed with riffraff in buckskins and bright calicos, a motley throng from many plains tribes, Cree and Blackfoot and Assiniboin. There were breeds and whites. There were French trappers who had penetrated here long before other whites. One or two escaped slaves caught his eye, along with two or three pink-cheeked easterners looking utterly out of place. They in turn stared at the wagon and the women. They'd never seen a wagon this far west, and the women inspired smiles, curiosity, and lust held in abeyance by Mister Skye's murderous gaze and reputation.

He stopped at the narrow portals of the fort, beneath its looming adobe brick walls and the slit-windowed corner blockhouse that covered the riverside entrance, and left Jawbone and Victoria to protect the women and Father Kiley.

"Skye!" rasped the bourgeois Alec Culbertson, "I heerd you was in these parts. Have a toddy."

Mister Skye gazed wistfully at the jug and its amber paradise and shook his head. "In a bit," he said. "I've got deliveries to make."

In a half hour it was settled. There were quarters within the fort suitable for the missionary women, and Culbertson and American Fur would delight in their company through the hard winter, and sell supplies to the men when they came in for them. There would be no doctor for Henrietta's delivery, but some fine Piegan midwives.

"I heer ye got Kiley with ye," Culbertson said when the other was settled.

"You hear a lot, mate. Maybe you've heard something else. A white girl, eleven or twelve, taken prisoner by Cut Nose and his Assiniboin."

"Nay, nary a thing, You lost her?"

"She was with us, got took berrying. She and Victoria and the parson's wife, Esmerelda. We got the rest back but they hid her. We never got a peek, and I can't say for sure she's alive. But that band, Cut Nose . . ."

Culbertson whistled. "That's no place for a little miss. Hope to God she's alive. Hope to God she's dead."

Mister Skye nodded. Alec Culbertson understood the realities.

"I've got a man riding to Fort Union today. I'll send the details along with him, and maybe they can trade her back. Maybe. It's happened. But never with Cut Nose."

"Never with Cut Nose," said Skye.

He told Culbertson everything he knew, described Miriam as best he could, while the bourgeois scratched it all down, dipping a quill pen into lampblack ink furiously.

"It'll go with the dispatch," Culbertson said. "Wish I could promise more. How are the parents taking it?"

"Mrs. Sample bore five or six children. They have one left."

Culbertson whistled, and shook his head.

"More grief than a man and woman can endure," Mister Skye added. "But maybe you'll hear. Word filters in here."

"The Injuns are the biggest gossips I ever run across," said the bourgeois. "I got a couple of surprises for Kiley stashed away here, a pair of lady penguins," he said. "Go git the porkeater."

Mister Skye glared. "He's blinded. If you hurt that man or pain his spirit, I'll wring your bloody neck."

The bourgeois grinned.

Mister Skye wheeled out of the rough log room, and the trader bolted up from his copperplate records and quill pens, and began barking something at his engagés.

Mister Skye found the priest waiting patiently on the wagon seat. "Culbertson wants to see you, mate. Says he's got something for you."

"I remember him well."

Skye led the Jesuit gently into the central yard. Off to the left the door of the windowless warehouse yawned, and the smell of dusty dry hides burdened the air. He guided the priest around some manure, and past a water trough and hitchrails. The bourgeois's quarters lay on the north side. To the east were the quarters of the engagés, and to the west, the kitchens, where rich smells emanated into the yard. On the remaining side were corrals and stables.

Inside Culbertson's chaotic rabbit warren stood the bulge-bellied factor himself, and two nuns, white and black, white and black, in a room made of leather and log and bare earth.

It startled Mister Skye to see nuns, immaculately cowled, here a thousand miles and more from anything resembling settled community. They must have come by fur company boat as far as Fort Union, and trailed the rest of the way here somehow.

"Dunstan Kiley," roared Culbertson. "You old varmint. I heerd you wiped out a passel of Cheyenne by wavin' your wand."

The priest went rigid.

"Arrgh, I got a leetle surprise for your old Jesuit hide."

A nervous sister tittered.

"Over hyar I got a pair of genuine, bottled and bonded Ursuline sisters."

Father Kiley peered where he could not see.

"I am Sister Monica, Father," said one of the women.

"And I'm Sister Jude," said the shorter one.

Something like a grin lifted the corners of Kiley's mouth. "Mister Culbertson," he said tartly. "Now that's a fine prank to play on a blind man. These ladies—these ladies are . . ."

"With your permission, Father," said Sister Monica. She took his hand in hers and led it to her face, and placed a finger on her white cowl.

"Here is the cowl across my forehead. Trace it with your finger. Follow it, like this, down the sides of my face. And touch my black cape. And now I will hand you my crucifix. We are Ursulines."

Father Kiley sobbed. There were no tears for the ducts had been burned from his head, but he sobbed.

"You are Godsent," said Sister Monica. "We have been sent by the order to see where schools and sisters and the Church are most needed. This is a place where the need is very great. Many of the French are here, and have received no sacraments, and are in great need of baptism and marriage and reconciliation."

Father Kiley was beyond speech.

"We have found a small log building that used to be a trading post upstream for a school and church. And beside it, a place for ourselves and the other Ursulines who will come. But we have no priest. I . . . I cannot tell you how valuable you are to us, how much everything we have started depends on you. I pray God the Society of Jesus will consent."

For minutes Father Kiley said nothing, his sanctified hands clasped by those of the two women. He sucked air into famished lungs. Then a change came upon him, and he stood upright, no longer stooped. The others stood transfixed.

"Mister Skye," he said softly. "I was dead and am alive, lost and now found. I was proud—I roamed the wild lands knowing how to survive in them, make meat, live free, needing no one, as independent as any of you men of the mountains. Now I am humbled. I am dependent on others for every mouthful of food I eat, for shelter. I must be led wherever I go. I cannot even—even—I cannot even take care of my bodily needs without help. And now, in my . . . humbling, I depend on God. On his church. On these religious . . . And that's not all, Mister Skye. I have always loved the thing Saint Paul wrote, that God can make all things work for the good. Even blindness, sir. Other priests might come here from duty, but I will be here from love, and a loving priest can tend his flock better than one who is only obedient."

"I won't forget you, Father," said Mister Skye. "And we'll remember Miriam."

Something like a grin lifted Kiley's face. "Sister Jude and Sister Monica. Find me a place where we may sing the Te Deum."

Later, Mister Skye clasped the priest's hands in his own and made his rough goodbye. He settled the missionary women in their quarters, and arranged for the pasturage of the oxen and storage of the wagon. At the last he shook hands with Henrietta and Alice, but Esmerelda hugged him fiercely and wept.

He found his women in the lodge, which they had set up on the west edge of the settlement. Victoria had gotten Mary nestled down in her robes. It would be days before she could travel horseback again, but he had things to do. He held her hand. She smiled and he kissed her softly.

He hugged Dirk. He turned Jawbone out upon the short grasses. The horses and mules all needed rest.

He counted his last bit of gold. There would be enough for a little powder and ball, some four-point blankets for Mary and Victoria to sew into winter capotes, a trinket for Dirk, and a good earthen jug of Fort Benton lightning.

Victoria eyed him narrowly, and muttered, but Mister Skye, with a certain gleam in his eye and a fine, building dryness of throat, rolled toward the fort.

Author's Note

Pine Leaf was a real Crow warrior woman whose prowess in battle was legendary. She was probably killed by the Gros Ventre in 1854, but I have exercised the novelist's prerogative and have extended her life a year. There is no evidence that she had the medicine powers I have given her here.

The Blackfeet buffalo dance described near the end of the book is an invention. Most plains tribes did have buffalo dances, but these were more commonly performed before the hunt rather than after it. The Blackfeet did, however, take pains to thank their most important deity, Sun, for buffalo and successful hunts.

The Reverend Pierre de Smet, S.J., proselytized the Blackfeet in the 1840s, and in the fall of 1846 held a Mass in a Piegan camp where more than two thousand lodges of Piegans, Bloods, Northern Blackfeet, and Gros Ventres had assembled, along with such Blackfeet enemies as Flatheads and Nez Perces. In the 1850s Father Albert Lacombe founded his famed mission Lac Ste. Anne and ministered to the Blackfeet. Later, when the Blackfeet Reservation was turned over to the Methodists by the government, Catholics were excluded from it. The nuns in my story were in Fort Benton well before nuns arrived in the territory that became Montana.

The Presbyterians were the first Protestants to proselytize the Blackfeet. In 1856 the Rev. Elkanah Mackey and his wife Sarah Armstrong Mackey arrived in Fort Benton, but didn't stay long. Mrs. Mackey was the first white woman to arrive at Fort Benton, and the first seen by the Blackfeet.

In 1857, the government complied with its 1855 treaty with the Blackfeet to establish a model farm at Sun River, along the lines advocated by Cecil Rathbone in this story. It failed. The Blackfeet were not interested in abandoning their nomadic buffalo and war-oriented life, and it became yet another of the noble experiments that had to be abandoned.

The presence of the Bloods, a northern Blackfeet tribe, on the Judith River around October 1855 is historical. A large portion of the Blackfeet nation gathered at the mouth of the Judith to ratify a peace treaty and receive annuity goods in October of that year.

Thus *Sun River* borrows from history, even though it is pure fiction.

My profound thanks to Dale L. Walker for sharing his vast fund of knowledge about the nineteenth century British navy. And to W. Michael Gear and Kathleen O'Neal Gear for sharing their encyclopedic knowledge of the Northwest and tribal culture. When I sought help from these friends, I received it abundantly.

Bannack

For Sue Hart

Chapter 1

Mister Skye lifted the new Henry, peered down the blued octagon barrel until the blade sight lined on the dusty glass eye of a royal elk, and squeezed the trigger. He was rewarded with a smooth hard click. Then he leveled the rifle at the low furry brow of the erect grizzly, with the late Mrs. Bullock's beflowered straw hat upon it, and squeezed again. Nothing happened. He had forgotten to lever the Henry. He levered it and aimed again and squeezed, and felt again the satisfying click. He loosed a fusillade at the grizzly, and deemed that he had stopped it in its tracks. Next he focused on the color lithograph of the Last Supper on the whitewashed plank wall behind Bullock's desk and he thought for a moment to dry-fire at Judas, who was holding the bag of silver, but he decided against it. Mister Skye was a reverent man.

Skye groaned, full of covet. "I'll take it, Bullock," he growled. His voice boomed too large for buildings, and anything he said rumbled through the gloomy cavern of the Fort Laramie sutler's store, cut down and measured.

Colonel Bullock sighed. He fidgeted beside his desk, florid-faced, white-haired, in a gray swallowtail coat. "Ah'm sorry, suh, but Ah can't sell it to you. You're over two hundred in arrears on your accounts, Mistuh Skye."

"Hold it for me, then!"

"Ah can't do that, either. I've a dozen officers on the post salivating, Mister Skye. This is the first one I've laid hands on. Only fifteen hundred made last year, and all snapped up by the army back in the states. This was made in January sixty-three, and just came in with the freight. Ah'm truly sorry, Mister Skye."

The post sutler, a retired Southern colonel, had chosen the North in the current conflict, knowing exactly where his hominy grits were buttered.

Again Skye groaned. The lever-action repeater held enough shining brass cartridges in its magazine to hold off a whole war party of Bug's Boys. And now some shavetail from West Point with a pocketful of gold would snatch it.

"I need it worse," Mister Skye argued. "Out there by myself, much worse than your soldier boys, mate. Stash it away and I'll find the plunder somehow."

The courtly sutler shook his head. "Ah wish I could. Ah'll hold it for an hour or two, but Ah can't hang on—"

Commotion erupted out on the parade. Another wagon train arriving, Mister Skye thought. And in moments, a horde of westering pilgrims would flood in, men in homespun shirts, square-toed boots, and baggy britches; women in ginghams and bonnets, looking to trade, buy, sell. This was the place for it, he thought. Bullock's cavernous emporium sheltered whole rolls of canvas and barrels of pickles and wagon ironwork and axes and coiled hemp rope and burlap sacks of green coffee beans, cotton bags of flour and sugar, and whole shelves of airtights.

A man as burly as Skye burst through the open front door, peered around in the brown gloom, and finally spotted Colonel Bullock and Mister Skye.

"Where's the commander?" he shouted. "I'm Porter, Jarvis Porter, captain of this train, and I've a military matter to put to him."

"Suh? At headquarters, suh," Bullock replied.

"You some damned Southerner? What are you doing in a Union fort?"

Colonel Bullock drew himself up quietly. "My loyalty is beyond your consideration," he said. "The fort is barely garrisoned, suh. The rest are out patrolling the Oregon Trail for the safety of parties such as yours. There's only a lieutenant here at the moment. The colonel is up at the Platte River Bridge. Perhaps, suh, you could state the nature of your . . . business?"

Porter oozed choler. He glared darkly at Bullock, and then at Mister Skye, staring at Skye's shoulder-length gray hair, black silk stovepipe hat screwed rakishly on his head, and fringed buckskins, elaborately quilled and beaded. He looked pained.

"You're not the army, but maybe you'll steer me. I've captained a large train this far, some for Oregon, some for Idaho. Decent salt-of-the-earth people, upright farmers and their families, God-fearing. Some of them desperate and miserable war refugees. Well, gents, just before we left from Independence, three more wagons attached themselves to our party. One was a couple named Riddle chaperoning some women, mail-order brides, bound for the Grasshopper diggings. Mean-tempered and too slow, not able to keep up, and troublemakers. I don't mind them so much, but the others . . . the others! The whole lot should be hanged from the nearest cottonwood."

"That what you want the army for, Porter? Enforce your discipline on the wagon train? Won't work, suh. The army never interferes in civilian conflicts unless there's— mayhem."

Porter glared, outraged. "One wagon is owned by a woman named Goldtooth, and she has with her several, ah, ladies, ah, whores, sir. She has whores of the lowest sort. The other wagon is also owned by this—this—this Goldtooth slattern. In it are a gambler with the stinking audacity to call himself Cornelius Vanderbilt, a man who would steal his grandmother's wedding ring. Not only that, but a black banjo singer—who corrupts my sons with scandalous music—and worse, a giant Chinese, seven feet tall, they call Seven-Story Chang. It wouldn't be so bad if they minded themselves, but these lowlifes set up shop—do business, to put it bluntly—on the trail, causing havoc in decent families. The tinhorn gambler has fleeced everyone in sight. And the women, the slatterns, have—deflowered my boys and offended my Stella.

"We've tried to rid ourselves of them. We've threatened death if they continue to attach themselves. We've—we've attempted . . . but that heathen Chinese is like a demon. And so we want the army, we want the army to detain them. Stop them. Throw the whole unsavory lot into your stockade. Stop them from preying on decent people."

"Are they with the train now, suh?"

"A mile behind. I've ordered my people to shoot, shoot their stock, their mules, if they get any closer."

"Should be rolling in about now, then," said Mister Skye. "I think I'll have me a look. Give me two hours, Colonel. Don't sell that Henry just yet."

The faintest smile peeked through the sutler's white beard. "Mistuh Porter, suh, you can tell it to the lieutenant, Bates is his name, over yonder down the row there, where the colors are flying. Go tell him your woe, suh, and let me know what the army says."

"I'll do that," snapped Porter. "But we're not leaving here with those lowlifes. We'll shoot them if there's no other justice out here. I'm not just talking; I mean it."

He stormed out, pushing through a crowd of people examining the sutler's wares and hoping to strike bargains.

Colonel Bullock slid out from behind his rolltop desk. His office squatted in a corner separated from the store by a banister. A flood of customers demanded attention, far more than his two sallow clerks could handle. "Excuse me, Mister Skye," he said.

"Why, if it isn't dear old Colonel Bullock!" exclaimed a sweet female voice.

The lady accosting him was brown-haired and doe-eyed and full-figured, and wearing a skimpy summer dimity with a scoop neck that revealed the tops of her lush golden breasts. When she smiled, a gold tooth caught the light from Bullock's window.

"Imagine finding you here," she said brightly. "It's a long way from Memphis!"

Mister Skye was grinning.

"I don't believe I know you, ah, madam."

"Of course you don't, honey. I was Ella Lou Jones then. Now they call me Goldtooth."

The colonel reddened and appeared flustered. "Ah don't believe—ah, how shall I address you . . . Miss? Mrs.?"

"Call me Honey."

The colonel nodded slightly.

"I'm havin' a little trouble, sweetie, and I'm a-lookin' for some help. This little old wagon train just won't let some working girls go along. The wagon master wears cast-iron pants. We're a-goin' to Bannack City, Grasshopper Creek, to do a little business, and we're having the hardest time. The wagon master just won't have us along and we have no protection."

Colonel Bullock had turned crimson, much to Mister Skye's delight. He'd never seen the colonel hued in any color other than sallow indoors-white.

"If you'll excuse me, ah, madam, I've customers waiting. Good day."

He fled toward a knot of calicoed women standing at the footwear shelves.

"He doesn't remember me," she said to Mister Skye. "He used to be our neighbor in Memphis. We lived—my parents lived—up on the Chickasaw heights. That was before I went into business on Beale Street."

"The wagon master, Porter, was just here spilling woe," said Mister Skye.

"Woe and fire and brimstone. I don't know how we'll get to the Grasshopper diggings without the protection of a wagon train," she said. Then her eyes focused at last on the burly barrel of a frontiersman before her. "Hey, aren't you something. Do you live out here? Those quilled buckskins! All you'd need to be an Injun is a warbonnet instead of that stovepipe hat. How come you wear that?"

"To remind myself and others that I'm mister. Mister Skye," he rumbled.

"What do you do, Mister Skye?"

"Milk wayfarers of their money."

"I'm in business too," she said. "Honey, I got portable merchandise and the shelf is never bare." She laughed. "Or maybe it is."

"How many are in your party?"

"Why, myself and three ladies, Big Alice Roque, Mrs. Parkins, and Juliet Picard. And in my other wagon, Cornelius—Cornelius Vanderbilt—he's a sporting man— and Blueberry Hill, my pianist and friend, and Seven-Story Chang. And there's another wagon the wagon master won't have, also going to Bannack City. Full of mail-order brides. Now Mister Skye, why do you ask? Is there something I can sell you?" She flashed a knowing smile.

"Let's go look," said Mister Skye.

"The Riddles and their ladies are over there," she said, pointing at the dry-goods counters. "That's Alvah," she said, pointing at a ferret-faced balding skinny man. "And that's Gertrude," she added, pointing at a potbellied jowly scraggly haired female with mean gray eyes. "They are very virtuous," she added wearily. "And those are the brides. I forget their names. The Riddles are marriage brokers, taking those poor little old things to the mining camps. They're like me, only they peddle new merchandise and I sell the used." She grinned. "Everything I sell is properly broken in."

They emerged from the post sutler's into a blinding June sun and hiked toward the riverbank, where wagons were gathered in a long string. "I didn't let my people come in," she said. "For obvious reasons, honey."

"Mister Skye."

"Mister Skye, honey. Now tell me true, what do you do?"

"I'm a guide when there's guiding."

"We don't need a guide. They tell me the trail's perfectly clear. What we need is protection. I'd like about ten soldiers."

"We'll get you through," said Mister Skye.

"Who's we, honey?"

"I'll discuss that after I see whether I wish to do business with you."

Three fine wagons hunkered separately, about two hundred yards east of the rest of the wagon train. Even at a distance Mister Skye could see that these were all mule-drawn, three spans apiece with spare mules and horses tied on. Faster and better than oxen, when there was good grass on the trail. Two of the wagons were lacquered a dazzling red, and the wagon sheets spread over the bows had been dyed blushing pink. The other wagon was lacquered green with gilt filigree work.

Advertisements, Mister Skye thought. Advertisements.

Standing beside the wagons were the lowlifes. "There

they are," said Goldtooth. "We're going to have the best parlor house in Bannack City. And mine all the gold in the gulch." She laughed amiably.

"What's in the wagons?"

"Why, in this one, nothing but the ladies and supplies. In my other one, some hogsheads of Kentucky bourbon, some vintage wine, and Cornelius's faro and roulette layouts."

Mister Skye experienced a stab of delight. Sometime along the trail, he'd tap a hogshead and disappear for a few days. Always assuming, of course, that he landed this business.

They were all staring at him, their gaze fastening on the silky stovepipe with the two bullet holes in it, his beefy face with the mashed and twisted prow that had been broken in a dozen brawls, at the golden-tanned skin garments, the shirt and leggins fringed, at his red-beaded loincloth, and heavy boots, as well as the Navy Colt holstered at his side and the battered heavy Sharps cradled in his arms. They saw, too, his sailor's roll, as if the earth were a pitching deck, and they sensed the menace about him. He could read it in their faces as he, in turn, surveyed this gaggle of outcasts.

"I want you-all to meet Mister Skye," said Goldtooth. "He's a guide just a-lookin' us over."

She introduced them all. Big Alice reached almost six feet, yellow-eyed and yellow-fleshed, and dressed entirely in lavender. Mrs. Parkins—Cleo Sylvanus Parkins— seemed a patrician blonde, dressed in a svelte summer yellow dress with a deep vee at the neck. Perhaps thirty. She studied him with calculating gray eyes. Juliet Picard turned out to be a young sable-haired beauty with a voluptuous figure and shining eyes, dimples, and pouty open lips made to kiss.

He had been unprepared for this. He had not expected such dazzling beauty, such bright eyes and good humor. He turned then toward the sporting gents, and Goldtooth introduced. The gambler wore a gray swallowtail. He was a cadaverous pocked gent with oily black hair combed straight back, and darting brown eyes that never steadied on anything. Crooked as hell, Mister Skye thought.

"What's your real name, Vanderbilt?" he rumbled.

The man started. It was a question never asked. He glanced into Mister Skye's blue eyes, and surrendered. "Donk. Homer Donk. Brooklyn, New York. But I'd just as soon that weren't bandied about because of, ah, troubles back there."

Mister Skye nodded.

Beside him slouched a graying black as burly as himself, with hair like iron shavings. He wore a collarless white shirt, a black broadcloth suit, and white spats over patent-leather shoes.

"Blueberry Hill, our pianist," Goldtooth was saying. "Blueberry takes good care of us and is very strong. When there's trouble, why, we just call on Blueberry and he throws the troublemakers out, don't you, honeybunch?"

Blueberry smiled. Mister Skye saw the telltale bulge of a shoulder holster, and decided the man would be formidable in a brawl.

"I keep the ladies from going stale," said Blueberry, revealing a row of even white teeth.

Mister Skye nodded.

"And this is Lui Chang, but we call him Seven-Story Chang," Goldtooth continued.

Of all the people in this party, Seven-Story Chang commanded Mister Skye's attention. Powerfully built, lean, and all muscle. He wore a long queue that swung easily across the small of his back. But he wore Western clothing—denim britches and open-throated gray Bedford cord shirt. A pair of holstered shining revolvers, a sheathed dagger, and on his great white horse a Spencer carbine in a scabbard.

"It is an honor to meet Mister Skye, who is plainly a fighting man," said Seven-Story. "As am I."

"Seven-Story is a mandarin from Peking and the son of an officer of the Imperial Guard," Goldtooth explained. "He's not really with us permanently. He's adventuring, and we—exchange services."

Mister Skye found himself believing Chang could whip him, fists, clubs, knives, anything. He had that look about him, at once serene and assured, as if nothing on earth save a coward's bullet from ambush would ever fell him. A one-man army, Skye thought. No wonder Goldtooth was glad to include him.

Mister Skye hadn't met the Riddles yet, but he thought he knew the type, and they didn't concern him. He had seen what he wanted to see. He could get this party safely to Bannack City, especially with Seven-Story Chang beside him.

"Five hundred dollars," said Mister Skye. "In gold."

"For what?" said Goldtooth, astonished.

"For delivering you safely to Bannack City. My services include those of my wives, who will make meat and scout."

"Wives?"

"Mary, my beautiful young Shoshone, and Victoria, my beloved Crow lady."

"We were looking for protection, not a guide."

Mister Skye sighed. "Inquire about me at the fort. Ask Colonel Bullock."

"Hire him," said Cornelius Vanderbilt. "It doesn't matter what he charges. He'll enjoy our sport."

"That's more than we can afford." She smiled coyly. "How about a hundred dollars—and services? We'd all love to share the merchandise, wouldn't we, ladies?"

"Five hundred in gold."

She shook her head. "We'll find someone else, I think."

"Try it," said Mister Skye.

Something in the way he said it gave her pause. "I don't know anything about you," she said.

"Ask."

Seven-Story Chang said, "Don't ask, Madam Jones. This is a man I have heard of. I hear of all such men. He is exactly what we need. I am pleased to make his acquaintance."

Goldtooth sighed. "Four hundred fifty in greenbacks. We haven't gold. I'll charge the Riddles a hundred fifty for their wagon, and pay three hundred for mine. They'll complain, but they'll pay rather than be left behind."

"Gold," said Mister Skye. "In advance. Gold you skinned from the wagon train."

"Two hundred in gold and the rest in merchandise. Honey, I have the best merchandise west of the Mississippi."

Mister Skye yawned. "Find someone else," he said, and turned to leave.

Seven-Story hissed something at her. "Wait!" she cried. She lifted her dimity skirts, revealing a splendid golden thigh, and extracted some greenbacks from a purse strapped to the glowing flesh.

"Here!" she said. "We're leaving in the morning. We have some business to do with the soldiers at the fort tonight. Be ready!"

Mister Skye was taken aback. He always made the decisions once he agreed to captain a party into the wilderness.

"Goldtooth," he rumbled, "the safety of this party depends on strict obedience to my direction at all times. We will be in a wilderness infested by bandits, outlaws, hostiles, disease such as cholera, rattlesnakes, and more. Your lives will depend on my knowledge. Is that understood?"

"I trust you-all, honey."

He nodded and trotted off to Bullock to pay his bill, buy the Henry, and boxes of those shining brass cartridges. There'd be enough left over for supplies, and treats for his wives.

Chapter 2

It wasn't the fine brick parlor on Beale Street, but it'd do, she thought. She was open for business and getting it here at this makeshift parlor house on the Platte, perhaps half a mile from Fort Laramie. Cornelius had his faro game laid out on a light folding table brought along for the purpose, with a pair of coal-oil lamps on poles for light. Her ladies, in their skimpy wrappers, lounged around their wagon, now partitioned into two cribs with a canvas sheet. Display the merchandise, she had always told them, and they were doing it, a knee or thigh golden in the firelight now and then. Blueberry, when he wasn't tending the bar, sat up on the tailgate of the other wagon, plucked his banjo and sang. Out in the dark somewhere, Seven-Story Chang stalked the night like a yellow cat, making sure all was well. Goldtooth herself tended the bar, drew reluctant blue-clad corporals and sergeants to the girls, and drummed up trade for

Cornelius. She envied her ladies—there were several of the Fort Laramie soldiers she'd have loved to bed.

It had gone on all evening. Cornelius, looking particularly sallow and pocked beneath the two lanterns, shuffled the greasy faro deck methodically and replaced it in the casebox and turned over the soda card and once again invited the troopers to lay coin on the oilcloth. But the pickings were slim. These soldiers drew eight dollars a month when they got paid at all. Cornelius knew that, of course, and traded chits for U.S.-issue boots and belts and holsters and anything else. He methodically milked them all, until a fine midden of army goods was heaped behind his layout.

Men and boys from the wagon train milled around too, mostly just looking because the ladies and Cornelius had long since skinned them all. And assorted Brulé Sioux from Squaw Town wandered through. They loved to gamble, but had little to wager with. Even so, Cornelius cleaned them out of their knives and blankets and belts and a few old revolvers, with his braced deck and his twitchy dealing. Every few minutes a spasm would rack him, and he'd suck on a tin cup of raw bourbon, and go back to dealing and keeping cases with the little black abacus beads on their wires. After each cleaning, he gazed dolefully at the shorn victim, his brown eyes blinking, and sympathized. "Have a little drink on Goldtooth," he said. "We want sporting men to go away happy." And she would dish up a well-watered dose of popskull.

The trouble came close to midnight when the crowd tapered to an edge and Goldtooth was about to fold up the tents and count the loot. Before leaving, she intended to trade as much of the U.S.-issue stuff with the sutler, dear old Colonel Bullock, for whatever she could get. It had been a splendid evening, she thought, except that she didn't get a chance to bed. That made her cross. She needed two or three good customers a day.

A rush of hooves rattled from the darkness, on the flats along the river. Several muffled shots. At almost the same moment, armed men materialized around her outdoor parlor house, all of them carrying rifles at the ready, which glinted in the firelight. She recognized most of them at once. They were the bearded patriarchs of the wagon train, and foremost among them was Jarvis Porter, the wagon master. And among them a sprinkling of blue cavalry shirts, many with two or three yellow chevrons on their sleeves, noncoms who could be out at night, away from the fort, without getting into trouble. Every one of them, over thirty in all, brandished rifles or drawn revolvers.

Worse, they were leading Seven-Story Chang from out of the darkness, his hands bound behind him. The giant Celestial peered calmly at his silent captors and Goldtooth, and smiled faintly. An ominous silence pervaded these night visitors. Mrs. Parkins stared, and dived into the wagon, along with Juliet. But Big Alice stared back defiantly in a black kimono with a giant red dragon on its back, a gift from Seven-Story. Easily, they prodded Blueberry and Cornelius Vanderbilt into their circle.

Something glinted in Porter's eye. "You've been warned," he whispered softly. "You've been warned but didn't heed. Now the price."

At a nod from him, rough-hewn men wheeled off in all directions recovering booty. The wagon master himself searched her, his giant rough hands probing everywhere, ripping greenbacks and coin from her pockets and purses, yanking at everything, ruthless and cruel.

When he finished, he shoved her into the grass. Cornelius endured the searching stoically, his hands in the air. Rough hands dug at his pockets, threw his hideout derringer into the grass, dropped his britches, ripped off his moneybelt, emptied the lining of his silk top hat. And then these silent avengers carried the U.S.-issue loot piled behind his faro layout off to a central collection depot near the wavering wind-whipped fire.

From inside the wagon came the screams of the ladies as others of these hard men probed and dug.

"I've had that all my life," cried Juliet Picard, from within.

"Shut up," came a voice.

Big Alice, still outside, simply opened her kimono and grinned. There was nothing underneath. God! thought Goldtooth, what great merchandise. Then one of them slapped her down, and she sat with a thud. Next they dug at Blueberry, yanking out his pockets, ripping off his black broadcloth coat.

"Where's it hid, nigger?" snapped one.

Blueberry said nothing.

They threw him to the ground.

Several of these silent avengers climbed into the supply wagon and rolled the hogsheads of bourbon out. They hit the ground with a hard thump. One cracked as it landed and began to leak. Porter himself caught up an axe and began to swing.

"Hold it," yelled a burly old sergeant, menace in his eye. "This here stuff is illegal in Injun country and I'm confiscating it for the army."

No one laughed. Cornelius managed a faint smirk. Seven blue-shirted noncoms with leveled revolvers held the vengeful wagon train men at bay.

From inside the wagon came the shrill voice of Mrs.

Parkins. "You sonofabitch, that's a family heirloom," she said.

Goldtooth wondered whether the Riddles were escaping this. They and their mail-order brides had camped a couple hundred yards away, far enough to get sleep. None of them showed up now, not that she expected them to. She sighed. She had been through something like this before, but not . . . this bad. Memphis had fallen to Union forces led by Charles Henry Davis just a year earlier, June 6, 1862, and business on Beale Street had at once tailed off under a reign of fear. But little by little the blue-clad army's curfew had relaxed, and in some small anemic way, the sporting crowd revived, sliding in and out of her house. Hard times. Food always ran short, and at times she couldn't squeeze spirits out of a drunk. Then more and more of the Union officers—the only ones who could afford her amazing prices—slipped in, magnetized by her stunning ladies. She thought she'd weather the war that way, taking in Union gold, but it was not to be. Davis closed her down for various reasons—money, demoralization, fear of disease, and above all, fear the Union Army secrets were divulged in the cribs of Beale Street and were finding their way into the ears of the army of the Confederacy—which was true. One night they came, polished officers and a smart squad of infantry, and ransacked the place—some of them the very men she'd entertained—and told her to shut down. But not before carrying off everything of value. She had wasted no time leaving Memphis then, with the safety of the Western camps the end of their odyssey. Until now.

Jarvis Porter had found two shovels, and these he handed to Cornelius and Seven-Story.

"Dig," he said curtly.

The sallow gambler paled. "You aren't—you can't—" he blustered.

"You were warned," said the captain of the wagon train.

Seven-Story took his shovel, and somehow it looked like a weapon in his hand, she thought. He began calmly to lift sod and set it carefully aside, his eyes less on what he was doing than upon those whose rifles bored in at him.

"You wouldn't!" she gasped.

"You were warned."

"But why the Chinese? He's not even one of our party!"

"He was with you. And there's no room here for the heathen, the Celestials."

"You'd kill him for that?"

"This land is given to the God-fearing."

"I suppose you'll murder us all."

"Only the men."

"Blueberry too?"

"Is that his name?"

"All he does is make music and serve drinks. What has he done to any of you?"

"Corrupted our sons," said a black-bearded man.

Blueberry's eyes, yellow in the amber firelight, peered from face to face, and then he sagged. "Never was much hope for a man of color," he muttered.

"And what's my fate? and my ladies'?"

"We are confiscating your mules and horses and harness to repay—debts. And burning your slut-wagons. What you choose to do after that is your business."

"That sounds about right!" she cried. "You're stealing about twenty times what was sold to you. And murdering three men."

For an answer, he booted her. The heavy brogan caught

her square in the ribs, a painful sickening jolt that shot nausea and fire through her. She thought, absurdly, that the bruise would turn yellow and purple and turn away trade.

Cornelius and Seven-Story dawdled with their spades, slowly lifting off turf but not producing holes.

"Get busy," snarled the wagon master, prodding Seven-Story with his rifle.

"If I am pleased to join my ancestors, then, gentleman, it makes no difference. You may have the honor of burying me." He bowed slightly and handed the shovel to the surprised Porter.

"Dig!" Porter handed back the spade.

"Ah, no, I will decline the great honor."

The wagon master pointed at Blueberry. "You—dig."

"I can't say that it makes much sense to dig my own grave," said Blueberry.

For a reply he got a wicked boot to the kidneys, and crumpled into the grass.

Vanderbilt thought otherwise, and dug feverishly, hoping Lady Luck might be kind.

"You and all your bible-thumpers are nothing but murderers," said Goldtooth. "And thieves."

Jarvis Porter grinned sallowly in the flickering light. "I'll wager that this sport here, Vanderbilt, has some hanging offenses behind him. As for the rest"—he shrugged—"they aren't whites."

Seven-Story's arcing spade landed on Porter's head with an awful thump, and the wagon captain toppled to earth. Several of the night visitors lifted rifles to shoot the Chinese, but shots crashing from the blackness burned their hands, shattered rifle stocks. They screamed. Others, especially the noncoms, wheeled toward the darkness, emptying revolvers at unseen targets.

Bodies slammed to earth, making themselves small. Blueberry flattened himself. Cornelius dove into the shallow hole that was to hold his bones. Goldtooth saw all this in a series of flashing impressions, and clutched the earth, bewildered.

From the blackness came the roar of a vaguely familiar voice. "Hands up, mates. Drop the guns." From out in the blackness came an insane shriek of a horse, eerie, unlike any horse Goldtooth had ever heard in her young life. Much to her astonishment the soldiers dropped their revolvers at once, all of them looking terrified. The wagon men were slower, some of them obeying but most of them firing blind into the night, a useless racket.

"Hands up, mates," came that rumble again, but from a different place. Now it became familiar, that voice. The guide she had hired, Mister Skye. Her heart hammered.

Still the wagon men clung to their rifles, peering into the darkness, many of them too stubborn and inept even to get out of the firelight that perfectly silhouetted them. Shots cracked again, shattering rifles, bloodying hands. More of the wagon men peered at their own bloodied hands and fingers, yelping in the night. And they surrendered.

A stretching silence. Goldtooth peered about and saw nothing. Closer at hand, disarmed men began to wrap shirting around hand wounds to stanch the blood.

"The two with the pistols in their holsters—pull them out and drop them," came the thunderous voice again. One of them did; the other tried to slip off into the night. A shot cracked. "Far enough, mate. Get back to the firelight."

Seven-Story stood, a commandeered revolver glinting in his hand.

Then at last a soft thump of hooves, and into the amber wind-whipped light rode an apparition, Mister Skye

on a giant ugly blue roan so scarred and battered that all
its furrows and pocks lay black-shadowed in the firelight.
Its cruel yellow eyes caught the light and glowed like
lanterns from hell, and its lips were drawn back around
murderous teeth that clacked and clicked and snapped.
What had she hired? What sort of hell-man and hell-horse
had she engaged to guide them?

"Why are you here?" she whispered.

"We were paid to protect you."

She didn't know who the others were.

He addressed the several noncoms. "You. Pick up the
government-issue and be glad you won't have to pay for
it. And collect what this gambler took from you. To the
penny."

"I won that fair and square," croaked Vanderbilt.

"With a braced deck, Homer Donk. Hand me the casebox."

Reluctantly the greasy cadaverous man handed the box
up to Mister Skye, who pulled out an ace of diamonds
and eight of clubs and held them up to the firelight. Pinpricks of light shone through. "Braced," he said. He pulled
the rest of the filthy cards and tossed them into the fire,
where they flared yellow.

The soldiers carefully claimed their goods and cash.

"You're square now," said Skye. "Go back. In the morning report it all.

"You—Porter—you've got three men with bloody hands
as a result of your little murderous games. Be glad you
are all alive."

The choleric wagon master glared. "There's over twenty
of us here. You think you can take us all?"

Two things happened. Mister Skye's giant blue roan,
Jawbone, lurched, his hard chest slamming into Porter

and toppling him again. And shots rang from the blackness, each plucking off a hat.

Mister Skye glared at them all. "Take what the gambler screwed out of you and not a penny more," he said. "You paid for the booze and you paid for the ladies, and they'll stay paid-for. Take what Donk here skinned out of you and get out. Go back to your families. Go nurse your fingers. If you sneak back here, you're dead."

Even as Skye addressed the night riders, Seven-Story emptied their rifles and revolvers of their charges and pried caps off nipples. He handed the weapons back to them. The wagon men stared reluctantly, and finally began sorting out their own possessions, under Goldtooth's watchful eye. The ladies joined her.

Ten minutes later it was done. The wagon-train elders skulked off to their wagons, and the night held only the music of the crickets. The terror left Blueberry's eyes. Goldtooth felt more at ease, except for the dull ache where she had been booted. She would remember that little calling card forever, she thought savagely.

"I do believe I am alive," muttered Blueberry. "It is a surprise."

Seven-Story Chang glided in from the darkness. "The mules and horses are all at hand and picketed," he said. He turned to Mister Skye. "I have the honor to be in your debt. You and the others who are still out there. Mister Skye, I had heard of you from the day I arrived in San Francisco. And all the stories are true."

Mister Skye nodded.

The fire was reduced to embers, and the camp grew dark. The guide seemed to like it that way. "Goldtooth," he said softly, "I will get you all to Bannack City safely. And once you get there you can do as you please. But on the trail, I will have certain rules. There'll be a lot of people on the trail to Oregon and California. We'll be mixing with various wagon trains, camping close to all sorts. I will have no trouble. You and your ladies will avoid married men and boys, youths. Are we agreed?"

Goldtooth nodded, reluctantly. What he doesn't know won't hurt him, she thought.

"And you, Donk. That faro layout stays in the wagon as long as you're under my protection. And so do all your thimble-rigged games. If I catch you skinning the pilgrims, you'll be in trouble with me. Do we have a meeting of minds, Donk?"

The gambler stared back, sullen. "I will do what I want. You've no authority over me," he replied.

Mister Skye grinned, his teeth catching the vague orange of the embers. "I will not protect you from the consequences of your acts, as I did tonight. You were almost the late Cornelius Vanderbilt."

"I've always fended for myself," the gambler retorted.

"Until tonight, mate. Go lie down in that hole."

"What are you talking about?"

"Lie down in that hole or feel my fists, mate."

The gambler stared, and then slowly dragged himself to the long slash gouged from hard clay, and lay down.

"Throw some dirt on him, Seven-Story."

The Chinese grinned, and began shoveling enthusiastically.

"You're dirtying my suit! My swallowtail coat!"

"It's no dirtier than the man inside."

The Chinese stopped after unloading several shovels.

"I'm fitting you for your future, Cornelius Vanderbilt." Skye's voice mocked the name as he pronounced it.

The last embers faded, and Mister Skye became an

unseen voice in the dark. "We'll be back 'round dawn. Be harnessed and ready. Have the others—the Riddles over yonder, and their women—ready too. If we get a fast start, we won't have to tangle with the wagon train you've managed to incite to murder."

"Amen, Mister Skye," muttered Blueberry. "I think I see stars up there."

Goldtooth smiled. Men like Mister Skye were hard to find. "Thank you, honey," she said. "You come visit."

Chapter 3

A lvah Riddle couldn't understand why he had been booted out of Porter's wagon train. Or, indeed, why he had been bounced from yet another train back on the coasts of Nebraska. To be sure, he was slow. He had to harness and hitch three span of mules each morning, and not a woman in his party helped him. And each evening he had to unhitch the six mules and pasture and picket them, also without help.

At first Porter had waited for him, but soon he hadn't, leaving the Riddles to fend for themselves and at the mercy of hostile Indians on the trail. Now, here he was, tied to some bawds and lowlifes for mutual protection, and he a respectable man, too. That Porter, now, he must have had some angle. People always had angles. Maybe someone in the wagon train had paid Porter off. Riddle figured he had just as much right to be in that train as anyone else, and a lot more right than those sluts, but they had all turned against him. Someone in that outfit had stirred up feelings against the Riddles, for sure. Probably some gain in it, someone who didn't want the Riddles to deliver their mail-order brides to Bannack City.

An angle lurked behind everything, anyone knew that. The train had been badly captained anyway—Porter hadn't the faintest idea how to run a wagon train. He bossed people around as if they were lackeys, and he continually made stupid decisions, such as driving the wagons far into the evenings, wearing down the footsore stock. Alvah figured if he'd been wagon boss, the whole party of forty-seven wagons would be better off.

He unrolled his bed each night under his enameled green wagon, mostly because all the women he chaperoned needed their privacy. And now, as usual, the early sun of June upended him long before the time they'd travel. Riddle had a protruding belly and bright glancing eyes that studied others and hunted the angles. The stubble on his face ran smoothly from his nose to his neck, without the interruption of a jaw. He hadn't slept well: he never slept well on the hard ground, and he'd explained to Porter that was why he was slow getting harnessed in the morning, but Porter kept playing some angle and wouldn't listen or sympathize.

Now he was stuck with the lowlifes, and that made him uneasy. Maybe when he rolled into Bannack City with his women, he'd try to be well ahead, or well behind, so the miners who had paid him good money to bring them respectable brides wouldn't get the wrong impression. Yes, he'd do that. Arrive separately. He had a wagonload of virgins and they had to be quarantined from those shopworn bawds. Not that he minded close contact with the bawds on the trail, though Gertrude and the brides complained. In fact that heathen Chinee might be a comfort. With him around, it would be like traveling with a squad of infantry. And he figured maybe that gambler and the black lowlife could be deadly if it came to that.

Yes, that would be his angle. Get what protection he could from them, but keep his distance. Three miners had contracted for the women, half down, half on delivery, and he intended to make sure they didn't have any angle that would work against him. It was hard enough making money in the bride business—finding the women and delivering them took all the string-pulling and sharp dealing he could muster—and the cost of delivery kept rising. Why, he'd have over a thousand of expenses and clear only two; less if any of the miners balked. Of course he'd written up an ironclad contract, empowering him to seize assets and keep the bride if they defaulted, but one never knew. The bride business bid fair to be troublesome because the husbands and brides sometimes recoiled when they met. But he had a default clause in his contracts, drawn up for him by the trickiest shyster in upstate New York, and if they defaulted he'd have them both over the barrel in any court.

It rankled him that this bawd, Goldtooth Jones, had gone and hired some lumbering guide to protect them en route, since they lacked the protection of a wagon train. A hundred fifty would reduce their profits all the more, and Gertrude would be peeved. Well, he hadn't paid Goldtooth, and didn't intend to. He would cook up his own angle to squirm out of it. Hadn't she struck the deal without his consent? She'd played the sucker. So he'd just profit. Who said madams were so smart? That guide had skinned her good, a whopping five hundred smackerinos for a little trip down the trail. He hadn't met this Mister Skye, but sort of admired him as a slick operator. If he could shoot, or haul in a little game, all the better. Alvah had heard there would be no game along the heavily traveled trail, except when they struck buffalo, so anything this slick frontier rube brought in would be a little bonus and fill the hollow bellies of those complaining women. They were eating up his profit, these women.

Life stammered within the wagon, and it rocked above him. That would be Drusilla Dinwiddie, always first up, and first to the bushes. She hadn't much in the beauty department, but in the dark they were all the same. That's what he told his clients. He told the women that, too. In the dark they were all the same. And of course his contract expressly stated that physical appearance would not be a ground to nullify the agreement. This one, Miss Dinwiddie, had taken a lot of persuading. New England bred, built like a pear, with a face like a mule. The blue-stocking had eyeglasses, liked to read, and even kept a diary. She had left thirty-one behind and looked desperate. That's when he had them over the barrel, when they got desperate. He'd had to go clear from his home in Skaneateles, New York, to Bennington, Vermont, to persuade her, and then pay for a hoity-toity first-class rail ticket to Council Bluffs, Ioway, before she'd consent. Not much profit in her.

She clambered down from the wagon in her long wrapper, stared owlishly at him, and headed for the Platte River brush. He rolled out of his blankets, rubbed the mouse-stubble on his cheeks and stood in the moist dawn air. He wouldn't scrape his whiskers today. Most days he didn't scrape. That was just another angle people played, scrape your chin to do good business. She returned, glaring at him.

"You haven't even got the mules harnessed or breakfast started," she snapped. "No wonder they kicked us out. No wonder I'm forced to associate with—I won't say the name. Women who are beneath words. If you weren't so lazy, this would be a better trip. But no, I had to get stuck with a no-account."

That was her angle, he figured. The more she complained and nagged and demanded, the more people jumped to her word. He grinned, thinking of the unlucky future husband, one Amos Rasmussen of Bannack City in the new territory of Idaho.

He had to harness the blasted mules, but that could wait. Now that they were no longer with the wagon train, they could set their own pace and tell the guide, this Skye, that a few miles a day were plenty. Save the mules. He calculated that he could sell the mules for a better price fat and healthy than he could trail-gaunted. That was an angle hardly anyone else thought of.

He waited for breakfast, irked because as usual Gertrude and these lazy women were dawdling in there long after sunup. He wanted his hotcakes, doused with the maple syrup they'd hauled clear from New York. She'd grumble at him because the fire wasn't built or the coffee on, but he couldn't see why he should be doing that kind of work, women's work. Here he was, supporting her, and filling the bellies of the merchandise, his shelf stock, and they would grumble because he didn't think it his duty or responsibility to build the fire. Women all had their angles too, and if you let them get away with it, they'd con a man out of his manhood. Let them build their own fire. He relented a moment and thought to fetch some wood, but hardened. He had enough burdens without adding that.

Next out, and predictably, he thought, was Flora Slade. He didn't like her. She lacked nineteen and thought the whole world should kiss her big toe. The war had wiped out her family and left her alone and destitute, and that was how he had cottoned onto her. Halfway pretty would describe her, but snobby as a dowager. Her father had been a slave broker, a slave auctioneer down somewhere in the South, but had been killed in the war, and her mother had died suddenly. What an evil thing, he thought, buying and selling flesh like that, brokering slaves. The father, Slade, deserved what he got. Alvah didn't hold with slavery. He suspected Flora was corrupted—she must have watched naked slaves bought and sold, and felt some sort of bizarre power and conceit, knowing her father could do that to people. Alvah could see it in her, a contempt for the world, a woman ready to buy and sell anything, up to and including God. Getting her north had been a problem, but Alvah had his angles. He'd picked her up in Council Bluffs. She had brought silks and satins, things utterly impractical for the trail, and he had been forced to buy other clothing. But he'd present a bill, padded generously thanks to a little token of esteem he gave the storekeeper, to Flora's fiancé, a placer miner named Yakima Cranston. Alvah didn't believe anyone would be baptized Yakima Cranston, and could hardly wait to find out what the man's angle was. If he balked at the clothing bill, Alvah would keep the bride and sell her elsewhere. That hunkered in the contract too, unusual expenses.

From within the wagon sheet arose a great caterwauling and snapping, and Alvah knew the last of his merchandise was awake. He'd gotten her cheap, right off the boat, though it took a small fee to another marriage broker to fetch her. Mary-Rita Flaherty was her moniker, redheaded, freckled, and plain as the snout of a pig. She'd arrived in Boston with scarcely a penny, and not much more than a pair of leather lungs and tonsils that howled at everything. He'd wormed the story out of her

soon enough: her family in Tipperary had scraped together her passage. It had taken the combined savings of
her father, uncles, aunts, plus her mother's gold wedding
ring to do it. Alvah thought that sounded rather touching,
a whole family sacrificing its last cent to let a lass fulfill
her dream of going to a new and better life in the New
World, until he found out that Mary-Rita hadn't wanted
to go. They had bodily hauled her to the boat and locked
her in, courtesy of the purser, who didn't open the door
until the ship plowed the sea. Alvah loved that. Those
micks always worked the angles. They'd simply got rid
of her with that ticket. After a while he understood why.
She had caterwauled her way clear across the continent.
It tickled Alvah to think he'd be foisting her off on some
poor unsuspecting Irish miner out there, fellow named
Tom O'Dougherty. Good thing he'd signed an ironclad,
airtight, hellacious contract. Well, Alvah thought, those
Papists deserved one another.

Alvah congratulated himself for setting up camp a
couple hundred yards away from the lowlifes. There'd
been wild times over there last night, even gunshots from
some hell-raisers, and the noise of it hadn't been so both-
ersome here. A good angle, camping apart. He'd do that
on the trail.

A voice from behind startled him. "Mister Riddle!"

Alvah turned, stared up at a man on a giant ugly blue
roan with evil yellow eyes. Alvah had never seen such a
man, built like a barrel, wearing dark buckskins and a
black-silk stovepipe hat, set rakishly on gray hair that hung
to his shoulders.

"I'm Mister Skye. I'll be guiding you and your ladies
to Virginia City. We'd best be off, mate. Time's flying."

"You're Skye?"

"Mister Skye."

"Heard of you," Alvah said, craftily, playing the best angle. The man before him was astonishing. He wore fringed leggins and a breechclout, like the savages, instead of pants, and some thigh flesh shone umber in the sun. Indecent. And he cradled a new rifle in his arm, as if he expected Alvah to be dangerous or something.

"On the trail we'll be moving one hour after first light without fail," said Skye. "I see your people are barely up, and your mules aren't harnessed. I'll help you today, mate, but after this . . ." Skye's voice trailed off.

"Now just a minute!" said Alvah. "I didn't hire you. And we're going to be moving slower. I got delicate women to think of. And no help for the harnessing."

Mister Skye stared unblinkingly, and Alvah withered under the gaze. At once he despised this man, this barbaric guide.

"On the trail you'll follow instructions from me or my wives. Your lives will depend on it."

"Wives? Wives?"

"Mary of the Shoshone, and Victoria of the Crow."

"I didn't hire you. Wouldn't ever hire some bigamist, squawman, lowlife," said Alvah. Resist Skye, that would be a good angle. Resist this wilderness oaf.

"Suit yourself," said Mister Skye. "The other two wagons are leaving in a few minutes. Join us or go alone." He peered amiably at Alvah.

So that is his angle! thought Alvah. Threaten to leave him behind and helpless, without protection, so he could have his way on the trail. Alvah stared back shrewdly. Still, it was probably a bluff. Alvah liked to ferret out a bluff.

"We've employed you; we'll make the decisions, and you'll obey them," he said airily.

Mister Skye yawned. "Suit yourself." He turned the ugly horse and trotted off.

"Wait!" cried Alvah. That man and the Chinese looked like a whole army to Alvah, safety on the trail. But oh, the price. "We'll harness. We'll forget breakfast. We'll be right there."

"Who says we'll forget breakfast?" yelled Mary-Rita Flaherty. "You idjit, who do you think you are, starving me?"

Mister Skye smiled. "I will help you harness, Mister Riddle," he said.

Alvah couldn't understand Skye's angle, helping him harness. It made him suspicious.

But the guide slid off that terrible horse, which stood quietly, trailing a single rope rein on the grass. The burly man lumbered toward Alvah's mules, unhobbled one and led it to the pile of black harness and slipped on the collar and buckled the bellyband, and soon had the animal ready for the tugs, even while Alvah and his women gaped. Secretly Alvah exulted. He'd have this dumb guide, who didn't mind work, harness the six mules each day.

"Grab a collar, mate," said Mister Skye. "I'll fetch the next one."

Alvah did nothing. Let the rube do the work, he thought. The man's accent bothered him. What was it? Sailor-talk, that's what. And the way the man walked, too, rolling the way they do on the deck of a ship. Alvah squinted. This guide had been a sailor, but was now a Western man. Some angle there, maybe fraud. He'd worm it out of Skye and maybe use it.

"You a sailor once, Skye?" Alvah asked, carefully doing no work.

"It's Mister Skye, mate. British navy, until I jumped ship. I was pressed right off a dock on the Thames."

Jumped ship! The confession delighted Alvah. He'd turn the big dumb guide in, and collect a reward. Contact some Canadian Crown officials.

In minutes, Mister Skye had two mules harnessed. These would be the wheelers, so he added breeching and backed them up to the singletrees, fastened the tugs, secured the wagon tongue between them, and tied up the reins.

"You oaf," yowled Mary-Rita, "I'm going to eat me porridge. And cover up your flesh, you—you wildman."

Alvah permitted himself a smile. Mary-Rita Flaherty was having a normal day.

"Suit yourself," said Mister Skye.

Alvah Riddle plucked a long stem of timothy grass and pressed it between his yellowed teeth. "Some nag you got there," he said, as Skye lumbered off to fetch another mule. "Older'n creation. Guess you can't afford better, guiding business bad as it is. Never seen one so scarred up." He ambled over toward Jawbone, who laid his ears back and bared his teeth.

The next thing Alvah knew, he catapulted to the ground, thrown hard by some terrible force hitting from behind. It belched the wind out of him. When he finally caught his breath and stared up, Mister Skye loomed over him.

"Sorry, mate," said Skye. "Don't ever go near that horse. You and your party, never get closer than ten or fifteen feet. Is that clear?"

Alvah was peeved. "He probably kicks. Fine thing, we have to live with an unsafe horse that kicks."

"No, Mister Riddle, he kills."

Alvah chose silence. Then Gertrude Riddle, who had

watched all this with alarm, helped Alvah up and faced Mister Skye. "We have decided to employ some other guide," she said primly.

"Now hold up, Gertie," said Alvah. "This fella must be hell on Injuns, and that's the kind we want."

"Take a whip to him," said Flora. "Some men just need whipping. Mister Riddle, if you don't whip this man, I will."

Alvah muttered unintelligibly.

Flora Slade lifted a long snaky plaited whip from the whipsocket on the fine enameled wagon, and cracked it a few times. "I'll teach hired men manners," she said, advancing on Skye.

Mister Skye unhobbled another brown mule and led it to the harness pile. He watched her coming. "I don't believe we've met," he said gently.

The tasseled whip snapped and hissed as she cracked it. "Flora Slade, and you will address me as miss," she said. The tassel hissed close to Mister Skye's face. The mule reared, frightened.

"Very well, Miss Slade," he said, patiently leading the mule.

The lash snapped angrily around Mister Skye's midriff, whacking the buckskin with an awful pop.

"Stop that, Flora," muttered Alvah, but not too forcefully. It seemed a good angle to be on record against it, even though a good whipping might teach the oaf manners.

Mister Skye ignored the lash, and tied the skittery mule to the wagon.

"I'm afraid you're frightening the mules, Miss Slade. Perhaps you'd care to whip me after they're harnessed."

He dropped the collar over the mule, and began to harness the twitching animal. Flora Slade gaped.

"We are ladies and gentlemen, Skye," she yelled. "You are a hired servant. You will do exactly what we tell you." She cracked the whip hard over his head for emphasis, knocking off his silk hat and denting it.

Mister Skye's gaze followed her. Then, like a giant cat he clawed out at her, trapped a small hand in his giant brown one and easily plucked the whip from her. "Save the whipping, Miss Slade, until after the mules are harnessed." He smiled amiably, and screwed his hat back down.

Flora Slade glared. The rest stared.

He addressed Alvah Riddle. "If you're coming with us, have your wagon at the other camp in five minutes."

Alvah decided he would. Where else could he get a savage lackey for free?

Chapter 4

Drusilla Dinwiddie hadn't yet made up her mind about Mister Skye. He behaved like any frontier oaf equipped with a pair of squaws to do his drudge work. That had been the lot of women, she knew—men had the fun and women drudged. Still, there seemed something competent about the man. He hefted that new repeater rifle as if he knew how to use it. In minutes he had done something Alvah Riddle couldn't do—organize this little party of three wagons into a small train and start westward on schedule.

She'd had more or less two months of experience with Alvah Riddle, and had come to conclusions about him.

The paunchy proud man with the chinless ferret face and balding head seemed crafty and nasty. Drusilla rode in a fine wagon pulled by three span of prime mules because Riddle was clever and didn't want breakdowns. But no other virtues manifested themselves. He repelled her now that she knew him. He'd gotten them kicked out of Jarvis Porter's disciplined wagon train, and its safety. She loathed him for that. Now they were forced to travel with two wagons of unspeakable lowlifes, and with no safety at all. They'd be easy prey to the restless Sioux or Cheyenne, prowling unhappily this year of 1863, especially since the frontier garrisons were gravely weakened by the great holocaust back East.

Still, this Skye, who insisted on being called mister but had a low-class British sailor twang to his voice, seemed commanding and competent, and her dread eased a bit. She knew nothing of weapons, but obviously a man with a repeater could do a lot of damage fast. He'd sent those squaws out on either flank as soon as they were clear of Fort Laramie and proceeding down the south bank of the Platte—or at least she thought they were, since the trail more and more distanced itself from the river and plunged through black hills covered with pine and cedar.

This Skye had done something else, too. He'd summoned that giant Chinese named Chang, who appeared to be of the warrior caste, and the two of them had ridden ahead of the procession, talking, taking the measure of each other. Behind Skye, who rode that awful blue roan horse, came several of Skye's mules, some with packs and others drawing travois with Skye's buffalo-skin lodge and lodgepoles on them. The squawman lived totally like an Indian. Drusilla peered ahead discreetly at Skye's breechclout and leggins and the bare flesh of the thigh.

She'd never seen a white man like this, and had never seen breechclouts until far out on the plains, when beggar Indians had shown up in Jarvis Porter's camps.

Next rolled Alvah's wagon, and after that the red wagon of that infamous Cyprian, Goldtooth, and her bawds. And behind that, bringing up the rear, came the other red wagon driven by that crook, Cornelius Vanderbilt, and Blueberry Hill, who usually walked beside it, his white spats gleaming in the prairie sun. Tied to the rear of that wagon was a span of spare mules. How perfectly disgusting to have to travel with such people, and she scorned Alvah for it.

She blamed herself for signing that contract with the potbellied weasel. She had read his character instantly when he showed up at her cottage in Bennington, floppy hat in hand, leering around crooked yellow teeth. She debated now what to do about it. She feared for her life. This little party would be easy prey for even a small hunting party of fierce Plains tribesmen. It would depend on Skye, she thought. If he proved as inept as Riddle, she'd just jump this party and join any wagon train they overtook, or that overtook them, contract or not. Staying alive was more important than contracts. One thing about Skye she liked: he seemed to handle that rodent Alvah as if he scarcely existed.

Late today, Mister Skye had told them, they'd pass Register Cliff. For two decades now immigrants had stopped there to paint or carve their names on its face, and before that, the mountain men did it. But he said they wouldn't stop; if they wanted to carve their names, they could do that at Independence Rock a few days ahead. Tonight they would stay at a warm springs where people usually scrubbed laundry on the trail, and he wanted this party to arrive there ahead of any wagon trains. That made

sense to her, although Alvah grumbled about Skye's re-
lentless speed, faster by far than Porter's train with its
ox-drawn wagons.

She'd do laundry then. And bathe, too, if she could
manage it without all those oafs and lowlifes peering.
Not that they'd want to peek at her anyway, she thought
bitterly. When it came to beauty, Nature had dealt her the
two of clubs. She'd grown so plain that her whole life had
been affected by it, and she despaired of ever enjoying
the normal pleasures and comforts of home and family
given to other women. She had only two assets, one of
them lustrous brown hair she wore long and divided at
the center and hanging in ringlets. The other a smooth
peachy complexion. Everything else was—dreadful. Her
face too long, and with too much jaw. Her eyes too small
and far-sighted, so that she wore rimless spectacles. Her
mouth naturally turned down, making her look sour no
matter how amiable her mood. From neck to waist she
stayed thin as a celery stalk, and almost without breasts,
but below her waist her hips flared to ungainly size, and
her legs swelled as thick as the variety that propped up
pianos. The very thought of all this plainness plunged her
into melancholy.

There were compensations, she thought. She read a
great deal, and had become particularly familiar with
the transcendentalists over in Massachusetts, especially
Emerson and Thoreau. She had completed an education
at Savoy Women's Academy, and could teach. She read
voraciously and knew without a doubt that she possessed
the best-informed and -educated mind of either sex in
this party, or maybe even in this vast territory. She wrote
melancholy poems, kept a diary with a lock on it so she
could record her savage thoughts about Alvah—and Gertrude, who dabbled in spiritualism, tarot cards, séances,

and the rest. And since Drusilla had the mental training to judge the worth of others, she did not hesitate to judge. She had no illusions at all about why she traveled here, on this wilderness trail, and why the other two brides were here as well, instead of back at their homes being courted and preparing for an amiable life. It embarrassed her faintly even to be in the same wagon with that howling immigrant girl and that incredible slave-seller's daughter. But that would pass, she told herself.

Alvah Riddle had shown up at a time of crisis, shortly after her father died, leaving her with a small Bennington cottage, a pittance of inheritance, and no means other than the possibility of a tiny living boarding somewhere else as a schoolmarm. The possibility of marriage had never occurred to her—she thought only of her plainness—until Alvah had discussed the miners in the Far West starving for a wife, any sort of respectable wife, of any description. Were any starved enough to marry the likes of her? It seemed so. Still, she thought the bulgy ferret was loathsome, and she appended all sorts of conditions, which Riddle reluctantly agreed to. Then she accepted. Men might make their destinies; why couldn't women? It scared her to think such bold thoughts. But the meeting, the confrontation at the end of this vast journey—that alarmed her even more. What if Amos Rasmussen stared, gasped—and embarrassed her?

Well, she thought, she'd deal with that when the time came. She didn't really want a consummated marriage anyway. That whole animal business seemed—messy. She'd be quite content to cook and sew and provide company, in exchange for his security. She felt indifferent about children. A good novel seemed better than a messy, sucking, demanding infant anyway. She wished she knew the means those soiled women used to prevent conception. Perhaps she'd nerve herself to find out before the trip was over. She'd read, write, live her own life of the intellect. If she got there alive, which she increasingly doubted.

They had toiled the last half hour up a long grade that took them away from the river and its valley. At the crest Mister Skye—why did she involuntarily call that oaf mister?—halted to let the mules blow. Drusilla clambered down from Alvah's enameled wagon and stood in the warm sun, enjoying the feel of the dry winds whipping her tan skirts. The wildness of the land struck her hard. From this vantage she could see the wide Platte coiling sleepily through a green valley, between arid blue hills dotted with silvery sage. Off on the western horizon rose purple saw-toothed mountains still capped with white, and another range stretched across the hazy north. And above her a sky so azure and intense that the color pierced into her spirit. Blue was the color of freedom, she thought. Those who loved liberty loved blue. Her colors were blue and white.

Mister Skye dismounted, and studied the members of this party. Drusilla had the feeling she would be observed, weighed, and—judged. It annoyed her. How dare he, a wilderness squawman, subject her to his judgment?

"What is it you don't like about me?" she said crossly.

The old guide gazed silently for a moment. "I don't rightly find any reason to dislike you, Miss Dinwiddie."

"Well, stop you staring, then. Am I too plain for you?"

Mister Skye grinned faintly. "I like to think I'm helping people make their dreams come true," he said quietly.

She would not buy his blarney. "I don't think so," she snapped. "I think you're studying each of us to see whether we're going to be helpful on the trail, or a problem you'll have to deal with."

The guide looked faintly surprised. "You may have something there," he admitted.

Drusilla felt the faint thrill she always did when her sharp mind had penetrated through to some truth, usually ill-concealed in the Aesopian language of someone else. She felt a strange power over this frontier oaf, Skye.

"Are we going to be safe in this wilderness?" she asked.

"There is no safety here."

That was not an answer she wanted to hear. "We're outcasts. No wagon master would have us. I'm sure you understand why."

"I do," he said. "But traveling this way has some advantages. Disease, for instance. It can burn through a large wagon train like a prairie fire, killing as it goes. There's no cholera this year, so far. And speed. This party with its mules can go much faster than ox-drawn wagons. And convenience. At the warm springs tonight you won't have to wait for others to wash ahead of you or worry about muddied water."

"But we're vulnerable—to even the smallest band of thieving Indians."

Skye grinned. "Depends how you look at it. Horse theft is a great honor among the Plains tribes. They will try us, for sure. And we'll try them."

"You mean you'd steal?" she asked indignantly.

"When in Rome, do as the Romans do," he replied.

"Where did you learn that?"

He grinned, saying nothing. Then, "We have four superb warriors and three others who might or might not fight. I think Blueberry Hill might stand up and be counted, but the others will set too much store on preserving their precious hide."

She peered around her at the others who stood near their wagons, enjoying the vast aching views. "I don't follow your counting," she said crossly.

"My wives are better warriors and sureshots than I am. Ruthless. Between them, they've taken a dozen scalps."

She shuddered.

"The younger one is Mary, of the Shoshone, or Snake people. She's excited because she'll be seeing her people this trip. And the older is Victoria, of the Crow." He eyed her amiably. "Get to know them. You might learn a thing or two."

That miffed her, the subtle insult. But she knew how to deal with the barbs of this man.

"I will teach them more than I learn from them," she said archly.

He nodded, smiling. "You will excuse me, Miss Dinwiddie. There are people in this party I don't yet know and wish to meet."

She felt suddenly alone. How could a big halfwit do that to her? She had formed no friendships on this long trek. The immigrant girl appalled her. The daughter of the slave dealer thought only of social position. Gertrude Riddle was . . . peculiar. Drusilla peered in the direction of the dumpy woman and found her perched on the wagon seat. Tarot cards in hand, eyes pressed firmly shut, and mouth forming inchoate sounds. No, she thought. There'd be no bonds formed with that bizarre creature. As for the rest, the lowlifes, she hadn't yet nerved herself even to talk with them, though she found herself curious. Perhaps she would try it sometime. Now, on the trail, would be the time to study the other side of life and draw conclusions about it. She could examine these women and put them in the display cases of her orderly mind, much the way butterfly collectors netted specimens and pinned them down in glass-covered chests.

Mister Skye approached Alvah, who industriously greased his axles with a brush and tar bucket.

"That's always a good move, mate," Skye rumbled.

Alvah peered up, sharply. "I know what you're up to, Skye, but your compliments don't signify anything."

"Your mules are in fine shape, Mister Riddle."

The chinless man straightened. "I fed out oats the first two hundred miles until two bags were used up. It pays," he said. "But don't think soft words will get you the upper hand of me, Skye."

"Mister Skye."

"Whatever," said Alvah.

"You haven't paid Goldtooth for my services yet, mate."

"I don't need your services. If she was sucker enough to pay you your fee without my consent, that's her problem."

"Pay her, Mister Riddle."

"Who are you to be giving orders, Skye?"

"I'd hate to see you and these young ladies out alone on the trail."

"You've got some angle, Skye. Are you getting a rake-off?"

"I guide and protect paying clients, mate."

The thought of being alone in Riddle's wagon chilled Drusilla.

Mister Skye stared off toward the dun horizon. "No, Mister Riddle. I've found that a party works together— defends itself better—when the burdens are shared properly."

"Don't ya fear for me, Skye. I got a loaded Spencer repeater. That'd cut a whole party of Injuns in two."

"An arrow travels far, Mister Riddle."

"I know your angle and I ain't buyin'."

"Then we will leave you behind in the morning," said Mister Skye softly with the whisper of steel in his voice.

"I know your angle!" the man croaked.

Drusilla grew alarmed. "Mister Skye, if that happens I wish to go with you and the—lowlifes."

The guide grinned. "It can be arranged," he said.

"You have a contract! I'll sue you from one end of the territory to the other!"

Drusilla peered at the rodent and smiled.

That was when Gertrude Riddle cried out from the wagon seat, and began to swoon. They all peered up at her. Riddle did nothing, and acted as if he'd seen all this before. The woman righted herself and stared out into blue space, as if she'd seen a specter. Others joined Drusilla now, Mary-Rita, and Flora, all of them staring at the woman clutching her chest and gasping up on the seat.

"You have another trance, Gertie?" asked Alvah.

"The cards. The cards!" she cried. "I asked the tarot cards about our safety. And the spirits replied. Yes, they answered!"

Drusilla yawned.

"Tell us," begged Flora.

The woman peered wildly around, her eyes on everything and nothing. "Trouble!" she cried. "Trouble aplenty. And . . . someone is going to die!"

They waited silently. Something wild and eerie possessed her, something commanding their attention and keening their senses.

"The spirits have told me that Mister Skye will not survive this trip."

A quick black silence. "Now, now, Gertie, half the time

that blasted board tells nonsense," said Alvah. "Did Skye put you up to this? There's some angle to this."

Drusilla peered furtively at Skye, who frowned but otherwise revealed nothing. Then his face relaxed, and the faintest smile appeared on his crevassed mouth.

"I am a fatalist," he said. "The wilderness is like a catamount in the night. The best-prepared men go under."

"It's all nonsense," snapped Drusilla. "The universe operates on rational principles."

In minutes they were off again, wending down long grades and around sharp curves through the black hills. Word of Gertrude's revelation spread swiftly to the lowlifes, and all of them kept a sharp lookout through the breezy afternoon. But no matter how hard they peered, they did not find death lurking anywhere. They followed the rutted trail, hammered into a wide highway by thousands of wagons before them, and in the long June evening they rounded a claw of land and approached the warm springs which were nestled between dark dry bluffs that flamed orange in the low sun.

Drusilla chose to walk the last mile. She grew impatient. She itched to wash her clothing—why were women always surrounded by rags and constantly scrubbing? Men were lucky. Maybe she'd bathe, too, if suitable awnings could be erected. But not in the same water with those—those fallen women. She might catch something, something terrible! She'd insist on bathing first, before those lowlifes so much as dipped one of their petticoats—if they wore any—into the water.

But as they approached the spring they found horses hobbled nearby, a dozen of them. Not mustangs, either, but good solid bays and sorrels and blacks with some size. Distant figures lolled around a campfire, and even at a distance Drusilla could see they were all male. Ahead of her, Mister Skye loosened the thong that pinned his revolver in his holster. Up on the sunlit bluff she spied Skye's two squaws, sitting quietly on their ponies, and suddenly Drusilla grew afraid.

Chapter 5

It gladdened Mister Skye's heart to see his two women sitting their ponies on the far bluff. This was sudden country, even so close to Fort Laramie, and when he sent his women out on the flanks to scout and hunt, it was always with the gnawing fear that he'd never see one or the other again. So much could and did happen to lone riders in country like this—such as captivity or death at the hands of hunting or war parties. Ponies had a way of coming up lame. There were always sudden encounters with grizzlies or rattlers, not to mention flash floods or hailstorms or bad water.

But there they were, a mile or so above them on the high bluff. Old Victoria seemed to have meat slung over the rump of her pony, though he couldn't tell for sure just what. Antelope, probably. He thought of her as old now, with her face like lined brown parchment, and her black hair shot with gray. She'd lost weight and gotten smaller too, but still rode her ponies with feist and ease. And Mary! A woman in her prime, thirty now, still flashing the smiles exuding the bright happiness that had first galvanized him when he discovered her among her Shoshone people. He loved her, and even though he pushed toward sixty, she still built a fine fire in him. Nowhere on earth were there two women wiser on the trail, more experienced, cautious, and able to fight like male warriors. Time and again they'd rescued him, rescued parties he had guided. They found food where none existed, and water where it didn't flow.

Now their presence on the cliff above the warm springs signaled trouble, he thought. For the moment, they would not come in, but would lurk like ghosts out of sight of whoever squatted there, able in an emergency to send a bullet out of the night, or out of the brush. Somehow they knew, instinctively, what to do, and Mister Skye had only to fathom their ways to have a hand full of aces in any trouble.

He felt glad, as he always did in moments of potential danger, that his son, Dirk, wasn't here. Twelve winters now, and in Missouri being schooled. There wasn't money enough, but somehow things had been arranged. Mister Skye had friends, some of them from the fur-trade days, who were eager to help. How his Mary had wept, and hugged the boy, when they had put him on the steamer at Fort Union, but how proud she'd been that the blocky golden child would learn the mysteries of white men's medicine, and read the talking signs on paper. She wept that day but never again, and after that redoubled her efforts to bring happiness and comfort to the man she loved.

They judged right to be cautious, he thought. Who knew what sort of men hunkered ahead? Those at the warm springs could not see his women, who had retreated behind a low ridge. As always, he lifted his black stovepipe and screwed it down again, as a signal. The three of them had never discussed the gesture, but they all understood it to say, I see you, and be wary—there could be trouble. He watched the tiny figures turn their ponies and disappear beyond a saddle. For the time being, they would be watching all that transpired at the warm springs.

He glanced at Seven-Story Chang, riding beside him, and noted that the mandarin had not missed anything.

"Mister Skye likes to improve upon the Fates," he said, pulling his white stallion apart from Jawbone, who stayed strangely docile around the mandarin's horse. It was an instinctive move for a warrior, separating so as not to bunch up and become an easy target.

Mister Skye and his wagons pulled up near the springs, which were set in totally barren hills. Any trees that had once grown there had been long since stripped off by immigrants seeking firewood. Nonetheless the eight young men present there had a smoky fire wavering in the low light, feeding on buffalo chips and brush hauled some great distance.

They looked to be civilians but Mister Skye knew at once they were an army in spite of their gray butternut shirts and britches and old laced high-top boots and floppy felt hats over long unkempt hair and beards. A single glance at the horses, with their U.S. brand, and at the saddles, some of which were McClellans, told him that. A closer look revealed muzzle-loading Springfield carbines in cavalry-issue saddle-scabbards. One of them, a burly auburn-bearded man, had a Colt's Army revolver at his waist, and a faded blue shirt with darker blue chevrons on an arm where the marks of rank had been torn off.

Veterans, then. Wounded veterans, discharged, heading for the West and its bonanzas, Mister Skye thought. But he saw no wounds among them. They all had four intact limbs. They peered at him now, their gaze raking him and the wagons, wagons enameled a startling red, with dyed wagon sheets. Then he knew: *deserters*.

Men who, if caught, could be thrown into stockades— or shot. Men trained to battle and arms, and probably well disciplined by this deserting sergeant into a smooth fighting force. Mister Skye studied the surrounding country, looking for a ninth or tenth, but didn't see one. The land was so barren it would ill conceal a sentry. Deserters. No wonder he had not seen them at Fort Laramie. They had skirted the fort and ducked its patrols. Even now they were tempting fate, resting here at a popular stopping point on the Oregon Trail, between garrisoned outposts.

The burly one's cold gray eyes studied the Henry cradled in Mister Skye's arms, raked the giant Chinese, and glanced briefly at the rest, dismissing Riddle but assessing Blueberry, and then the women of all sorts. Cornelius Vanderbilt had vanished, and was in fact spread flat in his wagon, derringer in hand.

"Light and set," the man said suddenly, a smile forming in his curly beard. "I'm Twill. Conrad Twill. The boys and I could use some company. We just stopped here to wash up a bit, and boil up some parched corn. If you've got some chow to spare, we'd be plumb grateful."

Mister Skye nodded. "You're cavalry," he said.

"You see the McClellans and the cavalry mounts, I reckon. Yep, we are. Fort Kearney, Nebraska. On a little private foray for Gen'l Harney. Can't tell ye about it."

"Harney? The retired General Harney, mate?"

"One and the same, fella. You got a little chow to spare? We ain't seen hide nor hair of game along this trail. All shot out or skeered off."

General William Harney had sat out the war, bitter because the Union Army gave him no commands, not trusting him because of his Southern origins. That was common enough gossip around Fort Laramie, and Mister Skye well knew of the fate of the old frontier warrior.

"Where are you headed, mate?"

Twill didn't answer. Instead, he studied Skye and Jawbone and the rest. "I don't think I caught your name," he said.

"I am Mister Skye."

The name meant nothing to Twill. It usually meant a great deal to men familiar with the Northwest frontier.

"Well, Skye, it's confidential army business."

"Mister Skye."

The man laughed, and so did the others. "Well, if you want to be 'mister,' no skin off my back," he said. "You sure got yourself a passel of females here."

"Yes. They've engaged me to protect them."

"Looks like some of them lovelies don't want your protectin' very much."

Several of Twill's young colleagues laughed. Most of them were boys, Mister Skye thought. Eighteen, nineteen, fuzz-faced young toughs who decided to give the army the slip. And all the more dangerous because of their lack of scruple. Their carbines were not in hand, but close by.

The women had emerged from the wagons behind him, and Mister Skye knew these deserters would quickly understand Goldtooth's profession. It showed plain in their gaudy dress, in their manners or lack of them. All except Mrs. Parkins, who dressed severely and looked like a deacon's wife. Riddle's ladies had emerged too, and Mister Skye could see them being dismissed with a glance.

"I am engaged to do what I must do," said the guide amiably.

"Now, don't be hasty, Mister Skye," said Goldtooth. "These look like fine sporting men to me."

He said nothing. He couldn't stop incautious people, especially out on these wilderness trails where the constraints of the East seemed to fly away like dry cocoons and people's hidden natures emerged.

Alvah spoke up. "The name's Riddle," he said. "I already got yourn, but not the rest of these soldier-boys. Mrs. Riddle and me, we're chaperoning these young ladies to Bannack City, where their fiancés await them. We just happened to get caught in this—this"—he waved toward the lowlifes—"this other party, mutual protection of course, and we'll be pleased to have a visit with you. The ladies here—they do want to wash."

Mister Skye thought that for a man obsessed with angles, Alvah Riddle was being rash. Or blind.

Goldtooth said, "You boys come visit in a little while. The gals and I, we've got some scrubbin' to do, and don't you stare too hard at the laundry." She laughed amiably. "We'd like to get the undies scrubbed up and drying before some big train rolls in. Then you all come visitin' a little later, and we'll have us some dessert."

"I like dessert," said one of them, a youngster with blond stubble over sunburnt cheeks, and an old six-gun hanging low.

"I'd sure take it kindly if you could spare some chow," said Twill again. "This parched corn ain't fit for hogs."

"It seems that General Harney didn't provision you properly, mate," said Mister Skye.

"This here's army business and you get your nose out, big fella. You hear me? Any more pushing and prodding and you'll get hurt."

Mister Skye grinned, feeling his pulse quicken as it

always did in moments like this. Chang had already vanished somewhere to the rear of these men, managing to be invisible even in open space.

Another one of them, thin with wary brown eyes, broke in. "We don't want trouble, Twill. Remember? This is a quiet little mission."

"This big galoot Skye is proddy, and I thought to show him some army steel," Twill muttered. "But like you say, Callaghan, we got a mission to do." He turned to Skye. "All right, Skye. You and this bunch of wimmin and low-lifes mind your own business, and we'll mind ours, and you won't get hurt."

"It's Mister Skye, mate."

Twill laughed. "Sure enough, Mister Skye. And Mister Riddle. And my respects to these Virgin Marys."

The women carted bundles of clothing to the springs, along with balls of lye soap and washboards. For once no social distinction cleaved them, brides and bawds on their knees beside the purling waters.

Mister Skye shrugged. He enjoyed a brawl, just to be brawling, and the odds were about right. Maybe later. A few bloodied noses might straighten out the army. He'd brawled in the toughest brawl college in the world, the decks of British men-o'-war, and he'd brawl again, even near age sixty. But for the moment there were horses to care for, mules to unharness, travois to untie.

"You! Skye!"

Mister Skye turned.

"The army's requisitioning food. That's the way it is in war. You got any objections?"

Skye ignored him, and the sergeant laughed. Trotting down a game path now were Victoria and Mary on their ponies. A slain antelope drooped over Victoria's horse, the blood from an arrow wound in its chest dark and congealed. On Mary's horse teetered a tied bundle of deadwood, gathered in some distant place.

"Well, look here," said Twill. "We got us some meat. We'll have lots of meat tonight. Looks like you're a squawman. Two squaws, one for slaving and one for sport. Maybe you'll share all the meat with the army, eh, Skye?"

"It's Mister Skye, mate."

Twill laughed, and the other deserters, emboldened now, laughed too.

Mister Skye lifted the blood-soaked pronghorn carcass from Victoria's mount, and squeezed her hand.

"Sonofabitch," she muttered, and dismounted, glaring at the strangers with fierce proud eyes.

There were no trees, so Mister Skye hung the carcass from a propped-up wagon tongue and Victoria and Mary skinned it skillfully with deft cuts and tugs. Mary glanced fearfully at the rough men watching her, and at Mister Skye, who simply screwed his hat down on his gray head.

"You got 'em well trained, Skye. Well-trained squaws are like well-trained mules," said one.

"Mister Skye, mate." Patience, he thought. He had people under his care. He'd try to get free of this scum at dawn, get his assorted ladies miles away before the others stirred much.

It took an hour to butcher and cook the antelope on the economical fire Mary and Victoria built, and when it turned brown it yielded a small meal for all, but not enough to allay the hunger of men who had toiled outdoors all day. Cornelius Vanderbilt never showed, and lay hidden in his wagon. He'd gone coward, Skye thought, or else he recognized some soldiers he'd skinned some time or other. Well, let the thimblerigger starve. Blueberry took his meat but sat apart, finding some sort of safety simply in distance. The deserters eyed him from time to time, obviously adding up odds, calculating costs, if there should be a little fracas. In the end, they dismissed him as unimportant or an unknown quality. That was good, Mister Skye thought. And as twilight settled into darkness Seven-Story evaporated again into the night somewhere in the vicinity of the mules. Maybe even inside Skye's lodge, judging from the way Jawbone stood with laid-back ears and an alert glare in his evil yellow eyes. Good enough, then.

"I could sure use some meat," said one whose name Mister Skye knew to be McMaster. They laughed. The bawds grinned.

The three brides and the Riddles pretended not to hear or understand. They were peculiarly silent. Flora Slade said not a word, afraid that her Southern tongue would provoke these Union soldiers, or reveal her hatred of them. Alvah peered at them all, yellow-eyed and nervous and afraid. Even Mary-Rita Flaherty held her sharp tongue. Goldtooth itched to open her store for business, and Mister Skye wished she wouldn't, for the simple reason that these deserters would be penniless and likely to take what they couldn't pay for. But that wasn't Goldtooth's way, and now she sat beside the embers in her scoop-necked pink gown, provoking whatever lusts she could. Big Alice grinned and locked smoldering gazes with one man after another. Juliet Picard found ways to display her assets. Only the patrician Mrs. Parkins, dressed primly in a high-necked turquoise summer calico, didn't seem to invite trade, and that only provoked a great deal of attention from the young toughs, who recognized social caste when they saw it.

The June night air eddied languorous, and scented with fresh sage. It played with the clothing hung from lines stretched between the wagons, making the bawds' under-things of bright pink and purple and gold and silk shimmy in the lavender twilight. Such gauds delighted Mary and Victoria, who had studied the bawd clothing rapturously, fingering silky things, giggling at frills and peekaboos and transparent nothings and black net.

"Mister Skye," said Mary, "gimme one of them." She stabbed at something made entirely from black lace. "I never saw stuff like that at the sutler's store. How come they don't got it?"

The guide bellowed.

Over at the green wagon of Alvah Riddle hung another type of clothing altogether, primly white, dancing like ghosts in the night.

Alvah stood. "Well, ladies, it's time to retire. Guess I'll check my Greener shotgun before I turn in," he said in a slightly loud voice. "I got a fine new one, loaded with buckshot," he announced loudly. "Out on the trail, a man has to figure angles."

Several of the young deserters grinned through their beards, their teeth gleaming yellow from the embers of the fire.

"That's not the only protection we got," boasted Alvah loudly. "Got things that'd wipe out an army—ah, of Injun warriors and such."

He shepherded his uneasy women toward their wagon, after some detours into the darkness.

"I would have liked to write in my journal," said Drusilla, sounding annoyed.

But a few moments later the wagon stopped creaking, and there was silence.

"Well, ain't we gonna have fun," said Twill.

"I can hardly wait, honeyboy," said Goldtooth. "My good Kentucky bourbon is two bits, and other merchandise starts at a fancier price, U.S. dollars or gold."

It was coming, thought Mister Skye. He nodded slightly, and Mary and Victoria disappeared into the lodge. Jawbone snorted in the darkness. The rest were still seated around the dead fire, starlit shadows, the deserters rank with sweat and grime.

"I don't think I got me a thin dime," said Twill. "You got some coin to lend a poor suffering sarge, boys?"

"Ain't got a cent. Eight bucks a month in this man's army, and it don't last through payday," came a voice in the dark.

Goldtooth replied, "Why, don't worry your poor heads about cash. I bargain, honeypots, for any old thing. Like those nice guns. We love to have guns, don't we, ladies. Big guns, little guns. Long as they shoot!"

"I think not," said Mister Skye softly, thinking how stolen army Springfields would look to any Union command inspecting wagons on the Oregon Trail. But he was trumped by Twill.

"Sorry, my little lady. We'll be keeping our Springfields. And our horses. And our saddles. We're the army, honey, and this is war, and we're just going to requisition everything we need."

"Yeah," came a voice from the dark. "Start dishing out that Kentuck, for starters. Get a jug of that, and we'll just have a fine old time."

"I think not," said Mister Skye.

The silence steepled. "Want to try us, Skye?" said Twill.

"I think you'll just turn in now," said the guide.

Chapter 6

A hard rough hand clamped over Mary-Rita Flaherty's mouth, even as a burly arm caught her in a vise, pinioning her arms to her side. She bolted awake in convulsed terror, and in seconds her heart slammed so fast and hard in her chest she thought she'd die. She twisted and wrenched in her white nightdress, the fear of death upon her. But the brutal force pressed her, and she lay trembling and helpless, feeling now the cold steel of a blade upon her throat.

Beside her she heard the others threshing helplessly, and knew that more than one attacker crawled inside the dark wagon, where the girls and Gertrude Riddle had pallets on top of a pile of supplies. She peered around wildly. Mrs. Riddle lay inert; she could see that much in the murky light.

"If you make a sound—you're dead," hissed a harsh male voice addressing them all. Then the brutal hands and arms hoisted her as if she were a feather, tossing her outside. The night air pierced through her thin white nightdress. Then all three brides emptied out of the wagon, trembling ghosts in the night. She saw Alvah pinioned to the ground beneath the wagon by three men. One of them hefted Alvah's glinting Greener shotgun. Others ransacked the wagon, no doubt hunting for money. One pinched coin in a purse and grunted. Then Mary-Rita was lifted bodily and hauled to a place where two others held saddled horses. She was thrown up over the withers of one, and a man who seemed a giant swung up behind her.

Just then Mister Skye's horse, Jawbone, shrieked cra-

zily, squealing in the night as no other horse she had ever
heard. The eerie howling frightened her worse than the
cruel arms that bound her like a band of steel. They bolted
off, the throb of the loping horse hard upon her soft
thighs. She tried to see whether anyone followed, whether
anyone would rescue or help, but when she twisted her
head he cuffed her hard, a blow so jarring that she cried.
She hadn't cried since she was a wee lass, but now she
bubbled tears and wished she were back in green Ireland
with her people.

Beside her raced other horses, and in the starlight—no
moon lit the way—she saw the ghostly white forms of
Drusilla and Flora, all of them being sped to their doom.
They'd be used brutally and killed; she knew it. She
knew she would be tormented and die. She tried muttering an Our Father but the words wouldn't form in her
head, and she fought back panic. The brutal riding never
stopped, the hard gait of the horse slamming into her,
making her sore. She wanted desperately to relieve herself. She wanted desperately just to be put down, just to
feel the earth beneath her bare feet. But it never stopped.
She bit her lip until she tasted blood. She began to weep,
and got cuffed for it, but wept anyway, even as the cuff-
ings rocked her head.

She had fallen asleep thinking she had nothing to fear
from these rough men. There had been one last drama,
which she and the others had watched unfold in the
darkness around the campfire, from the shadow of the
wagon sheet as they peered through the loosened puckerstring hole. The soldier men had tried to work their
will upon those sinful women, but Mister Skye had told
them to forget it, go to bed. The burly guide had stood
there, his gleaming repeater cradled in his arms, and

resisted. They had laughed, but a voice in the darkness—Blueberry Hill's—told them that the first one to move would die. And another voice—it belonged to that slimy gambler, Cornelius—had announced that they were covered. That astonished them—a voice they'd never heard, because the gambler had never shown himself the whole evening. To cap it off, something out of the dark brained two of the soldiers, who fell with a thud, never uttering a word, and so they knew the heathen Chinee, plainly a man to be reckoned with, skulked behind them. Mary-Rita had sniffed. Heathen Chinee shouldn't be braining good Christian white men. She had blessed herself at the sacrilege. And finally, even that contemptible Alvah under their wagon had yelled, "My Greener's on you, gents, jist in case you try playing the angles."

And that wasn't the end of it either. That sinful woman had a pearl-handled little lady's revolver snug in her hand, aimed steadily at the sergeant, Twill. She had laughed gaily. "Sorry, honeys, we all shoot."

Mister Skye had told them to rest peaceable, or some of them would rest eternal. Mary-Rita liked that. He spoke poetry, and it flamed romantically in her Irish heart. She thought Skye a disgusting beast, him with a British way of talking, too, but at that moment she became an admirer.

She had fallen into uneasy sleep then, feeling protected enough by brave men. Until she had been so brutally awakened. And now she knew she'd die, after being abused. Saints in heaven, if they abused her she'd have a baby. That's what always came of it, her ma had said. She'd have a baby and not even be married, and that would be shame, worse even than, than . . . she couldn't think of anything worse. She wouldn't even have the courage to confess it to the father—if any father existed in this place she was being taken to. If only her ma and pa could see her now!

Then they'd be sorry they stuffed her on the boat! If only they could see her now! All their fault!

"I have to go. Let me down," she said to the man behind her.

For an answer he cuffed her again, and her head rang with the noise of it.

"You . . . you swine!" she boiled. "You scum! You don't even know how to treat a lady. I'm a lady! I'll bite your ear off, I will! You think you'll have your way with me, but I'll fix you!" she bawled. For an answer she got socked so hard she tumbled, and was dragged back up onto the horse just before she slid off. She wept again. "You are a pig, is what!" She wheeled her head around and spat at him, seeing the glob of it land full in his bearded face.

"Bitch!" he muttered. "I'll take the starch out of you soon enough, you dumb mick."

She spat again and he slapped her.

"Don't you call me a mick, you swine."

She boiled clear through, and the mounting ache and chafing of her bare limbs only made her madder.

"Saint Joseph, Saint Jude, Saint Paul, Saint Peter," she howled.

"Saint Mary, Saint Rita, Saint Elizabeth, Saint Clare, Saint Teresa," she added.

"Jesus before me, Jesus behind me, Jesus beside me," she yelled for good measure.

"Shut up, you little bitch."

She got an arm loose, balled up a fist and smacked it into his gut, feeling the explosion of sour air as it landed. "I'll kill you," she yelled, howling like a demon on the moors.

This time an arm clamped around her neck and tightened, choking her until her breath bottled up, harder and harder.

"That's a lesson," came the voice behind her as the arm eased. She gasped fiery air into her lungs, sucked it in again, and slugged him.

"Goddamn you!" he cried.

"You got trouble with that mick, Leo?" Twill's voice, and a horse loomed beside.

"I can handle it. Little bitch needs a lesson," snarled the man clamping her.

"You need a little lesson, lady?" Twill's amused voice came to her in the darkness. "Why, in a little while we'll teach you lessons you won't forget, and you'll like them, too." He laughed. "But for now you be quiet. One more peep outa you, and we'll shoot you."

That seemed like a good idea to Mary-Rita, so she yelled, a fine lusty bawl into the night, a bawl just like all the ghosts and goblins and werewolves she'd heard prowling on All Souls' Eve back across the seas. She howled, a fine daffy howl, and when the crack came on her skull, she just kept on howling, dizzy or not. A hand clamped over her mouth and she bit it, tasting blood. It yanked away, and she heard cursing behind her, words she'd never heard before and which she knew would shock a priest if she used them.

She yelled them back at him, and could hear laughter in the night. So she yelled them louder, fine dirty words bayed into the night like wolf laughter, an endless stream of them, new dirty words that filled her mouth and rolled from her tongue. She wasn't sure of the meaning of them all, but she knew they were dirty and her ma'd wash her mouth out if she heard, but her ma lived across the seas and glad to be quit of her. So she howled and they laughed, and she could sense those other women staring. She peered around. It grew lighter now, with a crack of gray slitting the east. She saw the gray and knew they hauled her south, away from the Platte River, away from the man who would marry her, a man with a name as Irish as her own, and a Catholic too.

Now in the gloomy dawn she saw only the two others, Drusilla and Flora, white ghosts in their nightgowns, silent and terrified. So Gertrude Riddle wasn't here. And neither was that skunk Alvah who'd got her into this, bought her, he did. Just the three of them, and each one a pure virgin. At least for the moment. Her anger slipped away to despair. "Blessed Mother, Blessed Mother, protect me, protect me, spread your wings over me, Saint Mary . . ." she muttered, and finally she wept.

Flora Slade had grown up with horses, and she found her perch on the slight pommel of the McClellan saddle not at all uncomfortable. Her thin white nightdress rode high on her thighs, though, and she deplored that. But nothing seemed possible with that lout of a Yankee pinning her in place with arms of iron.

War, she thought. She'd never escape the war. War had reduced her whole life to rubble in months, and now it came back to haunt her after she thought she was free of it. Using her! The same as they used a slave, she thought, and it shocked her. She was being taken somewhere—she, a white woman—taken somewhere against her will! How dare they? Had these Yankee soldiers no decency?

Unlike Mary-Rita, who howled and caterwauled, or Drusilla, who simply sobbed, Flora sat cold and calm and thinking of murder and mayhem. She took after her father. Her father had been a calculating man, who smiled when the occasion called for it, not particularly a cheerful sort. Her father had perfected a calculating command of human nature, and knew exactly how much he could demand for a slave; knew exactly how to deal with sullen, rebellious slaves without destroying the merchandise. Oh, that had always been a sight, the disciplining of slaves, and Flora thought back on it with a certain electric pleasure through her back and loins.

Her father, Conan, had been a tall wiry man with jet hair, and a long face so chalky white that some believed the sun never touched it. In fact the sun touched it a great deal, but he neither tanned nor burned. Slaving waxed more than profitable, it became a bonanza, though a tricky thing because a lot of merchandise had been damaged. He had built, in Biloxi, a fine red-brick auction market with a raised covered dais on the street front, where crowds of buyers could gather on auction day. Inside hulked his offices, pens, and a few barred calls for particularly bestial brutes. Also a kitchen and some crude sanitary facilities: it wouldn't do for the place to stink too much, or for the merchandise to get ill. In the rear, cloistered from eye and ear, stood a small brick disciplinary room with things in it that always made Flora shiver. Occasionally slaves were shot there, either because they were weak or ill and not worth the care, or because they had turned into savage animals. But for the most part, they were whipped, after their arms and feet were pinioned to the walls with chained manacles. At first her father had shooed her away from these events, but she had sneaked back anyway, and eventually he gave up. So she knew exactly how to treat people beneath her, and knew all the special torments reserved for males, and other torments reserved for females.

The wealth generated by this lucrative trade had purchased a fine mansion with Doric columns in front, and a whole stable of blooded horses, some trained to saddle and some to driving, all with the ruthless discipline that had been applied to human beasts of burden in the auction yard. Flora knew, by the time she grew old enough to understand such things, that her family was richer than almost anyone save for a few plantation owners who rarely came to Biloxi anyway. She knew too that slavery was a great institution, not only the source of her family's comforts, but valuable to the whole South, and also a natural and beneficial way of life for the Africans themselves, who might otherwise be trapped in steaming jungles without the slightest enlightenment of religion and science.

By her teens, Flora had become a willful aristocrat who defied her soft and retiring mother, invited the courtship of numerous swain and beaux and gallants, promising and tantalizing and seducing them with endless adroitness, but actually giving them nothing at all save for an occasional chaste kiss. If a horse displeased her, she had it shot, until even her father protested the extravagance. But she always reminded him that he would do the same, and she took after him. She had her own retinue of slave women, none of whom pleased her for more than a few weeks, whereupon she caused them to be whipped or sold or sent back to the auction market to be sold, naked, to someone else. She enjoyed the power of it. Let any one of them become too familiar with her, and she would swiftly show them the differences of caste, class . . . and power.

Then the war changed everything. Almost at its debut, her father had been killed by a Union minié ball that had passed through his left eye and emerged from the base of his skull. A month after the black-garlanded caisson had drawn his Stars-and-Bars-draped casket to the family graveyard, and he had been laid to rest with full military honors befitting a colonel of the Mississippi cavalry, her mother had taken ill and begun a lingering decline that had lasted six months. Meanwhile men stripped the great house of horses for Confederate cavalry; income from the slave dealership had ceased, the grim brick fortress became a hospital for the wounded; and finally she found herself alone in an abandoned mansion, selling off the last of her furniture, staring at untilled fields, damning surly slaves who no longer jumped to her whip. That's when she began to think of escape to a better life, somewhere, somehow. Preferably shooting a few blue-shirted Union soldiers en route. If she killed a thousand of them, she had thought, it would not atone for the murder of her father, death of her mother, and present poverty.

And now one of those despicable Yank soldiers pinned her familiarly in her nightdress, taking her against her will, and intended to do to her exactly what a slave woman might expect. She was a slave! The thought astonished her. They would force her onto her back just like the lowest slave women, and they would have their sport with her! She seethed at the thought of it, seethed that a person of her caste would be treated like a slave by these barbaric Northern louts. But as she seethed, she realized that she had not been bred humble or dumb, and that her salvation lay in her hands. They'd find her no slave, submitting dumbly to their lusts. She knew where to strike them to double them up. Knew exactly where to jab with a knife to ruin their manhood forever. She'd seen slaves and other animals gelded, and she'd geld these Yank pigs one by one.

So Flora didn't struggle or howl vile obscenities the way that stupid immigrant girl did, or weep the way that toad of a New England woman did. She calculated. Her maidenhead for sixteen balls. The only trouble was, she hadn't the faintest idea how to wreak her revenge.

"You're smart," said a rough voice behind her. "Not like that dumb girl fresh off the boat."

"Yes, I'm smart. And I'll find ways to kill you," she retorted.

He laughed.

The endless ride had become painful, even for her. They were hastening south; she knew that from the light cracking the east. It occurred to her that she might die. These barbarians might simply use the women and kill them.

"Are you going to kill us?" she asked.

"Only if they're dumb enough to follow. If those low-lifes and that Skye come after you, we might."

She peered behind to look at him, now that enough gray light allowed her to see. Twill, the one whose blue shirt showed where sergeant's chevrons had once been.

"You're cowards and deserters," she said. "That's what Yankees are."

"It'll be a pleasure to enjoy a Reb lady," he replied. "In fact, this is as good a place as any."

"You had better kill me when you're done. Because I'm going to remember your face. And I'm going to have you tracked down. I'm going to find you, wherever you hide, and have you killed, but not before you lose your balls."

"My, my," said Twill. "I thought you Southern belles were all blushes and kisses."

"Try me," she said.

He stopped the horse, and dumped her unceremoniously into a patch of prickly pear. She yelped, sprang to her feet, and landed a petite foot in the chest of the cavalry horse, which reared up and began pitching, while Twill cursed.

The others had stopped, tossing the other brides to earth. They halted in an open arid meadow, a shallow valley. Stiff-legged men stomped life back into their saddle-bound limbs, while the women huddled and drew their thin nightdresses tight about them. The air lay chill.

"Well, who's first?" asked Twill, after he had gotten his mount under control.

"Loser gets the ugly one," said one. They laughed. Drusilla looked tormented, Flora thought. No trees, no shrubs, no brush grew here, and whatever happened would happen in full sight of everyone. Now terror and rage crawled through her, and she felt a need to vomit.

She had no weapons, not even long fingernails to claw with; not a shoe or a belt. Leering, Twill approached her, and yanked her to her feet. She scarcely realized that the other women were being yanked up by other men and dragged, like her, to a sandy place. Then a single brutal rip yanked the nightdress off and spun her to earth.

"Halfway pretty—for a Reb lady," he said.

A moment later he was on her, and she fought with knee and claw and teeth and muscles inspired by rage. But it failed her, even as her screaming gained her nothing as it pierced out into a dawn-gray wilderness. He laughed and fenced and finally clubbed her, so that her head rang, and still she evaded him, evaded the piercing, until at last she ran out of breath, pinioned by hands other than Twill's, and she felt herself hammered and invaded.

She scarcely heard the weird shrieking of Skye's horse Jawbone from afar, and scarcely knew why the thing that hadn't yet succeeded was abandoned, why Twill leapt to his feet and yanked at his clothing. She sprang at him, and with the only weapon she possessed, bit him exactly where she wanted, and spit out flesh.

Chapter 7

He thought he was too late. The women sprawled whitely in the dirt, somehow luminous in the murk of dawn. On second glance he changed his mind. Each of them thrashed violently, far from inert. At the sound of Jawbone's insane screech, deserters scrambled to their feet and lumbered toward their stolen cavalry mounts with the sheathed Springfields hanging from the saddles.

Jawbone wheeled to cut them off, his demonic screeching stirring the cavalry horses until they danced at the end of their pickets. The evil blue roan terrified horses as well as men. Mister Skye dropped the big rope rein and let the animal have its head. Easily he lifted the new Henry and sent a bullet into the earth just ahead of the deserter closest to the horses. He levered another cartridge and fired at one who was wrestling one of the women to her feet, taking care where he aimed. The slug missed, plowing dirt close to the man. He dropped the woman. A revolver cracked, and Skye saw that Twill had his side-arm out and was shooting with one hand, even while clutching his naked groin where blood leaked between the fingers of his other hand.

The picketed mounts pulled loose and skittered away from the deserters, and Skye turned Jawbone toward Twill, who grappled with the Slade girl. The deserter yanked her to her feet and slid behind her, making her a living shield of soft white flesh, while his revolver pressed into her skull above the ear.

"She dies, Skye. Drop that Henry or she dies!" he barked.

The man had sand, Mister Skye granted him that. The

sort of sand that had made him a sergeant. He leveled his Henry straight at the girl, straight at Sergeant Twill.

"If you kill her, mate, you'll die," he said softly.

One of the others had caught a horse and ripped the Army Springfield from its sheath. Skye swung slightly, shot, and the man's hands bloomed red even as the horse began pitching wildly from the splattering lead that had struck the sheath and carbine and sprayed in all directions, none fatal. Twill shot, and the slug tore Skye's hat off, along with some of his hair and the smallest furrow of scalp.

Now others were catching their horses, and that became the larger danger. He leapt free of Jawbone, who screeched his macabre howl and plummeted full tilt into the milling cavalry horses, bowling over deserters in the process. He wheeled through them, ears laid back, flailing hooves and teeth in every direction, spinning violently on any man who lifted himself from the ground.

Skye saw the other women, Drusilla and Mary-Rita, attempt to rise. "Stay low," he yelled, and they did. Twill was the problem. The sergeant shot again from behind the Slade girl, but it flew wild because she struggled. Mister Skye levered his Henry and lowered it again, straight at Flora Slade, straight at Sergeant Twill.

"She dies if you don't drop that rifle," snapped Twill.

"You die, Twill. If she dies, you die."

Skye crouched now, sliding in little panther steps toward the pair of them.

"Don't shoot me," screamed Flora. "You murderer, don't shoot me!" The terrible black bore of the Henry opened on her. The muzzle of the revolver shoved again into her skull above her ear.

"Miss Slade," said Skye quietly, "get out of the way."

She gaped at him. Eternities passed.

"Stop where you are, Skye—" barked Twill, swinging the revolver from Flora's head to shoot at Skye again. Flora wrenched suddenly, spoiling the shot, then dropped herself violently, wrenching free from Twill's arm and falling in a heap on the ground before him. Mister Skye aimed down the octagonal barrel and slowly squeezed the trigger. The Henry cracked, and Twill crumpled, dead from the hole in his forehead before he hit earth.

Flora flapped her mouth wordlessly. She sprang up and leapt at Mister Skye like a lioness, her claws raking him. "Murderer!" she cried. "You would have killed me. You stupid oaf."

He pulled the powerful girl off him and pinioned her with his free arm.

"Stand down, now," he said quietly. "You're alive and safe."

Several of the others crawled toward the milling horses, even as Jawbone paraded murderously between the men and the animals.

He snapped a bullet into the earth before the most active one.

"The next bullet will not miss," he thundered at them.

Behind him he heard the soft progress of a horse, and a swift glance revealed Seven-Story Chang on his white stallion. That would be about right, he thought. At Jawbone's first screech in the night, Skye had catapulted from his lodge, thrown on the saddle that was always at his lodge door, and loped off only a minute or two after the deserters had pillaged the Riddle wagon and fled into utter blackness. He'd given Jawbone his head. The horse would track through the blackness, using its nostrils and senses to follow a trail that Mister Skye could not pick out of the inky night. He knew Chang, the warrior mandarin, would be along soon enough. Skye sometimes probed so close to the deserters he could hear them talking and jesting ahead, but he and Jawbone hung back until dawn, when he could see what to do, and do it.

"I see I am not needed," said Chang as he turned his stallion toward the cowering deserters and leveled a long-barreled blue revolver upon them.

"Needed you plenty, and sooner," replied Skye.

Mary-Rita and Drusilla lay huddled and naked in the dirt. The Irish girl simply stared, but Drusilla wept softly and clutched her whiteness with her hands as if to ward off the gaze of male eyes. Three thin nightgowns lay in white ruin in the bunchgrass. Flora stood, no longer caring, and railed at Skye.

"I'll horsewhip you," she snapped. "Aiming that gun at me! I'll see you in hell! I'll cut you to pieces, you and your stupid squaws. You big idiot. You risked my life!"

She was, in a way, a beautiful woman with a fine full lithe figure turning golden in the dawn, and Mister Skye found it difficult to address her. "Was I too late?" he said softly.

"I don't know," she snapped. "Yes, you were hours too late. You should have been protecting us, you swine. You're a murderer. You killed that man. And stop staring at me."

"That is hard to do."

She picked up her gown, now confetti in her fingers.

"Now what am I going to do?"

Mister Skye addressed Miss Dinwiddie. "Was I too late?" he asked softly.

She shook her head and wept again.

"Was I too late?" he asked Mary-Rita Flaherty.

"Of course you was," she snapped. "Here am I, without a stitch on me body and men staring at me like I'm some common slut. And God in heaven and all the saints peering at me naked body and the shame of it. Oh, was you too late? If you had an ounce of decency, you wouldn't even ask a poor lass. And stop your starin'. I haven't got fine full breasts like that one has, just these little things that won't suckle a mouse, and you ask, was you too late?"

Mister Skye sighed. He could face arrows and guns. He could plunge into war. He could shoot to kill. The sight of gouting blood, his own or others', didn't faze him. But these women did, and he retreated from their glares.

"You," he said to one of the deserters. "You are going to donate your shirt and britches to the lady standing there."

"And what does that leave me in this wilderness?" the man muttered.

"That's your problem."

Reluctantly the man shed his shirt and wrestled with the buttons of his cavalry britches.

"Saints preserve us, there's enough nakedness to go around," yelled Mary-Rita. "Are ya daft, Skye?"

"Mister Skye," he said.

He carried the britches and shirt to Flora, who swiftly put them on, rolling up trouser legs.

"You!" barked Mister Skye. The man he pointed to reluctantly stood and began sliding out of his shirt and britches, and moments later Drusilla stood before them in clothing.

"You left me to last so you could feast your sinful eyes on me," snapped Mary-Rita. "You pig."

Moments later, another of the deserters doffed his shirt and britches, and Mary-Rita skinned them on, wallowing in the oversized garments. The third deserter had worn nothing underneath.

"I'll burn to death in this wilderness," he snapped.

"Three nightdresses over there, mates." He addressed Chang: "We may as well return the stolen mounts, saddles, and carbines to the army."

Chang began to round up the horses and the cavalry gear. In Twill's saddlebags he found a black pigskin purse laden with greenbacks and some double eagles. No doubt Riddle's. Mister Skye picked up his black stovepipe hat, discovered new ventilation in it, and screwed it down on his head.

"You'd leave us here on foot?" yelled one.

"Should have thought of all that before you deserted. The army can use the horses and carbines. Can't use you, though. Shoddy goods."

"We'll starve!" cried another.

"You'll have Twill's revolver and cartridge belt," Skye said. "Which is more than you're worth. I will take it with me for a half a mile or so, and then drop it for you."

Once they were clad, the women recovered their dignity and courage swiftly. Somehow it had come out well enough, though he felt unsure about Flora. Maybe the slave trader's snotty daughter deserved what she got.

He helped them mount, and adjusted the stirrups on the McClellan saddles.

"You!" he barked at the surviving deserters. "Lie down. I'll shoot the first one that stands, for as long as you're in the range of this rifle."

They glowered at him, but obeyed. Skye watched them from Jawbone's back while Chang and the women distanced themselves, driving the unridden horses ahead. Then he caught up.

Noon passed before they reached the warm springs camp on the Oregon Trail. Old Victoria, always alert, sat her pony on the bluff above the springs, watching them come. Mister Skye doffed his hat, and she turned her little bay down the easy slope. They rode in silently, amid the gapes of the fallen doves, Cornelius Vanderbilt, Blueberry Hill, and his own lithe and dusky Mary. But the Riddles clucked and fussed and asked questions. Alvah hadn't scraped razor over flesh; Gertrude luffed like a loose sail.

"High time, Skye," he said. "High time. These women look badly used. I'll hold you responsible for it. I'm glad they're alive, at any rate . . . Are they in good marriageable condition?"

"They are unharmed," said Mister Skye wearily.

"Indecent in men's clothing," snapped Gertrude. "Wash up. We won't have you dressed like that."

The three brides dismounted. They didn't need encouragement to head for the warm springs. All of them were caught in a melancholy silence.

"You poor dears," said Goldtooth. "We can help you. If you wish. Come along, ladies—we'll help these girls."

Drusilla nodded. Flora and Mary-Rita acquiesced, silently.

"Stay away from those women of mine. I know your angle, and I ain't a-gonna permit it," snapped Alvah.

But Goldtooth had taken charge. She snapped instructions to her ladies, who brought awning for a screen, and bottles of mysterious salves and ointments.

"It ain't right. Women like that messing with my brides," muttered Alvah.

"What happened?" asked Blueberry Hill. Mister Skye told them the whole story, and how he and Chang rescued the women.

"Damaged goods! The women has got carnal knowledge now because you didn't get there fast enough. I know your angle, Skye. You was fixing to break me. Where's my shotgun that they took? Where's my purse that they robbed? You keeping it?"

Mister Skye stared at the chinless, unshaven man. "I don't recollect that you employed me, Riddle."

"What do you mean by that?"

"I don't recollect that you paid Goldtooth, there, your share of my fee."

Riddle glanced around craftily. "So that's your angle. I should have known. Not an ounce of decency in you; not a shred of charity for these poor abducted women. Not a care in you about my business, bringing virtuous folk together to unite in eternal wedlock." Riddle peered narrowly up at Skye. "I suppose you'll keep my purse. I didn't contract for your services—there was no contract, no agreement—and now you'll pay yourself from it."

Mister Skye laughed. He slid heavily off Jawbone, tired from a dozen miles of night riding, and lumbered over to 'Twill's cavalry mount. He dug around in the saddlebags, found Riddle's purse, and held it up.

"This what you're looking for?"

"It is. And there was three hundred and seventeen dollars and twenty-seven cents in it, in currency and specie. If it ain't all there, Skye, I'll see you in court."

"Mister Skye."

The guide opened the black pigskin, and extracted a hundred fifty in greenbacks, and handed the rest to Riddle.

"That goes to the madam, who paid your share."

Alvah could scarcely contain his rage. "I didn't make that contract; she did. I knew you had an angle, you and her teaming up to sucker an honest businessman. I know your kind, Skye."

Mister Skye grinned. "All right then," he said. He stuffed the bills back into the purse and handed it to Riddle. "Here it is. Count it if you wish."

"What's your angle, Skye?" Riddle said suspiciously, even as he furtively flicked through the contents with adroit fingers.

"Well, if you aren't employing me, Riddle, I thought I'd just take the girls back and leave them with the deserters. Take your purse back, too."

"You wouldn't!"

"You haven't employed me, Riddle."

"It's a bluff. I know your angle. You'd never abandon decent women to them kind of men."

Mister Skye scratched his head. "I do believe you're right, mate. Guess I'll deliver them back to Laramie. I imagine there'd be a heap of soldiers, officers maybe, who'd like to tie the knot."

"You can't do that, Skye. They're my property!"

"Mister Skye," he said, leading Jawbone toward his lodge, which Mary and Victoria were dismantling.

"We gonna go down the road now?" Victoria asked.

"You are a beautiful lady."

"Sonofabitch," she muttered. "You getting crazy in old age, Chief Skye. If you ain't going down the road, I am. Pretty quick that wagon train with that Jarvis Porter is gonna roll in here, and then they see these sporting women and all hell busts loose. Maybe you'll get drunk, and I'll get mad."

Mister Skye laughed, and settled to earth in the glowing sun for a ten-minute snooze. That was the great thing about squaws, he thought. They did all the work and he had all the fun. He'd had a good life. The best of all lives, though it had begun brutally, when he'd been pressed into the British navy as a boy, and spent years as a virtual slave in a man-o'-war until he slid over the side one foggy night back in twenty-six, and swam to the south bank of the Columbia River, close to Hudson's Bay Company's

Fort Vancouver. Thirty-seven years now, a man of the mountains and prairies, a squawman, living a life beyond the wildest imaginings of the London youth who'd been shanghied on the banks of the Thames. And he didn't regret a moment of it, not even when the likes of Alvah Riddle temporarily blotted out the sun.

The burly guide cocked one eye open and rolled to a sitting position, feeling the soft buckskin shirt that had been Mary's shy gift to him slide over his barrel staves. The paunchy matchmaker shifted uneasily from one foot to the other, clearing his throat, which bobbled beneath a day's whiskers.

"I've been working the angles. Don't think you're pulling one over on me, because I'm wise to you, Skye. I know what you're up to, better than most. You're not worth a hundred fifty. This here is a well-marked trail and we don't need no guide. Mebbe worth a little for protection. Not any hundred fifty. But I'll make an agreement. I'll pay that—that—woman the price, but deduct the price of my shotgun, which was just under fifty dollars, leaving a hundred. You didn't protect my property, get my scatter-gun back, so I'll deduct that."

Mister Skye yawned, observing puffball June clouds in the aching blue beyond Riddle's head. "I've been paid. Deal with the madam."

Drusilla approached, encased now in a crisp gray cotton dress, her washed hair hanging lustrous and loose. "Mister Skye," she said, "I don't suppose anyone has thanked you. I wish to."

The guide nodded, peering up at a plain woman with intelligent soft eyes, hidden behind small gold spectacles.

"That—woman—who runs the parlor house . . ." She glanced helplessly at Mister Skye, and Riddle, and proceeded bravely on. "She says that no one was—damaged. Miss Slade is . . . intact. We all owe that to you."

Mister Skye felt embarrassed. He'd rather face a hunting party of Bug's Boys than this. He cleared his throat and flapped his lips. "We'll travel in fifteen minutes," was all he could manage. "Harness your mules, Riddle. I see that Blueberry and Vanderbilt have theirs all set to go."

"But—but, you're to harness the mules. That is part of it, Skye. You did it yesterday morning. That's part of it. Otherwise—"

Mister Skye stood and slapped tan dust from his leggins.

"Miss Dinwiddie. I'll be escorting you and Miss Slade and Miss Flaherty back to Fort Laramie, where you will have your freedom. I will leave instructions with the post sutler, Colonel Bullock, to attend to your needs on my account. I think you'll find a good new life there."

"I'll sue!" croaked Riddle. "These women are under bond, signed and sealed."

"Harness your mules," said Mister Skye.

"I'll pay the bawd her extortion," Riddle muttered.

Chapter 8

Blueberry Hill had a great fondness for mules. Goldtooth's mules were long brown creatures with bowed noses, floppy ears, and powerful bodies. Like himself, he thought. Mules were smarter and feistier than horses, and that reminded him of himself. He understood mule minds much better than horse minds. Mules were opportunists, finding feed and comfort at times when horses stared stupidly from harness and ignored the grass at their feet. That also reminded him of himself. He prospered with no visible means of support.

Technically he had been a slave all his life, but actually he lived in a delicate limbo, neither a freeman nor in servitude. He had never been manumitted, and hadn't a single paper declaring his ownership of himself. But neither did his masters, from outside Biloxi, ever pursue. In fact he was owned by an elderly widow and she had been rather fond of him, and not inclined to set the hounds after him. Still, that could change in an instant. He had drifted off, found refuge in the demimonde of Beale Street in Memphis, and had settled down in the parlor house and saloon of Goldtooth Jones. There he lived one day at a time, doing everything. He plucked his banjo and sang; learned to tickle tunes on the black and white levers of the pianoforte; learned to mix spirits and pour slightly watered bourbon; found himself evicting unruly white men from the confines; hauled water and toted bales and cared for Miss Jones's fine trotters and coach. For all this he was fed and sheltered, had his choice of the merchandise, and picked up occasional tips. He never seemed to lack funds, though he never seemed to have any to spare, either.

But it proved to be a delicate existence, especially when war came and with it the possibility of being conscripted into slave-labor battalions in the service of Confederate army engineers, digging sanitary trenches and breastworks, cutting and hauling firewood, and toiling for those who wished to keep him in bonds. So when Memphis fell to the Union forces early in the war, he had quietly rejoiced, until he found that they had similar designs on him, and a moralistic fervor that threatened the livelihood of his patroness, Goldtooth Jones, and thereby threatened him. So he felt perfectly content to be where he rode now, far west of the conflict and organized society, sitting in the madam's flaming red wagon, reining the mules and spitting occasionally at the footboards, targeting a knot midway between his black patent-leather shoes and the white spats over them.

Each dewy dawn he and Seven-Story Chang harnessed the twelve mules, with no help from Cornelius Vanderbilt, who considered such labor beneath him and in any case liked to sleep until the very last moment before they struck camp. The evening unharnessing fell easier, and Blueberry did that alone, picketing or hobbling each animal in good grass, near water if possible. Each hot day, Blueberry drove Goldtooth and her ladies, while Vanderbilt drove the second red wagon. The giant Chinese, who rode along for adventure rather than for the madam, simply mounted his great white stallion and vanished one way or another, often stopping to consult with Mister Skye at the front of the small procession.

Behind him this day the ladies lolled on their makeshift pallets beneath the pink wagon sheet. Heat blanketed the land, making breath come short. Usually they walked, or sat beside him as the wagon rolled down the long westering ruts, but today the sun forged so fierce and the air lay so heavy with blistering heat that they left Blueberry to his own devices. He coaxed the goldbricking mules along, cussing them with his gravelly voice, singing them love songs. They responded by rotating giant cupped ears backward, listening for the vinegar voice that meant whip or lash, and not hearing it. Today all three wagons ambled at the pace of an ox train.

Customarily he wore his black broadcloth suit coat everywhere, on this long trail as well as in camps, just as he wore it as a sort of uniform in the parlor house on Beale Street. But by mid-morning, the coat had turned into a furnace, and he felt his cotton shirt drenching across his back and belly, and sweat collect under his armpits. And so he gingerly wrapped six reins around some scalded ironwork and doffed the coat, folding it neatly beside him. The wily mules decided the faint tremor of the reins could be interpreted as a lax hand, and Blueberry admired them for their craftiness, a craftiness well understood by any black man who had ever worked cottonfields in heat like this. He felt a faint coolness as the sweated white shirt began to dry in the furnace breezes.

"Move your lazy ass," he said softly to the mules, recalling when the exact phrase had been spoken to him in his boyhood. Not once but too many times to remember. The mules quickened slightly, for a few yards, and imperceptibly slowed down again, and Blueberry grinned. Mules were realists, but had a great sense of theater. Mules were four-footed magicians, expert at illusions and abracadabra. Mules were mountebanks, standing eagerly in their traces but plotting skulk and sloth. He knew the inside of a mule soul, and they knew the inside of his.

"Were you referring to me?" asked Big Alice, putting a bawdy coloration on it. "When it's a little cooler, honey, I'll move it fast enough."

Big Alice's mind went only in one direction. From any starting point on the compass, it vectored toward sex. In that respect she was a soul mate of Blueberry's, seeing life groin-to-groin. She liked herself, enjoyed what she did, and had no intention of leaving the life until old age forced her to. In that respect also she was Blueberry's soul mate. Alicia Roque rose almost to six feet of high yellow, a fine amber nectar of French and Spanish and African, raised half wild in the bayous, where she dis-

covered her life's calling at age thirteen, and never looked
back. Big Alice's approach to her trade seemed exhausting, and he did not wish to exhaust himself after a broil-
ing day.

"I'm saving my virginity for Mrs. Parkins," he replied,
rattling the reins.

Mrs. Parkins did not reply.

Blueberry could neither scribble his name nor extract
sense from books and magazines and broadsides, except
for numbers. He knew the exact difference between a one-
dollar Confederate shinplaster and a ten. But he plumbed
souls, and knew precisely what anyone around him was
thinking. He constantly dumbfounded people by telling
them their private thoughts, and he had long since discovered a certain power in it, this ability he alone shared
with God. Thus he knew the minds of his mules. Not in
general terms, but specifically. Right now, for example,
the offside wheeler concentrated on murdering a horsefly
that had landed on its nose and was crawling toward a
nostril.

Blueberry closed his eyes for a moment, shutting out
the arid sagebrushed hills and the long blue mountains as
they approached the Platte River Bridge. He wanted to
know whether Mrs. Parkins would welcome him tonight.
He already knew everything else worth knowing about
her. The others always welcomed him, but Cleo Sylvanus
Parkins sometimes dithered. No more prominent families
ruled Memphis than those named Parkins and Sylvanus,
and no more beautiful belle resided in antebellum Memphis than young ice-blond Cleo Sylvanus. She crowned
and sceptered Goldtooth's ménage. In 1859 she had been
given in marriage to Hannibal Parkins, who had amassed
a fortune by massacring hardwoods, notably black walnut, and by age thirty-four, having slaughtered forests, he

built himself a fine porticoed red-brick manse on a slope of Chickasaw Heights overlooking the river town and the silvery river. Cleo had already discovered voluptuous pleasures, and supposed, as Hannibal carried her straight across the threshold to the fourposter upstairs, that she would now command an endless supply of this titillating commodity. But in fact nothing satiated her, and while Hannibal proved as virile as any man, she never felt satisfied. Given her position, she resigned herself to this state of affairs, except for minor flirting at balls. But with the onset of war, Hannibal became Colonel Parkins and marched off to slaughter Yankees. Cleo wasted no time, not even twenty-four hours, before finding satisfactions, and enjoying the game of it as well, as she flitted among young Confederate officers. In a trice she galvanized gossip. But people of her caste merely tut-tutted such things, and ignored her even while her conduct grew wanton.

Then Memphis fell, and with scarcely a breather Cleo seduced a Union Army captain, her thirty-eighth lover, to be precise. That set tongues wagging, so she invited him to move into the great red-brick house, just to make them wag harder. Hannibal was gone, and could not in fact return to Union-held Memphis. It all seemed amusing enough until the captain's wife appeared one day, trotting down the gangplank of a riverboat she had boarded at Dubuque, proceeded by carriage straight to the Parkins mansion, and shot the captain dead. Some said, dead in bed, with Cleo Parkins beside him. At that point, the tattered shreds of society in occupied Memphis froze Cleo out. She, in turn, chose a career that would fill her insatiable needs and let her thumb her nose at the silly snobs. She arrived in a liveried carriage one day before Goldtooth's door, and announced her intentions. Unlike most any other woman of her caste, she kept her full name out of spite. Business had been spectacular. Not every man had sampled high-society women. Goldtooth goosed the price to astronomical levels, fifty Union dollars a tickle, but the trade never slowed—and Cleo lusted more than ever.

Blueberry delighted as much as anyone else in the reckless fury of Mrs. Parkins's lovemaking. He closed his eyes, heard Cleo entertaining the prospect of a night with Blueberry, felt no objections emanating from the ice-blond bawd, and decided, with a small flick of his six reins, how he would spend the night.

Homer Donk had devoted his entire life to improving the odds. It was not just philosophy with him, it was religion. Look life over and find ways to bend Fate. It didn't really matter to him how Fate could be bent; only that the odds in his favor would multiply like rabbits.

He lacked the nature of a mule-driver or teamster, but Fate had decreed that he would drive Goldtooth's red wagon west, as the third and last wagon in the procession. Within the bowels of his wagon, fine stout oaken hogsheads of Tennessee bourbon clunked and whispered, along with his roulette wheel with the removable magnet under the seven, and faro layout. The wagon toted sundry other items that would elegantly furnish Goldtooth's next bordello, along with delicacies not available in Bannack City, such as tins of oysters. And beyond that, a supply of staples and trail foods for Goldtooth's entire ménage. The Celestial, Seven-Story Chang, had thrown his small affairs into the wagon as well. Blueberry possessed nothing and needed nothing, beyond a bedroll.

Homer Donk didn't like driving the last wagon. No guard marched behind to protect him from surprise. So he peered backward frequently, around one side and the other, staring past the wagon sheet sagging on its bows, beyond the saddle horses tied to the rear, and off to the dusty backtrail, where who knows what lurked. He had been doing that, looking over his shoulder, a long time, both as Homer Donk from Brooklyn, and Cornelius Vanderbilt. He had selected the name, Vanderbilt, as a classy way to hoist the odds. It didn't matter whether people took him for the famous financier; it festooned him with instant respect and recognition. It had a mellifluous ring, too, not at all like the dismal one he had inherited from his Dutch parents.

He meditated, with some satisfaction as the wagon seat battered his tailbone, that he had changed life's odds. He had been dealt deuces, and had managed to turn the business of living into jacks and queens. With luck, he might yet make kings and aces. There had been temporary setbacks, such as when Skye had snatched his braced faro deck from him at Fort Laramie, and burned it. He muttered. It would take a few days of painstaking labor to pinprick another deck, and thus restore the edge. Faro, when played square, offered the dealer only the slightest of odds, about half a percent or so. Plainly that needed improving if a man were to survive in the sporting world at all. The pinpricks allowed him a precise knowledge of what card lay just below the top one in the casebox, and then it was easy enough to palm one, or pluck seconds if the need arose, which it rarely did.

He thought from time to time to do something about his appearance, for life had dealt him deuces in that matter, also. The image in looking glasses had been a cadaverous, pale, pocked man possessed of a long horseface and aquiline nose with fur prospering around the nostrils. His jet hair grew straight as a shingle and looked greasy even after he had just scrubbed it with Castoria.

He had squinty furtive brown eyes that focused on nothing for more than a split second, but saw everything. He lacked the face or physique that would swoon a woman, so he had abandoned all thought of domestic life and had tackled his pleasures in the demimonde. He did, however, sport the attire of his profession, a swallowtail black coat, boiled shirt, luxurious maroon cravat with a flashy two-carat headlight diamond stuck on it. And on his fingers glinted four rings, each with solitaires, except for the one with the flat gold surface, polished into a convenient mirror.

He normally fanged himself with three derringers, a single-shot in a special boot holster; an over-and-under in his swallowtail coat pocket; and another single-shot in a small underarm holster. But this artillery was insufficient, in his estimation. He lacked speed. The odds needed improving, at least in certain high-stakes games against dangerous sports. So he had gone to a smith and had some personal armor made to specification from sheet steel of sufficient gauge to stop a lead bullet fired at close range. The thing was slightly curved to the contours of his chest. It covered about a square foot of vital area, protecting heart and lungs. It draped from leather straps over his shoulders, and weighed so much—seven and a half pounds can become a strain on the shoulders over a period of time—that he anchored it under his boiled shirt only when the occasion called for it. Once it had saved his life. He had been ruthlessly skinning a teamster when, with no warning at all, the man pulled a Colt Navy and fired a .36-caliber ball into Cornelius Vanderbilt's heart. But it gonged on steel and the gambler had calmly extracted the over-and-under from his coat pocket and made a loser of him. The others in that Saratoga Springs game had sat perfectly astonished, and for a brief while people had called him Gongs. Now a fine pucker dimpled the device, and Cornelius took to improving odds the way Baptists took to total immersion.

Cornelius did not favor the wilderness. Danger could come at him from any quarter, and he had no way to adjust the odds. He inclined toward corner seats in sporting houses, with log or rock walls projecting to either side of him. All this open space made him antsy. Try as he might—and he devoted whole days to it while the wagon seat hammered his hemorrhoids—he could discover no way to embellish odds out here. At the warm springs he had simply vanished into the bowels of the wagon, lying flat for several miserable hours while those deserters— one of whom he had skinned once—reveled. Now he debated whether to doff his swallowtail coat. The heat lanced his vitals. But he had worn that coat like a second skin through all kinds of weather, and he hated to doff it now, even though his flesh craved cooler air. It would reveal his shoulder holster to the world. He did not want Mister Skye to know of the holster. He distrusted Mister Skye, and expected trouble from the burly guide. He might in any case shoot the man, as a small billet-doux for burning his braced deck, and treating him as some sort of scum.

But the heat triumphed. Ahead, Blueberry had shed his suit coat, and finally Cornelius did likewise, neatly folding the coat so that the pocket with the over-and-under derringer lay on top, the gun instantly available. For a while the swift evaporation of his soaked and soiled shirt cooled him, but then the forbidding heat crushed him again. He would not shoot Skye en route, he thought— the guide provided certain comforts in his brute way as a species of infantry. But later, on the very skirts of Bannack

City, he'd have his revenge. He'd sidle up behind Skye and blow out the back of his head.

They had driven all that day along the south bank of the Platte, and the gumbo dust had bathed Cornelius in a fine powder, along with his mules, and the whole wagon. Another reason to despise Skye, who had put him at the tail end of the procession. Off to the left rose a high blue mountain, among the first of the Rockies, though ranges were now visible west and north as well. By late afternoon they had come to the Platte Bridge crossing, a toll operation run by toughs who were not inclined toward charity. They were raking in fifty cents per wagon, and lesser sums per animal.

There would be a wait. Ahead of them a wagon train spasmed forward, and many of the wagon owners harangued and argued fees with the ruddy-faced owners, who simply invited the objecting parties to swim or raft the river instead. Cornelius knew that Goldtooth would pay without even questioning the toll. Such things were of no consequence to her. Enterprise would recover whatever was lost. But that marriage broker would moan and connive, and that would be the day's entertainment. He studied the wagons ahead, concluding they were the usual westering riffraff, dullwits and their families planning to prong Mother Nature somewhere else. Easy marks, perhaps, if Skye would permit him a game or two, which he doubted. Another reason to get even with Skye when the right moment arrived. Maybe he could improve the odds a bit this evening, with a game or two on the sly. He could carry a whole shell game, not to mention a deck, in any pocket.

It looked like an hour wait. Sure enough, Riddle slithered ahead, tromping down to the riverbank looking for a ford, calculating angles. The weasel even waded into the Platte here and there, surprised by its sudden depth and the tug of its water. Sensible Blueberry unhitched a span of mules at a time and led them down to the river for a welcome drink on a scorching day. Riddle watched, apparently decided that was a good idea, and began to water his own mules. But that sort of stuff bored Cornelius, and he left his mules to stand, heads drooping, in the blistering sun while he ambled forward to case the wagon train ahead. In every train there was a mark or two.

Up ahead where the bridge operators extracted wealth, Skye stood listening. Riddle had caught up with him and was playing yet another angle as Cornelius arrived.

"Up to you to pay," said Alvah. "You're the guide, paid a mighty big fee to git us here, and you're the one should be paying these bloodsuckers. Else find us a ford somewheres."

"You can always build a raft, Riddle," boomed Mister Skye. Laughter rippled out. Any cottonwoods that had once prospered here had long since been stripped away. Some parties in this train had no cash, but that was commonplace on the Oregon Trail, and the tollmen accepted payment in kind. But it always took time to come to agreement about the worth of a highboy or barrel of flour or silver teapot, and more often than not, westering pioneers were driven to rage and their women to tears by the extractions.

An hour later they rattled over a crude wood bridge barely wide enough to accommodate a wagon, and were heading along the north bank through rough country. Two hours later, in June twilight, they halted at a likely camp spot already crowded with westering people. Mister Skye didn't like it. He hadn't missed the flinty stares at the red wagons and their inhabitants from the wagon master and various yeomen farmers. But the mules had played out in the heat. They'd have to compete for what remained of grass in this overgrazed spot. Skye pushed on a quarter of a mile or so beyond the wagon train, hoping for distance and grass, but bluffs hemmed the trail and he could go no farther. Cornelius could read Skye's mind easily enough, and from his wagon seat, laughed.

Chapter 9

Unlike some, this train of thirty-six wagons seemed to be a merry one. Drusilla wandered timidly among these people in the bright June evening, enjoying the sight of families eating or doing their chores, scampering boys, bearded men in trail-worn clothes out among the oxen and horses, weathered wagons with sun-bleached sheeting drooping between bows . . . and all of it an amiable cacophony with no shrill sounds of dissidence and rage in them, sounds she had picked up at once in other trains.

Some had gathered in a central place among the drooping wagons where a fiddler tuned up. People eyed her amiably, their gazes settling long on her rimless glasses, respectable tan dress, and the small book in her hand. No one bothered to talk; something about her discouraged approach. Drusilla knew only that she didn't really want to make small talk with these robust souls. She would simply satisfy her curiosity, retire to her own small camp with its disgusting denizens, and read her new Thoreau, *Excursions,* which she'd plucked from the stalls the day before she left Bennington. The sojourner at Walden Pond was dead, but this book had just appeared posthumously.

Thank heaven, she thought, Goldtooth and her bawds were discreet enough not to venture here and become a cynosure of shame. Blueberry had stayed away too, and the Chinese had simply vanished to prowl the country, as he often did. Not even his mandarin background would rescue him from savage treatment often accorded to Celestials in the Far West. But the Riddles were everywhere here, and Alvah rounded through the wagons like a rat terrier, sometimes leaving puzzled frowns behind him. She'd seen the gummy black gambler, Cornelius, sidle around the wagons, but now he was invisible.

What a disgusting thing to travel with such people, people so disreputable that they had to remain hidden away from the eyes of the virtuous, she thought. Perhaps all these people thought she was one of them! Mary-Rita had wandered through briefly and retreated to the wagon, but Flora wandered around somewhere, daring these people to make something of her Southern origins. Drusilla thought for a moment of retreating to her own camp, but she feared the bawds would be doing business over in their wagon, and maybe selling spirits to the men who sneaked over there. Unless she chose to crawl into her bedroll in the Riddle wagon, the options weren't good.

Earlier she'd witnessed a peculiar thing. After they'd made camp up against the bluff, Mister Skye had meandered toward the wagon train and had run into the wagon master, a perfectly disreputable man in grease-blackened buckskins with a salt-and-pepper beard and hair so long it draped over his shoulders. The pair of them had roared like young lions—she'd heard exactly such a roar when a circus with caged lions had rolled through Bennington— and embraced each other and hoorawed around until she

thought they were quite mad. Mister Skye had called the
wagon master Boudins, and seemed to know him from
somewhere. She stood mesmerized, seeing conduct that
would have been unthinkable in the East. Odder still, they
began to roar at each other in a tongue she barely recognized as English, though it was plain they were insulting
each other, calling each other ring-tailed coons and old
niggurs and things that shriveled her abolitionist soul.

And they growled and jabbered and proffered perfectly odd sentiments, such as "that's the way the stick
floats," and "hyar's damp powder and no way to dry it."
The phrase "gone under" rang frequently, and it dawned
on her they discussed the dead, dead comrades from some
time and place. It annoyed her, this unintelligible babble
of plews and skins and Hawkens and Bug's Boys and
bullboats and buffler and *aguardiente* and men named
Broken Hand and Blanket Jim. Worse, Mister Skye
had wrapped a giant paw around the shoulder of this
wagon master and dragged him back to the sordid little
camp and sat him down in front of Skye's conical skin
lodge, and then, as bold as you please, filled a crockery
jug from Goldtooth's hogshead, and sat at Victoria's fire,
passing the raw whiskey back and forth with Boudins,
all the while roaring and belching and—and relieving
themselves in sight of everyone and burping and reducing
themselves to pure savagery. Never had she seen such a
disgusting thing! And even his squaw Victoria muttering
"sonofabitch" and "now you gonna go away for a week,"
and "now I gotta run the wagons." Even the young squaw,
Mary, swilling from that awful jug, and giggling and
elbowing and—Drusilla's mind blanked—pawing Mister
Skye.

It frightened her. She couldn't read there, with those
two bull moose howling and baying. She felt her security

melt away. What safety resided in a party led by a howling drunkard? She'd be murdered in her bed by any red- or white-skinned predator.

So she felt homeless, at least until that awful guide and his awful wagon master friend had imbibed so much spiritous liquor that they fell into a stupor. She hoped they'd have a monstrous headache in the morning. The fiddler tortured his squealing fiddle now, with merry notes punctuated by shrill squeaks, and some of the wagon-train people had started to jig and hop and behave in a most undignified manner. She couldn't read there, either, amidst such chaos. Had the whole world gone mad here? Even the women, the wives and daughters, were circling and bowing and linking arms, as if an exhausting hot day on the trail were not enough for them!

Daylight lingered, and she would read until dusk and hope things would settle down. It would be dangerous to wander far from camp—awful things happened to lone women—and men—who wandered beyond a kind of circle of safety. But she had a clear view of barren bluffs, and she slipped toward the Platte River, found a large smooth boulder, still sun-warm, and pulled out her slim new Thoreau.

Peace at last.

"Where did you get that!" exclaimed a male voice. Drusilla peered up through her small spectacles and beheld the most awkward and plainest young man she'd ever seen. Like her, he wore rimless spectacles. She gaped at a high white forehead and a skull that seemed to bulge over his ears, all of it set on a delicate jaw perched on a long stem of neck, which convulsed behind a prominent Adam's apple. He seemed young, probably younger than she. He peered at her from intelligent hazel eyes that blinked as regularly as a watch tick.

"I didn't know that was published," he said.

"I found it the day I left."

They talked about Henry David Thoreau and *Walden* and Thoreau's civil disobedience, and she found him intelligent and literate, and best of all, not one to notice her plainness. Perhaps he couldn't because in that respect he was just as plain as she, she thought. He seemed to possess a mysterious knowledge, as if he knew things about the universe that no one else did, especially these wagon-train families. She itched to find out what he knew and didn't know.

"I don't believe I know your name," she said.

"I am Parsimony McGahan."

"Oh," she said. He did not ask hers, and perhaps that meant he wasn't interested. A chance meeting on the Oregon Trail. Let them be ships passing in the night.

"Where are you from?" he asked. "I know it is New England because of the way you talk."

"Vermont, Bennington."

His eyes lit. "I know the place. That is where William Lloyd Garrison's pamphlets come from."

"You are an abolitionist?" She itched with curiosity.

"Of course. Of course I am. And the tracts are printed in Bennington. What did you say your name is?"

"I didn't. I am . . . Drusilla Dinwiddie." She loathed her name and slid past it quickly.

"You don't look like your name. You should have been named Venus or Diana."

She gaped at him.

"If you are done with that book, I will buy it from you on the spot."

"No . . . it's something I treasure, Mister McGahan."

"Call me Parsimony. The name makes the person, and I am too frugal for my own good. Don't call me Parse—I loathe it. My parents picked the wrong virtue, so I am heading west."

"I—I don't follow."

"I should like to be called Abundance, or Generosity, or one of the warmer virtues. When I am in the new land, I will change my name to one or another. I'm going to Comstock, Virginia City, Nevada, to open a lending library. A reading room, actually. I will charge members five dollars a month."

"Virginia City? Oh. Nevada. I'm going to Bannack, in Idaho Territory, or maybe the new camp they're calling Alder Gulch. A lending library?"

"In my wagon are eight hundred books, weighing over one thousand pounds, half a ton of books and more. I asked myself, what do they need in the Far West? What might I bring for a living they don't have, and the answer was, knowledge. Books of course. I've heard they all starve for books, for the latest novels, for science and the higher arts, and practical advice. All of it well salted with abolitionist literature. I will have none of slavery, I assure you, and if you were on the other side, why, I would have long since made my excuses."

"Where are you from, Parsimony?" She detected a quaver in her voice, and felt mortified by it.

"Boston of course. My father is an immigrant from Ireland, a perfectly common man with a great heart and a natural hilarity I happen to love and admire. My mother is a Boston patrician, a puritan, a rebel of sorts, a Congregationalist, and very rich. I love her also. Now what can the son of a proper Bostonian mother, born on Beacon Street, and an Irish pappy, do but head west?"

He laughed, and she realized she'd never even seen him smile. He seemed almost handsome, and his face burst into sunlight when he laughed his Irish laugh.

"But Parsimony—why aren't you in the war, if you feel so strongly?"

"Ah, you pierce to the heart of things and turn over a man's weaknesses like a plow turns soil. I am a coward. Physically, that is. And a snob. I don't wish to subject a fine mind to minié balls. I am no coward in the realm of ideas—in fact I am a radical and willing to stand on my beliefs. But uniforms and marching and orders and all the rest—why, we purchased my relief from the forthcoming draft. There are advantages to family wealth. I am perfectly corrupt, except that I have an uncorrupted mind with which to corrupt others."

He laughed again, and she heard music in it.

In short order they discussed the war, the abominable Mister Lincoln, Harriet Beecher Stowe, *Uncle Tom's Cabin,* and sundry other matters of large importance to both. She hung on to his every word, but only part of her listened. The other part, a part she wouldn't admit to owning, examined him, hearing the tone and lilt of his voice rather than what he said, studying his richly made clothing, listening for idiosyncrasy or foible that would make him weak and foolish, glancing into eyes to see whether there might be mockery or malice in those windows of the soul. She grew dimly aware that he scrutinized her with quick glances, quiet observations, leading questions. It occurred to her that she desperately wanted to pass muster, to meet his approval.

It grew dark and blue light traced the ridges of the western mountains, and now a fire flared where the fiddler sawed and people swung their partners right and left. And still they sat.

"You haven't told me why you are going to Bannack City, Idaho—or have they organized the new territory yet?"

"It's Idaho, but back at Fort Laramie we heard they're talking of a new territory that will be called Montana. And just a few months ago it was called Washington, and before that, why, Oregon! I'm not sure I have it all straight."

"You were saying—"

"To visit a relative!" she blurted out. Then she blushed in the dark.

She never lied. It stung her conscience to lie. She couldn't imagine what wild impulse impelled her to lie. But she was made of stern stuff, and corrected herself at once.

"I—didn't put that correctly," she said softly. "I am betrothed to a man I have not met, who is either at Bannack or the new Alder Gulch diggings."

The slightest pause. "I rejoice in your happiness," he said softly.

"I don't know that I will be happy," she responded tartly. "I don't know the man. I entered into a contract . . . because my circumstances required it."

"I think you will find a good life," he said amiably. "What happens if this liaison doesn't happen?"

"The contract treats me as merchandise! I am the marriage broker's shelf goods, to be offered again! And yet again if that fails."

He grinned, and she caught his humor in the dark. "And you an abolitionist!"

"I am!" she cried. "You do not know the special slavery of being female. In some places I could not even have signed that contract because women are wards, in law."

"What's to prevent your simply abandoning the contract?"

She recoiled. She knew he had a weakness, and here it was. "Mister McGahan," she retorted icily. "I abide by the contracts I make. I entered into it knowingly and willfully. I will not act dishonorably or unethically. I will not casually toss aside, as a result of my whim or will, a solemn agreement!"

He laughed. "You are like my mother," he said. "You puritans are impossible."

"Maybe it's the people who don't keep their word or their bond who sully civilization!" she cried. "Mister McGahan, good night."

"Don't leave! This night is young. You are the first woman I've ever met that I could talk to."

"Are we all so dumb?" she snapped.

"No, but the interests of so many lie in domestic things, and I am not domestic."

She laughed. She couldn't help but like him.

"I haven't a domestic bone in my body."

"I wasn't suggesting you break the contract. I think the contract might be unconstitutional and certainly unenforceable, that if you had a good lawyer, you might put it to a test. That's very different from simply breaking an agreement."

She knew where all this would lead. In the space of three hours they had gotten so far as to be considering each other for wedlock. That's how she put it to herself— considering each other for wedlock. A cool and sanitary way of putting it. She disdained sentiment. Well, it would never happen. Some aspects of marriage she didn't look forward to: its endless drudgery, cleaning, babies, jumping to a man's will . . . She intended to turn the marriage she had agreed to into a kind of companionship that would permit her to have her own bookish life.

"Whatever I do will be in accordance with the highest standard of civilization," she said primly.

"Migawd, you puritans. I don't wish to marry. I wish to live in sin with a lady who loves books and liberty."

"Sir!"

"I told you—I'm a radical. I oppose bonds, including those of marriage."

"If your parents hadn't married you wouldn't be here," she retorted.

"Why, Drusilla, I'm not so sure about that."

"You are unthinkable and impossible—and I am going to retire."

"To the camp of the bawds and lowlifes. Oh, I listened to that Riddle when he skittered about."

In truth, she didn't want to return to her own camp and listen to the raucous laughter of the soiled doves and their men, or the wild fustian of the drunken guide and wagon master. She didn't want to stray an inch from Parsimony.

"When I went to my mother's church, I listened to long and brilliant sermons, the tenor of which was that I had to continually shape myself toward perfection to find favor with God. And when my pap slipped off to Mass with me, I learned that we were all going to sin, because of our nature, and if we went contritely to the communion rail, we would be cleansed. I don't know which I like better. I'm an abolitionist and a radical because I think the whole commonwealth, the people and our institutions, might be led toward wisdom and virtue. That's my puritan side. But I don't know whether it applies to persons. The thought of transforming myself into a moral paragon is simply—exhausting. I prefer to sin and find grace. That's my Catholic side. One thing my pap has is fun. He loves life."

Drusilla had never heard such talk.

"I think I am an agnostic anyway," he added.

That horrified her, but not terribly much after she'd thought about it.

"I don't think I wish to live . . . in scandalous circumstances with a man—no matter how pleasant a man. He would dishonor me by it."

"I thought so." He chuckled. "I also look like a frog. So we are ships passing in the twilight. Tomorrow you and your lowlifes will whip your mule teams and soon be far ahead of our ox-drawn train. And that will be the end of it. I'd like to write you, though. You're the only one. The only princess who would talk to an educated frog."

"We will probably lose track. My name is going to change, and you are going to change yours. I don't even know whether I'll be in Bannack, or the new Alder Gulch camp."

"I will always be Parsimony McGahan at the Virginia City, Nevada, post office. And you?"

"I am to become Mrs. Amos Rasmussen," she said slowly. "I understand him to be a pleasant and literate man."

"I will remember the name." He rose and stretched, and she realized he stood tall, like herself. "Drusilla, I am going to ask you a terrible question. . . . Would you like me to go to Alvah Riddle and propose to buy up the Rasmussen contract at a figure that would give Riddle more profit?"

"Parsimony!"

He laughed, infectiously, but hot tears welled up and she couldn't choke them back.

Chapter 10

Victoria knew she wouldn't be sleeping for a few days. Whenever Skye found the whiskey jug and disappeared to the other side for a while, everything fell to her. Now he was gone. He and Boudins had roared and guzzled at the campfire before Skye's buffalo-skin lodge, and now they sprawled. It was bad, she thought crossly. Mister Skye the guide, and Boudins the wagon master of the other people, passed-out drunk. And Skye only employed a few days, too. What would that madam say?

Mary slept heavily too, but that was all right. The young Shoshone had nothing to do now that the boy had been sent to St. Louis and put into a white men's school. She drank and laughed with Skye, and watched the stars spin. But Victoria was his Sits-Beside-Him-Wife. Now she was old and her flesh felt like dried and cracked rawhide, and she had nothing but old bones inside. Old Jawbone sagged like that too, but she doubted that Mister Skye noticed. He seemed to think Jawbone would last forever. But Jawbone's teeth grew long and his back sank and the ribs separated, and soon Jawbone would be gone. Like herself, like Skye.

She and Jawbone would watch camp, the way they always did when Mister Skye went over to the other side. She wouldn't sleep. She would go for days without real sleep, just tiny naps, her old brown eyes and leathery ears more alert than ever. They'd gotten this far through life, and she intended they'd get the rest of the way before being gathered into the spirit world. Mister Skye never apologized, or regretted these times. It was not in him. But he had given her a sawed-off double-barreled fowling piece, with many balls of lead in each barrel, for safety and comfort. It might be worth a hundred arrows. She had it in her lap now, as she peered into the windy night, and listened to the air move.

She knew Boudins from the old days, the times when he and Skye and she had trapped the beaver, and roamed the mountains and valleys, and every sun set on joy, except the times they ran into the Siksika, or Gros Ventre, or Arapaho. The names made a sour taste in her mouth, and she spat. It felt good to spit out hated names. Boudins had been a good trapper and got many plews, and had traded the plews for geegaws and that terrible stuff they drank at the rendezvous, with grain alcohol, peppers, and plugs of tobacco in it for flavor. Then, in debt for his next year's supplies, he roamed out into the hard mountains again, sometimes with Mister Skye and Victoria, sometimes with a girl of his own. Now he guided white men along trails, just like Mister Skye.

The rolling air cut sparks out of the embers and jammed them off like shooting stars. Nearby, Jawbone grew restless. She knew that without looking, but she peered back at him. His yellow eyes picked up light like glowing marbles, and his ears flattened back. That meant someone was coming, but not stealthily. When someone sneaked, he began his unearthly shrieking, and then she knew of trouble. She spotted a man, someone she'd seen with the wagon train. He peered behind him to see whether he walked alone, glanced briefly at her lodge and the sprawled figures before it, and at the green wagon that was silent and dark; then slipped onward to the red wagon with the red lantern hanging from it. Victoria laughed. He was going to hire a woman. Her people, the Absaroka, knew all about that. Many a warrior had hired out his squaw to the trappers at the rendezvous, but it was all fun and not so furtive as this. The white men acted sneaky about this, and that had always puzzled her. Sonofabitch, what a good thing those hired women stayed at their wagon and didn't go parading around the wagon train, getting them white women mad. Then there'd be trouble, and Skye and Boudins drunk as magpies, too.

She sniffed the air. There would be a hell of a damn big storm, soon, and then Skye would get wet. She laughed. Over at the red wagon, the women slipped out and stood around in thin wrappers, so thin she could damn well see right through, shadowy limbs in the lantern light.

They parleyed, he and Goldtooth, and he studied the women and talked, and finally he dug into his britches pocket and pulled out a sack and pressed something into Goldtooth's hand, and then he and two of the women, that Mrs. Parkins and that Juliet Picard, climbed into the red wagon. It shook, and not from the wind, and the other two, the madam and Big Alice, settled down in the grass outside, and she heard yelps and laughter. Sonofabitch, she wished she were young enough to have a good time like that. But she had become dried out as old leather now.

The stars burnt out. Off to the south the sky lit white and went black again. Pretty soon now, she thought, smelling dampness in the freshets of air. She eyed the dark terrain narrowly. This place might be no damn good in a storm. They camped at the foot of a long draw that snaked up the hills into the night. And too close to the Platte River. Mister Skye as crazy as a magpie, too.

Jawbone snarled. His ears cocked forward. Victoria didn't know what to make of that but she swung the fowling piece into the darkness where his ears pointed. Probably someone of this party, maybe that gambler Vanderbilt, or the black man Blueberry or the big Chinese. Sonofabitch, where did that yellow man go all the time? She liked him. He looked a little like the Absaroka, same eyes. A good man to cut throats or count coup.

Like a skunk one of the bride women padded to the green wagon. That startled her faintly. She'd kept track and thought they were all over there, Riddle and his medicine wife, and the women, all asleep. It was the strange one with the rimless spectacles. The one who carried a book all the time. Victoria pitied her because life pressed heavy upon her. She'd been having a damn bad time, she could see that from the way the woman walked, all slumped and weary. Dinwiddie, that was her name. Them whites had such funny names, no song, no music, no medicine in them. Just some damn sounds in the throat. Drusilla Dinwiddie stopped and stared at the red wagon and its lantern wavering in the wind, recoiled from some noise and the sight of half-covered women lounging in the night, and walked toward the green wagon. Something shone on her cheeks, wetness.

"Hey!" Victoria yelled. The woman turned, approached hesitantly. She stared uncertainly at the corpses of Boudins, Skye, and Mary.

"You're not feeling good. You sit down here and mebbe I can help."

She shook her head, but sat anyway, and Victoria waited. Lightning sheeted across the west now, and in the flashes she glimpsed towering thunderheads, the Thunder Spirits riding the bucking sky tonight.

"Them people over in the wagon train do something bad to you?" Victoria asked, squinting at the woman.

Drusilla shook her head, and Victoria waited.

"I met someone I care about. Someone who cares about me," Drusilla said. "It has never happened—and it will never happen again."

"How come that's bad?"

"Because I am under bond. I have made a contract."

"Go anyway. Go to this man and say you will be his woman."

"I can't. I am committed."

"Damn! You are a strange woman. I don't understand this stuff."

"My word is my bond."

"You go! Riddle, he ain't gonna come after you. You go to the other wagon train, and nothing will happen, and you'll be happy with this here man."

She shook her head slowly. "You don't understand. I don't suppose you—I mean, your background, I don't suppose—"

There she went, Victoria thought. Them whites always figured Indians were dumb, didn't know nothing about stuff.

"We got medicine vows," Victoria broke in. "Sometimes we lie like hell, and make big jokes against other Indians, against white men. But we got sacred vows too. When the men come back from battle, they tell what happened, how many scalps, how many times they count coup, they tell it all exactly true. We got people going on a vision-quest, making vows and doing them, mebbe die if they don't do what they vow. We got truth times, when our Spirit Helpers make us talk true and do what we say. You got a medicine vow, this contract, and you ain't gonna break it."

Drusilla stared. "You have said it very well, Mrs. Skye."

"Victoria, dammit."

"I'm a New England puritan, and it's the way I'm bred. I have given my word on paper, and I must keep it."

"You love this man over there?"

"I don't know what that word means. I know we could be lifelong friends and have a very good time."

"You keep your vow. I'm going to make medicine, love medicine. I'm gonna talk to my Helpers, and find out about you. I get a vision, I'll let you know, but I gotta have some time. The Helpers come when they come. You're doing good, young woman. Keep your sacred contract vow, and we'll see."

Drusilla smiled. "Nothing will come of it, I'm sure. But you are most kind." She rose.

"You whites never believe nothing. Thunder's coming, and the Thunder Spirits will tell me. Maybe they strike lightning on the Riddles."

Drusilla recoiled. "That is not what I wish," she replied sharply, and fled to her dark wagon.

That's a good woman, thought Victoria. Damn good woman who got ways to live and things figured good in her head. A woman like that made good medicine.

Lightning cannoned, scattering white glare off the land, and she knew she'd have to round up the mules swiftly before it was too late. She peered around sharply in the cavernous night. Yonder the red lantern swung. The man emerged from the red wagon and skittered off toward his own camp. The bawds snuffed the lamp, and darkness folded in, along with wind.

She set the fowling piece just inside the doorflap of her lodge, so it wouldn't get wet, and toiled up the slopes toward the mules. She'd have to both hobble and picket them, not only hers but all the rest. Lightning snapped, and she saw them all, restless and tugging on their pickets. A crackle like water snapping on a hot skillet came, and then the world turned white and an explosion rocked creation. It came too fast! Below, Jawbone shrieked. And

Skye lost on the other side. Where were all them white men? Didn't that Riddle know nothing? She reached a picket line with two mules on it and began tugging it downslope, fighting the nervous mules every step. Another jolt hit and she felt the blast of it, hot air whiffing past and hissing, and a white ball rolling along grass and up on the mules' ears. They bucked and shrieked and yanked free and went clattering up the slope again.

Maybe she would go to the Spirit Lands herself. It might be the time. She started up the slope again, up to the ridges where the mules gathered. They'd all pulled their picket lines now, and headed up where lightning hissed. Crazy, going where the Lightning Spirits would strike them. Sheets of white rattled off the clouds now, rattled like gourds, light making noise or noise making light. She stumbled into one black mule, one of Skye's, down lower and grabbed the halter. One anyway. But it jabbed its head up and down, its teeth bared in the blue light, and refused to budge. A white crack knocked her flat and she left the world a moment. When she came to, she smelled scorch, scorch in the grass and on her hair, and Skye's mule was sprawled on the grass. Sonofabitch, and him drunk down there.

She clambered painfully to her feet, winded and tired. The mules rolled off the ridge now, scattering into the hollows of the dunes. She rattled after them, against torrents of air that knocked her back and whistled around her skirts. She could scarcely push up the slope because of the icy air that the Thunder Spirits had thrown to earth like sky lances. She heard a new rattle, a thousand rattlesnakes rattling, and the first hail smashed wetly on her black hair, and others slapped her face. She glimpsed a specter up on the ridge, the Lightning Spirit riding a white charger. She'd never seen the Lightning Spirit before, and she clawed away her fear. Across the ridge it galloped, crackling blue bolts following in its wake, a spirit sowing lightning. She'd never seen anything like that.

With her own eyes she saw the Lightning Spirit. She fled downslope, tumbling, air hot and cold in her throat, hail clubbing her, hammering her shoulders and the back of her head. And behind her the Lightning Spirit galloped. She felt it coming, and when it fell upon her she glanced back at the specter and saw it was the Chinese, leading three wet mules. She sat in the grass and held her chest because the pain burst her in two.

"Go down!" the Chinese Lightning Spirit yelled.

She crawled, hail pummeling her back and haunches and splattering up into her face. Sonofabitch, the mules gone everywhere, maybe days away, and Skye sprawled down there. She raged. She'd kick that damn Skye and that damn Boudins awake. And kick Mary too, for good measure, good kick in her soft breasts.

The world whirled. Wind shrieked, and walls of water blurred the way down. She heard Jawbone shriek and wondered how that could be, and then the evil blue roan minced before her, clacking his teeth and snarling and nudging her with his powerful snout. She grabbed a leg and pulled herself up until she could clutch the mane, and then, from the high side of the slope, she crawled over his bony back and held on. He flew down the hill, gliding somehow instead of jolting. She turned cold, and the numbness penetrated from her clammy skin dress to her heart and bowels. Ice water sheeted down the knobs of her spine, dripped from her ears and collarbones, sloshed between her hard old breasts, pooled on her belly making her tremble, and then dripped off the fringes of her doeskin skirt. Hail clouted her hair, gouging at her like a Sioux scalping knife.

He slopped through a roaring bottom, the torrent un-
balancing him until he leapt powerfully to the far side, and
she knew the coulee ran, deluging the camp below. Near
her sat the Chinese Lightning Spirit on its white charger.

The lodge had been flattened, and lay in a clumsy sprawl
like a dead buffalo, lodgepole poking the sky, rain hammering on parfleches and horse gear and her fowling
piece. Jawbone shrieked, and danced around Skye and
Mary and Boudins, who lay stupefied by whiskey, pawing the air as if pestered by gnats. The lightning quit and
night closed black like a womb and she waited to be
born. Jawbone stopped, stood for her to slide off, and
then began nuzzling Skye with his snout, squealing
angrily. She splashed through a raging flow of water,
finding Skye first and lifting his head out of it. He coughed.
She couldn't pull him. She found a saddle in the blackness and propped his head up on it. She found Mary
next, and violently tugged her, got her face up out of the
racing water and propped on the saddle. She felt around
in the blackness for Boudins. The deluge plucked him,
rolled him. Sonofabitch, she'd need a rope. She couldn't
pull the heavy man, but she could keep him from being
washed into the Platte. She probed around the carcass of
the lodge, and finally grasped horsehair reins, and started
toward Boudins, or at least where Boudins should be. But
he wasn't there. Water had rolled him somewhere. She
waited for lightning but the Spirit hid in the blackness.
Her heart pattered through the cold winters of time and
the Lightning Spirits didn't come.

"Jawbone! Go find the man," she cried. The horse
shrieked and she heard him slopping around closer to the
river. Even the wide Platte boiled now, not a high flood but
a sprawling one. The horse whinnied like a night trum-
pet and she started toward the sound, but the current

snagged at her legs, and some drifting thing upended her. Then Jawbone was butting her, and she grabbed mane and let him drag her to higher ground. Maybe Boudins fell in the river, maybe Boudins had tumbled over to the Spirit Land.

She grew dimly aware of women's screams, but they seemed distant. Her own lodge and everything inside lay in a heap. She heard the melody of a lark and then a crow, and knew the Spirit Helpers walked the earth this night. She listened to the sweet warble of the meadowlark and remembered being a girl and walking through a sunny meadow near Arrow Creek, looking for breadroot and wild onions, and plucking yellow daisies and rubbing their soft pollen on her cheeks.

Lightning raked again, a hollow gray light that hung in curtains and let her see the world with the clarity of noon-sky. Her man and Mary sprawled in a foot of tugging water, their heads half under. Mister Skye roared and waved arms the thickness of tree limbs. Jawbone butted him furiously. Victoria found a woven rawhide lariat on the saddle, slipped the lasso end of it over Jawbone's withers, and wrapped the other end under Mister Skye's shoulders. Without command, Jawbone slid Skye toward higher ground until the man was out of the slop. Then Victoria dragged Mary to the higher earth the same way. She carried household goods, her parfleches, her fowling piece, Mister Skye's new Henry, soaked buffalo robes leaden with water, and the rest, until the lightning flickered out like a burnt candle. She rested, her heart banging, and heard cries in the blackness.

A faint flicker bared the rest of the camp to her. Riddle had double-reefed his wagon sheet, and his wagon stood upright but fifty yards from where it had been, being tugged mercilessly toward the rushing river a foot at a time by the flood tide from the coulee, up to the hubs of its wheels, and gusts of wind that yanked the unreefed middle of the wagon sheet like a sail, sucking and tugging the wagon to its doom. Under the naked bows at either end, desperate women clung to wood and cried piteously. The other wagons had been blown onto their sides and their pink wagon sheets whipped off into the night. Wind churned their high wheels, making them spin and chatter and vibrate. The wagon goods lay in a spill downwind of each wagon, and even as Victoria watched, wind spun a hogshead of whiskey and rolled it into the moil of water plummeting into the Platte. The bawds clung to the wagon bows like pink caterpillars, their thin wrappers plastered wetly to them so they seemed naked in the sheet lightning, and colder than the blue ice caves up in the Pryor Mountains. And their hair lay death-clamped over their skulls and shoulders. One by one, trunks and bundles floated off, propelled like dandelion fuzz by the gale and the water.

Sonofabitch, but nothing could she do for them. She still had to tie her rawhide lariat to her collapsed lodge to keep it from floating off, marshaling whatever last energy she could muster. With numb hands she slid the lariat loop around the lodgepoles that weren't buried in muck, and tugged. The massive weight of the water-soaked lodge anchored it to mud. The torrent of water now boiling over it added to its weight. She found the saddle in the gloom and found Jawbone, and saddled him. He stood patiently, ears back but obedient. She cinched up with all the energy left in her old cold body, dallied the lariat rope around the horn and barked a sharp command at the trembling horse, who dug into the slop and pulled steadily. The lariat sang and sprayed water but held, and slowly the soaked lodge slid up the gentle slope, one step at a time, until it was out of the clutches of the Platte and the demons.

She released Jawbone, unsaddled him, and sat in the downpour, drawing a soaked four-point Hudson's Bay blanket over her, trapping only cold. There was nothing she could do for the others. The pain in her own breast bloomed so large she thought she would soon go to the Beyond Land, but she didn't.

The storm faded, but the water cascading from the highlands mounted higher. In the fading flashes, she glimpsed the Chinese on his white horse dragging the Riddle wagon back from the Platte, and caught the panic of screaming women. Then weariness folded her soul, and she heard meadowlarks singing and the Spirit Helpers making jokes.

Chapter 11

The gibbous moon reminded him of a war lord flush with victory, fat on both sides and cold yellow. It had reappeared as suddenly as it had been eclipsed by cloud, casting wan beams upon the carnage below.

They called him a Celestial here and mocked as they said it. The allusion was to the Celestial Kingdom, the Middle Kingdom of his ancient people. It all sounded heathenish to them, but these pale barbarians did not understand the ancient ways. To build railroads they had virtually enslaved some of his race, the low Cantonese who didn't even speak the Mandarin of the imperial castes, and it amused him that the whites thought all of China was like Canton. Of the nine grades of mandarins, his family's was the highest, and he could wear the button of power and prestige on his dress cap. But they wouldn't know that here.

Everything he wore oozed water and his bones ached, but he ignored it. He knew of no way to kindle a fire. There wasn't a dry stick or dry tinder for leagues, and no place to lay a fire because the earth swam in slop and the shoulders of the land were still shrugging off water. The coulee cutting into the river bluff still roared and foamed like a hydrophobic lion. He sat his wet white stallion surveying the wreckage, and yawned. One had died, but it didn't matter. Boudins, the master of the nearby wagon train, or what was left of it, had vanished, drunk on spirits. Skye, as much a wolfish barbarian as Boudins, would have died too but for the old squaw. Even now he lay stupefied, along with his younger wife, sprawled on a wet slope.

He'd rescued the Riddle wagon. That weasel had reefed his wagon sheet, so the wagon stood while the others toppled, but the wagon had rested in the very throat of the coulee, careening toward perdition when Seven-Story had roped it and dallied the lariat around the horn of the saddle, the way these Western cattle herders caught a cow. While the stallion braced and held the rope taut, Chang had found slabs of rock and lowered them into a foot of raging water around the wagon wheels, stopping its progress. He offered to ferry the terrified women inside it to higher ground, but they wouldn't. Even now, a river moiled through the wheels, rocking the green wagon.

The bawds had fared worse. Blueberry Hill had known nothing about reefing wagon sheets, and both wagons had toppled in the vicious gusts. Orgasmic wind had tugged the canvas loose, billowed it out like a jib, and flipped the wagons over like a woman waiting. Moments later the canvas had whipped loose and sailed on down the Platte, leaving the bows naked in the night. The storm had spent itself upon the bawds' wagon. Most everything within vanished, the ladies' finery, bedrolls, stored food, tins of delicacies for the new parlor house, shoes and boots and parasols and blankets. All gone.

The other red wagon lost its sheet too, and everything inside. A fortune in whiskey gone, the hogsheads floating and banging their way down the Platte, intoxicating suckers and trout. Vanderbilt's faro layout vanished, cards and casebox and oilcloth. Likewise the furnishings for the parlor house, sconces and candelabra and percale and drapes. The things in his saddlebags survived, but his clothing and books in Vanderbilt's wagon didn't. For that matter, Vanderbilt had vanished, either caught in the other camp, or dead. Everything of the gambler's disappeared too, along with Blueberry's few things.

In the moonlight Chang and Blueberry had righted the wagons with the help of the stallion, but not the help of Alvah Riddle, who peered maliciously at them from his wagon box. Some of the harness vanished, but Blueberry had hung much of it from a broken limb of a tree, where it still draped. In the morning they would know how many spans of mules they could harness—if they found the mules.

Now the red wagons stood upright and their naked bows poked the moon. The bawds were bare. Their thin wet wrappers felt icier than bare flesh, so they'd stripped them and sat forlorn in their empty wagon box, their flesh dry and goosebumped, unmindful of Alvah Riddle's stare and the huffy mail-order brides who glared at them. Seven-Story enjoyed the sight, moonsprites in the box, their breasts light and shadow. He laughed softly. The ladies had nothing to wear, and that seemed a sublime joke of the storm spirits. Naked they would go to Bannack, advertising their sunburnt wares as they entered.

They were smarter than Riddle's virgins, who sat shivering in layers of soaked clothing, feeling morally superior. There'd be some sharing in the morning. Riddle and his ladies would drive a hard bargain and the sporting crowd would be gowned, at least if Goldtooth had any gold left. Maybe that had bottomed in the Platte too, enriching crawfish. Something would have to be done for Blueberry, now attired in soaked red long johns with a hanging trapdoor for the want of buttons. His black broadcloth suit and patent shoes and white spats rolled along the silty bottom of the Platte. Blueberry was not without resources. He stood up in his soaked wagon, peered at the ladies, and clambered over the side, splashing through muck, trapdoor flapping.

He lifted a foot to a hub and then catted into the red wagon.

"All right, ladies," he grated, "let's get warm."

There were amiable giggles and they all disappeared below the sideboards.

Seven-Story admired Blueberry. There lay a man to make the best of any calamity. He touched heels to the stallion and slopped across to Victoria, who huddled silent under a mud-soaked blanket.

"Sonofabitch," she muttered. "I'm going to kill Skye. In the morning I'm gonna kill Skye and kick Mary in the ass."

"A commendable idea," said Seven-Story. "But now we will put your lodge up and start it drying."

Jawbone eyed him narrowly, ears back.

"Bite your master," said Seven-Story.

Jawbone clacked teeth and snarled.

Chang dismounted and attempted to wrestle the lodge upright but it wouldn't budge. The thirteen buffalo cowhides in it slopped with water and one lodgepole had snapped. Victoria shed her blanket and helped him, tugging poles out of the mess until she had the good ones lying free. Then she found a straight seam in the moonlight and unlaced the soppy rawhide until the skins parted and the heavy cover lay flattened on a rise of land. He watched her, admiring the skills of this Indian woman, who looked so much like the peoples of Asia.

She retied the tops of the poles and soon had a conical frame resting on higher ground and poking toward the stars.

"No way to get that cover up," she muttered. "It weighs more than me and you can lift." But they tugged and wrestled anyway and in a few minutes they had yanked the sodden skins up a bit upon the frame, high enough so they could drain and dry. The result was a low hovel with a lot of night air poking around it.

"I got one more thing," she said. She dug into a parfleche and pulled out a bedroll canvas. "I'm gonna wrap them two in this and maybe they won't get sick and die."

Chang did even better. He lifted Mister Skye easily and carried him up to some relatively dry shelf-rock, and then Mary, and rolled the pair of them in the canvas.

Jawbone laid back his ears and followed, protecting Skye.

Mister Skye opened one eye and then the other. "Why, it's Mister Chang," he said. "Bloody imperial mandarin Chinese won't let a man sleep."

With that, Mister Skye passed back into his own world.

Victoria spat.

Seven-Story bowed amiably, boarded his stallion, and slopped his way east toward the wagon-train camp. There was yet a mystery, the fate of Cornelius Vanderbilt. Two mysteries: Vanderbilt and the scattered mules. He saw that the other camp had done better. Wagon sheets had been reefed and the wagons had stood. No coulee had disgorged water into their middle. People wore dry clothes, extracted from dry luggage. No fire flared here—no dry fuel anywhere—but several lanterns burned from wagon hooks, casting eerie beams across water-black earth. Work parties had organized, women repairing loose canvas and men checking harness and hunting for drifted stock in the pale light.

The hour was late, perhaps three, and not a soul slept. Chang rode quietly through the hubbub, wondering who to address, where to look for Cornelius, and who to tell about the death of Boudins.

A red-bearded man waylaid him. "You! Chinese!" he said in a sort of singsong. "You tellee where guidee is, chop-chop?"

Seven-Story Chang smiled amiably and reined his horse.

"Hey! Quick-quick, chop-chop, talkee, yes?"

Seven-Story knew the game, and smiled. It always led to such fun, except the time one ruffian got mad and pulled out a toadsticker.

Others gathered now, pushing toward him, glowering in the faint lantern light.

"Talk-talk, Chinaman, or we cuttee offee your pigtail."

Chang debated whether to respond with an Etonian inflection, or Cambridge, and decided on the latter. "Gentlemen," he said, "I bring you sad tidings. I believe your guide, the estimable Boudins, perished in the river."

They gaped. "He was intoxicated from spiritous liquor and was washed into the river," Chang added. "It is a pity. A most distinguished gentleman."

They stared narrowly. Boudins was dead? Dead? Tough old mountain man dead? Impossible.

"How'd it happen again?" snapped one.

"Mister Boudins and Mister Skye and the younger Mrs. Skye were napping after an amiable evening when a wall of water washed over them."

"Don't you use them fancy Chinee words," snapped one. "Most likely you slit his throat and took his coin, for opium. We know your kind, worshipin' idols, sittin' in joss houses. Slit his throat in a storm and pushed old Boudins in the river."

Chang smiled slightly and bowed from horseback. "I'm looking for the sporting man, Vanderbilt."

One of them jerked a thumb toward a wagon whose sagging wet sheet glowed from a wavering orange light inside. "He's one of your kind. Been in there all night playing poker and skinning some of our young men and bachelors. That there bunch, they hardly paid never no mind to the storm, just dealing and smoking, and him in there sitting with a derringer in his lap for all to see. . . . You're all the same kind, fancy-talking Chinee. You and that crook and the fancy women over yonder, all trouble for decent folks, and now you come telling us our guide is dead, washed away in a storm. We should string you all up!"

"Go back to China, Celestial," said another. "We'll go a-hunting Boudins and when we find him with a slit throat, we'll slit yours, and then Skye's for good measure."

"At your service, honorable gentlemen," said Chang, mocking.

He touched heels to his horse and threaded through them to the yellow-lit wagon.

From the front, Seven-Story could peer through the oval puckerstring hole into its smoky interior. A smudged lamp dangled from the middle bow, casting a jaundiced glow on six males, all of them seated on mounds of cargo. The wagon sheet oozed moisture but the inside of this haven remained virtually dry, including Cornelius Vanderbilt, who occupied a seat at the far end, his back to the rear puckerstring hole, where he could make a hasty exit. Not that a hasty exit would do much good on a moonlit night. The light caught Cornelius's sallow features and made him look oily and skeletal, his slicked-down hair glinting blue. They all looked yellow and purple and blue, like bruised flesh.

He dealt blue-backed cards with paisley patterns on them to the others, seven in all, and they plucked these up furtively from the hairy brown blanket beneath them. In the hollows of this metastasizing wool lay piles of gummy greenbacks, a few small gold pieces, mostly eagles, and little piles of dried peas, counters of some sort. But none of these skimpy piles equaled the hoard of green and gold that humped before Mister Vanderbilt, who fingered them idly after he had dealt.

The mood of this makeshift emporium edged toward sour, and seeped out even to Seven-Story, watching intently. In fact the glowers of these sleepless hostages of Fate grew malign, and Chang wondered whether Vanderbilt fathomed the trouble. Probably not, for he droned on, lips pulled back from yellow teeth, restless crabby fingers diddling the deck as he waited for these soldiers of fortune to make up their minds. The storm had come and gone with only the faintest acknowledgment in here. But shipwreck lay near.

"Mister Vanderbilt," said Chang from without, "the Sirens are singing and it is time to stop your ears."

Chang's presence thus penetrated to those within. The gambler peered into the night, startled, and perceived the moonlit Chang. Then he glanced at his hand and smiled thinly.

"Let them sing," he said.

A black-bearded man turned to him. "He's not going anywhere, Celestial, until we've a chance to win it back. We ain't caught him cheating, but that don't mean he don't. And when we catch him, we'll take care of it, and you, and the sluts and lowlifes, and the dirty Injuns and all the rest over there."

"Ah, Mister Vanderbilt, the Sirens sing, the music is in your ears," said Chang.

Now at last Vanderbilt paused. Here was a white horse to carry him off, and no others remained in this drenched camp. The betting had not begun. He sighed and peered at his cards.

"Gents, I will fold for the night. It grows late and tomorrow will be a wearisome day without sleep."

He set his hand down and waited for the others to do the same. Instead, one of them flipped Vanderbilt's cards over, baring four queens lying on their royal backs.

"Bigawd," he said, "your luck runs a little too strong, Vanderbilt. I think you'll just stay here a while. That or give it all back."

Vanderbilt's claws flicked and in no time he had stuffed his loot into the pocket of his black broadcloth. "As the gent said, you've nothing against me," the sporting man muttered. His other hand plucked the two-barrel derringer from his lap. "Let's have the cards, gents; it's my last deck."

None of them donated the pasteboards.

"The cards, gents. It's been a pleasant little game."

From outside, Seven-Story eased out his revolver, hoping it wasn't waterlogged. He would shoot out the light.

"You ain't going anywhere," said one. "Is he, boys?"

"The Sirens sing," said Seven-Story.

"It is my last deck," replied Cornelius. "My means."

Chang hated to shoot the lantern. It would arouse a camp that had finally quieted down.

"You are the Lamp of the Occident," said Chang.

But Vanderbilt paid no heed. His hand flicked up, and the two bores of the derringer pointed at a man whose fist bent seven cards.

"The deck," he said.

Chang thought to shoot the lantern, but things went too fast. Someone plucked the lantern from its bail and threw it at Chang. It exploded at the feet of the white stallion, scattering yellow flame. The horse leapt and plunged. Inside the blackened wagon, tumult and a muffled shot. Chang steadied his horse and raced to the rear, hoping Vanderbilt would exit. Instead, burly men bailed out of both ends, and dragooned the gambler out the front end with them.

They landed all over him, smacking him with blocky fists and square-toed boots, thumping him into a rag doll. He fought back but there were six. A fist knocked the gambler's head back. A knee rammed into his gut, doubling him up. A boot hit his thigh with an awful crack.

Chang glanced swiftly. The shot had awakened the camp, and heads peered from dark and ghostly wagons. A violent hand ripped Vanderbilt's coat off him, and with it the boodle. Another heavy hand, plow-hardened, yanked white shirt and the linen beneath with a fine shrill rip, baring cadaverous hollow hairless chest to the mocking moon.

A brawl, a thing to enjoy, thought Chang. He slid easily off the stallion onto catfeet, returning the revolver to its holster, and plunged into the melee, feeling the concealed lead weight woven into the bottom of his queue swinging behind him. Vanderbilt sank into the muck now as fists clubbed him. He swung back weakly, no match for the six stomping farmers with mean boots. A rough hand grabbed belt and yanked, popping leather and pulling away shrieking broadcloth. Except for his gummy black boots, the skinny gambler was shorn of wool.

Six Occidentals, about right for one mandarin, Chang thought as he waded in, making deft use of foot and the knife-edge of his hardened hands. Art, not muscle, would punish; the artful chop to the vulnerable point—the thing took years of study and practice, something young mandarins learned—the artful chop to the neck, and one fell poleaxed, and another, and now they wheeled toward him, having turned Vanderbilt into a mudball. And a good kick, yes, favor of the gods, a good kick and a little combination kick-feint-chop, and two more doubled up holding privates and coughing up the contents of their bellies.

Ah yes, the science of the warrior! And now one with a knife, quite expected, the point of it blurring past him a foot wide in the white moonlight, and the tripped oaf wallowed in the slop near Vanderbilt. Ah, these giants of the West! Chang laughed happily and caught the remaining one at the base of his skull with his fist, crumpling him over the carcasses of the others, and then quiet settled—for a moment. Yonder, ghostly wagons rocked and men in nightshirts and boots, carrying Dragoon Colts and barrel staves, came mucking through the slop.

"Cornelius, my friend, the Sirens sang and you are shipwrecked on the rocks. Or is it Blueberry down there?"

He heard only a moan.

"I shall have to sully my knickers," said Chang, plucking up the gambler, who slid in hand like a greased pig. He threw the gambler over the withers of the sidestepping unhappy stallion. Fortunately the gambler weighed less than a pronghorn. Seven-Story stepped into the saddle, steadying the slippery gambler all the while, and trotted toward Mister Skye's camp, nether cheeks before him, laughing softly. Behind, the cards lay scattered.

Chapter 12

The sun pained Mister Skye. He cocked an eye open and peered into a dome of transparent azure, washed clean of the last speck of dust. He felt parched and at the same time his bladder howled, as if his kidneys had sucked his carcass dry and transported everything downward. But canvas entombed him and he could scarcely wiggle. Rock mauled his backbone. He lifted his head and it throbbed, but he could see which way the burial sheet wound, and rolled himself free and stood up. And sat down again promptly as dizziness overwhelmed him. Oh, that had been lively whiskey, and now he would pay a fancy price.

It all seemed odd. Shimmering puddles everywhere, the glint lancing his head. The two red wagons lacked sheets. He lay on a rock bench. His lodge had been moved and squatted grotesquely in the sun, steaming. His silk stovepipe hat had vanished. The sporting girls wandered around shamelessly in translucent wrappers that did little to conceal their charms. Blueberry Hill lounged on his wagon seat in red long johns and needed little more than a trident and horns to look like the devil. But that was nothing compared to Cornelius Vanderbilt, who flaunted one of Mister Skye's own fringed buckskin shirts, which fell to his thighs and barely covered his ass. Beneath this attire two legs, white and green as celery stalks, projected downward into Vanderbilt's boots. Red and purple bruises marked them, as well as his arms and face, and he looked uncommonly scrubbed. Seven-Story Chang and Victoria had gone somewhere, and so had Jawbone. Even Jawbone!

From the Riddle wagon, lines splayed out toward tree limbs, and each line sagged under a vast array of women's things, flapping white and mauve and ice-green. Ah, but there came Mary, poking among parfleches and pulling out pemmican. He slipped behind his tilted lodge and released a great satisfying steam of last night's joy, and then found Mary smiling beside him. It all reminded him of the rendezvous of '36, except for the wagons.

"I'm thirsty," he said.

"There are no cups." She handed him some pemmican. He didn't want any and handed it back.

She looked solemn.

"Where's my hat? Where's my Henry?"

"The hat's gone. The Henry is at the lodge, drying."

"We must have had a rain. I see puddles."

The tears in Mary's eyes startled him. "Boudins is dead," she cried.

It did not register at once. Dead? "Who killed him?" he asked at last.

"The whiskey did. The rain did. We did."

Tears seeped down her brown cheeks now. "He got washed away in the water, in what you call a flash flood. He was drunk. We were drunk. We made our camp here at the bottom of that gulch."

Not Boudins. Not an old trapper tougher than grizzly

and a match for ten lions. Not Boudins. A man like that couldn't go under. A bullet or arrow maybe, but a flood, water . . .

Mister Skye groaned and ran a gnarled hand through his graying hair. "Not Boudins. He'll show up downstream. He swims better than beaver."

"He was drunk like you and me."

Mister Skye felt like a man with an arrow through the heart, and sat down heavily on wet rock. "We did it to him. We put him under," he muttered. "What else, Mary?"

"The sporting wagons, they got tipped over, and all they got was washed away. They got nothing."

"Where's Victoria? Where's Jawbone?" he asked sharply.

"Gone to find mules. Them and Seven-Story Chang. All the mules and horses busted loose, long time away."

He sat, feeling the throb in his forehead. "What else?"

"Victoria and Chang saved our lives. He pulled me and you up to here. Chang, he went everywhere. Victoria too. The brides, they're okeydokey. Riddle rolled up the canvas when the storm came. But the sporting ladies, they got nothing. Even the barrels of whiskey, all down the river."

Mister Skye observed the faint tremor in his hand.

"They got no food. Riddle got some but he ain't sharing. He and the brides, they say no food and no clothes for a mess of sluts and lowlifes."

Mister Skye pondered that. There had to be weighty meaning in it, but he couldn't grasp it at the moment.

"What else, Mary?"

"I got a damn headache. I shouldn't drink that stuff."

Cornelius Vanderbilt tottered around his wagon, and then Blueberry helped him up, baring his white buttocks.

"What about him?" Skye asked.

At last Mary smiled. "He was over in the other camp

playing poker all night until Chang went for him. But they got mad and beat the crap out of him and Chang brought him home. Now he got nuthing to wear. He's got a funny white behind. Every time he bends, his white behind shows. Chang says maybe the whole outfit there come after us and string us up. They don't like it, Boudins dead and Vanderbilt stealing money. I dug the wet powder out of the fowling piece and got dry in, and dry patch and balls, and I been sitting here waiting."

Mister Skye loped for his Henry, found it warm and dry to the touch, and loaded. But no targets presented themselves. His head throbbed. He felt naked without his hat.

Unsteadily, he trudged to the river and drank endlessly from cupped hands. It made him feel nauseous again. He found a cast-iron skillet half buried in muck, one he'd seen the sports use. He rescued it and wobbled over to their wagon. They sat desolately in the sun, barefoot, bareheaded, no doubt burning. Their wrappers hid little, but Mister Skye lacked the eye for it.

Goldtooth fumed. "You got us into this," she screamed. "Now I've got nothing. Not even clothes! We'll burn to death! Starve to death! My money's gone and I couldn't even buy clothing to save our lives from those bastards over there. And you did it, camping here at the foot of this coulee, getting drunk, you goddamn incompetent idiot."

Mister Skye nodded. His brain wasn't functioning yet.

"We don't have anything to cook with or eat from! We haven't a weapon between us, not even a knife! All my wealth went down the river. Five barrels of good whiskey! Every stitch of clothes we have! Half the harness! Our mules are gone! The wagon sheets tore off so we'll fry! No bedrolls, no blankets! All our jewelry! Mrs. Parkins's heirlooms! We're hungry! No one in the other camp will lift a finger for—women in the Life. We're going to die because you're incompetent, careless, stupid, drunk, addled, and—" She ran out of steam for a moment, and then wept. All four of them wept. Mister Skye almost wept.

"I found a skillet anyway," he mumbled, "and we can find more."

He summoned Blueberry and Cornelius.

"We'll search the riverbank for things," he said. "Maybe the heavy things will be caught in brush. Maybe even canvas and clothing."

"Mister Skye," said Blueberry, "those folks in the other camp, they'd shoot a black man in red long johns comin' along the shore. They'd horsewhip these ladies, wandering along the shore in little nothings."

"A lot of good a few odds and ends will do," said Goldtooth.

"Mizz Jones," said Mister Skye, "in a wilderness, a few small items can perform miracles."

"You goddamn idiot," she snapped.

"I think we've enough truck—Mary's and Victoria's and my things—to outfit two of you. I'll get it, and all of you get under the wagon and stay in shade."

"But it's muddy!" snapped Mrs. Parkins.

"Mud never hurt anyone. Sunburn will kill."

He pawed through the parfleches Victoria had rescued and found leggins, a breechclout, and an old gingham dress of Mary's. Also some jerky. A few minutes later, Goldtooth wore brown gingham and Blueberry had a breechclout and leggins over his red underwear.

"Find what you can. Salvage everything, no matter how useless it seems," Skye said. He handed them all some jerky.

His head ached but he had a lot of thinking to do. First and foremost he would deal with the threat from the

wagon-train camp. He surmised that the men were hunting stock that had strayed before the storm, so he would
have some time. The next question was whether he could
get the women and lowlifes to Bannack. They'd need everything: food, clothing, bedding, cooking utensils,
weapons. Once in Bannack they'd make up their losses
easily enough . . . He smiled faintly.

He had, he thought, exactly one eagle, ten dollars in
gold, with which to buy something from the other camp—
if they'd sell. Riddle and his women had things, and
Riddle might welcome a bit of gold. He'd see. Mules
and horses and harness would be a question mark. He'd
wait for Chang and Victoria, and meanwhile see what
was left of Goldtooth's stuff. But food would be something. There wasn't much of anything to hunt along the
Oregon Trail because the traffic drove animals far away,
dozens of miles away. Maybe this trail wasn't the way to
go . . . He and Jim Bridger had always thought wagons
could be taken up through the Bighorn Valley and west
on the Yellowstone. The pass into the Gallatin Valley
might be trouble, though. There'd be game on the Yellowstone but less in the Bighorn Valley. Might have to
eat mules or horses. That would not thrill Goldtooth or
Mrs. Parkins.

He felt a bit better now, but the death of Boudins lay
heavy in him, along with shame. One thing Mister Skye
had learned in the wilderness was to set aside guilt. His
task now would be to find the means to survive in the
present and future, and take his clients safely to the Bannack diggings.

At Alvah Riddle's wagon he found things in order.
Soaked clothing hung on lines, food had survived, and
Alvah had rolled the wagon sheet back over the bows,
where it baked in the sun. But the brides slumped about

in damp and drooping clothing, refusing even to doff a layer or two of petticoats to dry in the sun. They all eyed him narrowly as he approached.

"You did pretty well, Riddle."

"No thanks to you, Skye. You were drunk over there with your slut and that oaf—"

Mister Skye's thick arm caught Riddle across the chest and sent him sprawling into muck. The paunchy man leapt up sputtering.

"Are you crazy? What's your angle, Skye?"

"Mister Skye," he replied softly. "You never call Mary a slut again. If you do I will kill you. And you will never call Boudins an oaf. He stood as tall as the mountains."

Riddle caught something in Mister Skye's tone, and eye, and held himself in check. He reddened, muttering for a moment, and then subsided into his usual craftiness, glancing quick-eyed at Skye, the sporting women, the sprawled lodge, and Mary. "What are you going to do now, eh? They've got nothing over there. I know the angles and I saved everything here."

"With the help of Seven-Story Chang, who kept your wagon from sliding into the Platte. And who's even now hunting down the mules you failed to hobble before the storm. Along with my wife Victoria. You owe your lives to the Chinese. The mules probably scattered over a ten-mile circle, and if they are returned, you'll owe your future to Mister Chang and Mrs. Skye."

"I know your angle, Skye. You're trying to draw attention away from your drunk and irresponsible conduct last night. If you'd stayed sober, none of this would have happened."

The guide glared. "It's Mister Skye. And I don't walk on water or send down cloudbursts. As for the rest, you're right. I've come to borrow some food and clothing and I thought you'd be neighborly enough to supply it. With that, I'll get you all to Bannack City safely."

Riddle eyed him and calculated. "Well . . ." he said cautiously. "I figure that maybe we'll just join up with that other train. I don't cotton to your guiding much, and we'll be safer over there, with good respectable folk."

"Go ahead," Skye said.

Riddle seemed faintly startled. "Well, of course, those oxen, they're slower than snails, and we've got mules to make time with."

"Maybe you have mules. Maybe you won't."

"Well, I think I'll just mosey over there anyway, and let those respectable folks know that we've got respectable women here . . ."

"By all means," said Skye. "And now, I'd like to borrow some clothing for women who could die of exposure."

Riddle laughed nastily. "They got what they deserve. Good Lord's repaying them. I might sell them something—"

Drusilla said, "I have an old dress and a petticoat they may have, Mister Skye."

"Now see here," protested Riddle. "That's your dowry. I got a proper business interest in keeping you all dowered. If Skye or those females wish to pay me for it, I'll consider it. Might be worth a double eagle."

Drusilla glared at him icily. "It is not yours to dispose of." She began to remove a blue checked calico from one of the lines. Riddle leapt toward her. "We have a contract. Section Four, Clause Twelve, prohibits you from disposing—"

She ignored him, and lifted the damp dress and a petticoat from the line. Riddle snatched them from her. "We have a contract. We have a contract—" he snapped.

"I think the lady wishes to give some of her clothing

to a charitable cause," said Mister Skye gently. "Is that
not correct, Miss Dinwiddie?"

"The contract says that the party of the second part—
that's the bride—can dispose of her property only with
the permission of the party of the first part—that's me,"
said Alvah Riddle.

Mister Skye yawned. His head throbbed.

"They're suffering. I don't care what they are, they're
suffering," protested Drusilla.

Flora laughed. "Let 'em suffer," she said.

Mary-Rita said, "I don't think we should be helping
such flamin' sinners."

Riddle's eyes lit up. "There, you see, Skye? We're against
you. Respectable folk are against you. Now I'll just go on
over to that other train and see about things."

Drusilla said, "I'm sorry, Mister Skye. He does have
that right, and I am bound by my contract."

Riddle cackled nastily, enjoying his triumph.

Mister Skye yawned again. The morning sparkled but
he barely noticed. At his own wagon he found the canvas
he and Mary had been wrapped in, and took it over to the
ladies.

"Two of you roll up in this," he said.

He trudged down to the riverbank and found Goldtooth
and Blueberry hunting through the brush. They hadn't
found much, but they salvaged a pink wagon sheet, much
torn but usable, along with some frayed rope still attached
to it. He waved at the pair of them and dragged the sodden sheet back to the red wagon and enlisted Vanderbilt
to help pull it over the bows and tie it down. Minutes later,
the soiled doves had shade and shelter.

It was getting toward noon. Still no sign of Victoria
and Seven-Story Chang.

To Mary he said, "I'm going over to the other camp. I'd just as soon you keep that fowling piece handy."

She smiled and nodded. "I can maybe get a fire going now, and boil some jerky for the sporting women."

"You can make fires in the middle of blizzards using fingernails for fuel, Mary."

He had heard the bawling of oxen yonder and knew the other camp would soon pull out. He wanted to palaver before they got away. When he arrived there, he found them almost ready to go. The slow oxen hadn't been driven far by the storm, and most stood in their heavy wooden collars. He spotted other bunches up on the slopes, being choused down by men on foot.

They saw him coming and gathered around, their faces thunderous. "You're Skye, aren't you? The drunken guide of all those lowlifes yonder. Took our guide from us, right into the grave," said one.

"He was my best friend, and it grieves me more than I can say, mate," Skye replied.

"I bet it does," another snapped.

These were angry men, and they spoiled for trouble, such as maybe a good whipping.

"I came over to apologize about the gambler. He had instructions from me not to come here."

"I'll bet," a black-bearded one growled.

Mister Skye fixed him in the eye. "If you haven't the decency to take a man's word, mate, then have the courage to call me a liar."

It gave them pause.

"My wife and Mister Chang are rounding up stock, and will probably bring in horses of yours. I'd expect them anytime now."

"You lowlifes'll probably steal them from us."

Mister Skye's Henry swung casually toward the man. "I didn't hear you thanking us for the help, friend."

"Nothing to thank you for, far as I can figger," said another.

Here lay a stony wall, he thought. "I've a party that wants to join you," he said. "A man named Riddle and his wife, who are escorting some young women to Bannack."

"We know their kind."

"You don't rightly do," said Mister Skye. "Engaged to be married—Riddle's a matchmaker—and not what you're thinking."

"He the one we heard about at Laramie that couldn't get hisself harnessed up in the morning, complained constantly, and dragged down the whole outfit?"

Mister Skye ignored him. "They've had enough of travel with lowlifes, mates, and I thought you might welcome respectable folk to your train."

The last of the oxen trotted into camp now, and men broke from this gathering to yoke them and be off. Far up on a bluff, he saw something new, a herd of dark mules and multicolored horses winding its way downslope, driven by a man on a white stallion, and a tiny Indian woman, his Victoria, on an ancient, battered blue roan. The man on the white horse he esteemed. The woman and the blue horse he loved.

Chapter 13

Thirteen wagon-train horses were returned to their grateful owners, and hostility to Skye's party's evaporated with the rain puddles. A search party ranged three miles down the rough banks of the Platte, did not find Boudins, but salvaged a trunk of Goldtooth's full of gold corsets studded with purple rhinestones, pink-frilled nightgowns, black bloomers, green lisle stockings, and crimson garters with black roses embroidered on them, caught in bankside brush where a log snared the water. The muscular river had swept everything else beyond grasp.

Alvah Riddle sidled around the wagon train, smiling, howdying, whispering to men yoking oxen that he had grown weary of those . . . lowlifes. "Guess I'll join up with you. Make you a stronger party," he ventured to a busy choleric farmer.

The sweated man paused, his brow wet from dealing with fractious oxen, and glared at Alvah. "Heerd Porter's train had trouble with you," the man said and returned to his task.

"I don't get help from the women! But I got it figgered out now. I got it all figgered," Alvah allowed, confidentially.

"We're moving faster than Porter. Passed them some while back. Three, four, more miles a day than him when it's good. Boudins told us we had the best-disciplined outfit he'd ever guided. Mean to keep it that way. We've been out a long time, have it all down."

"Didn't know," Alvah mumbled. "Not quite what I figgered. You'll plumb wear out your stock. It's a good angle to slow down and keep it fat."

The drenched man paused. "We got land to clear, cabins to build, crops to put down, fences to build, all before snow, and you talk slow."

Alvah Riddle found no warmer reception elsewhere, and Mister Skye watched him skitter back to his wagon.

The bright-eyed wagon man who had fiddled the turns last night became, by common consent, the train's new captain, and he began at once to organize a small memorial service for Boudins. No one volunteered, but finally Parsimony McGahan, the atheist, pulled a King James from his barrels of books, and read the Twenty-Third Psalm and recited the Lord's Prayer, the Catholic version, which puckered women's faces. Mister Skye, Victoria, and Mary attended.

Just before the new captain, Gonzales Baer, pulled his train out into the soggy ruts of the trail, Mister Skye caught him.

His face reddened. "Say, mate, I could use some help. I've some naked women over there, lost everything. Need britches too."

"Why, that is their natural condition," said Baer.

"I've an eagle left for provisioning."

Something bright sparked in Baer's brown eyes, crinkling flesh. Then he laughed, like a cataract on a sunny afternoon. He walked back to the center of the line and gathered people around him.

"Mister Skye, here, informs me that certain of his party are without clothing. We're owing them for the horses they brought back, and I would like those women who can spare dresses and certain other things to donate them to a worthy cause. Also two pairs of men's britches, one skinny, one wide."

People laughed. This wagon train took life amiably.

"Polly," said one, "ain't you got a spare skirt or two?"

"Never thought it'd cover a Cyprian," she said, digging into a trunk.

"One tall and skinny, three mediums," said Mister Skye.

"You're tall and skinny, Della," said another.

"Well, I never," she retorted.

"Shoes, moccasins, food?" said Mister Skye.

At that they shook their heads. There would be no game along the trail, and barely food enough to last to Fort Hall. As for shoes, they were wearing them out at a fearsome rate trudging fifteen or seventeen miles a day.

"Looks like we can't help you there, Skye," said Baer.

"It's Mister Skye. Thanks for your help, mates."

He turned to leave, his arms draped with fabrics, but Parsimony McGahan stayed him.

"Sir," he said hastily. "Please take this to Miss Dinwiddie, with my compliments." He thrust a slim velour-bound book in the guide's hands, *Sonnets from the Portuguese,* by Elizabeth Barrett Browning.

"Whose compliments, mate?"

The young man swallowed. "Parsimony McGahan, sir. With my love, sir."

"I will do that, Mister McGahan. And where may she reach you?"

"She knows, sir. Virginia City, Nevada."

"I will do it," said Skye. He and Mary and Victoria watched as the men roared and whipped and cursed the oxen to life, and the heavy wagons hissed through furrowed gumbo. They would not go far this afternoon before the oxen played out, but only half a day remained anyway.

Mary and Victoria pawed through Goldtooth's trunk, giggling and pressing corsets to themselves.

"Mister Skye," said Mary solemnly, "if you would buy these things, I will wear these things."

"Mary, if you do, I will sell you."

"Mister Skye, that would be fun."

They carried the waterlogged trunk back to their camp, amid the sudden silence. Anger hung there like fog.

"We got these," said Mister Skye, dumping dresses and britches into the red wagon. The women pawed at them silently, dividing them by fit and pulling them on without bothering to hide themselves. Vanderbilt pulled on some butternut gray britches that fit at the waist but were short. Blueberry set his aside, content to wear Skye's leggins and breechclout. Big Alice encased herself in a blousy shapeless gray dress that could not eclipse her golden charms. Mrs. Parkins found an ice-blue that enhanced her blond beauty. Sable-haired Juliet wiggled into a too-small black twill and looked ravishing. Goldtooth pawed testily through the recovered trunk, cussing, and didn't try on charity.

In the grass before the red wagon lay everything Goldtooth and Blueberry had recovered from the river brush—precious little—and Skye studied it because Fate depended on it. A butcher knife, one tin cup, an empty steamer trunk, an axe, loose pieces of harness.

He sighed. Seven-Story herded the mules yonder, and Mister Skye trudged wearily in that direction, his head throbbing again.

"Five killed by lightning, one missing," said the Chinese.

"Whose?"

"You lost one. Goldtooth lost four. Riddle's is the one missing."

Skye nodded. "Has anyone checked harness?"

The mandarin shook his head.

Beneath a cottonwood Blueberry sorted out collars and bellybands. "We can harness three span proper, and I got stuff to make another if I got rope."

Mister Skye nodded. Victoria could cut strips from the bottom of the lodge if necessary.

The sun baked his head and his eyes ached without the shade of his silk hat. Maybe his eyes would ache anyway this morning, he thought. At his lodge he found a red bandana and tied it over his forehead, pinning his long hair.

"That should get you a new squaw," said Victoria. "Put an eagle feather in back. You're pretty dumb, drinking last night. Maybe I quit and go back to the Absaroka people. Maybe you getting too goddamn old for this."

"Hadn't seen that old coon Boudins for years," he muttered.

He needed to think, and toiled his way up a rise to a small plateau, overlooking the Platte. Below him his people busied, taking tucks in dresses, harnessing mules, dismantling the lodge, loading parfleches on panniers. He lacked a mule and the loads pressed heavier now on the others.

He sank down, thinking about Boudins, gone under. Right here, plenty of people around to help, and the pair of them stinking drunk, pair of old goddamn fur men piss-eyed and careless out where carelessness puts a man under. Should have been himself, not Boudins, not Boudins. Some poor-meat prayer by strangers and old Boudins plumb forgotten. Big Beaver that took plews out of ice water, waltzed with grizzlies, sucked the buffler gut that gave him his name. Come to think of it, he never knew Boudins by another. The man never seemed to have a Christian one, never a Peter or Joseph or Jedediah. No folks to tell about it either, just Boudins, with no strings going anywhere, no family save for a few temporaries out on the trail he'd bought for a few plews, or blankets, or a crowbait pony or two.

Skye mourned in the high sun for an hour, mourned and watched them break camp below. It would be an unspoken thing, but they'd turn back to Laramie. Of course, Riddle'd bide his time there and hook up with some train that didn't know about him. The sports would go into business temporarily and reoutfit. . . . In a few minutes they'd line up facing east, not west, and starve all the way back. Victoria probably had jerky or pemmican enough for a day, but they were twelve days out of Laramie. Some army garrisons in between, but they couldn't part with food and shoes.

He thought some about going back, giving up on this one he had botched. But he didn't like it. He'd never failed to get his clients to their destination. It ragged him, this defeat. They'd starve all the way back, too, and that bothered him.

Well, why go back at all? He and his women knew how to make do with a lot less. He inventoried what they had and what they'd need. It came down to sleeping robes, shoes or moccasins for the lowlifes. As for the food, there might be a way . . .

He sat there another half hour, working it through a brain still puddling from the night's debauch. Below, they'd finished harnessing and loading and were waiting for him irritably. He stood, feeling the warm brass of the Henry in his hand, and trudged down to his party.

They peered at him angrily. Goldtooth steamed. Alvah Riddle's gaze popped at him like the tassel of a whip. Victoria and Mary had turned surly and silent. Mrs. Parkins exuded frost. The only sign of warmth came from Seven-Story Chang, who grinned mockingly on his white stallion.

"We'll get you to Bannack," he said.

"We're returning to Fort Laramie, thanks to your stupidity," snapped Goldtooth Jones.

"Starve the whole way. No need for it."

"With what? How are you going to get us to Bannack when we have one cup, one knife, and an empty trunk? Where are shoes and bedrolls? Where's food?"

"All about us," said Mister Skye. "But not here on the Oregon Trail, where the game's been run off and everything's been picked over."

"You got us into this mess!" she raged.

"Do you want to go to Bannack?"

He could see the abacus beads of her mind skinning on the wires. "Soldiers earn eight dollars a month—when they're paid at all," she said wryly.

He stared. "You'll starve getting to Fort Laramie, and starve at Fort Laramie, and buck a lot of competition."

"This conversation is disgusting," said Gertrude Riddle.

"What's your angle, Skye?" whickered Alvah.

The mandarin sat on his horse, mocking.

"No need to starve, at least no longer than a day or two. No need for you to be barefoot either. No need to sleep cold in this high country either. No need to turn back. What do you think the Indians do to stay alive and warm, mates?"

"You'd better do something plenty damn fast, Skye, because I'm half starved," snapped Vanderbilt.

"I'll stuff you this evening, but you won't like the meat," Skye said. "It'll be more than you deserve."

"What's your angle, Skye? Me and my women, we're fixed good and can go back and hitch to another wagon train."

"And get tossed out again, Riddle. My friend Jim Bridger and I, we always figured there might be a wagon route through the Bighorn Basin, north of here. Then along the Yellowstone, and over a divide Blanket Jim and I know, and after that it's easy to Bannack or the new Alder diggings. Probably two, three hundred miles shorter, maybe more. Game all the way, once we get a few miles off this trail."

"Go where there's no road?"

"Fur company trails," replied Mister Skye. "Know it like the back of my hand."

"Barefoot!" snapped Goldtooth.

"Yonder, packed on that travois, is my lodge. Good cured cowhide skins for moccasins, made to order for your feet by my two ladies, who can outfit the whole lot of you in a day or two. We'll unstitch the hides, and you'll all have robes. If we find buffler along the trail— should be some north of here—we'll have hump roast and bones for kitchen ladles and such, robes we can start tanning, and rawhide for harness."

"What will we eat off of?"

"Wooden trenchers we'll cut from cottonwood and hollow in a day or two."

"Is there water?"

"There is. As it happens, this is a good enough place to leave the Oregon Trail and strike west. Maybe some will be brackish."

"I haven't a shovel for road building," said Blueberry.

"You will when we get some buffalo bones."

"What will we eat tonight?" said Vanderbilt.

"Mule steaks, if the wolves and coyotes haven't got to them. Victoria will cut the tail hair too, and weave new bridles and halters and even reins from it."

"You get drunk and me and Mary work our fingers off," growled Victoria.

Goldtooth laughed raucously.

It looked good, he thought. Blueberry had jury-rigged some harness from loose parts, and had two spans hooked to each wagon. Each red wagon had started with three, but now the wagons carried little. Riddle had five chocolate mules, two spans harnessed and one reserve tied to the rear.

"I'd suggest you and your women walk as much as possible, Riddle," he said. "You've all got shoes, unlike these others. Until it dries, it'll be hard pulling."

"I'll run my outfit as I please, Skye. I don't know what your angle is, but you rightly got nothing to say about it. Not after what you done to us all."

But even as Riddle replied, Drusilla clambered down, followed by Mary-Rita, and a reluctant Flora.

No one said yes. No one said anything, but Skye knew he had carried the day. They wanted to get to Bannack; they wanted food and shelter and comfort.

"One thing, Skye," said Vanderbilt. "I don't have a weapon. Blueberry doesn't have a weapon. These women don't have a weapon. How are we to protect ourselves? What if we have Indian trouble?"

Mister Skye smiled. "Henry repeater here. In my kit is an old Sharps buffalo gun. Colt's at my side. My women each have muzzleloaders. Double-barreled fowling piece, too. And Mister Riddle is not naked."

"I'll say not," said Alvah, "Spencer carbine, revolver. Might think twice about letting others use them though."

"That's not the end of it, Mister Vanderbilt. Each of my ladies has a bow of Osage orange, wrapped in fine sinew, and a full quiver of arrows with iron trade points, and a lifelong skill with them. Very handy for making meat when quiet is needed. I would add, Mister Vanderbilt, that only last night you were well armed with short-range weapons, but lost them because you are a sharper."

He turned to Blueberry. "You should have some protection at your wagons, Mister Hill. This evening we will lend you the fowling piece and some powder and buckshot. Directly, I will begin to make lances, war clubs, and shields, all from wood and bone and hide and stone. . . . You may wish to observe, Mister Riddle. That's an angle you hadn't angled."

"I'd be obliged, Mister Skye," said Blueberry.

He waited for objections. No one spoke.

He turned Jawbone toward a long dun coulee rising north, and behind him heard the sounds of hawing and whips, and the rattle of trace chains and harness, and the stammer of wagon wheels turning sharply. They would come, then. Ahead of him old Victoria rode her pony, hunched and small and dry as parchment. She would head for the carcasses of the mules and salvage meat before the predators and sun fouled it. And with a swift hack of her old Green River knife, cut an armload of tail hair which she would plait with dextrous old fingers into reins and halters and bridles. She could make those things more easily from the cured leather of their lodge, but that in the end meant more brutal work, tanning fresh lodge-skins. It would be trouble enough for the old woman to make moccasins from one hide, and separate the other hides for bedrolls.

Behind him wagons hissed through damp earth, extruding thin lines of shining clay behind them, and broken bunchgrass.

"Ow, goddamn sonofabitch," howled a female voice behind him, and he turned. Barefooted Big Alice muttered, limping, and just back of her lay a low clump of prickly pear. Mister Skye smiled. They would soon learn that moccasins would not defend them from the stickers either, and they would need to walk with care, as Indians did. But he didn't say anything then. She clambered into the red wagon beside Blueberry, and blued the vaults of heaven.

When they finally topped the bluff north of the Platte Valley, he could see a vast distance, clear to the Bighorns, baking distantly in July heat. He felt suddenly free. This was the empty West he knew, the untouched lands he had learned and loved as a young trapper. Along the Oregon Trail he had felt imprisoned. He always felt hemmed in by people, but suddenly those iron bands around his heart slipped away in the shimmer of the duned prairies. Here was life! Now the days would run and leap and sing! Off to the east he could see Chang scouting and hunting. Far ahead, Victoria dropped over a low ridge, and he knew when he saw her again she'd probably have a load of fly-bitten mule meat wrapped behind her, and enough hair to keep stiff old fingers busy for weeks. But he wanted something else, the shaggy brown beasts that never ventured close now to the Oregon Trail—buffalo, the food, shelter, weapons, and clothing of all the Plains tribes. He sucked sweet, sage-scented air into his lungs, and laughed.

Chapter 14

She had never been poor before. Her own family, the Sylvanuses, ranked among the Memphis elite. Then she had married Hannibal Parkins, who had more gold than Midas. At Goldtooth's parlor house she had used her perfect body, chiseled features, shining ash-blond hair, and twilight-gray hooded eyes to make herself independent, and it was all hers, too, not any man's.

Then that buckskinned idiot leading this brigade lost it all for her in one night. Everything she owned except for one li'l old white wrapper. And out in a wilderness too, where one couldn't simply call the dressmaker or order dinner at a restaurant. She scorned the lout, but even more did she dread the days ahead. She could scarcely imagine life without the things she had carefully packed in fragrant cedar-lined trunks, her silk gowns and pink frocks and black underthings, Wedgwood china, silver, fine damask table linens; a trunk of shining shoes and slippers, belts and yellow velvet ribbons, lavender scents, rouges, and English soaps.

Her inheritance here had been one li'l old sky-blue dimity dress, badly worn and busted out at the elbows, plus an unbleached-muslin petticoat that smelled of cat droppings. The translucent dimity let the slightest breeze through, as well as men's gazes, which amused her. But nothing more amused her. She wished to go back to Fort Laramie. She might easily have married a captain for a while, long enough to put her life together. She knew what she could do to men. Not that she'd have stayed at a crude army post for long.

That first afternoon had been ghastly. She craved food. Not a blanket remained in the wagon to cushion its bouncing over a roadless land, and she jolted and rolled until her whole torso felt bruised. But she found walking even worse because she lacked shoes and the whole mean ol' prairie contrived to stab her feet. Only Big Alice walked. The Creole woman had gone barefoot much of her life, and the rock and prickly pear and sagebrush sticks didn't bother her.

She was a prisoner. On the driver's seat, Blueberry slouched lazily, enjoying himself. He could enjoy himself in hell, she thought bitterly. Britches had been donated to him, but he preferred his faded red long johns, Mister Skye's leggins, and a breechclout. He too lacked shoes. Like Mister Skye and those squaws, Blueberry seemed to bloom the moment they left the Oregon Trail and started overland through an empty, endless, and desolate wilderness.

Mrs. Parkins peered toward the hazy horizons, deeply afraid. She'd been in cities all her life. What would they do for food? Clothing? Shelter? Would she eat grasshoppers or snakes with her filthy fingers? What would she do for soap and shoes and her monthly time? What if Indians came? Would this harsh dry climate bake her flesh and ruin her beauty, her living? On the Oregon Trail there might be help—garrisoned army posts every twenty miles, other wagon trains. But here . . . That evening the gray mule meat salvaged by one of the squaws had been ghastly. It crawled with green-bellied flies when she first saw it, and then the squaws roasted it harshly in open flame, burning it black on the outside. But she ate it ravenously with her fingers after it had cooled, there being nothing else. They all felt so starved they ate the whole of it, envying the Riddles and their mail-order brides who cooked from airtights.

Mrs. Parkins snorted. Where lay the difference between her and the mail-order brides? Nowhere, really. Some li'l old person would mumble over them, but after that a woman's life stayed the same, only she enjoyed it a hundred times more than they ever would. That's why she had entered the Life. She enjoyed it. All she wanted was a big ol' man! Lots and lots of them!

They had made ten good miles that afternoon, striking just north of west from the Oregon Trail, and Mister Skye camped in a shallow valley choked with brush and trees, on either side of a tiny alkaline creek. After that

awful meal, Mister Skye's younger squaw, Mary, beckoned her. Moments later, she found herself standing on a
buffalo cowhide that had been snipped out of Skye's
lodge, while Mary swiftly outlined her bitsy feet with a
stick of charcoal. Beside Mary, old Victoria cursed and
snipped leather and poked holes in it with an awl. By
twilight, the sporting ladies and Blueberry all had moccasins, crudely made but serviceable. And all of them
learned instantly that Indian moccasins didn't keep rocks
and sticks and thorns from biting their feet. They begged
for liners, and that helped. They could walk at last. Mrs.
Parkins felt less a prisoner now that she could at least
head for bushes without stabbing her feet.

Still muttering and cursing, Victoria snipped the sin-
ews that had bound the lodgeskins together in watertight
seams, and somehow separated four soft old hides for the
bawds before the night spun too far along. A sleeping
robe for each.

That Mister Skye, off in the creek brush, hacked a cottonwood limb with rhythmic whacks. By the time light
dimmed in this shallow dip in the plains, he had cut half
a dozen things that looked like thick shingles, oblongs of
creamy wood, perhaps two inches thick. He lowered
himself before the fire, which Victoria kept burning only
for light, and with a hatchet for a chisel deftly hollowed
out each slab of wood.

"Trenchers," he said, handing one to Mrs. Parkins. She
found herself staring at a serviceable plate.

"If you hadn't gotten drunk, we could be eating from
our tin camp things," she retorted nastily. She would
not let that irresponsible lout off so easily. He came from
the servant class, but scarcely knew it, and needed disciplining.

"Right you are, Mrs. Parkins," he replied amiably.

"You'd better make us some silverware. It's disgusting to eat with fingers," she added.

"Will when we take a buffler."

Across the fire, still muttering and cursing, old Victoria separated tail hair she had sliced from the lightning-struck mules into twisted strands, and plaited it. Did these squaws never sleep? she wondered. Victoria's hard brown eyes flicked at her man, and Mrs. Parkins saw embedded forgiveness there, the kind of thing that lasts and grows beyond lifetimes.

"This is all your idea. I trust you have some bitsy thing planned for breakfast, Mister Skye," she said tartly.

"Last of the jerky, Mrs. Parkins."

She could scarcely imagine anything worse. The hard, dried strips of buffalo eventually melted in the mouth, but never satisfied hunger.

Big Alice commandeered the butcher knife and was off slaying grass and carting armloads of it to the red wagon. Mrs. Parkins suddenly realized that might be a good idea, and helped. Eventually Goldtooth and Juliet helped too, and in a while a foot of soft, sweet-smelling dry grasses lined the wagon bed, along with pungent sage leaves. It dawned on Mrs. Parkins for the first time that comfort might be possible out here. The Indians managed it somehow. After that, she sank into a soft new bed beside the others, wrapped the cowhide robe about her, and slept better than she had hoped, except for the pimple that stung on her inner thigh.

The next day she enjoyed. She walked when she felt like it, learning to cope with moccasins, understanding what they could and couldn't do. And when she wearied of that, she rode in the grass-lined wagon bed relishing the fresh smell, somewhat insulated from the rude jolting, staring at the broad back of big ol' Blueberry and the drops of sweat that rolled down his heavy corrugated neck, darkening the faded long john.

She scarcely noticed the vast land they crossed, or the earth she trod upon. The red wagon and its frayed pink sheet had become a sort of island, a tiny dot of shade under an iron sun. This day she thirsted but they found no water anywhere. She peered through the rear pucker-hole, watching Vanderbilt stolidly drive the grimy red wagon behind, dressed now in ancient butternut britches that had probably been part of a Confederate uniform, his dull black boots, and a sagging mud-colored calico blouse he'd scrounged somewhere, maybe on the sly from that bride, Drusilla. Without his gambler uniform he looked odd, she thought. Like he ought to be pickin' cotton.

In the morning those squaws of Skye's had made a stew in a black kettle, with jerky and some white roots with brown skins they'd dug up, and even some prairie turnips they'd found, and added a bit of salt from Mister Skye's parfleches, and it'd been grand. And then during the nooning in willow shade, Seven-Story Chang had ridden in on his white horse with a blood-crusted antelope tied behind the cantle, and they feasted. She loved big ol' Chang. He always mocked her, and that made time fly. She looked up to any big ol' man who could tease her. She decided she'd have him tonight. Maybe Blueberry too. She thought about that big ol' Mister Skye, but he had his Mary. Maybe she could steal him from Mary.

For a moment she envied the Shoshone woman, but not much. So what if the squaw had flesh as smooth and colorful as rosy peaches, and shiny blue-black hair, plaited into two braids? So what if her doe eyes gleamed, and she had a row of even white teeth? Mary had a li'l old scar that started back from her forehead, and that marred her. Mrs. Parkins envied the beautiful soft tan doeskin blouse

that Mary wore, fringed at the hips and quilled across
the bodice in bold jags of rainbow color. She wore it over
a long skirt of red calico, with high beaded moccasins
below that, and all cinched at the waist with a black sash
she tied as a belt. Mary was lucky to be so beautiful. Mister
Skye was lucky too, but she'd show that big ol' man a trick
or two that Mary never learned. Mrs. Parkins lay back in
the jouncing wagon, stared at blue sky peeping through
furry holes in the wagon sheet, and thought about Mister
Skye's leggins and red-beaded breechclout.

The moment Mister Skye turned the wagons northwest,
away from the Oregon Trail, Mary rejoiced. She knew
Victoria rejoiced, too. They rode out upon a vast sun-
danced prairie, and she felt at home at once. An eagle
soared on summer drafts, and she felt free and clean. Far
ahead, Victoria scouted, a dark dot on a golden land, and
off to the right side Mary sometimes glimpsed the Chinese on his white medicine horse, dipping in and out of
hollows invisible to the eye.

She rode behind Mister Skye, keeping the packmules
in line and watching the travois with the lodgepoles and
what remained of the lodgecover upon it. She still had
enough skins to erect a small shelter for them if it stormed.
Mister Skye's back had changed too, straighter and more
erect now. He didn't like the trail either. He had become
like her people, even though he was a white man. Even
Jawbone looked happier, almost dancing along and gam-
boling like a colt.

She wasn't really afraid of the whites, except sometimes when hard-eyed ones came, but she could not
understand them. These had lost their things and talked
of going back. What a mystery! They thought they had to
go back because there would be nothing to eat or wear.

Were they blind, these white women? Here she could find everything to eat and wear. Here in this moon they called July grew roots and berries and herbs, wild onions and breadroot, raspberries and turnips. It had been thus with every party of whites they had taken out upon the breast of the Earth Mother. They walked through food and did not see it, saw clothing but did not know it. Passed weapons and implements and tools and their minds were shut to all of it.

There were dyes in rock and clay and berries and roots and bark; medicine everywhere in leaves and roots and the pulp of insects; and signs everyplace to tell who had come and gone. Even now, they rode over an oblique path of many small unshod hoofs, made since the big rain but dry and a day old. But she knew the whites had not seen this plain thing, even though Mister Skye had. The white people had great medicine and made guns and pots and wheels, but they didn't see or know.

Mister Skye paused to examine the tracks, and the fresher one of a shod horse beside them. Mary paused too. It had been a hunting party, too small for war. No travois furrowed the earth, but a dog ran with them. They had spare ponies that paused to nip bunchgrasses beside the main trail. The prints were light and that meant the ponies carried no meat. The Chinese had found them, and started northeast along their trail, just to check upon them. They scouted for buffalo, just as Mister Skye hunted for a valley black with them.

She did not talk much to Mister Skye. She had little to say, especially when she knew his thoughts before he spoke them. She knew when he would come to her robes and make her happy. She knew when she made him happy, too. He seemed happy now, crossing the wide grassland ahead of the wagons and far from the Oregon Trail. She

remembered when they had made Dirk. It was not at
night, but at noon in the mountain lands on a day much
like this. They made Dirk beside a raucous creek on the
other side of the Bitterroot Mountains, and she knew it at
once, and knew Dirk would be a good-medicine child.
She missed him now, but her task was done. The boy had
wept but she didn't when they had put him on a white
steamer at Fort Benton in the care of a rich Frenchman
named Chouteau who was a friend of Mister Skye's.

Now he learned the medicine of the white men, the
little figures on the paper, their stories and their way of
adding things up. It was good, but she hoped Dirk would
not lose the wisdom of her people. He had gone on a
vision-quest beforehand, and had come back laughing,
with a small medicine bundle dangling from his neck.
She would not ask, and he would not say, what sacred
things he carried. But he knew who his medicine helper
was: the red fox. Good! Dirk would have his helper-fox,
even back in the place called Independence; even among
the blackrobes who would teach him things. Mister Skye
had old friends among the blackrobes, especially Father
Kiley, who had made all the arrangements.

She did not want ever to see Independence.

These whites were the strangest Mary had ever known.
Two wagons of outcast whites, and another wagon of
ones who judged the others, and they barely spoke to
each other. The outcasts were friendlier to her. She could
talk to the ones who sold themselves to men, and she
loved to be around Chang or Blueberry, but the women
in the other wagon ignored her or addressed her curtly,
as if she were a Cheyenne. The ones in the Riddle wagon
would not share with the others, and that shocked her.
The man, Riddle, talked about angles, and it took her
time to understand his meaning, but then she knew he

made evil and contrived to take advantage of everyone. He had tried right off to take advantage of Mister Skye, not doing anything in the mornings, thinking that would force Mister Skye to harness his mules for him. But Mister Skye knew how to handle such a person. Just once he asked Mister Riddle to be ready in the morning. But that weasel-man wasn't. He intended to sit back and smirk and leer and feel lordly and make Mister Skye harness. So Mister Skye had gathered Riddle's six mules and tied them all behind the red wagons, and had driven out, leaving Riddle and his women with a bare wagon, openmouthed behind them.

Riddle learned the lesson. Mary giggled, remembering how the weasel-man raved and yelled and cried theft when Skye returned an hour later. Not that it changed Mister Riddle. The white man spent hours trying to get Mary and Victoria, or someone else, to do things he could easily have done for himself with half the effort. But that was the way of Riddle, very lazy but very energetic about pressuring others. He would be no help at all in a fight, and would hide in his wagon.

Mister Skye knew that too. She saw it in her man's face whenever he looked at Riddle. What a strange party! Nobody helping anybody! It scandalized her. Her Snake people helped one another. In war, there could be no greater honor than to rescue a wounded or endangered comrade. No chief stood tall unless he made sure the least widow woman of the band was fed and sheltered. Mary sat tall in her saddle, proud of her people and aware of the terrible shortcomings of whites.

Mister Skye looked strange to her without his black hat. He wore a red bandana over his forehead now, knotted at the back, holding his long white-shot hair in place and looking like a chief of her people rather than a white man. It pleased her. His black hat came from the other world.

Far off she spotted Victoria galloping toward them, slouched lightly over her sweated brown pony. She never raced unless trouble neared. Mister Skye saw her at once, and loosened the thong of his revolver scabbard. He turned, nodded to Mary, who knew what to do. She wheeled her pony and trotted back to the Riddle wagon.

"Mister Skye say trouble," she announced curtly. Alvah glanced narrowly around, saw nothing, and smiled lazily.

She trotted back. "Mister Skye say trouble," she said to Blueberry. He peered sharply, lifted the fowling piece, and also a small poke full of shot, and a powderhorn. It made a slim defense. In a hard fight, he'd scarcely be able to reload the two barrels before being swept under.

She continued back to Vanderbilt. "Mister Skye say trouble," she announced. But he shrugged. She remembered he lacked weapons, save for some willow staves Mister Skye had cut for him at the last camp.

She rode up to the Riddle wagon. "The sporting man has no gun," she said to Riddle.

"He's plumb in a fix," Riddle said. "Wish I could help."

The brides scurried into the hot shade of the wagon sheet, and spread themselves below the plank box, a thin inch of hardwood between themselves and bullets. Mary-Rita moaned, scared witless.

No good arguing with Riddle, so she trotted forward again. Victoria hung immobile on her racing pony. She weighed scarcely a hundred pounds now, and rode a light grass-stuffed pad which her pony carried effortlessly, but she lost ground to what raced behind her, a dozen bronzed and naked men raising a long plume of dust like running elk on the drying prairie.

Mister Skye stopped now, and the wagons behind him. He peered not at Victoria, but along the horizon to the north, looking for Chang and not seeing him.

"The gambler man has no gun," Mary said to him.

He glanced back. Vanderbilt had abandoned his wagon and was dodging across the prairie, looking for a rabbit hole. The trotting mules dragged the empty wagon farther and farther off, its body and naked bows shrinking into a red dot on the horizon.

Victoria raced in, saying just one word: Arapaho.

Chapter 15

Eleven, and they were not painted. A hunting party then, looking for sport and finding it. They paused, just beyond rifleshot, assessing their chances, seeing Vanderbilt's naked red wagon far from the others, seeing only two males, Mister Skye and Blueberry.

Beneath him Jawbone pawed and shrieked, ears back, clenched for war and blood. Mister Skye pressed his palm against Jawbone's withers, a signal, and the horse quieted.

"Hunters," he said.

"Sonofabitch," muttered Victoria. He heard her pulling her muzzleloader from its sheath. He knew Mary was crouched back of the mule with the travois, the big Sharps resting on the pack.

The warriors began to spread out now, one party heading for the flank and the other nerving itself for the run. So . . . they would take scalps and count coup this fine summer day. They looked to be boys and young men, he thought, but couldn't be sure. Age had done things to his sight.

They would not be far from an Arapaho village that followed the buffalo. Out yonder, the bronze riders paused to make medicine, each in his own way. They hadn't the advantage of surprise, so this would be no sweeping howling assault, but an orchestrated dance of daring, braving the rifles of the whites.

Seven with bows, four with carbines, of what sort he couldn't imagine. He felt the gleaming new Henry in his hands, with more cartridges in its long belly than there were warriors out there. Beneath him Jawbone shivered.

Two of them raced toward Vanderbilt's red wagon now. That would be the first prize, and a shelter to shoot from.

"Mary," he said.

She swung the big Sharps toward them, and squeezed. The throaty boom echoed in the afternoon. The recoil jolted Mary. It had twice the range of his Henry.

A pony collapsed, red flowering its chest, and the rider leapt free as it sank.

Mister Skye glanced behind him, noting Blueberry at the ready. Alvah Riddle had vanished, but now a gleaming blue barrel poked through a small port in the side of his wagon. Another of Riddle's angles, he thought, and not a good one, blindsided as he was.

The main body of the Arapaho spread into a skirmish line now and trotted fast.

"Mister Riddle," he said, "do not shoot to kill unless they are upon you. They are hunters having sport, and we will avoid war. We'll likely go to their village directly."

No answer.

He nodded to Victoria, and she crept toward Riddle's barrel, pressing hard against the side of Riddle's wagon.

She would do what Plains Indians were gifted at doing with tumescent barrels.

The unhorsed warrior crabbed toward the abandoned wagon. The others closed in.

He focused on the sweated chest of the lead pony and squeezed. The Henry bucked. He missed. He levered and fired again, dropping a horse and catapulting its rider. He levered and hit another horse, which kept running, stumbling, falling along a declining trajectory. A whinny pierced the afternoon. He smelled gunsmoke. He heard a flat shot from out there, and another. But they stayed too far away for arrows. He levered and shot, grazing a rump, and the horse bucked violently, crowhopped, head down, spilling a rider.

Behind him the Sharps boomed and the most distant of the ponies stumbled. The several dismounted warriors lay flat. From Riddle's wagon a rifle barked and a warrior's arm blossomed red.

Mister Skye cursed.

The horse warriors milled now, then dashed toward their unmounted brothers, who leapt up gracefully as the hunting ponies trotted by, seating themselves behind the riders.

Mister Skye held his fire. Behind him Victoria grasped the barrel of Riddle's rifle, jammed it inward, knocking the butt into Riddle's teeth, and yanked outward violently. Inside, Alvah Riddle howled and women screamed. Victoria darted under his wagon with the rifle.

"You didn't listen to me, Mister Riddle, and now there's a man wounded out there and maybe war."

No reply.

A warrior had gained the empty red wagon and whipped up the mules. Another darted straight toward the bunch-grassed slope where Vanderbilt had flattened himself to earth. Bad business.

He slid brass cartridges into the Henry's magazine and waited. They lurked just beyond Henry range, making medicine again. They wrapped the arm of the wounded one, who sat in shock on the sunstruck earth.

On the flank, one of them spotted Vanderbilt. The gambler sprang up and lumbered in, with the warrior gliding behind him, scalping knife glinting. Mister Skye nodded to Mary, and the Sharps boomed, geysering dirt and rock just ahead of the warrior. He got the message. Vanderbilt puffed in and scrambled under Blueberry's wagon, wheezing and wild-eyed.

They hadn't expected a repeater. They barely understood the seven-shot Spencers and had never experienced a Henry. Mister Skye raised the weapon over his head and touched heels to Jawbone, who snorted and minced toward the warriors, ears flattened and teeth bared. Behind him, Mary and Victoria lay prone, their rifles resting solidly on packs, ready to back their man.

The Arapaho sat their ponies or stood like cemetery statues in a prairie graveyard, naked except for moccasins and breechclouts, bows and rifles canted but ready. Mister Skye rode steadily, hoping he would not have to do what he might have to do. But they had not left their village as a war party, and their sport had vanished with the dead ponies, probably good buffalo runners.

He reined Jawbone some thirty yards from them, and watched. The recognition came to them then. They knew Jawbone, the bad-medicine horse familiar to all the Plains tribes, a source of terror. Those who had never seen the horse nonetheless knew him by description, the scarred evil blue roan with the yellow eyes narrowly set, owned by a barrel of a man with a black stovepipe hat . . .

They studied Skye's head. No hat, but a red bandana. But this horse could only be the terrible one, and this man Mister Skye. He knew none of them, but their eyes knew him. They lowered their weapons cautiously, well aware of the reach of the big buffalo gun back at the wagons.

They stood immobile, waiting. Arapaho, he thought. Dog-eaters, the other Plains people called them, speaking a tongue close to the Atsina, or Gros Ventre, and similar to the Cheyenne. They roamed this land, here close to the North Platte.

He waited too, sniffing out treachery, ticking off time to see whether he could cradle his Henry in his lap and make his big hands flash the signs. He decided he could. I am Mister Skye, the guide, he told them, making the sign for the heavens. Known to all the tribes by the sign of the sky. I am passing through; looking for buffalo. I am peaceful. I had shot only ponies, not men, and had stopped the one in my party who'd shot to kill. His blunt brown hands slashed air as harshly as his voice did.

They nodded.

Did they want war? he asked.

One among them said no; not war against Mister Skye. They had been out for sport. Buffalo grazed nearby. But now they lacked ponies. Three of the dead ones were good buffalo runners. They would keep the red wagon and mules they had captured.

No, said Mister Skye, they would not. He would take back the wagon and mules. But maybe when he found buffalo he would leave many carcasses for them. He would shoot them with his big Sharps from a distance, the way of the white buffalo hunters, and would drop

many before the herd even stirred, and all but one would
be theirs. He would take four hides and the meat of one
carcass. But if they wanted war, he would give them war,
much more war than they ever imagined.

They muttered, and turned at last to the one on the
ground holding his arm, and Mister Skye realized the
wounded one was their leader. He looked older, perhaps
forty, with a bit of white lacing his parted and braided jet
hair. The warrior lolled in shock.

Cover him, Skye signaled. But they had little to cover
him with. Their ponies had grass-filled pad saddles and
no blankets.

My woman will care for him, Mister Skye signaled.
He would not turn his back on them, tempting them to
shoot him and take his Henry. But he signaled, and Victoria rode forward, hunched lightly over her pony. She
said nothing, always understanding his wishes, and slipped
off her pony, carrying with her a kit that had been rolled
on the pad saddle behind her. Her eyes glinted hard
black, and her face grew grave, as it always did among
the enemies of the Absaroka people. But she covered the
man with her blanket and then pressed herbs under his
tongue.

The wash of blood on his arm had gone brown in the
hot sun, but his face looked pale and moist. She felt of
his arm, and he groaned.

"Broken," she said.

Damn that Riddle, he thought. He'd be the death of
them all.

His hands flashed again. No wood here for splints, but
under one of the pad saddles lay a piece of tanned hide.
He asked for it, and Victoria wound it tightly around the
bullet-mangled arm, tying it deftly with rawhide thong.

Where is your village? Skye's hard hands asked.

They pointed and signed. Half a day west.

We will go there, Skye's hands said.

It would be all right, he thought, if he could disarm Riddle and keep the women of all sorts halfway calm. But even as he thought it, he knew there'd be trouble aplenty. One of the warriors had already started westward with Goldtooth's second red wagon.

He and Victoria rode back to the wagons, his back itching.

"We are going to their village," he said. "Riddle, hand me your revolver."

"You think I'm crazy, Skye?"

"Yes."

That nonplussed Riddle. "What's your angle?" he said at last. "I want my carbine back. I defend my women and your squaw bashes in my lips with my own Spencer."

"Hand me the revolver or I'll come in there after it."

"Try it. I'll shoot you first, Skye."

The women in the wagon cringed.

Mister Skye slid off Jawbone and leapt in the wagon with one cat-spring, knocking Riddle's revolver up even as he pulled the trigger. Inside the wagon the report was deafening. Women screamed.

"You beast!" screamed Flora.

"I am saving your lives," said Mister Skye.

Riddle lay sprawled over trunks and barrels, cursing. Skye plucked up the revolver and backed out, his eye hard upon the milling Arapaho.

"Now I'm defenseless!" cried Alvah. "What's your angle—killing us?"

Mister Skye didn't answer. Drusilla sobbed.

He spotted Vanderbilt under the bawds' wagon. "Gambler! Drive this green wagon."

The command brooked no delay, and Vanderbilt slunk

out from under Goldtooth's wagon and sidled into the seat of Riddle's wagon.

"I want my wagon back, you idiot!" snarled Goldtooth.

Mister Skye handed Riddle's weapons to Blueberry. "We are going on a peaceful visit, make meat," he said. "There will be maybe a hundred lodges of Arapaho yonder. They can be friendly or they can take scalps. If we had won this skirmish, we'd have lost the war."

It was all the message Blueberry needed.

Riddle bawled and raged, and his women wept. Mister Skye stopped again at his wagon.

"Mister Riddle," he said. "When I give an instruction in dangerous circumstances, you will bloody well follow it. If you'd killed that warrior, what's left of your hair would be hanging from a medicine tripod tonight. Along with the sausage curls of your wife, these women, and everyone else here."

He didn't wait for an answer.

They veered due west, steering wagons over rolling dunes of sandy prairie. Arapaho warriors flanked the wagons and rode ahead. One of them drove Goldtooth's red wagon far ahead, almost out of sight, lashing the mules recklessly. No doubt that man's first experience with harnessed animals, Mister Skye thought. Might smash the wagon.

He peered sharply at these Arapaho. Their carbines had been sheathed, arrows returned to quiver. But often coup-seekers wanted to make medicine against Skye, the medicine legend. For the moment all seemed well. The older one with the wounded arm looked less pale, and more alert. He rode in close to Mister Skye now, his good-arm fingers asking questions, his bad-arm fingers making tiny motions.

Mister Skye replied. The finger-language of the plains

required short answers. They were going far to the north-west, he said. Beyond the spine of the mountains to the land of the Bannacks. The women in the green wagon would be brides for the men there. The women in the red wagon sold themselves for money. The men with them were a gambler and bartender . . .

Which reminded him that he had not seen Chang. That worried him. They had veered west, and Chang might miss them . . . if he lived.

Had the Arapaho seen a man on a white horse? he asked.

Surprised, the Arapaho gazed about, studied horizons, and then shrugged.

They didn't know about Chang, Skye thought, still mystified.

"Where are the buffalo?" he asked.

"North," the Arapaho replied.

"How are you called?"

"Crow Killer."

Just behind Skye, Victoria huddled deeper in her saddle and her eyes turned hard.

Crow Killer urged his pony closer and closer to Jaw-bone, who laid his ears back and began to mince. In one fluid move, Crow Killer raised his good arm, smacked a hand on Mister Skye's hair and wheeled away on his buffalo pony even as Jawbone exploded, shrieking and snapping.

"You don't count coup on guests and friends," Skye said. "So you have told me you are enemies."

Crow Killer shrugged. The flanking warriors reached for arrows and nocked them.

"You have stolen medicine and I will make your med-icine bad," Mister Skye said, his Henry leveled in the crook of his arm. "My brothers the buffalo bulls will kill you soon."

Crow Killer laughed.

Three tense hours later they found themselves looking into a shallow, wide trough in the prairie with a silvery creek oxbowed through it. On a verdant meadow along the creek stood scores of Arapaho lodges, their smoke-blackened windflaps a dark forest in the glare of afternoon. The dog soldiers, or village guards, had long since spotted them and now escorted them in. Ahead rolled Goldtooth's empty wagon driven by the warrior and surrounded now by the curious, who had boiled out of the village to see this amazing sight. Town criers announced their presence. Before a larger lodge, painted with bright yellow medicine symbols, stood a chief, one Mister Skye did not recognize.

Behind him was pure fear. He could smell Alvah's sweat and the women's terror. Fear always stank. Blueberry looked drawn. Vanderbilt as taut-strung as a fiddlestring. Mary-Rita sobbed and bawled imprecations. Jawbone didn't like it, and walked with flat ears and bared teeth.

Yellow and gray dogs, some half wolf, snapped and yapped and howled. Some of them would be tonight's stew, Skye thought. Women with wide cheekbones glared. Naked boys peered, drew mock bows and loosed mock arrows, and fled behind lodges. A sharp breeze flapped orange buffalo-hide lodges, ballooning them and tugging them from the circles of white boulders that pinned them to dun earth. Before many lodges stood tripods with medicine bundles hanging from them, and black-haired scalps, and feather bundles. Squat bronze men with powerful builds trotted beside, carrying deadly lances with black tips. And everywhere rose cacophony, dogs yapping and howling, horses shrieking, children screaming, women chattering.

Mister Skye did not like the feel of it. Neither did Mary and Victoria behind him, who peered flint-eyed and solemnly at all this familiar village life. These were ancient enemies of both the Crows and Shoshones. The warriors among them pointed sullenly at Skye, at Jaw-bone, and at Skye's brass-framed repeater, which kindled something wary in their eyes.

They wound past a circle of tipis and into a central plaza before the looming lodge of the chief, which stood at its west side, its doorflap pointed ritually east, as did every doorflap here. The man stood in ceremonial finery, wearing a medicine shirt of elkskin from which dangled human hair, mostly black but blond and red and brown as well. Around his neck hung a rawhide string of dried human ears, separated by elk's teeth. Skye knew the man but had never met him: Old Bull, squat, wedge-shouldered, glint-eyed, and with the arced nose of a hawk above thin cruel lips. Skye had only a moment to glance at this legendary war-prone chief before his gaze was drawn elsewhere, to a familiar white stallion, a giant Chinese who stood with mocking eye, and beside him a young Arapaho woman. A beautiful tall woman.

"Ah, Mister Skye," said Chang. "You were a long time arriving in Paradise."

Old Bull motioned for Skye to dismount.

The guide preferred to sit. Beneath him Jawbone trembled and snarled. Skye's hands flashed: Will you smoke?

The question. If Old Bull would smoke the peacepipe, they were guests. If not . . . captives.

Old Bull nodded. He had the calumet in hand, inside of a soft doeskin bag decorated with fine bonework.

Mister Skye's hands flashed. One of your number,

Crow Killer there, counted coup with his hand upon my head, after inviting us here as guests. His medicine is bad. Soon the buffalo bulls will kill him.

Crow Killer laughed, but it had been said. Others who read the hand-signs stared at Skye, and at Crow Killer, noting his wounded arm. Mister Skye felt content. Medicine prophesy could be suggestive. He had learned that long ago. Say it, and self-fulfilling doom would begin. Crow Killer sneered, but Skye read the quake in it.

I will smoke the pipe with the great chief Old Bull, said Mister Skye through his hands. And we will talk. If any here can speak English or Crow or Shoshone, we will talk with our tongues.

Mister Skye dismounted slowly, still cradling the Henry. It would be too large a temptation for those outside the lodge, even though stealing from guests in a village ranked among the most shameful of deeds among many of the Plains tribes.

He turned. "Mister Riddle. Mister Vanderbilt. Mister Hill. And ladies. These people will not harm you if you do not harm them. They will expect presents soon. I will explain that later. Be firm but amiable. Is that understood, Mister Riddle? If you knew the angles, Mister Riddle, then you brought twists of tobacco for these moments . . . I am going to smoke with Old Bull, and then we shall see."

Riddle, subdued and frightened, nodded.

Chang laughed. "When the honors are done, Mister Skye, come meet my high-priced bride."

Chapter 16

The barbaric menace of Old Bull's village was too much for a poor colleen only weeks off the boat from Tipperary. Mary-Rita peered bug-eyed at these naked yellow savages and thought her life would come to an abrupt end. She blessed herself, repeated every form of contrition she knew of, and fumed because no priest was on hand for extreme unction. She'd been mad through and through for three months now, but that was nothing new. She'd been born mad at the world.

Mary-Rita Flaherty had orange hair and midnight tongue, and some of her brothers and sisters thought she was a witch. Her hair was her glory. In misty sun it shone gold, and in lamplight it shone carrot colored and leapt from darkness like a blaze. As for the rest, she wasn't so fortunate. She had distrustful green eyes, a wide wavery pink mouth, and a snotty pig-nose sprinkled with lavender freckles. She stood tall and had a fine willowy figure except for thick white ankles. No one in the Arapaho village had seen blazing hair like hers. And so they crowded about her, almost-naked men with wide cheekbones and black hair hanging loose or in braids, reaching out, touching hair the color of rising suns.

She bawled at them. "You idjits! Leave me hair alone! You blasted savages, get away now! You smell like rotten potatoes."

They smiled and probed and touched the orange filaments and inspected her freckles. Their touch felt rough and dry.

"You're the dumbest things! Haven't you got a brain in your idjit heads? Saints preserve me. Saint Patrick get your blasted sword out! Smite the heathen right and left! Blessed Saint Bridget, carry me back to Tipperary!"

She wasn't all that sure she wanted to go back to misty Ireland. Not after what her own ma and pa and Tommy and Peggy and Sean and Martin had done to her. They were all idjits. Sean didn't know which end of a red cow to milk. Peggy grew so lazy she wouldn't even pull up her blue stockin's. Tommy would spend hours hunkering behind the stone shed and scratching his brown britches where he wasn't supposed to touch, and smoke and talk about stranglin' Englishmen and the hoity-toity rich. But he wasn't half so bad as Martin, the parish quarter-wit, babbling about taking vows with the brown-robed Benedictines and warning Mary-Rita to get down on her knees all the time. And that wasn't half so bad as her watery-eyed pa, who kept them all starving and hardly a potato to spare, or her ghost-pale ma with black-shadowed eyes, who kept nagging and never quit.

But all that was nothing compared to the rest. For half a year they said nary a word to her, no matter how much she shouted at them. Idjit silence all the time, like they were all daft or something. The quieter they got, the more she'd railed, and the more she bawled, the more they turned away like she was the divil's own she-child. And then Pa, he told her she would go on a trip. She yelled at him she didn't want to go on any trip, but they all made her pack a bag—not that she had anything. But Pa gave her a battered black valise he had, and they all stood around solemn, and Pa made the sign of the cross and they hiked into Tipperary, and Pa and Martin and Tommy, they came along jist to make sure, while Ma and Peggy just stared, and they got a carmine coach to Waterford and next she knew she trotted the deck

of a big gray clipper. Pa's eyes leaked and she'd never
seen that.

"Mary-Rita," he said all solemn, "this passage was a
scrape and it took even your ma's ring. When you get to
the other side of the sea, maybe you'll learn to say a kind
thing."

"I'm not ever going to see you again," she wailed.

They filed out and closed the door to this rusty place,
and it clicked. She felt the ship roll under her, and hammered on the door. When the idjit purser sprung her,
nothing remained but the green swelling sea.

She arrived with three shillings and a sixpence, too
mad to be frightened. She didn't know what she'd do.
They herded her through a cavernous smelly brickpile in
Boston and then she was free to walk through a var-
nished door into a world she didn't know. That's when a
man approached her. He could arrange a good Irish and
Catholic marriage for her. And next thing, she met another man, Alvah Riddle, and he said a miner out in the
west, Tom O'Dougherty, wanted to marry a sweet colleen like herself, and in the church too. She could barely
read or write, but she painfully inscribed her name,
Mary-Rita Flaherty, on the line, and added a small cross
for good measure, like the priests did.

And now she stood here, clutching her wood beads
and getting ready to be burned at the stake like Saint
Joan, or beheaded or scalped or . . . like saints. . . . or . . .
Aw, these idjits!

"Mary-Rita, stop bawling like a loon," said Alvah. "All
they want is to see your hair. You'll get us all slaughtered
carrying on like that."

"You idjit! You got me into this, you Protestant heathen pig. You crook. You miserable worm. You son of
the divil. You heretic skinflint sneaky dim-witted swine!

You pink chinless bald fool! You smelly potbellied con-
niver! You dirty-fingered lazy—you can't even harness
the mules—you stupid conniving . . . Protestant!"

Mary-Rita didn't run out of breath. "Get these creatures
away from me. Heathen! Savages! Murderers! They'll slice
my flesh and wring my neck! Saint Brendan, Saint Peter,
Saint Patrick, Saint Bartholomew, Saint Teresa, Saint Patrick, Saint Elizabeth, Saint Patrick, Saint Benedict, Saint
Francis . . . Pa before me, and beside me, Tommy behind
me, Jesus above me, Peggy beneath me . . ."

Old Bull and Mister Skye and others emerged from
the chief's lodge, the pipe ceremony completed. Old Bull
saw her and stared, hard brown eyes peering straight at
that flaming hair. He rolled toward her on legs bandied
by a long life on horse, and gazed, taking her all in, his
eyes studying the hair, her freckles, her little breasts—oh,
the scandal!—and her hips. Oh how he stared and stared.

"Get this heathen away from me!" she bawled at Mister Skye.

Mister Skye said, "He likes the look of you, Miss
Flaherty. He understands a little English too. This band
winters over on the South Platte, near Denver City and
Auraria."

"What's that supposed to mean?"

"Bridle your tongue, Miss Flaherty."

"Why should I? I want to get out of here. These heathen! These smelly savages! These pagan idjits!"

Old Bull said something to Skye's squaw, Victoria,
who repeated something to Mister Skye. It dawned on
Mary-Rita that the chief knew Crow, and talked to
their idjit drunken guide by speaking Crow to Victoria,
who translated. They talked a long time, and Old Bull
kept staring at Alvah Riddle, and at her, and back at
Riddle.

Finally Mister Skye turned to her, a faint mocking on his leathery face. "Old Bull would like to marry you," he said. "He likes your hair."

"Marry me? Marry me?" Mary-Rita cried, thunderstruck. "Why, I'd sooner go to bed with the divil! Yes, the divil! Marry me! I'm to be wed to the miner, Tommy O'Dougherty, I am. A good Catholic man. Yes I am, you idjit!"

The guide turned to Riddle. "I've explained your part in this to Old Bull. He wishes me to tell you he'll offer a good bride price. Twenty tanned robes, a dozen prime ponies, and a ceremonial elkskin shirt, fringed, with quill and bead trim. And he'll adopt you as a son, and make you a blood brother of the Arapaho."

Alvah Riddle peered at Old Bull, his eyes darting hither and yon, his mind whirling. "I'll have to consider the angles," Riddle muttered. "Got a contract with O'Dougherty."

"Over me dead body! Saints preserve and defend me!" howled Mary-Rita.

Riddle peered craftily. "Kinda hint to me, Mister Skye. Kinda slip it to me, so the old chief don't catch it—but how much would those tanned robes fetch in Bannack among the miners? And the fat ponies?"

Some vast delight suffused Mister Skye's face. "Why, Riddle, that's easy. Mining camps are plumb starved for anything usable, and a good robe should fetch maybe thirty dollars in dust. Ponies, why, they'll vary. Fifty or hundred each. Lots of miners would like them to pack with."

Alvah Riddle's face twisted with excitement. "Skye, get the old chief to throw in some packsaddles, the kind them miners want, for the bride."

Mister Skye and Victoria conveyed Riddle's request,

and there began a long powwow with Old Bull in a tongue Mary-Rita thought sounded like jail bars clanging.

"Mister Riddle." This time Drusilla spoke, and her tone was withering. "You have a contract. A most solemn agreement between Miss Flaherty and yourself and Mr. O'Dougherty. If you are going to violate a sacred contract, why, why—"

"I won't mary that heathen goat!" yelled Mary-Rita.

"Got a clause, a forfeit clause," said Alvah Riddle. "Fourteen B. It says that in the event party of the first part—that's me—can't deliver the merchandise—ah, bride—I get to deduct expenses and return the residue. O'Dougherty paid me five hunnert and is to pay another five hunnert on delivery. But I spent, let's see, over five hunnert getting her here, at twelve cents a mile . . . I wouldn't have to return anything to O'Dougherty; just not take his second payment, is all."

"I'm not a slave! You can't buy and sell me! I'm Irish!"

"Old Bull'll supply two packsaddles with panniers," said Mister Skye.

"What'll they fetch in Bannack?"

"Whatever the market'll bear. Should be pretty scarce, though. He wants the copper-haired young lady for any price."

"Figure a hunnert. Twenty tanned robes times thirty-five is seven hunnert. Horses might fetch five hunnert. Packsaddles maybe a hunnert. That shirt, maybe twenty. But I got to rent that empty wagon from Goldtooth. Figger a hunnert expenses . . . Tell my old friend and brother Old Bull it's a deal. Yes, I'd be plumb honored to give the hand of Miss Flaherty to a great chief of the Arapaho."

"You're cheating Mister O'Dougherty. And you've made a slave of Mary-Rita. I'm an abolitionist and I will see you in Hades for it," snapped Drusilla.

"Got a clause in the contract," bubbled Alvah. "Maybe I could fetch a price for you, too." He laughed nastily.

"You made a contract with me but now you're going to sell me into slavery, to a heathen," Mary-Rita blubbered. She was beyond anger, and unfamiliar tears oozed from her green eyes.

Goldtooth raged at that slimy gray-fleshed gambler, Vanderbilt. The coward had abandoned the red wagon and it had become the booty of an Arapaho warrior and maybe she'd never get it back. The warrior had unharnessed the mules and driven them off to the village herd, and now the wagon stood forlornly here, its naked bows against the azure sky, harness heaped in its bed.

"I had plans for that wagon," she stormed. "I was going to divide it into two cribs for business while we waited for a proper place to be built. But now look! You get that back or I'll kill you, and I mean it!"

"Luck turns," he said blithely. "Life is a turn of the card. Tomorrow you'll have it all back."

"Get out of this wagon," she snapped.

Vanderbilt clambered down and vanished into a crowd of staring Arapaho villagers who eyed his sallow sour face and stepped aside.

A milling crowd gathered around her wagon, fingering harness, touching the skittery mules so that Blueberry had to tug on the lines repeatedly, peering boldly into the wagon bed, their eyes fastening on the only thing of consequence in there, the salvaged black trunk of sporting duds.

"We'd better smile, ladies," she said to her three companions.

Her girls looked all scared, taut as fiddle strings. Mister Skye had disappeared into the chief's skin lodge with

several of the elders, plus Victoria and Mary. She wondered why the squaws had gone inside. Blueberry was a
comfort, sitting there on the wagon seat like a black boulder, slapping blue flies. And over in the crowd she found
even more comfort in Seven-Story, whose arm encircled
a stunning young Arapaho woman with black braids, high
cheekbones, golden flesh, and a long slim figure. Goldtooth
eyed the glowing girl with professional envy. Seven-Story
caught her eye, nodded slightly, and mocked Goldtooth
with his wicked eyes.

Goldtooth felt so unraveled and despondent she barely
noticed the press of the crowd. Everything lost because
of that stupid drunken guide. Rags to wear. All the gilded
and velvet things to furnish her parlor house. Her ladies
desperate and near tears and hungry, dependent on that
barbarian. And now the wagon, too, thanks to that cra-
ven slinking worm of a Vanderbilt with his oily black hair
and gray flesh and sunken shadowed eyes and dirty fingernails. Oh, she'd scratch his eyes out!

"I keep having the feeling they want something from
us," said Mrs. Parkins. "Nasty things. Full of lice, I suppose. Probably pluck them from their greasy hair and eat
them. Oh, why did we evah leave ol' Memphis?"

Goldtooth had wondered that herself a hundred times
in the last days, now that they were reduced to utter poverty. It wasn't all bad, she thought. They could all do business anywhere, anytime, right here before the chief's lodge
if it came to that. The thought amused her.

Some of them milled around Blueberry, touching his
skin, poking and probing. One woman wanted him to pull
off his shirt, wanted to see if all of him had burnt black.
He obliged, and they touched and probed and studied his
black torso, and peered at his lighter palms.

"Guess they want to see how much of me got toasted,"

he said. A gray old woman urged him to drop his britches, tugged at his rope belt, but he declined. "You're too old, woman," he said, chuckling. Over at the mail-order-bride wagon, they glared at him. "No ma'am," he muttered testily to an Arapaho woman, "it do not rub off. Try burnt cork."

Some of them began unbuckling harness. Mule-snatchers, she thought, suddenly alarmed. She had to keep her mules! "Blueberry, stop them!" she cried. "The mules are all we have left!"

He slid off the wagon and into their midst. The almost-naked men and boys were unbuckling harness. The women, mostly in cooler calico tradecloth, voluminous skirts, and long white blouses tied at the waist with a sash, were busy too, unbuckling, loosening, while the big mules pranced and sidled.

"Here now," bawled Blueberry, threading through them.

"Stop them!" cried Goldtooth.

"Not rightly an easy thing without getting us scalped," said Blueberry.

Goldtooth leapt up from the wagon seat and crawled back through the rocking wagon to the trunk. The trunk! She dragged it over the grass bedding and robes from Skye's lodge, and sprung the latch. On the very top lay the gold brocade corset, studded with purple rhinestones, whore's armor. She snatched it out.

"Here, y'all," she cried, waving it like a guidon. "Lookit this, sweeties, look here, slut stuff." She laughed, jumped down among them. She found a young woman and wrapped the corset around her and tied it down the front, compressing the figure over her red calico skirts. "Look at that!" Goldtooth cried. "How's that for class. You'd make a great sporting woman, little lady!"

The Arapaho matron beamed, fondling the fat purple lumps of glass, smoothing a hand over the gold brocade, giggling and dancing while her sisters exclaimed and clucked and cackled and honked and clapped hands. The woman whirled, her jet braids flying, sun spraying off the golden girdle. She giggled. The mules were forgotten, and Blueberry hastily buckled the harness back.

"Ayaa," squealed the Arapaho woman, and ran off somewhere, with a crowd of Arapahos following her.

"Belle of the ball," said Blueberry.

A lithe dusky girl hung back, peering up at Goldtooth hungrily. She was a young thing, barely at womanhood, Goldtooth thought. And wanting something. Goldtooth dug into her trunk and found the pea-green lisle stockings and the black garter belt with crimson hearts.

"Come here, honeychile," she said.

The girl sidled up shyly.

"How's this, sweetie?" Goldtooth said, holding the loot. The girl looked puzzled.

"Up here, honey. In here. I'll fix you up."

Hestitantly the girl clambered into the wagon, and in moments Big Alice and Juliet rolled the green stockings up her legs, hoisted her doeskin skirt, and fastened the gaudy garter belt at her waist. Then they showed the girl how to hook the stockings onto the clips. The girl squealed and leapt back to the earth, and danced around, lifting her doeskin skirts, showing green stockings, black garters, golden thighs.

"She keeps that up and I'm going to get myself scalped by her pappy," muttered Blueberry.

The woman who flaunted the gold corset returned, burdened by something that filled her arms. Before Goldtooth she spread out an exquisitely tanned buffalo robe of light color and summer weight, and presented it to her. Goldtooth Jones exclaimed. So did her ladies.

"I nevah saw such a fine robe," said Mrs. Parkins. "I'd sure like that velvet under my bare back. It'd be like makin' love from both di-rections."

It was dawning on Goldtooth. It took a while, like a bubble rising through cold molasses, but when it finally surfaced in her mind with a pop, she chortled. Wealth. She pawed through the trunk restlessly. There was a ton of it, some a bit water-damaged. A dozen naughty corsets, like the one on top, all black lace with red ribbons running through; or the next one of silver, that tied down the front, and had peekaboos all over it, each the size of a silver dollar. And below that, frilly things in purples, pinks, oranges, fleshtones, and yellows. A pile of skimpy black stockings and black garters. Frilly nothings, black chemises, naughties, slut things for Memphis whores. Riches galore, beyond imagining.

In business! She dragged out the trunk and held up each rainbow thing, one by one, before the enchanted throng, now mostly women. Blueberry sweated and studied the mules and slapped flies. The Arapaho women giggled, tried them all on, sometimes dropping whatever clothes they wore to do it, and snorted and pirouetted and howled, and for each selection they made, they scurried off to their lodges and returned with fine robes, or quilled skin dresses, or exquisite moccasins, masterfully crafted in the tribal style and beauteous upon foot and ankle. Others shyly brought white or blue blanket capotes trimmed with ermine or mink or wolf.

One by one, the ladies put on their new finery and paraded through the village, black and silver corsets, black stockings on garters, purple silk robes, red bloomers, pink bloomers, lavender bloomers. Never had the village of Old Bull been so gaily decorated, nor giggles and laughter so thick through a spacious afternoon.

Seven-Story watched it all, wild mockery in his face, holding his Arapaho lady in hand. But Goldtooth ignored him. For one large trunk of bawd's costumes, she had thirty-two perfect robes, a dozen tanned skirts and shirts, twelve pairs of moccasins in every size, a heavy bag of pemmican, a warbonnet with eagle feathers and weasel-skin pendants, a woman-sized Osage bow and a quiver of arrows, five fired clay jars, a waterbag, and two belts with fine bone designwork on them.

When at last Old Bull and his elders emerged from the lodge, along with Mister Skye and his squaws, the chief's eyes beheld a transformation of his women; beheld Goldtooth and her bawds, now attired like Arapaho princesses, and his face crinkled up. That's when he saw the fiery hair of Mary-Rita. And when Mister Skye lost his aplomb.

"Sonofabitch!" said Victoria, and giggled.

Chapter 17

The joke had gone too far. Riddle had leapt at the chance to make an extra few hundred. Mary-Rita sobbed on the wagon seat. If she knew she would be Old Bull's fourth wife, and no doubt maltreated by the senior ones, she'd cry all the more, Mister Skye thought. He could have stopped it earlier, but Mary-Rita's barbed tongue had stung everyone in the caravan, and she could use a little humbling.

Riddle had been predictable. It would be a better

angle. His slippery contracts let him do whatever he pleased, and treat his brides as absolute slaves. But it took courts and law to enforce contracts, and those civilized things didn't exist here. The brides would be Riddle's slaves only if Mister Skye let them be.

Mister Skye gazed at the sobbing girl, and his own memories flooded back. Long ago, so long it lay as a blur in the back of his mind, he'd been a slave. He'd been a boy on the banks of the Thames, son of a merchant, when the press gang found him, snatched him, hauled him bodily aboard a teak-decked man-o'-war and made him a powder monkey, living in conditions so brutal he barely survived until he learned to brawl and fight for his gray porridge.

It had made him strong and wily. He had learned courage and ferocity. He'd learned distrust and hate. That crucible had fired every weakness out of him, and had given him the means to live in this wild blue land. So good had come from that terrible thing. His family surely thought him dead, and now his only family was the one he had created here in the vastness of North America. Good had come from slavery, and good might come to Mary-Rita from slavery. Old Bull and his wives would bridle her tongue soon enough. He'd seen pale boys become sun-blistered soldiers and sailors of the Crown, and come out of it men. It was true enough that women were often given away in marriage, and had no say in it. And most of those marriages turned out fine, too. In Mary-Rita's own Ireland, fathers and brothers and priests were all matchmakers for sisters and daughters and parishioners. And yet . . . he could not permit this. The thought of enslaving an adult competent human being rankled him. In Drusilla, abolition formed a principle, an ideal. In Mister Skye, once a slave, it flared as a rage. He pitied the weeping girl so new to this raw land and thought she'd probably die of heartbreak even if Old Bull treated her well. What a sorry thing it'd be to leave her here to sob and die, to shrivel within. No matter how kind to her the Arapaho might be, this would be more than the lass could bear.

"I think not, Mister Riddle," he said.

"Stay out of my business, Skye. My contract—"

"Judge Henry enforces contracts here, Mister Riddle. Sixteen decisions at a time."

The ferret-faced man with red veins in his pointy nose peered craftily about. "The great chief and I have come to an agreement. He'll have something to say, Skye, and so will his warriors."

"Judge Henry's first decision might go against you, Riddle."

"You—you wouldn't!"

"You beast!" yelled Mary-Rita at Skye. "Kill a man, would you? Heathen savage! Your skull is as thick as your body. I know how you talk; like a heretic Englishman. Killin' your own kind indeed!"

Mister Skye cocked a graying eyebrow. "Victoria, tell Old Bull that the lady is promised, and not available, and thank him for the offer. Tell him he has a fine eye for women, with an especially sharp knowledge of their souls and character."

Victoria translated to Crow, while Old Bull listened intently and Alvah Riddle peered about him.

Through Victoria Old Bull replied that the bargain was sealed. He fancied the white woman with the hair the color of fire. He would have his squaws bring the robes and packsaddles. He would take the bride-man out to pick his ponies. There would be a ceremony of adoption. The tears of the fire-haired woman told him she would be a good squaw.

"You heard all that, Miss Flaherty. Will it be Chief Old Bull or Tommy O'Dougherty?" asked Mister Skye.

"Heretics and heathen! That's all there is here. Don't you be tellin' me what to do, you drunk. Chinless fools and drunken guides and savages, and what's a girl to do? It's not every lass gets proposed to by a chief. Fancy a lass bein' a queen, or at least a princess. You idjit, you stay out of this."

Mister Skye caught Seven-Story Chang at one side of a gathering circle of villagers, mocking as usual.

"Mister Riddle," Skye said, "how do you propose to take all these robes to Bannack? I don't know whether we'll have Mrs. Jones's second wagon. I will discuss the matter with Old Bull, but it's going to be tricky. That's a prize of battle, and whichever warrior got it, he's not likely to give it up, or the mules. And even if I get it back, I haven't heard you making an agreement with Goldtooth to rent it."

"You'd better get it back!" snapped Goldtooth from the edge of the crowd. "You big drunk. If you hadn't climbed into your jug, we'd still be safe on the Oregon Trail and I wouldn't have lost a thing!"

"I imagine a storm had something to do with your difficulties," Mister Skye said amiably.

"What do ya take me for, Skye? A rube? I got that angle figured out first off." Riddle preened a bit. "What do you think I got the packsaddles thrown in for? Five ponies, plus two packsaddles, ten robes to a packsaddle. I don't need that slut's wagon."

Old Bull had had enough of the babble. He abruptly motioned to his squaws. One graying thin Arapaho woman, and three stout ones with glossy black hair and massive hips scurried into his lodge, and emerged with piles of robes. One by one they spread these out on the

grass. Each looked soft and tanned, with thick dark—
almost black—winter hair.

"Not as good as Crow robes," muttered Victoria nastily.

"I'm not marrying that savage. I'm worth more than a
bunch of flea-bit robes," yelled Mary-Rita. "I want
Tommy O'Dougherty and a priest, you idjit!"

The women brought Riddle a soft creamy elkskin
shirt, fringed on the bottom and sleeves, and decorated
with orange and black-dyed quills in a crosshatch pat-
tern.

"Pretty fine stuff. I know Indian stuff. This here'll
fetch plenty if I play it right," announced Alvah.

Finally they brought two rawhide yellow packsaddles
with buffalo-hide panniers and laid them on the pile.

The chief stared, waiting, daring Riddle to reject any
of it. Riddle smirked. The chief nodded abruptly, and
Riddle clambered from his muddy green wagon and followed Old Bull out beyond the village, across a tawny
bunchgrass meadow where youths watched the horse herd
continuously.

Mister Skye followed, along with Victoria and several
headmen. They continued onward to a separate band of a
hundred or so spotted and solid-colored ponies, buckskins, sorrels, paints, guarded by a sour-looking hard-
eyed warrior, his torso laced with white scars. He hefted
a new Spencer carbine. The chief waved a gnarled brown
hand at the animals.

"Warned you, Riddle," said Mister Skye quietly.

Riddle ignored him, and plunged in, squint-eyed, poking and probing, lifting tan hoofs, peering at grass-
stained black teeth, hunting for saddle galls. In an hour
he had his five, all solid-colored, and with a sharp command Old Bull had them separated out by the hard-eyed
warrior. Riddle looked ecstatic.

In the larger herd stood Goldtooth's four mules, shining harness marks on their hair, and watching them a
thin, concave-chested warrior, their captor. Mister Skye
studied the man, memorizing him, noting the hard flesh
and the hawknose and the shoulder-length loose blue-
black hair and the red bandana, like his own, holding it
to the warrior's skull. Their eyes caught. The warrior's
glittered, daring Mister Skye to try it, try taking these
brown prizes, these coups of battle.

Mister Skye stared back unblinking, and not smiling.

They trooped back to the village, Riddle tugging his
ponies behind him on picket lines, the chinless pink man
almost prancing with glee. He sidled up to Mister Skye.

"To get ahead, you got to play the angles. I come out
like a rose. Likely make five, six hundred more dollars.
That's a year's income! Saved me the cost of renting that
bawd's wagon, too. Now these ponies—solid colors, Skye,
all solids—I'll break them to harness along the way, too,
put one at a time in the traces with the mules until they
know what's what. So I got two and a half new span,
added to my two and a half mulespan, and I'll get the
women to riding, and save wear on the harness mules.
How's that for angles, Skye? I turned your drunk into a
bonanza here."

"If they let you leave the village, mate. I don't rightly
trust Old Bull. And you'd better not trust me."

"What do you mean by that?"

"You'll know soon enough," said Mister Skye, as they
trudged past skin lodges and barking yellow mutts. "Better tell your women. They're going to have a feast tonight, boil a few dogs. Then tomorrow they hunt the
buff. They've been following a big herd for days."

"Dogs!"

"Better eat it. They don't take kindly to someone

scorning their stewpots. They'd just as soon throw a little white man in, too."

At his lodge, Old Bull barked a command, and the hefty squaws approached Riddle's wagon like oxen on the prod. One of them beckoned to Mary-Rita.

"Go away, you filthy things!" she bawled. "I'm not going to marry some heathen. Go away!"

Drusilla arose, a gray-clad wraith, addressing the chief's women. "This woman has not consented," she said quietly. "Take back the robes and things."

They didn't understand the words, but they understood her message.

Flora tittered nervously, and the chief studied her as well, discovering beauty he'd missed earlier. He approached the wagon and motioned her to stand.

"I don't stand up for red niggers," she said coolly.

He reached abruptly into the wagon seat and dragged her out of it with a powerful grip. She screamed.

"Let go of me! Do you know who I am? My father bought and sold better ones than you!"

He tugged at the yellow ribbon that gathered her hair, and it fell loose around her neck. He stared at one bride, then the other, and finally his eyes settled on Flora. "Maybe I like you better," he said in sudden English. He nodded toward Mary-Rita. "She got bad mouth. You're mean, but I fix that."

He turned to Alvah, who was tugging his prizes toward his wagon.

"Maybe I'll switch," he said, in words Alvah understood instantly.

It had taken a while for Blueberry Hill to understand about Flora Slade of Biloxi. The recognition came slow. He had seen her only from the inside of a cage, and she was much younger. But she hadn't changed any in the eight years, except for a fine woman's figure and a lushness of body that inspired lust.

That's when her father had sold him, naked, on the raised auction block fronting the red-brick slave mart that had housed him in a stinking cage for several days prior. The bids reached two thousand thirty-seven dollars, and four bits. Plus one dollar for feed and title. Her father had called him a fine, strapping young nigger, no diseases, tractable and hardworking, a perfect field hand. They'd all stared at him, mostly white men but a few women too, including Miss Slade, who simply delighted in hopping around the auctions, whatever her father's wishes may have been, and lording it over other flesh and blood.

So he fetched that much. That much and no more for his flesh and bone, his vision, his hearing, his blood. For his fingers that plucked banjo strings and pounded ivory and black keys, and his brain that remembered songs and spoke words. That much and no more. More indeed than this chief of the Arapaho was offering for Miss Slade, whose value equaled twenty thirty-dollar robes, five ponies worth perhaps four hundred, and odds and ends. Her price came to maybe half his own. It didn't please him to think it: she was quite beautiful.

He watched amiably as the old chief yanked her off the wagon seat, walked with measured gait around her like a buyer of fine horseflesh, poked and probed at her while she raged. It was familiar, and yet different. If he'd raged while they prodded his flesh, he'd have been whipped brutally. The memory made him sweat. Any one of these whites could take him at gunpoint, bind him up and deliver him back to Biloxi, and claim a reward. He might survive the whipping, and might not. The old white mistress who let him wander and had been kind might be dead now; her sons would be a different matter.

"Sorry, my friend, Chief Old Bull. She's not for sale. I got a contract to deliver her. You take this here one with the flame hair," said Alvah, his lips spouting words from his chinless pink face. "Yessir, she's worth a lot more. And we had us a little shake-hand deal, friend."

Old Bull eyed him flatly. "How much more?"

Riddle's Adam's apple bobbled and his eyes darted around. "Why, Flora looks to be ten robes more," he said, hopping about. "She cost me more to fetch up from the South, middle of the war."

"I'll kill you, you slimy thing," yelled Flora. "I've bought and sold better than you."

That, thought Blueberry, was quite true.

"Mister Riddle," snapped Drusilla. "You have made contracts in good faith. If you do not honor them, I'll see to it that your business is ruined. My pen is mightier than swords."

Riddle squinted up at her, a sudden caution on him. Then he leered. "Not likely," he said. "I know your angle and it isn't worth spit."

Flora started to run toward Mister Skye, the only hope she knew, but Old Bull caught her easily. "I'll take this one," he said and wheeled her into the hands of his burly squaws, who dragged her shouting and cursing wild oaths into his lodge. A moment later all sound ceased.

"But you can't— You owe . . . ten robes!" said Alvah, dancing like a boy needing an outhouse.

Old Bull grunted.

Drusilla began weeping. Mary-Rita sobbed. From over at their wagon, the bawds stared, horrified.

"He can't just take her like that!" cried Juliet.

Blueberry found himself feeling sorry for the girl.

He'd been bought and sold several times, made to work for nothing—no pay, no hope, no chance of home or family, no future except to toil all his days and then die broken and used. He'd been ripped from a girl he loved, hauled where he would not go, manacled with chains, told his body wasn't his own. He'd been called dumb because he was careful not to be too bright around masters, laughed at for the rags he wore, cast out because of his color. And so he felt sorry for this daughter of a man who'd sold him, knowing she would be taken where she would not go, into a life she did not will.

But not entirely sorry. Some part of him gloated.

"Let it go, Riddle," said Mister Skye sharply. "Unless you want to get us all in more trouble than you ever dreamed of. They know how to peel your skin slow, and burn you with little pine-stick embers so you die a little bit at a time."

"Old Bull and I had us a contract and he cheated," bawled Riddle. "He plum cheated. Crookedest stinking Injun I ever did see."

Mister Skye's slap sent the pink man sprawling into dun earth. He rolled over and sputtered.

"Get into your wagon and stay there, Riddle."

The crowd clamored at this, squaws clucking and staring. Old Bull watched with flat black eyes, his face empty. The women wept, the remaining brides and the bawds alike.

"Old Bull," said Mister Skye, "I mean to powwow with you."

The chief nodded, seeing something akin to murder in Skye's small hooded eyes.

With a short slashing gesture he summoned his elders and shamans and a squat powerful warrior into his lodge. The guide and his squaw Victoria followed. At the flap,

Skye's eyes found Blueberry. "Go make camp wherever they want you to. Take Riddle. Take Chang. Stay out of trouble."

Then he vanished inside, and a quietness settled over the villagers, the way breath stops before a trap is sprung or a guillotine blade falls. No one moved. All were awaiting the result of the conference within the quiet lodge. Blueberry hadn't the faintest idea what Mister Skye might be saying or doing. The whores drifted back to their red wagon, thoroughly subdued. Blueberry spotted Vanderbilt, gray-fleshed and sour.

"Cornelius, reckon you'd better drive Riddle's wagon. We'll make us a camp."

No one moved. Riddle hid within his wagon. Vanderbilt stood rooted to earth. Blueberry clambered to his seat and cracked the whip over his mules, sawing on the offside line to turn them, but the Arapahos did not make way, and Blueberry had a sense of being in an island, surrounded by murderous seas. Near the chief's lodge Jawbone stood, ears flat back, murder-eyed, and yellow teeth bared, grunting softly and snapping when anyone edged within ten or so feet.

"Ah, Blueberry, a wild free land filled only with emptiness and here you are trapped like a rat," said Seven-Story Chang. "It is a puzzle, yes? Something to contemplate. Slave and free, free and slave."

The mock suffused Chang's bony face, but Blueberry found no humor in it. Everything here had struck too close to home.

"Come meet my bride," said Chang.

Fearfully, Blueberry slid off the red wagon, feeling earth shiver beneath him in this terrible silence.

"This is Madame Chang," said Seven-Story, "the fairest maiden on the steppes of North America. I wandered in here only this morning, and was taken for divinity. Something about the way I look, I suppose. I seem to be a great Arapaho creation story come true. They promptly brought me to the most beautiful maiden in the village and offered her to the deity in their midst. Do I look like a god? I suppose I do. I bowed, said, yes the lady would make an acceptable wife for any god stalking North America, and she promptly became mine.

"She's delighted with the proposition, and so am I, my friend. She's the daughter of a subchief and medicine giver, a man who eyed my mandarin face, queue, white horse, and pronounced me divine, as far as I could gather. I didn't dally, Blueberry. I proffered her father a twist of tobacco since I don't exactly know how Arapaho gods behave, and he solemnly accepted. So the deed was done. Her name is Buffalo Whiskers. We have yet to communicate, except by those gentle squeezes of hand that tell her I am smitten blind. Tonight I shall give a nuptial feast—or rather my in-laws will, with my contributions—and then, Blueberry, we shall see. We shall see."

She stood unusually tall for this tribe, smiled serenely at Blueberry, and touched his hand with hers. Her jet hair parted at the center and hung in glossy braids to her breast, encased in soft white doeskin decorated with angling sheaths of tiny hollow bones. Her almond eyes were chocolate and soft, lying above prominent cheekbones that widened her face, and all of her colored a rich light umber that set Blueberry's heart to beating. And plainly she brimmed with joy to be a bride of so great a warrior and lord as this. What she offered Chang could not be bought for gold or any price.

Blueberry bowed. "Madame Chang, I am honored," he muttered.

She smiled, revealing perfect white teeth, and plucked

his hand and held it in hers for a moment, eyeing Chang eagerly.

"She bestows her favors generously," said Chang, eyes mocking again. "Ah, how the campfires will change as we forge ahead. If we forge ahead," Chang added.

"Buffalo Whiskers," said Blueberry earnestly, "you are the most exquisite female my sight has seen. You are Venus herself, Minerva and Diana as well. Your sun makes every other lady a moon . . ."

She smiled and pulled Seven-Story close to her side.

For the next hour, all was still. Then at last the flap of Old Bull's lodge parted, and Arapaho men emerged, sub-chiefs, shamans, and a camp crier. Next, Mister Skye and Victoria. Then Old Bull, carrying a staff of office with eagle feathers flapping from it in the late afternoon breeze. And finally Old Bull's squaws. But not Flora.

They stood solemnly in the racing breeze, long sun shadowing them in orange light. They all looked calm, Blueberry thought. He didn't see mayhem and massacre in these faces. From within the green wagon, Alvah Riddle peered furtively, hiding in the shadow of his wagon sheet.

Mister Skye found Goldtooth and addressed her. "I will hunt buffalo tomorrow with my Sharps. If I am able to drop thirty and help haul them here, I will buy back your wagon and mules. We will be using the wagon to haul the carcasses, two at a time—about a ton and a half a load for cows. I will shoot. Every man of us will help hoist the carcasses into the wagon, deliver them here, un-load, and drive back out to the buffalo grounds. This village wants fifty buffalo, thirty of them the price for the wagon and mules. They will save their own scarce bul-lets for the future.

"Riddle," he barked. "I could not get Miss Slade back.

She's his now and that is that. Old Bull wishes you—and the rest—to know that if another word is spoken about it, or there is any trouble at all, the men of our party won't leave here alive, and the women will become slaves."

Drusilla and Mary-Rita began weeping. Gertrude Riddle managed a tear.

"I don't know how that little ol' southern gal can live here," muttered Goldtooth. "It's downright sinful, I think. A wife of red Indians. Poor thing, poor thing . . ."

"Old Bull says that Miss Slade will be comfortable. Perhaps that is more courtesy than she ever knew how to give."

Blueberry said, "You are correct, Mister Skye."

Chapter 18

A sadness fell upon him as he rode Jawbone north-east, accompanied by the hard-eyed warrior who captured the red wagon, and others of the tribe. They were taking him to the herds scattered a few miles from the village. His new Henry stayed sheathed, and in hand was his old Sharps buffalo gun. Among his possibles was a box of paper cartridges, and the caps for them.

As he grew old, he lost his taste for this thing, this taking of life, this reduction of a live, sensate creature breathing the clean air, drinking the sweet water, watching the sunlit prairies with bright eyes, to dead and bloody meat. All the while he had led the fur brigades and trapped beaver, he did what he had to, making meat and drowning beaver, but advancing years had somehow changed all that, and now he largely left the hunting to his women.

He would do what he had to. It consoled him that every scrap of meat and hide and bone would be put to good use by these people. There was no joy in him of slaughter, and men who slaughtered for sport or excitement or trophies puzzled and disgusted him. They were butchers and in their souls lurked something dark and evil. He had shot many an animal over a long life in this empty wilderness, but not a one for the killing. In hard times, starving times, he'd eaten strange food, muskrat and eagle and porcupine and even prairie dog. He was a carnivore and would eat what he would eat, and would kill what he had to kill.

It didn't matter that nature was red in tooth and claw; that wolves prowled the buffalo herds, snaring the old and the very young; that lions and coyotes and wolves and eagles ate fawns and dropped does. Death from his bullets came faster and easier than death from the jaws of wolves tearing out an animal's entrails while it yet lived, but that didn't ease the sorrow Mister Skye had come to feel these recent years about the taking of life.

This day, if he could, he would kill fifty-one animals, one for his own people and the rest for the village that held them all but captive. The young men of the village, primed for a hunt on fleet buffalo ponies, resented him, resented Old Bull's decision to send out Skye. But with summer came war and raids. White men's bullets were always scarce, and Old Bull saw a way to save precious cartridges and arrows and preserve horses, even while gaining more meat than his warriors and hunters could slaughter alone. And so he had commanded it to be. And the one who captured the red wagon, Bad Elk, would have the great honor of distributing meat to the whole band. It would be a high honor, well worth the surrender of the wagon and mules, which were all but useless to his people anyway.

There blew the softest of breezes this morning, lazy air out of the west. He had thrown a handful of grass to the air to test it, and had watched it scatter a few feet east. Now he and Bad Elk and two other warriors rode a large circle compassing the herds, so they might approach from the southeast. The sun lay heavy on the dun dry prairie and no cloud troubled the sky. To the north the Bridger Mountains huddled blue.

They topped a soft rise and the first band of them hove into view half a mile away, thirty or forty. Beyond, similar grazing herds dotted the dun land like dark ponds. This time of year they rarely coalesced into vast migratory herds, but roamed through the lush dry bunchgrasses, fattening in small companies. Their summer hair grew lighter, almost cinnamon at times, and contrasting with the dark hairy collar over their shoulders and hump.

The riders quickly pulled back below the brow of prairie and left their horses hidden from the grazing herd. The buffalo had a keen sense of smell but poorer vision and hearing, and did not observe Mister Skye and the Arapahos with him. He spotted a sentinel bull, but that one didn't worry him. He wanted to find the lead cow, the one who would decide to whip the band away if she sensed trouble. If he could kill her first, or nearly first, he could drop the other beasts one by one and scarcely upset the herd. If these stampeded, they might trigger the distant bands too, and the hunt would be ruined.

They studied the herd for minutes while the sun ticked up the sky. He studied one cow who ate, peered around with weak eyes, ate, and peered again. He would try her

first. With a flash of hand and finger, he signed to one of
the warriors to have the red wagon that would carry
these carcasses back to camp brought near here by the
white men. An Arapaho nodded and slipped away on his
pony. With a heaviness of spirit that was rare in him,
Mister Skye picked up his shooting sticks and possibles
and began the crawl that would take him closer, in this
case to a slight hummock a hundred fifty yards ahead
and down-slope. He'd be exposed all the way but the
gain of yardage would be valuable. He crawled and
stopped, crawled and stopped. Sweaty work in the sun's
early forge. Three gray wolves noticed him and slid toward his left flank. Always the cruel wolves circled the
herds.

The restless cow stared in his direction and he froze.
She resumed cropping, and he slid the rest of the distance
fast. The hummock would be a good place, he thought.
He spread the sticks, which had been tied at their centers
with thong, making an X of them, and rested the barrel
of the big Sharps in the vee. The range was ideal for the
heavy Sharps, but very long for his Henry or the carbines
of the Arapaho. He sweated, and now the bad moment
fell upon him as always, the moment when he didn't want
to shoot.

He gazed at the cows, twenty or twenty-five of them
here. Their summer hides would be scraped clean of hair
and would make lodge covers and summer robes. The
hides of the bulls would make war shields that could turn
arrows and often bullets; horse tack, winter moccasins,
and lots more.

The bad moment passed as it always did. He lined the
blade sight upon the heart-lung area just behind the shoulder of the cow he thought was the leader, and squeezed.
The Sharps roared and its butt slammed into his thick

shoulder. Before the day ended his shoulder would be battered and so sore it would take a week to heal.

The shot went true; the cow staggered four steps forward and fell, its legs pawing for a minute and then slowly freezing in place. The others peered dully at the sound and then resumed their cropping. He slid a paper cartridge into the slant breech and positioned a paper cap and was ready again. He selected a smaller cow, also close, but she turned suddenly, denying him the heart shot he wanted. Two others were facing him, heads low, grazing. He spotted a more distant cow who stood broadside, and lined his sight on her carefully. He squeezed again and the throaty boom of the Sharps disturbed the plains again, and his shoulder hurt again. The cow stood, peered around, shook her head violently. He watched. A dark glout blossomed on her side, a little behind the ideal target area. She sawed her head up and down, walked forward, and gently sank to earth.

He shot a bull next. Bull meat was poorer but could be jerked. His Arapaho hosts would want a few bulls and many cows, he knew. The bull bellowed in its death throes, and now the rest of the herd peered restlessly. But it lacked a leader. Mister Skye had found the lead cow right off, so this band did nothing more than mill a bit, and sniff the downed animals curiously. He shot three more cows. One took two cartridges. The big Sharps grew too hot to touch, too hot to load in a paper cartridge, and he let it cool. But it did not cool fast enough so he urinated into its barrel, smelling his water and his sweat and the grimy stink of his own buckskins. The nipple had fouled. He picked at it, and ran a patch through the crusted barrel.

Last evening they had cooked a dog feast, and he had eaten the mushy meat solemnly, and so had the others,

although Mary-Rita gagged on it, and Mrs. Parkins managed only a bite or two and looked pale. Flora never appeared and Old Bull's lodge had been guarded by one or
another of the dog soldiers. He pitied her, and pondered
what he might do.

Tonight there would be a buffalo feast, hump roast of
tender red meat more delicious than the standing rib
roasts of cattle. And that would be only the beginning.
There'd be delicious tenderloin, which most people
swore far excelled anything taken from cattle; buffalo
tongue, a great delicacy; and sausages of buffalo gut
stuffed with minced tenderloin meat and the tasty fat of
the animal. Buffalo fat itself was tastier and more palat-
able than beef fat, especially that long cord of it that ran
down the spine of the animal; a part that was carefully
recovered and stored as a delicacy by all the Plains
tribes. Nor would that be the end of delights. They'd
sample hot marrow, too, sweet and juicy, cooked deli-
ciously right in the thigh bone of the animal. The hot
bone would be brought from the cook-fires, hit adroitly
with the back of an axe, and broken open to reveal the
succulent treasure within. Before this day was done, everyone in the village, along with his own party, would
gorge themselves on several pounds of meat, and find a
kind of ecstasy in it. People who considered a pound of
meat filling in the East would eat five or six pounds here,
and think nothing of it.

In the days following there'd be endless stews sea-
soned with herbs, boiled or roasted tongue, which kept
well on the trail, and all the rest, including succulent
dark liver, delicious raw. Some men of the mountains
claimed that if a coon could eat buffler liver, he didn't
need greens, and Mister Skye had found it so.

Beginning today, every squaw in the village would be

busy scraping hides staked out on the earth with small pegs, tanning them with a mixture of brains and liver, cutting meat into thin slices and hanging them on racks to dry in the hot sun, layering thin meat and fat and berries into pemmican, throwing offal to the howling dogs, and saving those bones that would be scraped and hewn into implements.

Green-bellied flies had found him and swarmed around his sweating face, crawling over the gummy stock of his Sharps and even along the hot barrel. The sun rolled high and his own body smelled rank. With the cooled Sharps he sighted on another cow, a distant one this time, and his rifle thundered. He was lucky, he knew: this band had not fled. He felled seven more before the survivors, sniffing restlessly at the black sunbaked carcasses smeared with brown blood, finally trotted over a gentle rise. Mister Skye creaked to his feet and signaled to the observers on the rise behind him. Wearily he trudged up the rise and found on the other side an army of squaws with ponies and travois, ready to butcher and haul meat and hide. Among them, the red wagon with Blueberry reining the mules. Vanderbilt sat beside him, looking gray and dour, and nearby Chang on his white horse, his face forever mocking. His bride had not come. Mister Skye studied the entourage, looking for something and not finding it: Alvah Riddle had weaseled out of the hard work.

He summoned them. The small butcher army scattered out among the dark carcasses and began its swift bloody work under a brass sun. In minutes the women were covered with gore and filth. They slit open the bellies of the beasts and eviscerated them, setting gray gut aside along with the bright red livers. Bold black and

white magpies flocked among them robbing carrion almost from the women's hands.

The air was thick with blood-smell and dust and urine,
drawing swarms of flies. Arapaho women had been doing this thing for as long as anyone could remember,
and very efficiently now that they had white men's knives
rather than bone and stone cutting tools. Mister Skye
watched, vaguely repelled by the red nakedness of the
carcasses as hide after hide was ripped and tugged off.
That such noble animals could be reduced to such red
and white nakedness, to such indignity, troubled him.

Blueberry pulled up his mules near the first carcass,
where three squaws hacked ruthlessly, and soon he and
Vanderbilt were dragging and hoisting heavy quarters of
cow buffalo into the wagon. On each fresh hide the women
piled boudins, liver, heart, tongue, and other parts, and
then made a sort of carrying bag of the carcass. Seventeen downed buffalo sprawled here.

Two blood-soaked squaws approached a cow on the
farthest side and began slicing its brisket. The animal
flayed violently, hoofs catching one woman and spinning
her off. She fell on her knife, and began wailing. The other,
also thrown by the thrashing animal, lay inert for a moment, shook herself, and crawled toward the wounded
one. Mister Skye lumbered down the red slope past carnage and flies and gore, and found a mean gash on the
thigh of the wounded woman, bleeding bright and copi-
ously. With his filthy bandana he fashioned a tourniquet
and summoned Blueberry. The wagon groaned with raw
red meat anyway, and they'd take the sobbing woman back
to her village. At some point in all of this, the cow had
stopped breathing. The squaws who had gathered around
their wounded sister slowly returned to their bloody work,

sawing and slicing and wrestling slippery gray gut, and loading it in bundles on travois hanging from ponies driven mad by flies.

Seventeen. Mister Skye clambered wearily onto Jawbone and steered the blue roan northward to the next bunch. The herds had drifted north, away from the butchery, and a half hour lapsed before he found the next group, ranged along the slope of a gentle rise peppered with gray rock and sun-scorched dun bunchgrass. The sun arced high, sucking water out of him, suffocating him. Furnace wind from the west kept the stink of him away from the buffalo. Many of these lay in the grass, waiting out the heat before they returned to cropping. One or two stood, a bull and a cow, staring weak-eyed straight at him. There wasn't a single good lung-shot.

He steered Jawbone directly toward them. There'd be no worthwhile shooting until they stood. But when they stood they'd all stare at him face-on. He might drop them that way if he were lucky, but it would be less certain and he'd waste precious cartridges. He was two hundred miles from a place where he could resupply. The bull saw him and turned belligerent, lowering its massive head, pointing its small curved horns, pawing earth and bellowing. He stopped Jawbone and let the bull bellow. The others in the bunch swung their heads toward him. None rose. He waited, feeling sweat trickle down his neck and chest. The big sun-hot Sharps blistered his hands.

Nothing. The animals lay inertly in the midday heat. He slid off Jawbone, feeling the heat of the horse, and felt his legs give under him as he touched ground. He knew why he felt weary. He walked a hundred yards straight toward the watching bull, and then settled on an ant-bitten slab of clay. He spread his sticks and lowered the barrel of the Sharps into the vee, and fired at the bull. It bawled, sprayed crimson blood from its mouth, shook its head, and then rumbled toward him. He reloaded swiftly, singeing his fingers on hot metal. His lungs sucked powdersmoke and prairie dust and his own stink. The bull tumbled fifty yards from him. Behind the bull, a dozen of the dozing animals jacked themselves to their feet, two legs at a time. He studied them, without an inkling of what animal might be the boss cow.

The standing animals turned more or less to face him. He preferred to shoot from another quarter, so he clambered back on Jawbone and wheeled the reluctant horse to the east. The heatstruck buffalo watched but did nothing, which is what he had hoped. Ten minutes later he was shooting again, waiting long periods between shots for the Sharps to cool, dropping black and tan cows. Seven humped on the ground, three inert and four spasming and flaying legs, when the entire herd rose and fled, as if warned by the hand of God. It was one of the mysteries of nature. He walked out among the dark dead animals, smelling brass blood and the urine and green fecal matter that leaked from the doomed. One saw him and in a final rage tried to clamber to her feet, struggling, and then gave up with a long sigh. Death, he thought. Death. Flesh to feed my flesh, Arapaho flesh.

Seven here, seventeen yonder. Less than half. He felt weary, more weary than if he had been ripping and slashing and sweating the carcasses yonder. He struggled back to Jawbone, and it took him two bounces to board the animal. Jawbone turned, curious. He rode south and west, and met the squaws and their ponies and travois, heading toward the echoing booms of his Sharps. He pointed the way, and the women passed him, staring hard at this man whose medicine and legend they all knew. He spat, scraping his gums to find the juice to do it.

He rode slowly toward the village, following the furrows of innumerable travois poles that had gouged the dusty earth with their passage. He passed several squaws and ponies heading back to the carnage for new loads. Ahead rolled the red wagon, also returning after a long trip. It was not efficient. The travois and the ponies and the squaws moved meat and gut and hide and bone faster, he thought. He tugged gently on Jawbone's rope rein, and waited.

Blueberry tugged the mules to a halt beside him, and wordlessly handed Mister Skye a waterskin. He drank, feeling warm water trickle down his esophagus and spread loosely through his gut. Blueberry was alone. Vanderbilt had vanished this trip.

"How many?" asked Blueberry.

"Twenty-four. Enough for one day. All the squaws can handle, too."

"Not half," said Blueberry.

"No, not half. You want to try it? I'll lend the Sharps."

The man shook his head. "I'm in no rush. Getting to like the village, now that they didn't slit my throat last night."

"We'll see," said Mister Skye.

"We saw Flora Slade," said Blueberry. "Out cutting buff, near the chief's lodge. Right between those two beefy squaws of Old Bull's. Big mamas. Every time she slowed down, they whopped her. I mean whopped. Sprawled her in the gore. There's a dog soldier hovering around there too, just in case Riddle gets notions."

"How'd she look?"

"She ain't dead yet."

"How'd she look, Blueberry?"

"Too mean for tears. Her face is a mess, though. Soft, all that conceit and snob pounded out of it. Whenever

one or another of us got near, she started yelling. Says
she's going to kill you; that you got her into it. Says she'll
escape someday and then come hunting. Better watch
your backside, Mister Skye."

"I better had," he agreed.

"I'm not minding it a whole lot," said Blueberry. "Slade
sold me once. Ripped me away from my sweetheart and I
never saw her again. He said this nigger would make a
great field hand. My price, Mister Skye, added up to about
twice hers. Good strong slaves have all the luck."

"You sure are lucky," agreed Mister Skye.

He rode slowly toward the village, past dog soldiers
patrolling, past gore-soaked squaws slicing red meat,
past mutts vomiting up gore and guts, past girls pegging
out a hide with tiny stakes, toward his own camp, his
Victoria and Mary. He stank. He was filthy inside and
out. He would wash with sand in the warm creek, wash
until he abraded his flesh, scour his body and soul.

Chapter 19

The wagon stank. In its bed lay offal and guts, now
crawling with larvae and coppered with a black
mass of flies that swirled in green whirlpools.

Mister Skye found Cornelius Vanderbilt. "Clean that
thing. Drive it into the creek and scrub it down. I won't
have that flybait around my camps."

Vanderbilt peered back at him indolently. The man
puzzled Mister Skye. Without his cards and faro layout, without his gambler's attire, he had ceased to be a

person. He had caved into a sallow hulk, sullen and de-
nuded.

"I have nothing to clean it with," he replied. "I'll find
Blueberry Hill to help you."

Blueberry tackled the job happily because the noisome rank odor of the wagon pervaded their whole
camp. He harnessed a pair of mules to it and clattered
down to the creek trailing a cloud of winged things while
Arapaho children watched. Mister Skye followed, hunting for a smooth piece of sandstone, remembering how
often he had holy-stoned the teak decks of royal men-o'-
war. Blueberry Hill was a good man, he thought.

In three days he'd fulfilled the contract, recovered
Goldtooth's spare wagon, supplied the whole village
with meat and hide with his overheated Sharps, and
downed one last cow for his own party. The evidence
of it lay at every hand: willow-pole racks sagged under
jerked meat. Hides were staked to the ground everywhere, being fleshed or brain-tanned by patient squaws.
Camp dogs lazed dolorously, gorged on offal. Buffalo
heads and horns were being worked for ceremonial
purposes; bone had become awls and knives and forks
and ladles. The air swam with the odor of putrefying
meat, turning the place foul. The Arapaho had been
here too long, and fecal odor eddied among the lodges.
The grass wasted down to nothing and the pony herd
grazed farther and farther out. Mister Skye itched to
be off.

But there was still business to attend. It had come hard
to him to do it, but he knew he had to. He padded past
cheerful people rejoicing in this buffalo-wealth, toward
Old Bull's lodge and waited patiently at the doorflap. He
thought briefly about fetching Victoria to translate, but
the old chief knew enough English, and he could sign the

rest with fingers and hands. A hard thing, what he would do, but the need and duty of it would not go away.

He waited several minutes. It amused chiefs to let business wait and guests stand. But eventually one of the beefy squaws let him into the translucent shade of the lodge. With a curt wave of hand, the chief dismissed the women, including Flora Slade. They rose to leave, but Mister Skye stayed Flora.

"This is about her. I'd like her here," he said.

The chief acquiesced, and Flora settled uncertainly in a far place near the doorflap. She had dark circles beneath her eyes, but her hauteur radiated from her. His eyes caught hers and locked, and he saw no warmth in them.

Old Bull amiably prepared a pipe and lit it with a sulphur match, since the cookfire burned outside in warm weather. The village was tallowed with meat; his lodgepoles groaned with it.

"You will be leaving today," said Old Bull at last. "We will leave in a day or two."

"We'll be off soon. I've come to trade one last thing," said Mister Skye.

The chief peered at him, curious.

"This for her."

He thrust the gleaming new Henry, its brass frame glowing dully in the orange light of the lodge, into the chief's hands. He hefted it, opened the magazine and slid out the cartridges, one after another, counting, and then stuffed them back again and jacked the lever.

"First one in this country," said Mister Skye. "Sixteen shots and one in the chamber, gives you something no chief of any tribe possesses. This plus the two and a half cartons of cartridges I have left . . . over a hundred."

The chief ran his gnarled brown hands down the blued barrel, sighted, felt the balance, and smiled.

"Where will I get cartridges?" he asked.

"Denver City. Maybe Fort Laramie. Maybe Fort Bridger or Fort Hall."

"For her."

"That's what I'm offering."

She spoke from behind him. "It is no use, Mister Skye. You are too late. Two days too late."

A severity he'd never seen hardened her face, and a determination.

Old Bull said, "I will do it. You will take her. This is a good thing. Give me the cartridges now, and take her."

Mister Skye handed over the boxes, feeling something precious slip from his fingers. Now he would be low on ammunition as well as firepower. He'd used scores of the Sharps cartridges and had barely fifty left, tucked in a parfleche.

"Good. Take her," said Old Bull. "I don't need a new wife. But she's a good one, made me happy."

"Come along, then, Flora," he said.

Across her face emotions eclipsed. She peered misty-eyed at him, then hard. Her lips smiled and then drew taut.

"No. I will not go. I am a chief's bride. I am married. I have—been with him. I have entered a new life and don't wish to go back to the other. I am no longer a—maiden. I no longer wish to have a white husband—who'd be my second."

"Come along, Flora. Let's get out in the sun and on the trail."

Old Bull watched closely, fondling his new Henry. "I have given her to you," he repeated.

Mister Skye understood.

Flora's face softened. "I know what the trade meant to you," she said gently. "And I thank you. I am worth one

Henry. Also, twenty robes and five ponies plus a few things. I would have been glad of it two days ago. But this man, my chief, has—taken me into . . . a new world. What happened, I enjoyed. I wish to be his woman."

"His fourth woman," said Mister Skye.

"His fourth woman."

"Your mind is set?"

"Yes."

"You are free to come with us. You won't regret it later?"

Her face softened again. "Of course I will. I'll miss everything I am used to, including speaking in my own tongue. And everything is strange and alien. But I am the wife of Chief Old Bull, and I'll be loyal to him."

She smiled at Old Bull, who returned the gaze amiably.

"I have given her. I will keep the Henry. You take her," said Old Bull. "And a good pony. I will add that."

"You will be alone. We will be off in an hour. Who will you talk with?"

"Mister Skye. How often you've spoken against slavery. I'm here of my own free will now. Not at first, but now I am. Will you violate my decision, my choice?"

Mister Skye saw the lay of it and sighed. No, he thought, he would not violate an intelligent, competent, adult woman's will. His hands felt empty, deprived of the comfort and nurture of the rapid-firing rifle. He opened and closed them around nothing. It had all been for nothing.

"Very well then," he said abruptly. "You are made of steel, Flora Slade. I admire that."

He addressed the chief. "We part as friends. I thank you for your hospitality."

Old Bull nodded and stood. Mister Skye squeezed his heavy bulk through the lodge door and into a glaring day. He didn't know what to do with empty hands. What impelled a man to do such things? Why had he given away advantage and perhaps the protection of himself and all under his care, for a woman who deserved nothing? He had put her in her dilemma, that's why.

They were waiting for him at the edge of the village. Mary and Victoria had recovered their lodgeskins from the bawds and sewn the lodge back together, adding a new skin to replace the one cut into moccasins. Now it lay on one travois, with bundles of lodgepoles on another. His mules were loaded. Goldtooth's spare wagon was clean and harnessed, with Vanderbilt driving. Blueberry Hill sat on the seat of Goldtooth's wagon, now loaded with robes and riches, including buffalo dorsal-bone knives and spoons and forks that Seven-Story's wife, Buffalo Whiskers, had ground and carved for the women.

Alvah Riddle sat upon his wagon, now harnessed to three span again, the middle span consisting of a trained mule and one of his new ponies. The remaining ponies were loaded with Riddle's wealth, and tied behind. Mister Skye stared dourly at Riddle, and knew that the paunchy pink man was far more responsible than himself for losing Flora.

And far ahead, Chang on his white mount and his bride on a fat pony waited. Mister Skye sighed, found Jawbone saddled and ready, and mounted, turning the surly half-starved animal north and west. Behind him he heard the sullen rattle of wagons over roadless wastes. There were few to see them off: the women of the village were processing meat as fast as possible before it spoiled, and scraping hides. But the town crier waved, and the dog soldiers saluted Chang and his bride. The mandarin smiled.

Victoria rode beside Mister Skye, watching him sharply. She handed him his old Sharps. "You traded, but no good," she said. She always had it right, a supreme realist, he thought.

"No good," he muttered.

"Plenty good," she said. "Sonofabitch, you are a big man, Mister Skye. You made the medicine but now you kick yourself. I'm gonna cook up buffalo hump tonight and then kick Mary out of the lodge and hug you good."

For days they rode northwest through a duned land, seeing no one, feeling the wind. The rare brackish creeks were easy to cross, and they often discovered buffalo trails down one bank and up the other that the wagons could follow.

Buffalo were plentiful, and Seven-Story Chang shot one daily. He and Buffalo Whiskers usually skinned and butchered on the spot, returning to the caravan with the hump and tongue and liver, wrapped in the hide. Seven-Story found himself immersed in an idyllic life here on these endless steppes of North America, wandering daily forward with his Arapaho bride beside him on a stout bay pony. She was exquisite—far more so than the Peking beauties she resembled in a dusky way—and guileless. She spoke exactly what lay on her mind, contrary to any humans he had known in China, who approached things with mannered indirection. She was equally unlike these Europeans invading this empty land, more natural and without artifice.

They had swiftly learned to communicate, mastering a certain patois composed of English, Arapaho, and such finger-language as Seven-Story had acquired in his months on the prairies. He occasionally added a Mandarin word as well, or a Mandarin inflection of an English word. She laughed and shook her head. They were helped in camp by

Victoria and Mary, who knew enough Arapaho to supply details and nuances. Buffalo Whiskers belonged to an enemy tribe, but both of Mister Skye's women accepted her at once, even as she accepted her new friends. Evenings, the three of them industriously haired and fleshed the new hides, and crudely tanned them with brain for a few days at least, keeping them rolled in wet heaps while they traveled. They had a gift in mind for Chang.

They found their private moments far from the caravan, beneath a rare cottonwood, or in a hidden hollow. And there he held her and she clung to him, with a mutual joy that made his spirit sing. He was too much the warrior to dally for long, and always he leapt up and peered intently at empty horizons, and then slipped down to her side once again. Neither in China nor Europe, nor in the settled portion of this continent, had he experienced such indolent isolation. He didn't care if he ever saw the bright-hued palaces of Peking again, or any city. This place transformed a man's spirit into its most primitive and true nature. Someday he would write poetry about this poetic land.

Behind them the wagons toiled. Mister Skye looked serene, except that a lack of ammunition lay on his mind. The newly rich bawds had become content. They wore exquisite Arapaho doe- and elkskin dresses now, moccasins that Skye's squaws and Buffalo Whiskers made as other pairs wore out, and were more handsomely attired—and beautiful—than when they wore sweat-stained, soiled calico and dimity and twill. The French girl, Juliet Picard, was transformed into an Indian by her clothing. Big Alice had always looked like one, and the ash-blond Mrs. Parkins presented an electric contrast in her skin clothes. Except for iron pots they had everything they needed now, plus a wealth in robes to trade when they arrived at Bannack. They were swiftly learning from their Indian mentors how to find edible roots and herbs along creek banks, the meaty biscuit-root, the high-summer berries that added nourishment to pemmican as well as their daily meals. And withal, they felt a lot less helpless than they had in the wake of the storm.

The day before they pierced into the Bridgers along a trail pioneered by old Jim Bridger and Mister Skye himself, the women readied their surprise for Chang. They had made a wagon sheet of half-tanned cowhide sewn together with sinew. At camp one evening they hoisted the heavy skin rectangle over the hickory bows of Goldtooth's wagon and then anchored it with thong thrust through holes awled in its edges. The stiff hide would be difficult to reef in a gale, but usable even so, especially if the thongs that anchored it could be undone swiftly.

Chang stood admiring. "We'll chase Vanderbilt and Hill off and move in," he said. "We have a house."

No sooner did they anchor down the cover than Alvah Riddle sidled up to Goldtooth Jones. "Say," he said, "mind if I store my robes in there? It'll save packsaddling my ponies and unsaddling them each day. Speed us all up."

"Fifty dollars, Riddle," said Goldtooth amiably, watching the shapeless lips on the chinless face pucker over her pickle.

"So that's your angle," he said. "People in your profession, they never do anything free. Never neighborly."

Goldtooth laughed.

For the first time, these sunny days, the brides made timid contact with the bawds. Drusilla paused to admire Juliet Picard's quilled doeskin dress, and shared her Elizabeth Barrett Browning book with Goldtooth. Mary-Rita ventured to ask Big Alice what it felt like to sin every day. Gertrude Riddle didn't approve. She sat like a mound of gum arabic beside the green wagon, and scolded her charges about it.

"What's your angle?" Riddle asked Drusilla. "How come you're lending that book? That's part of your dowry and I shouldn't let you do that, taint yourself like that. In the contract."

"Is kindness in your contract?" Drusilla retorted shortly.

"So that's your angle," he said. "Not bad, not bad. Now she'll owe us. Yes, good, something to use. Call in the marker when we need it."

"You are disgusting, Mister Riddle," she said.

Chang, who had witnessed the contretemps, laughed softly. Riddle reminded him of a certain kind of peasant found commonly in the hinterlands of his country.

Mister Skye pulled Chang aside that evening. "I get bad feelings," he said. "So does Victoria. There's not much space separating us from trouble. Maybe Cheyenne, maybe Sioux. But I got the skincrawls I usually get. Jawbone's showing it too, mate. Now, I'm so short of cartridges for my Sharps I don't have an hour of fight, much less something to get to Bannack with. The women have plenty of powder and shot for their longrifles, but that's plumb slow. Riddle's well armed, rifle and revolver and cartridges, but he's about as useless as wet powder in a fight. Now I'm thinkin', Chang, if trouble comes, we've got to highjack his carbine, leave him the revolver. That's all I'm thinkin', mate. Just give it your attention."

"Ah, Mister Skye, you can hold off a painted war party with medicine alone," Chang said. "Jawbone is worth ten rifles."

"I'm going to cut your queue, Chang," muttered Mister Skye.

It amused him. At the first sign of trouble, he would assault Riddle's wagon.

Later he caught Drusilla in a place beyond hearing. "Ah, Miss Dinwiddie," he said. "Would you be so kind as to tell me just where in your wagon the esteemed Mister Riddle stores his arms and ammunition?"

She peered through darkness at him. "I will do better," she said quietly. "If the need arises, I will hand them to you. I would feel far more protected if they were in anyone's hands but Mister Riddle's. They are across the front, just behind the seat."

"Leave his revolver for him," said Chang, lightly.

"That's my angle," she replied, and laughed.

They crawled up an alluvial fan the next day, and into a throat of red granite, salted with juniper and silvery sage. The path seemed easy enough for mountain country, but they were occasionally slowed by the need to pull brush and boulders aside. They traversed a hot, dry, sunny wash, but there were springs, and at noon they watered the sweated stock and themselves as one. An hour later they rounded a bend, and came out on a ridge where they could survey the vast plains behind them. They were a thousand feet higher, but could see a vast distance into the haze of nothingness. The plains looked less empty to them then, for below, three snakes of dust marked human passage. Mister Skye pointed and grinned.

They pushed ahead into a narrowing red-rock chasm, where sage grew thicker and movement slowed. Above, along either cliffside, juniper sentinels made a living from rock. It was up-and-down country. Chang and Buffalo Whiskers rode ahead, studying defiles. There could be no scouting on the flanks here, only ahead of the toiling caravan.

Behind them, mid-afternoon, they heard the tattoo of carbines, and then the staccato of shots driving at themselves, gouging earth and shattering rock. Chang turned his horse back, but painted warriors blocked the way.

Chapter 20

"**A**tsina!" snapped Victoria.

It always mystified him, how Indians could instantly identify each other. He had asked her once, and she had shrugged.

"Maybe Piegan," she added, puzzled. She squinted at darting figures above. "Sarsi? Sonofabitch!" She spat.

A bullet whanged off his pommel. He heeled Jawbone, cursing. He should have had Mary and Victoria flanking the red ridges, he thought. Maybe not. They'd be dead . . .

"Keep moving," he bellowed. "Don't stop for anything. Whip those mules!"

Trapped in a bad place, no defense at all, a bloody defile with Gros Ventre or Piegan or whatever the hell they were peeping and crawling from every pink granite boulder and squat juniper bush up there, and a dozen more vermilioned warriors darting toward them on the trail dead ahead, blurred brown shapes. Broncos, he thought. Mixed bunch of young ones, hating the reservations, hell on whites.

"Hill! Vanderbilt! Whip those mules!"

The bawds were whickering and braying in the red wagon. Behind, Mary-Rita invoked saints in a keening voice, including some he'd never heard of.

Mary and Victoria kicked their ponies, drawing clumsy longrifles from their sheaths, poor weapons for this. A shot creased Jawbone's stifle and he shrieked insanely, kicking at invisible hornets and twisting crazily. Mister Skye hung on, for a moment an impossible target, but also unable to shoot.

He didn't know what lay ahead, but stopping would slaughter them all in seconds. Behind, the green wagon careened to a halt. No one in the driver's seat.

"Riddle!" he roared. "Keep moving, whip those mules!"

Gertrude Riddle wailed like a leaky bellows. Bullets ripped through wagon sheets, feral noises. Above, short bronze naked warriors darted up, fired fusils, loosed arrows, and vanished behind rocks. A bullet smacked a travois pack, bonging a frying pan.

"Sonofabitch!" yelled Victoria, huddling low. One of Goldtooth's lead mules slumped and died in the traces, sighing down. Another shot brained the off-lead mule, and the wagon stopped, forcing Vanderbilt behind to stop. Hill jumped down, shotgun in hand, and began unhooking traces. Three warriors above popped up, aiming for him. Mister Skye methodically unloaded his Colt at them. Only the one-shot Sharps loaded now, and he wished to hell he had his Henry.

Riddle had vanished, and now the blue pecker of his revolver poked through that gunport of his in the side of his wagon.

"Riddle!" roared Mister Skye.

Blueberry jerked spastically, and blood blossomed on his upper arm. He tugged frantically. Mister Skye leveled his Sharps at a warrior upslope aiming at Hill. The warrior flipped and fell on his back, began crawling behind rock. Red rock cascaded.

Ahead, a dozen silent shapes daubed with white chevrons were darting and weaving closer, all scorpion-footed and as elusive as fawns.

Hill got traces loose from the offside mule. Skye rammed home another paper cartridge and cap, and fired again. Hill was the key to everything. The broncos knew it, and five of them rushed him now, dodging and darting to within twenty yards. Hill quit tugging at harness, and blew both barrels of his scattergun at them, bloodying two. One took a ball in the neck but came on, seeing Hill unarmed and pouring fresh powder down a smoking hot barrel. Two others kept coming.

Drusilla suddenly emerged in the seat of Riddle's wagon, Riddle's carbine in hand. She aimed unsteadily at the warrior closing on Hill, and shot. The recoil threw her back. The bullet hit the closest warrior's throat. He fell at Blueberry Hill's feet, leaking blood from neck and mouth. The bawds whickered. Goldtooth leapt out and grabbed the warrior's old carbine, and sprang back into the wagon. Hill got one barrel of the shotgun recharged when the others sprang for him. He fired and caught two, but only one fell. One came on, sheeting red across his chest.

Vanderbilt jumped down from his seat, stone-headed war club in his belt, jabbing the staff Mister Skye had cut for him. The staff knocked the attacker sideways. An arrow gashed Vanderbilt's calf, and he limped convulsively. Mister Skye swore. Victoria snarled.

Mister Skye and Mary fired simultaneously at the darting greased warriors swarming downslope from dead ahead, winging two. Mary threw powder, wad, and ball down her flintlock. Victoria fired at one aiming at Skye, who was fumbling a fresh paper cartridge home. Jawbone shrieked. A magpie exploded from a cedar.

Send him, he thought. He grabbed his possibles from the cantle and sprang off Jawbone. The murderous old blue roan laid ears back, shrieked, exploded like a plugged howitzer, and avalanched into the advancing warriors. He bit one's shoulder, kicked another at the breechclout, folding him in two, stomped on the leg of a downed warrior and broke it with a loud snap, spun into one peering down his rifle, sending him sprawling. He knocked down three with flailing legs. One yellow-daubed giant jabbed a knife into Jawbone's rump before Jawbone caught him with a shod hoof. Jawbone wheeled and charged straight up a slope impossible to horses and chased three warriors from the cover of a juniper thicket. Mister Skye shot the one still standing through a shoulder.

Behind, Skye glimpsed Hill back on his wagon seat, steering his remaining two mules around the dead. Vanderbilt jabbed his willow staff at one springing warrior, but another whirled in with a glinting knife. Drusilla shot him just as his arm thrust out. The blow in his back sprawled him under the wagon wheel, blocking its progress. Hill whipped the two mules mercilessly. They strained, and the wheel rose and dropped over the warrior's buttocks, leaving an indented gray path. A knee rose and the body twitched and defecated. His mouth hollowed and leaked blood.

Three broncos with high scalplocks rushed the blind side of Riddle's wagon. One trotted along just behind Drusilla and sprang up, knocking her sideways. Vanderbilt's stone war club caught him just as he reached for the reins, leaving a caved-in skull with white bone and white pulp poking through jet hair. The gambler wheeled, too late. An arrow hit at the left kidney and pierced clear through, its trade-goods iron point projecting from his abdomen. He slumped silently to earth, staring at his reddening shirt. Drusilla shot again, and a warrior dotted with white clay and grease careened into another, blood gouting from his armpit. They fell and the wagon pulled ahead.

Something heavy clobbered Mister Skye above the ear. He went blind, and the earth rushed up. His Sharps clattered off. Then he saw again, and a wide-cheeked green-greased warrior who shone like an archangel was drawing a sinew-wrapped bow above him, his eyes alight with the knowledge. Mister Skye rolled but the bow followed him. The arrow struck his revolver belt like a sledge and winded him. He found his knife and sprang up, feeling his knees tremble. His knife sliced meat off the arm and the warrior shrieked. Skye twisted, and kicked the bow aside. He found his Sharps and possibles and reloaded. Jawbone's chest gouted red. Skye's breath scraped in sharp hot gasps, and his heart rattled beneath his barrel staves.

From the ridge above he caught a glimpse of a dancing white horse, and the mandarin, laughing wildly, coolly firing his pair of Navy revolvers and reloading with spare cylinders. Around Skye, warriors turned, spotted this flanking menace, and scattered. Chang held protected high ground in a natural purple-rock and silvery cedar fortress. His wild laugh sent chills through Skye, who sat exhausted on the hard earth, the battle whirling around him. But he was not a part of it for a moment. He watched Mary's breasts slide beneath her doeskin blouse, and wanted her. She was alive but where was Victoria?

The wagons were rolling again, now coming past him.

Victoria materialized. "Get up, dammit," she yelled. "You stopping the wagons."

Riddle's wagon rattled by, Drusilla whipping mules and Mary-Rita whining like a sawmill blade in a knot. Mary shot a warrior about to scalp Vanderbilt. He grabbed his crotch and howled.

Goldtooth's wagon careened next, with Hill, sweating rivers and blood-soaked, whipping two weary mules with his good arm. His pants were wet.

The mules of the driverless third wagon followed unbidden. Vanderbilt sat stupidly, watching blood ooze down his britches. Skye trotted that way, and lifted him bodily into the empty wagon, beneath the new skin wagon sheet, which let in pink sunlight like a colander now.

"Five aces," said Vanderbilt.

From above, Chang poured lead and Chinese imprecations at broncos, dancing on a skillet. Warriors broke into flanking parties then and darted upward, tightening the noose. Below, Jawbone butted an aiming warrior and somersaulted him into a ravine. A bullet splintered wagon wood just above Skye's head. A red sliver hung from Skye's vast nose. Three warriors speckled with white dots and ochre heads rushed. He grabbed the burning barrel of the Sharps and scythed, knocking one back and glancing off the burly shoulder of the second. Then the third one was on him, piling him backward. The wagons rolled ahead of him now, upslope, leaving him behind. He kneed the one on him and felt stale air erupt from a wide mouth. The warrior's knife tunneled down. Skye twisted. The blade spanged earth exactly below his armpit, nicking his underarm.

"Smell right, mate?" Skye muttered, rolling hard and throwing off the warrior. A foot caught Skye's groin, and he felt nausea boil up and his remaining strength leak. His bladder emptied into his loincloth. He butted the warrior, feeling warpaint and grease smear on him. He found the man's throat and clamped with his big square blunt hands. The warrior thrashed and stopped thrashing. His tongue went purple, and a green fly landed on it.

Skye lay on his back, willing the nausea away. Above, they closed on Chang. Buffalo Whiskers was visible now, darting toward him with a bow and quiver. The wagons had spun two hundred yards up the grade. Making it, he thought. Getting out. A wounded warrior daubed with yellow clay around each eye spotted him, lifted his dirty fusil. Skye stood up and kicked the black-eyed Susan and picked up the smoothbore. The warrior vomited.

Mary staggered toward him. "Mister Skye," she cried, her eyes leaking.

"I'm here," he muttered.

She dragged him forward toward the train. They were isolated here. A calf bawled ahead, and it puzzled him.

Above, a death-angel swung a blue barrel toward them. The shot hit Mary's moccasin and destroyed her big toe. She danced on blood. She sobbed and staggered forward. Skye set down his unarmed Sharps, and lifted the fusil he'd retrieved. He let his lungs and heart quiet. Another shot from above seared by. Skye shot. The ball hit purple rock an inch below the blue barrel, spraying chips. Someone howled and the barrel vanished. Skye dropped the empty fusil and loaded his Sharps. His possibles bag had vanished and he found one of three spares in the pocket of his fringed shirt. The paper turned pink in his fingers. His breechclout stank.

He searched wildly for his possibles, which contained the other Sharps cartridges. The wagons ahead pulled away. Mary turned stoic and strode deliberately, putting pain squarely on her torturing foot. Skye found his possibles bag, and began trotting. Above, Chang was in deep trouble.

Riddle's peckerpiece popped, and a horse died, but the warrior on top rolled off and bounded toward the rolling wagon. He yanked Riddle's revolver as it ejaculated. Riddle's hand came with it and then darted back in. Skye threw his knife. It caught the warrior's cheek and popped out the opposite cheek. The skinny warrior yanked it out and jabbed at Riddle's porthole, and Riddle shrieked. Skye's boot caught the warrior in the buttocks and drove the warrior's arm into the wagon, up to the shoulder. Skye sledged, the warrior careened sideways, his trapped arm broken and white bone saluting the sun. Skye picked up Riddle's revolver. Jogging ahead, he handed it to Drusilla. Her face shone.

" 'How do I love thee? Let me count the ways,' " she said, and sobbed. "I've murdered," she cried brokenly.

Skye slid to his knees, rested his Sharps on a wind-twisted cedar limb, waited for the barrel to steady and his hands to calm. He sighted on a black-daubed giant who was drawing his bow at Chang. The Sharps vomited and the bow flew up. Chang wore some kind of war vest, thick leather rosetted with shining steel. Three arrows struck it simultaneously. One hung; two fell. Chang danced. A white cloud above unfolded a vision of Buddha. Buffalo Whiskers drove an arrow into the belly of an Atsina cousin. The warrior sat heavily. He wore a crucifix, and he began making the sign of the cross.

Mister Skye rummaged in his possibles for a cartridge. A fly crawled into the breech just before he rammed home the cartridge and slid up the next cap. He jammed the slant-block shut, shearing off the paper to expose the powder to the cap. Chang wrestled three warriors, one of them black and yellow stripes from head to foot. No good shot. Mary's foot would hurt for weeks. The fly emerged from the muzzle and climbed up on the blade sight, resting bluely. A greased warrior careened backward from a chop administered by Chang, Chang-chop. The broncos fled now, scattering through red boulders.

The wagons had rounded a bend and vanished. He felt sticky blood dripping over his ear. He heard the soft thump of Victoria's muzzleloader, and behind him a stark naked warrior with greased blue genitals and arm chevrons sat suddenly and clutched his reddening calf. A black horsefly sucked blood.

Where was Victoria? She was too old for this. Chang ducked a scything captured cavalry saber and ripped upward with a filagreed gold dagger, releasing gray and red guts. The last bronco fled, holding his belly, Chang stood, red at one ear, bleeding from both forearms. The arrow dangled.

He saw Victoria now, a wizened elf pouring fresh black powder down the barrel, ramming home a lead ball in a red patch made from old long johns. She hunched halfway up the pink granite slope, looking like ancient cedar. Safe. For years he had wondered when the end would come. Mary, or Victoria, or himself. But their medicine had been strong once again. One more time.

He reloaded his Sharps and his revolver. The possibles bag seemed awfully light. Jawbone stood in the sun, his ears perked upward, his flanks red gore. This bunch needed following and punishing, he thought. Broncos, looking for trouble, moochers of the plains, fighting and stealing, visiting relatives until they were booted out, then off to find new trouble and more loot.

It took him three tries to board Jawbone. The blue roan shivered beneath him. "Got to finish it up," he muttered. He turned the horse upslope in the direction of the vanishing band.

"I am going to kill them."

"Sonofabitch," snapped Victoria. She padded off toward the wagons ahead. Her old cheeks glistened wet.

"Fix Mary," he said. "Find a place up there."

Chang and Buffalo Whiskers joined him, Chang laughing. He let the arrow dangle from his war vest. The horses sagged, weary, especially old Jawbone, who limped a bit from his stifle wound. They followed a red-speckled trail down a defile and up the other side, and at the cedar-crusted ridge they spotted the retreating broncos a thousand yards ahead, doubled on ponies, carrying several limp forms. Sharps range, he thought.

He slid off and found a benchrest of gnarled gray cedar, and sighted down the blued barrel. The Sharps felt peculiarly heavy. He fired, and nothing happened. The retreating party urged tired horses into an uphill trot. Skye fired again, and nothing happened. He shot one more time, missing.

"I'll kill them all," he said.

Chang's eyes mocked but he said nothing.

"Cut your queue," Skye muttered.

"That's original," said Chang.

"Serve 'em notice anyway," said Mister Skye.

He had seven Sharps cartridges left. And they were several hundred miles from Bannack. He slid the gummy weapon into his saddle scabbard.

"Who's alive?" asked Chang.

"Don't know about the women. Vanderbilt's dead. A lot of wounds. Hill for sure, maybe that damned Riddle. Mary's hurt. Drusilla showed blood. You. Me. Jawbone here." He peered at Buffalo Whiskers. "Don't know how you escaped," he muttered.

"They're cousins with Gros Ventre," Chang said, and Skye shrugged, knowing.

Victoria had halted the caravan on a sloping plateau a mile ahead, near the summit. It could be defended, with long fields of fire. Moist July grass too, and the remaining stock was gorging on it. Water dripped from a crack in red granite a hundred yards distant. Mister Skye let Jawbone drink from a natural pool. He splashed his face, his fingers gingerly exploring the clotted furrow above his left ear. Jawbone's wounds leaked red and crusted brown.

Victoria doctored in camp. The ball had amputated Mary's toe and Victoria was preparing to cauterize the leaking stump. Mary looked drawn. Dirt crusted the paths of her tears.

"I'll live, Mister Skye," she said, but she looked like she might not.

Vanderbilt lay on his side in the wagon, still alive. Flies clustered around the two wounds. "Busted hand," said the gambler. "Deuces all my life. Born Homer Donk, two of clubs." Bitter tears welled from his shocked eyes. He couldn't lift an arm to wipe his sallow cheeks.

"We'll make you comfortable," said Mister Skye. He found Chang. They'd get the arrow out and let Vanderbilt die on his back, facing God. Chang sawed at the shaft.

"Godalmighty," said Vanderbilt. "If there is a God." A sob convulsed him.

The iron point fell off.

"Hold him," said Skye. Chang crawled behind and pinioned the gambler. Mister Skye pulled hard. The arrow wouldn't come. Vanderbilt groaned and fainted. "Stretch him flatter," said Skye. He tugged again, wiggling the shaft, and it greased out. "We'll plug the holes, not that it'll do any good." Not much blood leaked from either one. They patched him with his filthy calico shirt and stretched him out in the perforated shade of the wagon.

"He might last a day," Mister Skye muttered.

Mary screamed. The smell of burnt flesh hung in the air. She wept softly, clutching her calf, the pain too large.

Alvah Riddle peered into Vanderbilt's wagon. "Is he dead yet? I'd kinda like the boots. My size, I figure. Mine getting worn through, all this walking."

"Riddle," snapped Mister Skye, "get out of my sight."

Chapter 21

Only moments ago, Alvah Riddle had been congratulating himself. He had come out of it almost unscathed because he had figured all the angles. Gertrude had been wounded. An arrow had ricocheted into her sagging right breast, and fallen out. The women had bound it tight and she was lying quietly in the green wagon. He counted seventeen perforations in the wagon sheet, and seven white-splintered gouges in the green-enameled sides of the wagon box. A wheel spoke had been shattered, but he could fashion a splint. A mule's ear had been shot off. A bullet had furrowed the neck of another. A rein had been severed, and a trace weakened by a shot through its center. A small water cask hanging from the rear of his wagon had absorbed a shot, and bled a third of its water. Three iron-tipped arrows lay inside the wagon, one of them with blood on it.

His shirt was ripped where the warrior who thrust a hand into his gunport had cut it. But no harm had befallen him. Those little gunports on each side made a perfect defense, he thought, congratulating himself. He'd employed a carpenter to cut the six-inch ports before they started, and fashion pivoting metal covers for the holes. When trouble came, he hunkered on the wagon bed, surrounded by high barrels and trunks, and fired in perfect safety. It wasn't perfect: he couldn't see along the flanks. The warrior who had grabbed his revolver surprised him, even as Skye's squaw had surprised him earlier. He'd do something about that: drill tiny peepholes here and there in the box.

"Miss Dinwiddie," he said. "You had no business whipping those mules. Your duty was to find safety among the barrels and goods and not expose yourself. Why, what if you'd been killed or wounded? The ah, contract, ah, expressly provides that a bride place herself under my direction for the duration of the journey. If you'd been ah, killed, we could not deliver you to your husband. Not only that, you commandeered my carbine and used it without permission, and just at a time when I might need it."

The woman's hair sprayed out, half free of her bun. She glared at him through her small rimless spectacles, and turned away. Her gray dress dripped filth and it looked like she had soiled herself. Great wet stains in the skirts. What a loathsome-looking thing, he thought. He suddenly rejoiced that his contract was airtight. She did not reply, but stared at him from a drawn face.

"Clean yourself and start cooking. Poor Gertrude can't cook," he said. "Nobody to help me unhitch the mules and unload the packhorses. No one to help Gertrude, either. Say, isn't it grand that we came out of it in one piece? Let us all give thanks for this blessing. No one badly hurt."

She closed her eyes and that seemed strange to him. He was feeling cocky, having proved to himself that he knew the angles in Indian fighting. He licked a chapped lip and grinned. "You'll feel better in clean duds," he said. "War is hell."

She plucked his Spencer from the wagon seat and started for the spring.

"Leave that here!" he commanded. He'd worked angles to get that Spencer because the army was eating them all. And she was treating it as her own.

She ignored him.

He let her go. Maybe there'd be a savage lurking over there. He had recharged his revolver and wore it now. The woman lacked obedience, but he was too elated now to fuss about it. How good to be alive! How fine to smell the sweet sage, and feel the brassy sun on him! How marvelous his Gertie could shrug off an arrow wound! Every breath that filled his lungs gave him joy.

Skye and that heathen were off somewhere, still chasing the redskins, whatever tribe it was. When Skye got back, Alvah intended to cuss him out for coming this way and endangering their lives. But just now, feeling himself lord of this camp, he wanted to celebrate victory, and relive his clever defense.

The lowlifes were wandering about now. Hill had a blood-soaked white bandage tied tightly over his upper left arm. The sluts headed for the spring. Alvah sidled over to the second red wagon and found Vanderbilt within, slumped against the plank wall and staring at him, at his arrow, at nothing. Riddle found a twig and held it against Vanderbilt's boots, taking a measure. They were slightly larger than his own. Vanderbilt stared grayly, saying nothing.

The red box was splintered in a dozen places, he noted. That hide cover the squaws had made let sun through to speckle the inside. One beam struck Vanderbilt's nose.

Nothing in the wagon but Vanderbilt and blood and a thousand flies. Alvah took a last look at the boots, gauging them keenly for width. He thought to take them now, but that didn't seem a good angle with Vanderbilt still alert. Alvah smiled at the man.

Skye, Chang, and that Arapaho slut rode down a long red slope, and Alvah scuttled away.

"You. Riddle," came an iron voice behind him. Skye's old squaw. "Sonofabitch, unhitch those mules of yours. They need water. And get them ponies on grass, too. One needs sewing up. Got a crease."

He glared back. "I didn't hire you and I don't take orders from squaws," he said loftily. He didn't know about the wound, and sidled around behind his bedraggled wagon. A bay pony had a long red gash across its chest. It slumped beneath its pack load. He cursed Skye for the wound. He'd find some angle to get even. He always did. He began unharnessing, and led his mules and ponies to some thick bunchgrass where Hill had picketed his. The women were at the spring, so he'd water the animals later. His brides and those sluts, they were there together, he noted.

He peered into his own wagon. It stank of urine.

"How are you, Gertrude?" he asked methodically. He liked to humor her.

"Poorly," she said. "I saw it all coming. The spirit writing. Last night on my slate the hand wrote, 'The living dead, the dead living.' You will have to cook, Alvah. Or get these worthless girls to do it."

"You're a brave woman, Gertie, and I'm proud of you."

No flaw marred the sky and the blue scraped these humped red ridges. He peered around him, enjoying the coolness of the mountains after the July heat of the prairies. They'd have a lot of patching to do here, three or four days probably. He'd have the ladies sew up his wagon sheet and mend harness and cook. The whole wagon stank, and he would have them scrub it out, too. He would be busy, but maybe he'd find time to bore some peepholes in his wagon box with his auger. Ahead, that old squaw Victoria—most annoying old hag—had kindled a tiny fire, not two hands wide, and had a knife blade in it. Fool savage, he thought, ruining the temper of the steel like that. The young squaw lay on her back in the bunchgrass, one foot bared and the red pulpy stump of a big toe projecting, along with tan bone.

The old hag stared at the wound and touched the bone. Mary gasped.

"Got to get the bone," she muttered. She peered up at Alvah. "You. Sit on the leg."

She found two jagged pieces of granite and handed them to Mary. "Hold on tight," she said. Mary nodded.

"I have important work to do," said Alvah, backing off.

Victoria opened a barlow knife and stood. "Hold down the leg or I'll cut you to ribbons," she said.

She made him nervous. The old squaw just might. He peered around wildly. Skye and Chang were at Vanderbilt's wagon. Alvah sat gingerly on top of the leg, facing away from the wound. He didn't know which would be worse—staring at Mary's face, or staring at the surgery. Sweat drenched her honey-colored cheeks.

Victoria grunted. The leg spasmed violently, bucking Riddle high. Mary sobbed and clutched the rocks in her hand. Victoria muttered again, and Mary's golden leg shuddered beneath him.

"Good," said the old crone. Alvah peeped around, and she was holding a shattered piece of bone, yellow and red.

The wound gouted blood again. "Now hold leg down again," she said.

He heard sizzling. Mary screamed. The acrid smell of burnt flesh scoured his nostrils. Quite unwillingly, he twisted around and saw the heated blade pressed hard against the wound, making purple smoke and blackening flesh. Victoria grunted.

"Sonofabitch," she said. Riddle sprang up and fled, leaving burnt flesh and Mary's sobs behind him.

If they'd fought his way, with total protection, no one would have been hurt, he thought.

Mister Skye approached him that evening, and Riddle began to cringe. "There's a big hot springs two or three days from here. We're going there and rest up. Shoshone place; maybe Mary's people will be there. She needs that right now . . . We're going to need those ponies of yours, Riddle. Goldtooth lost two more mules, and I lost one. You got one of the ponies harness-broke, and we'll break the others, yoking them with the harness mules. Harness one pony as a wheeler on each wagon. That'll be safe enough, and break them fast. And I need a packhorse. You can throw your loads into Vanderbilt's wagon."

Riddle puffed out. "I didn't hire you and I don't take orders. Them lowlifes can suffer, far as I'm concerned. We can stay right here and rest up. When Vanderbilt's dead, that wagon can be ditched anyway. Besides, Skye, one span's enough to pull an empty wagon."

The guide's blue eyes burned brightly. "Vanderbilt might last a week."

Alvah shrugged. "One span's enough. One of those sluts can drive it."

Mister Skye, still bloody and haggard, glared back. "I'm going to harness your ponies in the morning."

"I'll swear out warrants in Bannack," shouted Alvah.

"I'm not under your orders. By the time we get there you'll wish you didn't have me along. You like to got us killed, running instead of forting. Now you're wearing down my ponies for those sluts and lowlifes."

Mister Skye's patience was gone; the blow caught Riddle's chinless pink jaw and spiraled him into grass. He sat dizzily for a moment, then sat up. He never got mad, but he felt a little cross. His revolver nestled in its holster. Not a good angle to pull it now, but later he'd catch Skye and pull the trigger. He'd have to get the squaws too, or they'd kill him.

Mary lay in the rocking wagon for two days, watching the sunlight from the bullet and arrow holes knife bright ribbons within. She had wanted to ride her pony after her foot was cauterized, and no one stopped her from trying. But as soon as she had climbed on, that next morning, she felt faint with pain. Her wounded foot throbbed, and shot an ache up her leg and back, until it exploded in her head. Her Shoshone people had always endured such things, and she intended to, but Victoria frowned and Mister Skye had carried her back to the wagon. In his arms, she was glad.

Now she lay next to the wounded gambler, who was taking his time about dying, and who smelled so vile she could barely stand to be next to him. The women who sold themselves had piled the robes they traded from the Arapahos into the wagon, and Mary and the gambler rode comfortably on these. The one they called Big Alice drove, and had no difficulty with the three mules and unbroke pony that Mister Skye and Blueberry Hill had harnessed each morning.

As long as Mary lay quietly with her foot up, the throbbing could be borne. But the moments when she left the wagon to attend to her needs, or just to escape the rank odor of the rattle-throated gambler, which poisoned all the air inside, she gasped at her hurt. The caravan had topped the Bridgers, lurched on down along a small creek into the Bighorn basin, and rolled toward the great hot spring, Bah-que-wana. That pleased her. It would be a place to wash and heal. It was a favorite medicine place for her people, the Snakes. Maybe, just maybe, some would be there, and the thought excited her. She hadn't seen any of them for three winters.

The gambler said nothing the first day. He lay awake and aware, but lolled quietly, his sallow face dark with fatigue and fever. No one had cleaned him because he would be dead soon, when the rest of his blood poured into his belly. But he lingered and stank, and finally Victoria washed him, cursing all the while. No one cared about the man. Mary thought a foul and sick spirit resided in his mind, and it made his body foul too. Victoria had poured a warm stew into him. He could swallow, but lay inertly, his shallow breath wheezing. Then she and Blueberry Hill had tugged his soiled clothing off, changed the bandages on his suppurating wounds, and clothed him in some britches of Blueberry's. The stink retreated then, and Mary no longer felt like vomiting. Occasionally Big Alice peered in, smiled, and spat.

"I hope you make it, Cornelius," she said amiably. "You old sweetie."

After that bawds came regularly, Goldtooth especially, smiling at Vanderbilt and patting him gently. "You ol' dear," she exclaimed. "You get well now."

On the third day they abandoned the mountains and circled west and south over rugged sage-covered foothills through brutal heat. She knew they were close to the healing place. Game never tarried here, but Chang managed to shoot an antelope two of the three days. Victoria brought them both a broth made from the marrow, saying it would heal. She peered narrowly at Vanderbilt, who seemed neither better nor worse.

"I'm slow to die," he said to Mary that morning. "It's inconvenient. No need to bury me. Let the coyotes clean my bones."

"When a person goes to the Spirit Land, he should be buried properly, as he wants. Some people want the earth. Many of the Indian people want the scaffold, high above, where they give themselves to the great sun," she replied.

"It doesn't matter," he muttered, coughing desperately.

She felt indignant. "Of course it matters! Who are you to scorn the Great One above? Do you think the Great One doesn't care? You must find what honor you can, and present yourself to Him with honor. If you can't think how you want to go, I will tell you. We will make a place in a tree, a cottonwood, and lash many poles there with rawhide, and place you on your back so you face Sun and the One Above, and He can see you. And you will be wrapped up, so nothing eats at your flesh and no animal below, wolf or fox or coyote or skunk, eats of you. Then it will be right and you will be given honor."

"Makes no difference," he muttered. "Not for Homer Donk."

"You have given yourself a new name," she said. "That is good. Our people give themselves many names, and sometimes our medicine men give names to people. The new name is good, and gives a new self. What does Cornelius Vanderbilt mean? It is hard to pronounce."

The gambler lay quietly, panting hard and convulsing, until she thought he'd drifted off, maybe to die. But then he said, "I named myself for a very powerful and wealthy man, who earned a lot of—money, gold—and put it to use, making great boats to sail the seas and take things from place to place. They call him Commodore, which is a name for ones who are the chiefs on the boats . . . I didn't take his name to be like him, but to confuse people into thinking I might be him."

"You took a great name," she said. "A man with much medicine. And so his medicine worked in you. It is good, as I say. You saved the life of Blueberry Hill. You had only a lance, a staff Mister Skye calls it, and a war club, but you got down from your wagon and saved the life of your friend."

"I don't have any friends."

"Now you do," she replied. "Blueberry comes here all the time to help feed and wash you. We must bury you with honor for the One Above. You counted coup twice, and saving a life counts for more, and you are a fine warrior."

"Waste of energy," he said. "It got me killed."

"No. Mister Skye says that if you hadn't helped Blueberry when he was unhitching the mules, Blueberry would have been killed, the dead mules would not have been unhitched, and the wagons would all have been stopped in that narrow place, and everyone would be dead now. So, Vanderbilt, you must die good now; you tell us how. Mister Skye, he's got the black book and will read those things of your people."

"I'm Homer Donk," he said, and closed his eyes.

She lay on her robes, wondering about him, about the unclean yellow-tinged man beside her, and the sickness that ate at him. The close breathless heat of midday passed. The mule teams were sweated and white-caked with alkali dust. No shade sheltered, no water flowed where they nooned; only fragrant sage that had snagged the

wagon wheels as they rolled over it, and a furnace-hot
earth that scorched and dehydrated them all.

Late in the afternoon she knew they were growing
close. They struck the Bighorn River and rolled southward over lush green grasses in its bottoms, back into
the jaws of the red mountains. Ahead would be a strange
dark canyon with layers of red and purple and pink
rock, and dun rock at higher levels, an evil place where
this river had pierced through. On the other side, whites
called it Wind River. Here, the Bighorn. But before they
arrived, they would strike the hot springs, Bah-que-wana,
the medicine place of her people, except sometimes the
Crows were there, and they would fight.

The gambler studied her. "You're excited about something. We getting to this place?"

"Yes!" she said. "Springs so large the whole side of a
hill boils with them, and so hot you can't touch the water.
The hot water runs south, over white terraces for a little
way, and then into the Bighorn River. And there are many
places to bathe and wash, where the water is cool enough.
It is a great medicine place. Do you see? It has powers
from the Unseen Ones. I can feel the powers, and so can
Victoria and her Absaroka people, and so can Mister
Skye. We will take you to the place and let the medicine
powers heal you. You have lived this far; maybe the One
Above wants you to make good medicine here."

"Healed for what?" he asked.

"To be what you will be. You need a new name. Vanderbilt was a good name, but now we need a name that says
you saved us. You came out of your wagon cave like a
bear, a sleeping bear. I will name you Sleeping Bear. No
man disturbs a sleeping bear, but walks softly around."

Cornelius smiled at her. She had never seen him smile.

"Maybe I did better than Riddle," he said. "We're both hidey-hole types, but I got out of my hole. Makes me feel not so bad about kicking off."

Mary heard excitement ahead, exclamations and a quickening of the pace, and then they were there, at this familiar sacred place. From the base of a steep sage-covered hill waters gushed from sandstone lips, steaming even on this hot day, and spraying an acrid odor upon the breeze. She clambered up now beside Big Alice, enjoying the scenes, noting the small medicine cairns left here by her people and other people: feathers, small skins, a hawk's head, shining white stones. The sacredness infused her with a rush. She felt the holiness in a ball just under her lungs. This was where Earth Mother and the One Above brought Snake people to heal body and soul. Mary's eyes glowed.

Game didn't visit here, though sometimes a doe might be taken in the bottoms, or an antelope, so people did not stay long. But she hoped to collect greens and herbs from the Bighorn River bottoms, especially the wild asparagus. She frowned. She could not walk. But it made little difference. Victoria would. The white people were dropping from their wagons now, staring at this place of the hot waters, testing with their fingers.

She felt the power of this place infuse her, and turned to the gambler. "Maybe these waters will heal you," she said.

"Royal flush," the gambler whispered.

This was a hard-used place, without grass or game. The dun earth lay naked. Mister Skye doubted there'd be an antelope or mule deer or duck or a rabbit within miles, a worrisome thing with most of his party depending entirely on game. Nor would there be vegetables and herbs because it all had been picked over. He thought some of tarrying here an hour or two, and then rolling on down the Bighorn to good grass. But he gave up the thought as fast as it formed in his mind. This party needed these springs and a chance to heal.

A few shallow pools, inches deep, hoarded water cool enough for bathing, but these were as naked as everything else here. The women looked longingly at the delicious water, and turned instead to laundering. They would bathe tonight. Drusilla emerged from her wagon with a small washboard, a ball of orange lye soap, and a pile of filthy clothes. The bawds, wearing fine doeskin dresses and skirts, were less in need, but thought to wash what they could. Mrs. Parkins appeared in her thin wrapper, and proceeded to splash into the middle of a pool. The white wrapper clung translucently to her, and stirred Mister Skye's loins. Mary-Rita clucked and scolded at the sight, finally silenced by Mrs. Parkins's raucous laugh.

Mister Skye sighed. He felt tired and filthy himself, and brown blood crusted the gouge above his ear. He found Blueberry Hill unhitching the mules and ponies from red wagons.

"No grass. We'll have to drive them down the bottoms until we find some, graze them until dusk under guard, and then picket them here," he said. His beaten and wounded animals wouldn't get much of a meal tonight.

Blueberry nodded. "Lots of hours to dark," he said. "They'll get a bellyful. You want me to guard?"

"We'll divide that. There's you, me, Riddle, and Victoria to do it, and I don't trust Riddle. Chang's out hunting and scouting. We'll be lucky if he makes meat. I'd just as soon let Victoria tend to Mary and Vanderbilt and keep things in order here. So it's you and me, Mister Hill."

Riddle's mules and ponies remained hitched, and the man had disappeared toward the springs. Mister Skye found him sitting slightly above the woman, gawking at Mrs. Parkins.

"Unhitch your stock, Riddle. It's a mile or so to grass."

"Mine to do with as I want. You got no right—"

Mister Skye grabbed a handful of sweaty shirt and yanked Riddle upright. "We will walk in one of two directions. Up above there, where the springs boil up, or down to your stock. If we walk up there, I will sit you in a pool and boil your meat."

Riddle grabbed at his holstered Remington, but Skye batted his pink arm away.

"You got no right!" Riddle said. "I'm going to let them graze tonight where there's grass."

"You'd likely never see them again."

"Who says? You think you know everything, but you haven't got half the angles. I'll picket them down there. You can guard if you're so worried about it. They'll be in river brush. Who'll see them?"

Mister Skye dragged Riddle toward the hottest pools.

"You're making extry work. Walking them clear to grass, then back down here. I got enough to do without all that extry—"

They'd reached a hot steaming pool just below the cliff-slope. The steam smelled slightly of minerals. Mister Skye poised the paunchy pink man on the lip, and he shrank from the heat.

"You're trying to kill me!"

"That's about right. Put a finger in, Riddle. The rest of you will follow."

Riddle sank down, and jabbed a finger in, and yanked it out.

"I'll move my stock," he said sourly. "Not that it makes a bit of sense. You make work for everyone here, don't know how to deal with savages—"

Mister Skye shoved him, and Riddle staggered.

"I'll kill you, Skye."

"It's Mister Skye."

They trudged a long way to grass, but eventually the mules and horses spread out on lush yellow-dried bottom grass in an area thick with brush. Riddle complained the whole distance.

"I'll take the first watch," said Blueberry. "I'm feeling poorly, and I'll get this over with."

He carried the double-barreled scattergun. "You need more," Mister Skye said. "Riddle here will lend you his revolver."

"My property! Don't you touch—"

But Mister Skye's massive hands had already pinioned the man and were undoing the belt. He tossed it to Blueberry.

"Here's a few more, for a jam," he said. "I'll be here in a couple of hours." He peered around sharply, studying the low bluffs on both sides. Jawbone looked bad to him, limping slightly and crusted with blood in three places. "Eat," he said to the animal. Jawbone did not lift his head from the grass. In about two hours, the horse would appear in camp. "Jawbone will come in when he wants," Skye said to Blueberry.

Riddle stomped sullenly all the way back.

The women had bathed, and sundry items of clothing lay whitely over sage bushes, leached by dry air and a plummeting sun. Seven-Story Chang and Buffalo Whiskers had returned to camp empty-handed. Mary had scrubbed herself clean and rested before Mister Skye's lodge.

"Riddle," he said. "Maybe you'd be willing to share some airtights and your staples tonight."

"Why should I share—those lowlifes—" he sputtered.

"Didn't hear you refusing when we brought in buffler days on end."

"That's different. You're being paid to—"

"We'll do without, then."

"Now I didn't say that. Didn't say that. Just seems like a little trade here, a little exchange, that's the fair thing. A robe. A robe for—"

"We'll do without. I'd like to borrow your auger and a five-eighths bit."

"What in tarnation do you want that for? What are you offering for the use?"

"Protection, Riddle. Protection."

He didn't wait for an answer, but clambered into Riddle's wagon, pawed among barrels and crates until he found Riddle's toolbox, and the auger and bit he wanted. When he emerged, Riddle hopped from one foot to the other.

"You got no right!" he raged.

"I'll return it directly." Mister Skye turned away.

He found Victoria. "I'm going to need a heap of firewood from someplace," he said. She eyed the auger curiously but said nothing. Then she padded toward the river.

She would find fuel, Mister Skye knew. She found it where others found only rock. He would need plenty of it.

He found Vanderbilt sprawled in the red wagon, smelling bad.

"You up to a bath, mate?"

"Makes no difference whether I die dirty or clean. The wounds aren't closed. Might as well let water in as blood out."

"I'm thinking you won't die. That arrow missed your lights and you've got most of your blood."

"Let's go then."

Mister Skye carried the gambler to a pool and set him in gently. Vanderbilt was too weak to sit up, and lolled back, his head resting on whited rock.

"The flow will do the work, mate."

"Stings the wounds, but who cares . . . Say, Skye? When I kick off, put me up on a scaffold. Mary gave me a name I like, Sleeping Bear. Say a kind word about Sleeping Bear."

"She told me," said Mister Skye. "It's a name you earned. You did a fine brave thing, Sleeping Bear. Think about living."

"Water feels good, except for the stings. I must stink. Maybe it's in my flesh and won't wash out. Souls stink too."

"I'll be back or send someone in a few minutes. If you get too hot in there, speak up."

The gambler peered up, face gray, and nodded.

Mister Skye sagged on his feet, and his head wound throbbed. He'd dip into the pool himself later, after his guard shift with the stock, and after he had taken care of other matters. He found the camp axe and set off toward the river, passing Victoria, who had miraculously accumulated a pile of small sticks. Everything here had been stripped by passing bands. He found a small cottonwood at last, its lower limbs hacked off to the height of a man on horseback. He ratcheted his way up between two trunks, to a fork in one, and then hacked at a four-inch limb until it dropped. He chopped off two feet of it and abandoned the rest. In camp he skinned two opposite sides flat with the axe and then drilled a dozen short holes in one flattened side, each hole bored five-eighths inch deep.

Seven-Story watched. "You Occidentals are inscrutable," he said. "You must be saving face."

"Something like that," said Mister Skye. He drilled a dozen more holes on the other flat side.

The time arrived for his shift. Victoria was back and soon would have some jerky and herbs boiling into some kind of thin soup, but he would wait. "I'll need some dry wood later," he reminded her. "Relieving Blueberry now. Maybe I can collect some while I guard."

She peered up at him, at his strange stick, and grinned.

It seemed a long walk down the river bottoms in long light, and he felt wearier than he could remember. The fight with the Gros Ventre still lay heavily on him, sapping something vital from him. He'd gotten them through. Vanderbilt might well live. All the other wounds would heal. But he grew tired, tired of guiding greenhorns and pork-eaters and pilgrims, tired of dealing with people like Riddle who showed up in some parties. He'd had a full life, had taken his fill of it, and not much mattered now . . .

He found the mules and horses cropping quietly, some of them hidden by brush. No sign of Blueberry. "Hill," he said softly in a voice that would jab through dusk, "it's Skye. Watch your trigger finger."

Silence.

He heard a rustle of hoof, and Jawbone emerged from a thicket, his jaw working methodically.

He didn't like it much. He unfastened his holster, and checked his Sharps. He had one paper cartridge chambered, and his last six cartridges in a pocket.

He prowled the twilight, through grassy parks dotted with thickets of brush. The horses and mules cropped peacefully. Most were free-herded, but Riddle had hobbled his Indian ponies.

"Over here, Mister Skye."

"I didn't see you in the twilight."

"White people don't see blacks."

"There's something wrong with you." Hill lay heavily against an ancient cottonwood trunk decaying in the grass.

"I reckon that's so," said Hill. "It's hitting me bad now."

Mister Skye squatted down, suddenly filled with foreboding.

"I got the distemper of the blood," said Hill. "From the wound. The streaks coming out from it, both sides of the gouge. I've seen those streaks before. It's the distemper. Streaks shooting out."

"Let me see," said Mister Skye. The arm had swollen and Blueberry had slit his sleeve to accommodate it. The guide unwrapped the bandage and stared at the pulpy furrow. Even in twilight it looked angry. "I don't think it's mortifying. It doesn't smell mortifying," he said.

"Nope. Not the gangrene. It's the bad blood, making me hot and sucking everything out of me."

"My friend Jim Bridger always says, 'Meat don't spile in the mountains,' Blueberry. I'll take you back in. Maybe Victoria's got something. She's got herbs . . ."

"I don't rightly think I can make it. I won't get to the

mountains, Mister Skye. Not the real ones. Not the ones off west, with snow on the roof, that we've been seeing all day. Maybe up there meat don't spoil, but here it does."

"The Absarokas," said the guide. "The roof of the world, the mountain men call them."

"I'm not going to see them. Not with the distemper of the blood."

"You didn't say anything. How long . . . ?"

"Started to get bad yesterday. No, I didn't say anything. I wanted to do my share and more."

"More? You're the most valuable man I've got."

"Worth more than two thousand dollars?"

Mister Skye nodded. The light was fading fast.

"I don't rightly figure I was a free man until we got west of Fort Laramie. I never knew who'd tie me up and haul me back. Lots of Southerners out here. But after Laramie, and after you took us up, I got to thinking this is how it is, this owning myself at last. But I've been studying and observing, Mister Skye. Long as I didn't own myself, I did as little as possible—just enough to escape the whip and beating. But there wasn't a reason in the wide world to do more, you see? But men who own themselves, they've got to work hard. No one's going to take care of them but themselves. So a free man has got to treat his own property good. I figured I would have to get rid of a whole lifetime of doing as little as possible, and start doing as much as I could so's to make myself valuable. I started that, some, working for Goldtooth, but I wasn't really free there. I figured maybe if I could be valuable, she'd maybe hide me out if they came after me . . . but I wasn't owning myself yet."

"It's not over, mate. You're my best man. We'll get you to the wagon now. You should have said something—"

Blueberry Hill didn't respond for a while. "No, I can tell I got to be a freeman for a few weeks, and got to taste the burden of it. Freemen got a burden on them, fierce weight. No one takes care of them. They can starve and die too easy. Not sure I want all this freedom and weight on my shoulders, Mister Skye."

The guide made his decision. He found Jawbone and led him to Blueberry. He hoisted the burly black onto his horse's back, staggering under the man's inert weight. But Blueberry, too weak to hang on, started to slide off. It wasn't going to work. He lifted Blueberry off and settled him next to the fallen cottonwood again.

"I'm going to move camp to here," he said. "I'll bring back Victoria directly."

He clambered wearily onto Jawbone, and tried to herd the mules back to the hot springs, but they wanted to graze, and dodged around the tired man and tired horse. He finally caught one of Riddle's hobbled ponies, unhobbled it and led it back to camp.

He found Victoria before their lodge. Mary lay there too, on a robe.

"Blueberry's in a bad way," he said.

Wordlessly the tired old woman rose, and ducked into the lodge. He heard her rummaging. He collected halters and picket lines, and saddled Jawbone, who slouched wearily, the feist out of him. Darkness crept close, save for the tiny fire Victoria had built of twigs. Then the weary guide and his tired woman rode down the bottoms of the Bighorn River, to the herd, and Blueberry. She slid off the pony and pressed her palm to Hill's forehead.

"He is very hot. Get him some water," she said. "I will need a fire to see . . ."

He trudged toward the river with a skin waterbag, while

she examined his wound in the darkness. By the time he returned she had gathered kindling from the profuse thickets here, and was striking flint to steel, directing sparks into a tiny ball of cottony tinder. In a few minutes she had a small blaze, and examined the swollen arm. Blueberry watched inertly, aware but not wasting energy on words.

"Sonofabitch!" she exclaimed crossly.

The tired guide bridled six mules and dragged them back to the hot spring.

"We're moving camp about a mile," he said shortly. "Seven-Story, I'd be grateful if you'd harness Goldtooth's wagons."

The mandarin sprang silently to work.

"Not me. We're settled for the night," protested Riddle.

Mister Skye didn't have the strength to argue. "All right then. The rest of us are moving, Riddle, and you can stay here alone."

"Now wait a minute! What's your angle, Skye?"

Mister Skye didn't answer. He hunkered down beside Mary, slipping his hard hand into her tiny one. "I'm going to put you back in the wagon for a bit, and all our truck, too. The lodge and the poles and the parfleches. Hate to do it."

She smiled, and hugged him as he lifted her wearily. "I am glad you are here to hold me," she whispered. "You will tell me soon why we do this."

"Blueberry's dying."

While Chang harnessed, he loaded his whole lodge into the wagon, finding room around Mary and Vanderbilt.

Riddle danced around doing nothing. "Seems to me, you can be harnessing me up, seeing as how you're making the extry work," he said.

Mister Skye addressed Riddle's women. "You will be safer coming with us," he said.

Drusilla and Mary-Rita came at once, and clambered into the bawds' wagon, sitting beside Big Alice.

"Now see here—" yelled Riddle, but the rest rode out into solemn darkness, with only starlight to guide them. Mister Skye rode quietly beside Chang and Buffalo Whiskers, who were driving a red wagon.

"Our friend Blueberry has the fevers and bad blood. Sinking fast. I couldn't get him back here, so we're going there."

Chang said nothing. There was only the soft clop of mule hoofs on the hardpan. "Yin and yang," he muttered at last.

They made a dark camp by the sliver of a moon, on a flat near the river, but far enough back so they could hear the sounds of the night. Mister Skye carried Blueberry Hill from the thicket where he lay, and lowered him onto a robe before his lodge. Victoria muttered and despaired. The swollen arm had a poultice of herbs over it, but Blueberry was sinking.

At last they were settled, and Mister Skye hunkered down beside Blueberry.

"Anyone you want to know? Any message you've got?" he asked harshly.

Blueberry sighed, words coming hard. "Hardly know my parents. I got taken away and sold at ten. They wouldn't know me. No more than a cow knows a calf after a few years. The girl . . ." He paused. "Lou. Bought by Spiller. I don't know the rest. Two counties west, is all . . . No. A slave gets born alone, lives alone, dies alone . . ."

"Not alone," said Mister Skye tightly.

"Alone," said Blueberry. He closed his eyes and wouldn't talk.

An hour later, Riddle drove in and made camp. At dawn, Blueberry lay unconscious. He lingered on for three days, feverish and delirious at first, and finally quiet, hot, and barely breathing. While Blueberry Hill slipped into his death agony, the party rested and healed. Hours on end, Goldtooth held his hand in her own while tears rimmed her eyes. Big Alice, too, hovered over him, caressing him with rough warm fingers. The third night, Blueberry's breathing became shallow and irregular. Then, near dawn, it stopped. Across that morning, Mister Skye built a scaffold. He and Chang wrapped Blueberry tightly in a good robe and laid him on his back, eight feet above the earth, his face toward the sun. Mister Skye found his ancient Bible and read from the last chapter of Deuteronomy. It struck him that Blueberry had left slavery behind and headed for his Promised Land, only to die with his goal in sight. Drusilla led a prayer of her own creation, one she had penned that morning. Her voiced trembled.

Sleeping Bear, propped up in the wagon so he could see, wept bitter tears.

Chapter 23

For two more days they tarried in the bottoms of the Bighorn while stock fattened and healed. Victoria liked the place, except for the swarms of insects, especially the big stinging horseflies. Seven-Story Chang and Buffalo Whiskers rode out each day to scout and hunt, but returned empty-handed. Mister Skye had done a little better. Downriver he found a slough with mud hens, and shot seven with his scattergun. Here the herbs and roots had escaped squaw baskets, and Victoria was able to make a stew to sustain them.

Each day she had escorted the women back to the hot springs to bathe and wash clothing, hovering nearby on her pony and well armed. The barriers between these strange white women had broken down, and the ones who sold themselves mingled with the ones who didn't. Even Gertrude Riddle came along the second day, bathing silently. Victoria watched keenly for visitors, but the hot springs remained deserted in the ruthless July sun.

She thought about the morning that Mister Skye had lifted Blueberry Hill to his scaffold, and the gambler Vanderbilt had started to weep. That was a strange thing. She thought she'd never understand white people. But he wept, lying in his hot wagon with tears leaking from his eyes and flies crawling over him. What sort of dark spirits possessed a soul like that? No one could know, she thought.

At her lodge, things became happier. She had rolled up the cover to let the breezes through, and had built a brush arbor beside it, where she worked. Mary lay on a robe, making moccasins for the women. Mister Skye rested too. Like all of them, he had bathed and freshened his clothing. The red bandana that held his hair also covered his scalp wound, and Victoria had scrubbed it until there was no blood or grime staining it.

That morning he gathered bone-dry sticks and built a hot fire between some rocks he had gathered. He borrowed her frying pan, dropped a bar of galena into it, and waited until the lead slowly dissolved into silvery hot liquid. Then he carefully poured it into each of the holes he had drilled in the cottonwood stick. It spat and smoked, and the lead slowly hardened while he watched.

Now she understood.

"I got seven paper cartridges left, and it's getting worrisome," he muttered as he waited for the lead to cool.

"No mould for this .60 Sharps, but here you have to make do, make do."

When the lead seemed solid, he rapped his stick sharply, and the bullets fell into the grass. He still could not touch them, but he filled his bored holes a second time.

When he could pick them up at last, he studied each one, rejecting two that seemed slightly oval. With his knife he pared the front ends into smooth cones. "Five-eighths bit should yield a sixty-two caliber bullet," he muttered. He slid open the slant breech of his Sharps and nestled a heavy bullet into the bore. It resisted. He jammed harder but the bullet wouldn't seat. "Too large," he said. "The lead burned out the wood. It didn't work."

She understood little of the arithmetic. No bullets. He'd tried to protect her, as he always did. He had medicine to make everything work, made do with anything and everything on the trail, but this time he'd failed. She studied him darkly.

Irritably he tried a half-inch auger, but it proved too small. Nothing worked, and he gave up. "Seven shots for the Sharps," he growled. "I'd better buy a sixty-caliber mould when we get there and not rely on paper cartridges."

Over at the Riddle wagon, Alvah seemed uncharacteristically busy. He had stripped off the wagon sheet and had set his three women to sewing up the holes in it. He had heated up the remaining tar in his bucket, and the women daubed each mend with it to waterproof the canvas. He spent a morning fashioning a sort of splint for the bullet-shattered wheel spoke by wrapping it in soaked rawhide he got from Victoria. It dried into a bandage of steel.

At Goldtooth's red wagon, the women likewise worked on the wagon sheet and their clothing and moccasins.

They had no needles and thread, having lost them in the
storm, but Victoria proffered an awl and thong and the
bawds put them to good use. They didn't bother with
Vanderbilt's wagon, or the bullet holes in its cowhide
cover. Once in a while Victoria heard him weeping there,
or muttering to himself, and she knew dark spirits possessed him. She didn't want to go near him or meet this
evil of his.

Still, at noon she took him a bowl of broth, and he
drank it gratefully. "You are good. Skye's lucky," he said.

"Sonofabitch, but you got the bad medicine in you,"
she said, tarrying beside this strange white man.

"A good man died and I live," he muttered. "He was a
good man. I am a coward."

"Sleeping Bear came out of his cave and fought."

"Names. I'm Homer Donk. Born and raised near the
United States Naval Yard in Brooklyn, third largest city
in the United States, and they didn't miss me a bit."

"This name you don't like. Homer. What is this name?"

"Bad name to saddle a boy with. All the boys called
me Homer the Donkey. They teased and teased, and beat
me up. But I got even. I learned to skin them good, get
their marbles and jackstraws out of them."

"What is this name, Homer?" Victoria persisted.

Sleeping Bear lay back, his eyes soft. "Homer was a
great man long ago, long long ago. He made poems, the
Iliad, the *Odyssey* . . ." He paused, seeing incomprehen-
sion. "He sang songs about the stories of his people, the
greatness and courage of his people, and their foolishness too. He was the one to keep their history for them."

"Ah, we have those too. We have the ones to keep the
past and tell it. They are sacred ones among us. But we
don't call them Homers. They are the holy ones, among

the Absaroka. If you are named for a holy one, how come you don't like it?"

"I was a boy. Boys are cruel . . . They teased until I hated being Homer."

"Sonofabitch," she muttered. "How could that be? You got a good name and you got ashamed of it. What is Donk?"

"Dutch. That's Dutch."

"What is Dutch? I never heard Dutch. Are they bad people?"

He shook his head. "No, it's just a funny name. Strange name. Vanderbilt is Dutch too."

"Why do you weep?"

"Because I can't stop it. I took an arrow and should be up on that platform. All I did. All I skinned. All I took. I should be up there."

"You don't like it that you gambled bad?"

He shook his head and the tears came again. "Wasted life," he muttered. "Skinned a thousand people, even the poor, took as I could."

She shook her head. This was a strange thing. "Can you walk as far as my lodge?"

She supported him as he staggered toward the brush arbor she had built, and soon helped settle him on a robe there.

She eyed him sharply. "We got to make big medicine now, drive away the bad spirits."

She bustled out, gathering sweetgrass and stalks of sage.

Mary stopped lacing up a moccasin and watched, approval in her soft brown eyes. Victoria kindled a tiny fire in the shade of the arbor, and let it burn hotly for a while.

"Now, Homer Donk," she said. "I burn the sweetgrass and sage and you lean over the smoke, make the sweet smoke flow around your body. You do that, and make the sour go away."

She threw grass and sage into the hot coals and white smoke billowed up, pungent and scented sweet. She beckoned. He stared, uncertainly, and then crawled over and bathed his yellowish torso in the smoke for a moment. Then he pulled back.

"No. Stay in the smoke," she said sharply.

"Now," she droned, "the smoke of the clean sage and the sweetgrass is bathing you, making you clean. Spirits making you clean. Now the One Above likes the scent. Now the One Above looks kindly on you . . ."

For an hour she made her medicine. She painted him with umber clay mixed with grease. She daubed white clay on his chest in the shape of a cross, the white men's medicine symbol. She found her gourd rattles and rattled away the demon spirits. And when she finished, Sleeping Bear was asleep, and his face looked peaceful.

"We make him a child, and he starts over," she muttered. "He's damn sorry about the old self. We give him a new one."

Wearily, she packed up her paints and rattles, and trudged through the hot of the afternoon until she found Blueberry's scaffold.

There she sat. "You," she said. "You had a good spirit and now you gone to the other side. Before you go, you gave it to Sleeping Bear, hey? I watch. I watch all the people Mister Skye guides. You worked the hardest. Never complained. Always helping those women, or the rest. I'm gonna remember you, Blueberry Hill."

She felt an ineffable sadness as she sat there in the shadow of the scaffold. It was good to feel a sadness. That meant that he had made his way into her soul. She sat in the quietness, and at some time Mister Skye joined her.

They sat quietly in the shadow of Blueberry, and he held Victoria's hand, loving her.

They rolled north, along the west bank of the Bighorn, encountering few difficulties except for an occasional draw that forced them to detour around its head. Often Mister Skye took them a mile or so west of the river, which lay greenly off to the right. The sun blazed hot, and dun alkali dust lifted into the air by metal tires covered them all. They found no shade in these rolling sage-dotted plains, and the noonings under the hammering July sun were quiet and miserable. The air became so suffocating that Mister Skye let them dally for two or three hours midday, but pushed them onward in the long summer evenings.

Drusilla had taken to driving Vanderbilt's wagon, and within a day Mary-Rita had joined her. They both had come to loathe Alvah Riddle so intensely that it was a relief to slip away from his green wagon and the increasingly peculiar Gertrude.

"That's a good angle," he said at last. "Lightens the load on my stock. Yes, good angle. But when we get to Bannack, I don't want you driving any red wagon or being anywhere near those lowlifes."

"Respectability is where you find it," Drusilla replied.

She had taught herself to harness, and each day unhobbled or unpicketed three of Goldtooth's mules and one of Riddle's ponies and readied them.

It enraged Alvah. "If you kin do that for the lowlifes, you kin do it for me. I got enough work, without any help from you. The contract says you're under my direction—"

Drusilla wearied of contracts. They made less sense here in these vast alkali flats. Life imposed larger contracts, she thought, obligations to one another here where the well-being of each affected the others. She had simply turned her back and continued to settle collars over necks, tighten surcingles, slip on bridles, and hook animals into the traces.

"I forbid it!" cried Alvah, but he addressed the wind.

With Blueberry gone, Big Alice had taken to driving the bawds' wagon, handling the chores just as easily as Blueberry had. Mary was riding again and ignoring the throb in her foot, herding Mister Skye's pack and travois animals. Victoria scouted ahead and left, while Seven-Story and Buffalo Whiskers probed along the river bottoms to the right, scouting and hunting game. They'd found very little. It seemed as if every deer and antelope in the basin had fled to the mountains until the heat broke. Riddle grumbled about using up his stores. They turned in the evenings back to the river, and there Victoria managed to find roots and herbs, wild onions and turnips, to fill out rabbit or duck or sage-hen stews.

While Drusilla drove, Vanderbilt recovered strength daily, and felt able to attend to his needs and join the others for meals. He said nothing, and Drusilla was in no mood to encourage talk. Her thoughts settled constantly on Parsimony McGahan, wending his way toward far Nevada and the Comstock. She thought also of her husband-to-be in Bannack, and subdued her yearnings with the knowledge that she would be well wed at last, and fortunate for it.

She enjoyed Mary-Rita's company, pleased that the Irish girl kept quiet and held her mean tongue. This vast hot dry land, wild Indians and peculiar Americans, had been so strange to her that she had finally quieted, having run out of words.

"You drive the mules well," Mary-Rita ventured one day, and the kind word surprised Drusilla.

"Would you like to try it? I'll walk a little," she replied.

Fearfully Mary-Rita took the eight lines, and Drusilla stepped down into the dust and began stretching her legs. Her skirts caught on sagebrush, but she had no trouble keeping up with the lagging animals on this furnace of a day.

The next day Vanderbilt asked if he might join them on the seat, and soon he tried the lines for a while, until he tired.

"Perhaps you can advise me," he said abruptly to Drusilla. "I wish to begin a new profession, or living, and I don't know what I'm fitted for. I have no skills, but I have fast hands."

"You might tend bar in a saloon," said Drusilla.

"I would rather not, Miss Dinwiddie," he replied, and she felt sorry. She had suggested something respectable enough, but he hoped to escape the sporting life altogether.

She tried to think. He hadn't the muscled body of a farmer or teamster, and probably couldn't handle heavy labor. "Perhaps a clerk, Mister Vanderbilt."

He smiled softly. "I'd take it kindly if you'd call me Sleeping Bear. The name reminds me of something in me I didn't know was there."

"I will do that."

"There will be many camps who will know me—a gambler and a . . . tinhorn. I don't suppose anyone will let me try to be something else . . ."

"I will put my mind to it, Mister—Sleeping Bear. I don't know what trades and services are needed in these camps."

"I've never thought about it," he said. "I only know I took an arrow clear through, and I'm alive to tell about

it. I suppose if there's a God, he had something to do
with it."

Mary-Rita blessed herself. "It was a saint, some saint,"
she muttered. "Looking out. I don't know the patron saint
of gamblers."

Clear across the northern horizon lay a featureless
blue mountain, and to the east the Bighorns edged closer
and closer as if to herd them west. But off to the west lay
formidable peaks still topped with white in late July.
Now at last Mister Skye left the Bighorn River, and that
night they reached an alkaline slow river he called the
Greybull. They crossed it with surprising difficulty, mir-
ing in a soft gumbo that sucked at hoofs and wheels.
They were heading for Pryor Gap, Mister Skye had explained, and once through that, they'd be in Yellowstone
country, and back in the best game area in the Far West,
including buffalo.

No Indians disturbed their passage and it dawned on
Drusilla that the Indians, like migratory creatures, would
be in cooler country this time of year. She learned they
were passing through the lands of the Absaroka, or Crow,
Victoria's people, but she saw no sign of anticipation on
Victoria's face.

One nooning, as she lay indolently in the open shade
beneath the wagon, she realized she had changed. In fact
they had all changed for better or worse. This hard free
land of long peaces and short terrors had annealed her
body and soul. She had walked across much of a continent, and now her legs were hard and her ungainly hips
much reduced. Her bust and shoulders were fuller and
her arms strong. In fact her proportions had found a balance, which pleased her. But beyond that, the rigors of
the trail had made her different, more tolerant. She had
long since stopped sniffing at Mister Skye and his women.

She admired them as models for all who pierced into the wilderness. She had befriended bawds and found them not at all what she had thought. She had always thought that women were forced into that degraded life by desperation, but now she discovered that some women sought it and enjoyed it. Indeed, both Goldtooth and Mrs. Parkins had come from comfortable circumstances. And she suspected that Juliet Picard had a similar background. It surprised her. There was so much that she, in her New England puritan way, had never known and never dreamed.

Sleeping Bear, whose ordeal still crushed him, was being transformed by it, and she felt curious about how he would turn out; whether he'd slip back into his old ways at Bannack. Blueberry Hill had changed, too, becoming industrious and eager and steadfast as the days rolled by. For a while she grieved his loss, coming just as he had blossomed open to the western winds. Mary-Rita, lying beside her, had become subdued and was making some tentative gestures toward accepting others. Would she, too, revert after she married into a vicious-tongued harridan? And Chang. Ah, there was a mystery. She didn't fathom him, and therefore was not sure how this vast exodus across an empty dangerous land had changed him. He was a hard and competent warrior when he began, perhaps as much at home here as upon the deserts and steppes of central Asia. But happy he was, and his bride had become a partner, a unity, with him. Drusilla thought of them riding off each day, beyond the vision of this little caravan, and she knew they found some small Eden and made love there, day after day. The thought quickened her pulse and filled her with some unfathomable yearning for that mystery to unfold in her. For a moment she felt loss.

Curious about herself, she found her looking glass

among her things, and stared, barely recognizing the image. Her flesh golden and her cheeks suffused with color. She had gone from soft and white and pinch-faced, to lean and brown. Her lips no longer compressed into lines of disapproval and superiority. Even her hair, sunbleached, seemed softer and looser than when it was severely brushed, parted, and bunned. Oh, if only Parsimony could see her now!

The very thought saddened her, but she dealt well with fragile if-onlys, and thought resolutely instead of the abstract man awaiting her at the end of this journey. It had never occurred to her she had become beautiful, but she knew she was as hard as granite.

A few days later they toiled through Pryor Gap into the Yellowstone country, and the world around her transformed. Here raced icy clear creeks among verdant stretching meadows, and jackpined slopes and yellow rim-rock. And the dome of heaven rose bluer than sapphires. They were all wondrously changed, and especially Victoria, who had been reincarnated as a bold young woman.

Chapter 24

Was there ever such a land? Did ever the Absaroka people want for anything in a land like this? This homecoming infused Victoria with an elementary joy that she could not hold within her small withered frame. Each day, as they probed deeper into the Yellowstone country, Victoria grew younger and brighter, until she seemed a shining-eyed girl to those around her.

She had not expected to see her land ever again, or her people, the Kicked-in-the-Bellies band of the mountain Crows. She was old and life perilous, and Mister Skye not as strong and wary as he once had been. So she had made her peace with the future, knowing that someplace unexpected, she would cross over to the Other Side without knowing what children had been born in her village, or who had gone to the Other Side, or who had counted coup against the Siksika, or who had become a war chief or headman.

But here they were, toiling over vast hills that spurred out of the blue mountains to the south, in the land of her fathers and mothers. Almost imperceptibly, she assumed the task of guiding these white people through the tumbled country she knew in her bones and flesh. Each sunny day she rode out ahead of the wagons, finding a path through a tumultuous land full of rushing creeks of clear snowmelt, lush green bottoms, long ridges black with ponderosa pine, and long plateaus of gnarled cedar and purple sagebrush. She spotted game everywhere, does and bucks parading along cottonwood groves or up in aspen, antelope in white-rumped bunches darting down ridges, and grizzly too, although she saw only the awesome scratches on trees, taller than a man could reach. Absaroka! Abundant land! Plain and mountain, buffalo and berries, cool and warm!

This was tricky country for wagons, and often she sat on a ridge, crystalline air playing with the mane of her pony, while far below they double-teamed a wagon to haul it up a steep grade. On top of these vast slopes, they could survey the whole universe, the shoulders of the Absaroka Mountains rearing to the south and west, and the tumbled dun plains north and east, and sometimes the distant tawny cut of the river the whites called Yellowstone, but her people called the Elk. Not the slightest haze dulled this clean air, and sometimes they could look to the edge of the world. Mister Skye called it a hundred miles.

She grew impatient with them and their cumbersome wagons, and at every rise she scanned her world eagerly, with keen old eyes, hunting sign of her people. She would find them eventually. She would cut a trail of ponies, or the furrows of travois, or run into young warriors out stealing horses, or find medicine symbols of feather or hair or birdbone on cairns, or dangling from trees, telling her in their mysterious ways who had come here or what had happened or where someone had gone.

In the camps each evening they noticed the change in her and teased her, and Mister Skye grinned, knowing everything there was to know about her. Meat became abundant, and they grew strong on the best cuts of elk and deer. Even the gambler, Sleeping Bear, flourished on red meat, up and about several hours each day, doing what chores he could. He was harnessing his wagon without help now, and unharnessing evenings, which spread the burdens.

Still her Kicked-in-the-Bellies eluded her, and she decided they were farther west this summer, maybe in the dreaming intimate valley of the Boulder or one of its branches, where game grew thick and the summer breezes flowed cool. She herself left signs of their passage now, the sign for Skye they all knew, the sign for the trapper and guide white man who had become a friend and occasional war ally of the Absaroka people. She felt secure here, even though the terrible Siksika sometimes raided deep in Absaroka, and others as well—the Teton Dakota, the Assiniboin, and even the Cheyenne. They reached the Stillwater on a hot day early in the moon her husband called August. She crossed several trails but they were old and sunwashed and told her only that her people had stayed upstream earlier. But she had come close, and the nearness of her tribe and clan-family infused her. Her medicine toyed with her, delaying the moment she could hug her sisters and babble half a night in the lodges of her brothers, and pay her respects to Many Coups.

Sonofabitch! she thought. How would she explain these strange people to her own? There weren't good Absaroka words to describe the brides, or their chaperones. This man is not their father? they would say. How can that be? The others, the women who sold themselves, she could explain. That practice the Absaroka people knew all about. Her people professed virtue and enjoyed lust. From the days of the fur trappers, husbands had sold wives to white men, often for the price of a cup of mountain whiskey—grain alcohol, diluted with water, with a plug of tobacco and some pepper for taste—or beads or foofaraw. Victoria laughed. Absaroka women had sat at the campfires of these white men and told them the bawdiest imaginable jokes, stories that left the white men gaping at them. She had done it herself. Even now, she could make Mister Skye turn red. Well, what was winter for, if not to steal wives and seduce husbands? She giggled. Her people would understand the bawds, and maybe try them out. But white women were less valuable than whiskey. They'd trade anything for that, and she suddenly felt glad none remained in this caravan. The whiskey hurt her people, but the women would not.

Late that night, when the smell of dew on the grass hung heavy in the air, every mule and pony disappeared. Their night sentinel, Jawbone, shrieked and whinnied beside their lodge, and Mister Skye, Mary, and she sprang up instantly, rushing into a moonless dark, hearing the soft scuff of retreating hoofs. The evil blue roan stood quivering in the night, snorting, awaiting his master's direction.

"Maybe Absaroka," she growled, and the thought mortified her. A terrible thing to think of.

Mister Skye saddled Jawbone swiftly as Victoria threw kindling in the coals to give him light. Then, without waiting to pull on his buckskin shirt, he grabbed his Sharps and his possibles and rode off, letting Jawbone pick the way. Victoria's heart lay leaden in her, heavy with the shame, for the thieves were surely her people, and most likely Kicked-in-the-Bellies. But they would recognize Mister Skye, and they all knew about Jawbone, the great medicine horse.

Dawn broke, and a gray haze rimmed the northeast. Victoria could wait no longer.

"Mary, goddamn, you make the white people stay calm while I'm gone. They gonna go crazy, especially that Riddle. The thieves got Chang's stallion and the Arapaho pony too, and we ain't got anything. But I'll fix it. Fix it good."

Grimly she gathered a sausage of pemmican, a knife, and spare moccasins, and began walking west, along a trail she sensed and smelled more than saw in the ghostly gray of first light. She trotted easily, as she had done as a thin girl and in an hour she had covered a vast distance through tangled hills. Twice she forded rushing creeks, soaking her feet in ice water. The trail grew clearer now, and anyone but a tenderfoot white man could follow it. She found Jawbone's prints and knew Mister Skye rode ahead of her, closing in. Once she found where one of the raiders had dismounted. Yes, Absaroka moccasins! The discovery shamed her. What would Mister Skye think? His mules and ponies, and every mule and pony of the others, driven hard toward her own village?

She trotted west and south, scarcely noticing that the long slopes became harder to climb. She pushed each leg ahead methodically, as she had done as a girl, not thinking of her gray hair or the crevasses lining her weathered brown face. Then at last the sun rose, giving color to a gray world, turning a white sky azure. Muffled on the morning air thumped a single shot, and it filled her with dread. They were cutting across valleys, each a drainage leading from the vast gray and black mountains on down to the Yellowstone River. Still she trotted, perhaps fifteen miles now, by Mister Skye's reckoning. Ahead the thieves were gaining on her; their prints drier now to her keen eye. She topped a long ridge, threaded through loose-knit stubby ponderosa, and down a dun sandstone grade. Ahead lay a mound on the brown grass, and beside it, Mister Skye. Horror rose in her. Now she ran until her lungs ached and her old heart clattered, and still she loped.

The two of them sprawled in a sandy boulder-strewn bottom, surrounded by copses of dark pine, and groves of bright aspen. Jawbone lay inert on his side, his lungs heaving shallowly and his teeth curled back in a death grin. Mister Skye sat mutely, tears leaking down his dark face, one arm cast possessively over Jawbone's trembling belly. She had never seen him cry, except once, when that mad Siksika, Moon-Hides-the-Sun, had struck Mary what seemed a mortal blow in the head.

Stunned, she stopped and stared at the terrible sight, at Mister Skye's torment, at the scarred blue roan gasping. She made her legs sidle closer. She made her feet walk around to Jawbone's chest, where she could see the hole and the froth of blood around it as heaving lungs expelled and sucked red air. She saw no exit wound. The horse's tongue hung in the sand, and its eyes focused on nothing. Jawbone wept from dimming eyes.

"It had to come sometime," Mister Skye muttered. "I just wasn't ready for it."

She groaned with a sorrow beyond words, beyond what her soul could contain. She made her small feet walk the remaining distance to her man, and made her hands take his. He barely noticed.

"I guess I have to do it. Don't have the will for it," he muttered.

He slowly pulled his old Navy out of its holster and stood. He wore only his breechclout and leggins, and she noticed something, that the hair of his chest grew gray. She had not known that his chest was gray. He cocked the Colt and pressed it behind the ear of Jawbone and closed his eyes. Time ticked by, and Victoria wished he would shoot, but he didn't. The horse trembled beneath the muzzle. Jawbone turned his head back, and caught Mister Skye's eye. Jawbone still wept.

"I can't," said Mister Skye hoarsely. "I don't have it in me to do that."

He holstered the revolver and sat heavily beside the trembling horse, beginning his terrible vigil. He seemed lost and forlorn, the smallest speck in a vast wilderness. Her heart ached for him, ached for Jawbone in his pain and dying. She peered narrowly about this place. They perched on a steep slope leading to a sharp cedar-choked bluff. An ambush place. One of them had waited above, shot down the steep incline, hitting Jawbone in the chest. Mister Skye should have been more alert, she thought. The way to her village led through lower hills to the right, not this way to ambush.

Jawbone lay panting irregularly, a horrible wheezing

in his chest, leaking blood from his wound. Victoria loved the old gallant horse that had rescued them so often, from so many desperate moments. Softly her old hand found Jawbone's neck, and slid along under the mane. She wished she had medicine in her fingers to heal the animal, medicine to plug the hole and heal the terrible damage within, medicine to pluck out that leaden ball buried in him. Then she knew that her hand did have medicine: her touch along the great stallion's neck transmitted something to the old blue roan, and his breathing steadied and he closed his eyes.

"He knows we love him," she said.

She found Jawbone's half-shot-off ear, and toyed with it, stroked it. Jawbone grew very quiet, eyes closed, awaiting the end.

"Come, Mister Skye," she said. "We must go to my village and see who has done this thing."

He said nothing, sitting heavily, turning old before her eyes. She had never seen Old Man in him, but now Old Man peered from within his haggard face. He could not stop touching Jawbone.

"See?" she said softly. "His eyes are closed and he does not know we are here now. We must go."

He saw it now. He saw that Jawbone had gone to the Other Land. She tugged at his hand. He stood, not wanting to, not wanting to tear himself away from the animal he had trained from weaning day by day to become the greatest war-horse, medicine horse, the people of the plains had ever known. With humans, with herself, he could be taciturn and at loss for words, but between Mister Skye and Jawbone communication had been perfect, and so had love. Through all the years the terrible blue roan whickered his joy at Mister Skye's presence, and Mister Skye's voice and hand and eyes had returned love.

Victoria had delighted in this thing, and she had watched it over the long years, this love of man and horse.

"Come along," she said sharply. "We go now."

He followed, unresisting. She did not take him up the trail and over the bluff, but to the north on softer land, and around, picking up the trail again a mile ahead as they descended into an intimate valley curling between sage-crowned hills, not far from the dark flanks of the mountains. And there, ahead, lay a band of blue haze from the cookfires of her people, the Kicked-in-the-Bellies. She would have been so glad. Her heart would have burst. She would have run around the bend ahead, until the poles of the lodges were a forest before her and the people she loved spilled out of the village with open arms to hug her. But she could not run.

They stumbled ahead along the bottoms. The camp police, at this time the Kit Fox Society, aware of them now. The crier racing to spread the word through her village. Now at last her people did boil out to them, and she saw nieces and nephews, a sister and two brothers, a score of friends, all graying now, and far ahead, at the great lodge whose door faced east toward the rising sun, old Many Coups, her cousin. But all of these, her friends and family, the little children she'd never seen, the old ones, the sharp-eyed medicine men, the elders, they saw, and turned suddenly quiet. Once Mister Skye had told her about a man in his black book named Moses, who had been in the presence of God, and whose face was so filled with the presence of God that he had to wear a veil because his face had become too terrible to behold. Mister Skye's face was too terrible for her people to behold. He had not seen God, but he had seen death, and his face became as terrible as the face of Moses, she thought. They knew without being told, and the women wailed.

Never in memory had such shame come upon the Kicked-in-the-Bellies.

She tugged Mister Skye along, through a tunnel of silent people, until at last they stood before old Many Coups, who stood on bowed legs with his ceremonial staff in hand, in somber silence.

"My dear cousin and Mister Skye, we welcome you," he said at last. "Only a while ago, our young ones returned in victory, with many prizes, telling us they had ambushed one who followed on a blue horse and killed the horse. Now our victory has turned to ashes. Come, if you will, for the pipe."

They entered his lodge then, and sat in their appointed places, and the elders and medicine men filed in also and seated themselves quietly. It was light within because the cover had been rolled up off the grasses to let the breezes run. Victoria's heart had never been so heavy. She ached for Mister Skye, for old Jawbone, for Many Coups, and for all of her people, who would never forget the shame of this day. Many Coups sighed heavily and extracted his long red pipe from its soft bag of unborn buffalo calf. Silence lay heavy, as he tamped tobacco and lit it with a coal brought to him. The pipe made its passage, and the smoke hung low upon the grass and would not rise.

"Tell us your story," said Many Coups at last.

Mister Skye could not, though he spoke enough Absaroka to do it. So Victoria did.

"Jawbone is dead?"

"He passed to the Other Land before we left," she replied.

The ancient medicine man, Red Turkey Wattle, peered sharply at her, lifted a pinch of dust and let it sift back to earth.

For many minutes no one spoke.

Then, "The young men grieve. They will return what they have taken, and give to you all that they own. The one who shot Jawbone is making a sweat lodge, and when he is sweated he will go into the mountains and fast for four days and four nights, as is the way with us."

Mister Skye nodded.

"I wish to give you my best war-horse, Fastrunner, and your pick of my horses. As many as you will. All of them, if you will."

Mister Skye replied softly. "I am honored by the great gift of Fastrunner, and he will make a good horse for me. We need a few others, humble ones for packs, and for these we would thank you, Many Coups."

The chief nodded. "As many as you need," he said. "I too will enter this lodge and fast, and my face will not see the sun for four days."

"You do us great honor, Many Coups, and return more than was taken away. We—Victoria and I—are friends and kin here."

Red Turkey Wattle said, "I will take my medicine bundle and I will go to Jawbone and help him in his passage to the Other World and bring to his spirit the sorrows of the Kicked-in-the-Bellies."

The old shaman arose then, and walked out into the sun. Victoria watched him slip into his own tiny lodge—everything he possessed, including each meal, was given to him by the village people—and emerge with his medicine bundle and shuffle slowly off. The village watched solemnly as he left. No medicine had more power than the red throat of the wild turkey.

"The Kit Fox Society will escort you back to your wagon people, and drive the mules and ponies. Take my gifts, and those of the young men, and bring your white people here if you would."

The chief turned to Victoria. "I have not seen you, and thought I never again would," he said. "But now I have seen you, and I say welcome, and say goodbye, because now I will fast."

Her heart grew heavy.

They filed out solemnly into the August sun, and Many Coups had his war-horse brought, and gave it to Mister Skye, who took the unfamiliar rein in hand awkwardly. The powerful buckskin with bulging stifles nudged him hard with its nose. Then they took Mister Skye out to the pony herd, upstream, and there he selected three serviceable ponies that had been broken to pack or carry travois.

"You have taken very little, and do me little honor," said Many Coups darkly.

"I have taken your greatest gift, the best war-horse in the village," replied Mister Skye.

The chief nodded, and began to prepare for his long and mortifying fast. Victoria stayed, but Mister Skye and the Kit Fox Society warriors began the long funereal procession of horses and mules back to the wagons.

Chapter 25

The buckskin war-horse stood small for a man of his weight, but carried him eagerly and responded instantly to the slightest command. Mister Skye scarcely noticed. He rode silently through the afternoon, along with six Kit Fox Society warriors who herded the horses and mules. It dawned on Mister Skye that they were not following any route that wagons could travel. The Kicked-in-the-Bellies had camped high in the roots of the mountains, on a creek that burrowed through canyons, amidst cliffs and bluffs black with ponderosa. The village stood maybe fifteen miles southwest of the wagon train near the Yellowstone River. No, he thought, he would not bring the wagons to the village.

Off to the south a mile stretched the canyon where he'd been ambushed and where Jawbone had died. None of that was visible from where they rode, nor did Mister Skye wish to glimpse the stiffening corpse of the great blue horse. The shaman would be there bringing the medicine of the wild turkey to Jawbone, and that would be enough. Someday, when he could bear it, he'd go back there and bury Jawbone's clean-picked bones, and maybe set a rock up at the place to mark it. He wished he could put sentences together well. He would write the story of that horse. But no one would believe it, he thought heavily. Horses never ran toward trouble; they always ran away from it. Who would believe a horse would fight like that?

Another thought formed in his mind across that solemn afternoon, too. He would urge Victoria to stay with her people for a while. He would come for her after he had delivered his party to Bannack. She had thought she'd never see her village again, and when she finally did, it came in the middle of shame and sorrow. No. She should not come to Bannack. She should stay until her village brightened again, and she could chatter with her family and friends, and meet the little ones. Anyway, he wanted to be solitary now. She would want to comfort him and be with him, and yet it would be the wrong thing for a while. He wanted to crawl inside of his own mortality and meet death alone. We die alone, he thought. Even if we are surrounded by others, we die alone, even as Jawbone died alone while he and Victoria stared help-lessly. Now he wanted to prepare for his own dying.

On a hilltop half a mile from the wagons they saw a flash of metal and then the rising figure of Seven-Story Chang. It stirred the Crow warriors briefly, but Mister Skye quieted them. Chang and his tall sweetheart trotted downslope toward them, and Mister Skye could see their eyes were riveted on the buckskin under him.

"Jawbone is dead," he said roughly.

"I have lost an esteemed friend," said Chang. He did not ask for details. Something of the events conveyed it-self to him.

"It is Victoria's village and she's there," Mister Skye said, forestalling the question.

At the forlorn wagons the others waited, gladness upon them as they spotted their herd of mules and ponies. Gold-tooth beamed. Drusilla and Mary-Rita grinned. Even the inert Gertrude managed a smile at the sight of so many horses.

"I never thought you'd do it, honey. I expected to camp here till— You sure got the magic, Mister Skye," said Goldtooth.

"You dear ol' man. You come fetch your reward any-time," Mrs. Parkins added.

"Royal flush!" proclaimed Sleeping Bear. "How'd you do it?"

Alvah Riddle fairly danced at the sight of his stock, but cast worried eyes at the six powerful Crow warriors who rode solemnly forward, carbines at the ready, and a hard light in their eyes.

"Riddle," said Mister Skye, "these are Victoria's kin and friends."

"You got extry horses. They forked over extrys by way of apologizing. I know Injuns, Skye. That's exactly what they did. Which ones are mine? They paid us all for takin' the stock."

Mister Skye did not feel like answering.

"Say, where's Jawbone? You leave him back with the savages?"

"Dead," said Mister Skye.

He saw Mary's hand fly to her mouth, and tears form; their eyes locked, and they silently exchanged their grief.

"Too bad," replied Riddle. "Pretty decent horse. Might have traded him for something younger but for all those scars."

Mister Skye turned his back. Vanderbilt—Sleeping Bear, he remembered—took charge of the animals now, along with Mary and Chang, who looked over his white stallion and Buffalo Whiskers's Arapaho pony. Big Alice, too, caught Goldtooth's mules and picketed them.

"You didn't say which of these new ones are mine, Skye," persisted Riddle.

"They were a gift to me," Mister Skye replied curtly.

"So that's your angle. Just like I figured. They give us a gift, and you hog it all to yourself. Well, I'm going to take those two there," he said, pointing at a bay pony and black mare. "Ought to pack good. Fetch something in Bannack."

Mister Skye slid off the buckskin and caught the pink man by the scruff of the neck.

"You didn't hear me, Riddle."

The man squirmed in his fist, and tried to swing his Spencer around. Mister Skye let go, and Riddle staggered to earth.

Drusilla exploded. "Can't you see the Crows tried to pay back Mister Skye for Jawbone? Can't you see that, Alvah?"

"That's his story," Riddle muttered.

"Riddle. You point a gun at me again, and you will be dead," whispered Mister Skye.

"If he succeeds, I'll kill him," said Sleeping Bear.

Mary said nothing. When Riddle looked up, it was into the black bore of Mary's cocked fusil. He crabbed sideways, but the bore followed him.

"Tell your squaw to be careful!"

"I understand your English," she retorted.

Riddle peered around, this time into the bores of six Crow carbines, the bore of Chang's carbine, and the twin caverns of Sleeping Bear's scattergun.

"I didn't do anything," he mumbled, terror in his eyes.

Mister Skye lifted his face to the hills. The sun lay low, knifing the land before him into slices, blazoning westerly slopes gold and easterly ones blue. A breeze toyed with his hair and his buckskin's mane. This Yellowstone country . . . if Jawbone had to die, he rejoiced that it happened here, amid clear cold creeks and forested slopes and long grassy plateaus, and huge outcrops of dun rock.

They all stood expectantly.

"I am going back to the village tonight," he said. "It is a long way, over four hours. I will be back in the morning, mid-morning, and we'll start rolling then. You'll be safe here. My dear Mary will keep you comfortable. My friend Mister Chang is a mighty warrior, and wise in the wilderness."

"You abandoning us?" asked Riddle from the earth.

Mister Skye turned wearily, and with a nod he and the Kit Fox warriors rode southward. He knew some of them slightly. They were the cream of all the warriors in the village, and counted many coups between them.

In the blue last light he found Victoria in her brother's lodge. The August nights were chill here, and the covers were rolled to the ground now. Many of the lodges glowed orangely, like dim streetlights through the village, as firelight pierced softly through the cowhide covers. He found a terrible quietness here, and all the familiar joy and cacophony of an Indian village absent. He waited to be invited in, and in a moment he was offered the place of honor, and elk rump stew. He wasn't hungry at all, and declined, with thanks.

Six sat within. Victoria's brother, Arrow Giver, her two sisters, Makes-the-Lodge and Quill-Dye-Woman, a young woman, and two somber youths.

In halting Crow, accompanied by his big hands, Mister Skye asked Arrow Giver to shelter Victoria for a moon or so, while he took people to the mining camp and came back. Victoria could visit her people. Happier days soon. It would be a good visit for them all. He wished to be alone for a little while.

Victoria stared, and then her old face went soft, and its umber creases gentled.

"Sonofabitch!" she exclaimed in English, and hugged him. "How are you going to get along? Cooking, Mary's no damn good. Me, I keep you fat."

"I need it," he said.

"I know."

His business done, he settled into the woven backrest chair given him, and thought of sleep. But he felt an expectancy here, and after a bit he sat up again and waited for whatever would be.

"These young men are my nephews," said Victoria. "They were with—the raiding party. They are like dead men inside of themselves. They wish to—undo what was done. Neither of them pulled the trigger. The one who pulled the trigger waits outside."

She nodded, and one of the young men, a very thin

one, rose and slowly lifted the medicine bundle that hung on his chest up and over his head, and handed it to Mister Skye. And the other youth did likewise.

Frightful, terrible gifts. In his hands lay the small leather pouches that contained the most sacred things, sometimes a small stone, or something from the spirit animal that was the youth's guide and protector. These were sacrifices of self, of protection, of help, of courage, of faith, of identity, of tribal connection, of vision-quest and purpose. Mister Skye felt the cold heaviness of these things, gathered now in his hands. These young men had made themselves nameless and had stripped themselves of all that might protect and guide them. He felt the heaviness, and the terribleness, and then knew what he must do.

"The medicine of these young men goes into my heart," he said. "And now, I wish to give the sacred bundles back, each to the one whose medicine it is. They have made Mister Skye happy, and have healed his wound."

He walked over to each, and slipped the thong back over the neck of each, while they gazed at him with wide dark eyes.

He returned to his seat. "There is no greater gift an Absaroka can give," he added.

Victoria nodded. "The other waits outside."

Outside the doorflap stood six ponies and a pile of things hard to discern in the dark. Moccasins, a shirt, a bow and full quiver, a battered muzzleloader—the weapon that had killed Jawbone, he knew—a shield with some-one's private medicine daubed in white clay upon it, and more. And off to one side, sitting cross-legged, a youth naked save for a breechclout. The killer of Jawbone.

The boy's entire worldly possessions rested here. Again Mister Skye felt the weight. He could not refuse these gifts and sacrifices for a wrong done. The flap of the lodge closed behind him, and he met the dark. In all politeness Victoria's family would avoid listening, and would talk of other things within their lodge. Mister Skye examined the ponies one by one, and carefully studied the pile of goods, the fine sinew-wrapped bone bow, the skin clothing. Then at last he sat down heavily, directly opposite the youth.

"What is your name?" he asked in his faltering Crow.

"I was named Tobacco Dancer."

"It is a good name. I know of the sacred ceremony of the tobacco."

"I have dishonored the name and now I have none."

"I will give you a new one soon. You have brought me many gifts. All that you have."

"I took away all that you have."

"Much, but not all. I have Victoria, of your people. Mary, of the Shoshone. And my son, Dirk. And more."

"I have had a sweat. Now I must go high upon the mountain and seek the vision. I would like to go now."

The youth twisted uneasily, but Mister Skye did not want him to leave. Not just yet. He stared upward into the mystery of the heavens, wanting guidance. His own spirit lay so heavy he could scarcely decide what to do.

"Red Turkey Wattle has left the village, but is there another medicine man here?"

"There is Little People's Voice."

"We will go see Little People's Voice. Bring along the best pony."

The youth stared sharply at him, and then selected a dun with white stockings, and they walked through the softly lit silent village. Lodge flaps hid those within, and yet Mister Skye felt that the whole village knew exactly where he and the killer of Jawbone were walking.

They stopped at a small dark lodge at the rim of the village, and waited.

"I have expected you," said a reedy voice. "Come in."

They settled down inside a pitch-black lodge.

"You have brought me a pony. We will have a smoke," said the ancient voice.

Mister Skye heard a rustling, and finally a scratch of a sulphur match, and in the matchlight he glimpsed a cragged and seamed face, dark as a saddle. Little People's Voice looked very old. If he was the voice of the miniature people the Absarokas called Nimimbi, protectors of the Crow people, then the old man's medicine was sacred indeed.

He sucked on the long pipe, and passed it to Mister Skye, who drew a breath, and passed it to the youth. The pipe slowly circled among them until the entire charge of tobacco had burned, and the shaman knocked the ashes out. Time for business.

"I wish to adopt this young man as my son, and to give him a new name. I have come to you for the name-giving, and for the blessing."

Silence thickened in the blackness of the lodge. He wished he could see the youth's face. He waited for what seemed an eternity before the old shaman spoke.

"It is good. I am pleased to have the gift of the pony."

The silence folded in again, but Mister Skye sat easily. Careful deliberation was the way of all the Indian people he had known.

He lost track of time in the closed darkness, and heard nothing save for the occasional rasp of breath from the old man. Then at last the shaman spoke. "I see that this young man will be away from the village much of the time. He will often be among the whites learning their ways. I will name him Half Absaroka, or in your tongue, Half Crow."

"That is a good name. Now, Half Crow, in the presence of our esteemed friend Little People's Voice, I adopt you as my own son, with all the honor that I bestow upon my own son, Dirk."

The youth said, "I did not know this would happen. I am very honored. I will always strive to be a good son to Mister Skye."

"Now, a father likes to give good gifts to his son," continued Mister Skye in his faltering Crow. He could not use his hands in this blackness, and the words came slowly. "So I will give you what you gave me, and something more which I will bring back from the mining camp of Bannack in about a moon. Give me your hand, Half Crow."

The boy's hand found his in the blackness, and he held it in his own.

"It is good," said the old man. "Now, Half Crow, give me your medicine bundle. It is dead."

The youth obliged.

"Now, Half Crow, go meet your family. Your new mother is in the lodge of Arrow Maker. Then after you have met your new kin, go up this very night upon the mountain, and begin a vision-quest, and pray that the One Above will send you a vision. If you receive the vision, we will make a new medicine bundle for you."

He dismissed them and they walked back through the quiet village to the lodge of Arrow Maker, and were invited in. Victoria's nephews had left.

"Victoria," he said softly, "meet your new son Half Crow."

"Sonofabitch!" exclaimed the old woman. She stood and peered into the youth's tense face. "Sonofabitch!" she muttered, completely circling him.

"I hope I am acceptable to my new mother," the youth said in Crow.

"Ah!" she cried, her seamed face softening. She hugged Half Crow. And then the others did too, congratulating him, and themselves, and Mister Skye.

"Half Crow will now go up to the mountain for four days, seeking the vision that will give him new medicine," said Mister Skye. "Little People's Voice has declared it."

"I am proud to be the son of Mister Skye, and my mother Victoria," he said, and left.

"Sonofabitch," said Victoria, and hugged Mister Skye.

In the morning Victoria grew cross with him, snapping at everything he said, and serving breakfast rudely. It was her way of saying goodbye, he knew. She couldn't bear any other mood when she and Mister Skye were to be parted for a while. He pressed her to him anyway, and said he'd be back swiftly, and to take care of her new son, giving him gifts.

"Ha!" she bellowed. "You think I don't know what to do!"

He cinched his Crow-made pad saddle over the buckskin while she watched, and when she handed him a small sack of pemmican and berries for the trail, her old brown cheeks were wet. Mysteriously, word of the adoption of Half Crow had spirited through the village, and many people, less solemn now, saw him off. The shame upon the village had lifted. The Kit Fox warriors accompanied him a mile or so, and then resumed their patrolling and policing.

He rode alone. The horse beneath him was not Jawbone. There blew a hint of autumn on the air, but the sun banished it by mid-morning. It was a familiar thing, this aloneness. This vast continent did that to him. Ever since he had jumped ship near Fort Vancouver as a young man, he had encountered this aloneness. He was a Yank now, but not a part of them, and had scarcely seen their civilization, except for one trip to St. Louis. The separateness rose keen in him with Jawbone dead. For many years the horse had been a companion, and they had talked without words. There remained some of the Cambridge-bound merchant's son in him, the youth who buried himself in books, and it was a rare occasion out here that he found anyone who had read the same books and wished to talk of them. This land and its people spoke another language, which he knew and loved, but he rarely found anyone from the East who understood it, or cared about it. So he walked alone among Easterners, and alone among his friends out in this wild.

He rode through a grand and open land, not noticing it this day, once again passing the side canyon where Jawbone lay. His mind went numb and he refused to think about it.

Mary would be waiting, and would share his grief. She gave herself to smiles and tears, and these things of the heart flowed freely from her, while they always caught up in his own throat. He rode into the wagon camp and found it peaceful. The wagons were harnessed and the animals stood patiently in their traces, lashing flies and nipping at each other in their leather prisons. He stared at them irritably, these whites. Over the years in the wilderness he had become more Indian than white. In the village he had understood the feelings, knew what to do, and approved of all that had been done. But here among these people thoughts turned private and sometimes opposite what appeared on their faces. He spotted Drusilla, looking remarkably tanned and handsome, and read pleasure in her eye. He must not judge, he thought. There were people here he would willingly protect with his life.

"You are a fine and brave man, Mister Skye," she said softly.

"Let's be on our way," he said, and heard the wagons begin to roll behind him.

Chapter 26

Sleeping Bear marveled that he was alive. The holes in his belly and back had sealed over and healed into tender dimples. The blood that had reddened his urine had long since disappeared. Day by day the terrible weakness had vanished, and now somehow he felt stronger and healthier than he had been. The sallow yellow-gray of his flesh had turned to tan, and the night-cast of his face had become a ruddy wind-chapped brightness.

He had never seen country like this. Before, he had been indifferent to nature, but now he could scarcely drink in enough. They had struck the Yellowstone River after a hard two days toiling down rugged pine-dotted hills south of the river. Now before him lay a broad tawny valley curling between the great wall of the Rockies to the south, and a jagged separate range to the northwest. The wide clear river rolled between thick green bands of cottonwood that were rife with game, but Mister Skye led them across open grassy bottoms, often a half mile from the stream. The going was easier, he said, and there was less possibility of an ambush.

They were shorthanded now, and Mister Skye and Mary occasionally had a time of it with the loose herd of ponies given to him by the Crows. Sleeping Bear would have liked to help them, but wasn't up to horseback riding yet. So he drove the red wagon, with one of Mister Skye's new ponies as a wheeler, surrounded by well-broke mules and ponies. Another of Mister Skye's green ponies was locked in the traces of Goldtooth's wagon. Sometimes he glimpsed Chang and Buffalo Whiskers far ahead, Chang usually on the hills south of the broad valley, and the Arapaho woman skirting along the river and its thickets.

This land seemed wondrous to him, and he felt like a child in it, seeing it for the first time, noticing gray bluffs, admiring the way low sun sharpened distant black and white peaks, feeling the arch of a limitless and mysterious blue heaven over him. He had never looked into the sky before, or limned its aching distances against his small-ness. When white-rumped antelope herds burst away, they enchanted him. When Mister Skye had spotted a prowling grizzly along the river and had given it wide berth, it fascinated him. Why had he never seen or even imagined these things before? How had he crossed a continent without knowing what lay about him?

But most of all he had come to love driving this red wagon, steering it around small barriers, little gullies and boulders, the soft earth of a prairie-dog town, unex-pected potholes. He had learned to anticipate, see the earth ahead in terms of his team and his wagon, and choose paths that were easiest on both. Often Drusilla and Mary-Rita joined him on the seat. They couldn't stand Alvah, they said at first, but then it became another reason: the three of them were having fun. Never before had any white women enjoyed his company, and when it dawned on him, it amazed him for hours. Always before, he had bought female companionship for brief imper-sonal businesslike moments.

They bounced across a rock-strewn tributary river

Mister Skye called the Boulder, in a place where wooded islands dotted the Yellowstone and creeks poured in from the opposite bank. Signs of traffic on this great highway lay everywhere, but they saw no one these long August days. Mister Skye had warned of raiding Blackfeet, and even raiding Sioux, far from their home country. From high points now they could see a blue barrier clear across the west, dead ahead. They would cross these formidable mountains by a pass he knew, Mister Skye said. Just before that, the river would swing south, pierce through a mountain gate, and head for the land of the geysers.

A day after they'd crossed the Boulder, Mister Skye led them closer to the Yellowstone until he came to a stretch where the river ran wide and slow, and the gravelly banks were almost horizontal.

"We'll cross here, mates," he said. "Ahead is a narrows I don't want to tackle with these wagons. Might make it, might not. But I want to get on over to the north side anyway. There's a hot springs on that side for those who want to wash. Tomorrow we'll cross. I've seen buffler cross here, and I think we'll have no trouble."

"How deep is the channel, Skye?" asked Riddle.

"Mister Skye."

Riddle was annoyed. "I can't even get an answer to a civil question."

"Uncivil," said Skye. "You'll have to swim the teams and float the wagons. Double-teamed, you'll be all right."

"My wagon doesn't float. I got my shooting ports cut in the sides. All my supplies and robes will get soaked."

Mister Skye seemed to stop a retort in his throat. "I suppose we can put your truck in one of Goldtooth's wagon boxes, if they're tight."

"They should be," said Goldtooth Jones. "I bought the best I could, cash and merchandise." She laughed. "Maybe I ought to charge you for hauling your truck over dry, Alvah."

"So that's your angle," Riddle muttered. "All conspired up against me."

Goldtooth laughed, and soon the others did too. "I might even lend you a team for the double-teaming, Alvah," she added.

They camped in an open grove of majestic cottonwoods beside the cold river, below a small shelf that would conceal firelight. Mister Skye always selected campsites that would hide fires from night-eyes as much as possible. The women slipped down to the gravel bank of the cold-running Yellowstone for their ablutions, with Mary and the scattergun for protection. Sleeping Bear unhitched both teams, watered and picketed the stock. Riddle did the same, in huffy silence. He had set up his camp at a small defiant distance from Mister Skye's lodge and the red wagons. Chang had brought in a doe, and now it hung from a limb while he methodically yanked back hide and butchered. It was amazing, Sleeping Bear thought, how much work Victoria had done. Not until she had left this party had he or anyone else, except Mister Skye, understood what the old woman's industry meant to them all.

"You gonna share some of that doe, Chang?" asked Riddle.

Chang laughed.

Sleeping Bear found Mister Skye off in deep bunch-grass, combing the buckskin and muttering all the while.

"Need some help?" he asked.

Mister Skye peered up sharply. "No, I guess not. I'm just getting introduced to this bloody horse."

"Is he a good one?"

"He's a horse," said Mister Skye shortly. Then something softened in him. "He's a good horse. Good pony."

"I like this country," said Sleeping Bear.

"Best there is. Heart of Absaroka."

"Why don't you live here? I'm sure Victoria would like that."

The guide stared off into the dusky western hills. "I don't rightly have an answer for that," he said. He finished rubbing the buckskin stallion, and began examining its feet. The animal resisted. Sleeping Bear grabbed the halter rope and held tight while the guide lifted one hoof after another, and checked pasterns and cannons and hocks for heat.

"Thanks, friend," he said. "You know what you're going to do when we get to Bannack? Get a new faro layout?"

"No . . . no. I thought I'd try to buy the wagons and teams from Goldtooth after we hit Bannack, start freighting. Fort Hall, Salt Lake. Maybe Fort Benton."

"Hell of a lot to learn about freighting, mate. Competition, dirty tricks, harassment, Indian trouble, drunken teamsters, ruined goods, breakdowns, bad river crossings, hail, snow, feed that sickens the stock, alkali water . . . and road agents. I've heard talk of road agents around Bannack."

"What else would you have me do then, Mister Skye?"

The guide was visibly startled. "Why, damn, Sleeping Bear. Why, mate, that's a good plan. It'll take sand. Red wagons—they'll be . . . a target. Sleeping Bear, freighting is harder than gambling . . . but . . ."

"I don't know if I can do it either."

"But you're going to try."

The women straggled back to camp, wet-haired and

fresh-scented, in twos and threes that revealed no sign of earlier divisions. Soon their laundry draped from limbs and brush, and they were tackling a supper. Sleeping Bear corraled Goldtooth and led her over to the dark river.

"I've got a business proposition," he began.

"Honey, I'm always open for business, and never turned down a proposition." She laughed heartily.

"I'd like to buy your wagons when we get there. And the stock too."

"Now how are you going to do that, Cornelius?"

"I'd like you to call me Sleeping Bear now. It means something to me. I was hoping—I thought maybe I'd work off the debt with profits."

"Profits?"

"I thought I'd freight for a living."

"Why, Sleeping Bear—now there's a name for a cathouse, Sleeping Bear—I thought you'd be my houseman, now that Blueberry is gone. You silly old thing. You'll have plenty of time to deal faro on the side. I'll stake you to a layout. I mean, after we turn a few tricks and get going. Might put one in my house if I've got room for a saloon."

"Goldtooth, no. I'd like to freight."

She frowned. "You going bluenose on me, sonnyboy?"

"Look, Goldtooth, I've got a new lease on life, and when I lay in that wagon sick of myself, sick of what I was, half dead, I just started to see—"

"Bluenose," she said. "Some people get that way. No, I won't sell the wagons or the stock. I like my wagons. We're almost to Bannack, and they got us here. Tell you what, honey. If you want to start freighting, I'll go fifty-fifty on the earnings. Your business, my wagons and stock. Or are you too bluenosey now to be partners with a madam?"

"Hell no!" he said, and kissed her. It was dark here, and she kissed back, and didn't stop.

"I like being partners," she said.

"**W**e're doing fine, Gertie," said Alvah the next morning. "Why, with Flora sold off, and Skye's people bringing in so much meat, we're going to be ahead. You bet. We'll have airtights and such to sell in Bannack or that new Alder Gulch camp, and they'll fetch fortunes. Sell the wagon and stock and robes too, and we can head back in style, on Holladay's Overland stages."

"The girls are coming along," said Gertrude amiably. "Drusilla is looking nicer each day, and Mary-Rita's holding her tongue. But oh, I'm weary of this."

"It'll be over pretty soon, Mother. We won't be rich, but we'll have comforts. We'll turn heads in Skaneateles. I'm aiming to buy a black surrey and some trotters."

She frowned. "My spirit writers have vanished. I hold the chalk on the slate and nothing happens. Do you suppose that's a bad sign?"

Alvah shrugged. He didn't hold with that nonsense.

He spotted Goldtooth and headed toward her, a little business in mind.

"Say, madam, I'd like to stow my truck in your spare wagon for the crossing. It'll float dry. And of course I'll lend you a team, so we can double-team them across."

"Why Alvah, honey, I've already got two teams."

So that was her angle, he thought. "Well, madam, I thought maybe I could trade two or three airtights for the use. Got some tomatoes and corn."

"Why, honey, the hunters and Mister Skye's ladies have brought so much meat and greens, why, we just don't need—"

"Thought it might be a good angle to trade," he said shortly.

Goldtooth laughed. "Alvah Riddle, you goose. Of course you can use the spare wagon. We all help each other here."

"Well, that's a good thing," he said. "Now I'd like you people to unload my wagon while I harness up. You ladies, and Vanderbilt, Chang, and Skye, why we can do it in no time."

Goldtooth laughed again, and didn't reply. He decided to try Vanderbilt.

"Say, Vanderbilt. I'm borrowing Goldtooth's wagon to float my stuff over, and I sure could use some help unloading and loading. I reckon I could pay you a couple of airtights."

The former gambler looked up from the log where he sat attacking his breakfast. He started to shake his head, and then stopped. "I've changed my name, Alvah," he said mildly. "I'll be there in a minute. If you'd get your team harnessed and pull your wagon next to mine, it'd help."

"That sounds fine, but let's agree on a price first," said Alvah.

Sleeping Bear shook his head. "For help in wilderness, Alvah, there is no price."

Riddle couldn't figure the man's angle, but he didn't argue. He was tempted to ask help harnessing, but decided not to push his luck. In half an hour, the gambler had lifted everything out of Riddle's wagon and set it into the red one, while Alvah directed.

Big Alice harnessed both of Goldtooth's teams, and now they slouched in the traces of Goldtooth's wagon. Alvah thought it was a good angle to let her go first. He'd see how it went before risking his stuff. On the bank

Mister Skye waited, and it startled Alvah to see Mary over on the north bank, wringing water from her doeskin skirt. All of the guide's animals were dripping water and shaking their packs loose over there. Somehow the guide had driven the loose stock across too, including Alvah's ponies.

"Need help, Alice?" asked Sleeping Bear.

"It's my first really big crossing," she said. "Maybe if you'd sit beside me—"

The pair of them drove the loaded red wagon with its ragged sheet down the flat gravel bank and into the swift water, which curled and churned around legs and wheels. As the powerful river pushed and tugged, the going got heavier even for the eight horses and mules. Water crept higher on the wheels, plucking and tilting the wagon, crept up on the red box, splashing and pushing on the upstream side, sucking on the other. The lead team stepped into nothing, splashed almost under, and swam, necks and heads showing. The channel shrank, they found bottom, and bounded in powerful surges toward the far shore, while the teams behind still swam, and the wagon veered crazily downstream, threatening to tip.

The red wagon hit bottom sideways, but the gambler swung the double teams upstream and gradually angled out until the wagon and teams stood dripping in the sun. It worried Alvah. On the far shore, Vanderbilt—what an absurd name he had now—unhitched the teams, clambered up on the lead mule, and swam them back again with Goldtooth and Big Alice whipping the reluctant animals into the water. On the far shore, Drusilla and Mary-Rita emerged from the tarts' wagon. They'd crossed without his permission!

Cussing, he waited for the gambler. In a few minutes the man had the teams hooked to the red wagon, and Alvah drove into the water. His angle was to steer the teams slightly upstream to keep the current from twisting the floating wagon around behind them. It worked. The wagon lurched and bucked beneath him, and at moments the heads of his team dipped clear under water. Horses coughed and sputtered, but eventually he eased the wagon up and let the dripping animals rest. He squirmed back into the wagon to see if his truck was dry. There'd been a small leak, some robes were wet, but he'd dry them out soon enough.

"I'm plumb tuckered out, Vanderbilt. Do you think you could fetch the green wagon for me?" he said, testing his luck.

The soaked gambler stared. "I haven't all my strength back," he said. He shrugged. "What the hell. This is going to be my business, and I'd better learn it."

Triumphantly, Alvah watched from the wagon seat as Vanderbilt unhooked one team and walked it to the gravel bank.

But Mister Skye intervened. "You've had enough, mate," he said to Sleeping Bear. "Riddle, what's back there? An empty wagon?"

"Empty except for Gertrude."

"One team should do," the guide said. He trotted his buckskin into the water, the pony moving calmly under Skye's firm command. Alvah watched the guide swim the pony back to the south bank and then clamber into the wagon seat. He thought he glimpsed Gertrude poke her head out. Mister Skye eased the team into the water, while the buckskin swam along on the downstream side. When water boiled into the box through the gunports Gertrude lumbered out onto the seat next to Skye, and a few minutes later they were across. They'd tackled the wide Yellowstone and won. Alvah exulted. He'd find some angle to make them reload his green wagon—delay usually would do it—and he would get away scot-free.

Water sluiced out of the wagon, down to his gunholes. But the last eight inches lay trapped in his tight wagon box. That was an angle he hadn't thought of. He peered around irritably. Some of the women hustled into dry clothing behind bushes. On the far north bluffs, Chang and his Indian slut sat their horses, watching. Mister Skye pulled off his leggins and twisted the river out of them.

"Say, Vanderbilt. You mind helping me?"

The gambler trotted over, spotted Lake Riddle, and hoorawed.

"I don't see any trout," he yelled.

That drew the rest, and they all flocked to view Alvah's lake.

"Looks like you'll be our water wagon, Riddle," said the guide solemnly.

"Those gunholes are the best angle I ever had," Alvah retorted. He spotted a sandy hump ahead and whipped his team up it until the wagon hung crazily and water gushed from a hole. That drained half of it. Muttering, Alvah dug through his truck in the red wagon, extracted his auger and bit, and drilled two holes in opposite corners through the bed of the green wagon.

The next day, Mister Skye led them wide of the river, around some ravined hills, and then down into the dun valley again. Ahead squatted a vast impenetrable barrier of mountains the guide called the Belts, and Alvah Riddle knew he'd need double teams again, and that meant borrowing, and he bridled at the thought.

Chapter 27

"**H**ey, Celestial! Git! Out! Chop-chop! And take that squaw, too. We don't want your kind in here," said the saloonkeeper.

"I can understand the sentiment," replied Seven-Story. "In Peking, we don't look kindly on white barbarians."

The man gaped through his beard, which rolled in salty waves to his chest.

"How'd you git to talk whiteman like that?"

"When among barbarians, do as the barbarians do," mocked Chang. "You have a crude language, but expressive."

"Well, that don't cut no ice here. We don't fancy the yellow race, horning in on our placers and practicing heathen ways."

"A familiar melody. Has no one another tune? You are most unimaginative."

Seven-Story glanced amiably about this saloon and general store, hastily built of massive logs and without windows for want of glass. The open door plus a single lantern supplied quirky light that cast odd shadows.

The sharp-eyed keep studied him distrustfully, his lips forming words under the straggle of his beard. "I don't cotton to what you're saying," he said. "But maybe you're being high and mighty for a Celestial. Git now, chop-chop. We got a boneyard out back to bury your kind."

"Most cordial of you," said Chang. "Western hospitality is legend."

The barkeep reached beneath his crude bar of rough-sawn slab wood and lifted a sawed-off scattergun.

"Most cordial," said Chang.

"You're a big 'un, but that just means you take more buckshot. Now git, chop-chop."

"You certainly speak a peculiar English," said Chang. "Words that have eluded the Oxford lexicographers. Do you suppose you might offer wayfarers some advice? Or sell an item or two?"

"You got dust?"

"Better than that, I have an eagle and double eagles."

The black bore of the weapon, which had never quite reached Seven-Story's chest, wavered downward.

"Well, be quick about it. Don't want you seen in here, understand. You buy quickie, chop-chop, vamoose, yes?"

"Vamoose is more or less Spanish," said Chang. "This is Gallatin City, is it not? We're with a caravan of wagons bound for Bannack City. We'd thought to go down the Jefferson River, and the Beaverhead, but back ten miles we struck a wagon road heading down the Madison valley. Perhaps you could enlighten us?"

"All of you Celestials? I ain't about to sic dogs on a town."

"Ah, I wish they were all Chinese. But I must report that the caravan has less superior stock. A parlor-house madam and her ladies, from Memphis; some brides and their chaperones from all over; and a stray dog or two."

"Whites then. Come down from Benton," the barkeep said.

"No, up the Yellowstone from Fort Laramie."

"Horseapples, Chinaman. There's no wagon road thataway." He swung his scattergun around.

"It is just as you say," said Seven-Story. "Now then, since you are a perspicacious gentleman, perhaps you will divulge—"

"Cut them Chinee words, or I'll cut your queue."

"Say, now that is original!"

The barkeep peered at Chang, and lowered the weapon. "Sure, take that trail south down the Madison. It heads for the new digs at Alder Gulch. Big strike. They called it Varina, after Jeff Davis's wife. But I heered tell Doc Bissell—he's the miners' judge there—said it ain't gonna be named for a Secesh first lady, and he's labeled it Virginia City, nice and Northern. Go there, and if they don't string up Chinee and squaws, there's a good new wagon road west on the Stinking Water and Beaverhead to Bannack City. Hell of a lot better'n hacking down the Jefferson."

"Much obliged, sir."

"Heered tell there's road agents plundering along there. Likely get your gold and string you up. Unless I do it first."

"You barbarians have a fine sense of humor. I am looking for a few provisions. Some cartridges for a Sharps sixty-caliber; some Spencer cartridges. Potatoes or cabbage for the scurvy. A quart of red-eye, popskull, rattlesnake juice—"

"Show me your gold first."

"Ah, you've heard of quartz gold. Well, I have colt's gold and it'll fill your purse chop-chop. That is an interesting term, chop-chop. I try to master your tongue."

"You makin' fun of me, Celestial."

"Well, if you don't want my trade . . ."

The man sighed, tucked his shotgun in his arm, and began collecting goods. "Got no Sharps sixty, but here's the Spencer. One box. Got no potatoes, but here's cabbage. Two dollars a head. Three dollars for Celestials. How many?"

"Six, at white prices."

"I charge what I charge."

"No tickee, no shirtee," said Chang. He nodded at Buffalo Whiskers, who had been peering wide-eyed into the hostile gloom.

"Hold on, Chinee!" The barkeep was lifting his scattergun. "You kin pay me for my advice."

Chang's shot splintered the stock and bloodied the man's hand. He howled.

"At your service," said Chang. "Most cordial visit."

They rode easily out of the somnolent hamlet. His shot had racketed inside the great log walls, and no one slowed their passage. In moments they escaped the settlement, trotting southeasterly, back to the wagon-road fork where Mister Skye and his party waited.

Gallatin City lay at the three forks of the Missouri, in a breathtaking intermountain valley filled with thick grasses turning dun in the dryness of August. Even now, the tips of the blue ranges that circumscribed the vast basis shone white with last winter's snow. The day shone finer than polished jade, and he heeled his horse into a rack. His smiling bride rode easily beside him through zephyrs—a tall, exquisite woman with features chiseled by the gods, but the whites were too blind to see that. In his arms, she became demanding, mad and delirious, and sometimes comic. Ah, what wouldn't they give for her in the courts of the emperor?

Mister Skye had taken them up a long gentle pass that began just where the Yellowstone curved south into the belly of the mountains, and the teams stood it well as long as they were rested frequently. Near the summit they had double-teamed the wagons the last half mile. On the west slope the descent was so easy they had scarcely paused to lock wheels, but a final sharp grade choked with trees had slowed them. They'd driven along a steep slope that threatened to topple the wagons, and then emerged one sunny afternoon into this valley of the gods. Even Alvah Riddle had exclaimed about the grand vistas, after whining his way up, and whining his way down the mountains.

They were waiting on a sun-swept meadow beside the ruts.

"This goes down the Madison River to the new Alder Gulch camp they're calling Virginia City," Seven-Story explained to Mister Skye. "From there, there's a good wagon road on over to Bannack, down the Stinking Water and up the Beaverhead. No problem except for road agents."

"You get any truck there?"

"We had a slight problem."

Mister Skye grinned. "You solved it satisfactorily?"

"Call me Bloody Hand. Call me Empty Hand. You barbarians are quite expressive in your naming. An improvement over our Lotus Flowers and Crystal Jades. Here's your eagle back. No popskull, no Sharps loads."

"I'm dry as August prairie," Mister Skye muttered. "Well, mates, we'll head for this Alder Gulch digging— Virginia City—and maybe meet up with a husband or two. If not, we'll keep on going to Bannack City. Wagon roads now all the way."

Even Alvah Riddle nodded cheerfully. The man had taken to bouncing and beaming, and inspecting his robes, and peering happily at his tanned and golden brides these last few days.

They drove easily across a shimmering wide valley, and not even the rushing clear creeks dicing the land slowed them in this last rush toward their destinations, and destinies. Chang and Buffalo Whiskers meandered ahead, less alert for hostile Indians here, although the Blackfeet prowled. In the dappled shade of quaking aspens beside a purling white creek, they made tumultuous love, the thunder music of howitzers, then lay stupefied, staring at humped puff clouds. When Chang looked up, it was into the alert shining eyes of three buffalo cows. They camped beside the Madison that night. At dinner, they feasted on tender hump roast, boiled tongue, boudins stuffed with spiced tallow and meat, and wild carrots and onions and camas root Mary scrounged from the verdant land.

This adventure was coming to an end. Chang had no idea what he'd do next, but his golden-bellied beauty would be with him. The earth was vast and wild, and he was unready to become a dutiful courtier in the shadow of the Manchu emperor. Someday he'd spin his tales of this endless wilderness and its wild peoples, and they'd lift fans to lips and whisper him a liar. He laughed easily. Mongol blood coursed his veins, blood that would boil even in the cool shadows of the palace of T'ung Chi.

But first he'd see Goldtooth to Bannack. He'd promised her that, and she'd sealed the contract her own delicious way. There were yet perils, from what the oaf in Gallatin City had told him, and his blood raced at the thought of another fine brawl or three. In the settling dusk, he pulled Buffalo Whiskers to him. He'd change her name when at last they crossed the wide Pacific, and hope the emperor wouldn't steal her.

Mary-Rita was subdued. The moment of truth was racing down upon her. What would Tommy O'Dougherty think? Was he rich? Did this endless land bleed his Irish soul, so he'd become something else? He was probably ugly as sin and mean as a lord, or he wouldn't have got himself a bride by mail. Well, if so, she'd give him a piece of her mind, and if he guzzled ale, she'd have a thing or two to say about it.

Still . . . an Irishman here! She stared nervously at her tanned arms with a summer's gold trapped in them. She'd borrowed Drusilla's ivory-handled looking glass and barely recognized herself. Sunbleached red hair tumbled about her now, and hardship and hunger had chiseled her rectangular face into sharp planes, narrowed her nose and turned her freckles into a single tan mass. Her eyes glistened with light caught from the sunny prairies and long blue mountains. She'd become too good-looking for him! She wouldn't let the likes of a Tommy O'Dougherty, up to his knees in muck, touch a beautiful lass like herself! She'd not say a word to some common potato of a man, no matter what that Alvah Riddle might try to do. She'd find a lord and save herself for him. She'd be a lady, and no blarney from some grubby red-faced mucker would turn her cheek!

Her ma told her once to keep her legs crossed and nothing bad would happen. She practiced crossing her legs, and squeezing her thighs together, back and forth, banging her knees. It'd take more than that mean Tommy O'Dougherty to pry them apart, she thought savagely. And probably not a priest in the whole place. She would just keep her, legs tight, that's what she'd do. It'd take a rich man or a sheriff or official, Catholic, of course . . .

"There's some bushes up there. I'll stop if you want," said Sleeping Bear.

"None of your business!" she howled.

The trail took them over a tumult of low grassy hills, and down into the vast valley of the Madison River, arching south and flanked by long chains of mountain to either side. Puffy clouds dawdled on the peaks to the west, a range Mister Skye called the Tobacco Roots. The trail veered to the western edge of this vast trough, and turned up the valley of a creek barely two feet wide that raced between long grassy slopes dotted with cedar and sagebrush. The land lay naked, and game stayed distant. She'd never seen such a vast tumbled country, and she felt about the size of an ant in it.

They encountered a hard-looking man named Slade building a toll gate at a rocky choke point. A stone cabin stood upslope.

"Four bits a wagon. I cut this road through," he said.

"You're a long way from the Platte," said Skye.

"You're Skye," said Slade.

"Mister Skye."

Slade nodded and let them pass without paying.

The man scared Mary-Rita witless. They probed through hills so barren and foreboding that she thought the world had ceased to be, or maybe this corner was forgotten by God. She blessed herself. At the low divide they paused to rest. Ahead some vast distance lay black mountains, a devil's kingdom for sure. Mister Skye led them toward hell. Massed gray clouds lowered over those mountains, and the high ridges to the south, sawing them off, bellying down upon the gray land like squatting heathen goddesses. Gold! That's what heathen hunted. Father O'Reilly had warned her about greed, and now she smelled greed everywhere. And Tommy O'Dougherty swirled gold there.

They curled down a sharp slope, rough-locking the wagon wheels to slow their descent. From upland grasses they plunged into gulches of alder, lined with pine, and sweeping around one last curve they beheld an astonishing sight, sprawled cabins and huts, dugouts, a main street with a stone building up and scores of board-and-batt ones being erected, steep-roofed with false fronts.

Virginia City. A whole metropolis in September, where none had existed in May.

Everywhere below them men and horses, teams and wagons, swarmed like insects. The sound of hammering lifted to them, and Mary-Rita spotted workmen crawling along walls and beams. She wondered where the sawn wood had come from. Alder Gulch itself curved past the lower end of town, an avenue of bright green alders that shaded the fevered sluicing and panning and rocking of thousands of rough men. Not even the lowering black clouds stayed the feverish swarming of the tiny men below her, gouging gold, guiding giant three-hitch trains drawn by twenty-mule teams from Salt Lake City, throwing together shelter against oncoming winter, buying and selling with a golden dust for money, worth much more than Mister Lincoln's greenbacks.

Somewhere below, Tommy O'Dougherty would probably be washing the gravels. Or maybe he lingered still at Bannack City if he had a good claim there. She had no intention of staying for an hour in this horrible raw place. She'd give him that for starters, she would! Where could she find a priest? She was getting tired of crossing her legs.

Over in the next wagon, Goldtooth laughed. "Oh, we are about to get rich and have fun," she cried. "But maybe Bannack City is bigger and richer. We'll see."

Mrs. Parkins turned wild, peering hot-eyed into the gulch as she stood up the slope in her beautiful doeskin blouse and skirt. Big Alice and Juliet Picard gaped happily.

The shame of it! thought Mary-Rita. And likely Tommy O'Dougherty would prefer such ones to her! Oh, she'd read him her mind, she would! He'd been patronizing them, those evil creatures, instead of saving himself for her. She just knew it! Squandering his gold, wasting his fortune, and not saving a bit of it for her! Oh, she would scold him. He'd have to show her a whole mountain of gold before she'd consent to the sacrament of holy matrimony!

Alvah Riddle's nasal bark snapped her out of her reverie. "You get out of that red wagon, Mary-Rita. We're going in separate. Skye and the sluts, Chang and all, can wait behind. From now on, you keep clear of the bawds and squaws and Chinese and all like that."

Sleeping Bear, beside her, laughed. But it made sense. Lord God in heaven and all the holy saints, she didn't want to ride into this Virginia City in a red wagon!

Alvah skipped around his green wagon, unlocking the braked wheel, and they clattered recklessly into town. Amazingly, Mister Skye halted the rest above town. Mary-Rita felt ashamed—it was almost like betraying friends—but relieved too. Now she was in respectable company, the respectable Drusilla beside her, and the Riddles. Protestants, but she'd escape that soon enough. She pressed her knees together so tight her bladder hurt.

Wallace Street, a crude sign said. There was another rutted thoroughfare running parallel down in a shallow gulch to her right; still others lining the hill to her left. Riddle's mules and horses jangled down the rutted street, past raw plank buildings, log saloons and cabins, an astonishing mercantile called Pfouts and Russell, made of hewn rock. Gusts of icy rain dashed her face but she refused to crawl under the wagon sheet. Alvah Riddle was fairly dancing on the seat, smiling and whistling. Miner and workmen spotted the women and crowded close, galvanized by the sight of white women here, only months after this had been utter wilderness. Bale of Hay Saloon. Dance and Stuart. Idaho Hotel, a squat log structure.

Full of bedbugs, she thought. Another one, the Virginia
Hotel, still roofless, its walls wet with rain but the sign in
front new and silvery with water. Mud stuck to wheels
now, making them hiss. Rough bearded men in shapeless
black pants, slouched hats, flannel shirts with faded red
underwear peeking from the throat, and square-toed
brogans. All staring. Ox teams drooped in their yokes,
chained to battered wagons with rain-sagged gray sheets.
Whirls of cold water splashed her face, but still Alvah
drove, his itchy fingers making his mules mince, showing
off, flaunting the rarest merchandise in the wilderness, in
this camp.

"Whatcha got there, friend?" yelled an amiable young
man whose blond hair glowed even in the gray light. He
walked lithely beside the wagon now, peering first at
Mary-Rita, then Drusilla, then the Riddles, his eyes never
stopping.

"Brides!" crowed Alvah like an inflated rooster.
"Spoken-for brides from the states. All spoken-for, fella,
but I'll take your name and put it on the list. And robes—
I've got buffler robes, two ounces of dust for a whole
robe, ounce and a half for a split."

"Name's Ives, George Ives. Put me on your list. And
yours?"

"Riddle," Alvah replied. "Here or in Bannack City."

Mary-Rita and Drusilla glanced at each other. The
lithe blond man wasn't named O'Dougherty or Rasmussen. Drusilla looked tense, with worry lines radiating
from her mouth. Like Mary-Rita, she refused to take
cover, and gaped at this wild raw place half horrified,
half fascinated, water dripping from her chin and turning her sun-streaked hair black.

On they went, down the gentle slope. New York Clothing Store. Variety Store. Gohn and Kohrs butcher shop.

A turnoff with a dripping sign pointing toward Highland, Pine Grove, and Summit, up the gulch. Nevada, Central, Adobetown, Junction City down the gulch. Mechanical Bakery. Morier's Saloon. California Blacksmith and Wagon Shop. Gem Saloon. Fairweather District. Oliver Stagecoach Line. Peabody and Caldwell. At the base of Wallace, Riddle swung his team around while three blue-jacketed Celestials watched, and onto the lower street, Cover, gawking, hunting miners' shacks and dugouts. But this was not a respectable place. Dusky women lolled here under porches, veiled only by water. He wheeled the wagon up a cross-street, Van Buren, to the safety of Wallace, and pulled up before the Idaho Hotel, which lay squat and cold under the sheeting deluge. He glimpsed Mister Skye and his squaw, the bawds, the Chinese, swinging over to Cover Street, and Daylight Gulch.

Clouds rolled through them now, and Mary-Rita wondered what Alvah would do. He needed to find both of two men, both miners. Men who owed him five hundred dollars in gold, upon delivery. Mary-Rita found herself clenching Drusilla's icy wet hand for comfort.

Chapter 28

Fresh snow bleached the surrounding black peaks and even the lower barren hills, reminding Goldtooth that winter would soon grip this high country of far northwest Idaho Territory. So much to do, and she scarcely knew where to start. She'd trade the robes first, she thought. The ladies needed dresses and underthings, flour and sugar, coffee and tea.

What a mad, vibrant, fascinating raw place! Some called it Fourteen Mile City, because miners toiled from the head of Alder Gulch clear down to the Stinking Water River, with Virginia City somewhere near the middle. A place where a sporting lady could mint a fortune in weeks, but also a place that might not last. These placer camps vanished as fast as they sprang to life, after miners had panned and sluiced and gouged nugget gold and dust from the gravels and bars.

Last night, in the midst of that violent storm, Mister Skye took them into town, his face pinched and suspicious. She could see he didn't like places like this. Mary looked fearful and ill at ease. Sheeting cold rain had chased men off the streets, but those who braved the wet stared at Goldtooth's wagons and the women in the seats, uncertainty written on their faces. Were these women in water-blackened skin dresses and beaded skin blouses respectable? The gawking men couldn't tell, and it amused Goldtooth. Let them wonder for a bit. She read the yearning in their eyes though, and their wants pierced to her. Mister Skye had squinted narrowly through the drip, his gaze clashing with mercantiles and miners, ox teams and log cabins. Upslope from the main street rose the beginnings of permanent homes. Down on the next muddy street to the right, though, squatted lines of shanties and tents. He swung that way.

This gummy street was different. A hurdy-gurdy, the Virginia Dance, stretched back from the thoroughfare, wet logs and a peaked canvas roof, and an ornate sign promoting four-bit dances. Goldtooth laughed. What a way to make a living! Those poor dears clung to respectability they didn't have, and wore themselves out for pennies. She found the line across Daylight Creek: shacks, tents, and a few larger houses half built. Icy rain had chased the girls inside like the whine of a street preacher, and the travelers splashed through the raw and sullen district appalled.

She wondered whether she could even find men to build her a parlor house. The thought of her gorgeous red-brick building in Memphis brought pangs of regret. How could she afford such a thing here? How could she and her ladies even find comfort in a place like this with winter lowering over them? Maybe Bannack City, almost two years old now, might be better. Still, countless males tore at gravel here, thousands of men and almost no women, and most of these burly rough men had leather pokes full of dust. She laughed. There was no call to be gloomy, not when a fortune lay at hand!

Mister Skye found a small bench of level land just west of town, near the road to Nevada City, that night. His face became a hard mask as he studied the town, its toughs, the shanties of flinty miners around the edges, and the hardness didn't soften until they were a few hundred yards out. The bench had been grazed hard, and little was left for the mules and horses, but it'd have to do. No one except Chang had money for a livery barn or feed.

"I'd suggest you stay here in the lodge tonight," the guide said. "Too cold and wet to cook out there, and your wagons will be plenty chill even if you sleep under robes. In the morning, when it's warmer and drier, do your dickering or whatever you need to do."

That seemed agreeable to them all. Mary and Buffalo Whiskers managed to find firewood in a gulch, peeling back wet bark to make kindling from dry wood underneath. Only Chang prowled, and had returned quickly after a look at the main street. He seemed uncommonly silent to Goldtooth.

"Have a bad time, honey?"

"I tried to buy feed at Boyd and Smith Livery," he said after a moment's silence.

No one spoke for a while.

"It'll take Riddle a day or two to find out whether those husbands are in this camp or Bannack," the guide said. "That'll leave you time to get at your own business. In the morning we'll make camp back away from town, find grass. The farther back, the better we'll be."

He glanced solemnly at Mary and Buffalo Whiskers, who were drying their hair close to the lodgefire.

Goldtooth marveled at the warmth and comfort of the tipi, and understood at last how a man like Mister Skye could choose to live in a skin tent like this. She drifted to sleep easily, and the last thing she remembered was Mister Skye sitting up in the glow of the embers, his Sharps across his lap. No Jawbone lived to warn him, and he wasn't taking chances.

In the bright morning, with ice glinting like diamonds from every shrub, tree, and building, she and Sleeping Bear drove the red wagon up Wallace to Dance and Stuart's big log mercantile for some trading. Men stared but obviously didn't know what to make of the buckskin-clad twosome. Let them wonder! she thought.

They entered a long narrow log cavern, gloomy after the glare of the sun. Few shelf goods lined the walls, and even the rough tables down the center were bare: the camp devoured everything as fast as freight teams hauled it almost four hundred miles from Salt Lake City. All the better, she thought. If this, the town's biggest emporium had nothing, the smaller places would have less. At one side a bootblack stand projected into the narrow building, presided over by a cadaverous clubfooted dirty man with stained fingers. He studied Goldtooth with calculating eyes.

"I'm Dance," said a brown-bearded young man in a gray flannel shirt. "Need help?" He stared at Goldtooth, unable to make up his mind about her. Sleeping Bear puzzled him just as much.

"Do you trade, honey?"

Dance's eyes went flat and cautious. "Likely," he replied.

"I have a dozen tanned robes. A few pair of moccasins and some fringed elkskin shirts, all Arapaho."

"I can sell pretty near anything here. Good robes fetch three or four dollars at Benton. The shirts—I'll have to look."

"No," she said. "Not three or four for the robes. I'll sell them off my wagon in the streets for much more, honey."

He stared at her. "Let's go look. That your red outfit there?"

"All mine, honey."

She held back robes for herself and her girls and sold everything else. He offered her ten a robe, and twenty-five dollars for the rest, if she'd take it all out in trade rather than cash.

"Suits me, honey," she said. The storekeep became more and more edgy.

"I'll fetch George Lane to help," he said. Dance, the lame bootblack, and Sleeping Bear carted robes to his plank counters while Goldtooth prowled the two aisles, finding little she wanted. In the end she settled for bolts of navy and gray woolen broadcloth, muslin for petticoats, canvas, needles and thread, small sacks of beans, sugar, flour, coffee, a few sprouting potatoes, and ready-made highbutton shoes for herself, in black, and a pair for Mrs. Parkins, who wore her size.

"Is there a dressmaker here?" she asked.

Dance shook his head. "No . . . might be one or two

women who could fashion a dress, but Bannack City's the place. Several fine ladies there—" He cut himself off suddenly.

"I run a parlor house, honey. Which place, Bannack or here, is the place to be?"

Dance stiffened, flustered, and peered about the empty store, seeking the funneling ears of customers and finding none.

"This is a rich strike," he said. "Never seen the like. No telling how long it'll last, though. These placer diggings don't settle into keeper towns like quartz mines. Bannack's got quartz, and lots of gold still, though half the town stampeded over here last June. Depends on what you want, ah, ma'am. Fast money here, comfort over there. Maybe they'll find quartz here soon."

"Thanks a bunch, honeypie," she said. She felt Dance relaxing behind her as she and Sleeping Bear clambered into the red wagon and set off for the line.

They halted the mules before the only substantial building, a narrow log affair with lime mortar, a sawn-wood-roofed porch, and a peaked plank roof covered with tar-coated canvas. The morning had scarcely begun and she knew she'd awaken someone. But the Life never stopped for sleep. A place was always open; a lady always available. Leaving Sleeping Bear with the wagon and team, she dodged a puddle and entered. A single tiny window doled grudging light upon a cramped front parlor sided by wooden benches, like a jail cell. The door triggered a small bell, but then silence struck her. She smelled sour whiskey and lilac.

She sat on a bench. Back there, the madam or one of the girls would struggle awake, throw on a wrapper, and scuff in slippers out here to see what sort of male wanted sport at eight in the morning.

A buxom blond materialized, sleepy-eyed, in an open gray wrapper. She seemed surprised to find a woman.

"I'm Nell. Nellie. Strumpet Nellie," she said. "My house here. You here on business or pleasure or both?"

"Goldtooth Jones, from Memphis, honey," she said, rising. "I'm in the Life. I have three ladies out in a wagon."

"I can use you. Always need more girls," said Nell. "Are they pretty?"

Goldtooth grinned. "Knockouts. And they all love the life and won't go running off. But honey, I'm just here to find out stuff, if you don't mind. Like what's the best place to be, Bannack or here? And how can I get a place of my own built?"

Nell laughed sleepily. "Look, sister, you can't get a place built. No workmen will build it. Every goddamn one is building stores or miner cabins or outhouses or driving freight wagons or putting up saloons . . . You think I make money? I do, sister. More dust than I ever seen, but I'm in the hole. I got a note on this place I can't pay off in two years, just because I had to bribe workers—fifty dollars a day, fifty dollars!—to throw this dump up. Makes me want to go back to Bannack. This damned dump. I still got my place there, but it'd be slow now—"

"You've a place in Bannack?"

"Yeah, nice log building, parlor in front all fixed up, cozy little bar to serve spirits, six cribs, plus my private quarters, barn in back for horse and carriage, plus a room there for my houseman. I sure don't know why I left, especially with winter coming on."

"Would you rent, honey?"

"I'd prefer to sell. Long as I'm here, I don't see hanging on to property there. Bannack's down to a thousand people now."

"I'm interested, honey. We lost everything on the trail and I can't pay at once. But in six months—"

"I've heard that song before, Mrs. Jones. I want dust, and now. But if you stick around here, that's just more competition . . . Tell you what: I can tell from the girls. Bring the girls over and let me see the merchandise, and I'll tell you what I'll do. Maybe I'll rent. I've got a man there keeping the place. Some miner who couldn't pan gold out of his navel. Amos Rasmussen. He came to me almost busted after scraping dust off a poor digging, and spent his poke on my girls. So I'm paying him a dollar a day to keep the place. Maybe I'll rent. You'll need a man anyway, I suppose."

Rasmussen's name seemed vaguely familiar to Goldtooth. He would solve another problem, now that Sleeping Bear wasn't available and poor Blueberry lay on his scaffold.

"I'll rent," she said. "And buy in six months, Nell. And we'll be in Bannack, not competing with you here."

Nell retreated into herself. "So damned early I don't have my head on," she muttered. "I'll sell. You pay me five hundred a month for five months and it's yours."

"That's a lot. And I haven't even seen it—"

"Take it or leave it." She yawned.

Goldtooth took it. Five rough months. But she knew exactly what she'd do. Parade Mrs. Parkins through this camp and Bannack until they knew of her from one end of Idaho to the other. And then charge three or four ounces of dust.

Alvah put them up in the Idaho Hotel. He hated to squander the cash, but he wanted the girls bathed and fresh and healthy, and besides, Gertie begged him for the comfort.

It'd be a good angle, though, to make them grateful. "I don't normally waste money like this," he said to Drusilla. "But we got some celebrating to do, and I guess Alvah Riddle can afford to put his brides up comfortable. You just remember that I never stint on comforts. Now I'll pay the extry four bits for a hot bath—you and Mary-Rita can share—and you can git yourselves all fixed up, dresses flatironed and all, whilst I go hunt for Rasmussen and O'Dougherty, if they're in this camp."

Drusilla nodded curtly, and Alvah skittered out to find a livery for his mules and horses. At Morier's Saloon he invested in popskull, privately cussing the two-dollar price, and the price of everything in this camp, and beckoned the barkeep.

"Say, my friend," he whispered confidentially, "I'm new to the diggings, and I've some special merchandise for two men—one named Rasmussen, and the other O'Dougherty. Now how does a gent find these boys in a place like this? I'll make it worth your while," he added craftily.

"Buster, there's three, four thousand men in this gulch and more pouring in daily. It runs from the summit, way the hell south of here, down to the Stinking Water. You'll just have to start at the top and start asking. Might take a few days."

"No message place?" asked Alvah. "No one leaves his name anywheres?"

The barkeep shrugged. "Never heard of either one. You might try the other saloons. Gem, Bale of Hay . . ."

"I'll get cracking," said Alvah. "Say, if I can't find these boys, I've some hot merchandise here. Brides. Both guaranteed respectable, unsullied, know what I mean. Now, for a price I'll—you be thinking of the right customers, eh? I got the rarest thing in the whole camp, and

I don't make matches cheap. Understand? I'll pay you a finder's fee."

The barkeep stared. Alvah downed his popskull and sidled out. At the Bale of Hay he got lucky.

"O'Dougherty? Sure, there's one here, man. Thomas. Tommy. He spreads a little dust in here most evenings. He's staked one of the best bars in the gulch, half a mile up from here. In fact, just above Bill Fairweather's discovery claim. Big brown-haired fellow, happy as a king. He's got so much dust he stores it in Dance and Stuart's safe."

"That's the one!" exclaimed Alvah. "I've got something special for him, yes, special merchandise. Say, you've never heard of this Rasmussen?"

"Can't say as I have. You got special merchandise for him, too?"

"Brides!"

He trotted back to the hotel, and pounded on the women's cubicle. "Be ready, Mary-Rita," he cried. "I'll take you to O'Dougherty in the morning."

"I'll tell her," said Drusilla wearily, through the door. "She's in the bath parlor out back."

After a night of no-quarter bloodletting, in which the bedbugs emerged victorious, Alvah shepherded Mary-Rita up a raw road gouged out of red earth, to the gravel bar worked by her intended. He permitted no one else to come, not wanting troubles or diversions. Mary-Rita never opened her mouth, and followed along dutifully in a fresh-pressed pink dimity dress, scrubbed and tanned.

"Now you be nice, Mary-Rita. Remember, I'm Cupid."

He found O'Dougherty easily enough. He had the look of a boxer, and worked shirtless even in the cool air.

"Yas, I'm Tommy O'Dougherty," he boomed in a laughing basso voice. His bright eyes swept Mary-Rita, who stood shivering and speechless.

"I'm Riddle. The broker. The little old matchmaker and happiness man. Well now, I've brought the little lady. Here she be, clear across the continent. Straight from Ireland. Unspoiled—you can have her examined at your expense, and then tie the knot. Of course, I'll need my contract fee first, five hundred in dust, plus a few minor expenses—"

But O'Dougherty's eyes were on Mary-Rita, his gaze sweeping from her sun-gilded carrot hair to the square tanned and freckled planes of her upthrust face, to the fine silky curves that filled out her dress. A grin crinkled his tanned face. White even teeth showed. His brown eyes danced.

"Would you be marrying a rich mick, Mary-Rita Flaherty?" he asked, some comic light in his voice.

"Tommy O'Dougherty, I wouldn't marry you for all the silk in China. Imagine my marrying a man with no shirt! Shame upon you, you ugly beast. I'll not marry the likes of you, you blasted miserable pig."

O'Dougherty laughed.

"And furthermore there's no priest, and you'll have me living in sin, you would. I won't do it, me pure and all, keeping me legs crossed three thousand miles, and now you want to be hauling me off and making babies without even—"

"Why, Mary-Rita, that's a good thing. There's a priest rode into camp a few days ago, held a Mass first thing and married up six miners and their women in holy matrimony. He's a Jesuit, Joseph Giorda, and he's in town. Why, lass, we'll go visit him directly."

"Not on your life!" she cried. "You build me a house first, with glass and lace curtains and doilies on the stuffed chairs."

"Why, Mary-Rita Flaherty, I've done it. I've hired it built while I've mucked gold. Would you come see it, lass?"

"Don't you touch me," she said. "I'd rather die. You take a bath first. Imagine kissing the likes of you, Tommy O'Dougherty!"

Alvah Riddle danced on one foot and then the other, and needed a bush to relieve himself. "Now just a minute, just a minute. I can't release this little lady until I'm paid. Cupid's fee," he said, chortling.

"Where are you from, Mary-Rita Flaherty?"

"Tipperary, and what's it to you? What's wrong with Tipperary, may I ask? Aren't I good enough? You, putting on airs, spending your dust on scarlet women, throwing away money on fancy houses, and drinking yourself into a wreck of a man. I know all about you, Tommy O'Dougherty!"

The miner laughed, a fine roar up from the belly, and he slipped his hard brown hand around her slim one.

"I'm a lost soul, sure I am," he replied. "I think I'm going to love you, Mary-Rita Flaherty."

"I won't love you until after we're married," she replied. "And then you'll stop drinking, stop smoking, and stop going to the Bale of Hay Saloon."

"Let's find the priest," he said, reaching for his shirt. "I've got to pay Cupid here, so we'll be walking to Dance and Stuart's."

"I'll give the bride away!" cried Alvah.

"That won't be necessary, Cupid," replied Tommy O'Dougherty. "I'll pay you now, and that'll be it."

Chapter 29

Drusilla wept through the wedding, more for herself than for Mary-Rita, who beamed pugnaciously through it all. The bride looked ferociously happy, and the groom kept grinning and winking at his mining pals, who had gathered in Tommy O'Dougherty's fine cabin to help him solemnize a union.

Father Giorda looked faintly skeptical about all this, but rattled his way through the ceremony and the Mass with aplomb, after a private hour counseling the betrothed. Alvah Riddle, polished up to a fine gloss and sporting his Sunday suit, smelling of camphor, fairly floated, enjoying his roll as matchmaker and Cupid and successful entrepreneur. Gertrude had spiffed up too, and sat at the rear, a dowager lump, faintly put off by the Romish mumbo jumbo. Mister Skye, Mary, and Sleeping Bear had come to the celebration, but the sporting women stayed discreetly away, and Chang, who had encountered rank hostility in the camp, found other things requiring his attention.

Alvah had plenty to crow about, Drusilla thought bitterly. That morning, just before he was about to ride up and down the gulch seeking Rasmussen, Goldtooth had pulled him aside with her news. A gent named Amos Rasmussen was in Bannack, a caretaker for an empty house of ill fame. The news hit Drusilla like a dropping guillotine blade. In the crumbling moments that followed, all her dreams and hopes disintegrated into dust. The dream of love, of respect, of a good marriage with pleasures of the heart, of companionship, of joy of soul and body, of a part in a new community, a happy home, a place for her

books, a hand to hold in the night, a kiss at dawn, a sharing of all that she was, a husband in whom she might find
pride . . . all gone in one sagging, caving minute.

She had not known whether she could bear to watch
Mary-Rita's wedding, but the girl pressed her, and Drusilla
had come with soul and limbs heavier than lead. She'd
started this long journey an ugly duckling expecting
nothing much, and resigned to a bluestocking life. But
along the trail her hopes had risen, not only because her
face and figure had changed, but because the long trek
had to lead to something good. Surely a woman who had
set her small world aside for this, a woman who dared and
dreamed, would find goodness and mercy and love at the
end of this long rainbow. But no. She grieved. She was
widowed before she was wedded. Shorn, doomed. She
barely managed to compose herself through the ceremony, and sometimes she failed, and dabbed wet cheeks
with a lilac-scented handkerchief from her dowry trunk.

It never occurred to her to break the contract. That
wasn't in her. The best she might manage would be a
shameful divorce and escape to nowhere, her life a ruin.
Even as Mary-Rita and Tom exchanged vows, Drusilla's
mind turned to Parsimony McGahan, and suddenly she
craved him. Ruthlessly she'd driven every vagrant
thought of him from her mind. She managed days on the
trail when she didn't think of Parsimony at all. But now
the image of him flooded her soul, and she remembered
his every word, and the light in his eyes, and the dimming flame when she told him she had committed herself. Now she had only the book of Browning poems to
console herself. It was something anyway. After this, she
would flee to the wagon and read them, and remember
him. He was so far away, far far away, in a place with the
same name as this . . .

Then they were all congratulating the bride and groom, handshakes and hugs. Drusilla watched, as if from a distant planet, in a fog of despair. She drifted to the door of Tom O'Dougherty's solid cottage and stepped into bright sun, but Mary-Rita caught her there, hugged her and wept.

"I'll miss you," cried the bride. "We came a long way together, we did, and it all worked out. It'll all work out for you, Drusilla."

"No, it won't work out."

"Come visit. The O'Doughertys will be servin' tea any afternoon."

Drusilla summoned the courage then to congratulate the groom, smile, and slip into the silence of the day. Mister Skye, Mary, and Sleeping Bear all stared at her, she knew, for they had heard Goldtooth's news.

They all drifted toward the wagons. Nothing kept them in Virginia City now. Alvah Riddle danced and skittered behind them, beaming at passersby, doffing his brushed black bowler, smiling his toothy smile from distended pink cheeks.

The lithe blond man who had waylaid them in the rain caught up with Alvah now.

"Looks like you found one of the grooms and had a little wedding," he said amiably.

"Indeed I did," boasted Alvah. "Thomas O'Dougherty, on up the gulch. I believe he's a solid citizen."

"Indeed he is," said the golden-haired man. "He's staked one of the richest bars in the gulch, and coining money."

"He sure is! Paid me my whole fee without a quibble. I charge plenty, you know. He handed over all that dust because I brought him a great bride. Only the best. What did you say your name was?"

"Ives. George Ives," said the man. "Come from Wisconsin, little place you never heard of called Racine."

"Well, Ives," said Alvah. "I have the other groom located in Bannack City. Rasmussen. I tell you, this is a great business if you have the knack and know the angles. Why, my Gertie and me, we'll clear a young fortune, more than most men earn in three years. Brides, and a fine sideline, picked up prime buffalo robes. I sold those for a premium price, too, lots of dust."

"You'd better be careful," said Ives. "This camp has its toughs and thugs. When you get to Bannack, you look up the sheriff, Henry Plummer. He'll look after you."

"Good idea," said Alvah. "That's what the law is for, protecting folks."

George Ives grinned, raked Drusilla with veiled eyes, and ambled off.

Drusilla peered up the long slope at O'Dougherty's cottage, saw the bride and groom standing in the door seeing the last of their guests off. Then the door closed, and Mr. and Mrs. O'Dougherty were alone inside. Drusilla wept, tears sweeping her cheeks as they reached Wallace Street.

"Come along, little lady," said Alvah. "I'll fetch my wagon from the livery barn, while you get your things together at the Idaho. Cheer up now; bliss will be yours in no time."

She sighed, wanting somehow to stay close to Mister Skye.

"Want to talk with you later," said the guide.

She nodded, and made her feet go toward the hotel, walking beside Gertrude. Across Wallace, Goldtooth and Mrs. Parkins promenaded in their beautiful Arapaho doeskin clothing, richly beaded and quilled, turning male heads with every step. Goldtooth was grinning;

Mrs. Parkins leveled smoldering gray eyes upon stupefied burly men who didn't know what to make of the pair.

An hour later Mister Skye's entourage swung west down Alder Gulch, with Alvah Riddle's wagon a discreet hundred yards behind because he didn't want to associate too closely with the red wagons and packmules and travois-laden horses ahead. Drusilla did not sit out on the seat. She curled into her blankets in the shadow of the wagon, and hid her tears from Alvah and Gertrude.

He led them along a good stagecoach road that ran down the alder-strewn gulch between barren broad hills. The bottoms swarmed with rough bearded men, panning, gouging, shoveling gravel into wooden rockers and long toms. They rolled through Nevada City and Central; past Adobetown and the Granite Creek district. On a wide flat, they pulled aside to let a Peabody and Caldwell Concord stage rattle through, swaying on its leather braces. From above, the shotgun messenger stared at them from flinted eyes.

Mister Skye sank into melancholy. The men who gouged these gravels gouged his heart. Settlement would arrive on the heels of these industrious diggers, and something dear to Mister Skye would be forever lost. He'd never been a part of the United States, and hadn't even seen it except for one journey to the frontier city of St. Louis. He'd left Victoria's England behind, but was no more a Yankee than Chang. But the bloody Yanks were swarming, both Northern and Southern varieties.

There'd be no game for miles in either direction. He knew some of these people did nothing but supply the camp with meat they shot in distant hills. The bawds had grub now, and he and Mary would sup at their table, along with Chang. Mister Skye had hung on to his thin eagle. It'd buy Sharps cartridges in Bannack, but little more. He hoped there'd be enough to lubricate his parched throat, just a bit. He'd lost everything this trip. Bullock would extend him a little credit back in Laramie, but that was all he could count on. Maybe, just maybe, he'd winter with Victoria and the Kicked-in-the-Bellies. His wives would love that.

The thought turned his mind to Jawbone, and the bitterness seeped through him again, the bitterness of losing that great horse and treasured friend to the Crows, to Victoria's own people. The buckskin pony he rode was a good horse, carrying him smoothly along this final stretch, but it wasn't Jawbone, and wouldn't go to war like Jawbone. He knew, hollowly, that Jawbone would not be replaced. He felt too old to start training a colt the way he'd trained Jawbone long ago.

Chang and his tall bride rode close now, subdued by the rank hostility he'd discovered in Virginia City. The mandarin's face had become secretive and Mister Skye privately raged. Civilization brought hatreds and divisions. His memory whirled back to the sprawling rendezvous of the mountain men, wild times among happy barbarians as varied and colored as Joseph's Coat, and as bonded as brawling brothers. Ending, all of it faded away now, amidst these swarms of pick-and-shovel men crawling the gulch, bunched along this road.

They reached Pete Daley's ranch and stagecoach stop at twilight, and he decided to camp there for the night. Daley's place was a two-story log affair with a roofed verandah on one side. Tough-looking gents lounged about the porch. The upstairs room seemed to be a dance hall of some sort. The scratch of fiddle music drifted to him, and in the ambered windows he caught glimpses of bearded men and scrawny women. He wondered where the women had come from and what sort of place this might be.

Two of the loungers unfolded from the verandah and floated across the twilight.

"You putting up here?" asked one. Mister Skye peered into the flat eyes of a rough dark giant. The other was younger and lighter.

"We thought we might."

"Pasture's grazed down, but we have prairie hay. The stagecoach stock takes all we can get. Four bits an animal. You'll have to makeshift the rest. Place there's a saloon and dance hall. Ladies welcome."

Some sharp intuition stole through Mister Skye. "I guess we'll go on ahead a way," he said. "Most of us don't have scratch for a feed bill."

"Now hold up, Skye," yelled Alvah. "This here's a lively looking place, and a bit of civilization isn't going to hurt anyone after months on the trail. Right, Gertie?"

Mister Skye ignored him, and addressed the heavy rough one: "What did you say your name was?"

The man stared at him. "Boone Helm. This other is Jack Gallagher."

He'd never heard of either, but he knew the type.

"I reckon we'll go ahead to grass."

"Mister Skye," said Goldtooth, "we don't have a plugged nickel for hay, but maybe we could make a little ol' bargain with these gents. Listen to the fiddle!"

The guide didn't like it a bit. Beside him Mary frowned, and Chang and Buffalo Whiskers sat their horses silently. "We'll go on ahead a mile or so for grass," he said abruptly.

But here, away from wilderness and back among people, his command had evaporated.

"Boone Helm," Goldtooth said cheerily, "if you're feelin' your oats, honey, we'll make us a little trade, oats for oats."

"Let's go with Mister Skye," said Drusilla sharply from the green wagon.

"Now hush, little lady," said Alvah. "I'll buy some feed, and we'll just have us a whirl up there. I'll show you off, just in case this Rasmussen fellow can't come up with—"

"I do not wish to be shown off."

"Now see here. It's in the contract that—"

"I'm coming with you, Mister Skye," she said, stepping down from the wagon. Riddle caught her but she wrenched free.

"Well, honeys, me and the ladies are stayin' for a little light entertainment, and the Riddles too. I guess we'll see you down the trail a bit in the morning."

"As you wish," said Mister Skye curtly.

Trouble here. His nerves tingled with it. He touched heels to his buckskin and rode into the thickening night, with the amber lights fading behind him. Drusilla walked because the three wagons stayed at Daley's.

A mile ahead he pulled off the two-rut road into a star-washed meadow beside the Stinking Water. It seemed a good enough place, with grass and firewood, and enough open space to prevent surprises. Under a sliver moon, Mary silently erected the lodge, while Chang and Buffalo Whiskers made camp.

Too late, Skye remembered the bawds had whatever grub there was. There might be some jerky in one of Victoria's parfleches, but that'd be it.

Chang approached softly. "I'm going back. But not on the white stallion. Mind if I borrow one of your dark ponies?"

"One Chinese against many."

"One mandarin warrior."

"Helm's a murderer."

"How do you know that?"

"I know it."

Chang stared into the murk. "My little adventure must end happily. What point is there in protecting these ladies of the night across fifteen hundred miles of wilderness only to fail them among the barbarians?" The mock was back in his voice.

"It's Riddle who's in trouble."

Chang laughed. "How do you keep such a one out of trouble?"

He saddled a bay that stood like a shadow in the dark, and rode quietly back, on unshod hooves.

Skye picketed the horses and dug through the parfleches, finding nothing, and hunkered into the cool grass.

"We're going hungry," he said to Drusilla.

"I can bear it."

"Then you're stronger that I am. Miss Dinwiddie, I want to talk."

"About Rasmussen."

"No, not really. About slavery, and contracts that most courts would throw out the window."

"I'm obligated—" she began.

"I'm not going to let it happen, if it comes to that. I don't think it will. The man apparently squandered his last dime, and hasn't the will or the means to make a living."

"In that case, Mister Riddle has the right to find another—maybe someone better—"

Mister Skye laughed heartily. "You're no abolitionist, but I sure am," he said. "I run my own underground railroad."

A wry smile spread across her moon-touched face. "A few weeks ago I would have stormed at you. I would have insisted on meeting my obligations . . . and ending my life." She paused, flinging herself back on the grass. "Railroad me, Mister Skye."

They laughed quietly, until Mary sat down, frowning, mystified. And then all three laughed. Buffalo Whiskers emerged from the lodge, joined them, and laughed because the others did.

Nothing happened.

The night-peace was broken by two hastening riders going west. With Jawbone dead, Mister Skye's mountain senses had gradually returned, and he slept cat-light, wakening at the slightest change of rhythm in the gloom.

A Bannack-bound Oliver coach awakened him just at sunrise. He pulled aside his doorflap to watch it rumble off into the morning silence. His belly protested its hollowness and made him sour.

An hour or so later, not long after Mary had broken his camp and loaded the lodge on the travois, the wagons rolled in, Big Alice and Sleeping Bear driving the red ones, Alvah the other. Alvah looked gray. Big Alice and Sleeping Bear looked weary and bag-eyed. Chang rode with them, looking taut.

"You missed the fun, Skye," said Alvah. "Not the most respectable place in the world, but we all had a whirl."

"Is that what you call it?" said Goldtooth, yawning. "Mister Skye, honey, you missed the party. I'd sure like to sleep in this mornin', but that damned Sleeping Bear made us all git—"

"It's a long way to Bannack City," growled Mister Skye. He pulled out ahead of them, leading the weary caravan one more leg. His stomach hurt, but that was nothing new. A thousand times, in the high country, cold and hot, his stomach had demanded food.

His sleep-robbed party strung out behind him, Drusilla

back in the green wagon and looking brighter, Chang, Buffalo Whiskers, and Mary dozing in their saddles, Big Alice
and Sleeping Bear rocking half-awake in their seats. They
forded the Stinking Water, cut west, passed another stage
stop, and nooned near Dempsey's ranch, in a broad valley
guarded by blue ramparts now dusted white. With some of
the bawds' grub in his gut, he felt better. The drawn look of
hunger had slipped away from the faces of his women, too.
Goldtooth joked about how her ladies had paid for hay and
spirits, while Gertrude Riddle listened dourly.

"It sure enough was fun," concluded the madam.
"You're just an old worrywart, Mister Skye."

"That's what you employed me to be."

In fact he was worrying more than ever. He alone in
this party stayed alert and ready. The others weaved
in their seats, reins loose in hand, scarcely caring whether
they rolled anywhere. Even Chang catnapped on his white
stallion.

The guide didn't like it, this vulnerable procession
spread out loosely behind him because no one remained
alert enough to keep the wagons close. He fought back
sleep himself, wiped his face with cold water from springs
and creeks, and finally trotted back to the wagons, growling at the drivers, demanding the customary care and
wariness. He stomped out of his mind the bad feeling
choking him, the sense of trouble crawling down his gut.
Only yawns cleaved the afternoon. Maybe he worried
too much, he thought, eyeing the still blue peaks and the
quiet dun grasslands cupped in the valley.

Late that day they struck the rippling Beaverhead and
followed it south along well-worn ruts. A Virginia-bound
Peabody stage creaked by, followed by a party of Ger-
man miners leading packmules, who saluted them in a
strange tongue.

Ahead loomed a squat craggy landmark, Beaverhead Rock, or Point of Rock as it was called sometimes. The giant rockpile reared up in the dry valley as if thrown from some distant mountain by a god. The sun lay flat, and the pile of rock flared into orange and black chevrons. Nothing moved in this dry sage-packed bottom. He would camp up the Beaverhead a way, and they'd be lucky to scrounge enough dead sagebrush to build a decent cook-fire.

An innocuous crease of land near the river came alive. Masked men swarmed out, six of them on blanketed ponies, just as the last of Skye's caravan, Riddle's wagon, straggled by. Skye cursed. They had the drop on him, six-guns leveled on him, on each driver, on Chang. Their hair lay hidden by wide-brimmed hats jammed down hard and blue bandanas rode high over their noses. And in between, mean cold eyes surveyed each of them.

"If you reach for your guns, you're dead," grated a voice. "You in the green wagon—you step down, slow and careful."

Chapter 30

Alvah Riddle froze, too anguished to do anything.

A shot blistered air inches from his nose. He startled, and trembling, clambered down on shaky legs.

"You. Big one. Drop it." Another shot slashed into Mister Skye's pommel, bloodying his hand. He let his revolver slip to earth, and slowly, slowly raised his arms.

"You! Chinese. Up with 'em. Up with the paws or you're a yellow-skinned dead man." A bullet crashed past Chang's chest. He bowed slightly and raised his hands.

"What you grinning at, heathen?"

"It's a jolly afternoon, Mister Helm," said Chang, mockery in his voice.

The masked road agent lifted his blue revolver, steadied, and pulled the trigger. A black hole in Chang's forehead. Gray and red splattering from the rear of his skull. He sighed, toppled, hit earth with a rolling thud, sprawled on his back. Buffalo Whiskers screamed, wild keening, piercing the sky. Blue powdersmoke curled. Shakily she slid off her pony, ran, sobbing, to Chang, threw herself upon him, hands clutching his chest, her cheeks sheeting with tears of sorrow.

The shot jarred Mister Skye. He rotated his head slowly to see behind him. Buffalo Whiskers sighed, slumped heavily over Chang's still body, twitched and lay quiet, blood leaking from her soft Arapaho skin shirt.

"Don't like colored trash," the road agent said.

Mary sobbed, slumped in her saddle, convulsing with terror and anguish. Mister Skye feared she would be next, but the agent had other things in mind.

Drusilla wept, trembling on the seat of Sleeping Bear's wagon. "You're scum!" she cried. "You're filthy scum! Murderers!"

From behind the dirty red bandana, black eyes glittered at her, and the bore of a heavy Walker Colt steadied on her.

"Go ahead, Boone Helm! Go ahead! I don't want to be in a world with the likes of you!"

"Don't," snapped another one from behind his mask.

Drusilla trembled violently. "Scum! Scum! Scum!" she cried.

The bigger agent nodded to another. "The heathen had

gold. Get it, Red." A wiry man with a bit of carrot hair poking from his hat pawed through Chang's saddle kit, snatched out a sack. Then he flipped Buffalo Whiskers off Chang, leaving her in a crumple, and dug another sack from Chang's britches.

"I'm going to track you down. I'll track you down if it's the last thing I do!" yelled Drusilla, trembling.

Mister Skye winced. Miss Dinwiddie had the courage of the deranged.

A shot seared past her nose, making her start.

Alvah Riddle folded into the ground, trembling too violently to stand.

Goldtooth's dander was up. She peered out of the rear puckerstring hole of her wagon. "I know you, Boone Helm," she snapped.

A shot seared through the sheet, just above her. She jerked back inside. Within, women sobbed and choked. Big Alice sat like a statue holding the reins.

"Get up, Cupid," said the big agent. Alvah couldn't manage it. His muscles had turned to jelly. A shot sprayed dirt in front of him and he bounded up, his hands trembling so violently he couldn't control them.

"Fetch Cupid's arrows," came the dry voice behind the bandana.

A dark one with brown almond eyes pawed into Riddle's coat and extracted a heavy leather pouch.

"No, don't . . ." moaned Riddle. "That's everything I've got."

Helm just nodded, and the dark one clambered inside. Gertrude squawked like a mad hen. "How dare you!" she cried. Chests and cases and barrels flew out of the wagon, popping open, spraying clothing and airtights. A flour bag burst white over sagebrush. Wind plucked every bit of clothing Drusilla owned, and tugged it across the prairie, where things snagged on sage. A sack of sugar burst, revealing a dark poke.

"There's the sweets," said the road agent. He plucked it up and peered inside. "You lied to me, Cupid. It wasn't everything. Do you know what we do to liars?" He lowered the revolver.

Riddle spasmed.

"Company," said an agent, pointing. A party of walking men, miners leading mules, materialized on the southwestern horizon.

The leader stared, and walked over to Goldtooth's wagon. "Give it to me," he said. "Last night's take."

Goldtooth handed him the dust they'd gotten at Daley's.

"The wages of sin is death," said the agent. The others laughed roughly. They clambered onto powerful fast horses, and trotted off, taking everything with them but sorrow.

Mister Skye's rigid muscles eased, and the bile settled back in his belly. He stared at his wet-cheeked Mary, and a shudder racked him. A squaw, nothing, annoyance to them. He stepped shakily off the buckskin and caught her in his big arms and hugged her. She trembled and wept and clutched him, in the tight circle of his arms.

"I can't cope with this, I can't cope with this . . ." Drusilla droned, on and on.

They all slumped, stupefied, too shattered to move. The party of miners found them that way, and took time, in the twilight, to shovel out a shallow grave for Chang and Buffalo Whiskers.

Mister Skye watched silently as the miners shoveled tan earth over Chang's chest and face, over Buffalo Whiskers's soft breast, and into her open mouth. Then they disappeared under the earth.

"Road agent work," said one of the miners, a graying

man, leaning on his shovel. "Lots of it. You look pretty bushed. Guess I'll say some words. Heathen, but I'll say some anyway."

They gathered bareheaded in the dusk, and the miner read sonorously, and then they stood quietly, on into the darkness. Goldtooth and Big Alice sobbed softly. Vagrant thoughts hovered and whispered in Mister Skye's mind, and it came to him that he would attempt to contact Chang's family at the Imperial Court; and to bear the news to the Arapahos. They all camped together for protection beside the Beaverhead.

Alvah recovered his wits enough to bluster. "Everything I had, everything I had, except for what Rasmussen owes. You should have defended us, Skye. That's what you're paid for."

Mister Skye walked away.

"He did!" snapped Drusilla, barely containing rage. "He told you—told Goldtooth—not to stop there. But you stopped and had your fun. And it cost lives! Your money doesn't matter. Two lives matter!"

"He should have told me plainer," Alvah whined.

Mister Skye wasn't so sure of Drusilla's view. That Ives, asking questions back in Virginia . . . they knew all about Riddle. It would have happened somewhere.

As fast as gray dawn broke, they set off over frosty ground for Bannack City, the last lap. No one spoke. Drusilla and the Riddles had salvaged what they could. Mister Skye had inherited Chang's Spencer, three boxes of cartridges, his Colt revolver, a fine white stallion, and a bay pony. The trail cut west from the Beaverhead River, climbed steep dry hills, wove through tumbled grassy mountains as barren as death, and settled into an endless downgrade that wound into a hollow cut slashed by Grasshopper Creek. They toiled past Rattlesnake Ranch, a seedy stage stop, but didn't halt. Hard men watched them pass. A Kiskidden Company freight train, twenty ox teams on a three-hitch load, met them. No one felt like talking, but Mister Skye paused briefly to warn the bullwhackers what might lie ahead. They nodded solemnly.

They passed turnoffs into the hamlets of Spring Gulch and Centerville, on Grasshopper Creek below Bannack. Passed Jim's bar, and White's bar, rich diggings. Under a broken sky, with autumnal clouds scudding under the sun now and then, they rolled slowly down a grade into a white and black town, whitewashed plank and black logs, set deep in a hollow surrounded by barren long slopes. The place thrummed. In spite of the rush to Alder, a thousand argonauts gouged gravel here along four miles of the creek. They passed a cemetery hulking on a hill. Below lay Yankee Flats. Two-rut roads cut over slopes to Horse Prairie, and other hamlets in the district.

Mister Skye paused, leaning over the buckskin, staring at an outpost of civilization, such as it was. A ditch had been cut to the left, sluice water, and beside it ran a row of shanties. Storefronts and signs: Chrisman's Store. City Bakery. Bank Exchange Saloon. Skinner's Saloon. Goodrich Hotel, two stories and log. Oliver's Express Office. Aults Hall. Clothing. Pony Express Mail, four bits to Salt Lake. Off at Yankee Flat across the creek, a segregated row of solid log buildings, squatting silently in the cool sun. The line, he thought. He led them there directly, since both Riddle and Goldtooth were heading for the same place. Bannack bustled with freighters and coaches, horses tied to hitch rails, and bearded men hurrying along boardwalks. No one stared at the bedraggled newcomers, except to eye Mary and her travois ponies, an odd sight there.

A wooden bridge, knocking hollowly beneath them, carried them to the edge of town, over to the line slouching on Yankee Flats.

He pulled up before a bald ruddy man of indeterminate age, taking sun on a roofed verandah of a dark and silent rectangle of log.

"Looking for Nell's Place," he yelled.

The rocking stopped, then started again. The gent spat a long brown gob of chaw out upon the dust.

"Guess you found it," he said. "But it's shut down. She's off to Alder."

His blue rheumy eyes took in the red wagons, Goldtooth and Big Alice and Juliet, settled a long moment on Mrs. Parkins, glanced briefly at Sleeping Bear, gazed blankly at Drusilla and the Riddles, and sharply at Mary and her travois. He yawned, stood, revealing a hairy white belly, gaping out of a dirt-grayed buttonless flannel shirt.

"I'm the caretaker, Rasmussen," he said. "You got some business or other?"

Drusilla's face turned to gray granite.

"Home sweet home, honeys," said Goldtooth. "Mister, we're buyin' this ol' place from Nell. We'll just wander in—"

"How do I know that?" asked Rasmussen.

"Right here, honey," said Goldtooth, thrusting a sale agreement before him.

He stared blankly. "Don't rightly know that. My eyes a little weak. Maybe you could read it, eh?"

Drusilla closed hers, tightly.

Alvah Riddle brushed off his dusty clothing, inflated himself, and stepped lightly to Rasmussen.

"My fine friend, I have brought you a great treasure. Yes, Cupid has arrived with a quiver of love darts. Yes, indeed. My name, Rasmussen, is—Riddle!"

The bald man licked lips, and chewed. "Don't recollect it," he muttered.

"The marriage contract. The bride! I've brought the bride to warm your little nest!"

Rasmussen's belly quaked. Hoarse laughter. A wheeze and another brown gob splattered dust. "Aw, shit, I forgot. That's the little lady?"

"You have your fee waiting, of course," said Alvah.

Rasmussen rocked on the balls of scuffed boots. "Haven't got a dime. No gold in my gravel, lot of work for nothing. Sorry, pal."

Something eased in Drusilla's face.

"You can't pay? Can't pay? But you contracted—"

"Go to hell, Riddle." Rasmussen yawned, followed the bawds inside.

"Well, then, little lady, I have the right to make another match. Get you married off. One thousand. Yes, one thousand is my fee. Lots of gold-grubbers got it. Prepare to meet your man, little lady!"

"No," said Drusilla quietly. "No, no, no."

"The contract—"

"You heard her, Riddle," said Mister Skye softly.

"But we have a signed and sealed—"

"Free territory, not slave. Go on home, Riddle. Back to Skaneateles."

"Drusilla, you are obliged to come—"

"No, Riddle."

"I'll sue you in every court. I'll set the hounds baying. I'll—"

He yanked his revolver from its holster. Skye landed on him, driving him back, toppling him hard into dust. The revolver skittered into grass.

"Warned you," whispered Mister Skye, sitting hard on Riddle.

Drusilla screamed.

He rolled off. Riddle lifted his jarred body from the dirt and brushed himself. The guide collected the revolver, and Riddle's Spencer, unloaded them, and handed them to him.

"I think I want to see the inside of this place," said Drusilla.

"It's not respectable. You'll become a slut like the others," said Riddle.

The rest had wandered in. She and Mister Skye climbed the steps, leaving Gertrude and Alvah staring huffily from their wagon. Lampless gloom. A parlor with a bar at the side stretched across the front. Dark and barren now, with the rough plank floor echoing hollowly under their feet. A black hallway stretched back to the rear of the building. On the left, madam's quarters, a two-room apartment with a door into the bar. Whitewashed log, tiny high windows. Behind, six small cribs, bedless and dark, echoing night. Nell's Place sang its sadness.

"Home sweet home," said Goldtooth, unenthused. "Beats livin' in a tent in the middle of Idaho winter. Beats having Union Army bluenoses shutting me down."

"We'll fix this li'l ol' place up," said Mrs. Parkins. "Oh, I wish I had my stuff. But I guess I can replace it fast enough."

At the rear, a door. And down a path, necessary rooms, and a bathhouse with a stove and four-clawed tub. Mary stared at it, clambered inside, sat down and giggled. The bawds laughed. They all drifted back to the front parlor and found it empty. Rasmussen had returned to his rocker on the verandah.

Goldtooth slipped an arm through Sleeping Bear's. "Honey, I know you're leavin' the sporting life. But could you help us get settled in? I want to get rid of that Rasmussen. Definitely not the type for my parlor house. Before you start up the freightin', would you stay, and maybe help find me a good man?"

The former gambler paused, uncertainly. "I'll help you get going, Goldtooth."

"Oh, honey, that's grand! Now first thing, we'll have us a little ride through town. We're gonna sashay up and down Bannack. Take off the wagon sheet! Ladies, we'll get all polished up! Sleeping Bear, you can unload the sleeping robes and things. Haven't got money for beds and ticks and pillows yet, but who cares? We'll open tonight! Money, money, money!"

She turned at last to Mister Skye, Drusilla, and Mary. "Why, honey, you got us here. You got us here, all that long way. You got us through wilderness and hostile Indians and everything. Mister Skye, honey, you're welcome here anytime, for free."

Barnaby Skye laughed.

"What're you going to do, honey?" she asked Drusilla.

"I don't know. Yes I do know. I will find work. And I will save, and buy passage to—a place."

"Well, honey, you need help, you let me know." She turned to the guide. "Goodbye, dear Mister Skye. We'll remember you."

She hugged him. He felt her arms embrace him, felt not lust, but something larger. The others hugged him too, Big Alice, grinning, Juliet Picard, smiling mysteriously, and Mrs. Parkins, who pressed against him too hard.

"Sweetie, I've got treats in the cookie jar for you," she whispered.

Mister Skye laughed, and let her go.

Sleeping Bear caught his hand and pressed hard. The

man wept. "Thank you," he said softly. "I'm proud to have known you."

"You were reborn in this free West," said Mister Skye. "Everything is possible for you, Sleeping Bear. You're a good man."

They stepped into blinding sun, leaving tears behind them. The Riddles had driven off, dropping Drusilla's trunk forlornly on the bare earth. The autumnal sky lowered cobalt upon the barren slopes.

"You're penniless. Not even four bits for a cheap room. Trunk sitting here. I've got an eagle I've been saving since Fort Laramie. Meant to buy some cartridges with it, but I don't need them now that I've got Chang's Spencer. Meant to buy—" He thought of the bottle he wanted so badly, to wet his parched throat. "Want you to have it. It'll keep you a week in a respectable rooming house, give you time to find something. Mary and I'll make do, get back to Victoria, spend a fat winter with the Kicked-in-the-Bellies."

"I'd like that. You'll be at Fort Laramie? I'll return the ten dollars when I can."

"Of course, you can stay with us. I hate like blazes leaving you here alone, prey to any—"

"Mister Skye," she retorted. "Look at me. Do I look like prey? After two thousand miles?" She laughed, throwing her loose sunbleached hair back, her eyes shining brightly from the tan planes of her face.

He hoisted her trunk onto a travois, and they rode toward the town, Drusilla walking beside them. The line squatted two hundred yards and two thousand miles from the rest of Bannack, and when they thrummed over the bridge, something in Drusilla's face relaxed.

On the main street they spotted a familiar green wagon, with ponies on a picket line behind it. Alvah, talking to a man with a sheriff's badge shining on his black suit, spotted them.

"There!" he cried. "That's the one. That woman's got contract obligations with me. He's stealing her. Already lost everything I got to road agents, and now that man—Skye—he's nipping her away! Don't know how we'll get back to New York, less I get my contract rights!"

Mister Skye found himself staring into the bland face of a compact elegantly dressed man, who studied him thoughtfully, his eyes glancing too casually to Mister Skye's fringed shirt, holstered Colt, and the Spencer he now cradled in his arm. Then at Mary. And then his gray eyes studied Drusilla, admiration kindling in them.

"I'm Plummer. Henry Plummer. You have a very beautiful woman there, Mister Skye. This gent says he has a contract, but that's a civil matter and out of my hands."

"Civil matter! That Skye almost killed me!"

Plummer turned to Riddle. "As I was saying. I see a thousand dollars here in the wagon, the mules, the ponies and harness. They command fine prices here, where things are short. Try Oliver's over there. Enough to get you and Mrs. Riddle home. Passage to Salt Lake is seventy-five each. And east on Holladay's Overland . . . you'll have enough. But watch out. Those road agents are a problem, so guard your poke."

Plummer smiled, dismissing the Riddles. "Now, Mister Skye, Miss Dinwiddie, if I may be of service . . ."

"Need a rooming house for the young lady. Say, where can I trade ponies? Forgot I had ponies to trade."

"Indeed, Gibson's very respectable, over in that block there—and any livery barn. Oliver's . . ."

They turned onto a side street, with Mary and her travois ponies drawing stares, and eyes curious upon the burly guide on the buckskin horse, leading a long picket line, and the tall woman striding boldly beside him.

Two workmen on ladders were bolting a gilded sign onto a log building with a rough-sawn board front, white-washed fresh. McGahan's Books. Drusilla gasped. Something feral caught up in her throat, erupting in a cry that shivered Mister Skye's flesh and spun Mary's head.

Drusilla Dinwiddie raced. But she'd been seen by a young man inside, who erupted from the door. They caught each other in the middle of the sunny street, caught and whirled, speechless.

"Parsimony!" she wept. "Parsimony! Parsimony!"

"I turned off at Fort Hall. Couldn't stand the thought of the Comstock. Thought I'd have a chance. Thought I might pay Riddle, outbid—thought I'd better find the woman I love, only woman I'll ever love . . ." he babbled.

Drusilla clutched him and sobbed.

"I love you, Parsimony McGahan. I want you, now, with or without clergy. Married or not. Right now, for-ever . . ." She buried her face in his chest, wetting his suit with flowing tears.

" 'How do I love thee? Let me count the ways,' " he whispered and she clutched him.

Burly men stared. Mister Skye coughed. Mary un-loaded Drusilla's trunk and hauled it into the store, gawk-ing at shelves of books. They all strolled into his store and found it half put together, books in barrels, books in stacks, books tumbling across white enameled floor-boards. Lamps glowing, smell of leather and paper.

"Oh, Parsimony. What a place! What a good life of the mind you have!" cried Drusilla.

"Do you like it? It's yours, my darling."

A battered black top hat perched on a stack of books in a dark corner, looking forlorn and homeless. Barnaby

Skye stared at it, recognition coming slowly. His own hat. The mark of an English gentleman, the very hat that separated him from these Americans, the topper that fit his head so well that gales couldn't dislodge it.

"My hat," he said, picking it up and clamping it down. Neither Parsimony nor Drusilla heard him.

"My hat!" he exclaimed.

"Found it," muttered Parsimony, never taking his eyes from the woman he loved.

"Where? How?" demanded Barnaby Skye.

He got no answer.

Mister Skye twisted it slightly, until it canted to starboard. "Haw!" he roared.

Mary giggled.

An hour later, Mister Skye and Mary rode east, up the long dry slopes out of Bannack City. His elkskin shirt was wet with Drusilla's tears. Beside him rode Mary, smiling, and behind them a picket string of ponies. Minus one he had traded at a livery for the grub that now burdened his parfleches. And a crockery jug corked tight, for the moment.

"Looking forward to tonight," he said, and she beamed.

Chapter 31

Outside the lodge, a horse stopped.

He and Mary were five hours east of Bannack, camping in a wooded draw among barren slopes. She'd scarcely gotten the parfleches put away. He sat in the dusk. Later he'd pull the cork. At the sound, he lifted the Spencer.

"Sonofabitch," yelled Victoria, outside. "You too close to the road, too easy to find. Get your horses stole."

He peered out, astonished. His Sits-Beside-Him-Wife materialized in the lavender twilight.

He hugged her, his mind full of questions.

In the wavering light of a smoky new fire, she settled herself quietly and grinned smugly, saying nothing.

Wait her out. He knew the game.

He yawned, scratched his belly, and formed in his mind the things he'd tell her, good and bad, bright and tragic, about what had happened since they parted. But why was she here?

"Yes, Victoria?" he asked, driven to surrender.

"Sonofabitch! Look here!" She dropped a flattened lead ball into his hand. He stared at it, finding no meaning.

"From Jawbone. He's feeling pretty good. Gonna be fine when we get back. Red Turkey Wattle, he made big medicine. He found the ball, down under the skin, between Jawbone's front legs, and he told bad medicine to come out. Jawbone, he's coming along. Half Crow, our Half Crow, he takes care of Jawbone like a mother. Jawbone likes Half Crow. You come on back now, and we'll stay with my people, and in the spring Jawbone will be good as new, right, Mister Skye?"

She grinned, but Mister Skye couldn't see her through the blur welling over his eyes.

She spotted his hat, picked it up, turned it around, and screwed it down on his head, scolding the wind.